By Stephen King and published by
Hodder & Stoughton

FICTION:
Carrie
'Salem's Lot
The Shining
Night Shift
The Stand
The Dead Zone
Firestarter
Cujo
Different Seasons
Cycle of the Werewolf
Christine
The Talisman (with Peter Straub)
Pet Sematary
It
Skeleton Crew
The Eyes of the Dragon
Misery
The Tommyknockers
The Dark Half
Four Past Midnight
Needful Things
Gerald's Game
Dolores Claiborne
Nightmares and Dreamscapes
Insomnia
Rose Madder
Desperation
Bag of Bones
The Girl Who Loved Tom Gordon
Hearts in Atlantis
Dreamcatcher
Everything's Eventual
From a Buick 8
Cell
Lisey's Story
The Dark Tower I: The Gunslinger
The Dark Tower II: The Drawing of the Three
The Dark Tower III: The Waste Lands
The Dark Tower IV: Wizard and Glass
The Dark Tower V: Wolves of the Calla
The Dark Tower VI: Song of Susannah
The Dark Tower VII: The Dark Tower

By Stephen King as Richard Bachman
Thinner
The Running Man
The Bachman Books
The Regulators
Blaze

NON-FICTION:
Danse Macabre
On Writing (A Memoir of the Craft)

STEPHEN KING

DUMA KEY

A Novel

HODDER &
STOUGHTON

Grateful acknowledgement is made for permission to
reprint excerpts from the following copyrighted material:

'Animals' from THE COLLECTED POEMS OF FRANK O'HARA,
by Frank O'Hara, edited by Donald Allen copyright © 1971 by
Maureen Granville-Smith, Administratrix of the Estate of Frank O'Hara.
Used by permission of Alfred A. Knopf, a division of Random House, Inc.

Permission to use lyrics from 'Dig' by Shark Puppy (R. Tozier, W. Denbrough),
granted by Bad Nineteen Music, © 1986

First published in Great Britain in 2008 by Hodder & Stoughton
An Hachette Livre UK Company

A CIP catalogue record for this title is
available from the British Library

ISBN 978 0 340 95219 1

Typeset in Bembo by
Palimpsest Book Production Limited, Grangemouth, Stirlingshire

Printed and bound by Clays Ltd, St Ives plc

Hodder Headline's policy is to use papers that are natural,
renewable and recyclable products and made from wood grown
in sustainable forests. The logging and manufacturing processes
are expected to conform to the environmental regulations
of the country of origin

Hodder & Stoughton
338 Euston Road
London NW1 3BH

www.hodder.co.uk

For Barbara Ann and Jimmy

Memory . . . is an internal rumor.
— GEORGE SANTAYANA

Life is more than love and pleasure,
I came here to dig for treasure.
If you want to play you gotta pay
You know it's always been that way,
We all came to dig for treasure.
— SHARK PUPPY

How to Draw a Picture (I)

Start with a blank surface. It doesn't have to be paper or canvas, but I feel it should be white. We call it white because we need a word, but its true name is nothing. Black is the absence of light, but white is the absence of memory, the color of can't remember.

How do we remember to remember? That's a question I've asked myself often since my time on Duma Key, often in the small hours of the morning, looking up into the absence of light, remembering absent friends. Sometimes in those little hours I think about the horizon. You have to establish the horizon. You have to mark the white. A simple enough act, you might say, but any act that re-makes the world is heroic. Or so I've come to believe.

Imagine a little girl, hardly more than a baby. She fell from a carriage almost ninety years ago, struck her head on a stone, and forgot everything. Not just her name; everything! And then one day she recalled just enough to pick up a pencil and make that first hesitant mark across the white. A horizon-line, sure. But also a slot for blackness to pour through.

Still, imagine that small hand lifting the pencil . . . hesitating . . . and then marking the white. Imagine the courage of that first effort to re-establish the world by picturing it. I will always love that little girl, in spite of all she has cost me. I must. I have no choice.

Pictures are magic, as you know.

1

1 – My Other Life

i

My name is Edgar Freemantle. I used to be a big deal in the building and contracting business. This was in Minnesota, in my other life. I learned that my-other-life thing from Wireman. I want to tell you about Wireman, but first let's get through the Minnesota part.

Gotta say it: I was a genuine American-boy success there. Worked my way up in the company where I started, and when I couldn't work my way any higher there, I went out and started my own. The boss of the company I left laughed at me, said I'd be broke in a year. I think that's what most bosses say when some hot young pocket-rocket goes off on his own.

For me, everything worked out. When Minneapolis-St Paul boomed, The Freemantle Company boomed. When things tightened up, I never tried to play big. But I did play my hunches, and most played out well. By the time I was fifty, Pam and I were worth forty million dollars. And we were still tight. We had two girls, and at the end of our particular Golden Age, Ilse was at Brown and Melinda was teaching in France, as part of a foreign exchange program. At the time things went wrong, my wife and I were planning to go and visit her.

I had an accident at a job site. It was pretty simple; when a pickup truck, even a Dodge Ram with all the bells and whistles, argues with a twelve-story crane, the pickup is going to lose every time. The right side of my skull only cracked. The left side was slammed so hard against the Ram's doorpost that it fractured in three places. Or maybe it was five. My memory is better than it used to be, but it's still a long way from what it once was.

The doctors called what happened to my head a contracoup injury, and that kind of thing often does more damage than the original hit. My ribs were broken. My right hip was shattered. And

3

although I retained seventy per cent of the sight in my right eye (more, on a good day), I lost my right arm.

I was supposed to lose my life, but didn't. I was supposed to be mentally impaired thanks to the contracoup thing, and at first I was, but it passed. Sort of. By the time it did, my wife had gone, and not just sort of. We were married for twenty-five years, but you know what they say: shit happens. I guess it doesn't matter; gone is gone. And over is over. Sometimes that's a good thing.

When I say I was mentally impaired, I mean that at first I didn't know who people were – even my wife – or what had happened. I couldn't understand why I was in such pain. I can't remember the quality of that pain now, four years later. I know that I suffered it, and that it was excruciating, but it's all pretty academic. It wasn't academic at the time. At the time it was like being in hell and not knowing why you were there.

At first you were afraid you'd die, then you were afraid you wouldn't. That's what Wireman says, and he would have known; he had his own season in hell.

Everything hurt all the time. I had a constant ringing headache; behind my forehead it was always midnight in the world's biggest clock-shop. Because my right eye was fucked up, I was seeing the world through a film of blood, and I hardly knew what the world was. Nothing had a name. I remember one day when Pam was in the room – I was still in the hospital – and she was standing by my bed. I was extremely pissed that she should be standing when there was a thing to sit on right over in the cornhole.

'Bring the friend,' I said. 'Sit in the friend.'

'What do you mean, Edgar?' she asked.

'The *friend*, the *buddy*!' I shouted. 'Bring over the fucking *pal*, you dump bitch!' My head was killing me and she was starting to cry. I hated her for that. She had no business crying, because she wasn't the one in the cage, looking at everything through a red blur. She wasn't the monkey in the cage. And then it came to me. 'Bring over the chum and sick *down*!' It was the closest my rattled, fucked-up brain could come to *chair*.

I was angry all the time. There were two older nurses that I called Dry Fuck One and Dry Fuck Two, as if they were characters in a dirty Dr Seuss story. There was a candystriper I called Pilch Lozenge

4

– I have no idea why, but that nickname also had some sort of sexual connotation. To me, at least. When I grew stronger, I tried to hit people. Twice I tried to stab Pam, and on one of those two occasions I succeeded, although only with a plastic knife. She still needed a couple of stitches in her forearm. There were times when I had to be tied down.

Here is what I remember most clearly about that part of my other life: a hot afternoon toward the end of my month-long stay in an expensive convalescent home, the expensive air conditioning broken, tied down in my bed, a soap opera on the television, a thousand midnight bells ringing in my head, pain burning and stiffening my right side like a poker, my missing right arm itching, my missing right fingers twitching, no more Oxycontin due for awhile (I don't know how long, because telling time is beyond me), and a nurse swims out of the red, a creature coming to look at the monkey in the cage, and the nurse says: 'Are you ready to visit with your wife?' And I say: 'Only if she brought a gun to shoot me with.'

You don't think that kind of pain will pass, but it does. Then they ship you home and replace it with the agony of physical rehabilitation. The red began to drain from my vision. A psychologist who specialized in hypnotherapy showed me some neat tricks for managing the phantom aches and itches in my missing arm. That was Kamen. It was Kamen who brought me Reba: one of the few things I took with me when I limped out of my other life and into the one I lived on Duma Key.

'This is not approved psychological therapy for anger management,' Dr Kamen said, although I suppose he might have been lying about that to make Reba more attractive. He told me I had to give her a hateful name, and so, although she looked like Lucy Ricardo, I named her after an aunt who used to pinch my fingers when I was small if I didn't eat all my carrots. Then, less than two days after getting her, I forgot her name. I could only think of boy names, each one making me angrier: Randall, Russell, Rudolph, River-fucking-Phoenix.

I was home by then. Pam came in with my morning snack and must have seen the look on my face, because I could see her steeling herself for an outburst. But even though I'd forgotten the name of the fluffy red rage-doll the psychologist had given me, I remembered how I was supposed to use it in this situation.

'Pam,' I said, 'I need five minutes to get myself under control. I can do this.'

'Are you sure— '

'Yes, now just get that hamhock out of here and stick it up your face-powder. I can do this.'

I didn't know if I really could, but that was what I was supposed to say. I couldn't remember the fucking doll's name, but I could remember *I can do this.* That's clear about the end of my other life, how I kept saying *I can do this* even when I knew I couldn't, even when I knew I was fucked, I was double-fucked, I was dead-ass-fucked in the pouring rain.

'I can do this,' I said, and God knows how I looked because she backed out without a word, the tray still in her hands and the cup chattering against the plate.

When she was gone, I held the doll up in front of my face, staring into its stupid blue eyes as my thumbs disappeared into its stupid yielding body. 'What's your name, you bat-faced bitch?' I shouted at it. It never once occurred to me that Pam was listening on the kitchen intercom, she and the day-nurse both. Tell you what, if the intercom had been broken they could have heard me through the door. I was in good voice that day.

I began to shake the doll back and forth. Its head flopped and its synthetic *I Love Lucy* hair flew. Its big blue cartoon eyes seemed to be saying *Oouuu, you nasty man!* like Betty Boop in one of those old cartoons you can still see sometimes on the cable.

'What's your name, bitch? What's your name, you cunt? What's your name, you cheap rag-filled whore? Tell me your name! Tell me your name! *Tell me your name or I'll cut out your eyes and chop off your nose and rip out your—*'

My mind cross-connected then, a thing that still happens now, four years later, down here in the town of Tamazunchale, state of San Luis Potosí, country of Mexico, site of Edgar Freemantle's third life. For a moment I was in my pickup truck, clipboard rattling against my old steel lunchbucket in the passenger footwell (I doubt if I was the only working millionaire in America to carry a lunchbucket, but you probably could have counted us in the dozens), my

6

PowerBook beside me on the seat. And from the radio a woman's voice cried '*It was RED!*' with evangelical fervor. Only three words, but three was enough. It was the song about the poor woman who turns out her pretty daughter as a prostitute. It was 'Fancy', by Reba McEntire.

'Reba,' I whispered, and hugged the doll against me. 'You're Reba. Reba-Reba-Reba. I'll never forget again.' I did – the following week – but I didn't get angry that time. No. I held her against me like a little love, closed my eyes, and visualized the pickup truck that had been demolished in the accident. I visualized my steel lunchbucket rattling against the steel clip on my clipboard, and the woman's voice came from the radio once more, exulting with that same evangelical fervor: '*It was RED!*'

Dr Kamen called it a breakthrough. He was excited. My wife seemed a good deal less excited, and the kiss she put on my cheek was of the dutiful variety. I think it was two months later that she told me she wanted a divorce.

ii

By then the pain had either lessened or my mind had made certain crucial adjustments when it came to dealing with it. The headaches still came, but less often and rarely with the same violence; it was no longer *always* midnight in the world's biggest clock-shop between my ears. I was always more than ready for Vicodin at five and Oxycontin at eight – could hardly hobble on my bright red Canadian crutch until I'd swallowed those magic pills – but my rebuilt hip was starting to mend.

Kathi Green the Rehab Queen came to Casa Freemantle in Mendota Heights on Mondays, Wednesdays, and Fridays. I was allowed an extra Vicodin before our sessions, and still my screams filled the house by the time we finished up. Our basement rec room had been converted into a therapy suite, complete with a handicap-accessible hot tub. After two months of torture, I was able to make it down there on my own in the evenings to double up on my leg exercises and begin some abdominal work. Kathi said doing that stuff a couple of hours before bed would release endorphins and I'd sleep better.

7

It was during one of these evening workouts – Edgar in search of those elusive endorphins – when my wife of a quarter-century came downstairs and told me she wanted a divorce.

I stopped what I was doing – crunches – and looked at her. I was sitting on a floor pad. She was standing at the foot of the stairs, prudently across the room. I could have asked her if she was serious, but the light down there was very good – those racked fluorescents – and I didn't have to. I don't think it's the sort of thing women joke about six months after their husbands have almost died in accidents, anyway. I could have asked her why, but I knew. I could see the small white scar on her arm where I had stabbed her with the plastic knife from my hospital supper tray, and that was really the least of it. I thought of telling her, not so long ago, to get that hamhock out of here and stick it up her face-powder. I considered asking her to at least think about it, but the anger came back. In those days what Dr Kamen called *inappropriate anger* was my ugly friend. And hey, what I was feeling right then did not seem inappropriate at all.

My shirt was off. My right arm ended three and a half inches below the shoulder. I twitched it at her – a twitch was the best I could do with the muscle that was left. 'This is me,' I said, 'giving you the finger. Get out of here if that's how you feel. Get out, you quitting birch.'

The first tears had started rolling down her face, but she tried to smile. It was a pretty ghastly effort. 'Bitch, Edgar,' she said. 'The word is *bitch*.'

'The word is what I say it is,' I said, and began to do crunches again. It's harder than hell to do them with an arm gone; your body wants to pull and corkscrew to that side. 'I wouldn't have left *you*, that's the point. I wouldn't have left *you*. I would have gone on through the mud and the blood and the piss and the spilled beer.'

'It's different,' she said. She made no effort to wipe her face. 'It's different and you know it. I couldn't break you in two if I got into a rage.'

'I'd have a hell of a job breaking you in two with only one amp,' I said, doing crunches faster.

'You stuck me with a knife.' As if that were the point. It wasn't, and we both knew it.

8

'A plastic rudder knife is what it was, I was half out of my mind, and it'll be your last words on your fucking beth-dead, "Eddie staffed me with a plastic fife, goodbye cruel world."'

'You choked me,' she said in a voice I could barely hear.

I stopped doing crunches and gaped at her. The clock-shop started up in my head; bang-a-gong, get it on. 'What are you saying, I choked you? I never choked you!'

'I know you don't remember, but you did. And you're not the same.'

'Oh, quit it. Save the New Age bullshit for the . . . for the guy . . . your . . .' I knew the word and I could see the man it stood for, but it wouldn't come. 'For that bald fuck you see in his office.'

'My therapist,' she said, and of course that made me angrier: she had the word and I didn't. Because her brain hadn't been shaken like Jell-O.

'You want a divorce, you can have a divorce. Throw it all away, why not? Only go do the alligator somewhere else. Get out of here.'

She went up the stairs and closed the door without looking back. And it wasn't until she was gone that I realized I'd meant to say crocodile tears. Go cry your crocodile tears somewhere else.

Oh, well. Close enough for rock and roll. That's what Wireman says.

And I was the one who ended up getting out.

iii

Except for Pam, I never had a partner in my other life. Edgar Freemantle's Four Rules for Success (feel free to take notes) were: never borrow more than your IQ times a hundred, never borrow from a man who calls you by your first name on first acquaintance, never take a drink while the sun's still up, and *never* take a partner you wouldn't be willing to embrace naked on a waterbed.

I did have an accountant I trusted, however, and it was Tom Riley who helped me move the few things I needed from Mendota Heights to our smaller place on Lake Phalen. Tom, a sad two-time loser in the marriage game, worried at me all the way out. 'You don't give up the house in a situation like this,' he said. 'Not unless the judge kicks you out. It's like giving up home field advantage in a playoff game.'

I didn't care about home field advantage; I only wanted him to watch his driving. I winced every time a car coming the other way looked a little too close to the centerline. Sometimes I stiffened and pumped the invisible passenger brake. As for getting behind the wheel again myself, I thought never sounded about right. Of course, God loves surprises. That's what Wireman says.

Kathi Green the Rehab Queen had only been divorced once, but she and Tom were on the same wavelength. I remember her sitting cross-legged in her leotard, holding my feet and looking at me with grim outrage.

'Here you are, just out of Death's Motel and short an arm, and she wants to call it off. Because you poked her with a plastic hospital knife when you could barely remember your own name? Fuck me til I cry! Doesn't she understand that mood-swings and short-term memory loss following accident trauma are *common?*'

'She understands that she's scared of me,' I said.

'Yeah? Well, listen to your Mama, Sunny Jim: if you've got a good lawyer, you can make her pay for being such a wimp.' Some hair had escaped from her Rehab Gestapo ponytail and she blew it back from her forehead. 'She *ought* to pay for it. Read my lips: *None of this is your fault.*'

'She says I tried to choke her.'

'And if so, being choked by a one-armed invalid must have been a pants-wetting experience. Come on, Eddie, make her pay. I'm sure I'm stepping way out of my place, but I don't care. She should not be doing what she's doing.'

'I think there's more to it than the choking thing and the butter-knife thing.'

'What?'

'I can't remember.'

'What does *she* say?'

'She doesn't.' But Pam and I had been together a long time, and even if love had run out into a delta of passive acceptance, I thought I still knew her well enough to know that yes – there had been something else, there was *still* something else, and that was what she wanted to get away from.

iv

Not long after I relocated to the place on Lake Phalen, the girls came to see me – the young women. They brought a picnic hamper. We sat on the piney-smelling lakeporch, looked out at the lake, and nibbled sandwiches. It was past Labor Day by then, most of the floating toys put away for another year. There was also a bottle of wine in the hamper, but I only drank a little. On top of the pain medication, alcohol hit me hard; a single beer could turn me into a slurring drunk. The girls – the *young women* – finished the rest between them, and it loosened them up. Melinda, back from France for the second time since my argument with the crane and not happy about it, asked me if all adults in their fifties had these unpleasant regressive interludes, did she have that to look forward to. Ilse, the younger, began to cry, leaned against me, and asked why it couldn't be like it was, why couldn't we – meaning her mother and me – be like *we* were. Lin told her this wasn't the time for Illy's patented Baby Act, and Illy gave her the finger. I laughed. I couldn't help it. Then we all laughed.

Lin's temper and Ilse's tears weren't pleasant, but they were honest, and as familiar to me as the mole on Ilse's chin or the faint vertical frown-line, which in time would deepen into a groove, between Lin's eyes.

Linnie wanted to know what I was going to do, and I told her I didn't know. I'd come a long distance toward deciding to end my own life, but I knew that if I did it, it must absolutely look like an accident. I would not leave these two young women, just starting out in their lives, carrying the residual guilt of their father's suicide. Nor would I leave a load of guilt behind for the woman with whom I had once shared a milkshake in bed, both of us naked and laughing and listening to the Plastic Ono Band on the stereo.

After they'd had a chance to vent – after a *full and complete exchange of feelings*, in Dr Kamen–speak – my memory is that we had a pleasant afternoon, looking at old photo albums and reminiscing about the past. I think we even laughed some more, but not all memories of my other life are to be trusted. Wireman says when it comes to the past, we all stack the deck.

11

Ilse wanted us all to go out to dinner, but Lin had to meet someone at the Public Library before it closed, and I said I didn't feel much like hobbling anywhere; I thought I'd read a few chapters of the latest John Sandford and then go to bed. They kissed me – all friends again – and then left.

Two minutes later, Ilse came back. 'I told Linnie I forgot my keys,' she said.

'I take it you didn't,' I said.

'No. Daddy, would you ever hurt Mom? I mean, now? On purpose?'

I shook my head, but that wasn't good enough for her. I could tell by the way she just stood there, looking me in the eye. 'No,' I said. 'Never. I'd—'

'You'd what, Daddy?'

'I was going to say I'd cut my own arm off first, but all at once that seemed like a really bad idea. I'd never do it, Illy. Leave it at that.'

'Then why is she still afraid of you?'

'I think . . . because I'm maimed.'

She hurled herself into my arms so hard she almost knocked us both onto the sofa. 'Oh, Daddy, I'm so sorry. All of this is just so *sucky*.'

I stroked her hair a little. 'I know, but remember this – it's as bad as it's going to get.' That wasn't the truth, but if I was careful, Ilse would never know it had been an outright lie.

A horn honked from the driveway.

'Go on,' I said, and kissed her wet cheek. 'Your sister's impatient.'

She wrinkled her nose. 'So what else is new? You're not overdoing the pain meds, are you?'

'No.'

'Call if you need me, Daddy. I'll catch the very next plane.'

She would, too. Which was why I wouldn't.

'You bet.' I put a kiss on her other cheek. 'Give that to your sister.'

She nodded and went out. I sat down on the couch and closed my eyes. Behind them, the clocks were striking and striking and striking.

v

My next visitor was Dr Kamen, the psychologist who gave me Reba. I didn't invite him. I had Kathi, my rehabilitation dominatrix, to thank for that.

Although surely no more than forty, Kamen walked like a much older man and wheezed even when he sat, peering at the world through enormous horn-rimmed spectacles and over an enormous pear of a belly. He was a very tall, very black black man, with features carved so large they seemed unreal. His great staring eyeballs, ship's figurehead of a nose, and totemic lips were awe-inspiring. Xander Kamen looked like a minor god in a suit from Men's Wearhouse. He also looked like a prime candidate for a fatal heart attack or stroke before his fiftieth birthday.

He refused my offer of refreshment, said he couldn't stay, then put his briefcase aside on the couch as if to contradict that. He sank full fathom five beside the couch's armrest (and going deeper all the time − I feared for the thing's springs), looking at me and wheezing benignly.

'What brings you our this way?' I asked him.

'Oh, Kathi tells me you're planning to bump yourself off,' he said. It was the tone he might have used to say *Kathi tells me you're having a lawn party and there are fresh Krispy Kremes on offer.* 'Any truth to that rumor?'

I opened my mouth, then closed it again. Once, when I was ten and growing up in Eau Claire, I took a comic book from a drugstore spin-around, put it down the front of my jeans, then dropped my tee-shirt over it. As I was strolling out the door, feeling jacked up and very clever, a clerk grabbed me by the arm. She lifted my shirt with her other hand and exposed my ill-gotten treasure. 'How did *that* get there?' she asked me. Not in the forty years since that day had I been so completely stuck for an answer to a simple question.

Finally − long after such a response could have any weight − I said, 'That's ridiculous. I don't know where she could have gotten such an idea.'

'No?'

'No. Sure you don't want a Coke?'

13

'Thanks, but I'll pass.'

I got up and got a Coke from the kitchen fridge. I tucked the bottle firmly between my stump and my chest-wall – possible but painful, I don't know what you may have seen in the movies, but broken ribs hurt for a long time – and spun off the cap with my left hand. I'm a southpaw. Caught a break there, *muchacho*, as Wireman says.

'I'm surprised you'd take her seriously in any case,' I said as I came back in. 'Kathi's a hell of a physical therapist, but a head-shrinker she's not.' I paused before sitting down. 'Neither are you, actually. In the technical sense.'

Kamen cupped an enormous hand behind an ear that looked roughly the size of a desk drawer. 'Do I hear . . . a ratcheting noise? I believe I do!'

'What are you talking about?'

'It's the charmingly medieval sound a person's defenses make when they go up.' He tried an ironic wink, but the size of the man's face made irony impossible; he could only manage burlesque. Still, I took the point. 'As for Kathi Green, you're right, what does she know? All she does is work with paraplegics, quadriplegics, accident-related amps like you, and people recovering from traumatic head injuries – again, like you. For fifteen years Kathi's done this work, she's had the opportunity to watch a thousand maimed patients reflect on how not even a single second of time can ever be called back, so how could she *possibly* recognize the signs of pre-suicidal depression?'

I sat in the lumpy easy chair across from the couch and stared at him sullenly. Here was trouble. And Kathi Green was more.

He leaned forward . . . although, given his girth, a few inches was all he could manage. 'You have to wait,' he said.

I gaped at him.

He nodded. 'You're surprised. Yes. But I'm not a Christian, let alone a Catholic, and on the subject of suicide my mind is open. Yet I'm a believer in responsibilities, I know that you are, too, and I tell you this: if you kill yourself now . . . even six months from now . . . your wife and daughters will know. No matter how cleverly you do it, they'll know.'

'I don't—'

He raised his hand. 'And the company that insures your life – for a very large sum, I'm sure – they'll know, too. They may not be able to prove it . . . but they'll try very hard. The rumors they start will hurt your girls, no matter how well-armored against such things you may think they are.'

Melinda was well-armored. Ilse, however, was a different story. When Melinda was mad at her, she called Illy a case of arrested development, but I didn't think that was true. I thought Illy was just tender.

'And in the end, they may prove it.' Kamen shrugged his enormous shoulders. 'How much of a death-duty that might entail I couldn't guess, but I'm sure it would erase a great deal of your life's treasure.'

I wasn't thinking about the money. I was thinking about a team of insurance investigators sniffing around whatever I set up. And all at once I began to laugh.

Kamen sat with his huge dark brown hands on his doorstop knees, looking at me with his little *I've-seen-everything* smile. Except on his face nothing was little. He let my laughter run its course and then asked me what was so funny.

'You're telling me I'm too rich to kill myself,' I said.

'I'm telling you not now, Edgar, and that's all I'm telling you. I'm also going to make a suggestion that goes against a good deal of my own practical experience. But I have a very strong intuition in your case – the same sort of intuition that caused me to give you the doll. I propose you try a geographical.'

'Beg pardon?'

'It's a form of recovery often attempted by late-stage alcoholics. They hope that a change of location will give them a fresh start. Turn things around.'

I felt a flicker of something. I won't say it was hope, but it was something.

'It rarely works,' Kamen said. 'The old-timers in Alcoholics Anonymous, who have an answer for everything – it's their curse as well as their blessing, although very few ever realize it – like to say, "Put an asshole on a plane in Boston, an asshole gets off in Seattle."'

'So where does that leave me?' I asked.

15

'Right now it leaves you in suburban St Paul. What I'm suggesting is that you pick someplace far from here and go there. You're in a unique position to do so, given your financial situation and marital status.'

'For how long?'

'At least a year.' He looked at me inscrutably. His large face was made for such an expression; etched on King Tut's tomb, I believe it might have made even Howard Carter consider. 'And if you do anything at the end of that year, Edgar, for God's sake – no, for your *daughters'* sake – make it look good.'

He had nearly disappeared into the old sofa; now he began to struggle up again. I stepped forward to help him and he waved me away. He made it to his feet at last, wheezing more loudly than ever, and took up his briefcase. He looked down at me from his height of six and a half feet, those staring eyeballs with their yellowish corneas made even larger by his glasses, which had very thick lenses.

'Edgar, does anything make you happy?'

I considered the surface of this question (the only part that seemed safe) and said, 'I used to sketch.' It had actually been a little more than just sketching, but that was long ago. Since then, other things had intervened. Marriage, a career. Both of which were now going or gone.

'When?'

'As a kid.'

I thought of telling him I'd once dreamed of art school – had even bought the occasional book of reproductions when I could afford to – and then didn't. In the last thirty years, my contribution to the world of art had consisted of little more than doodles while taking telephone calls, and it had probably been ten years since I'd bought the sort of picture-book that belongs on a coffee table where it can impress your friends.

'Since then?'

I considered lying – didn't want to seem like a complete fixated drudge – but stuck to the truth. One-armed men should tell the truth whenever possible. Wireman doesn't say that; I do. 'No.'

'Take it up again,' Kamen advised. 'You need hedges.'

'Hedges,' I said, bemused.

'Yes, Edgar.' He looked surprised and a little disappointed, as if I had failed to understand a very simple concept. 'Hedges against the night.'

vi

A week or so later, Tom Riley came to see me again. By then the leaves had started to turn color, and I remember the clerks putting up Halloween posters in the Wal-Mart where I bought my first sketchpads since college . . . hell, maybe since high school.

What I remember most clearly about that visit is how embarrassed and ill-at-ease Tom seemed.

I offered him a beer and he took me up on it. When I came back from the kitchen, he was looking at a pen-and-ink I'd done – three palm trees silhouetted against an expanse of water, a bit of screened-in porch jutting into the left foreground. 'This is pretty good,' he said. 'You do this?'

'Nah, the elves. They come in the night. Cobble my shoes, draw the occasional picture.'

He laughed too hard and set the picture back down on the desk. 'Don't look much like Minnesota, dere,' he said, doing a Swedish accent.

'I copied it out of a book,' I said. I had actually used a photograph from a Realtor's brochure. It had been taken from the so-called 'Florida room' of Salmon Point, the place I had just leased for a year. I had never been in Florida, not even on vacation, but that picture had called to something deep in me, and for the first time since the accident, I felt actual anticipation. It was thin, but it was there. 'What can I do for you, Tom? If it's about the business—'

'Actually, Pam asked me to come out.' He ducked his head. 'I didn't much want to, but I didn't feel I could say no. Old times' sake, you know.'

'Sure.' Tom went back to the days when The Freemantle Company had been nothing but three pickup trucks, a Caterpillar D9, and a lot of big dreams. 'So talk to me. I'm not going to bite you.'

'She's got herself a lawyer. She's going ahead with this divorce business.'

'I never thought she wouldn't.' It was the truth. I still didn't

17

remember choking her, but I remembered the look in her eyes when she told me I had. And there was this: once Pam started down a road, she rarely turned around.

'She wants to know if you're going to be using Bozie.'

I had to smile at that. William Bozeman III was a dapper, manicured, bow-tie-wearing sixty-five, wheeldog of the Minneapolis lawfirm my company used, and if he knew Tom and I had been calling him Bozie for the last twenty years, he would probably have suffered an embolism.

'I hadn't thought about it. What's the deal, Tom? What exactly does she want?'

He drank off half his beer, then put the glass on a bookshelf beside my half-assed sketch. His cheeks had flushed a dull brick red. 'She said she hopes it doesn't have to be mean. She said, "I don't want to be rich, and I don't want a fight. I just want him to be fair to me and the girls, the way he always was, will you tell him that?" So I am.' He shrugged.

I got up, went to the big window between the living room and the porch, and looked out at the lake. Soon I would be able to go out into my very own 'Florida room', whatever that was, and look out at the Gulf of Mexico. I wondered if it would be any better, any different, than looking out at Lake Phalen. I thought I would settle for different, at least to begin with. Different would be a start. When I turned back, Tom Riley didn't look himself at all. At first I thought he was sick to his stomach, and then I realized he was struggling not to cry.

'Tom, what's the matter?' I asked.

He tried to speak and produced only a watery croak. He cleared his throat and tried again. 'Boss, I can't get used to seeing you this way, with just the one arm. I'm so sorry.'

It was artless, unrehearsed, and sweet: a straight shot to the heart. I think there was a moment when we were both close to bawling, like a couple of Sensitive Guys on *The Oprah Winfrey Show*.

That idea helped me get myself under control again. 'I'm sorry, too,' I said, 'but I'm getting along. Really. Now drink your damn beer before it goes flat.'

He laughed and poured the rest of his Grain Belt into the glass.

'I'm going to give you an offer to take back to her,' I said. 'If she likes it, we can hammer out the details. Do-it-yourself deal. No lawyers needed.'

'Are you serious, Eddie?'

'I am. You do a comprehensive accounting so we have a bottom-line figure to work with. We divide the swag into four shares. She takes three – seventy-five per cent – for her and the girls. I take the rest. The divorce itself . . . hey, Minnesota's a no-fault state, after lunch we can go out to Borders and buy *Divorce for Dummies*.'

He looked dazed. 'Is there such a book?'

'I haven't researched it, but if there isn't, I'll eat your shirts.'

'I think the saying's "eat my shorts".'

'Isn't that what I said?'

'Never mind. Eddie, that kind of deal is going to trash the estate.'

'Ask me if I give a shit. Or a shirt, for that matter. I still care about the company, and the company is fine, intact and being run by people who know what they're doing. As for the estate, all I'm proposing is that we dispense with the ego that usually allows the lawyers to swallow the cream. There's plenty for all of us, if we're reasonable.'

He finished his beer, never taking his eyes off me. 'Sometimes I wonder if you're the same man I used to work for,' he said.

'That man died in his pickup,' I said.

vii

Pam took the deal, and I think she might have taken me again instead of the deal if I'd offered – it was a look that came and went on her face like sunshine through clouds when we had our lunch to discuss the details – but I didn't offer. I had Florida on my mind, that refuge of the newly wed and the nearly dead. And I think in her heart of hearts, even Pam knew it was for the best – knew that the man who had been pulled out of his ruined Dodge Ram with his steel hardhat crushed around his ears like a crumpled pet-food can wasn't the same guy who'd gotten in. The life with Pam and the girls and the construction company was over; there were no other rooms in it to explore. There were, however, doors. The one marked SUICIDE was currently a bad option, as Dr Kamen had pointed out. That left the one marked DUMA KEY.

19

One other thing occurred in my other life before I slipped through that door, though. It was what happened to Monica Goldstein's Jack Russell Terrier, Gandalf.

viii

If you've been picturing my convalescent retreat as a lakeside cottage standing in splendid isolation at the end of a lonely dirt road in the north woods, you better think again – we're talking your basic suburbia. Our place by the lake stood at the end of Aster Lane, a paved street running from East Hoyt Avenue to the water. Our closest neighbors were the Goldsteins.

In the middle of October, I finally took Kathi Green's advice and began to walk. These were not the Great Beach Walks I took later, and I came back from even these short outings with my bad hip crying for mercy (and more than once with tears standing in my eyes), but they were steps in the right direction. I was returning from one of these walks when Mrs Fevereau hit Monica's dog.

I was three-quarters of the way home when the Fevereau woman went past me in her ridiculous mustard-colored Hummer. As always, she had her cell phone in one hand and a cigarette in the other; as always she was going too fast. I barely noticed, and I certainly didn't see Gandalf dash into the street up ahead, concentrating only on Monica, coming down the other side of the street in Full Girl Scout. I was concentrating on my reconstructed hip. As always near the end of my short strolls, this so-called medical marvel felt packed with roughly ten thousand tiny points of broken glass.

Then tires yowled, and a little girl's scream joined them: '*GANDALF, NO!*'

For a moment I had a clear and unearthly vision of the crane that had almost killed me, the world I'd always lived in suddenly eaten up by a yellow much brighter than Mrs Fevereau's Hummer, and black letters floating in it, swelling, getting larger: **LINK-BELT**.

Then Gandalf began to scream, too, and the flashback – what Dr Kamen would have called *a recovered memory*, I suppose – was gone. Until that afternoon in October four years ago, I hadn't known dogs *could* scream.

20

I broke into a lurching, crabwise run, pounding the sidewalk with my red crutch. I'm sure it would have appeared ludicrous to an onlooker, but no one was paying any attention to me. Monica Goldstein was kneeling in the middle of the street beside her dog, which lay in front of the Hummer's high, boxy grille. Her face was white above her forest-green uniform, from which a sash of badges and medals hung. The end of this sash was soaking in a spreading pool of Gandalf's blood.

Mrs Fevereau half-jumped and half-fell from the Hummer's ridiculously high driver's seat. Ava Goldstein came running from the front door of the Goldstein house, crying her daughter's name. Mrs Goldstein's blouse was half-buttoned. Her feet were bare.

'Don't touch him, honey, don't touch him,' Mrs Fevereau said. She was still holding her cigarette and she puffed nervously at it.

Monica paid no attention. She stroked Gandalf's side. The dog screamed again when she did – it *was* a scream – and Monica covered her eyes with the heels of her hands. She began to shake her head. I didn't blame her.

Mrs Fevereau reached out for the girl, but changed her mind. She took two steps back, leaned against the high side of her Hummer, and looked up at the sky.

Mrs Goldstein knelt beside her daughter. 'Honey, oh honey please don't.'

Gandalf lay in the street, in a pool of his spreading blood, howling. And now I could also remember the sound the crane had made. Not the *meep-meep-meep* it was supposed to make (its backup warning had been broken), but the juddering stutter of its diesel engine and the sound of its treads eating up the earth.

'Get her inside, Ava,' I said. 'Get her in the house.'

Mrs Goldstein got an arm around her daughter's shoulders and urged her up. 'Come on, honey. Come inside.'

'Not without *Gandalf*!' Monica was eleven, and mature for her age, but in those moments she had regressed to three. 'Not without my *doggy*!' Her sash, the last three inches now sodden with blood, *thwapped* against the side of her skirt and a long line of blood spattered down her calf.

'Monica, go in and call the vet,' I told her. 'Say Gandalf's been hit by a car. Say he has to come right away. I'll stay with your dog while you do.'

Monica looked at me with eyes that were more than grief-stricken, more than shocked. They were crazy. I knew that look well. I'd seen it often in my own mirror. 'Do you promise? Big swear? Mother's name?'

'Big swear, mother's name. Go on.'

She went with her mother, casting one more look back over her shoulder and uttering one more bereft wail before starting up the steps to her house. I knelt beside Gandalf, holding onto the Hummer's fender and going down as I always did, painfully and listing severely to the left, trying to keep my right knee from bending any more than it absolutely had to. Still, I voiced my own little cry of pain, and I wondered if I'd be able to get up again without help. It might not be forthcoming from Mrs Fevereau; she walked over to the left-hand side of the street with her legs stiff and wide apart, then bent at the waist as if bowing to royalty, and vomited in the gutter. She held the hand with the cigarette in it off to one side as she did it.

I turned my attention to Gandalf. He had been struck in the hindquarters. His spine was crushed. Blood and shit oozed sluggishly from between his broken rear legs. His eyes turned up to me and in them I saw a horrible expression of hope. His tongue crept out and licked my inner left wrist. His tongue was dry as carpet, and cold. Gandalf was going to die, but maybe not soon enough. Monica would come out again soon, and I didn't want him alive to lick her wrist when she did.

I understood what I had to do. There was no one to see me do it. Monica and her mother were inside. Mrs Fevereau's back was still turned. If others on this little stub of street had come to their windows (or out on their lawns), the Hummer blocked their view of me sitting beside the dog with my bad right leg awkwardly outstretched. I had a few moments, but only a few, and if I stopped to think about what I was doing, my chance would be lost.

So I took Gandalf's upper body in my arms and without a pause I'm back at the Sutton Avenue site, where The Freemantle Company is getting ready to build a forty-story bank building. I'm in my pickup truck. Reba McEntire's on the radio, singing 'Fancy'. I suddenly realize the crane's too loud even though I haven't heard any backup beeper and when I look to my right the part of the world that should be in that window is gone. The world on that side has been replaced by yellow. Black letters float there: **LINK-BELT**. They're swelling. I spin the Ram's wheel to the left, all the way to the stop, knowing I'm too late. The scream of crumpling metal starts, drowning out the radio and shrinking the inside of the cab right to left because the crane's invading my space, *stealing* my space, and the pickup is tipping. I'm trying for the driver's-side door, but it's no good. I should have done that right away but it got too late real early. The world in front of me disappears as the windshield turns to frozen milk shot through with a million cracks. Then the building site is back and still turning on an axle as the windshield pops out. Pops out? It *flies* out bent in the middle like a playing-card, and I'm laying on the horn with the points of both elbows, my right arm doing its last job. I can barely hear the horn over the crane's engine. **LINK-BELT** is still moving in, pushing the passenger door, closing the passenger-side footwell, splintering the dashboard in tectonic chunks of plastic. The shit from the glove-compartment floats around, the radio goes dead, my lunchbucket is tanging against my clipboard, and here comes **LINK-BELT. LINK-BELT** is right on top of me, I could stick out my tongue and lick the fucking hyphen. I start screaming because that's when the pressure starts. The pressure is my right arm first pushing against my side, then spreading, then splitting open. Blood douses my lap like a bucket of hot water and I hear something breaking. Probably my ribs. It sounds like chicken-bones under a boot-heel.

I held Gandalf against me and thought *Bring the friend, sit in the friend, sit in the fucking PAL, you dump bitch!*

And now I'm sitting in the chum, sitting in the fucking *pal*, it's at home but home doesn't feel like home with all the clocks of Europe ringing inside my cracked head and I can't remember the name of the doll Kamen gave me, all I can remember is boy names: Randall, Russell, Rudolph, River-fucking-Phoenix. I tell her to leave me alone when she comes in with the fruit and the fucking college cheese, I tell her I need five minutes. *I can do this*, I say, because it's the phrase Kamen gave me, it's the out, it's the *meep-meep-meep* that says watch it, Pammy, Edgar's backing up. But instead of leaving she takes the napkin from the tray to wipe the fret off my forehead and while she's doing that I grab her by the throat because in that moment it seems to me it's her fault I can't remember my doll's name, *everything* is her fault, including **LINK-BELT**. I grab her with my good left hand. For a few seconds I want to kill her, and who knows, maybe I try. What I do know is I'd rather remember all the accidents in this round world than the look in her eyes as she struggles in my grip. Then I think *It was RED!* and let her go.

I held Gandalf against my chest as I had once held my infant daughters and thought, *I can do this. I can do this. I can do this.* I felt Gandalf's blood soak through my pants like hot water and thought, *Go on, you sad fuck, get out of Dodge.*

I held Gandalf and thought of how it felt to be crushed alive as the cab of your truck eats the air around you and the breath leaves your body and the blood blows out of your nose and those snapping sounds as consciousness flees, those are the bones breaking inside your own body: your ribs, your arm, your hip, your leg, your cheek, your fucking skull.

I held Monica's dog and thought, in a kind of miserable triumph: *It was RED!*

For a moment I was in a darkness shot with that red; then I opened my eyes. I was clutching Gandalf to my chest with my left arm, and his eyes were staring up at my face—

No, past it. And past the sky.

'Mr Freemantle?' It was John Hastings, the old guy who lived two houses up from the Goldsteins. In his English tweed cap and sleeveless sweater, he looked ready for a hike on the Scottish moors. Except, that was, for the expression of dismay on his face. 'Edgar? You can let him go now. That dog is dead.'

'Yes,' I said, relaxing my grip on Gandalf. 'Would you help me get up?'

'I'm not sure I can,' John said. 'I'd be more apt to pull us both down.'

'Then go in and see if the Goldsteins are okay,' I said.

'It is her dog,' he said. 'I was hoping . . .' He shook his head.

'It's hers,' I said. 'And I don't want her to come out and see him like this.'

'Of course, but—'

'I'll help him,' Mrs Fevereau said. She looked a little better, and she had ditched the cigarette. She reached for my right armpit, then hesitated. 'Will that hurt you?'

It would, but far less than staying the way I was, so I told her no. As John went up the Goldsteins' walk, I got a grip on the Hummer's bumper. Together we managed to get me back on my feet.

'I don't suppose you've got anything to cover the dog with?'

'As a matter of fact, there's a rug remnant in the back.'

'Good. Great.'

She started around to the rear – it would be a long trek, given the Hummer's size – then turned back. 'Thank God it died before the little girl got back.'

'Yes,' I said. 'Thank God.'

ix

It wasn't far back to my cottage at the end of the lane, but getting there was a slow chug just the same. By the time I arrived, I had developed the ache in my hand that I thought of as Crutch Fist, and Gandalf's blood was stiffening on my shirt. There was a card tucked in between the screen and the jamb of the front door. I pulled it out. Below a smiling girl giving the Girl Scout salute was this message:

A FRIEND FROM THE NEIGHBORHOOD CAME
TO SEE YOU WITH NEWS OF DELICIOUS GIRL
SCOUT COOKIES!
ALTHOUGH SHE DIDN'T FIND YOU IN TODAY,
Monica WILL CALL AGAIN!
SEE YOU SOON!

Monica had dotted the *i* in her name with a smiley-face. I crumpled the card up and tossed it into the wastebasket as I limped to the shower. My shirt, jeans, and blood-spotted underwear I tossed into the trash. I never wanted to see them again.

25

x

My two-year-old Lexus was in the driveway, but I hadn't been behind the wheel of a vehicle since the day of my accident. A kid from the nearby juco ran errands for me three days a week. Kathi Green was also willing to swing by the closest supermarket if I asked her, or take me to Blockbuster before one of our little torture sessions (afterward I was always too wiped out). If you had told me I'd be driving again that fall, I would have laughed. It wasn't my bad leg; the very idea of driving put me in a cold sweat.

But not long after my shower, that's what I was doing: sliding behind the wheel, keying the ignition, and looking over my right shoulder as I backed down the driveway. I had taken four of the little pink Oxycontin pills instead of the usual two, and was gambling they'd get me to and from the Stop & Shop near the intersection of East Hoyt and Eastshore Drive without freaking out or killing anyone.

I didn't tarry at the supermarket. It wasn't grocery shopping at all in the normal sense, just a quick bombing-run – one stop at the meat-case followed by a limping jaunt through the ten-items-or-less express lane, no coupons, nothing to declare. Still, by the time I got back to Aster Lane I was officially stoned. If a cop had stopped me, I never would have passed a field sobriety test.

None did. I passed the Goldsteins' house, where there were four cars in the driveway, at least half a dozen more parked at the curb, and lights streaming from every window. Monica's mom had called for backup on the chicken-soup hotline, and it looked like plenty of relatives had responded. Good for them. And good for Monica.

Less than a minute later I was turning in to my own driveway. In spite of the medication, my right leg throbbed from switching back and forth between the gas and the brake, and I had a headache – a plain old-fashioned tension headache. My main problem, however, was hunger. It was what had driven me out in the first place. Only hunger was too mild a word for what I was feeling. I was ravenous, and the leftover lasagna in the fridge wouldn't do. There was meat in it, but not enough.

I lurched into the house on my crutch, head swimming from the Oxycontin, got a frypan from the drawer under the stove, and slung

26

it onto one of the burners. I turned the dial to HIGH, barely hearing the *flump* of igniting gas. I was too busy tearing the plastic wrap from a package of ground sirloin. I threw it in the frypan and mashed it flat with the palm of my hand before scrabbling a spatula out of the drawer beside the stove.

Coming back into the house, shucking my clothes and climbing into the shower, I'd been able to mistake the flutters in my stomach for nausea – it seemed like a reasonable explanation. By the time I was rinsing away the soap, though, the flutters had settled into a steady low rumble like the idle of a powerful motor. The drugs had damped it down a little bit, but now it was back, worse than ever. If I'd ever been this hungry in my life, I couldn't remember when.

I flipped the grotesquely large meat-patty and tried to count to thirty. I figured a thirty-count on high heat would be at least a nod in the direction of what people mean when they say 'cooking meat'. If I'd thought to flip on the fan and vent the aroma, I might have made it. As it was, I didn't even get to twenty. At seventeen I snatched a paper plate, flipped the hamburger onto it, and wolfed the half-raw ground beef while I leaned against the cabinet. About halfway through I saw the red juice seeping out of the red meat and got a momentary but brilliant picture of Gandalf looking up at me while blood and shit oozed from the wrecked remains of his hindquarters, matting the fur on his broken rear legs. My stomach didn't so much as quiver, just cried impatiently for more food. I was hungry.

Hungry.

xi

That night I dreamed I was in the bedroom I had shared for so many years with Pam. She was asleep beside me and couldn't hear the croaking voice coming from somewhere below in the darkened house: '*Newly wed, nearly dead, newly wed, nearly dead.*' It sounded like some mechanical device stuck in a groove. I shook my wife but she just turned over. Turned away from me. Dreams mostly tell the truth, don't they?

I got up and went downstairs, holding the banister to compensate for my bad leg. And there was something odd about how I was

27

holding that familiar length of polished rail. As I approached the bottom of the staircase, I realized what it was. Fair or not, it's a rightie's world – guitars are made for righties, and school desks, and the control panels on American cars. The banister of the house I'd lived in with my family was no exception; it was on the right because, although my company had built the house from my plans, my wife and both our daughters were right-handers, and majority rules.

But still, my hand was trailing down the banister.

Of course, I thought. *Because it's a dream. Just like this afternoon. You know?*

Gandalf was no dream, I thought back, and the voice of the stranger in my house – closer than ever – repeated 'Newly wed, nearly dead' over and over. Whoever it was, the person was in the living room. I didn't want to go in there.

No, Gandalf was no dream, I thought. Maybe it was my phantom right hand having these thoughts. *The dream was killing him.*

Had he died on his own, then? Was that what the voice was trying to tell me? Because I didn't think Gandalf had died on his own. I thought he had needed help.

I went into my old living room. I wasn't conscious of moving my feet; I went in the way you move in dreams, as if it's really the world moving around you, streaming backward like some extravagant trick of projection. And there, sitting in Pam's old Boston rocker, was Reba the Anger-Management Doll, now grown to the size of an actual child. Her feet, clad in black Mary Janes, swung back and forth just above the floor at the end of horrible boneless pink legs. Her shallow eyes stared at me. Her lifeless strawberry curls bounced back and forth. Her mouth was smeared with blood, and in my dream I knew it wasn't human blood or dog's blood but the stuff that had oozed out of my mostly raw hamburger – the stuff I had licked off the paper plate when the meat was gone.

The bad frog chased us! Reba cried. *It has TEEF!*

xii

That word – *TEEF!* – was still ringing in my head when I sat up with a cold puddle of October moonlight in my lap. I was trying

28

to scream and producing only a series of silent gasps. My heart was thundering. I reached for the bedside lamp and mercifully avoided knocking it on the floor, although once it was on, I saw that I'd pushed the base halfway out over the drop. The clock-radio claimed it was 3:19 a.m.

I swung my legs out of bed and reached for the phone. *If you really need me, call me,* Kamen had said. *Any time, day or night.* And if his number had been in the bedroom phone's memory, I probably would've. But as reality re-asserted itself – the cottage by Lake Phalen, not the house in Mendota Heights, no croaking voice downstairs – the urge passed.

Reba the Anger-Management Doll in the Boston rocker, and grown to the size of an actual child. Well, why not? I *had* been angry, although at Mrs Fevereau rather than at poor Gandalf, and I had no idea what toothy frogs had to do with the price of beans in Boston. The real question, it seemed to me, was about Monica's dog. Had I killed Gandalf, or had he just expired?

Or maybe the question was why I'd been so hungry afterward. Maybe that was the question.

So hungry for meat.

'I took him in my arms,' I whispered.

Your arm, you mean, because now one is all you've got. Your good left.

But my memory was taking him in my *arms*, plural. Channeling my anger

(*it was RED*)

away from that foolish woman with her cigarette and cell phone and somehow back into *myself,* in some kind of crazy closed loop . . . taking him in my arms . . . surely a hallucination, but yes, that was my memory.

Taking him in my *arms.*

Cradling his neck with my left elbow so I could strangle him with my right hand.

Strangle him and put him out of his misery.

I slept shirtless, so it was easy to look at my stump. I only had to turn my head. I could wiggle it, but not much more. I did that a couple of times, and then I looked up at the ceiling. My heartbeat was slowing a little.

'The dog died of his injuries,' I said. 'And shock. An autopsy would confirm that.'

Except no one did autopsies on dogs that died after being crushed to bones and jelly by Hummers driven by careless, distracted women.

I looked at the ceiling and I wished this life was over. This unhappy life that had started out so confidently. I thought I would sleep no more that night, but eventually I did. In the end we always wear out our worries.

That's what Wireman says.

How to Draw a Picture (II)

Remember that the truth is in the details. No matter how you see the world or what style it imposes on your work as an artist, the truth is in the details. Of course the devil's there, too — everyone says so — but maybe truth and the devil are words for the same thing. It could be, you know.

Imagine that baby girl again, the one who fell from the carriage. She struck the right side of her head, but it was the left side of her brain that suffered the worst insult — contracoup, remember? The left side is where Broca's area is — not that anyone knew that in the 1920s. Broca's area processes language. Smack it hard enough and you lose your language, sometimes for a little while, sometimes forever. But — although they are closely related — saying is not seeing.

The little girl still sees.

She sees her five sisters. Their dresses. How their hair is crazy-combed by the wind when they come in from outside. She sees her father's mustache, now threaded with gray. She sees Nan Melda — not just the housekeeper but the closest thing to a mother this little girl knows. She sees the scarf Nanny wraps around her head when she cleans; she sees the knot in the front, at the very top of Nan Melda's high brown forehead; she sees Nan Melda's silver bracelets, and how they flash starpoints in the sunshine that falls through the windows.

Details, details, the truth is in the details.

And does seeing cry out to saying, even in a damaged mind? A wounded brain? Oh, it must, it must.

She thinks My head hurts.

She thinks Something bad happened, and I don't know who I am. Or where I am. Or what all these bright surrounding images are.

She thinks Libbit? Is my name Libbit? I used to know. I could talk in the used-to-know, but now my words are like fish in the water. I want the man with the hair on his lip.

She thinks That's my Daddy, but when I try to say his name I call

31

'Ird! Ird!' instead, because one flies past my window. I see every feather. I see its eye like glass. I see its leg, how it bends like broke, and that word is *crookit*. My head hurts.

Girls come in. Maria and Hannah come in. She doesn't like them the way she likes the twins. The twins are little, like her.

She thinks I called Maria and Hannah the Big Meanies in the used-to-know *and realizes she knows again. It's another thing that's come back. The name for another detail. She will forget again, but the next time she remembers, she will remember longer. She's almost sure of it.*

She thinks When I try to say Hannah I say 'Ird! Ird!' When I try to say Maria I say 'Wee! Wee!' And they laugh, those meanies. I cry. I want my Daddy and can't remember how to say him; that word is gone again. Words like birds, they fly and fly and fly away. My sisters talk. Talk, talk, talk. My throat is dry. I try to say thirsty. I say 'First! First!' But they only laugh, those meanies. I'm under the bandage, smelling the iodine, smelly the sweaty, listening to them laugh. I scream at them, scream loud, and they run away. Nan Melda comes, her head all red because her hair is wrapped in the snarf. Her roundies flash flash flash in the sun and you call those roundies *bracelets*. I say 'First, first!' and Nan Melda doesn't know. So then I say 'Ass! Ass!' and Nan makes me go potty even though I don't need to go potty. I'm on the potty and see and point. 'Ass! Ass!' Daddy comes in. 'What's this shouting about?' with all white bubbles on his face except for one smoothie. That's where he slid the thing that makes the hair go away. He sees how I point. He understands. 'Why she is thirsty.' Fills up the glass. The room is full of sunny. Dust floats in the sunny and his hand goes through the sunny with the glass and you call that pretty. I drink every drink. I cry more afterwards, but from better. He kiss me kiss me kiss me, hug me hug me hug me, and I try to say him – 'Daddy!' – and still can't. Then I think around sideways to his name, and John is there, so I think that in my mind and while I think John I 'Daddy!' out my mouth and he hug me hug me some more.

She thinks Daddy is my first word on this side of the bad thing. *The truth is in the details.*

2 – Big Pink

i

Kamen's geographical worked, but when it came to fixing what was wrong with my head, I think the Florida part was coincidental. It's true that I lived there, but I never really *lived* there. No, Kamen's geographical worked because of Duma Key, and Big Pink. For me, those places came to constitute their own world.

I left St Paul on November tenth with hope in my heart but no real expectations. Kathi Green the Rehab Queen came to see me off. She kissed me on the mouth, hugged me hard, and whispered 'May all your dreams come true, Eddie.'

'Thanks, Kathi,' I said. I was touched even though the dream I fixed on was of Reba the Anger-Management Doll, grown to the size of an actual child, sitting in the moonlit living room of the house I'd shared with Pam. *That* dream coming true I could live without.

'And send me a picture from Disney World. I long to see you in mouse ears.'

'I will,' I said, but I never got to Disney World. Sea World, Busch Gardens, or Daytona Speedway, either.

When I left St Paul, flying in a Lear 55 (successful retirement has its privileges), it was twenty-four and spitting the first snowflakes of another long northern winter. When I landed in Sarasota it was eighty-five and sunny. Even crossing the tarmac to the private air terminal, still clumping along on my trusty red crutch, I thought I could feel my hip saying thank you.

When I look back on that time, it's with the strangest stew of emotions: love, longing, terror, horror, regret, and the deep sweetness only those who've been near death can know. I think it's how Adam and Eve must have felt. Surely they looked back at Eden, don't you think, as they started barefoot down the path to where

33

we are now, in our glum political world of bullets and bombs and satellite TV? Looked past the angel guarding the shut gate with his fiery sword? Sure. I think they must have wanted one more look at the green world they had lost, with its sweet water and kind-hearted animals. And its snake, of course.

ii

There's a charm-bracelet of keys lying off the west coast of Florida. If you had your seven-league boots on, you could step from Longboat to Lido, from Lido to Siesta, from Siesta to Casey. The next step takes you to Duma Key, nine miles long and half a mile wide at its widest, between Casey Key and Don Pedro Island. Most of it's un-inhabited, a tangle of banyans, palms, and Australian pines with an uneven, dune-rumpled beach running along the Gulf edge. The beach is guarded by a waist-high band of sea oats. 'The sea oats belong,' Wireman once told me, 'but the rest of that shit has no business growing without irrigation.' For much of the time I spent on Duma Key, no one lived there but Wireman, the Bride of the Godfather, and me.

Sandy Smith was my Realtor in St Paul. I had asked her to find me a place that was quiet – I'm not sure I used the word *isolated*, but I may have – but still within reach of services. Thinking of Kamen's advice, I told Sandy I wanted to lease for a year, and price wasn't an object, as long as I wasn't getting skint too bad. Even depressed and in more or less constant pain, I was averse to being taken advantage of. Sandy fed my requirements into her computer, and Big Pink was what came out. It was just the luck of the draw.

Except I don't really believe that. Because even my earliest pictures seem to have, I don't know, something.

Something.

iii

On the day I arrived in my rental car (driven by Jack Cantori, the young man Sandy Smith had hired through a Sarasota employment agency), I knew nothing about the history of Duma Key. I only knew one reached it by crossing a WPA-era drawbridge from Casey Key. Once over this bridge, I observed that the northern tip of the island was free of the vegetation that tangled the rest. Instead there was actual landscaping (in Florida this means palms and grass undergoing nearly constant irrigation). I could see half a dozen houses strung along the narrow, patchy band of road leading south, the last one of them a huge and undeniably elegant hacienda.

And close by, less than a football field's length from the Duma Key end of the drawbridge, I could see a pink house hanging over the Gulf.

'Is that it?' I asked, thinking *Please let that be it. That's the one I want.* 'It is, isn't it?'

'I don't know, Mr Freemantle,' Jack said. 'I know Sarasota, but this is the first time I've ever been on Duma. Never had any reason to come here.' He pulled up to the mailbox, which had a big red **13** on it. He glanced at the folder lying between us on the seat. 'This is it, all right. Salmon Point, number thirteen. I hope you're not superstitious.'

I shook my head, not taking my eyes off it. I didn't worry about broken mirrors or crossing black cats' paths, but I'm very much a believer in . . . well, maybe not love at first sight, that's a little too Rhett-and-Scarlett for me, but instant attraction? Sure. It's the way I felt about Pam the first time I met her, on a double date (she was with the other guy). And it's the way I felt about Big Pink from the very first.

She stood on pilings with her chin jutting over the high-tide line. There was a NO TRESPASSING sign slanting askew on an old gray stick beside the driveway, but I guessed that didn't apply to me. 'Once you sign the lease, you have it for a year,' Sandy told me. 'Even if it's sold, the owner can't kick you out until your time is up.'

Jack drove slowly up to the back door . . . only with its face hanging over the Gulf of Mexico, that was the only door. 'I'm surprised they were ever allowed to build this far out,' he said. 'I suppose they did things different in the old days.' To him the old days probably meant the nineteen-eighties. 'There's your car. Hope it's okay.'

The car drawn up on the square of cracked pavement to the

right of the house was the sort of anonymous American mid-size the rental companies specialize in. I hadn't driven since the day Mrs Fevereau hit Gandalf, and barely gave it a glance. I was more interested in the boxy pink elephant I'd rented. 'Aren't there ordinances about building too close to the Gulf of Mexico?'

'Now, sure, but not when this place went up. From a practical standpoint, it's all about beach erosion. I doubt if this place hung out that way when it was built.'

He was undoubtedly right. I thought I could see at least six feet of the pilings supporting the screened porch – the so-called Florida room. Unless those pilings were sunk sixty feet into the underlying bedrock, eventually the place was going into the Gulf of Mexico. It was only a matter of time.

As I was thinking it, Jack Cantori was saying it. Then he grinned. 'Don't worry, though; I'm sure you'll get plenty of warning. You'll hear it groaning.'

'Like the House of Usher,' I said.

His grin widened. 'But it's probably good for another five years or so. Otherwise it'd be condemned.'

'Don't be so sure,' I said. Jack had reversed to the driveway door, so the trunk would be easy to unload. Not a lot in there; three suitcases, one garment bag, a steel hardcase with my laptop inside, and a knapsack containing some primitive art supplies – mostly pads and colored pencils. I traveled light when I left my other life. I figured what I'd need most in my new one was my checkbook and my American Express card.

'What do you mean?' he asked.

'Someone who could afford to build here in the first place could probably talk a couple of B-and-C inspectors around.'

'B-and-C? What's that?'

For a moment I couldn't tell him. I could *see* what I meant: men in white shirts and ties, wearing yellow hi-impact plastic hardhats on their heads and carrying clipboards in their hands. I could even see the pens in their shirt pockets, and the plastic pocket-protectors to which they were clipped. The devil's in the details, right? But I couldn't think of what B-and-C stood for, although I knew it as well as my own name. And instantly I was furious. Instantly it seemed that making my left hand into a fist and driving it sideways into the unprotected Adam's apple of the young man sitting beside me was the most reasonable thing in the world. Almost imperative. Because it was his question that had hung me up.

'Mr Freemantle?'

'Just a sec,' I said, and thought: *I can do this.*

I thought of Don Field, the guy who had inspected at least half of my buildings in the nineties (or so it seemed), and my mind did its crosspatch thing. I realized I'd been sitting bolt upright, my hands clenched in my lap. I could see why the kid had sounded concerned. I looked like a man having a gastric episode. Or a heart attack.

'Sorry,' I said. 'I had an accident. Banged my head. Sometimes my mind stutters.'

'Don't worry about it,' Jack said. 'No biggie.'

'B-and-C is Building and Code. Basically they're the guys who decide if your building is going to fall down or not.'

'You talking about bribes?' My new young employee looked glum. 'Well, I'm sure it happens, especially down here. Money talks.'

'Don't be so cynical. Sometimes it's just a matter of friendship. Your builders, your contractors, your building-code inspectors, even your OSHA guys . . . they usually drink in the same bars, and they all went to the same schools.' I laughed. 'Reform schools, in some cases.'

Jack said, 'They condemned a couple beach houses at the north end of Casey Key when the erosion there sped up. One of em actually *did* fall into the drink.'

'Well, as you say, I'll probably hear it groaning, and it looks safe enough for the time being. Let's get my stuff inside.'

I opened my door, got out, then staggered as my bad hip locked up. If I hadn't gotten my crutch planted in time, I would have said hello to Big Pink by sprawling on her stone doorstep.

'*I'll* get the stuff in,' Jack said. 'You better go in and sit down, Mr Freemantle. A cold drink wouldn't hurt, either. You look really tired.'

iv

The traveling had caught up with me, and I was more than tired. By the time I eased into a living room armchair (listing to the left, as usual, and trying to keep my right leg as straight as possible), I was willing to admit to myself that I was exhausted.

Yet not homesick, at least not yet. As Jack went back and forth, stowing my bags in the bigger of the two bedrooms and putting the laptop on the desk in the smaller one, my eye kept being drawn to the living room's western wall, which was all glass, and the Florida room beyond it, and the Gulf of Mexico beyond that. It was a vast blue expanse, flat as a plate on that hot November afternoon, and even with the sliding glass window-wall shut, I could hear its mild and steady sighing. I thought, *It has no memory.* It was an odd thought, and strangely optimistic. When it came to memory – and anger – I still had my issues.

Jack came back from the guest room and sat on the arm of the couch – the perch, I thought, of a young man who wants to be gone. 'You've got all your basic staples,' he said, 'plus salad-in-a-bag, hamburger, and one of those cooked chickens in a plastic capsule – we call em Astronaut Chickens at my house. I hope that's okay with you.'

'Fine.'

'Two per cent milk—'

'Also fine.'

'—and Half-n-Half. I can get you real cream next time, if you want it.'

'You want to clog my one remaining artery?'

He laughed. 'There's a little pantry with all kinds of canned shi . . . stuff. The cable's hooked up, the computer's Internet-ready – I got you WiFi, costs a little extra, but it's way cool – and I can get satellite installed if you want it.'

I shook my head. He was a good kid, but I wanted to listen to the Gulf, sweet-talking me with words it wouldn't remember a minute later. And I wanted to listen to the house, see if it had anything to say. I had an idea maybe it did.

'The keys're in an envelope on the kitchen table – car keys, too – and a list of numbers you might need are on the fridge. I've got classes at FSU in Sarasota every day except Monday, but I'll be carrying my cell, and I'll be coming by Tuesdays and Thursdays at five unless we make a different arrangement. Is that okay?'

'Yes.' I reached in my pocket and brought out my money-clip. 'I want to give you a little extra. You've been great.'

He waved it away. 'Nah. This is a sweet gig, Mr Freemantle. Good pay and good hours. I'd feel like a hound taking any extra.'

That made me laugh, and I put my dough back in my pocket. 'Okay.'

'Maybe you ought to take a nap,' he said, getting up.

'Maybe I will.' It was odd to be treated like Grandpa Walton, but I supposed I'd better get used to it. 'What happened to the other house at the north end of Casey Key?'

'Huh?'

'You said one went into the drink. What happened to the other one?'

'Far as I know, it's still there. Although if a big storm like Charley ever hits this part of the coast dead-on, it's gonna be like a going-out-of-business sale: everything must go.' He walked over to me, and stuck out his hand. 'Anyway, Mr Freemantle, welcome to Florida. I hope it treats you real well.'

I shook with him. 'Thank you . . .' I hesitated, probably not long enough for him to notice, and I didn't get angry. Not at him, anyway. 'Thanks for everything.'

'Sure.' He gave me the smallest of puzzled looks as he went out, so maybe he did notice. Maybe he did notice, at that. I didn't care. I was on my own at last. I listened to shells and gravel popping under his tires as his car started to roll. I listened to the motor fade. Less, least, gone. Now there was only the mild steady sighing of the Gulf. And the beat of my own heart, soft and low. No clocks. Not ringing, not bonging, not even ticking. I breathed deep and smelled the musty, slightly damp aroma of a place that's been shut up for a fairly long time except for the weekly (or bi-weekly) ritual airing. I thought I could also smell salt and subtropical grasses for which I as yet had no names.

Mostly I listened to the sigh of the waves, so like the breath of some large sleeping creature, and looked out through the glass wall that fronted on the water. Because of Big Pink's elevation, I couldn't see the beach at all from where I was sitting, fairly deep in the living room; from my armchair I might have been on one of those big tankers that trudge their oily courses from Venezuela to Galveston. A high haze had crept over the dome of the sky, muting the pinpricks of light on the water. To the left were three palm trees silhouetted against the sky, their fronds ruffling in the mildest of breezes: the subjects of my first tentative post-accident sketch. *Don't look much like Minnesota, dere,* Tom Riley had said.

Looking at them made me want to draw again – it was like a dry hunger, but not precisely in the belly; it made my mind itch. And, oddly, the stump of my amputated arm. 'Not now,' I said. 'Later. I'm whipped.'

I heaved myself out of the chair on my second try, glad the kid wasn't there to see the first backward flop and hear my childish ('Cunt-*licker!*') cry of exasperation. Once I was up I stood swaying on my crutch for a moment, marveling at just how tired I was. Usually 'whipped' was just something you said, but at that moment it was exactly how I felt.

Moving slowly – I had no intention of falling in here on my first day – I made my way into the master bedroom. The bed was a king, and I wanted nothing more than to go to it, sit on it, sweep the foolish decorative throw-pillows (one bearing the likenessness of two cavorting Cockers and the rather startling idea that MAYBE DOGS ARE ONLY PEOPLE AT THEIR BEST) to the floor with my crutch, lie down, and sleep for two hours. Maybe three. But first I went to the bench at the end of the bed – still moving carefully, knowing how very easy it would be to tangle my feet and fall when I was at this level of exhaustion – where the kid had stacked two of my three suitcases. The one I wanted was on the bottom, of course. I shoved the one on top to the floor without hesitation and unzipped the front pocket of the other.

Glassy blue eyes looked out with their expression of eternal disapproving surprise: *Oouuu, you nasty man! I been in here all this time!* A fluff of lifeless orange-red hair sprang from confinement. Reba the Anger-Management Doll in her best blue dress and black Mary Janes.

I lay on the bed with her crooked between my stump and my side. When I had made an adequate space for myself among the ornamental pillows (it was mostly the cavorting Cockers I'd wanted on the floor), I laid her beside me.

'I forgot his name,' I said. 'I remembered it the whole way out here, then forgot it.' Reba looked up at the ceiling, where the blades of the overhead fan were still and unmoving. I'd forgotten to turn it on. Reba didn't care if my new part-time hired man was Ike, Mike, or Andy Van Slyke. It was all the same to her, she was just rags stuffed into a pink body, probably by some unhappy child laborer in Cambodia or fucking Uruguay.

'What is it?' I asked her. Tired as I was, I could feel the old dismal panic setting in. The old dismal anger. The fear that this would go on for the rest of my life. Or get worse! Yes, possible! They'd take me back into the convalescent home, which was really just hell with a fresh coat of paint.

Reba didn't answer, that boneless bitch.

'I can do this,' I said, although I didn't believe it. And I thought: *Jerry. No, Jeff.* Then *You're thinking about Jerry Jeff Walker, asshole. Johnson? Gerald? Great Jumping Jehosaphat?*

Starting to drift away. Starting to drift into sleep in spite of the anger and panic. Tuning in to the mild respiration of the Gulf.

I can do this, I thought. *Crosspatch. Like when you remembered what B-and-C stood for.*

I thought of the kid saying *They condemned a couple beach houses at the north end of Casey Key* and there was something there. My stump was itching like a mad bastard. But pretend that's some other guy's stump in some other universe, meantime chase that thing, that rag, that bone, that connection—

—*drifting away*—

Although if a big storm like Charley ever hits this part of the coast dead-on—

And bingo.

Charley was a hurricane, and when hurricanes struck, I peeked at The Weather Channel, like the rest of America, and their hurricane guy was . . .

I picked up Reba. She seemed to weigh at least twenty pounds in my soupy, half-asleep state. 'The hurricane guy is Jim Cantore,' I said. 'My help-out guy is *Jack* Cantori. Case fuckin closed.' I flopped her back down and closed my eyes. I might have heard that faint sigh from the Gulf for another ten or fifteen seconds. Then I was asleep.

I slept until sundown. It was the deepest, most satisfying sleep I'd had in eight months.

41

v

I had done no more than nibble on the plane, and consequently woke up ravenous. I did a dozen heel-slides instead of the usual twenty-five to loosen my hip, made a quick trip to the bathroom, then lurched toward the kitchen. I was leaning on my crutch, but not as heavily as I might have expected, given the length of my nap. My plan was to make myself a sandwich, maybe two. I hoped for sliced bologna, but reckoned any lunchmeat I found in the fridge would be okay. I'd call Ilse after I ate and tell her I'd arrived safely. Ilse could be depended upon to e-mail everyone else with an interest in the welfare of Edgar Freemantle. Then I could take tonight's dose of pain medication and explore the rest of my new environment. The whole second floor awaited.

What my plan hadn't taken into account was how the westward view had changed.

The sun was gone, but there was still a brilliant orange band above the flat line of the Gulf. It was broken in only one place, by the silhouette of some large ship. Its shape was as simple as a first-grader's drawing. A cable stretched taut from the bow to what I assumed was the radio tower, creating a triangle of light. As that light skied upward, orange faded to a breathless Maxfield Parrish blue-green that I had never seen before with my own eyes . . . and yet I had a sense of déjà vu, as if maybe I had seen it, in my dreams. Maybe we all see skies like that in our dreams, and our waking minds can never quite translate them into colors that have names.

Above, in the deepening black, the first stars.

I was no longer hungry, and no longer wanted to call Ilse. All I wanted to do was draw what I was looking at. I knew I couldn't get all of it, but I didn't care – that was the beauty part. I didn't give Shit One.

My new employee (for a moment I blanked on his name again, then I thought Weather Channel, then I thought Jack: case fuckin closed) had put my knapsack of art supplies in the second bedroom. I flailed my way out to the Florida room with it, carrying it awkwardly and trying to use my crutch at the same time. A mildly curious breeze lifted my hair. The idea that such a breeze and snow in St

Paul might exist at the same time, in the same world, seemed absurd to me – science fiction.

I set the sack down on the long, rough wooden table, thought about snapping on a light, and decided against it. I would draw until I couldn't see to draw, and then call it a night. I sat in my awkward fashion, unzipped the bag, pulled out my pad. ARTISAN, it said on the front. Given the level of my current skills, *that* was a joke. I grubbed deeper and brought out my box of colored pencils.

I drew and colored quickly, hardly looking at what I was doing. I shaded up from an arbitrary horizon-line, stroking my Venus Yellow from side to side with wild abandon, sometimes going over the ship (it would be the first tanker in the world to come down with yellow jaundice, I reckoned) and not caring. When I had the sunset band to what seemed like the right depth – it was dying fast now – I grabbed the orange and shaded more, and heavier. Then I went back to the ship, not thinking, just putting a series of angular black lines on my paper. That was what I saw.

When I was done, it was almost full dark.

To the left, the three palms clattered.

Below and beyond me – but not so far beyond now, the tide was coming back in – the Gulf of Mexico sighed, as if it had had a long day and there was more work to do yet.

Overhead there were now thousands of stars, and more appearing even as I looked.

This was here all the time, I thought, and recalled something Melinda used to say when she heard a song she really liked on the radio: *It had me from hello.* Below my rudimentary tanker, I scratched the word **HELLO** in small letters. So far as I can remember (and I'm better at that now), it was the first time in my life I named a picture. And as names go, it's a good one, isn't it? In spite of all the damage that followed, I still think that's the perfect name for a picture drawn by a man who was trying his best not to be sad anymore – who was trying to remember how it felt to be happy.

It was done. I put my pencil down, and that was when Big Pink spoke to me for the first time. Its voice was softer than the sigh of the Gulf's breathing, but I heard it quite well just the same.

I've been waiting for you, it said.

43

vi

That was my year for talking to myself, and answering myself back. Sometimes other voices answered back as well, but that night it was just me, myself, and I.

'Houston, this is Freemantle, do you copy, Houston?' Leaning into the fridge. Thinking, *Christ, if this is basic staples, I'd hate to see what it would look like if the kid really decided to load up – I could wait out World War III.*

'Ah, roger, Freemantle, we copy.'

'Ah, we have bologna, Houston, that's a go on the bologna, do you copy?'

'Roger, Freemantle, we read you loud and clear. What's your mayo situation?'

We were a go for mayo, too. I made two bologna sandwiches on white – where I grew up, children are raised to believe mayonnaise, bologna, and white bread are the food of the gods – and ate them at the kitchen table. In the pantry I found a stack of Table Talk Pies, both apple and blueberry. I began to think of changing my will in favor of Jack Cantori.

Almost sloshing with food, I went back to the living room, snapped on all the lights, and looked at *Hello*. It wasn't very good. But it was interesting. The scribbled afterglow had a sullen, furnacey quality that was startling. The ship wasn't the one I'd seen, but mine was interesting in a spooky sort of way. It was little more than a scarecrow ship, and the overlapping scribbles of yellow and orange had turned it into a ghost-ship, as well, as if that peculiar sunset were shining right through it.

I propped it atop the TV, against the sign reading THE OWNER REQUESTS THAT YOU AND YOUR GUESTS DO NOT SMOKE INDOORS. I looked at it a moment longer, thinking it needed something in the foreground – a smaller boat, maybe, just to lend the one on the horizon some perspective – but I no longer wanted to draw. Besides, adding something might fuck up what little charm the thing had. I tried the telephone instead, thinking if it wasn't working yet I could call Ilse on my cell, but Jack had been on top of that, too.

I thought I'd probably get her machine – college girls are busy

44

girls – but she answered on the first ring. 'Daddy?' That startled me so much that at first I couldn't speak and she said it again. 'Dad?'

'Yes,' I said. 'How did you know?'

'The callback number's got a 941 area code. That's where that Duma place is. I checked.'

'Modern technology. I can't catch up. How are you, kiddo?'

'Fine. The question is, how are *you*?'

'I'm all right. Better than all right, actually.'

'The fellow you hired—?'

'He's got game. The bed's made and the fridge is full. I got here and took a five-hour nap.'

There was a pause, and when she spoke again she sounded more concerned than ever. 'You're not hitting those pain pills too hard, are you? Because Oxycontin's supposed to be sort of a Trojan horse. Not that I'm telling you anything you didn't already know.'

'Nope, I stick to the prescribed dosage. In fact—' I stopped.

'What, Daddy? What?' Now she sounded almost ready to hail a cab and take a plane.

'I was just realizing I skipped the five o'clock Vicodin . . .' I checked my watch. 'And the eight o'clock Oxycontin, too. I'll be damned.'

'How bad's the pain?'

'Nothing a couple of Tylenol won't handle. At least until midnight.'

'It's probably the change in climate,' she said. 'And the nap.'

I had no doubt those things were part of it, but I didn't think they were all of it. Maybe it was crazy, but I thought *drawing* had played a part. In fact, it was something I sort of knew.

We talked for awhile, and little by little I could hear that concern going out of her voice. What replaced it was unhappiness. She was understanding, I suppose, that this thing was really happening, that her mother and father weren't just going to wake up one morning and take it back. But she promised to call Pam and e-mail Melinda, let them know I was still in the land of the living.

'Don't you have e-mail there, Dad?'

'I do, but tonight you're my e-mail, Cookie.'

She laughed, sniffed, laughed again. I thought to ask if she was crying, then thought again. Better not to, maybe.

'Ilse? I better let you go now, honey. I want to shower off the day.'

'Okay, but . . .' A pause. Then she burst out: 'I *hate* to think of you all the way down there in Florida by yourself! Maybe falling on your ass in the shower! It's not *right!*'

'Cookie, I'm fine. Really. The kid – his name's . . .' *Hurricanes*, I thought. *Weather Channel.* 'His name's Jim Cantori.' But that was a case of right church, wrong pew. 'Jack, I mean.'

'That's not the same, and you know it. Do you want me to come?'

'Not unless you want your mother to scalp us both bald,' I said. 'What I want is for you to stay right where you are and TCB, darlin. I'll stay in touch.'

''Kay. But take care of yourself. No stupid shit.'

'No stupid shit. Roger that, Houston.'

'Huh?'

'Never mind.'

'I still want to hear you promise, Dad.'

For one terrible and surpassingly eerie moment I saw Ilse at eleven, Ilse dressed in a Girl Scout's uniform and looking at me with Monica Goldstein's shocked eyes. Before I could stop the words, I heard myself saying, 'Promise. Big swear. Mother's name.'

She giggled. 'Never heard that one before.'

'There's a lot about me you don't know. I'm a deep one.'

'If you say so.' A pause. Then: 'Love you.'

'Love you, too.'

I put the phone gently back into its cradle and stared at it for a long time.

vii

Instead of showering, I walked down the beach to the water. I quickly discovered my crutch was no help on the sand – was, in fact, a hindrance – but once I was around the corner of the house, the water's edge was less than two dozen steps away. That was easy if I went slow. The surge was mild, the incoming wavelets only inches high. It was hard to imagine this water whipped into a destructive hurricane frenzy. Impossible, actually. Later, Wireman would tell me God always punishes us for what we can't imagine.

That was one of his better ones.

I turned to go back to the house, then paused. There was just enough light to see a deep carpet of shells – a *drift* of shells – under the jutting Florida room. At high tide, I realized, the front half of my new house would be almost like the foredeck of a ship. I remembered Jack saying I'd get plenty of warning if the Gulf of Mexico decided to eat the place, that I'd hear it groaning. He was probably right . . . but then, I was also supposed to get plenty of warning on a job site when a heavy piece of equipment was backing up.

I limped back to where my crutch leaned against the side of the house and took the short plank walk around to the door. I thought about the shower and took a bath instead, going in and coming out in the careful sidesaddle way Kathi Green had shown me in my other life, both of us dressed in bathing suits, me with my right leg looking like a badly butchered cut of meat. Now the butchery was in the past; my body was doing its miracle work. The scars would last a lifetime, but even they were fading. Already fading.

Dried off and with my teeth brushed, I crutched into the master bedroom and surveyed the king, now divested of decorative pillows. 'Houston,' I said, 'we have bed.'

'Roger, Freemantle,' I replied. 'You are go for bed.'

Sure, why not? I'd never sleep, not after that whopper of a nap, but I could lie down for awhile. My leg still felt pretty good, even after my expedition to the water, but there was a knot in my lower back and another at the base of my neck. I lay down. No, sleep was out of the question, but I turned off the lamp anyway. Just to rest my eyes. I'd lie there until my back and neck felt better, then dig a paperback out of my suitcase and read.

Just lie here for awhile, that was . . .

I got that far, and then I was gone again. There were no dreams.

viii

I slipped back to some sort of consciousness in the middle of the night with my right arm itching and my right hand tingling and no idea of where I was, only that from below me something vast was *grinding* and *grinding* and *grinding*. At first I thought it was machinery, but it was too uneven to be machinery. And too *organic*, somehow. Then I thought of teeth, but nothing had teeth that vast. Nothing in the known world, at least.

Breathing, I thought, and that seemed right, but what kind of animal made such a vast grinding sound when it drew in breath? And God, that itch was driving me *crazy*, all the way up my forearm to the crease of the elbow. I went to scratch it, reaching across my chest with my left hand, and of course there was no elbow, no forearm, and I scratched nothing but the bedsheet.

That brought me fully awake and I sat up. Although the room was still very dark, enough starlight came in through the westward-facing window for me to see the foot of the bed, where one of my suitcases rested on a bench. That locked me in place. I was on Duma Key, just off the west coast of Florida – home of the newly wed and the nearly dead. I was in the house I was already thinking of as Big Pink, and that grinding sound—

'It's shells,' I murmured, lying back down. 'Shells under the house. The tide's in.'

I loved that sound from the first, when I woke up and heard it in the dark of night, when I didn't know where I was, who I was, or what parts were still attached. It was mine.

It had me from hello.

3 – Drawing on New Resources

i

What came next was a period of recovery and transition from my other life to the one I lived on Duma Key. Dr Kamen probably knew that during times like that, most of the big changes are going on inside: civil unrest, revolt, revolution, and finally, mass executions as the heads of the old regime tumble into the basket at the foot of the guillotine. I'm sure the big man had seen such revolutions succeed and seen them fail. Because not everyone makes it into the next life, you know. And those who do don't always discover heaven's golden shore.

My new hobby helped in my transition, and Ilse helped, too. I'll always be grateful for that. But I'm ashamed of going through her purse while she was asleep. All I can say is that at the time I seemed to have no choice.

ii

I woke up the morning after my arrival feeling better than I had since my accident – but not so well I skipped my morning pain cocktail. I took the pills with orange juice, then went outside. It was seven o'clock. In St Paul the air would have been cold enough to gnaw on the end of my nose, but on Duma it felt like a kiss.

I leaned my crutch where I'd leaned it the night before and walked down to those docile waves again. To my right, any view of the drawbridge and Casey Key beyond was blocked out by my own house. To the left, however—

In that direction the beach seemed to stretch on forever, a dazzling white margin between the blue-gray Gulf and the sea oats. I could

49

see one speck far down, or maybe it was two. Otherwise, that fabulous picture-postcard shore was entirely deserted. None of the other houses were near the beach, and when I faced south, I could only see a single roof: what looked like an acre of orange tile mostly buried in palms. It was the hacienda I had noticed the day before. I could block that out with the palm of my hand and feel like Robinson Crusoe.

I walked that way, partly because as a southpaw, turning left had come naturally to me my whole life. Mostly because that was the direction I could see in. And I didn't go far, no Great Beach Walk that day, I wanted to make sure I could get back to my crutch, but that was still the first. I remember turning around and marveling at my own footprints in the sand. In the morning light each left one was as firm and bold as something produced by a stamping-press. Most of the right ones were blurry, because I had a tendency to drag that foot, but setting out, even those had been clear. I counted my steps back. The total was thirty-eight. By then my hip was throbbing. I was more than ready to go in, grab a yogurt cup from the fridge, and see if the cable TV worked as well as Jack Cantori claimed.

Turned out it did.

iii

And that became my morning routine: orange juice, walk, yogurt, current events. I became quite chummy with Robin Meade, the young woman who anchors Headline News from six to ten a.m. Boring routine, right? But the surface events of a country laboring under a dictatorship can appear boring, too – dictators like boring, dictators *love* boring – even as great changes are approaching beneath the surface.

A hurt body and mind aren't just like a dictatorship; they *are* a dictatorship. There is no tyrant as merciless as pain, no despot so cruel as confusion. That my mind had been as badly hurt as my body was a thing I only came to realize once I was alone and all other voices dropped away. The fact that I had tried to choke my wife of twenty-five years for doing no more than trying to wipe the sweat off my forehead after I told her to leave the room was the very least of it. The fact that we hadn't made love a single time in the months between the accident and the separation, didn't even try, wasn't at the heart of it, either, although I thought it was suggestive of the larger problem. Even the sudden and distressing bursts of anger weren't at the heart of the matter.

That heart was a kind of pulling-away. I don't know how else to describe it. My wife had come to seem like someone . . . other. Most of the people in my life also felt *other*, and the dismaying thing was that I didn't much care. In the beginning I had tried to tell myself that the otherness I felt when I thought about my wife and my life was probably natural enough in a man who sometimes couldn't even remember the name of that thing you pulled up to close your pants – the *zoomer*, the *zimmer*, the *zippity-doo-dah*. I told myself it would pass, and when it didn't and Pam told me she wanted a divorce, what followed my anger was relief. Because now that *other* feeling was okay to have, at least toward her. Now she really *was* other. She'd taken off the Freemantle uniform and quit the team.

During my first weeks on Duma, that sense of *otherness* allowed me to prevaricate easily and fluently. I answered letters and e-mails from people like Tom Riley, Kathi Green, and William Bozeman III – the immortal Bozie – with short jottings (*I'm fine, the weather's fine, the bones are mending*) that bore little resemblance to my actual life. And when their communications first slowed and then stopped, I wasn't sorry.

Only Ilse still seemed to be on my team. Only Ilse refused to turn in her uniform. I never got that *other* feeling about her. Ilse was still on my side of the glass window, always reaching out. If I didn't e-mail her every day, she called. If I didn't call her once every third day, she called me. And to her I didn't lie about my plans to fish in the Gulf or check out the Everglades. To Ilse I told the truth, or as much of it as I could without sounding crazy.

I told her, for instance, about my morning walks along the beach, and that I was walking a little farther each day, but not about the Numbers Game, because it sounded too silly . . . or maybe obsessive-compulsive is the term I actually want.

Just thirty-eight steps from Big Pink on that first morning. On

51

my second one I helped myself to another huge glass of orange juice and then walked south along the beach again. This time I walked forty-five steps, which was a long distance for me to totter crutchless in those days. I managed by telling myself it was really only nine. That sleight-of-mind is the basis of the Numbers Game. You walk one step, then two steps, then three, then four, rolling your mental odometer back to zero each time until you reach nine. And when you add the numbers one through nine together, you come out with forty-five. If that strikes you as nuts, I won't argue.

The third morning I coaxed myself into walking ten steps from Big Pink *sans* crutch, which is really fifty-five, or about ninety yards, round-trip. A week later and I was up to seventeen . . . and when you add all *those* numbers, you come out with a hundred and fifty-three. I'd get to the end of that distance, look back at my house, and marvel at how far away it looked. I'd also sag a little at the thought of having to walk all the way back again.

You can do it, I'd tell myself. *It's easy. Just seventeen steps, is all.*

That's what I'd tell myself, but I didn't tell Ilse.

A little farther each day, stamping out footprints behind me. By the time Santa Claus showed up at the Beneva Road Mall, where Jack Cantori sometimes took me shopping, I realized an amazing thing: all my southbound footprints were clear. The right sneaker-print didn't start to drag and blur until I was on my way back.

Exercise becomes addictive, and rainy days didn't put a stop to mine. The second floor of Big Pink was one large room. There was an industrial-strength rose-colored carpet on the floor and a huge window facing the Gulf of Mexico. There was nothing else. Jack suggested that I make a list of furniture I wanted up there, and said he'd get it from the same rental place where he'd gotten the down-stairs stuff . . . assuming the downstairs stuff was all right. I assured him it was fine, but said I wouldn't need much on the second floor. I liked the emptiness of that room. It called to my imagination. What I wanted, I said, was three things: a plain straight-backed chair, an artist's easel, and a Cybex treadmill. Could Jack provide those things? He could and did. In three days. From then until the end it was the second floor for me when I wanted to draw or paint, and it was the second floor for exercise on days when the weather closed in. The single straight-backed chair was the only real piece of furniture that ever lived up there during my tenure in Big Pink.

In any case, there weren't that many rainy days – not for nothing is Florida called the Sunshine State. As my southward strolls grew longer, the speck or specks I'd seen on that first morning eventually resolved into two people – at least, on most days it was two. One was in a wheelchair and wearing what I thought was a straw hat. The other pushed her, then sat beside her. They appeared on the beach around seven a.m. Sometimes the one who could walk left the one in the wheelchair for a little while, only to come back with something that glittered in the early sun. I suspected a coffeepot, a breakfast tray, or both. I further suspected they came from the huge hacienda with the acre or so of orange tiled roof. That was the last house visible on Duma Key before the road ran into the enthusiastic overgrowth that covered most of the island.

iv

I couldn't quite get used to the *emptiness* of the place. 'It's supposed to be very quiet,' Sandy Smith had told me, but I had still pictured the beach filling up by midday: couples sunning on blankets and slathering each other with tanning lotion, college kids playing volley-ball with iPods strapped to their biceps, little kids in saggy swim-suits paddling at the edge of the water while Jet-Skis buzzed back and forth forty feet out.

Jack reminded me that it was only December. 'When it comes to Florida tourism,' he said, 'the month between Thanksgiving and Christmas is Morgue City. Not as bad as August, but still pretty dead. Also . . .' He gestured with his arm. We were standing out by the mailbox with the red **13** on it, me leaning on my crutch, Jack looking sporty in a pair of denim cut-offs and a fashionably tattered Tampa Devil Rays shirt. 'It's not exactly tourist country here. See any trained dolphins? What you got is seven houses, counting that big 'un down there . . . and the jungle. Where there's another house falling apart, by the way. That's according to some of the stories I've heard on Casey Key.'

'What's *with* Duma, Jack? Nine miles of prime Florida real

estate, a great beach, and it's never been developed? What's up with that?'

He shrugged. 'Some kind of long-running legal dispute is all I know. Want me to see if I can find out?'

I thought about it, then shook my head.

'Do you mind it?' Jack looked honestly curious. 'All the quiet? Because it'd get on my nerves a little, to tell you the God's honest.'

'No,' I said. 'Not at all.' And that was the truth. Healing is a kind of revolt, and as I think I've said, all successful revolts begin in secret.

'What do you do? If you don't mind me asking?'

'Exercise in the mornings. Read. Sleep in the afternoons. And I draw. I may eventually try painting, but I'm not ready for that yet.'

'Some of your stuff looks pretty good for an amateur.'

'Thank you, Jack, that's very kind.'

I didn't know if kind was all he was being or if he was telling me his version of the truth. Maybe it didn't matter. When it comes to things like pictures, it's always just someone's opinion, isn't it? I only knew that something was going on for me. *Inside* me. Sometimes it felt a little scary. Mostly it felt pretty goddam wonderful.

I did most of my drawing upstairs, in the room I'd come to think of as Little Pink. The only view from there was of the Gulf and that flat horizon-line, but I had a digital camera and I took pictures of other things sometimes, printed them out, clipped them to my easel (which Jack and I turned so the strong afternoon light would strike across the paper), and drew that stuff. There was no rhyme or reason to those snapshots, although when I told Kamen this in an e-mail, he responded that the unconscious mind writes poetry if it's left alone.

Maybe *sí*, maybe *no*.

I drew my mailbox. I drew the stuff growing around Big Pink, then had Jack buy me a book – *Common Plants of the Florida Coast* – so I could put names to my pictures. Naming seemed to help – to add power, somehow. By then I was on my second box of colored pencils . . . and I had a third waiting in the wings. There was aloe vera; sea lavender with its bursts of tiny yellow flowers (each possessing a tiny heart of deepest violet); inkberry with its long spade-shaped leaves; and my favorite, sophora, which *Common Plants of the Florida Coast* also identified as necklace-bush, for the tiny pod-like necklaces that grow on its branches.

I drew shells, too. Of course I did. There were shells everywhere, an eternity of shells just within my limited walking distance. Duma Key was made of shells, and soon I'd brought back dozens.

And almost every night when the sun went down, I drew the sunset. I knew sunsets were a cliché, and that's why I did them. It seemed to me that if I could break through that wall of been-there-done-that even once, I might be getting somewhere. So I piled up picture after picture, and none of them looked like much. I tried overlaying Venus Yellow with Venus Orange again, but subsequent efforts didn't work. The sullen furnace-glow was always missing. Each sunset was only a penciled piece of shit where the colors said *I'm trying to tell you the horizon's on fire.* You could undoubtedly have bought forty better ones at any sidewalk art show on a Saturday in Sarasota or Venice Beach. I saved some of those drawings, but I was so disgusted with most of them that I threw them away.

One evening after another bunch of failures, once again watching the top arc of the sun disappear, leaving that flush of Halloween color trailing behind, I thought: *It was the ship. That was what gave my first one a little sip of magic. How the sunset seemed to be shining right through it.* Maybe, but there was no ship out there now to break the horizon; it was a straight line with darkest blue below and brilliant orange-yellow above, fading to a delicate greenish shade I could see but not duplicate, not out of my meager box of colored pencils.

There were twenty or thirty photo printouts scattered around the feet of my easel. My eye happened on a close-up of a sophora necklace. Looking at it, my phantom right arm began to itch. I clamped my yellow pencil between my teeth, bent over, picked up the sophora photo, and studied it. The light was failing now, but only by degrees – the upper room I called Little Pink held light for a long time – and there was more than enough to admire the details; my digital camera took exquisite close-ups.

Without thinking about what I was doing, I clamped the photo to the edge of the easel and added the sophora bracelet to my sunset. I worked quickly, first sketching – really nothing more than a series of arcs, that's sophora – and then coloring: brown overlaying black, then a bright dab of yellow, the remains of one flower. I remember my concentration being fined down to a brilliant cone, the way it sometimes was in the early days of my business, when every building (every bid, really) was make or break. I remember clamping a pencil in my mouth once again at some point, so I could scratch at the arm that wasn't there; I was always forgetting the lost part of me. When distracted and carrying something in my left hand, I sometimes reached out with my right one to open a door. Amputees forget, that's all. Their minds forget and as they heal, their bodies let them.

What I mostly remember about that evening is the wonderful, blissful sensation of having caught an actual bolt of lightning in a bottle for three or four minutes. By then the room had begun to dim out, the shadows seeming to swim forward over the rose-colored carpet toward the fading rectangle of the picture window. Even with the last light striking across my easel, I couldn't get a good look at what I'd done. I got up, limped around the treadmill to the switch by the door, and flipped on the overhead. Then I went back, turned the easel, and caught my breath.

The sophora bracelet seemed to rear over the horizon-line like the tentacle of a sea creature big enough to swallow a supertanker. The single yellow blossom could have been an alien eye. More important to me, it had somehow given the sunset back the truth of its ordinary I-do-this-every-night beauty.

That picture I set aside. Then I went downstairs, microwaved a Hungry Man fried chicken dinner, and ate it right down to the bottom of the box.

v

The following night I lined the sunset with bundles of witchgrass, and the brilliant orange shining through the green turned the horizon into a forest fire. The night after that I tried palm trees, but that was no good, that one was another cliché, I could almost see hula-hula girls and hear ukes strumming. Next I put a big old conch shell on the horizon with the sunset firing off around it like a corona, and the result was – to me, at least – almost unbearably creepy. That one I turned to the wall, thinking when I looked at it the next day it would have lost its magic, but it hadn't. Not for me, anyway.

I snapped a picture of it with my digital camera, and attached it to an e-mail. It prompted the following exchange, which I printed out and stowed in a folder:

EFree19 to KamenDoc
10:14 AM
December 9

Kamen: I told you I was drawing pictures again.
This is your fault, so the least you
can do is look at the attached and tell me
what you think. The view is from my place down
here. Do not spare my feelings.

Edgar

KamenDoc to EFree19
12:09 PM
December 9

Edgar: I think you are getting better. A LOT.

Kamen

P.S. In truth the picture is amazing. Like an undiscovered Dalí. You have clearly found something. How big is it?

EFree19 to KamenDoc
1:13 PM
December 9

Don't know. Big, maybe.
EF

KamenDoc to EFree19
1:22 PM
December 9

Then MINE IT!
Kamen

57

Two days later, when Jack came by to ask if I wanted to run errands, I said I wanted to go to a bookstore and buy a book of Salman Dalís art.

Jack laughed. 'I think you mean *Salvador* Dalí,' he said. 'Unless you're thinking about the guy who wrote the book that got him in so much hot water. I can't remember the name of it.'

'*The Satanic Verses*,' I said at once. The mind's a funny monkey, isn't it?

When I got back with my book of prints – it cost a staggering one hundred and nineteen dollars, even with my Barnes & Noble discount card, good thing I'd saved a few million out of the divorce for myself – the MESSAGE WAITING lamp of my answering machine was flashing. It was Ilse, and the message was cryptic only at first listen.

'Mom's going to phone you,' she said. 'I did my best talking, Dad – called in every favor she owed me, added my very best pretty-please and just about begged Lin, so say yes, okay? Say yes. For me.'

I sat down, ate a Table Talk pie I'd been looking forward to but no longer wanted, and leafed through my expensive picture-book, thinking – and I'm sure this wasn't original – *Well hello, Dalí*. I wasn't always impressed. In many cases I thought I was looking at the work of a talented smartass who was doing little more than passing the time. Yet some of the pictures excited me and a few frightened me the way my looming conch shell had. Floating tigers over a reclining nude woman. A floating rose. And one picture, *Swans Reflecting Elephants*, that was so strange I could barely look at it . . . yet I kept flipping back to look some more.

And what I was really doing was waiting for my soon-to-be-ex-wife to call and invite me back to St Paul, for Christmas with the girls. Eventually the phone rang, and when she said *I'm extending this invitation against my better judgment* I resisted the urge to smash that particular hanging curveball out of the park: *And I'm accepting it against mine.* What I said was *I understand that.* What I said was *How does Christmas Eve sound?* And when she said *That's fine,* some of the I'm-covered-up-and-ready-to-fight had gone out of her voice. The argument that might have nipped Christmas with the Family in the bud had been averted. Which did not make this trip back home a good idea.

MINE IT, Kamen had said, and in big capital letters. I suspected that by leaving now I might kill it, instead. I could come back to Duma Key . . . but that didn't mean I'd get my groove back. The walks, the pictures. One was feeding the other. I didn't know exactly how, and I didn't need to know.

But Illy: *Say yes. For me.* She knew I would, not because she was my favorite (Lin was the one who knew that, I think), but because she had always been satisfied with so little and so seldom asked for anything. And because when I listened to her message, I remembered how she'd started to cry that day she and Melinda had come out to Lake Phalen, leaning against me and asking why it couldn't be the way it was. *Because things never are,* I think I replied, but maybe for a couple of days they could be . . . or a reasonable facsimile thereof. Ilse was nineteen, probably too old for one last childhood Christmas, but surely not too old to deserve one more with the family she'd grown up with. And that went for Lin, too. Her survival skills were better, but she was flying home from France yet again, and that told me something.

All right, then. I'd go, I'd make nice, and I would be sure to pack Reba, just in case one of my rages swept over me. They were abating, but of course on Duma Key there was really nothing to rage against except for my periodic forgetfulness and shitty limp. I called the charter service I'd used for the last fifteen years and confirmed a Learjet, Sarasota to MSP International, leaving at nine o'clock a.m. on the twenty-fourth of December. I called Jack, who said he'd be happy to drive me to Dolphin Aviation and pick me up again on the twenty-eighth. And then, just when I had all of my ducks in a row, Pam called to tell me the whole thing was off.

vi

Pam's father was a retired Marine. He and his wife had relocated to Palm Desert, California, in the last year of the twentieth century, settling in one of those gated communities where there's one token African-American couple and four token Jewish couples. Children and vegetarians are not allowed. Residents must vote Republican and own small dogs with rhinestone collars, stupid eyes, and names that end in *i*. Taffi is good, Cassi is better, and something like Rififi

59

is the total shit. Pam's father had been diagnosed with rectal cancer. It didn't surprise me. Put a bunch of white assholes together and you're going to find that going around.

I did not say this to my wife, who started off strong and then broke down in tears. 'He's started the chemo, but Momma says it might already have metas . . . mesass . . . oh, whatever that fucking word is, I sound like you!' And then, still sniffing but sounding shocked and humbled: 'I'm sorry, Eddie, that was terrible.'

'No, it wasn't,' I said. 'It wasn't terrible at all. And the word is metastasized.'

'Yes. Thank you. Anyway, they're doing the surgery to take out the main tumor tonight.' She was starting to cry again. 'I can't believe this is happening to my Dad.'

'Take it easy,' I said. 'They do miracles these days. I'm Exhibit A.'

Either she didn't consider me a miracle or didn't want to go there. 'Anyway, Christmas here is off.'

'Of course.' And the truth? I was glad. Glad as hell.

'I'm flying out to Palm tomorrow. Ilse is coming Friday, Melinda on the twentieth. I'm assuming . . . considering the fact that you and my father never really saw eye to eye . . .'

Considering the fact that we had once almost come to blows after my father-in-law had referred to the Democrats as 'the Commiecrats', I thought that was putting it mildly. I said, 'If you're thinking I don't want to join you and the girls for Christmas in Palm Desert, you're correct. You'll be helping financially, and I hope your folks will understand that I had something to do with that—'

'I hardly think this is the time to drag your goddam *checkbook* into the discussion!'

And the anger was back, just like that. Jack, almost out of his stinking little box. I wanted to say *Why don't you go fuck yourself, you loudmouth bitch.* But I didn't. At least partly because it would have come out *loudmouf birch* or maybe *broadmouth lurch.* I somehow knew this.

Still, it was close.

'Eddie?' She sounded truculent, more than ready to get into it if I wanted to.

'I'm not dragging my checkbook into anything,' I said, carefully listening to each word. They came out all right. That was a relief. 'I'm just saying that my face at your father's bedside would not be

60

likely to speed his recovery.' For a moment the anger – the *fury* – almost added that I hadn't seen his face at mine, either. Once more I managed to stop the words, but by then I was sweating.

'All right. Point taken.' She paused. 'What *will* you do for Christmas, Eddie?'

Paint the sunset, I thought. *Maybe get it right.*

'I believe that if I'm a good boy, I may be invited to Christmas dinner with Jack Cantori and his family,' I said, believing no such thing. 'Jack's the young fellow who works for me.'

'You sound better. Stronger. Are you still forgetting things?'

'I don't know, I can't remember,' I said.

'That's very funny.'

'Laughter's the best medicine. I read it in *Reader's Digest.*'

'What about your arm? Are you still having phantom sensations?'

'Nope,' I lied, 'that's pretty well stopped.'

'Good. Great.' A pause. Then: 'Eddie?'

'Still here,' I said. And with dark red half-moons in the palms of my hands, from clenching my fists.

There was a long pause. The phone lines no longer hiss and crackle as they did when I was a kid, but I could hear all the miles sighing gently between us. It sounded like the Gulf when the tide is out. Then she said, 'I'm sorry things turned out this way.'

'I am, too,' I said, and when she hung up, I picked up one of my bigger shells and came very close to heaving it through the screen of the TV. Instead, I limped across the room, opened the door, and chucked it across the deserted road. I didn't hate Pam – not really – but I seemed to still hate something. Maybe that other life.

Maybe only myself.

vii

ifsogirl88 to EFree19
9:05 AM
December 23

.

Dear Daddy, The docs aren't saying a lot but I'm not getting a real good vibe about Grampy's surgery. Of course that might

61

only be Mom, she goes in to visit Grampa every day, takes Nana and tries to stay 'upbeat' but you know how she is, not the silver lining type. I want to come down there and see you. I checked the flights and can get one to Sarasota on the 26th. It gets in at 6:15 PM your time. I could stay 2 or 3 days. Please say yes! Also I could bring my prezzies instead of mailing them. Love . . .

Ilse

P.S. I have some special news.

Did I think about it, or only consult the ticking of instinct? I can't remember. Maybe it was neither. Maybe the only thing that mattered was that I wanted to see her. In any case, I replied almost at once.

EFree19 to ifsogirl88
9:17 AM
December 23

Ilse: Come ahead! Finalize your arrangements and I'll meet you with Jack Cantori, who happens to be my own Christmas Elf. I hope you will like my house, which I call Big Pink. One thing: do not do this w/o your mother's knowledge & approval. We have been through some bad times, as you well know. I am hoping those bad times are now in the past. I think you understand.

Dad

Her own reply was just as quick. She must have been waiting.

ifsogirl88 to EFree19
9:23 AM
December 23

Already cleared it w/ Mom, she says okay. Tried to talk Lin into

it, but she'd rather stay here before flying back to France. Don't hold it against her.

Ilse

PS: Yippee! I'm excited!! ☺

Don't hold it against her. It seemed that my If-So-Girl had been saying that about her older sister ever since she could talk. Lin doesn't want to go on the weenie roast because she doesn't like hot dogs . . . but don't hold it against her. Lin can't wear that kind of sneakers because none of the kids in her class wear hightops anymore . . . so don't hold it against her. Lin wants Ryan's Dad to take them to the prom . . . but don't hold it against her. And you know the bad part? I never did. I could have told Linnie that preferring Ilse was like growing up lefthanded – something over which I had no control – and that would only have made it worse, even though it was the truth. Maybe *especially* because it was the truth.

viii

Ilse coming to Duma Key, to Big Pink. Yippee, she was excited, and yippee, I was, too. Jack had found me a stout lady named Juanita to clean twice a week, and I had her make up the guest bedroom. I also asked her if she'd bring some fresh flowers the day after Christmas. Smiling, she suggested something that sounded like creamus cackus. My brain, by then quite comfortable with the fine art of cross-connection, was stopped by this for no more than five seconds; I told Juanita I was sure Ilse would love a Christmas cactus.

On Christmas Eve I found myself re-reading Ilse's original e-mail. The sun was westering, beating a long and brilliant track across the water, but it was still at least two hours to sundown, and I was sitting in the Florida room. The tide was high. Beneath me, the deep drifts of shell shifted and grated, making that sound that was so like breath or hoarse confidential speaking. I ran my thumb over the postscript – *I have some special news* – and my right arm, the one that was no longer there, began to tingle. The location of that

63

tingle was clearly, almost exquisitely, defined. It began in the fold of the elbow and spiraled to an end on the outside of the wrist. It deepened to an itch I longed to reach over and scratch.

I closed my eyes and snapped the thumb of my right hand against the second finger. There was no sound, but I could *feel* the snap. I rubbed my arm against my side and could feel the rub. I lowered my right hand, long since burned in the incinerator of a St Paul hospital, to the arm of my chair and drummed the fingers. No sound, but the sensation was there: skin on wicker. I would have sworn to it in the name of God.

All at once I wanted to draw.

I thought about the big room upstairs, but Little Pink seemed too far to go. I went into the living room and took an Artisan pad off a stack of them sitting on the coffee table. Most of my art supplies were upstairs, but there were a few boxes of colored pencils in one of the drawers of the living room desk, and I took one of those, as well.

Back in the Florida room (which I would always think of as a porch), I sat down and closed my eyes. I listened to the waves do their work beneath me, lifting the shells and turning them into new patterns, each one different from the one before. With my eyes shut, that grating was more than ever like talk: the water giving tempo-rary tongue to the edge of the land. And the land itself was tempo-rary, because if you took the geological view, Duma wouldn't last long. None of the Keys would; in the end the Gulf would take them all and new ones would rise in new locations. It was prob-ably true of Florida itself. The land was low, and on loan.

Ah, but that sound was restful. Hypnotic.

Without opening my eyes, I felt for Ilse's e-mail and ran the tips of my fingers over it again. I did this with my right hand. Then I opened my eyes, brushed the e-mail printout aside with the hand that was there, and pulled the Artisan pad onto my lap. I flipped back the cover, shook all twelve of the pre-sharpened Venus pencils onto the table in front of me, and began to draw. I had an idea I meant to draw Ilse − who had I been thinking of, after all? − and thought I'd make a spectacularly bad job of it, because I hadn't attempted a single human figure since starting to draw again. But it wasn't Ilse, and it wasn't bad. Not great, maybe, not Rembrandt (not even Norman Rockwell), but not bad.

It was a young man in jeans and a Minnesota Twins tee-shirt. The number on the tee was 48, which meant nothing to me; in my old life I used to go to as many T-Wolves games as I could, but I've never been a baseball fan. The guy had blond hair which I knew wasn't quite right; I didn't have the colors to get the exact darkening-toward-brown shade. He was carrying a book in one hand. He was smiling. I knew who he was. He was Ilse's special news. That was what the shells were saying as the tide lifted them and turned them and dropped them again. *Engaged, engaged.* She had a ring, a diamond, he had bought it at—

I had been shading the young man's jeans with Venus Blue. Now I dropped it, picked up the black, and stroked the word

ZALES

at the bottom of the sheet. It was information; it was also the name of the picture. Naming lends power.

Then, without a pause, I dropped the black, picked up orange, and added workboots. The orange was too bright, it made the boots look new when they weren't, but the *idea* was right.

I scratched at my right arm, scratched *through* my right arm, and got my ribs instead. I muttered 'Fuck' under my breath. Beneath me, the shells seemed to grate a name. Was it Connor? No. And something was wrong here. I didn't know where that sense of wrong-ness was coming from, but all at once the phantom itch in my right arm became a cold ache.

I tossed back the top sheet on the pad and sketched again, this time using just the red pencil. Red, red, *it was RED!* The pencil raced, spilling out a human figure like blood from a cut. It was back-to, dressed in a red robe with a kind of scalloped collar. I colored the hair red, too, because it looked like blood and this person felt like blood. Like danger. Not for me but—

'For Ilse,' I muttered. 'Danger for Ilse. Is it the guy? The special-news guy?'

There was something not right about the special-news guy, but I didn't think that was what was creeping me out. For one thing, the figure in the red robe didn't look like a guy. It was hard to tell for sure, but yes – I thought . . . female. So maybe not a robe at all. Maybe a dress? A long red dress?

I flipped back to the first figure and looked at the book the special-news guy was holding. I threw my red pencil on the floor and colored the book black. Then I looked at the guy again, and suddenly printed

HUMMINGBIRDS

in scripty-looking letters above him. Then I threw my black pencil on the floor. I raised my shaking hands and covered my face with them. I called out my daughter's name, the way you'd call out if you saw someone too close to a steep drop or busy street.

Maybe I was just crazy. *Probably* I was crazy.

Eventually I became aware that there was – of course – only one hand over my eyes. The phantom ache and itching had departed. The idea that I might be going crazy – hell, that I might have already gone – remained. One thing was beyond doubt: I was hungry. Ravenous.

ix

Ilse's plane arrived ten minutes ahead of schedule. She was radiant in faded jeans and a Brown University tee-shirt, and I didn't see how Jack could keep from falling in love with her right there in Terminal B. She threw herself into my arms, covered my face with kisses, then laughed and grabbed me when I started listing to port on my crutch. I introduced her to Jack and pretended not to see the small diamond (purchased at Zales, I had no doubt) flashing on the third finger of her left hand when they shook.

'You look *wonderful*, Daddy,' she said as we stepped out into the balmy December evening. 'You've got a tan. First time since you built that rec center in Lilydale Park. And you've put on weight. At least ten pounds. Don't you think so, Jack?'

'You'd be the best judge of that,' Jack said, smiling. 'I'll go get the car. You okay to stand, boss? This may take awhile.'

'I'm good.'

We waited on the curb with her two carry-ons and her computer. She was smiling into my eyes.

'You saw it, didn't you?' she asked. 'Don't pretend you didn't.'

'If you mean the ring, I saw. Unless you won it in one of those quarter drop-the-claw games, I'd say congratulations are in order. Does Lin know?'

'Yep.'

'Your mother?'

'What do *you* think, Daddy? Best guess.'

'My best guess is . . . not. Because she's so concerned about Grampy right now.'

'Grampy wasn't the only reason I kept the ring in my purse the whole time I was in California – except to show Lin, that is. Mostly I just wanted to tell you first. Is that evil?'

'No, honey. I'm touched.'

I was, too. But I was also afraid for her, and not just because she wouldn't be twenty for another three months.

'His name's Carson Jones, and he's a divinity student, of all things – do you believe it? I love him, Daddy, I just love him so much.'

'That's great, honey,' I said, but I could feel dread climbing my legs. *Just don't love him* too *much*, I was thinking. *Not* too *much. Because—*

She was looking at me closely, her smile fading. 'What? What's wrong?'

I'd forgotten how quick she was, and how well she read me. Love conveys its own psychic powers, doesn't it?

'Nothing, hon. Well . . . my hip's hurting a little.'

'Have you had your pain pills?'

'Actually . . . I'm stepping down on those a little more. Plan on getting off them entirely in January. That's my New Year's resolution.'

'Daddy, that's wonderful!'

'Although New Year's resolutions are made to be broken.'

'Not you. You do what you say you're going to do.' Ilse frowned. 'That's one of the things Mom never liked about you. I think it makes her jealous.'

'Hon, the divorce is just something that happened. Don't go picking sides, okay?'

'Well, I'll tell you something else that's happening,' Ilse said. Her lips had thinned down. 'Since she's been out in Palm Desert, she's seeing an awful lot of this guy down the street. She says it's just coffee and sympathy – because Max lost *his* father last year, and Max really likes Grampy, and blah-blah-blah – but I see the way she looks at him and I . . . don't . . . care for it!' Now her lips were almost gone, and I thought she looked eerily like her mother. The thought that came with this was oddly comforting: *I think she'll be all right. I think if this holy Jones boy jilts her, she'll still be okay.*

I could see my rental car, but Jack would be awhile yet. The pickup traffic was stop-and-go. I leaned my crutch against my midsection and hugged my daughter, who had come all the way from California to see me. 'Go easy on your mother, okay?'

'Don't you even care that—'

'What I mostly care about these days is that you and Melinda are happy.'

There were circles under her eyes and I could see that, young or not, all the traveling had tired her out. I thought she'd sleep late tomorrow, and that was fine. If my feeling about her boyfriend was right – I hoped it wasn't but thought it was – she had some sleep-less nights ahead of her in the year to come.

Jack had made it as far as the Air Florida terminal, which still gave us some time. 'Do you have a picture of your guy? Enquiring Dads want to know.'

Ilse brightened. 'You bet.' The picture she brought out of her red leather wallet was in one of those see-through plastic envelopes. She teased it out and handed it to me. I guess this time my reac-tion didn't show, because her fond (really sort of goofy) smile didn't change. And me? I felt as though I'd swallowed something that had no business going down a human throat. A piece of lead shot, maybe.

It wasn't that Carson Jones resembled the man I'd drawn on Christmas Eve. I was prepared for that, had been since I saw the little ring twinkling prettily on Ilse's finger. What shocked me was that the photo was almost exactly the same. It was as if, instead of clipping a photo of sophora, sea lavender, or inkberry to the side of my easel, I had clipped this very photograph. He was wearing the jeans and the scuffed yellow workboots that I hadn't been able to get quite right; his darkish blond hair spilled over his ears and

68

his forehead; he was carrying a book I knew was a Bible in one hand. Most telling of all was the Minnesota Twins tee-shirt, with the number 48 on the left breast.

'Who's number 48, and how did you happen to meet a Twins fan at Brown? I thought that was Red Sox country.'

'Number 48's Torii *Hunter*,' she said, looking at me as if I was the world's biggest dummox. 'They have a huge TV in the main student lounge, and I went in there one day last July when the Sox and Twins were playing. The place was crammed even though it was summer session, but Carson and I were the only ones with our Twins on – him with his Torii tee-shirt, me with my cap. So of course we sat together, and . . .' She shrugged, to show the rest was history.

'What flavor is he, religiously speaking?'

'Baptist.' She looked at me a little defiantly, as though she'd said *Cannibal*. But as a member in good standing of The First Church of Nothing in Particular, I had no grudge against the Baptists. The only religions I don't like are the ones that insist their God is bigger than your God. 'We've been going to services together three times a week for the last four months.'

Jack pulled up, and she bent to grab the handles of her various bags. 'He's going to take spring semester off to travel with this really wonderful gospel group. It's an actual tour, with a booker and everything. The group is called The Hummingbirds. You should hear him – he sings like an angel.'

'I'll bet,' I said.

She kissed me again, softly, on the cheek. 'I'm glad I came, Daddy. Are you glad?'

'More than you could ever know,' I said, and found myself wishing she'd fall madly in love with Jack. That would have solved everything . . . or so it seemed to me then.

x

We had nothing so grand as Christmas dinner, but there was one of Jack's Astronaut Chickens, plus cranberry dressing, salad-in-a-bag, and rice pudding. Ilse ate two helpings of everything. After we exchanged presents and exclaimed over them – everything was *just what we wanted!* – I took Ilse upstairs to Little Pink and showed her most of my artistic output. The drawing I'd done of her boyfriend and the picture of the woman (if it *was* a woman) in red were tucked away on a high shelf in my bedroom closet, and there they would stay until my daughter was gone.

I had clipped about a dozen others – mostly sunsets – to squares of cardboard and leaned them against the walls of the room. She toured them once. Stopped, then toured them again. It was might by then, my big upstairs window full of darkness. The tide was all the way out; the only way you even knew the Gulf was there was by its soft continual sighing as the waves ran up the sand and died.

'You really did these?' she said at last. She turned and looked at me in a way that made me uncomfortable. It's the way one person looks at another when a serious re-evaluation is going on.

'I really did,' I said. 'What do you think?'

'They're good. Maybe better than good. This one—' She bent and very carefully picked up the one that showed the conch sitting on the horizon-line, with yellow-orange sunset light blazing all around it. 'This is so fu . . . excuse me, so damn creepy.'

'I think so, too,' I said. 'But really, it's nothing new. All it does is dress up the sunset with a little surrealism.' Then, inanely, I exclaimed: 'Hello, Dalí!'

She put back *Sunset with Conch*, and picked up *Sunset with Sophora*. 'Who's seen these?'

'Just you and Jack. Oh, and Juanita. She calls them *asustador*. Something like that. Jack says it means *scary*.'

'They're a little scary,' she admitted. 'But Daddy . . . this pencil you're using will smudge. And I think it'll fade if you don't do something to the pictures.'

'What?'

'Dunno. But I think you ought to show these to someone who *does* know. Someone who can tell you how good they really are.'

I felt flattered but also uncomfortable. Dismayed, almost. 'I wouldn't know who or where to—'

'Ask Jack. Maybe he knows an art gallery that would look at them.'

'Sure, just limp in off the street and say, "I live out on Duma

70

Key and I've got some pencil sketches – mostly of sunsets, a very unusual subject in coastal Florida – that my housekeeper says are *muy asustador.*" '

She put her hands on her hips and cocked her head to one side. It was how Pam looked when she had no intention of letting a thing go. When she in fact intended to throw her current argument into four-wheel drive.

'Father—'

'Oh boy, I'm in for it now.'

She paid no mind. 'You parlayed two pick-ups, a used Korean War bulldozer, and a twenty-thousand-dollar loan into a million-dollar business. Are you going to stand there and tell me you couldn't get a few art gallery owners to look at your pictures if you really set your mind to it?'

She softened.

'I mean, these are good, Daddy, *Good*. All I've got for training is one lousy Art Appreciation course in high school, and *I* know that.'

I said something, but I'm not sure what. I was thinking about my frenzied quick-sketch of Carson Jones, alias The Baptist Hummingbird. Would she think that one was also good, if she saw it?

But she wasn't going to. Not that one, and not the one of the person in the red robe. No one was. That was what I thought then.

'Dad, if you had this talent in you all the time, where was it?'

'I don't know,' I said. 'And how much talent we're talking about is still open to question.'

'Then get someone to tell you, okay? Someone who knows.' She picked up my mailbox drawing. 'Even this one . . . it's nothing special, except it *is*. Because of . . .' She touched paper. 'The rocking horse. Why'd you put a rocking horse in the picture, Dad?'

'I don't know,' I said. 'It just wanted to be there.'

'Did you draw it from memory?'

'No. I can't seem to do that. Either because of the accident or because I never had that particular skill in the first place.' Except for sometimes when I did. When it came to young men in Twins tee-shirts, for instance. 'I found one on the Internet, then printed—'

'Oh shit, I smudged it!' she cried. 'Oh, *shit!*'

'Ilse, it's all right. It doesn't matter.'

71

'It's *not* all right and it *does* matter! You need to get some fucking *paints*!' She replayed what she'd just said and clapped a hand over her mouth.

'You probably won't believe this,' I said, 'but I've heard that word a time or two. Although I have an idea that maybe your boyfriend . . . might not exactly . . .'

'You got that right,' she said. A little glumly. Then she smiled. 'But he can let out a pretty good gosh-darn when somebody cuts him off in traffic. Dad, about your pictures—'

'I'm just happy you like them.'

'It's more than liking. I'm amazed.' She yawned. 'I'm also dead on my feet.'

'I think maybe you need a cup of hot cocoa and then bed.'

'That sounds wonderful.'

'Which?'

She laughed. It was wonderful to hear her laugh. It filled the place up. 'Both.'

xi

We stood on the beach the next morning with coffee cups in hand and our ankles in the surf. The sun had just hoisted itself over the low rise of the Key behind us, and our shadows seemed to stretch out onto the quiet water for miles.

Ilse looked at me solemnly. 'Is this the most beautiful place on earth, Dad?'

'No, but you're young and I can't blame you for thinking it might be. It's number four on the Most Beautiful list, actually, but the top three are places nobody can spell.'

She smiled over the rim of her cup. 'Do tell.'

'If you insist. Number one, Machu Picchu. Number two, Marrakech. Number three, Petroglyph National Monument. Then, at number four, Duma Key, just off the west coast of Florida.'

Her smile widened for a second or two. Then it faded and she was giving me the solemn stare again. I remembered her looking at me the same way when she was four, asking me if there was any magic like in fairy tales. I had told her yes, of course, thinking it was a lie. Now I wasn't so sure. But the air was warm, my bare feet were in the Gulf, and I just didn't want Ilse to be hurt. I thought she was going to be. But everyone gets their share, don't they? Sure. Pow, in the nose. Pow, in the eye. Pow, below the belt, down you go, and the ref just went out for a hotdog. Except the ones you love can really multiply that hurt and pass it around. Pain is the biggest power of love. That's what Wireman says.

'See anything green, sweetheart?' I asked.

'No, I was just thinking again how glad I am that I came. I pictured you rotting away between an old folks' retirement home and some horrible tiki bar featuring Wet Tee-Shirt Thursdays. I guess I've been reading too much Carl Hiaasen.'

'There are plenty of places like that down here,' I said.

'And are there other places like Duma?'

'I don't know. Maybe a few.' But based on what Jack had told me, I guessed that there were not.

'Well, you deserve this one,' she said. 'Time to rest and heal. And if all this' – she waved to the Gulf – 'won't heal you, I don't know what will. The only thing . . .'

'Ye-ess?' I said, and made a picking-out gesture at the air with two fingers. Families have their own interior language, and that includes sign-language. My gesture would have meant nothing to an outsider, but Ilse knew and laughed.

'All right, smarty. The only fly in the ointment is the sound the tide makes when it comes in. I woke up in the middle of the night and almost screamed before I realized it was the shells moving around in the water. I mean, that's it, right? Please tell me that's it.'

'That's it. What did you think it was?'

She actually shivered. 'My first thought . . . don't laugh . . . was skeletons on parade. Hundreds, marching around the house.'

I'd never thought of it that way, but I knew what she meant. 'I find it sort of soothing.'

She gave a small and doubtful shrug. 'Well . . . okay, then. To each his own. Are you ready to go back? I could scramble us some eggs. Even throw in some peppers and mushrooms.'

'You're on.'

'I haven't seen you off your crutch for so long since the accident.'

'I hope to be walking a quarter-mile south along the beach by the middle of January.'

She whistled. 'A quarter of a mile and *back*?'

I shook my head. 'No, no. Just a quarter of a mile. I plan to glide back.' I extended my arms to demonstrate.

She snorted, started toward the house again, then paused as a point of light heliographed in our direction from the south. Once, then twice. The two specks were down there.

'People,' Ilse said, shading her eyes.

'My neighbors. My *only* neighbors, right now. At least, I think so.'

'Have you met them?'

'Nope. All I know is that it's a man and a woman in a wheelchair. I think she has her breakfast down by the water most days. I think the tray is the glinty thing.'

'You should get yourself a golf cart. Then you could buzz down and say hi.'

'Eventually I'll *walk* down and say hi,' I said. 'No golf cart for the kid. Dr Kamen said to set goals, and I'm setting em.'

'You didn't need a shrink to tell you about setting goals, Daddy,' she said, still peering south. 'Which house do they belong to? The big one that looks like a rancho in a western movie?'

'I'm pretty sure, yes.'

'And no one else lives here?'

'Not now. Jack says there are folks who rent some of the other houses in January and February, but for now I guess it's just me and them. The rest of the island is pure botanical pornography. Plants gone wild.'

'My God, *why*?'

'Haven't the slightest idea. I mean to find out − to try, anyway − but for now I'm still trying to get my feet under me. And I mean that literally.'

We were walking back to the house now. Ilse said, 'An almost empty island in the sun − there should be a story. There almost *has* to be a story, don't you think?'

'I do,' I said. 'Jack Cantori offered to snoop, but I told him not to bother − thinking I might look on my own.' I snagged my crutch, fitted my arm into its two steel sleeves − always comforting after spending time on the beach without its support   and started thumping up the walk. But Ilse wasn't with me. I turned and looked back. She was facing south, her hand once more shading her eyes. 'Coming, hon?'

'Yes.' There was one more flash from down the beach – the breakfast tray. Or a coffeepot. 'Maybe *they* know the story,' Ilse said, catching up.

'Maybe they do.'

She pointed to the road. 'What about that? How far does it go?'

'Don't know,' I said.

'Would you like to drive down it this afternoon and see?'

'Are you willing to pilot a Chevy Malibu from Hertz?'

'Sure,' she said. She put her hands on her slim hips, pretended to spit, and affected a Southern drawl. 'I'll drive until yonder road runs out.'

xii

But we didn't get even close to the end of Duma Road. Not that day. Our southward exploration began well, ended badly.

We both felt fine when we left. I'd had an hour off my feet, plus my midday Oxycontin. My daughter had changed to shorts and a halter top, and laughed when I insisted on anointing her nose with zinc oxide. 'Bobo the clown,' she said, looking at herself in the mirror. She was in great spirits, I was happier than I'd been since the accident, so what happened to us that afternoon came as a total surprise. Ilse blamed lunch – maybe bad mayo in the tuna salad – and I let her, but I don't think it was bad mayo at all. Bad mojo, more like it.

The road was narrow, bumpy, and badly patched. Until we reached the place where it ran into the overgrowth that covered most of the Key, it was also ridged with bone-colored sand dunes that had blown inland from the beach. The rental Chevy thudded gamely over most of these, but when the road curved a little closer to the water – this was just before we reached the hacienda Wireman called *Palacio de Asesinos* – the drifts grew thicker and the car waddled instead of bumping. Ilse, who had learned to drive in snow country, handled this without complaint or comment.

The houses between Big Pink and *El Palacio* were all in the style I came to think of as Florida Pastel Ugly. Most were shuttered and the driveways of all but one were gated shut. The driveway of the one exception had been barred with two sawhorses, bearing this faded stenciled warning: **MEAN DOGS MEAN DOGS**. Beyond the Mean Dog house, the grounds of the hacienda commenced. They were enclosed by a sturdy faux-stucco wall about ten feet high and topped with orange tile. More orange tile – the roof of the mansion inside – rose in slants and angles against the blameless blue sky.

'Jumping jeepers,' Ilse said – that was one she must have gotten from her Baptist boyfriend. 'This place belongs in Beverly Hills.'

The wall ran along the east side of the narrow, buckled road for at least eighty yards. There weren't any NO TRESPASSING signs; given that wall, the owner's stance on door-to-door salesmen and proselytizing Mormons seemed perfectly clear. In the center was a two-piece iron gate, standing ajar. And sitting just inside its open halves—

'There she is,' I murmured. 'The lady from down the beach. Holy shit, it's The Bride of the Godfather.'

'*Daddy!*' Ilse said, laughing and shocked at the same time.

The woman was seriously old, mid-eighties at least. She was in her wheelchair. An enormous pair of blue Converse Hi-Tops were propped up on the chrome footrests. Although the temperature was in the mid-seventies, she wore a gray two-piece sweatsuit. In one gnarled hand a cigarette smoldered. Clapped on her head was the straw hat I'd seen on my walks, but on my walks I hadn't realized how enormous it was – not just a hat but a battered sombrero. Her resemblance to Marlon Brando at the end of *The Godfather* – when he's playing with his grandson in the garden – was unmistakable. There was something in her lap that did not quite look like a pistol.

Ilse and I both waved. For a moment she did nothing. Then she raised one hand, palm out, in an Indian *How* gesture, and broke into a sunny and nearly toothless grin. What seemed like a thousand wrinkles creased her face, turning her into a benign witch. I never even glimpsed the house behind her; I was still trying to cope with her sudden appearance, her cool blue sneakers, her delta of wrinkles, and her—

'Daddy, was that a *gun*?' Ilse was looking into the rear-view mirror, wide-eyed. 'Did that old lady have a *gun*?'

The car was drifting, and I saw a real possibility of clipping the hacienda's far corner. I touched the wheel and made a course correction. 'I think so. Of a kind. Mind your driving, honey. There ain't much road in this road.'

She faced front again. We'd been driving in bright sunshine, but that ended with the hacienda's wall. 'What do you mean, of a kind?'

'It looked like . . . I don't know, a crossbow-pistol. Or something. Maybe she shoots snakes with it.'

'Thank God she smiled,' Ilse said. 'And it was a *great* smile, wasn't it?'

I nodded. 'It was.'

The hacienda was the last house on Duma Key's open north end. Beyond it, the road swung inland and the foliage crowded up in a way I found first interesting, then awesome, then claustrophobic. The masses of greenery towered to a height of twelve feet at least, the round leaves streaked a dark vermilion that looked like dried blood.

'What is that stuff, Daddy?'

'Seagrape. The green stuff with the yellow flowers is called wedelia. It grows everywhere. There's also rhododendron. The trees are mostly just slash pine, I think, although—'

She slowed to a crawl and pointed to the left, craning to look up through the corner of the windshield to do so. 'Those are palms of some kind. And look . . . right up there . . .'

The road bent still farther inland, and here the trunks flanking the road looked like knotted masses of gray rope. Their roots had buckled the tar. We'd be able to get over now, I judged, but cars passing this way a few years hence? No way.

'Strangler fig,' I said.

'Nice name, right out of Alfred Hitchcock. And they just grow wild?'

'I don't know,' I said.

She bumped the Chevy carefully over the tunneling roots and drove on. We were down to no more than five miles an hour. There was more strangler fig growing out of the masses of seagrape and rhododendron. The high growth cast the road into deep shadow. It was impossible to see any distance at all on either side. Except for

77

an occasional wedge of blue or errant sunray, even the sky was gone. And now we began to see sprays of sawgrass and tough, waxy fiddle-wood growing right up through cracks in the tar.

My arm began to itch. The one that wasn't there. I reached to scratch it without thinking and only scratched my still-sore ribs, as I always did. At the same time the left side of my head started to itch. That I could scratch, and did.

'Daddy?'

'I'm okay. Why are you stopping?'

'Because . . . I don't feel so great myself.'

Nor, I realized, did she look it. Her complexion had gone almost as white as the dab of zinc oxide on her nose. 'Ilse? What is it?'

'My stomach. I'm starting to have serious questions about that tuna salad I made for lunch.' She gave me a sickly coming-down-with-the-flu smile. 'I'm also wondering how I'm going to get us out of here.'

Not a bad question. All at once the seagrape seemed to be pushing in and the interweaving palms overhead seemed thicker. I realized I could smell the growth around us, a ropy aroma that seemed to come to life halfway down my throat. And why not? It *came* from live things, after all; they were crowded in on both sides. And above.

'Dad?'

The itch was worse. It was red, that itch, as red as the stink in my nose and throat was green. That itch you got when you were stuck in the *burn*, stuck in the *char*.

'Daddy, I'm sorry but I think I'm going to vomit.'

Not a *burn*, not a *char*, it was a *car*, she opened the door of the car and leaned out, holding onto the wheel with one ham, and then I heard her sowing up.

My right eye came over red and I thought *I can do this. I can do this. I just have to get my poor old shit together.*

I opened my door, reaching cross-body to do it, and got out. *Lurched* out, holding the top of the door to keep from sprawling headfirst into a wall of seagrape and the interwoven branches of a half-buried banyan. I itched all over. The bushes and branches were so close to the side of the car that they scraped me as I made my way up to the front. Half my vision

(RED)

78

seemed to be bleeding scarlet, I felt the tip of a pine-bough scrape across the wrist of – I could have sworn it – my right arm, and I thought *I can do this, I MUST do this* as I heard Ilse vomit again. I was aware that it was much hotter in that narrow lane than it should have been, even with the greenroof overhead. I had enough mind left in my mind to wonder what we'd been thinking, coming down this road in the first place. But of course it had seemed like nothing but a lark at the time.

Ilse was still leaning out, hanging onto the wheel with her right hand. Sweat stood on her forehead in clear beads. She looked up at me. 'Oh boy—'

'Push over, Ilse.'

'Daddy, what are you going to do?'

As if she couldn't see. And all at once both the words *drive* and *back* were unavailable to me, anyway. All I could have articulated in that moment was *us*, the most useless word in the English language when it stands by itself. I felt the anger rising in my throat like hot water. Or blood. Yes, more like that. Because the anger was, of course, *red*.

'Get us out of here. Push over.' Thinking: *Don't you get mad at her. Don't you start shouting no matter what. Oh for Christ's sake, please don't.*

'Daddy, you can't—'

'Yes. I can do this. Push over.'

The habit of obedience dies hard – especially hard, maybe, between fathers and daughters. And of course she was sick. She pushed over and I got behind the wheel, sitting down in my clumsy stupid backwards fashion and using my hand to lift in my rotten right leg. My whole right side was buzzing, as if undergoing a low-level electric shock.

I closed my eyes tightly and thought: *I CAN do this, goddammit, and I don't need any stuffed rag bitch to see me through, either.*

When I looked at the world again, some of that redness – and some of the anger, thank God – had drained out of it. I dropped the transmission into reverse and began to back up slowly. I couldn't lean out as Ilse had done, because I had no right hand to steer with. I used the rear-view instead. In my head, ghostly, I heard: *Meep-meep-meep.*

79

'Please don't drive us off the road,' Ilse said. 'We can't walk. I'm too sick and you're too crippled-up.'

'I won't, Monica,' I said, but at that moment she leaned out the window to vomit again and I don't think she heard me.

xiii

Slowly, slowly, I backed away from the place where Ilse had stopped, telling myself *Easy does it* and *Slow and steady wins the race.* My hip snarled as we thumped back over the strangler fig roots burrowing under the road. On a couple of occasions I heard seagrape branches scree along the side of the car. The Hertz people weren't going to be happy, but they were the least of my worries that afternoon.

Little by little the light brightened as the foliage cleared out overhead. That was good. My vision was also clearing, that mad itch subsiding. Those things were even better.

'I see the big place with the wall around it,' Ilse said, looking back over her shoulder.

'Do you feel any better?'

'Maybe a little, but my stomach's still sudsing like a Maytag.' She made a gagging noise. 'Oh God, I should never have said that.' She leaned out, threw up again, then collapsed back onto the seat, laughing and groaning. Her bangs were sticking to her forehead in clumps. 'I just shellacked the side of your car. Please tell me you have a hose.'

'Don't worry about that. Just sit still and take long, slow breaths.'

She saluted feebly and closed her eyes.

The old woman in the big straw hat was nowhere in evidence, but the two halves of the iron gate were now standing wide open, as if she was expecting company. Or knew we'd need a place to turn around.

I didn't waste time considering that, just backed the Chevy into the archway. For a moment I saw a courtyard paved with cool blue tiles, a tennis court, and an enormous set of double doors with iron rings set into them. Then I turned for home. We were there five minutes later. My vision was as clear as it had been when I woke

80

up that morning, if not clearer. Except for the low itch up and down my right side, I felt fine.

I also felt a strong desire to draw. I didn't know what, but I *would* know, when I was sitting in Little Pink with one of my pads propped on my easel. I was sure of that.

'Let me clean off the side of your car,' Ilse said.

'You're going to lie down. You look beat half to death.'

She offered a wan smile. 'That's just the better half. Remember how Mom used to say that?'

I nodded. 'Go on, now. I'll do the rinsing.' I pointed to where the hose was coiled on the north side of Big Pink. 'It's all hooked up and ready to go.'

'Are you sure *you're* all right?'

'Good to go. I think you ate more of the tuna salad than I did.'

She managed another smile. 'I always was partial to my own cooking. You were great to get us back here, Daddy. I'd kiss you, but my *breath* . . .'

I kissed *her*. On the forehead. The skin was cool and damp. 'Put your feet up, Miss Cookie — orders from headquarters.'

She went. I turned on the faucet and hosed off the side of the Malibu, taking more time than the job really needed, wanting to make sure she was down for the count. And she was. When I peeked in through the half-open door of the second bedroom, I saw her lying on her side, sleeping just as she had as a kid: one hand tucked under her cheek and one knee drawn up almost to her chest. We think we change, but we don't really — that's what Wireman says.

Maybe *sí*, maybe *no* — that's what Freemantle says.

xiv

There was something pulling me — maybe something that had been in me since the accident, but surely something that had come back from Duma Key Road with me. I let it pull. I'm not sure I could have stood against it in any case, but I didn't even try; I was curious.

My daughter's purse was on the coffee table in the living room. I opened it, took out her wallet, and flipped through the pictures inside. Doing this made me feel a little like a cad, but only a little.

It's not as if you're stealing anything, I told myself, but of course there are many ways of stealing, aren't there?

Here was the photo of Carson Jones she'd shown me at the airport, but I didn't want that. I didn't want him by himself. I wanted him with her. I wanted a picture of them as a couple. And I found one. It looked as if it had been taken at a roadside stand; there were baskets of cucumbers and corn behind them. They were smiling and young and beautiful. Their arms were around each other, and one of Carson Jones's palms appeared to be resting on the swell of my daughter's blue jeans-clad ass. Oh you crazy Christian. My right arm was still itching, a low, steady skin-crawl like prickly heat. I scratched at it, scratched through it, and got my ribs instead for the ten thousandth time. This picture was also in a protective see-through envelope. I slid it out, glanced over my shoulder – nervous as a burglar on his first job – at the partially open door of the room where Ilse was sleeping, then turned the picture over.

I love you, Punkin!
'Smiley'

Could I trust a suitor who called my daughter Punkin and signed himself Smiley? I didn't think so. It might not be fair, but no – I didn't think so. Nevertheless, I *had* found what I was looking for. Not one, but both. I turned the picture over again, closed my eyes, and pretended I was touching their Kodachrome images with my right hand. Although pretending wasn't what it felt like; I suppose I don't have to tell you that by now.

After some passage of time – I don't know exactly how long – I returned the picture to its plastic sleeve and submerged her wallet beneath the tissues and cosmetics to approximately the same depth at which I had found it. Then I put her purse back on the coffee table and went into my bedroom to get Reba the Anger-Management Doll. I limped upstairs to Little Pink with her clamped between my stump and my side. I think I remember saying 'I'm going to make you into Monica Seles' when I set Reba down in front of the window, but it could as easily have been Monica Goldstein; when it comes to memory, we all stack the deck. The gospel according to Wireman.

I'm clearer than I want to be about most of what happened on Duma, but that particular afternoon seems very vague to me. I know that I fell into a frenzy of drawing, and that the maddening itch in my nonexistent right arm disappeared completely while I was working; I do *not* know but am almost sure that the reddish haze which always hung over my vision in those days, growing thicker when I was tired, disappeared for awhile.

I don't know how long I was in that state. I think quite awhile. Long enough so I was both exhausted and famished when I was finished.

I went back downstairs and gobbled lunchmeat by the fridge's frosty glow. I didn't want to make an actual sandwich, because I didn't want Ilse to know I'd felt well enough to eat. Let her go on thinking our problems had been caused by bad mayonnaise. That way we wouldn't have to spend time hunting for other explanations.

None of the other explanations I could think of were rational.

After eating half a package of sliced salami and swilling a pint or so of sweet tea, I went into my bedroom, lay down, and fell into a sodden sleep.

xv

Sunsets.

Sometimes it seems to me that my clearest memories of Duma Key are of orange evening skies that bleed at the bottom and fade away at the top, green to black. When I woke up that evening, another day was going down in glory. I thudded into the big main room on my crutch, stiff and wincing (the first ten minutes were always the worst). The door to Ilse's room was standing open and her bed was empty.

'Ilse?' I called.

For a moment there was no answer. Then she called back from upstairs. 'Daddy? Holy crow, did you do this? *When* did you do this?'

All thought of aches and pains left me. I got up to Little Pink as fast as I could, trying to remember what I'd drawn. Whatever it

83

was, I hadn't made any effort to put it out of sight. Suppose it was something really awful? Suppose I'd gotten the bright idea of doing a crucifixion caricature, with The Gospel Hummingbird riding the cross?

Ilse was standing in front of my easel, and I couldn't see what was there. Her body was blocking it out. Even if she'd been standing to one side, the only light in the room was coming from that bloody sunset; the pad would have been nothing but a black rectangle against the glare.

I flicked on the lights, praying I hadn't done something to distress the daughter who had come all this way to make sure I was okay. From her voice, I hadn't been able to tell. 'Ilse?'

She turned to me, her face bemused rather than angry. 'When did you do this one?'

'Well . . .' I said. 'Stand aside a little, would you?'

'Is your memory playing tricks again? It is, isn't it?'

'No,' I said. 'Well, yeah.' It was the beach outside the window, I could tell that much but no more. 'As soon as I see it, I'm sure I'll . . . step aside, honey, you make a better door than a window.'

'Even though I am a pain, right?' She laughed. Rarely had the sound of laughter so relieved me. Whatever she'd found on the easel, it hadn't made her mad, and my stomach dropped back where it belonged. If she wasn't angry, the risk that I might get angry and spoil what had, on measure, been a pretty damned good visit went down.

She stepped to the left, and I saw what I'd drawn while in my dazed, pre-nap state. Technically, it was probably the best thing I'd done since my first tentative pen-and-inks on Lake Phalen, but I thought it was no wonder she was puzzled. I was puzzled, too.

It was the section of beach I could see through Little Pink's nearly wall-length window. The casual scribble of light on the water, achieved with a shade the Venus Company called Chrome, marked the time as early morning. A little girl in a tennis dress stood at the center of the picture. Her back was turned, but her red hair was a dead giveaway: she was Reba, my little love, that girlfriend from my other life. The figure was poorly executed, but you somehow knew that was on purpose, that she wasn't a real little girl at all, only a dream figure in a dream landscape.

All around her feet, lying in the sand, were bright green tennis balls.

Others floated shoreward on the mild waves.

'When did you do it?' Ilse was still smiling – almost laughing. 'And what the heck does it mean?'

'Do you like it?' I asked. Because *I* didn't like it. The tennis balls were the wrong color because I hadn't had the right shade of green, but that wasn't why; I hated it because it felt all wrong. It felt like heartbreak.

'I *love* it!' she said, and then *did* laugh. 'C'mon, when did you do it? Give.'

'While you were sleeping. I went to lie down, but I felt queasy again, so I thought I better stay vertical for awhile. I decided to draw a little, see if things would settle. I didn't realize I had *that* thing in my hand until I got up here.' I pointed to Reba, sitting propped against the window with her stuffed legs sticking out.

'That's the doll you're supposed to yell at when you forget things, right?'

'Something like that. Anyway, I drew the picture. It took maybe an hour. By the time I was finished, I felt better.' Although I remembered very little about making the drawing, I remembered enough to know this story was a lie. 'Then I lay down and took a nap. End of story.'

'Can I have it?'

I felt a surge of dismay, but couldn't think of a way to say no that wouldn't hurt her feelings or sound crazy. 'If you really want it. It's not much, though. Wouldn't you rather have one of Freemantle's Famous Sunsets? Or the mailbox with the rocking horse! I could—'

'This is the one I want,' she said. 'It's funny and sweet and even a little . . . I don't know . . . ominous. You look at her one way and you say, "A doll." You look another way and say, "No, a little girl – after all, isn't she standing up?" It's amazing how much you've learned to do with colored pencils.' She nodded decisively. 'This is the one I want. Only you have to name it. Artists have to name their pictures.'

'I agree, but I wouldn't have any idea—'

'Come on, come on, no weaseling. First thing to pop into your mind.'

I said, 'All right – *The End of the Game.*'

85

She clapped her hands. 'Perfect. *Perfect!* And you have to sign it, too. Ain't I bossy?'

'You always were,' I said. '*Très* bossy. You must be feeling better.'

'I am. Are you?'

'Yes,' I said, but I wasn't. All at once I had a bad case of the mean reds. Venus doesn't make that color, but there was a new, nicely sharpened Venus Black in the gutter of the easel. I picked it up and signed my name by one of back-to doll's pink legs. Beyond her, a dozen wrong-green tennis balls floated on a mild wave. I didn't know what those rogue balls meant, but I didn't like them. I didn't like signing my name to this picture, either, but after I had, I jotted *The End of the Game* up one side. And what I felt was what Pam had taught the girls to say when they were little, and had finished some unpleasant chore.

Over-done with-gone.

xvi

She stayed two more days, and they were good days. When Jack and I took her back to the airport, she'd gotten some sun on her face and arms and seemed to give off her own benevolent radiation: youth, health, well-being.

Jack had found a travel-tube for her new picture.

'Daddy, promise you'll take care of yourself and call if you need me,' she said.

'Roger that,' I said, smiling.

'And promise me you'll get someone to give you an opinion on your pictures. Someone who knows about that stuff.'

'Well—'

She lowered her chin and frowned at me. When she did that it was again like looking at Pam when I'd first met her. 'You better promise, or else.'

And because she meant it — the vertical line between her eyebrows said so — I promised.

The line smoothed out. 'Good, that's settled. You deserve to get better, you know. Sometimes I wonder if you really believe that.'

'Of course I do,' I said.

Ilse went on as if she hadn't heard. 'Because what happened wasn't your fault.'

I felt tears well up at that. I suppose I *did* know, but it was nice to hear someone else say it out loud. Someone besides Kamen, that is, whose job it was to scrape caked-on grime off those troublesome unwashed pots in the sinks of the subconscious.

She nodded at me. 'You *are* going to get better. I say so, and I'm *très* bossy.'

The loudspeaker honked: Delta flight 559, service to Cincinnati and Cleveland. The first leg of Ilse's trip home.

'Go on, hon, better let em wand your bod and check your shoes.'

'I have one other thing to say first.'

I threw up the one hand I still had. 'What *now*, precious girl?'

She smiled at that: it was what I'd called both girls when my patience was finally nearing an end.

'Thank you for not telling me that Carson and I are too young to be engaged.'

'Would it have done any good?'

'No.'

'No. Besides, your mother will do an adequate job of that for both of us, I think.'

Ilse scrunched her mouth into an ouch shape, then laughed. 'So will Linnie . . . but only cause I got ahead of her for once.'

She gave me one more strong hug. I breathed deep of her hair – that good sweet smell of shampoo and young, healthy woman. She pulled back and looked at my man-of-all-work, standing considerately off to one side. 'You better take good care of him, Jack. He's the goods.'

They hadn't fallen in love – no breaks there, *muchacho* – but he gave her a warm smile. 'I'll do my best.'

'And he promised to get an opinion on his pictures. You're a witness.'

Jack smiled and nodded.

'Good.' She gave me one more kiss, this one on the tip of the nose. 'Be good, father. Heal thyself.' Then she went through the doors, festooned with bags but still walking briskly. She looked back just before they closed. 'And get some paints!'

87

'I will!' I called back, but I don't know if she heard me; in Florida, doors whoosh shut in a hurry to save the air conditioning. For a moment or two everything in the world blurred and grew brighter; there was a pounding in my temples and a damp prickle in my nose. I bent my head and worked briskly at my eyes with the thumb and second finger of my hand while Jack once more pretended to see something interesting in the sky. There was a word and it wouldn't come. I thought *borrow*, then *tomorrow*.

Give it time, don't get mad, tell yourself you can do this, and the words usually come. Sometimes you don't want them, but they come, anyway. This one was *sorrow*.

Jack said, 'You want to wait for me to bring the car, or—'

'No, I'm good to walk.' I wrapped my fingers around the grip of my crutch. 'Just keep an eye on the traffic. I don't want to get run down crossing the road. Been there, done that.'

xvii

We stopped at Art & Artifacts of Sarasota on our way back, and while we were in there, I asked Jack if he knew anything about Sarasota art galleries.

'Way ahead of you, boss. My Mom used to work in one called the Scoto. It's on Palm Avenue.'

'Is that supposed to mean something to me?'

'It's *the* hot-shit gallery on the arty side of town,' he said, then re-thought that. 'I mean that in a nice way. And the people who run it are nice . . . at least they always were to my Mom, but . . . you know . . .'

'It *is* a hot-shit gallery.'

'Yeah.'

'Meaning big prices?'

'It's where the elite meet.' He spoke solemnly, but when I burst out laughing, he joined me. That was the day, I think, when Jack Cantori became my friend rather than my part-time gofer.

'Then that's settled,' I said, 'because I am definitely elite. Give it up, son.'

I raised my hand, and Jack gave it a smack.

88

xviii

Back at Big Pink, he helped me into the house with my loot – five bags, two boxes, and a stack of nine stretched canvases. Almost a thousand dollars' worth of stuff. I told him we'd worry about getting it upstairs the next day. Painting was the last thing on earth I wanted to do that night.

I limped across the living room toward the kitchen, meaning to put together a sandwich, when I saw the message light on the answering machine blinking. I thought it must be Ilse, saying her flight had been cancelled due to weather or equipment problems.

It wasn't. The voice was pleasant but cracked with age, and I knew who it was at once. I could almost see those enormous blue sneakers propped on the bright footplates of her wheelchair.

'Hello, Mr Freemantle, welcome to Duma Key. It was a pleasure to see you the other day, if only briefly. One assumes the young lady with you was your daughter, given the resemblance. Have you taken her back to the airport? One rather hopes so.'

There was a pause. I could hear her breathing, the loud, not-quite-emphysemic respiration of a person who has probably spent a great deal of her life with a cigarette in one hand. Then she spoke again.

'All things considered, Duma Key has never been a lucky place for daughters.'

I found myself thinking of Reba in a very unlikely tennis dress, surrounded by small fuzzy balls as more came in on the next wave.

'One hopes we will meet, in the course of time. Goodbye, Mr Freemantle.'

There was a click. Then it was just me and the restless grinding sound of the shells under the house.

The tide was in.

How to Draw a Picture (III)

Stay hungry. It worked for Michelangelo, it worked for Picasso, and it works for a hundred thousand artists who do it not for love (although that may play a part) but in order to put food on the table. If you want to translate the world, you need to use your appetites. Does this surprise you? It shouldn't. There's nothing as human as hunger. There's no creation without talent, I give you that, but talent is cheap. Talent goes begging. Hunger is the piston of art. That little girl I was telling you about? She found hers and used it.

She thinks No more bed all day now. I go Daddy room, Daddy's study. Sometimes I say study, sometimes I say groody. It has a nice big window. They sit me in the char. I can see down up. Birds and nice. Too nice for me, so it makes me sat. Some clouds have wings. Some have blue eyes. Every sunset I cry from sat. Hurts to see. Hurts the down up in me. I could never say what I see and that makes me sat.

She thinks SAD, that word is SAD. Sat is for how you feel in the char.

She thinks If I could stop the hurt. If I could get it out like weewee. I cry and beg beg beg to say what I mean. Nan can't hep. When I say 'Color!' she touch her face and smile and say 'Always was, always will be.' Big girls don't help either. I'm so mad at them, why don't you listen, YOU BIG MEANIES! Then one day the twins come, Tessie and Lo-Lo. They talk special to each other, listen special to me. They don't understand me at first, but then. Tessie bring me paper. Lo-Lo bring me pencil and I 'Ben-cil!' out my mouth and it makes them claff and lap their hands.

She thinks I CAN ALMOST SAY THE NAME OF PENCIL!

She thinks I can make the world on paper. I can draw what the words mean. I see tree, I make tree. I see bird, I make bird. It's good, like water from a glass.

This is a little girl with a bandage wound around her head, wearing a

91

little pink housecoat and sitting beside the window in her father's study. Her doll, Noveen, lies on the floor beside her. She has a board and on the board is a piece of paper. She has just succeeded in drawing a claw that actually does bear a resemblance to the dead loblolly pine outside the window.

She thinks I will have more paper, please.

She thinks I am ELIZABETH.

It must have been like being given back your tongue after you thought it had been stilled forever. And more. Better. It was a gift of herself, of ELIZABETH. Even from those incredibly brave first drawings, she must have understood what was happening. And wanted more.

Her gift was hungry. The best gifts – and the worst – always are.

4 – Friends with Benefits

i

On New Year's afternoon, I woke from a brief but refreshing nap thinking of a certain kind of shell – the orangey kind with white speckles. I don't know if I dreamed about it or not, but I wanted one. I was ready to start experimenting with paints, and I thought one of those orange shells would be just the thing to plop down in the middle of a Gulf of Mexico sunset.

I began prospecting southward along the beach, accompanied only by my shadow and two or three dozen of the tiny birds – Ilse called them peeps – that prospect endlessly for food at the edge of the water. Further out, pelicans cruised, then folded their wings and dropped like stones. I wasn't thinking of exercise that afternoon, I wasn't monitoring the pain in my hip, and I wasn't counting steps. I wasn't thinking of anything, really; my mind was gliding like the pelicans before they spotted dinner in the *caldo largo* below them. Consequently, when I finally spotted the kind of shell I wanted and looked back, I was stunned at how small Big Pink had become.

I stood bouncing the orange shell up and down in my hand, all at once feeling the broken-glass throb in my hip. It started there and went pulsing all the way down my leg. Yet the tracks I saw stretching back toward my house hardly dragged at all. It occurred to me then that I'd been babying myself – maybe a little, maybe quite a lot. Me and my stupid little Numbers Game. Today I had forgotten about giving myself an anxious mini-physical every five minutes or so. I'd simply . . . gone for a walk. Like any normal person.

So I had a choice. I could baby myself going back, stopping every now and then to do one of Kathi Green's side-stretches, which hurt like hell and didn't seem to do much of anything else, or I could just walk. Like any normal unhurt person.

I decided to go with that. But before I started, I glanced over

93

my shoulder and saw a striped beach chair a ways farther south. There was a table beside it with an umbrella, striped like the chair, over it. A man was sitting in the chair. What was only a speck glimpsed from Big Pink had become a tall, heavyset guy dressed in jeans and a white shirt with sleeves rolled to the elbows. His hair was long and blowing in the breeze. I couldn't make out his features; we were still too far apart for that. He saw me looking and waved. I waved back, then turned and began trudging for home along my own footprints. That was my first encounter with Wireman.

ii

My final thought before turning in that night was that I'd probably find myself hobbling through the second day of the New Year almost too sore to walk. I was delighted to find that wasn't true; a hot bath seemed to take care of the residual stiffness.

So of course I struck off again the following afternoon. No set goal; no New Year's resolution; no Numbers Game. Just a guy strolling on the beach, sometimes veering close enough to the mild run of the waves to scatter the peeps aloft in a smutchy cloud. Sometimes I'd pick up a shell and put it in my pocket (in a week I'd be carrying a plastic bag to store my treasures in). When I got close enough to make out the heavyset guy in some detail – today wearing a blue shirt and khakis, almost certainly barefoot – I once again turned and headed back to Big Pink. But not before giving him a wave, which he returned.

That was the real beginning of my Great Beach Walks. Every afternoon they got a little longer, and I saw the heavyset man in his striped beach chair a little more clearly. It seemed obvious to me that he had his own routine; in the mornings he came out with the old lady, pushing her down a wooden tongue of decking that I hadn't been able to see from Big Pink. In the afternoons he came out on his own. He never took off his shirt, but his arms and face were as dark as old furniture in a formal home. Beside him, on his table, were a tall glass and a pitcher that might have held ice water, lemonade, or gin and tonic. He always waved; I always waved back.

One day in late January, when I had closed the distance between us to not much more than an eighth of a mile, a second striped chair appeared on the sand. A second glass, empty (but tall and terribly inviting), appeared on the table. When I waved, he first waved back and then pointed at the empty chair.

'Thanks, but not yet!' I called.

'Hell, come on down!' he called back. 'I'll give you a ride back in the golf cart!'

I smiled at that. Ilse had been all in favor of a golf cart, so I could go racing up and down the beach, scaring the peeps. 'Not in the game-plan,' I yelled, 'but I'll get there in time! Whatever's in that pitcher – keep it on ice for me!'

'You know best, *muchacho!*' He sketched a little salute. 'Meantime, do the day and let the day do you!'

I remember all sorts of things Wireman said, but I believe that's the one I associate with him the most strongly, maybe because I heard him say it before I knew his name or had even shaken his hand: *Do the day and let the day do you.*

iii

Walking wasn't all Freemantle was about that winter; Freemantle started to be about living again. And that felt fucking great. I came to a decision one windy night when the waves were pounding and the shells were arguing instead of just conversing: When I knew this new way of feeling was for real, I was going to take Reba the Anger-Management Doll down to the beach, douse her with charcoal lighter-fluid, and set her ablaze. Give my other life a true Viking funeral. Why the hell not?

In the meantime there was painting, and I took to it like peeps and pelicans take to water. After a week, I regretted having spent so much time farting around with colored pencils. I sent Ilse an e-mail thanking her for bullying me, and she sent me one back, telling me she hardly needed encouragement in that department. She also told me that The Hummingbirds had played a big church in Pawtucket, Rhode Island – sort of a tour warm-up – and the congregation had gone wild, clapping and shouting out hallelujahs. 'There was a good deal of swaying in the aisles,' she wrote. 'It's the Baptist substitute for dancing.'

That winter I also made the Internet in general and Google in particular my close personal friends, pecking away one-handed. When it came to Duma Key, I found little more than a map. I could have dug deeper and harder, but something told me to leave that alone for the time being. What I was really interested in were peculiar events following the loss of limbs, and I found a mother-lode.

I should tell you that while I took all the stories Google led me to with a grain of salt, I didn't reject even the wildest completely, because I never doubted that my own strange experiences were related to the injuries I'd suffered – the insult to Broca's area, my missing arm, or both. I could look at my sketch of Carson Jones in his Torii Hunter tee-shirt anytime I wanted to, and I was sure Mr Jones had purchased Ilse's engagement ring at Zales. Less concrete, but just as persuasive to me, were my increasingly surreal drawings. The phone-pad doodles of my previous life gave no hint of the haunted sunsets I was now doing.

I wasn't the first person to lose a body-part only to gain something else. In Fredonia, New York, a logger cut off his own hand in the woods and then saved his life by cauterizing the spouting stump of his wrist. The hand he took home, put in a jar of alcohol, and stored in the cellar. Three years later the hand that was no longer south of his wrist nevertheless began to feel freezing cold. He went downstairs and discovered a cellar window had broken and the winter wind was blowing in on the jar with his preserved hand floating inside. When the ex-logger moved the jar next to the furnace, that sense of freezing cold disappeared.

A Russian peasant from Tura, deep in Siberia, lost his left arm up to the elbow in a piece of farming equipment and spent the rest of his life as a dowser. When he stood over a spot where there was water, his left hand and arm, although no longer there, would grow cool, with an accompanying sensation of wetness. According to the articles I read (there were three), his skills never failed.

There was a guy in Nebraska who could predict tornadoes by the corns on his missing foot. A legless sailor in England who was used by his mates as a kind of human fish-finder. A Japanese double amputee who became a respected poet – not a bad trick for a fellow who'd been illiterate at the time of the train accident in which he lost his arms.

Of all the stories, maybe the strangest was that of Kearney Jaffords of New Jersey, a child *born* without arms. Shortly after his thirteenth birthday, this formerly well-adjusted handicapped child became hysterical, insisting to his parents that his arms were 'hurting and buried on a farm'. He said he could show them where. They drove two days, finishing up on a dirt road in Iowa, somewhere between Nowhere and Nowhere in Particular. The kid led them into a cornfield, took a sighting on a nearby barn with a MAIL POUCH advertisement on the roof, and insisted that they dig. The parents did, not because they expected to find anything but because they hoped to set the child's mind and body at rest again. Three feet down they found two skeletons. One was a female child between twelve and fifteen. The other was a man, age undetermined. The Adair County Coroner estimated these bodies had been in the ground approximately twelve years ... but of course it could have been thirteen, which was the span of Kearney Jaffords's life. Neither body was ever identified. The arms of the female child's skeleton had been removed. Those bones were mixed with the bones of the unidentified man.

Fascinating as this story was, there were two others that interested me even more, especially when I thought of how I'd gone rooting through my daughter's purse.

I found them in an article called 'They See with What's Missing', from *The North American Journal of Parapsychology*. It chronicled the histories of two psychics, one a woman from Phoenix, the other a man from Río Gallegos, Argentina. The woman was missing her right hand; the man was missing his entire right arm. Both had had several successes in helping the police find missing persons (perhaps failures as well, but these were not set out in the piece).

According to the article, both amputee psychics used the same technique. They would be provided with a piece of the missing person's clothes, or a sample of his handwriting. They would shut their eyes and visualize touching the item with the missing hand (there was a hugger-mugger footnote here about something called the Hand of Glory, aka the Mojo Hand). The Phoenix woman would then 'get an image', which she would relay to her interlocutors. The Argentinian, however, followed up his communings with brief, furious spates of automatic writing with his remaining hand, a process I saw as analogous to my paintings.

And, as I say, I might have doubted a few of the wilder anecdotes

I ran across during my Internet explorations, but I never doubted something was happening to me. Even without the picture of Carson Jones, I think I would have believed it. Because of the quiet, mostly. Except when Jack dropped by, or when Wireman − ever closer − waved and called 'Buenos días, muchacho!' I saw no one and spoke to no one but myself. The extraneous dropped away almost entirely, and when that happens, you begin to hear yourself clearly. And clear communication between selves − the surface self and the deep self is what I mean − is the enemy of self-doubt. It slays confusion.

But to be sure, I settled on what I told myself was an experiment.

iv

EFree19 to Pamorama667
9:15 AM
January 24

Dear Pam: I have an unusual bequest for you. I've been painting, and the subjects are odd but kind of fun (at least I think so). Easier to show you what I mean than describe, so I will attach a couple of jpegs to this e-mail. I have been thinking about those gardening gloves you used to have, the ones that said HANDS on one glove and OFF on the other. I would love to put those on a sunset. Do NOT ask me why, these ideas just come to me. Do you still have them? And if you do, would you send them to me? I will happily send them back if you want.

I'd just as soon you didn't share the pix with any of the 'old crowd'. Bozie in particular would probably laugh like a look if he saw THESE things.

Eddie

PS: If you don't feel good about sending the gloves, perfectly O.K. It's just a wind.

E.

98

This response came that evening, from a Pam who was by then back home in St Paul:

Pamorama667 to EFree19
5:00 PM
January 24

Hello Edgar: Ilse told me about yr pictures of course. They certainly are different. Hopefully this hobby will last longer than yr car restoration thing. If not for eBay that old Mustang would still be behind the house I think. Yr right about it being an odd request but after looking at yr pix I can sort of see what yr up-to (putting different things together so people will look at them in new ways, right) and I'm ready for a new pr anyway so 'knock yrself out'. I'll send them UPS only ask that you send me a jpg of the 'Finnish Product' ☺ if there ever is one.

Ilse sd she had a terrific time. I hope she sent a Thank-You card and not just an e-mail, but I know her.

One more thing to tell you, Eddie, altho I don't know how much you will like it. I sent a copy of yr e-mail and jpg pictures to Zander Kamen, you remember him I'm sure. I thought he would like to see the pix, but mostly I wanted him to see the e-mail and find out if it was cause for concern, because you are doing in yr writing what you used to do in yr speaking: 'bequest' for 'request', 'laugh like a look' for 'laugh like a loon'. At the bottom you wrote 'It's just a wind' and I don't know what that means but Dr Kamen says maybe 'whim'.

I'm just thinking of you.

Pam

PS: My father is a little better, came through the operation well (the doctors say they might have 'got all of it' but I bet they always say that). He seems to be handling the chemo well and is at home. Walking already.
Thanks for yr concern.

Her PS zinger was a perfect example of my ex-wife's unlovelier side: lie back . . . lie back . . . lie back . . . then *bite* and 'make yrself scarce'. She was right, though. I should have told her to pass on best wishes from the Commiecrat when she spoke to her old man on the phone. That ass-cancer's a bitch.

The whole e-mail was a symphony of irritation, from the mention of the Mustang that I'd never had time to finish to her concerns about my mistaken word-choices. Said concerns delivered by a woman who thought *Xander* came with a *Z*.

And with that petty spleen out of my system (spoken to the empty house, and in loud tones, if you must know), I did review the e-mail I'd sent her, and yes, I was worried. A little, anyway.

On the other hand, maybe it was just the wind.

v

The second striped beach chair had become a fixture at the heavyset guy's table, and as I drew closer to it, we sometimes shouted a little conversation back and forth. It was a strange way to strike up an acquaintance, but pleasant. The day after Pam's e-mail, with its surface concerns and buried subtext (*You could be as sick as my father, Eddie, maybe even sicker*), the fellow down the beach yelled: 'How long before you get here, do you think?'

'Four days!' I yelled back. 'Maybe three!'

'You that set on making a round trip?'

'I am!' I said. 'What's your name?'

His deeply tanned face, although growing fleshy, was still handsome. Now white teeth flashed there, and his incipient jowls disappeared when he grinned. 'Tell you when you get here! What's yours?'

'It's on the mailbox!' I called.

'The day I stoop to reading mailboxes is the day I start getting my news from talk radio!'

I gave him a wave, he gave me one in turn, called '*Hasta mañana!*' and turned to look at the water and the cruising birds once more.

When I got back to Big Pink, the flag of my computer mailbox was sticking up, and I found this:

100

KamenDoc to EFree19
2:49 PM
January 25

Edgar: Pam sent me copies of your latest e-mail and your pictures. Let me say first and foremost that I am STUNNED by the rapidity of your growth as an artist. I can see you shying away from the word with that patented sidelong frown of yours, but there is no other word. YOU MUST NOT STOP. Concerning her worries: there's probably nothing to them. Still, an MRI would be a good idea. Do you have a doctor down there? You're due for a physical – soup to nuts, my friend.

Kamen

EFree19 to KamenDoc
3:58 PM
January 25

Kamen: Good to hear from you. If you want to call me an artist (or even an 'artiste'), who am I to argue? I currently have no Florida sawbones. Can you refer me to one or would you rather I went through Todd Jamieson, the doc with his fingers most recently in my brain?

Edgar

I thought he'd refer, and I might even keep the appointment, but right then a few dropped words and linguistic oddities weren't a priority. Walking was a priority, and reaching the striped beach chair that had been set out for me was also sort of a priority, but my main ones as January waned were Internet searches and painting pictures. I had reached *Sunset with Shell No. 16* only the night before.

On January twenty-seventh, after turning back only two hundred yards or so shy of the waiting beach chair, I arrived at Big Pink to find UPS had left a package. Inside were two gardening gloves, one with HANDS printed in faded red on the back and the other similarly printed with OFF. They were beat-up from many seasons in the garden but clean – she'd laundered them, as I had expected. As I had, in fact, hoped. It wasn't the Pam who had worn them during the years of our marriage that I was interested in, not even the Pam who might have worn them in the Mendota Heights garden the past fall, while I was out at Lake Phalen. That Pam was a known quantity. But . . . *I'll tell you something else that's happening,* my If-So-Girl had said, unaware of how eerily like her mother she had looked when she was saying it. *She's seeing an awful lot of this guy down the street.*

That was the Pam I was interested in – the one who had seen an awful lot of the guy down the street. The guy named Max. *That* Pam's hands had laundered these gloves, then picked them up and put them in the white box inside the UPS package.

That Pam was the experiment . . . or so I told myself, but we fool ourselves so much we could do it for a living. That's what Wireman says, and he's often right. Probably too often. Even now.

vi

I didn't wait for sunset, because at least I didn't fool myself that I was interested in painting a picture; I was interested in painting *information.* I took my wife's unnaturally clean gardening gloves (she must have really rammed the bleach to them) up to Little Pink and sat down in front of my easel. There was a fresh canvas there, waiting. To the left were two tables. One was for photos from my digital camera and various found objects. The other stood on a small green tarpaulin. It held about two dozen paint-tubes, and several jars partly filled with turpentine. It was quite the messy, busy little work-station.

I held the gloves in my lap, closed my eyes, and pretended I was touching them with my right hand. There was nothing. No pain, no itching, no sense of phantom fingers caressing the rough, worn fabric. I sat there *willing* it to come – whatever *it* was – and got more nothing. I might as well have been commanding my body to shit when it didn't need to. After five long minutes, I opened my eyes again and looked down at the gloves on my lap: HANDS . . . OFF.

Useless things. Useless fucking things.

Don't get mad, get even, I thought. And then I thought, *Too late. I am mad. At these gloves and the woman who wore them. As for getting even?*

'Too late for that, too,' I said, and looked at my stump. 'I'll never be heaven again.'

The wrong word. Always the wrong word, and it would go on like that for-fucking-ever. I felt like knocking everything off my stupid goddam play-tables and onto the floor.

'Even,' I said, deliberately low and deliberately slow. 'I'll never be *eeee*-ven again. I'm odd-arm-out.' That wasn't very funny (or even very sensible), but the anger started seeping away just the same. Hearing myself say the right word helped. It usually did.

I turned my thoughts from my stump to my wife's gloves. HANDS OFF, indeed.

With a sigh − there might have been some relief in it, I don't remember for sure, but it's likely − I set them on the table where I put my model objects, took a brush out of a turp jar, cleaned it with a rag, rinsed it, and looked at the blank canvas. Did I mean to paint the gloves anyway? Why, for fuck's sake? *Why?*

All at once the idea that I had been painting at all seemed ridiculous. The idea that I didn't know how seemed a hell of a lot more plausible. If I dipped this brush in black and then put it on that forbidding white-space, surely the best I'd be able to do would be a series of marching stick figures: *Ten little Indians went out to dine, One drowned her baby self, Then there were nine. Nine little Indians, Stayed up very late—*

That was spooky. I got up from my chair, and fast. Suddenly I didn't want to be here, not in Little Pink, not in Big Pink, not on Duma Key, not in my stupid pointless limping retired retarded life. How many lies was I telling? That I was an artist? Ridiculous. Kamen could cry STUNNED and YOU MUST NOT STOP in his patented e-mail capitals, but Kamen specialized in tricking the victims of terrible accidents into believing the pallid imitations of life they were living were as good as the real thing. When it came to positive reinforcement, Kamen and Kathi Green the Rehab Queen were a tag-steam. They were FUCKING BRILLIANT, and most of their grateful patients cried YOU MUST NOT STOP. Was I telling myself I was psychic? Possessed of a phantom arm capable of seeing into the unknown? That wasn't ridiculous, it was pitiful and insane.

There was a 7-Eleven in Nokomis. I decided I would try my driving skills, pick up a couple of six-packs, and get drunk. Things might look better tomorrow, through the haze of a hangover. I did not see how they could look much worse. I reached for my crutch and my foot – my left one, my good foot, for Christ's sake – caught under my chair. I stumbled. My right leg wasn't strong enough to hold me up and I fell full-length, reaching out with my right arm to break my fall.

Just instinct, of course . . . except it did break my fall. It did. I didn't see it – my eyes were squeezed shut, the way you squeeze them when you know you're going to take one for the team – but if I hadn't broken my fall, I would almost certainly have done myself significant damage, carpet or no carpet. I could have sprained my neck, or even broken it.

I lay there a moment, confirming to myself that I was still alive, then got to my knees, my hip aching fiercely, holding my throbbing right arm up in front of my eyes. There was no arm there. I set my chair up on its legs, leaned on it with my left forearm . . . then darted my head forward and bit my right arm.

I felt the crescents of my teeth sink in just below the elbow. The pain.

I felt more. I felt the flesh of my forearm against my lips. Then I drew back, panting. 'Jesus! Jesus! What's happening? What *is* this?'

I almost expected to see the arm swirl into existence. It didn't, but it was there, all right. I reached across the seat of my chair for one of my brushes. I could feel my fingers grasp it, but the brush didn't move. I thought: *So this is what it's like to be a ghost.*

I scrambled into the chair. My hip was snarling, but that pain seemed to be happening far downriver. With my left hand I snatched up the brush I'd cleaned and put it behind my left ear. Cleaned another and put it in the gutter of the easel. Cleaned a third and put that in the gutter, as well. Thought about cleaning a fourth and decided I didn't want to take the time. That fever was on me again, that hunger. It was as sudden and violent as my fits of rage. If the smoke detectors had gone off downstairs, announcing the house was on fire,

I would have paid no attention. I stripped the cellophane from a brand new brush, dipped black, and began to paint.

As with the picture I'd called *The End of the Game*, I don't remember much about the actual creation of *Friends with Benefits*. All I know is it happened in a violent explosion, and sunsets had nothing to do with it. It was mostly black and blue, the color of bruises, and when it was done, my left arm ached from the exercise. My hand was splattered with paint all the way to the wrist.

The finished canvas reminded me a little of those *noir* paperback covers I used to see back when I was a kid, the ones that always featured some roundheels dame headed for hell. Only on the paper-back covers, the dame was usually blond and twenty-twoish. In my picture, she had dark hair and looked on the plus side of forty. This dame was my ex-wife.

She was sitting on a rumpled bed, wearing nothing but a pair of blue panties. The strap of a matching bra trailed across one leg. Her head was slightly bent, but there was no mistaking her features; I had caught her BRILLIANTLY in just a few harsh strokes of black that were almost like Chinese ideograms. On the slope of one breast was the picture's only real spot of brightness: a rose tattoo. I wondered when she'd gotten it, and why. Pam wearing ink seemed as unlikely to me as Pam racing a dirtbike at Mission Hill, but I had no doubt whatever that it was true; it was just a fact, like Carson Jones's Torii Hunter tee-shirt.

There were also two men in the picture, both naked. One stood at the window, half-turned. He had a perfectly typical body for a white middle-class man of fifty or so, one I imagined you could see in any Gold's Gym changing room: poochy stomach, flat little no-cheeks ass, moderate man-tits. His face was intelligent and well-bred. On that face now was a melancholy she's-almost-gone look. A nothing-will-change-it look. This was Max from Palm Desert. He might as well have been wearing a sign around his neck. Max who had lost *his* father last year, Max who had started by offering Pam coffee and had ended up offering her more. She'd taken him up on the coffee and the more, but not all the more he would have given. His face said that. You couldn't see all of it, but what you could see was a lot more naked than his ass.

The other man leaned in the doorway with his ankles crossed,

105

a position that pressed his thighs together and pushed his considerable package forward. He was maybe ten years older than the man at the window, in better shape. No belly. No lovehandles. Long muscles in the thighs. His arms were folded below his chest and he was looking at Pam with a little smile on his face. I knew that smile well, because Tom Riley had been my accountant – and my friend – for thirty-five years. If it had not been custom in our family to ask your father to be your best man, I would have asked Tom.

I looked at him standing naked in the doorway, looking at my wife on the bed, and remembered him helping me move my stuff out to Lake Phalen. Remembered him saying *You don't give up the house, that's like giving up home field advantage in a playoff game.*

Then catching him with tears in his eyes. *Boss, I can't get used to seeing you this way.*

Had he been fucking her then? I thought not. But—

I'm going to give you an offer to take back to her, I'd said. And he had. Only maybe he'd done more than make my offer.

I limped to the big window, not using my crutch. Sunset was still hours off, but the light was westering strongly, beating a reflection off the water. I made myself look directly into that glaring track, wiping my eyes repeatedly.

I tried to tell myself the picture might be no more than a figment of a mind that was still trying to heal itself. It wouldn't wash. All my voices were speaking clearly and coherently to one another, and I knew what I knew. Pam had fucked Max out there in Palm Desert, and when he had suggested a longer, deeper commitment, she had refused. Pam had also fucked my oldest friend and business associate, and might still be fucking him. The only unanswered question was which guy had talked her into the rose on her tit.

'I need to let this go,' I said, and leaned my throbbing forehead against the glass. Beyond me, the sun burned on the Gulf of Mexico. 'I really need to let this go.'

Then snap your fingers, I thought.

I snapped the fingers of my right hand and heard the sound – a brisk little click. 'All right, over-done with-gone!' I said brightly. But then I closed my eyes and saw Pam sitting on the bed – some bed – in her panties, with a bra-strap lying across her leg like a dead snake.

Friends with benefits.

Fucking friends, with fucking benefits.

vii

That evening I didn't watch the sunset from Little Pink. I left my crutch leaning against the corner of the house, limped down the beach, and walked into the water until I was up to my knees. The water was cold, the way it gets a couple of months after hurricane season has blown itself out, but I hardly noticed. Now the track beating across the water was bitter orange, and that was what I was looking at.

'Experiment, my ass,' I said, and the water surged around me. I rocked unsteadily on my feet, holding my arm out for balance. 'My fucking ass.'

Overhead a heron glided across the darkening sky, a silent long-neck projectile.

'Snooping is what it was, snooping is *all* it was, and I paid the price.'

True. If I sort of felt like strangling her all over again, it was nobody's fault but my own. *Peek not through a keyhole, lest ye be vexed*, my dear old mother used to say. I peeked, I was vexed, end of story. It was her life now, and what she did in it was her business. My business was to drop it. My *question* was whether or not I could. It was harder than snapping your fingers; even than snapping the fingers of a hand that wasn't there.

A wave surged in, one big enough to knock me down. For a moment I was under, and breathing water. I came up spluttering. The backrun tried to pull me out with the sand and shells. I pushed shoreward with my good foot, even kicking feebly with my bad one, and managed to get some purchase. I might be confused about some things, but I didn't want to drown in the Gulf of Mexico. I wasn't confused about that. I crawled out of the water with my hair hanging in my eyes, spitting and coughing, dragging my right leg behind me like so much soaked luggage.

When I finally got to dry sand, I rolled over and stared up into the sky. A fat crescent moon sailed the deepening velvet above Big

Pink's roofpeak. It looked very serene up there. Down here was a man who felt the opposite of serene: shaking and sad and angry. I turned my head to look at the stump of my arm, then up at the moon again.

'No more peeking,' I said. 'The new deal starts tonight. No more peeking and no more experiments.'

I meant it, too. But as I've said (and Wireman was there before me), we fool ourselves so much we could do it for a living.

5 – Wireman

i

The first time Wireman and I actually met he laughed so hard he broke the chair he was sitting in, and I laughed so hard I almost fainted – did in fact go into that half-swooning state that's called 'a gray-out'. That was the last thing I would have expected a day after finding out that Tom Riley was having an affair with my ex-wife (not that my evidence would have stood up in any court of law), but it was an augury of things to come. It wasn't the only time we laughed together. Wireman was many things to me – not least of all my fate – but most of all, he was my friend.

ii

'So,' he said, when I finally reached his table with the striped umbrella shading it and the empty chair across from his own. 'The limping stranger arriveth, bearing a bread-bag filled with shells. Sit down, limping stranger. Wet thy whistle. That glass has been waiting for some days now.'

I put my plastic bag – it was indeed a bread-bag – on the table and reached across to him. 'Edgar Freemantle.'

His hand was short, the fingers blunt, the grip strong. 'Jerome Wireman. I go by Wireman, mostly.'

I looked at the beach chair meant for me. It was the kind with a high back and a low fanny-sling, like the bucket seat in a Porsche.

'Something wrong with that, *muchacho*?' Wireman asked, raising an eyebrow. He had a lot of eyebrow to raise, tufted and half-gray.

'Not as long as you don't laugh when I have to get out of it,' I said.

109

He smiled. 'Honey, live like you got to live. Chuck Berry, nineteen sixty-nine.'

I positioned myself beside the empty chair, said a little prayer, and dropped. I leaned left as always, to spare my bad hip. I didn't land quite square, but I grabbed the wooden arms, pushed with my strong foot, and the chair only teetered. A month before I would have spilled, but I was stronger now. I could imagine Kathi Green applauding.

'Good job, Edgar,' he said. 'Or are you an Eddie?'

'Pick your poison, I answer to either. What might you have in that pitcher?'

'Iced green tea,' he said. 'Very cooling. Try some?'

'I'd love to.'

He poured me a glass, then topped up his own and raised it. The tea was only faintly green. His eyes, caught in fine nets of wrinkles, were greener. His hair was black, streaking in white at the temples, and quite long indeed. When the wind lifted it, I could see a scar at the top of his hairline on the right side, coin-shaped but smaller. He was wearing a bathing suit today, and his legs were as brown as his arms. He looked fit, but I thought he also looked tired.

'Let's drink to you, *muchacho*. You made it.'

'All right,' I said. 'To me.'

We clinked glasses and drank. I'd had green tea before and thought it was okay, but this was heavenly – like drinking cold silk, with just a faint tang of sweetness.

'Do you taste the honey?' he asked, and smiled when I nodded. 'Not everyone does. I just put in a tablespoonful per pitcher. It releases the natural sweetness of the tea. I learned that cooking on a tramp steamer in the China Sea.' He held up his glass and squinted through it. 'We fought off many pirates and mated with strange and dusky women 'neath tropic skies.'

'That sounds a trifle bullshitty to me, Mr Wireman.'

He laughed. 'I actually read about the honey thing in one of Miss Eastlake's cookery books.'

'Is she the lady you come out with in the mornings? The one in the wheelchair?'

'Indeed she is.'

And without thinking much about what I was saying – it was her enormous blue sneakers propped up on the chrome footrests of her wheelchair I was thinking about – I said: 'The Bride of the Godfather.'

Wireman gaped, those green eyes of his so wide I was about to apologize for my *faux pas*. Then he *really* began to laugh. It was the kind of balls-to-the-wall bellowing you give out on those rare occasions when something sneaks past all your defenses and gets to the sweet spot of your funnybone. I mean the man was busting a gut, and when he saw I didn't have the slightest idea what had gotten him, he laughed even harder, his not inconsiderable belly heaving. He tried to put his glass back on the little table and missed. The glass plummeted straight down to the sand and *stuck* there, perfectly upright, like a cigarette-butt in one of those urns of sand you used to see beside the elevators in hotel lobbies. That struck him even funnier, and he pointed at it.

'I couldn't have done that if I was *trying!*' he managed, and then was off again, gale upon gale, heaving in his chair, one hand clutching his stomach, the other planted on his chest. A snatch of poetry read in high school, over thirty years before, suddenly came back to me with haunting clarity: *Men do not sham convulsion, Nor simulate a throe.*

I was smiling myself, smiling and chuckling, because that kind of high hilarity is catching, even when you don't know what the joke is. And the glass falling that way, with every drop of Wireman's tea staying inside . . . that *was* funny. Like a gag in a Road Runner cartoon. But the plummeting glass hadn't been the source of Wireman's hilarity.

'I don't get it. I mean I'm sorry if I—'

'She sort of *is!*' Wireman cried, cackling so crazily he was almost incoherent. 'She sort of *is*, that's the thing! Only it's *daughter*, of course, she's The *Daughter* of the Godfa—'

But he had been rocking from side to side as well as up and down – no sham, authentic throe – and that was when his beach chair finally gave up the ghost with a loud *crrrack*, first snapping him forward with an extremely comical look of surprise on his face and then spilling him onto the sand. One of his flailing arms caught the post of the umbrella and upended the table. A gust of wind

111

caught the umbrella, puffed it like a sail, and began to drag the table down the beach. What got me laughing wasn't the bug-eyed look of amazement on Wireman's face when his disintegrating beach chair tried to clamp on him like a striped jaw, nor his sudden barrel-roll onto the sand. It wasn't even the sight of that table trying to escape, tugged by its own umbrella. It was Wireman's glass, still standing placidly upright between the sprawling man's side and left arm.

Acme Iced Tea Company, I thought, still stuck on those old Road Runner cartoons. *Meep-meep!* And that, of course, made me think of the crane that had done the damage, the one with the fucked-up beeper that hadn't beeped, and all at once I saw myself as Wile E. Coyote in the cab of my disintegrating pickup truck, eyes bugged in bewilderment, frazzled ears sticking off in two opposite directions and maybe smoking a little at the tips.

That did it. I laughed until I rolled bonelessly out of my own chair and plopped onto the sand beside Wireman . . . but I also missed the glass, which still stood perfectly upright like a cigarette-butt in an urn of sand. It was impossible for me to laugh any harder, but I did. Tears gushed down my cheeks and the world had begun to dim out as my brain went into oxygen-deprivation mode.

Wireman, still howling, went crawling after his runaway table, locomoting on knees and elbows. He made a grab for the base and it skittered away as if sensing his approach. Wireman plowed face-first into the sand and came up laughing and sneezing. I rolled over on my back and gasped for breath, on the verge of passing out but still laughing.

That was how I met Wireman.

iii

Twenty minutes later the table had been placed in a rough approximation of its original position. That was all very well, but neither of us could look at the umbrella without breaking into fits of the giggles. One of its pie-wedges was torn, and it now rose crookedly from the table, giving it the look of a drunken man trying to pretend he's sober. Wireman had moved the remaining chair down to the

112

end of the wooden walk, and had taken it at my insistence. I was sitting on the walk itself, which, although backless, would make getting up an easier (not to mention more dignified) proposition. Wireman had offered to replace the spilled pitcher of iced tea with a fresh one. I refused this, but agreed to split the miraculously unspilled glass with him.

'Now we're water-brothers,' he said when it was gone.

'Is that some Indian ritual?' I asked.

'Nope, from *Stranger in a Strange Land*, by Robert Heinlein. Bless his memory.'

It occurred to me that I'd never seen him reading as he sat in his striped chair, but I didn't mention it. Lots of people don't read on the beach; the glare gives them headaches. I sympathized with people who got headaches.

He began to laugh again. He covered his mouth with both hands – like a child – but the laughter burst through. 'No more. Jesus, no more. I feel like I sprung every muscle in my stomach.'

'Me too,' I said.

For a moment we said nothing more. The breeze off the Gulf was cool and fresh that day, with a rueful salt tang. The rip in the umbrella flapped. The dark spot on the sand where the iced tea pitcher had spilled was already almost dry.

He snickered. 'Did you see the table trying to escape? The fucking *table?*'

I also snickered. My hip hurt and my stomach-muscles ached, but I felt pretty good for a man who had almost laughed himself unconscious. '"Alabama Getaway",' I said.

He nodded, still wiping sand from his face. 'Grateful Dead. Nineteen seventy-nine. Or thereabouts.' He giggled, the giggle broadened into a chuckle, and the chuckle became another bellow of full-throated laughter. He held his belly and groaned. 'I can't, I have to stop, but . . . Bride of the Godfather! *Jesus!*' And he was off again.

'Don't you ever tell her I said that,' I said.

He quit laughing, but not smiling. 'I ain't that indiscreet, *muchacho*. But . . . it was the hat, right? That big straw hat she wears. Like Marlon Brando in the garden, playing with the little kid.'

It had actually been as much the sneakers, but I nodded and we laughed some more.

'If we crack up when I introduce you,' he said (cracking up again, probably at the idea of cracking up; it goes that way when the fit is on you), 'we're gonna say it's because I broke my chair, right?'

'Right,' I said. 'What did you mean when you said she sort of is?'

'You really don't know?'

'No clue.'

He pointed at Big Pink, which was looking very small in the distance. Looking like a long walk back. 'Who do you think owns your place, *amigo*? I mean, I'm sure you pay a real estate agent, or Vacation Homes Be Us, but where do you think the balance of your check finally ends up?'

'I'm going to guess in Miss Eastlake's bank account.'

'Correct. Miss Elizabeth Eastlake. Given the lady's age – eighty-five – I guess you could call her Ole Miss.' He began laughing again, shook his head, and said: 'I have to stop. But in fairness to myself, it's been a long time since I had anything to belly-laugh about.'

'Same here.'

He looked at me – armless, all patchy-haired on one side – and nodded. Then for a little while we just looked out at the Gulf. I know that people come to Florida when they're old and sick because it's warm pretty much year-round, but I think the Gulf of Mexico has something else going for it. Just looking into that mild flat sunlit calm is healing. It's a big word, isn't it? *Gulf*, I mean. Big enough to drop a lot of things into and watch them disappear.

After awhile Wireman said, 'And who do you think owns the houses between your place and this one?' He jerked his thumb over his shoulder at the white walls and orange tile. 'Which, by the way, is listed on the county plat-maps as *Heron's Roost* and I call *El Palacio de Asesinos*.'

'Would that also be Miss Eastlake?'

'You're two for two,' he said.

'Why do you call it Palace of Assassins?'

'Well, it's "Outlaw Hideout" when I think in English,' Wireman said with an apologetic smile. 'Because it looks like the place where the head bad guy in a Sam Peckinpah Western would hang his hat.

Anyway, you've got six rather nice homes between Heron's Roost and Salmon Point—'

'Which I call Big Pink,' I said. 'When I think in English.'

He nodded. '*El Rosado Grande*. Good name. I like it. You'll be there . . . how long?'

'I have the place for a year, but I honestly don't know. I'm not afraid of hot weather – I guess they call it the mean season – but there's hurricanes to consider.'

'Yep, down here we all consider hurricane season, especially since Charley and Katrina. But the houses between Salmon Point and Heron's Roost will be empty long before hurricane season. Like the rest of Duma Key. Which could as easily have been called Eastlake Island, by the way.'

'Are you saying this is all hers?'

'That's complicated even for a guy like me, who was a lawyer in his other life,' Wireman said. 'Once upon a time her *father* owned it all, along with a good swatch of the Florida mainland east of here. He sold everything in the thirties except for Duma. Miss Eastlake does own the north end, of that there is no doubt.' Wireman waved his arm to indicate the northern tip of the island, the part he would later characterize as being as bald as a stripper's pussy. 'The land and the houses on it, from Heron's Roost – the most luxurious – to your Big Pink, the most adventurous. They bring her an income she hardly needs, because her father also left her and her siblings *mucho dinero*.'

'How many of her brothers and sisters are still—'

'None,' Wireman said. 'The Daughter of the Godfather is the last.' He snorted and shook his head. 'I have to quit calling her that,' he said, more to himself than to me.

'If you say so. What I really wonder about is why the rest of the island isn't developed. Given the never-ending housing and building boom in Florida, that's seemed insane to me from the first day I crossed the bridge.'

'You speak like a man with specialized knowledge. What are you in your other life, Edgar?'

'A building contractor.'

'And those days are behind you now?'

I could have hedged – I didn't know him well enough to put

myself on the line – but I didn't. I'm sure our mutual fit of hysterics had a lot to do with that. 'Yes,' I said.

'And what are you in this life?'

I sighed and looked away from him. Out at the Gulf, where you could put all your old miseries and watch them disappear without a trace. 'Can't tell yet for sure. I've been doing some painting.' And waited for him to laugh.

He didn't. 'You wouldn't be the first painter to stay at Salm . . . Big Pink. It has quite an artistic history.'

'You're kidding.' There was nothing in the house to suggest such a thing.

'Oh yes,' he said. 'Alexander Calder stayed there. Keith Haring. Marcel Duchamp. All back before beach erosion put the place in danger of falling into the water.' He paused. 'Salvador Dalí.'

'No shucking way!' I cried, then flushed when he cocked his head. For a moment I felt all the old frustrated rage rush in, seeming to clog my head and throat. *I can do this*, I thought. 'Sorry. I had an accident awhile back, and—' Then I stopped.

'Not hard to figure that one out,' Wireman said. 'In case you didn't notice, you're short a gizmo on the right side, *muchacho*.'

'Yes. And sometimes I get . . . I don't know . . . aphasic, I guess.'

'Uh-huh. In any case, I tell no lie about Dalí. He stayed in your house for three weeks in nineteen eighty-one.' Then, with hardly a pause: 'I know what you're going through.'

'I seriously doubt that.' I didn't mean to sound harsh, but that was how it sounded. That was how I felt, actually.

Wireman said nothing for a little while. The torn umbrella flapped. I had time to think, *Well this was a potentially interesting friendship that's not going to happen*, but when he next spoke, his voice was calm and pleasant. It was as if our little side-trip had never occurred.

'Part of Duma's development problem is simple overgrowth. The sea oats belong, but the rest of that shit has no business growing without irrigation. Somebody better investigate, that's what I think.'

'My daughter and I went exploring one day. It looked like outright jungle south of here.'

Wireman looked alarmed. 'Duma Key Road's no excursion for a guy in your condition. It's in shit shape.'

'Tell me about it. What I want to know is how come it isn't four

116

lanes wide with bike-paths on both sides and condos every eight hundred yards.'

'Because no one knows who owns the land? How about that, for a start?'

'You serious?'

'Yup. Miss Eastlake has owned from the tip of the island south to Heron's Roost free and clear since 1950. About that there's absolutely no doubt. It was in the wills.'

'*Wills?* Plural?'

'Three of them. All holographic, all witnessed by different people, all different when it comes to Duma Key. All of them, however, make the north end of Duma a no-strings bequest to Elizabeth Eastlake from her father, John. The rest has been in the courts ever since. Sixty years of squabbling that makes *Bleak House* look like Dick and Jane.'

'I thought you said all Miss Eastlake's siblings were dead.'

'They are, but she has nieces and nephews and grandnieces and grandnephews. Like Sherwin-Williams Paint, they cover the earth. *They're* the ones doing the squabbling, but they squabble with each other, not her. Her only mention in the old man's multiple wills had to do with this piece of Duma Key, which was carefully marked off by two surveying companies, one just before World War II and one just after. This is all a matter of public record. And do you know what, *amigo*?'

I shook my head.

'Miss Eastlake thinks that's exactly what her old man wanted to happen. And, having cast my lawyerly eye over copies of the wills, so do I.'

'Who pays the taxes?'

He looked surprised, then laughed. 'I enjoy you more and more, *vato*.'

'My other life,' I reminded him. I was already liking the sound of that other-life thing.

'Right. Then you'll appreciate this,' he said. 'It's clever. All three of John Eastlake's last wills and testaments contained identical clauses setting up a trust fund to pay the taxes. The original investment company administering the trust has been absorbed since then – in fact the *absorbing* company has been absorbed—'

117

'It's the way America does business,' I said.

'It is indeed. In any case, the fund has never been in danger of going broke and the taxes are paid like clockwork every year.'

'Money talks, bullshit walks.'

'It's the truth.' He stood up, put his hands in the small of his back, and twisted it. 'Would you like to come up to the house and meet the boss? She should be arising from her nap just about now. She has her problems, but even at eighty-five she's quite the babe.'

This wasn't the time to tell him I thought I already had met her – briefly – courtesy of my answering machine. 'Another day. When the hilarity subsides.'

He nodded. 'Walk down tomorrow afternoon, if you like.'

'Maybe I will. It's been real.' I held out my hand again. He shook it again, looking at the stump of my right arm as he did so.

'No prosthesis? Or do you just leave it off when you're not among the hoi polloi?'

I had a story I told people about that – nerve-pain in the stump – but it was a lie, and I didn't want to lie to Wireman. Partly because he had a nose attuned to the delicate smell of bullshit, but mostly because I just didn't want to lie to him.

'I was measured for one while I was still in the hospital, of course, and I got the hard sell on it from just about everyone – especially my physical therapist and this psychologist friend of mine. They said the quicker I learned to use it, the quicker I'd be able to get on with my life—'

'Just put the whole thing behind you and go on dancing—'

'Yes.'

'Only sometimes putting a thing behind you isn't so easy to do.'

'No.'

'Sometimes it's not even right,' Wireman said.

'That isn't it, exactly, but it's . . .' I trailed off and seesawed my hand in the air.

'Close enough for rock and roll?'

'Yes,' I said. 'Thanks for the cold drink.'

'Come on back and get another one. I only take the sun between two and three – an hour a day is enough for me – but Miss Eastlake either sleeps or rearranges her china figurines most of the after- noon, and of course she never misses *Oprah*, so I have time. More than I know what to do with, actually. Who knows? We might find a lot to talk about.'

'All right,' I said. 'Sounds good.'

Wireman grinned. It made him handsome. He offered his hand and I shook with him again. 'You know what I think? Friendships founded on laughter are always fortuitous.'

'Maybe your next job will be writing the fortunes in Chinese cookies,' I said.

'There could be worse jobs, *muchacho*. Far worse.'

iv

Walking back, my thoughts turned to Miss Eastlake, an old lady in big blue sneakers and a wide straw hat who just happened to own (sort of) her own Florida Key. Not the Bride of the Godfather after all, but Daughter of the Land Baron and, apparently, Patroness of the Arts. My mind had done another of those weird slip-slides and I couldn't remember her father's name (something simple, only one syllable), but I remembered the basic situation as Wireman had outlined it. I'd never heard of anything similar, and when you build for a living, you see all sorts of strange property arrangements. I thought it was actually rather ingenious . . . if, that was, you wanted to keep most of your little kingdom in a state of undeveloped grace. The question was, why?

I was most of the way back to Big Pink before I realized my leg was aching like a bastard. I limped inside, slurped water directly from the kitchen tap, then made my way across the living room to the main bedroom. I saw the light on the answering machine was blinking, but I wanted nothing to do with messages from the outside world right then. All I wanted was to get off my feet.

I lay down and looked at the slowly revolving blades of the overhead fan. I hadn't done very well explaining my lack of a fake arm. I wondered if Wireman would've had better luck with *What's a lawyer doing as a rich old spinster's houseman? What kind of other life is that?*

Still considering this, I drifted off into a dreamless and very satisfying nap.

119

V

When I woke up, I took a hot shower, then went into the living room to check my answering machine. I wasn't as stiff as I had expected, given my two-mile walk. I might get up tomorrow hobbling, but for tonight I thought I was going to be all right.

The message was from Jack. He said his mother had connected him with someone named Dario Nannuzzi, and Nannuzzi would be happy to look at my pictures between four and five p.m. on Friday afternoon – could I bring no more than ten of those I considered best to the Scoto Gallery? No sketches; Nannuzzi only wanted to see finished work.

I felt a tickle of unease at this—

No, that's not even close to what I felt.

My stomach cramped and I could have sworn my bowels dropped three inches. Nor was that the worst. That half-itch, half-pain swarmed up my right side and down the arm that was no longer there. I told myself such feelings – which amounted to three-days-in-advance flop-sweat – were stupid. I had once made a ten-million-dollar pitch to the St Paul City Council, which at that time had included a man who'd gone on to become the Governor of Minnesota. I'd seen two girls through first dance recitals, cheer-leading tryouts, driving lessons, and the hell of adolescence. What was showing some of my paintings to an art gallery guy compared to that?

Nevertheless, I made my way up the stairs to Little Pink with leaden heels.

The sun was going down, flooding the big room with gorgeous and improbable tangerine light, but I felt no urge to try and capture it – not this evening. The light called to me, just the same. As the photograph of some long-gone love, happened on by accident while going through an old box of souvenirs, may call to you. And the tide was in. Even upstairs I could hear the grinding voice of the shells. I sat down and began poking at the clutter of items on my junk-table – a feather, a water-smoothed stone, a disposable lighter rinsed to an anonymous gray. Now it wasn't Emily Dickinson I thought of, but some old folk-song: *Don't the sun look good, Mama, shinin through the trees.* No trees out there, of course, but I could put one on the horizon if I wanted to. I could put one out there for the red sunset to shine through. Hello, Dalí.

I wasn't afraid of being told I had *no* talent. I was afraid of Signor Nannuzzi telling me I had a *leetle* talent. Of having him hold his thumb and forefinger maybe a quarter of an inch apart and advising me to reserve a space at the Venice Sidewalk Art Festival, that I would certainly find success there, many tourists would surely be taken by my charming Dalí imitations.

And if he did that, held his thumb and forefinger a quarter of an inch apart and said *leetle*, what did I do then? Could some stranger's verdict take away my new confidence in myself, steal my peculiar new joy?

'Maybe,' I said.

Yes. Because painting pictures wasn't like putting up shopping malls.

The easiest thing would be just to cancel the appointment . . . except I'd sort of promised Ilse, and I wasn't in the habit of breaking the promises I made to my children.

My right arm was still itching, itching almost hard enough to hurt, but I barely noticed. There were eight or nine canvases lined up against the wall to my left. I turned toward them, thinking I'd try to decide which ones were best, but I never so much as looked at them.

Tom Riley was standing at the head of the stairs. He was naked except for a pair of light blue pajama pants, darker at the crotch and down the inside of one leg, where he had wet them. His right eye was gone. There was a matted socket full of red and black gore where it had been. Dried blood streaked back along his right temple like war paint, disappearing into graying hair above his ear. His other eye stared out at the Gulf of Mexico. Carnival sunset swam over his narrow, pallid face.

I shrieked in surprise and terror, recoiled, and fell off my chair. I landed on my bad hip and yelled out again, this time from pain. I jerked and my foot struck the chair I'd been sitting in, knocking it over. When I looked toward the stairs again, Tom was gone.

vi

Ten minutes later I was downstairs, dialing his home number. I had descended the stairs from Little Pink in the sitting position, thumping down one riser at a time on my ass. Not because I'd hurt my hip falling off the chair, but because my legs were trembling so badly I didn't trust myself on my feet. I was afraid I might take a header, even going down backward so I could clutch the banister with my left hand. Hell, I was afraid I might faint.

I kept remembering the day at Lake Phalen I'd turned to see Tom with that unnatural shine in his eyes, Tom trying not to embarrass me by actual bawling. *Boss, I can't get used to seeing you this way . . . I'm so sorry.*

The telephone began to ring in Tom's nice Apple Valley home. Tom, who'd been married and divorced twice, Tom who had advised me against moving out of the house in Mendota Heights – *It's like giving up home field advantage in a playoff game,* he'd said. Tom who'd gone on to enjoy my home field quite a little bit himself, if *Friends with Benefits* were to be believed . . . and I *did* believe it.

I believed what I'd seen upstairs, too.

One ring . . . two . . . three.

'Come on,' I muttered. 'Pick the motherfucker up.' I didn't know what I'd say if he did, and didn't care. All I wanted right then was to hear his voice.

I did, but on a recording. 'Hi, you've reached Tom Riley,' he said. 'My brother George and I are off with our mother, on our annual cruise – it's Nassau this year. What do you say, Mother?'

'That I'm a Bahama Mama!' said a cigarette-cracked but undeniably cheerful voice.

'That's right, she is,' Tom resumed. 'We'll be back February eighth. In the meantime, you can leave a message . . . when, George?'

'At the *zound* of the *zeep*!' cried a male voice.

'Right!' Tom agreed. 'Zound of the zeep. Or you can call my office.' He gave the number, and then all three of them said '*BON VOYAGE!*'

I hung up without saying anything. It hadn't sounded like the outgoing message of a man contemplating suicide, but of course he

122

had been with his nearest and dearest (the ones who, later on, were most apt to say 'He seemed fine'), and—

'Who says it's going to be suicide?' I asked the empty room . . . and then looked around fearfully to make sure it *was* empty. 'Who says it might not be an accident? Or even murder? Assuming it hasn't happened already?'

But if it had already happened, someone would probably have called me. Maybe Bozie, but most likely Pam. Also . . .

'It's suicide.' This time telling the room. 'It's suicide and it hasn't happened yet. That was a warning.'

I got up and crutched into the bedroom. I'd been using the crutch less lately, but I wanted it tonight, indeed I did.

My best girl was propped against the pillows on the side of the bed that would have belonged to a real woman, if I'd still had one. I sat down, picked her up and looked into those big blue peepers, so full of cartoon surprise: *Ouuuu, you nasty man!* My Reba, who looked like Lucy Ricardo.

'It was like Scrooge getting visited by the Ghost of Christmas Yet-To-Come,' I told her. '"These are things that *may* be."'

Reba offered no opinion on this idea.

'But what do I do? That wasn't like the paintings. That wasn't like the paintings at all!'

But it was, and I knew it. Both paintings and visions originated in the human brain, and something in my brain had changed. I thought the change had come about as a result of just the right combination of injuries. Or the wrong one. Contracoup. Broca's area. And Duma Key. The Key was . . . what?

'Amplifying it,' I told Reba. 'Isn't it?'

She offered no opinion.

'There's something here, and it's acting on me. Is it possible it even called me?'

The notion made me break out in gooseflesh. Beneath me, the shells ground together as the waves lifted them and dropped them. It was all too easy to imagine skulls instead of shells, thousands of them, all gnashing their teeth at once when the waves came in.

Was it Jack who had said there was another house somewhere out there in the toolies, falling apart? I thought so. When Ilse and I tried to drive that way, the road had gone bad in a hurry. So had

Ilse's stomach. My own gut had been okay, but the stink of the encroaching flora had been nasty and the itch in my missing arm had been worse. Wireman had looked alarmed when I told him about our attempted exploration. *Duma Key Road's no excursion for a guy in your condition*, he'd said. The question was, exactly what was my condition?

Reba went on offering no opinion.

'I don't want this to be happening,' I said softly.

Reba only stared up at me. I was a nasty man, that was *her* opinion.

'What good are you?' I asked, and threw her aside. She landed facedown on her pillow with her bottom up and her pink cotton legs spread, looking quite the little slut. *Ouuuu you nasty man*, indeed.

I dropped my head, looked at the carpet between my knees, and rubbed the nape of my neck. The muscles there were tight and knotted. They felt like iron. I hadn't had one of my bad headaches in awhile, but if those muscles didn't loosen soon, I'd be having a whopper tonight. I needed to eat something, that would be a start. Something comforting. One of those calorie-stuffed frozen dinners sounded about right – the kind where you slice the wrapping over the frozen meat and gravy, blast it for seven minutes in the microwave, then chow down like a motherfucker.

But I sat still awhile longer. I had many questions, and most were probably beyond my ability to answer. I recognized that and accepted it. I had learned to accept a lot since the day I'd had my confrontation with the crane. But I thought I had to try for at least one answer before I could bring myself to eat, hungry as I was. The phone on the bedtable had come with the house. It was charmingly old-fashioned, the Princess model with a rotary dial. It sat on a directory that was mostly Yellow Pages. I turned to the skinny white section, thinking I wouldn't find Elizabeth Eastlake listed, but I did. I dialed the number. It rang twice and then Wireman answered.

'Hello, Eastlake residence.'

There was hardly a trace in that perfectly modulated voice of the man who had laughed hard enough to break his chair, and all at once this seemed like the world's worst idea, but I saw no other option.

'Wireman? This is Edgar Freemantle. I need help.'

6 – The Lady of the House

i

The following afternoon found me once more sitting at the little table at the end of *El Palacio de Asesinos* boardwalk. The striped umbrella, although ripped, was still serviceable. A breeze chilly enough to warrant sweatshirts was blowing in off the water. Little scars of light danced across the table-top as I talked. And I talked, all right – for almost an hour, refreshing myself with sips of green tea from a glass Wireman kept filled. At last I stopped and for a little while there was no sound but the mild whisper of the incoming waves, breaking and running up the strand.

Wireman must have heard enough wrong in my voice the night before to concern him, because he'd offered to come in the *Palacio* golf cart immediately. He said he could stay in touch with Miss Eastlake via walkie-talkie. I told him it could wait a little. It was important, I said, but not urgent. Not in the 911 sense, at least. And it was true. If Tom were to commit suicide on his cruise, there was little I could do to prevent it. But I didn't think he'd do it as long as his mother and brother were with him.

I had no intention of telling Wireman about my furtive hunt through my daughter's purse; that was something of which I'd grown more rather than less ashamed. But once I started, beginning with **LINK-BELT**, I couldn't stop. I told him almost everything, finishing with Tom Riley standing at the head of the stairs leading up to Little Pink, pale and dead and minus an eye. I think part of what kept me going was the simple realization that Wireman couldn't commit me to the nearest lunatic asylum – he had no legal authority. Part of it was that, attracted as I was by his kindness and cynical good cheer, he was still a stranger. Sometimes – often, I think – telling stories that are embarrassing or even downright crazy is easier when you're telling them to a stranger. Mostly, though, I pushed

125

on out of pure relief: I felt like a man expressing snake-venom from a bite.

Wireman poured himself a fresh glass of tea with a hand that was not quite steady. I found that interesting and disquieting. Then he glanced at his watch, which he wore nurse-style, with the face on the inside of his wrist. 'In half an hour or so I really have to go up and check her,' he said. 'I'm sure she's fine, but—'

'What if she wasn't?' I asked. 'If she fell, or something?'

He pulled a walkie-talkie from the pocket of his chinos. It was as slim as a cell phone. 'I make sure she always carries hers. There are also Rapid Response call-buttons all over the house, but—' He tapped a thumb on his chest. 'I'm the real alarm system, okay? The only one I trust.'

He looked out at the water and sighed.

'She's got Alzheimer's. It's not too bad yet, but Dr Hadlock says it'll probably move fast now that it's settled in. A year from now . . .' He shrugged almost sullenly, then brightened. 'We have tea every day at four. Tea and *Oprah*. Why not come up and meet the lady of the house? I'll even throw in a slice of key lime pie.'

'Okay,' I said. 'It's a deal. Do you think she's the one who left that message on my answering machine about Duma Key not being a lucky place for daughters?'

'Sure. Although if you expect an explanation – if you expect her to even remember – good luck. But I can help you a little, maybe. You said something about brothers and sisters yesterday, and I didn't get a chance to correct you. Fact is, all Elizabeth's sibs were girls. All daughters. The oldest was born in 1908 or thereabouts. Elizabeth came onstage in 1923. Mrs Eastlake died about two months after having her. Some kind of infection. Or maybe she threw a clot . . . who's to know at this late date? That was here, on Duma Key.'

'Did the father remarry?' I still couldn't remember his name.

Wireman helped me out. 'John? No.'

'You're not going to tell me he raised six girls out here. That's just too gothic.'

'He tried, with the help of a nanny. But his eldest ran off with a boy. Miss Eastlake had an accident that almost killed her. And the twins . . .' He shook his head. 'They were two years older than Elizabeth. In 1927 they disappeared. The presumption is they tried

126

to go swimming, got swept away by an undertow, and drowned out there in the *caldo grande*.'

We looked at the water for a little while – those deceptively mild waves running up the beach like puppies – and said nothing. Then I asked if Elizabeth had told him all of this.

'Some. Not all. And she's mixed up about what she does remember. I found a passing mention of an incident that had to be the right one on a Web site dedicated to Gulf coast history. Had a little e-mail correspondence with a guy who's a librarian in Tampa.' Wireman raised his hands and waggled his fingers in a typing mime. 'Tessie and Laura Eastlake. The librarian sent me a copy of the Tampa paper from April 19th, 1927. The headline on the front page is very stark, very bleak, very chilling. Three words. THEY ARE GONE.'

'Jesus,' I said.

'Six years old. Elizabeth would have been four, old enough to understand what had happened. Maybe old enough to read a newspaper headline as simple as THEY ARE GONE. The twins dead and Adriana, the oldest, eloped off to Atlanta with one of his plant managers . . . no wonder John had had enough of Duma for awhile. He and the remaining three moved to Miami. Many years later, he moved back here to die, and Miss Eastlake cared for him.' Wireman shrugged. 'Pretty much as I'm caring for her. So . . . do you see why an old lady with onset-Alzheimer's might consider Duma a bad place for daughters?'

'I guess so, but how does an old lady with onset-Alzheimer's find the phone number of her new tenant?'

Wireman gave me a sly look. 'New tenant, old number, autodial function on all the phones back there.' He jerked his thumb over his shoulder. 'Any other questions?'

I gaped at him. 'She has me on *autodial*?'

'Don't blame me; I came in late on this movie-show. My guess is that the Realtor who handles things for her programmed the rental properties into the phones. Or maybe Miss Eastlake's business manager. He pops down from St Petersburg every six weeks or so to make sure she's not dead and I'm not stealing the Spode. I'll ask him the next time he shows up.'

'So she can call any house on the north end of the Key at the touch of a button.'

'Well . . . yeah. I mean, they *are* all hers.' He patted my hand. 'But you know what, *muchacho*? I think your button is going to have a little nervous breakdown this evening.'

'No,' I said, not even thinking about it. 'Don't do that.'

'Ah,' Wireman said, exactly as if he understood. And who knows, maybe he did. 'Anyway, that explains your mystery caller – although I have to tell you, explanations have a way of thinning out on Duma Key. As your story demonstrates.'

'What do you mean? Have you had . . . experiences?'

He looked at me squarely, his large tanned face inscrutable. The chilly late January wind gusted, blowing sand around our ankles. It also lifted his hair, once again revealing the coin-shaped scar above his right temple. I wondered if someone had poked him with the neck of a bottle, maybe in a bar fight, and tried to imagine someone getting mad at this man. It was hard to do.

'Yes, I've had . . . *experiences*,' he said, and hooked the first two fingers of each hand into little quotation marks. 'It's what makes children into . . . *adults*. Also what gives English teachers something to bullshit about in first year . . . *lit courses*.' Each time with the air-quotes.

Okay, he didn't want to talk about it, at least not then. So I asked him how much of my story he believed.

He rolled his eyes and sat back in his chair. 'Don't try my patience, *vato*. You might be mistaken about a few things, but you ain't nuts. I got a lady up there . . . sweetest lady in the world and I love her, but sometimes she thinks I'm her Dad and it's Miami circa nineteen thirty-four. Sometimes she pops one of her china people into a Sweet Owen cookie-tin and tosses it into the koi pond behind the tennis court. I have to get em out when she naps, otherwise she pitches a bitch. No idea why. I think by this summer she may be wearing an adult didey full-time.'

'Point?'

'The point is I know *loco*, I know Duma, and I'm getting to know you. I'm perfectly willing to believe you had a vision of your friend dead.'

'No bullshit?'

'No bullshit. *Verdad*. The question is what you're going to do about it, assuming you're not eager to see him into the ground for – may I be vulgar? – buttering what used to be your loaf.'

128

'I'm not. I did have this momentary thing . . . I don't know how to describe it . . .'

'Was it a momentary thing where you felt like chopping off his dick, then putting out his eyes with a hot toasting-fork? Was it *that* momentary thing, *muchacho*?' Wireman made the thumb and forefinger of one hand into a gun and pointed it at me. 'I was married to a Mexican lassie and I know jealousy. It's normal. Like a startle-reflex.'

'Did your wife ever . . .' I stopped, suddenly aware all over again that I'd only met this man the day before. That was easy to forget. Wireman was *intense*.

'No, *amigo*, not to my knowledge. What she did was die on me.' His face was perfectly expressionless. 'Let's not go there, okay?'

'Okay.'

'Thing to remember about jealousy is it comes, it goes. Like the afternoon showers down here during the mean season. You're over it, you say. You should be, because you ain't her *campesino* no more. The question is what you're going to do about this other thing. How you going to keep this guy from killing himself? Because you know what happens when the happy-family cruise is over, right?'

For a moment I said nothing. I was translating that last bit of Spanish, or trying to. You ain't her farmer no more, was that right? If so, it had a bitter ring of truth.

'*Muchacho?* Your next move?'

'I don't know,' I said. 'He's got e-mail, but what do I write to him? "Dear Tom, I'm worried you're contemplating suicide, please reply soonest"? I bet he's not checking his e-mail while he's on vacation, anyway. He's got two ex-wives, and still pays alimony to one of them, but he's not close to either. There was one kid, but he died in infancy – spina bifida, I think – and . . . what? *What?*'

Wireman had turned away and sat slouched in his chair, looking out at the water, where pelicans were diving for their own high tea. His body English suggested disgust.

He turned back. 'Quit squirming. You know damn well who knows him. Or you think you do.'

'Pam? You mean *Pam*?'

He only looked at me.

'Are you going to talk, Wireman, or only sit there?'

'I have to check on my lady. She'll be up by now and she's going to want her four o'clockies.'

'Pam would think I'm crazy! Hell, she *still* thinks I'm crazy!'

'Convince her.' Then he relented a little. 'Look, Edgar. If she's been as close to him as you think, she'll have seen the signs. And all you can do is try. *Entiendes?*'

'I don't understand what that means.'

'It means call your wife.'

'She's my ex.'

'Nope. Until your mind changes, the divorce is just a legal fiction. That's why you give a shit what she thinks about your state of mind. But if you also care about this guy, you'll call her and tell her you have reason to think he's planning to highside it.'

He heaved himself out of his chair, then held out his hand. 'Enough palaver. Come on and meet the boss. You won't be sorry. As bosses go, she's a pretty nice one.'

I took his hand and let him pull me out of what I presumed was a replacement beach chair. He had a strong grip. That was something else I'll never forget about Jerome Wireman; the man had a strong grip. The boardwalk up to the gate in the back wall was only wide enough for one, so I followed, limping gamely along. When he reached the gate – which was a smaller version of the one in front and looked as Spanish as Wireman's offhand patois – he turned toward me, smiling a little.

'Josie comes in to clean Tuesdays and Thursdays, and she's willing to keep an ear out for Miss Eastlake during her afternoon nap – which means I could come down and look at your pictures tomorrow afternoon around two, if that suits.'

'How did you know I wanted you to? I was still working up the nerve to ask.'

He shrugged. 'It's pretty obvious you want *someone* to look before you show them to the guy at that gallery. Besides your daughter and the kid who runs your errands, that is.'

'The appointment's on Friday. I'm dreading it.'

Wireman waggled his hand in the air and smiled. 'Don't worry,' he said. He paused. 'If I think your stuff is crap, I'm going to tell you so.'

'That works.'

He nodded. 'Just wanted to be clear.' Then he opened the gate and led me into the courtyard of Heron's Roost, also known as *Palacio de Asesinos.*

ii

I'd already seen the courtyard, on the day I'd used the front entrance to turn around, but on that day I'd gotten little more than a glance. I'd mostly been concentrating on getting myself and my ashen-faced, perspiring daughter back to Big Pink. I'd noticed the tennis court and the cool blue tiles, but had missed the koi pool entirely. The tennis court was swept and ready for action, its paved surface two shades darker than the courtyard tile. One turn of the chrome crank would bring the net taut and ready. A full basket of balls stood on wire stilts, and made me think briefly of the sketch Ilse had taken back to Providence with her: *The End of the Game.*

'One of these days, *muchacho,*' Wireman said, pointing at the court as we walked by. He had slowed down so I could catch up. 'You and me. I'll take it easy on you – just volley-and-serve – but I hunger to swing a racket.'

'Is volley-and-serve what you charge for evaluating pictures?'

He smiled. 'I have a price, but that ain't it. Tell you later. Come on in.'

iii

Wireman led me through the back door, across a dim kitchen with large white service islands and an enormous Westinghouse stove, then into the whispering interior of the house, which shone with dark woods – oak, walnut, teak, redwood, cypress. This was a *Palacio,* all right, old Florida style. We passed one book-lined room with an actual suit of armor brooding in the corner. The library connected with a study where paintings – not stodgy oil portraits but bright abstract things, even a couple of op-art eye-poppers – hung on the walls.

Light showered down on us like white rain as we walked the

131

main hall (*Wireman* walked; I limped), and I realized that, for all of the mansion's grandeur, this part of it was no more than a glorified dogtrot – the kind that separates sections of older and much humbler Florida dwellings. That style, almost always constructed of wood (sometimes scrapwood) rather than stone, even has a name: Florida Cracker.

This dogtrot, filled with light courtesy of its long glass ceiling, was lined with planters. At its far end, Wireman hung a right. I followed him into an enormous cool parlor. A row of windows gave on a side courtyard filled with flowers – my daughters could have named half of them, Pam all of them, but I could only name the asters, dayflowers, elderberry, and foxglove. Oh, and the rhododendron. There was plenty of that. Beyond the tangle, on a blue-tiled walk that presumably connected with the main courtyard, stalked a sharp-eyed heron. It looked both thoughtful and grim, but I never saw a one on the ground that didn't look like a Puritan elder considering which witch to burn next.

In the center of the room was the woman Ilse and I had seen on the day we tried exploring Duma Key Road. Then she'd been in a wheelchair, her feet clad in blue Hi-Tops. Today she was standing with her hands planted on the grips of a walker, and her feet – large and very pale – were bare. She was dressed in a high-waisted pair of beige slacks and a dark brown silk blouse with amusingly wide shoulders and full sleeves. It was an outfit that made me think of Katharine Hepburn in those old movies they sometimes show on Turner Classic Movies: *Adam's Rib,* or *Woman of the Year.* Only I couldn't remember Katharine Hepburn looking this old, even when she was old.

The room was dominated by a long, low table of the sort my father had had in the cellar for his electric trains, only this one was covered in some light wood – it looked like bamboo – rather than fake grass. It was crowded with model buildings and china figurines: men, women, children, barnyard animals, zoo animals, creatures of mythical renown. Speaking of mythical creatures, I saw a couple of fellows in blackface that wouldn't have passed muster with the N-double-A-C-P.

Elizabeth Eastlake looked at Wireman with an expression of sweet delight I would have enjoyed drawing . . . although I'm not sure anyone would have taken it seriously. I'm not sure we ever believe the simplest emotions in our art, although we see them all around us, every day.

'Wireman!' she said. 'I woke up early and I've been having such a wonderful time with my chinas!' She had a deep southern-girl accent that turned *chinas* into *CHA-nahs*. 'Look, the family's at home!'

At one end of the table was a model mansion. The kind with pillars. Think Tara in *Gone with the Wind* and you'll be fine. Or *fahn*, if you talk like Elizabeth. Around it were ranged almost a dozen figures, standing in a circle. The pose was strangely ceremonial.

'So they are,' Wireman agreed.

'And the schoolhouse! See how I've put the children outside the schoolhouse! Do come see!'

'I will, but you know I don't like you to get up without me,' he said.

'I didn't feel like calling on that old talkie-walkie. I'm really feeling very well. Come and see. Your new friend as well. Oh, I know who you are.' She smiled and crooked a finger at me to come closer. 'Wireman tells me all about you. You're the new fellow at Salmon Point.'

'He calls it Big Pink,' Wireman said.

She laughed. It was the cigarettey kind that dissolves into coughing. Wireman had to hurry forward and steady her. Miss Eastlake didn't seem to mind either the coughing or the steadying. 'I *like* that!' she said when she was able. 'Oh hon, I *like* that! Come and see my new schoolhouse arrangement, Mr . . . ? I'm sure I've been told your name but it escapes me, so much does now, you are Mr . . . ?'

'Freemantle,' I said. 'Edgar Freemantle.'

I joined them at her play-table; she offered her hand. It wasn't muscular, but was, like her feet, of a good size. She hadn't forgotten the fine art of greeting, and gripped as well as she could. Also, she looked at me with cheerful interest as we shook. I liked her for her frank admission of memory troubles. And, Alzheimer's or not, I did far more mental and verbal stuttering than I'd seen so far from her.

'It's good to know you, Edgar. I have seen you before, but I don't recall when. It will come to me. Big Pink! That's sassy!'

'I like the house, ma'am.'

'Good. I'm very glad if it gives satisfaction. It's an artist's house, you know. Are you an artist, Edgar?'

She was looking at me with her guileless blue eyes. 'Yes,' I said. It was the easiest, the quickest, and maybe it was the truth. 'I guess I am.'

'Of course you are, hon, I knew right away. I'll need one of your pictures. Wireman will strike a price with you. He's a lawyer as well as an excellent cook, did he tell you that?'

'Yes . . . no . . . I mean—' I was lost. Her conversation seemed to have developed too many threads, and all at once. Wireman, that dog, looked as if he were struggling not to laugh. Which made me feel like laughing, of course.

'I try to get pictures from all the artists who've stayed in your Big Pink. I have a Haring that was painted there. Also a Dalí sketch.'

That stopped any impulse to laugh. 'Really?'

'Yes! I'll show you in a bit, one really can't avoid it, it's in the television room and we always watch *Oprah*. Don't we, Wireman?'

'Yes,' he said, and glanced at the face of his watch on the inside of his wrist.

'But we don't have to watch it on the dot, because we have a wonderful gadget called . . .' She paused, frowned, and put a finger to the dimple in one side of her plump chin. 'Vito? Is it Vito, Wireman?'

He smiled. 'TiVo, Miss Eastlake.'

She laughed. 'TiVo, isn't that a funny word? And isn't it funny how formal we are? He's Wireman to me, I'm Miss Eastlake to him – unless I'm upset, as I sometimes am when things slip my mind. We're like characters in a play! A happy one, where one knows that soon the band will strike up and everyone in the company will sing!' She laughed to show what a charming idea it was, but there was something a little frantic in it. For the first time her accent made me think of Tennessee Williams instead of Margaret Mitchell.

Gently – very gently – Wireman said: 'Maybe we ought to go into the other room for *Oprah* now. I think you ought to sit down. You can have a cigarette when you watch *Oprah*, and you know you like that.'

'In a minute, Wireman. In just a minute. We have so little *company* here.' Then back to me. 'What kind of artist are you, Edgar? Do you believe in art for art's sake?'

'Definitely art for art's sake, ma'am.'

'I'm glad. That's the kind Salmon Point likes best. What do you call it?'

'My art?'

'No, hon − Salmon Point.'

'Big Pink, ma'am.'

'Big Pink it shall be. And I shall be Elizabeth to you.'

I smiled. I had to, because she was earnest rather than flirty. 'Elizabeth it is.'

'Lovely. In a moment or two we shall go to the television room, but first . . .' She turned her attention back to the play-table. 'Well, Wireman? Well, Edgar? Do you see how I've arranged the children?'

There were about a dozen, all facing the left side of the school-house. Low student enrollment.

'What does it say to you?' she asked. 'Wireman? Edward? Either?'

That was a very minor slip, but of course I was attuned to slips. And that time my own name was the banana peel.

'Recess?' Wireman asked, and shrugged.

'Of course not,' she said. 'If it were recess, they'd be *playing*, not all bunched together and gawking.'

'It's either a fire or a fire drill,' I said.

She leaned over her walker (Wireman, vigilant, grabbed her shoulder to keep her from overbalancing), and planted a kiss on my cheek. It surprised hell out of me, but not in a bad way. 'Very good, Edward!' she cried. 'Now which do you say it is?'

I thought it over. It was easy if you took the question seriously. 'A drill.'

'Yes!' Her blue eyes blazed with delight. 'Tell Wiring why.'

'If it was a fire, they'd be scattering in all directions. Instead, they're—'

'Waiting to go back in, yes.' But when she turned to Wireman, I saw a different woman, one who was frightened. 'I called you by the wrong name again.'

'It's all right, Miss Eastlake,' he said, and kissed the hollow of her temple with a tenderness that made me like him very much.

She smiled at me. It was like watching the sun sail out from behind a cloud. 'As long as he is still addressing one by one's surname, one knows . . .' But now she seemed lost, and her smile began to falter. 'One knows that . . .'

'That it's time to watch *Oprah*,' Wireman said, and took her arm. Together they turned her walker away from the play-table, and she began to clump with surprising speed toward a door in the far end of the room. He walked watchfully beside her.

Her 'television room' was dominated by a big flat-screen Samsung. At the other end of the room was a stack of expensive sound components. I hardly noticed either one. I was looking at the framed sketch on the wall above the shelves of CDs, and for a few seconds I forgot to breathe.

The sketch was just pencil, augmented by two scarlet threads, probably added with nothing more than a plain red ballpoint pen – the kind teachers use to grade papers. These not-quite-offhand scribbles had been laid along the horizon-line of the Gulf to indicate sunset. They were just right. They were genius writ small. It was *my* horizon, the one I saw from Little Pink. I knew that just as I knew the artist had been listening to the shells grind steadily beneath him as he turned blank white paper into what his eye saw and his mind translated. On the horizon was a ship, probably a tanker. It could have been the very one I'd drawn my first evening at Number 13 Duma Key Road. The style was nothing at all like mine, but the choice of subject-matter was damn near identical.

Scribbled almost carelessly at the bottom: *Salv Dalí.*

iv

Miss Eastlake – Elizabeth – had her cigarette while Oprah questioned Kirstie Alley on the always fascinating subject of weight-loss. Wireman produced egg salad sandwiches, which were delicious. My eyes kept straying to the framed Dalí sketch, and I kept thinking – of course – *Hello, Dalí.* When Dr Phil came on and began berating a couple of fat ladies in the audience who had apparently volunteered to be berated, I told Wireman and Elizabeth that I really ought to be getting back.

Elizabeth used the remote to silence Dr Phil, then held out the book the remote had been sitting on. Her eyes looked both humble and hopeful. 'Wireman says you'll come and read to me on some afternoons, Edmund, is that true?'

We're forced to make some decisions in a split second, and I made one then. I decided not to look at Wireman, who was sitting to Elizabeth's left. The acuity she'd exhibited at her play-table was fading, even I could see that, but I thought there was still quite a lot left. A glance in Wireman's direction would be enough to tell her that this was news to me, and she'd be embarrassed. I didn't want her to be embarrassed, partly because I liked her and partly because I suspected life would hold a great many embarrassments for her in the year or two ahead. It would soon be more than forgetting names.

'We've discussed it,' I said.

'Perhaps you'd read me a poem this afternoon,' she said. 'Your choice. I miss them so. I could do without *Oprah*, but a life without books is a thirsty life, and one without poetry is . . .' She laughed. It was a bewildered sound that hurt my heart. 'It's like a life without pictures, don't you think? Or don't you?'

The room was very quiet. Somewhere else a clock was ticking, but that was all. I thought Wireman would say something, but he didn't; she had rendered him temporarily speechless, no mean trick when it came to that *hijo de madre*.

'It can be your choice,' she said again. 'Or, if you've stayed too long, Edward—'

'No,' I said. 'No, that's all right, I'm fine.'

The book was simply titled: *Good Poems*. The editor was Garrison Keillor, a man who could probably run for governor and be elected in the part of the world I came from. I opened at random and found a poem by someone named Frank O'Hara. It was short. That made it a good poem in *my* book, and I waded in.

> *'Have you forgotten what we were like then*
> *when we were still first rate*
> *and the day came fat with an apple in its mouth*

137

'it's no use worrying about Time
but we did have a few tricks up our sleeves
and turned some sharp corners

'the whole pasture looked like our meal
we didn't need speedometers
we could manage cocktails out of ice and water . . .'

Something happened to me there. My voice wavered and the words doubled, as if the word water from my mouth had summoned some in my eyes. I looked up and said, 'Pardon me.' My voice was husky. Wireman looked concerned, but Elizabeth Eastlake was smiling at me with an expression of perfect understanding.

'That's all right, Edgar,' she said. 'Poetry sometimes does that to me, as well. Honest feeling is nothing to be ashamed of. Men do not sham convulsion.'

'Nor simulate a throe,' I added. My voice seemed to be coming from someone else.

She smiled brilliantly. 'The man knows his Dickinson, Wireman!'

'Seems to,' Wireman agreed. He was watching me closely.

'Will you finish, Edward?'

'Yes, ma'am.

'I wouldn't want to be faster
or greener than now if you were with me O you
were the best of all my days.'

I closed the book. 'That's the end.'

She nodded. 'What were the best of all your days, Edgar?'

'Maybe these,' I said. 'I'm hoping.'

She nodded. 'Then I'll hope, too. One is always allowed to hope. And Edgar?'

'Yes, ma'am?'

'Let me be Elizabeth to you. I can't stand being a ma'am at this end of my life. Do we understand each other?'

I nodded. 'I think we do, Elizabeth.'

She smiled, and the tears that had been in her own eyes fell. The cheeks they landed on were old and ruined with wrinkles, but the eyes were young. Young.

v

Ten minutes later, Wireman and I were standing at the end of the *Palacio* boardwalk again. He had left the lady of the house with a slice of key lime pie, a glass of tea, and the remote control. I had two of Wireman's egg salad sandwiches in a bag. He said they'd just go stale if I didn't take them home, and he didn't have to press me too hard. I also hit him up for a couple of aspirin.

'Look,' he said, 'I'm sorry about that. I was going to ask first, believe me.'

'Relax, Wireman.'

He nodded but didn't look directly at me. He was looking out at the Gulf. 'I just want you to know I didn't promise her anything. But she's . . . childish now. So she makes assumptions the way kids do, based on what she wants rather than on the facts.'

'And what she wants is to be read to.'

'Yes.'

'Poems on tapes and compact discs don't cut it?'

'Nope. She says the difference between recorded and live is like the difference between canned mushrooms and fresh ones.' He smiled, but still wouldn't look at me.

'Why don't you read to her, Wireman?'

Still looking out at the water, he said: 'Because I no longer can.'

'No longer . . . why not?'

He considered this, then shook his head. 'Not today. Wireman's tired, *muchacho*, and she'll be up in the night. Up and argumentative, full of rue and confusion, liable to think she's in London or St Tropez. I see the signs.'

'Will you tell me another day?'

'Yeah.' He sighed through his nose. 'If you can show yours, I suppose I can show mine, although I don't relish it. Are you sure you're okay to get back on your own?'

'Absolutely,' I said, although my hip was throbbing like a big motor.

'I'd run you in the golf cart, I really would, but when she's this way – Dr Wireman's clinical term for it is Bright Going On Stupid – she's apt to take it into her mind to wash the windows . . . or dust some shelves . . . or go for a walk without her walker.' At that he actually shuddered. It looked like the kind that starts out as burlesque and ends up being real.

'Everybody keeps trying to get me into a golf cart,' I said.

'You'll call your wife?'

'I don't see any other option,' I said.

He nodded. 'Good boy. You can tell me all about it when I come to look at your pictures. Any time'll work. There's a visiting nurse I can call – Annmarie Whistler – if the morning works better.'

'Okay. Thanks. And thanks for listening to me, Wireman.'

'Thanks for reading to the boss. *Buena suerte, amigo.*'

I set off down the beach and had gotten about fifty yards before something occurred to me. I turned back, thinking Wireman would be gone, but he was still standing there with his hands in his pockets and the wind off the Gulf – increasingly chilly – combing back his long graying hair. 'Wireman!'

'What?'

'Was Elizabeth ever an artist herself?'

He said nothing for a long time. There was only the sound of the waves, louder tonight with the wind to push them. Then he said, 'That's an interesting question, Edgar. If you were to ask her – and I'd advise against it – she'd say no. But I don't think that's the truth.'

'Why not?'

But he only said, 'You'd better get walking, *muchacho*. Before that hip of yours stiffens up.' He gave me a quick *seeya* wave, turned, and was gone back up the boardwalk, chasing his lengthening shadow, almost before I was aware he was leaving.

I stood where I was a moment or two longer, then turned north, set my sights on Big Pink, and headed for home. It was a long trip, and before I got there my own absurdly elongated shadow was lost in the sea oats, but in the end I made it. The waves were still building, and under the house the murmur of the shells had again become an argument.

How to Draw a Picture (IV)

Start with what you know, then re-invent it. Art is magic, no argument there, but all art, no matter how strange, starts in the humble everyday. Just don't be surprised when weird flowers sprout from common soil. Elizabeth knew that. No one taught her; she learned for herself.

The more she drew, the more she saw. The more she saw, the more she wanted to draw. It works like that. And the more she saw, the more her language came back to her: first the four or five hundred words she knew on the day she fell from the cart and struck her head, then many, many more.

Daddy was amazed by the rapidly growing sophistication of her pictures. So were her sisters – both the Big Meanies and the twins (not Adie; Adie was in Europe with three friends and two trusty chaperones – Emery Paulson, the young man she'll marry, had not yet come on the scene). The nanny/housekeeper was awed by her, called her la petite obéah fille.

The doctor who attended her case cautioned that the little girl must be very careful about exercise and excitement lest she take a fever, but by January of 1926 she was coursing everywhere on the south end of the Key, carrying her pad and bundled up in her 'puddy jacket and thumpums', drawing everything.

That was the winter she saw her family grow bored with her work – Big Meanies Maria and Hannah first, then Tessie and Lo-Lo, then Daddy, then even Nan Melda. Did she understand that even genius palls, when taken in large doses? Perhaps, in some instinctive child's way, she did.

What came next, the outgrowth of their boredom, was a determination to make them see the wonder of what she saw by re-inventing it.

Her surrealist phase began; first the birds flying upside-down, then the animals walking on water, then the Smiling Horses that brought her a small measure of renown. And that was when something changed. That was when something dark slipped in, using little Libbit as its channel.

She began to draw her doll, and when she did, her doll began to talk. Noveen.

141

By then Adriana was back from Gay Paree, and to begin with, Noveen mostly spoke in Adie's high and happy lah-de-dah voice, asking Elizabeth if she could hinky-dinky-parley-voo and telling her to ferramay her bush. Sometimes Noveen sang her to sleep while pictures of the doll's face – large and round and all brown except for the red lips – scattered Elizabeth's counterpane.

Noveen sings Frère Jacques, frère Jacques, are you sleepun? Are you sleepun? Dormay-voo, dormay-voo?

Sometimes Noveen told her stories – mixed-up but wonderful – where Cinderella wore the red slippers from Oz and the Bobbsey Twins got lost in the Magic Forest and found a sweetie house with a roof made of pepper-mint candy.

But then Noveen's voice changed. It stopped being Adie's voice. It stopped being the voice of anyone Elizabeth knew, and it went right on talking even when Elizabeth told Noveen to ferramay her bush. At first, maybe that voice was pleasant. Maybe it was fun. Strange, but fun.

Then things changed, didn't they? Because art is magic, and not all magic is white.

Not even for little girls.

7 – Art for Art's Sake

i

There was a bottle of single-malt in the living room liquor cabinet. I wanted a shot and didn't take it. I wanted to wait, maybe eat one of my egg salad sandwiches and plan out what I was going to say to her, and I didn't do that, either. Sometimes the only way to do it is to do it. I took the cordless phone out into the Florida room. It was chilly even with the glass sliders shut, but in a way that was good. I thought the cool air might sharpen me up a little. And maybe the sight of the sun dropping toward the horizon and painting its golden track across the water would calm me down. Because I wasn't calm. My heart was pounding too hard, my cheeks felt hot, my hip hurt like a bastard, and I suddenly realized, with real horror, that my wife's name had slipped my mind. Every time I dipped for it, all I came up with was *peligro*, the Spanish word for danger.

I decided there was one thing I *did* need before calling Minnesota.

I left the phone on the overstuffed couch, limped to the bedroom (using my crutch now; I and my crutch were going to be inseparable until bedtime), and got Reba. One look into her blue eyes was enough to bring Pam's name back, and my heartbeat slowed. With my best girl clamped between my side and my stump, her boneless pink legs wagging, I made my way back to the Florida room and sat down again. Reba flopped onto my lap and I set her aside with a thump so she faced the westering sun.

'Stare at it too long, you'll go blind,' I said. 'Of course, that's where the fun is. Bruce Springsteen, 1973 or so, *muchacha.*'

Reba did not reply.

'I should be upstairs, painting that,' I told her. 'Doing fucking art for fucking art's sake.'

No reply. Reba's wide eyes suggested to the world in general that she was stuck with America's nastiest man.

143

I picked up the cordless and shook it in her face. 'I can do this,' I said.

Nothing from Reba, but I thought she looked doubtful. Beneath us, the shells continued their wind-driven argument: *You did, I didn't, oh yes you did.*

I wanted to go on discussing the matter with my Anger-Management Doll. Instead I punched in the number of what used to be my house. No problem at all remembering that. I was hoping to get Pam's answering machine. Instead I got the lady herself, sounding breathless. 'Hey, Joanie, thank God you called back. I'm running late and was hoping our three-fifteen could be—'

'It's not Joanie,' I said. I reached for Reba and drew her back onto my lap without even thinking about it. 'It's Edgar. And you might have to cancel your three-fifteen. We've got something to talk about, and it's important.'

'What's wrong?'

'With me? Nothing. I'm fine.'

'Edgar, can we talk later? I need to get my hair done and I'm running late. I'll be back at six.'

'It's about Tom Riley.'

Silence from Pam's part of the world. It went on for maybe ten seconds. During those ten seconds, the golden track on the water darkened just a little. Elizabeth Eastlake knew her Emily Dickinson; I wondered if she also knew her Vachel Lindsay.

'What about Tom?' Pam asked at last. There was caution in her voice, deep caution. I was pretty sure that her hair appointment had left her mind.

'I have reason to believe he may be contemplating suicide.' I crooked the phone against my shoulder and began stroking Reba's hair. 'Know anything about that?'

'What do ... What do *I* ...' She sounded punched, breathless. 'Why in God's name *would* I ...' She began to gain a little strength, grasping for indignation. It's handy in such situations, I suppose. 'You call out of a clear blue sky and expect me to tell you about Tom Riley's state of mind? I thought you were getting better, but I guess that was wishful th—'

'Fucking him should give you some insight.' My hand wound

into Reba's fake orange hair and clutched, as if to tear it out by the roots. 'Or am I wrong?'

'That is *insane!*' she nearly screamed. 'You need *help*, Edgar! Either call Dr Kamen or get help down there, and *soon!*'

The anger – and the accompanying certainty that I would begin to lose my words – suddenly disappeared. I relaxed my hold on Reba's hair.

'Calm down, Pam. This isn't about you. Or me. It's about Tom. Have you seen signs of depression? You must have.'

No answer. But no hang-up click, either. And I could hear her breathing.

At last she said, 'Okay. Okay, right. I know where you got this idea. Little Miss Drama Queen, correct? I suppose Ilse also told you about Max Stanton, out in Palm Desert. Oh, Edgar, you *know* how she is!'

At that the rage threatened to return. My hand reached out and grasped Reba by her soft middle. *I can do this*, I thought. *It's not about Ilse, either. And Pam? Pam's only scared, because this came at her out of left field. She's scared and angry, but I can do this. I* have *to do this.*

Never mind that for a few moments I wanted to kill her. Or that, if she'd been there in the Florida room with me, I might have tried.

'Ilse didn't tell me.'

'Enough lunacy, I'm hanging up now—'

'The only thing I don't know is which one of them talked you into getting the tattoo on your breast. The little rose.'

She cried out. Just one soft cry, but that was enough. There was another moment of silence. It pulsed like black felt. Then she burst out: 'That bitch! She saw it and told you! It's the only way you could know! Well it means *nothing!* It proves *nothing!*'

'This isn't court, Pam,' I said.

She made no reply, but I could hear her breathing.

'Ilse *did* have her suspicions about this guy Max, but she doesn't have a clue about Tom. If you tell her, you'll break her heart.' I paused. 'And that'll break mine.'

She was crying. 'Fuck your heart. And fuck you. I wish you were dead, you know it? You lying, prying bastard, I wish you were dead.'

At least I no longer felt that way about her. Thank God.

145

The track on the water had darkened to burnished copper. Now the orange would begin to creep in.

'What do you know about Tom's state of mind?'

'Nothing. And for your information I'm not having an affair with him. If I *did* have one, it lasted for all of three weeks. It's over. I made that clear to him when I came back from Palm Desert. There are all sorts of reasons, but basically he's too . . .' Abruptly she jumped back. 'She must have told you. Melinda wouldn't've, even if she'd known.' And, absurdly spiteful: '*She* knows what I've been through with you!'

It was surprising, really, how little interest I had in going down that road with her. I was interested in something else. 'He's too what?'

'*Who's* too what?' she cried. 'Jesus, I hate this! This interrogation!'

Like I was loving it. 'Tom. You said "Basically he's too," then stopped.'

'Too moody. He's an emotional grab-bag. One day up, one day down, one day both, especially if he doesn't take—'

She ceased abruptly.

'If he doesn't take his pills,' I finished for her.

'Yeah, well, I'm not his psychiatrist,' she said, and that wasn't tinny petulance in her voice; I was pretty sure it was blue steel. Jesus. The woman I'd been married to could be tough when the situation called for it, but I thought that unforgiving blue steel was a new thing: her part of my accident. I thought it was Pam's limp.

'I got enough of that shrinky-dink shit with you, Edgar. Just once I'd like to meet a man who *was* a man and not a pill-popping Magic 8-Ball. "Cannot say now, ask later when I'm not feeling so upset."'

She sniffed in my ear, and I waited for the follow-up honk. It came. She cried the same way as always; some things apparently didn't change.

'Fuck you, Edgar, for fucking up what was actually a pretty good day.'

'I don't care who you sleep with,' I said. 'We're divorced. All I want is to save Tom Riley's life.'

This time she screamed so loud I had to hold the phone away from my ear. '*I'm not RESPONSIBLE for his life! WE'RE QUITS! Did you miss that?*' Then, a little lower (but not much): 'He's not even in St Paul. He's on a cruise with his mother and that gayboy brother of his.'

Suddenly I understood, or thought I did. It was as if I were flying over it, getting an aerial view. Maybe because I had contemplated suicide, cautioning myself all the while that it must absolutely look like an accident. Not so the insurance money would get paid, but so that my daughters wouldn't have to go through life with the stigma of everyone knowing—

And that was the answer, wasn't it?

'Tell him you know. When he gets back, tell him you know he's planning to kill himself.'

'Why would he believe me?'

'Because he *is* planning to. Because you know him. Because he's mentally ill, and probably thinks he's going around with a sign that says **PLANNING SUICIDE** taped to his back. Tell him you know he's been ditching his antidepressants. You do know that, right? For a fact.'

'Yes. But telling him to take them never helped before.'

'Did you ever tell him you'd tattle on him if he didn't start taking his medicine? Tattle to everyone?'

'No, and I'm not going to now!' She sounded appalled. 'Do you think I want everyone in St Paul to know I slept with Tom Riley? That I had a *thing* with him?'

'How about all of St Paul knowing you care what happens to him? Would that be so goddam awful?'

She was silent.

'All I want is for you to confront him when he comes back—'

'All you want! Right! Your whole life has been about all you want! I tell you what, Eddie, if this is such a BFD to you, then *you* confront him!' It was that shrill hardness again, but this time with fear behind it.

I said, 'If you were the one who broke it off, you probably still have power over him. Including – maybe – the power to make him save his life. I know that's scary, but you're stuck with it.'

'No I'm not. I'm hanging up.'

'If he kills himself, I doubt if you'll spend the rest of your life with a bad conscience . . . but I think you *will* have one miserable year. Or two.'

'I won't. I'll sleep like a baby.'

'Sorry, Panda, I don't believe you.'

It was an ancient pet name, one I hadn't used in years, and I don't know where it came from, but it broke her. She began to cry again. This time there was no anger in it. 'Why do you have to be such a bastard? Why won't you leave me alone?'

I wanted no more of this. What I wanted was a couple of pain pills. And maybe to sprawl on my bed and have a good cry myself, I wasn't sure. 'Tell him you know. Tell him to see his psychiatrist and start taking his antidepressants again. And here's the most important thing – tell him that if he kills himself, you'll tell everyone, starting with his mother and brother. That no matter how good he makes it look, everyone will know it was really suicide.'

'I can't do that! I *can't!*' She sounded hopeless.

I considered this, and decided I'd put Tom Riley's life entirely in her hands – simply pass it down the telephone wire to her. That sort of letting-go hadn't been in the old Edgar Freemantle's repertoire, but of course that Edgar Freemantle would never have considered spending his time painting sunsets. Or playing with dolls.

'You decide, Panda. It might be useless anyway if he no longer cares for you, but—'

'Oh, he does.' She sounded more hopeless than ever.

'Then tell him he has to start living life again, like it or not.'

'Good old Edgar, still managing things,' she said wanly. 'Even from his island kingdom. Good old Edgar. Edgar the monster.'

'That hurts,' I said.

'Lovely,' she said, and hung up. I sat on the couch awhile longer, watching as the sunset grew brighter and the air in the Florida room grew colder. People who think there is no winter in Florida are very mistaken. An inch of snow fell in Sarasota in 1977. I guess it gets cold everywhere. I bet it even snows in hell, although I doubt if it sticks.

ii

Wireman called the next day shortly after noon and asked if he was still invited to look at my pictures. I felt some misgivings, remembering his promise (or threat) to give me his unvarnished opinion, but told him to come ahead.

I set out what I thought were my sixteen best . . . although in the clear, cold daylight of that January afternoon they all looked pretty crappy to me. The sketch I'd made of Carson Jones was still on the shelf in my bedroom closet. I took it down, clipped it to a piece of fiberboard, and propped it at the end of the line. The penciled colors looked dowdy and plain compared to the oils, and of course it was smaller than the rest, but I still thought it had something the others lacked.

I considered putting out the picture of the red-robe, then didn't. I don't know why. Maybe just because it gave me the creeps. I put out *Hello* – the pencil sketch of the tanker – instead.

Wireman came buzzing up in a bright blue golf cart with sporty yellow pinstriping. He didn't have to ring the bell. I was at the door to meet him.

'You've got a certain drawn look about you, *muchacho*,' he said, coming in. 'Relax. I ain't the doctor and this ain't the doctor's office.'

'I can't help it. If this was a building and you were a building inspector, I wouldn't feel this way, but—'

'But that was your other life,' Wireman said. 'This be your new one, where you haven't got your walking shoes broke in yet.'

'That's about the size of it.'

'You're damn right. Speaking of your prior existence, did you call your wife about that little matter you discussed with me?'

'I did. Do you want the blow-by-blow?'

'Nope. All I want to know is if you're comfortable with the way the conversation turned out.'

'I haven't had a comfortable conversation with Pam since I woke up in the hospital. But I'm pretty sure she'll talk to Tom.'

'Then I guess that'll do, pig. *Babe*, 1995.' He was all the way in now, and looking around curiously. 'I like what you've done to the place.'

I burst out laughing. I hadn't even removed the no-smoking sign on top of the TV. 'I had Jack put in a treadmill upstairs, that's new. You've been here before, I take it?'

He gave me an enigmatic little smile. 'We've *all* been here before, *amigo* – this is bigger than pro football. Peter Straub, circa 1985.'

'I'm not following you.'

'I've been working for Miss Eastlake about sixteen months now, with one brief and uncomfortable diversion to St Pete when the Keys were evacuated for Hurricane Frank. Anyway, the last people to rent Salmon Point – pardon me, Big Pink – stayed just two weeks of their eight-week lease and then went boogie-bye-bye. Either they didn't like the house or the house didn't like them.' Wireman raised ghost-hands over his head and took big wavery ghost-steps across the light blue living room carpet. The effect was to a large degree spoiled by his shirt, which was covered with tropical birds and flowers. 'After that, whatever walked in Big Pink . . . *walked alone!*'

'Shirley Jackson,' I said. 'Circa whenever.'

'Yep. Anyway, Wireman was making a point, or trying to. Big Pink *THEN!*' He swept his arms out in an all-encompassing gesture. 'Furnished in that popular Florida style known as Twenty-First Century Rent-A-House! Big Pink *NOW!* Furnished in Twenty-First Century Rent-A-House, plus Cybex treadmill upstairs, and . . .' He squinted. 'Is that a Lucille Ball dolly I spy sitting on the couch in the Florida room?'

'That's Reba, the Anger-Management Queen. She was given to me by my psychologist friend, Kramer.' But that wasn't right. My missing arm began to itch madly. For the ten thousandth time I tried to scratch it and got my still-mending ribs instead. 'Wait,' I said, and looked at Reba, who was staring out at the Gulf. *I can do this*, I thought. *It's like where you put money when you want to hide it from the government.*

Wireman was waiting patiently.

My arm itched. The one not there. The one that sometimes wanted to draw. It wanted to draw then. I thought it wanted to draw Wireman. Wireman and the bowl of fruit. Wireman and the gun.

Stop the weird shit, I thought.

I can do this, I thought.

You hide money from the government in offshore banks, I thought. *Nassau. The Bahamas. The Grand Caymans.* And Bingo, there it was.

'Kamen,' I said. 'That's his name. Kamen gave me Reba. Xander Kamen.'

'Well now that we've got that solved,' Wireman said, 'let's look at the art.'

'If that's what it is,' I said, and led the way upstairs, limping on my crutch. Halfway up, something struck me and I stopped. 'Wireman,' I said, without looking back, 'how did you know my treadmill was a Cybex?'

For a moment he said nothing. Then: 'It's the only brand I know. Now can you resume the upward ascent on your own, or do you need a kick in the ass to get going?'

Sounds good, rings false, I thought as I started up the stairs again. *I think you're lying, and you know what? I think you know I know.*

iii

My work was leaning against the north wall of Little Pink, with the afternoon sun giving the paintings plenty of natural light. Looking at them from behind Wireman as he walked slowly down the line, sometimes pausing and once even backtracking to study a couple of canvases a second time, I thought it was far more light than they deserved. Ilse and Jack had praised them, but one was my daughter and the other my hired man.

When he reached the colored pencil drawing of the tanker at the very end of the line, Wireman squatted and stared at it for maybe thirty seconds with his forearms resting on his thighs and his hands hanging limply between his legs.

'What—' I began.

'Shhh,' he said, and I endured another thirty seconds of silence. At last he stood up. His knees popped. When he turned to face me, his eyes looked very large, and the left one was inflamed. Water – not a tear – was running from the inner corner. He pulled a hand-kerchief from the back pocket of his jeans and wiped it away, the automatic gesture of a man who does the same thing a dozen or more times a day.

'Holy God,' he said, and walked toward the window, stuffing the handkerchief back into his pocket.

'Holy God what?' I asked. 'Holy God *what?*'

He stood looking out. 'You don't know how good these are, do you? I mean you really don't.'

151

'Are they?' I asked. I had never felt so unsure of myself. 'Are you serious?'

'Did you put them in chronological order?' he asked, still looking out at the Gulf. The joking, joshing, wisecracking Wireman had taken a hike. I had an idea the one I was listening to now had a lot more in common with the one juries had heard . . . always assuming he'd been that kind of lawyer. 'You did, didn't you? Other than the last couple, I mean. Those're obviously much earlier.'

I didn't see how anything of mine could qualify as 'much earlier' when I'd only been doing pictures for a couple of months, but when I ran my eye over them, I saw he was right. I hadn't meant to put them in chronological order – not consciously – but that was what I had done.

'Yes,' I said. 'Earliest to most recent.'

He indicated the last four paintings – the ones I'd come to think of as my sunset-composites. To one I'd added a nautilus shell, to one a compact disc with the word **Memorex** printed across it (and the sun shining redly through the hole), to the third a dead seagull I'd found on the beach, only blown up to pterodactyl size. The last was of the shell-bed beneath Big Pink, done from a digital photograph. To this I had for some reason felt the urge to add roses. There were none growing around Big Pink, but there were plenty of photos available from my new pal Google.

'This last group of paintings,' he said. 'Has anyone seen these? Your daughter?'

'No. These four were done after she left.'

'The guy who works for you?'

'Nope.'

'And of course you never showed your daughter the sketch you made of her boyfr—'

'God, no! Are you kidding?'

'No, of course you didn't. That one has its own power, hasty as it obviously is. As for the rest of these things . . .' He laughed. I suddenly realized he was excited, and that was when I started to get excited. But cautious, too. *Remember he used to be a lawyer*, I told myself. *He's not an art critic.*

'The rest of these fucking things . . .' He gave that little yipping laugh again. He walked in a circle around the room, stepping onto

152

the treadmill and over it with an unconscious ease that I envied bitterly. He put his hands in his graying hair and pulled it out and up, as if to stretch his brains.

At last he came back. Stood in front of me. Confronted me, almost. 'Look. The world has knocked you around a lot in the last year or so, and I know that takes a lot of gas out of the old self-image airbag. But don't tell me you don't at least *feel* how good they are.'

I remembered the two of us recovering from our wild laughing fit while the sun shone through the torn umbrella, putting little scars of light on the table. Wireman had said *I know what you're going through* and I had replied *I seriously doubt that.* I didn't doubt it now. He knew. This memory of the day before was followed by a dry desire – not a hunger but an itch – to get Wireman down on paper. A combination portrait and still life, *Lawyer with Fruit and Gun.*

He patted my cheek with one of his blunt-fingered hands. 'Earth to Edgar. Come in, Edgar.'

'Ah, roger, Houston,' I heard myself say. 'You have Edgar.'

'So what do you say, *muchacho*? Am I lyin or am I dyin? Did you or did you not feel they were good when you were doing them?'

'Yeah,' I said. 'I felt like I was kicking ass and taking down names.'

He nodded. 'It's the simplest fact of art – good art almost always feels good to the artist. And the viewer, the *committed* viewer, the one who's really looking—'

'I guess that'd be you,' I said. 'You took long enough.'

He didn't smile. 'When it's good and the person who's looking opens up to it, there's an emotional bang. I felt the bang, Edgar.'

'Good.'

'You bet it is. And when that guy at the Scoto gets a load of these, I think he'll feel it, too. In fact, I'd bet on it.'

'They're really not so much. Re-heated Dalí, when you get right down to it.'

He put an arm around my shoulders and led me toward the stairs. 'I'm not going to dignify that. Nor are we going to discuss the fact that you apparently painted your daughter's boyfriend via some weird phantom-limb telepathy. I *do* wish I could see that tennis-ball picture, but what's gone is gone.'

'Good riddance, too,' I said.

153

'But you have to be very careful, Edgar. Duma Key is a powerful place for . . . certain kinds of people. It *magnifies* certain kinds of people. People like you.'

'And you?' I asked. He didn't answer immediately, so I pointed at his face. 'That eye of yours is watering again.'

He took out the handkerchief and wiped it.

'Want to tell me what happened to you?' I asked. 'Why you can't read? Why it weirds you out to even look at pictures too long?'

For a long time he said nothing. The shells under Big Pink had a lot to say. With one wave they said *the fruit*. With the next they said *the gun*. Back and forth like that. The fruit, the gun, the gun, the fruit.

'No,' he said. 'Not now. And if you want to draw me, sure. Knock yourself out.'

'How much of my mind can you read, Wireman?'

'Not much,' he said. 'You caught a break there, *muchacho*.'

'Could you still read it if we were off Duma Key? If we were in a Tampa coffee shop, for instance?'

'Oh, I might get a tickle.' He smiled. 'Especially after spending over a year here, soaking up the . . . you know, the rays.'

'Will you go to the gallery with me? The Scoto?'

'*Amigo*, I wouldn't miss it for all the tea in China.'

iv

That night a squall blew in off the water and it rained hard for two hours. Lightning flashed and waves pounded the pilings under the house. Big Pink groaned but stood firm. I discovered an interesting thing: when the Gulf got a little crazy and those waves really poured in, the shells shut up. The waves lifted them too high for conversation.

I went upstairs at the boom-and-flash height of the festivities, and – feeling a little like Dr Frankenstein animating his monster in the castle tower – drew Wireman, using a plain old Venus Black pencil. Until the very end, that was. Then I used red and orange for the fruit in the bowl. In the background I sketched a doorway, and in the doorway I put Reba, standing there and watching. I supposed Kamen would have said Reba was my representative in the world of the picture. Maybe *sí*, maybe *no*. The last thing I did was pick up the Venus Sky to color in her stupid eyes. Then it was done. Another Freemantle masterpiece is born.

I sat looking at it while the diminishing thunder rolled away and the lightning flashed a few goodbye stutters over the Gulf. There was Wireman, sitting at a table. Sitting there, I had no doubt, at the end of his other life. On the table was a bowl of fruit and the pistol he kept either for target practice (back then his eyes had been fine) or for home protection or both. I had sketched the pistol and then scribbled it in, giving it a sinister, slightly blobby look. That other house was empty. Somewhere in that other house a clock was ticking. Somewhere in that other house a refrigerator was whining. The air was heavy with the scent of flowers. The scent was terrible. The sounds were worse. The march of the clock. The relentless whine of the refrigerator as it went on making ice in a wifeless, childless world. Soon the man at the table would close his eyes, stretch out his hand, and pick a piece of fruit from the bowl. If it was an orange, he'd go to bed. If it was an apple, he would apply the muzzle of the gun to his right temple, pull the trigger, and air out his aching brains.

It had been an apple.

v

Jack showed up the next day with a borrowed van and plenty of soft cloth in which to wrap my canvases. I told him I'd made a friend from the big house down the beach, and that he'd be going with us. 'No problem,' Jack said cheerfully, climbing the stairs to Little Pink and trundling a hand-dolly along behind him. 'There's plenty of room in the – whoa!' He had stopped at the head of the stairs.

'What?' I asked.

'Are these ones new? They must be.'

'Yeah.' Nannuzzi from the Scoto had asked to see half a dozen pictures, no more than ten, so I'd split the difference and set out eight. Four were the ones that had impressed Wireman the night before. 'What do you think?'

155

'Dude, these are *awesome!*'

It was hard to doubt his sincerity; he'd never called me dude before. I mounted a couple more steps and then poked his blue-jeaned butt with the tip of my crutch. 'Make room.'

He stepped aside, pulling the dolly with him, so I could climb the rest of the way up to Little Pink. He was still staring at the pictures.

'Jack, is this guy at the Scoto really okay? Do you know?'

'My Mom says he is, and that's good enough for me.' Meaning, I think, that it should be good enough for me, too. I guessed it would have to be. 'She didn't tell me anything about the other partners – I think there are two more – but she says Mr Nannuzzi's okay.'

Jack had called in a favor for me. I was touched.

'And if he doesn't like these,' Jack finished, 'he's wack.'

'You think so, huh?'

He nodded.

From downstairs, Wireman called cheerfully: 'Knock-knock! I'm here for the field trip. Are we still going? Who's got my name-tag? Was I supposed to pack a lunch?'

vi

I had pictured a bald, skinny, professorial man with blazing brown eyes – an Italian Ben Kingsley – but Dario Nannuzzi turned out to be fortyish, plump, courtly, and possessed of a full head of hair. I was close on the eyes, though. They didn't miss a trick. I saw them widen once – slightly but perceptibly – when Wireman carefully unwrapped the last painting I'd brought, *Roses Grow from Shells.* The pictures were lined up against the back wall of the gallery, which was currently devoted mostly to photographs by Stephanie Shachat and oils by William Berra. Better stuff, I thought, than I could do in a century.

Although there *had* been that slight widening of the eyes.

Nannuzzi went down the line from first to last, then went again. I had no idea if that was good or bad. The dirty truth was that I had never been in an art gallery in my life before that day. I turned to ask Wireman what he thought, but Wireman had withdrawn and was talking quietly with Jack, both of them watching Nannuzzi look at my paintings.

Nor were they the only ones, I realized. The end of January is a busy season in the pricey shops along Florida's west coast. There were a dozen or so lookie-loos in the good-sized Scoto Gallery (Nannuzzi later used the far more dignified term 'potential patrons'), eyeing the Shachat dahlias, William Berra's gorgeous but touristy oils of Europe, and a few eye-popping, cheerfully feverish sculptures I'd missed in the anxiety of getting my own stuff unwrapped – these were by a guy named David Gerstein.

At first I thought it was the sculptures – jazz musicians, crazy swimmers, throbbing city scenes – that were drawing the casual afternoon browsers. And some glanced at them, but most didn't even do that. It was my pictures they were looking at.

A man with what Floridians call a Michigan tan – that can mean skin that's either dead white or burned lobster red – tapped me on the shoulder with his free hand. The other was interlaced with his wife's fingers. 'Do you know who the artist is?' he asked.

'Me,' I muttered, and felt my face grow hot. I felt as if I were confessing to having spent the last week or so downloading pictures of Lindsay Lohan.

'Good for *you*!' his wife said warmly. 'Will you be showing?'

Now they were all looking at me. Sort of the way you might look at a new species of puffer-fish that may or may not be the *sushi du jour*. That was how it felt, anyway.

'I don't know if I'll be snowing. Showing.' I could feel more blood stacking up in my cheeks. Shame-blood, which was bad. Anger-blood, which was worse. If it spilled out, it would be anger at myself, but these people wouldn't know that.

I opened my mouth to pour out words, and closed it. *Take it slow*, I thought, and wished I had Reba. These people would probably view a doll-toting artist as normal. They had lived through Andy Warhol, after all.

Take it slow. I can do this.

'What I mean to say is I haven't been working long, and I don't know what the procedure is.'

Quit fooling yourself, Edgar. You know what they're interested in. Not your pictures but your empty sleeve. You're Artie the One-Armed Artist. Why not just cut to the chase and tell them to fuck off?

That was ridiculous, of course, but—

But now I was goddamned if everyone in the gallery wasn't standing around. Those who'd been up front looking at Ms Shachat's flowers had been drawn by simple curiosity. It was a familiar grouping; I had seen similar clusters standing around the peepholes in board fences at a hundred construction sites.

'I'll tell you what the procedure is,' said another fellow with a Michigan tan. He was swag-bellied, sporting a little garden of gin-blossoms on his nose, and wearing a tropical shirt that hung almost to his knees. His white shoes matched his perfectly combed white hair. 'It's simple. Just two steps. Step one is you tell me how much you want for that one.' He pointed to *Sunset with Seagull*. 'Step two is I write the check.'

The little crowd laughed. Dario Nannuzzi didn't. He beckoned to me.

'Excuse me,' I said to the white-haired man.

'Price of poker just went up, my friend,' someone said to Gin-Blossoms, and there was laughter. Gin-Blossoms joined in, but didn't look really amused.

I noticed all this as though in a dream.

Nannuzzi smiled at me, then turned to the patrons, who were still looking at my paintings. 'Ladies and gentlemen, Mr Freemantle didn't come in to sell anything today, only for an opinion on his work. Please respect his privacy and my professional situation.' *Whatever* that *is*, I thought, bemused. 'May I suggest that you browse the works on display while we step into the rear quarters for a little while? Ms Aucoin, Mr Brooks, and Mr Castellano will be pleased to answer all your questions.'

'*My* opinion is that you ought to sign this man up,' said a severe-looking woman with her graying hair drawn back into a bun and a kind of wrecked beauty still lingering on her face. There was actually a smattering of applause. My feeling of being in a dream deepened.

An ethereal young man floated toward us from the rear. Nannuzzi might have summoned him, but I was damned if I knew just how. They spoke briefly, and then the young man produced a big roll of stickers. They were ovals with the letters NFS embossed on them in silver. Nannuzzi removed one, bent toward the first painting, then hesitated and gave me a look of reproach. 'These haven't been sealed in any way.'

'Uh . . . guess not,' I said. I was blushing again. 'I don't . . . exactly know what that is.'

'Dario, what you're dealing with here is a true American primitive,' said the severe-looking woman. 'If he's been painting longer than three years, I'll buy you dinner at Zoria's, along with a bottle of wine.' She turned her wrecked but still almost gorgeous face to me.

'When and if there's something for you to write about, Mary,' Nannuzzi said, 'I'll call you myself.'

'You'd better,' she said. 'And I'm not even going to ask his name – do you see what a good girl I am?' She twiddled her fingers at me and slipped through the little crowd.

'Not much need to ask,' Jack said, and of course he was right. I had signed each of the oils in the lower left corner, just as neatly as I had signed all invoices, work orders, and contracts in my other life: *Edgar Freemantle*.

vii

Nannuzzi settled for dabbing his NFS stickers on the upper right-hand corners of the paintings, where they stuck up like the tabs of file-folders. Then he led Wireman and me into his office. Jack was invited but elected to stay with the pictures.

In the office, Nannuzzi offered us coffee, which we declined, and water, which we accepted. I also accepted a couple of Tylenol capsules.

'Who was that woman?' Wireman asked.

'Mary Ire,' Nannuzzi said. 'She's a fixture on the Suncoast art scene. Publishes a free culture-vulture newspaper called *Boulevard*. It comes out once a month during most of the year, once every two weeks during the tourist season. She lives in Tampa – in a coffin, according to some wits in this business. New local artists are her favorite thing.'

'She looked extremely sharp,' Wireman said.

159

Nannuzzi shrugged. 'Mary's all right. She's helped a lot of artists, and she's been around forever. That makes her important in a town where we live – to a large extent – on the transient trade.'

'I see,' Wireman said. I was glad someone did. 'She's a facilitator.'

'More,' Nannuzzi said. 'She's a kind of docent. We like to keep her happy. If we can, of course.'

Wireman was nodding. 'There's a nice artist-and-gallery economy here on the west coast of Florida. Mary Ire understands it and fosters it. So if the Happy Art Galleria down the street discovers they can sell paintings of Elvis done in macaroni on velvet for ten thousand dollars a pop, Mary would—'

'She'd blow them out of the water,' Nannuzzi said. 'Contrary to the belief of the art snobs – you can usually pick them out by their black clothes and teeny-tiny cell phones – we're not venal.'

'Got it off your chest?' Wireman asked, not quite smiling.

'Almost,' he said. 'All I'm saying is that Mary understands our situation. We sell good stuff, most of us, and sometimes we sell great stuff. We do our best to find and develop new artists, but some of our customers are too rich for their own good. I'm thinking of fellows like Mr Costenza out there, who was waving his checkbook around, and the ladies who come in with their dogs dyed to match their latest coats.' Nannuzzi showed his teeth in a smile I was willing to bet not many of his richer clients ever saw.

I was fascinated. This was another world.

'Mary reviews every new show she can get to, which is most of them, and believe me, not all her reviews are raves.'

'But most are?' Wireman said.

'Sure, because most of the shows are good. She'd tell you very little of the stuff she sees is great, because that isn't what tourist-track areas as a rule produce, but good? Yes. Stuff anyone can hang, then point to and say "I bought that" without a quaver of embarrassment.'

I thought Nannuzzi had just given a perfect definition of mediocrity – I had seen the principle at work in hundreds of architectural drawings – but again I kept silent.

'Mary shares our interest in new artists. There may come a time when it would be in your interest to sit down with her, Mr Freemantle. Prior to a showing of your work, let us say.'

'Would you be interested in having such a showing here at the Scoto?' Wireman asked me.

My lips were dry. I attempted to moisten them with my tongue, but that was dry, too. So I took a sip of my water and then said, 'That's getting the harm before the force.' I paused. Gave myself time. Took another sip of water. 'Sorry. Cart before the horse. I came in to find out what *you* think, Signor Nannuzzi. You're the expert.'

He unlaced his fingers from the front of his vest and leaned forward. The squeak his chair made in the small room seemed very loud to me. But he smiled and the smile was warm. It brightened his eyes, made them compelling. I could see why he was a success when it came to selling pictures, but I don't think he was selling just then. He reached across his desk and took my hand – the one I painted with, the only one I had left.

'Mr Freemantle, you do me honor, but my father Augustino is the signor of our family. I am happy to be a mister. As for your paintings, yes, they're good. Considering how long you've been at work, they are very good indeed. Maybe more than good.'

'What *makes* them good?' I asked. 'If they're good, what makes them good?'

'Truth,' he said. 'It shines through in every stroke.'

'But most of them are only sunsets! The things I added . . .' I lifted my hand, then dropped it. 'They're just gimmicks.'

Nannuzzi laughed. 'You've learned such mean words! Where? Reading *The New York Times* art pages? Listening to Bill O'Reilly? Both?' He pointed to the ceiling. 'Lightbulb? Gimmick!' He pointed to his own chest. 'Pacemaker? Gimmick!' He tossed his hands in the air. The lucky devil had two to toss. 'Throw out your mean words, Mr Freemantle. Art should be a place of hope, not doubt. And your doubts rise from inexperience, which is not a dishonorable thing. Listen to me. Will you listen?'

'Sure,' I said. 'That's why I came.'

'When I say truth, I mean beauty.'

'John Keats,' Wireman said. '"Ode On A Grecian Urn." All we know, all we need to know. An oldie but still a goodie.'

Nannuzzi paid no attention. He was leaning forward over his desk and looking at me. 'For me, Mr Freemantle—'

'Edgar.'

'For me, Edgar, that sums up what all art is for, and the only way it can be judged.'

He smiled — a trifle defensively, I thought.

'I don't want to think too much about art, you see. I don't want to criticize it. I don't want to attend symposia, listen to papers, or discuss it at cocktail parties — although sometimes in my line of work I'm forced to do all those things. What I want to do is clutch my heart and fall down when I see it.'

Wireman burst out laughing and raised both hands in the air. '*Yes, Lawd!*' he proclaimed. 'I don't know if that guy out there was clutching his heart and falling down, but he surely was ready to clutch his checkbook.'

Nannuzzi said, 'Inside himself, I think he did fall down. I think they all did.'

'Actually, I do too,' Wireman said. He was no longer smiling.

Nannuzzi remained fixed on me. 'No talk of gimmicks. What you are after in most of these paintings is perfectly straightforward: you're looking for a way to reinvent the most popular and hack-neyed of all Florida subjects, the tropical sunset. You've been trying to find your way past the cliché.'

'Yes, that's pretty much it. So I copied Dalí—'

Nannuzzi waved a hand. 'Those paintings out there are nothing like Dalí. And I won't discuss schools of art with you, Edgar, or stoop to using words ending in *ism*. You don't belong to any school of art, because you don't *know* any.'

'I know buildings,' I said.

'Then why don't you *paint* buildings?'

I shook my head. I could have told him the thought had never crossed my mind, but it would have been closer to the truth to say it had never crossed my missing arm.

'Mary was right. You're an American primitive. Nothing wrong with that. Grandma Moses was an American primitive. Jackson Pollock was another. The point is, Edgar, you're talented.'

I opened my mouth. Closed it. I simply couldn't figure out what to say. Wireman helped me.

'Thank the man, Edgar,' he said.

'Thank you,' I said.

'Very welcome. And if you *do* decide to show, Edgar, please come

162

to the Scoto first. I'll make you the best deal of any gallery on Palm Avenue. That's a promise.'

'Are you kidding? Of course I'll come here first.'

'And of course I'll vet the contract,' Wireman said with a choirboy's smile.

Nannuzzi smiled in return. 'You should and I welcome it. Not that you'll find a lot to vet; the standard Scoto first-artist contract is a page and a half long.'

'Mr Nannuzzi,' I said, 'I really don't know how to thank you.'

'You already did,' he said. 'I clutched my heart – what's left of it – and fell down. Before you go, there's one more matter.' He found a pad on his desk, scribbled on it, then tore off the sheet and handed it to me like a doctor handing a patient a prescription. The word written on it in large slanting capitals even looked like a word you'd see on a doctor's prescription: **LIQUIN**.

'What's Liquin?' I asked.

'A preservative. I suggest you begin by putting it on finished works with a paper towel. Just a thin coat. Let it dry for twenty-four hours, then put on a second coat. That will keep your sunsets bright and fresh for centuries.' He looked at me so solemnly I felt my stomach rise a little toward my chest. 'I don't know if they're good enough to deserve such longevity, but maybe they are. Who knows? Maybe they are.'

viii

We ate dinner at Zoria's, the restaurant Mary Ire had mentioned, and I let Wireman buy me a bourbon before the meal. It was the first truly stiff drink I'd had since the accident, and it hit me in a funny way. Everything seemed to grow sharper until the world was drenched with light and color. The angles of things – doors, windows, even the cocked elbows of the passing waiters – seemed sharp enough to cut the air open and allow some darker, thicker atmosphere to come flowing out like syrup. The swordfish I ordered was delicious, the green beans snapped between my teeth, and the *crème brûlée* was almost too rich to finish (but too rich to leave). The conversation among the three of us was cheerful; there was plenty

163

of laughter. Still, I wanted the meal to be over. My head still ached, although the throb had slid to the back of my skull (like a weight in one of those barroom bowling games), and the bumper-to-bumper traffic we could see on Main Street was distracting. Every horn-honk sounded ill-tempered and menacing. I wanted Duma. I wanted the blackness of the Gulf and the quiet conversation of the shells below me as I lay in my bed with Reba on the other pillow.

And by the time the waiter came to ask if we wanted more coffee, Jack was carrying the conversation almost single-handed. In my state of hyper-awareness I could see that I wasn't the only one who needed a change of venue. Given the low lighting in the restaurant and Wireman's mahogany tan, it was hard to tell just how much color he'd lost, but I thought quite a bit. Also, that left eye of his was weeping again.

'Just the check,' Wireman said, and then managed a smile. 'Sorry to cut the celebration short, but I want to get back to my lady. If that's okay with you guys.'

'Fine by me,' Jack said. 'A free meal and home in time to watch *SportsCenter*? Such a deal.'

Wireman and I waited outside the parking garage while Jack went to get the rented van. Here the light was brighter, but what it showed didn't make me feel better about my new friend; in the glow spilling out of the garage, his complexion looked almost yellow. I asked him if he was okay.

'Wireman's as fine as paint,' he said. 'Miss Eastlake, on the other hand, has put in a few restless, shitty nights. Calling for her sisters, calling for her Pa, calling for everything but her pipe and bowl and fiddlers three. There's something to that full-moon shit. It makes no logical sense, but there it is. Diana calls on a wavelength to which only the tottering mind is attuned. Now that it's in its last quarter, she'll start sleeping through again. Which means I can start sleeping through again. I hope.'

'Good.'

'If I were you, Edgar, I'd sleep on this gallery thing, and for more than one night. Also, keep painting. You've been a busy bee, but I doubt if you have enough pictures yet to—'

There was a tiled pillar behind him. He staggered back against it. If it hadn't been there, I'm pretty sure he would have gone down.

The effects of the bourbon were wearing off a little, but there was enough of that hyper-reality left for me to see what happened to his eyes when he lost his equilibrium. The right one looked down, as if to check out his shoes, while the bloodshot and weepy left one rolled up in its socket until the iris was no more than an arc. I had time to think that what I was seeing was surely impossible, eyes couldn't go in two completely different directions like that. And that was probably true for people who were healthy. Then Wireman started to slide.

I grabbed him. 'Wireman? *Wireman!*'

He gave his head a shake, then looked at me. Eyes front and all accounted for. The left one was glistening and bloodshot, that was all. He took out his hankie and wiped his cheek. He laughed. 'I've heard of putting other people to sleep with a boring line of quack, but oneself? That's ridiculous.'

'You weren't dozing off. You were . . . I don't know *what* you were.'

'Don't be seely, dollink,' Wireman said.

'No, your eyes got all funny.'

'That's called going to sleep, *muchacho.*' He gave me one of his patented Wireman looks: head cocked, eyebrows raised, corners of the mouth dimpled in the beginnings of a smile. But I thought he knew exactly what I was talking about.

'I have to see a doctor, have a checkup,' I said. 'Do the MRI thing. I promised my friend Kamen. How about I make it a twofer?'

Wireman was still leaning against the pillar. Now he straightened up. 'Hey, here's Jack with the van. That was quick. Step lively, Edgar – last bus to Duma Key, leaving now.'

ix

It happened again, on the way back, and worse, although Jack didn't see it – he was busy piloting the van along Casey Key Road – and I'm pretty sure Wireman himself never knew. I had asked Jack if he minded skipping the Tamiami Trail, which is west coast Florida's engagingly tacky Main Street, in favor of the narrower, twistier way. I wanted to watch the moon on the water, I said.

165

'Gettin those little artist eccentricities, *muchacho*,' Wireman said from the back seat, where he was stretched out with his feet up. He wasn't much of a stickler when it came to seatbelts, it seemed. 'Next thing we know, you'll be wearing a beret.' He pronounced it so it rhymed with *garret*.

'Fuck you, Wireman,' I said.

'I been fucked to the east and I been fucked to the west,'Wireman recited in tones of sentimental recollection, 'but when it comes to the fuckin, yo mamma's the best.' With that he lapsed into silence.

I watched the moon go swimming through the black water to my right. It was hypnotic. I wondered if it would be possible to paint it the way it looked from the van: a moon in motion, a silver bullet just beneath the water.

I was thinking these thoughts (and maybe drifting toward a doze) when I became aware of ghostly movement above the moon in the water. It was Wireman's reflection. For a moment I had the crazy idea that he was jerking off back there, because his thighs appeared to be opening and closing and his hips seemed to be moving up and down. I shot a peek at Jack, but the Casey Key Road is a symphony of curves and Jack was absorbed in his driving. Besides, most of Wireman was right behind Jack's seat, not even visible in the rearview mirror.

I looked over my left shoulder. Wireman wasn't masturbating. Wireman wasn't sleeping and having a vivid dream. Wireman was having a seizure. It was quiet, probably *petit mal*, but it was a seizure, all right; I'd employed an epileptic draftsman during the first ten years of The Freemantle Company's existence, and I knew a seizure when I saw one. Wireman's torso lifted and dropped four or five inches as his buttocks clenched and released. His hands jittered on his stomach. His lips were smacking as though he tasted something particularly good. And his eyes looked as they had outside the parking garage. By starlight that one-up, one-down look was weird beyond my ability to describe. Spittle ran from the left corner of his mouth; a tear from his welling left eye trickled into his shaggy sideburn.

It went on for perhaps twenty seconds, then ceased. He blinked, and his eyes went back where they belonged. He was completely quiet for a minute. Maybe two. He saw me looking at him and said, 'I'd kill for another drink or a peanut butter cup, and I suppose a drink is out of the question, huh?'

'I guess it is if you want to make sure you hear her ring in the night,' I said, hoping I sounded casual.

'Bridge to Duma Key dead ahead,' Jack told us. 'Almost home, guys.'

Wireman sat up and stretched. 'It's been a hell of a day, but I won't be sorry to see my bed tonight, boys. I guess I'm getting old, huh?'

x

Although my leg was stiff, I got out of the van and stood next to him while he opened the door of the little iron box beside the gate to reveal a state-of-the-art security keypad.

'Thanks for coming with me, Wireman.'

'Sure,' he said. 'But if you thank me again, *muchacho*, I'm going to have to punch you in the mouth. Sorry, but that's just the way it's gotta be.'

'Good to know,' I said. 'Thanks for sharing.'

He laughed and clapped me on the shoulder. 'I like you, Edgar. You got style, you got class, you got the lips to kiss my ass.'

'Beautiful. I may cry. Listen, Wireman . . .'

I could have told him about what had just happened to him. I came close. In the end, I decided not to. I didn't know if it was the right decision or the wrong one, but I did know he might have a long night with Elizabeth Eastlake ahead of him. Also, that headache was still sitting in the back of my skull. I settled for asking him again if he wouldn't consider letting me turn my promised doctor's appointment into a double date.

'I will consider it,' he said. 'And I'll let you know.'

'Well don't wait too long, because—'

He raised a hand, stilling me, and for once his face was unsmiling. 'Enough, Edgar. Enough for one night, okay?'

'Okay,' I said. I watched him go in, then went back to the van.

Jack had the volume up. It was 'Renegade'. He went to turn it down and I said, 'No, that's okay. Crank it.'

167

'Really?' He turned around and headed back up the road. 'Great band. You ever heard em before?'

'Jack,' I said, 'that's Styx. Dennis DeYoung? Tommy Shaw? Where have you been all your life? In a cave?'

Jack smiled guiltily. 'I'm into country and even more into old standards,' he said. 'To tell you the truth, I'm a Rat Pack kind of guy.'

The idea of Jack Cantori hanging with Dino and Frank made me wonder – and not for the first time that day – if any of this was really happening. I also wondered how I could remember that Dennis DeYoung and Tommy Shaw had been in Styx – that Shaw had in fact written the song currently blasting out of the van's speakers – and sometimes not be able to remember my own ex-wife's name.

xi

Both lights on the answering machine next to the living room phone were blinking: the one indicating that I had messages and the one indicating that the tape for recording messages was full. But the number in the MESSAGES WAITING window was only 1. I considered this with foreboding while the weight with my headache inside it slid a little closer to the front of my skull. The only two people I could think of who might call and leave a message so long it would use up the whole tape were Pam and Ilse, and in neither case would hitting PLAY MESSAGES be apt to bring me good news. It doesn't take five minutes of recording-time to say *Everything's fine, call when you get a chance.*

Leave it until tomorrow, I thought, and a craven voice I hadn't even known was in my mental repertoire (maybe it was new) was willing to go further. It suggested I simply delete the message without listening to it at all.

'That's right, sure,' I said. 'And when whichever one it is calls back, I can just tell her the dog ate my answering machine.'

I pushed PLAY. And as so often happens when we are sure we know what to expect, I drew a wild card. It wasn't Pam and it wasn't Ilse. The wheezy, slightly emphysematic voice coming from the answering machine belonged to Elizabeth Eastlake.

168

'Hello, Edgar,' she said. 'One hopes you had a fruitful afternoon and are enjoying your evening out with Wireman as much as I am my evening in with Miss . . . well, I forget her name, but she's very pleasant. And one hopes you'll notice that I *have* remembered *your* name. I'm enjoying one of my clear patches. I love and treasure them, but they make me sad, as well. It's like being in a glider and rising on a gust of wind above a low-lying groundmist. For a little while one can see everything so clearly . . . and at the same time one knows the wind will die and one's glider will sink back into the mist again. Do you see?'

I saw, all right. Things were better for me now, but that was the world I'd woken up to, one where words clanged senselessly and memories were scattered like lawn furniture after a windstorm. It was a world where I had tried to communicate by hitting people and the only two emotions I really seemed capable of were fear and fury. One progresses beyond that state (as Elizabeth might say), but afterward one never quite loses the conviction that reality is gossamer. Behind its webwork? Chaos. Madness. The real truth, maybe, and the real truth is red.

'But enough of me, Edgar. I called to ask a question. Are you one who creates art for money, or do you believe in art for art's sake? I'm sure I asked when I met you – I'm almost positive – but I can't remember your answer. I believe it must be art for art's sake, or Duma should not have called you. But if you stay here for long . . .'

Clear anxiety crept into her voice.

'Edgar, one is sure you'll make a very nice neighbor, I have no doubts on that score, but you must take precautions. I think you have a daughter, and I believe she visited you. Didn't she? I seem to remember her waving to me. A pretty thing with blond hair? I may be confusing her with my sister Hannah – I tend to do that, I know I do – but in this case, I think I'm right. If you mean to stay, Edgar, you mustn't invite your daughter back. Under no circumstances. Duma Key isn't a safe place for daughters.'

I stood looking down at the recorder. Not safe. Before she had said not lucky, or at least that was *my* recollection. Did those two things come to the same or not?

'And your art. There is the matter of your art.' She sounded apologetic and a little breathless. 'One does not like to tell an artist what

169

to do; really, one *cannot* tell an artist what to do, and yet . . . oh dear . . .' She broke out in the loose, rattlebox cough of the life-long smoker. 'One does not like to speak of these things directly . . . or even know *how* to speak of them directly . . . but might I give you a word of advice, Edgar? As one who only appreciates, to one who creates? Might I be allowed that?'

I waited. The machine was silent. I thought perhaps the tape had run its course. Under my feet the shells murmured quietly, as if sharing secrets. *The gun, the fruit. The fruit, the gun.* Then she began again.

'If the people who run the Scoto or the Avenida should offer you a chance to show your work, I would advise you most strongly to say yes. So others can enjoy it, of course, but mainly to get as much of it off Duma as soon as you can.' She took a deep, audible breath, sounding like a woman preparing to finish some arduous chore. She also sounded completely and utterly sane, totally there and in the moment. '*Do not let it accumulate.* That is my advice to you, well-meant and without any . . . any personal agenda? Yes, that's what I mean. Letting artistic work accumulate here is like letting too much electricity accumulate in a battery. If you do that, the battery may explode.'

I didn't know if that was actually true or not, but I took her meaning.

'I can't tell you why that should be, but it is,' she went on . . . and I had a sudden intuition that she was lying about that. 'And surely if you believe in art for art's sake, the painting is the important part, isn't it?' Her voice was almost wheedling now. 'Even if you don't need to sell your paintings to buy your daily bread, sharing work . . . giving it to the world . . . surely artists care about such things, don't they? The giving?'

How would I know what was important to artists? I had only that day learned what sort of finish to put on my pictures to preserve them when I was done with them. I was a . . . what had Nannuzzi and Mary Ire called me? An American primitive.

Another pause. Then: 'I think I'll stop now. I've said my piece. Just please think about what I've said if you mean to stay, Edward. And I look forward to you reading to me. Many poems, I hope. That will be a treat. Goodbye for now. Thank you for listening to an old woman.' A pause. Then she said, 'The table is leaking. It must be. I'm so sorry.'

I waited twenty seconds, then thirty. I had just about decided that she'd forgotten to hang up on her end and was reaching to push the STOP button on the answering machine when she spoke again. Just six words, and they made no more sense than the thing about the leaking table, but still they brought gooseflesh out on my arms and turned the hair on the nape of my neck into hackles.

'My father was a skin diver,' Elizabeth Eastlake said. Each word was clearly enunciated. Then came the clear click of the phone being hung up on her end.

'No more messages,' the phone robot said. 'The message tape is full.'

I stood staring down at the machine, thought of erasing the tape, then decided to save it and play it for Wireman. I undressed, brushed my teeth, and went to bed. I lay in the dark, feeling the soft throb of my head, while below me the shells whispered the last thing she'd said over and over: *My father was a skin diver.*

8 – Family Portrait

i

Things slowed down for awhile. Sometimes that happens. The pot boils, and then, just before it can boil over, some hand – God, fate, maybe plain coincidence – lowers the heat. I mentioned this once to Wireman and he said life is like Friday on a soap opera. It gives you the illusion that everything is going to wrap up, and then the same old shit starts up on Monday.

I thought he'd go with me to see a doctor and we'd find out what was wrong with him. I thought he'd tell me why he'd shot himself in the head and how a man survives that sort of thing. The answer seemed to be, 'With seizures and a lot of trouble reading the fine print.' Maybe he'd even be able to tell me why his employer had a bee in her bonnet about keeping Ilse off the island. And the capper: I'd decide on what came next in the life of Edgar Freemantle, the Great American Primitive.

None of those things actually happened, at least for awhile. Life does produce changes, and the end results are sometimes explosive, but in soap operas and in real life, big bangs often have a long fuse.

Wireman did agree to go see a doctor with me and 'get his head examined', but not until March. February was too busy, he said. Winter residents – what Wireman called 'the monthlies', as if they were menstrual periods instead of tenants – would start moving into all the Eastlake properties the coming weekend. The first snowbirds to arrive would be the ones Wireman liked least. These were the Godfreys from Rhode Island, known to Wireman (and hence to me) as Joe and Rita Mean Dog. They came for ten weeks every winter and stayed in the house closest to the Eastlake estate. The signs warning of their Rotties and their Pit Bull were out; Ilse and I had seen them. Wireman said Joe Mean Dog was an ex–Green Beret, in a tone of voice which seemed to indicate that explained everything.

'Mr Dirisko won't even get out of his car when he has a package for them,' Wireman said. He was referring to the U.S. Postal Service's fat and jolly representative on the south end of Casey and all of Duma Key. We were sitting on the sawhorses in front of the Mean Dog house a day or two before the Godfreys were scheduled to arrive. The crushed-shell driveway was glistening a damp pink. Wireman had turned on the sprinklers. 'He just leaves whatever he's got at the foot of the mailbox post, honks, and then rolls wheels for *El Palacio*. And do I blame him? *Non, non*, Nannette.'

'Wireman, about the doctor—'

'March, *muchacho*, and before the Ides. I promise.'

'You're just putting it off,' I said.

'I'm not. I have only one busy season, and this be it. I got caught a little off-guard last year, but it's not going to happen this time around. It *can't* happen this time around, because this year Miss Eastlake's going to be far less capable of pitching in. At least the Mean Dogs are returners, known quantities, and so are the Baumgartens. I like the Baumgartens. Two kids.'

'Either of them girls?' I asked, thinking about Elizabeth's preju-dice concerning daughters and Duma.

'Nope, both the kind of boys who ought to have GOT IT MADE BUT DON'T HOLD IT AGAINST US stamped on their fore-heads. The people coming into the other four houses are all new. I can hope that none of them will be the rock-and-roll-all-night, party-every-day type, but what are the odds?'

'Not good, but you can at least hope they left their Slipknot CDs home.'

'Who's Slipknot? *What's* Slipknot?'

'Wireman, you don't want to know. Especially not while you're busy working yourself into a state.'

'I'm not. Wireman is just explaining February on Duma Key, *muchacho*. I'm going to be fielding everything from emergency queries about what to do if one of the Baumgarten boys gets stung by a jellyfish to where Rita Mean Dog can get a fan for her grand-mother, who they'll probably stash in the back bedroom again for a week or so. You think Miss Eastlake's getting on? I've seen Mexican mummies hauled through the streets of Guadalajara on the Day of the Dead who looked better than Gramma Mean Dog. She's got two basic lines of conversation. There's the inquisitive line – "Did you bring me a cookie?" – and the declarative – "Get me a towel, Rita, I think that last fart had a lump in it."'

I burst out laughing.

Wireman scraped a sneaker through the shells, creating a smile with his foot. Beyond us, our shadows lay on Duma Key Road, which was paved and smooth and even. Here, at least. Farther south was a different story. 'The answer to the fan problem, should you care, is Dan's Fan City. Is that a great name, or what? And I'll tell you something: I actually *like* solving these problems. Defusing little crises. I make folks a hell of a lot happier here on Duma Key than I ever did in court.'

But you haven't lost the knack for leading people away from the things you don't want to discuss, I thought. 'Wireman, it would only take half an hour to get a physician to look into your eyes and tap your skull—'

'You're wrong, *muchacho,*' he said patiently. 'At this time of year it takes a minimum of two hours to get looked at in a roadside Doc-in-the-Box for a lousy strep throat. When you add on an hour of travel time – more now, because it's Snowbird Season and none of them know where they're going – you're talking about three daylight hours I just can't give up. Not with appointments to see the air conditioning guy at 17 . . . the meter-reader at 27 . . . the cable guy right here, if he ever shows up.' He pointed to the next house down the road, which happened to be 39. 'Youngsters from Toledo are taking that one until March fifteenth, and they're paying an extra seven hundred bucks for something called Wi-Fi, which I don't even know what it is.'

'Wave of the future, that's what it is. I've got it. Jack took care of it. Wave of the father-raping, mother-stabbing future.'

'Good one. Arlo Guthrie, 1967.'

'Movie was 1969, I think,' I said.

'Whenever it was, *viva* the wave of the mother-raping, froggy-stabbing future. Doesn't change the fact that I'm busier than a one-legged man in an ass-kicking contest . . . plus come on, Edgar. You *know* it's going to be more than a quick tap and peek with the old doctor-flashlight. That's just where it starts.'

'But if you need it—'

'For the time being I'm good to go.'

'Sure. That's why I'm the one reading her poems every afternoon.'

'A little literary culture won't hurt you, you fucking cannibal.'

'I know it won't, and *you* know that's not what I'm talking about.' I thought – and not for the first time – that Wireman was one of the very few men I ever met in my adult life who could consistently tell me no without making me angry. He was a genius of no. Sometimes I thought it was him; sometimes I thought the accident had changed something in me; sometimes I thought it was both.

'I *can* read, you know,' Wireman said. 'In short bursts. Enough to get by. Medicine bottle labels, phone numbers, things like that. And I *will* get looked at, so relax that Type-A compulsion of yours to set the whole world straight. Christ, you must have driven your wife crazy.' He glanced at me sideways and said, 'Oops. Did Wireman step on a corn there?'

'Ready to talk about that little round scar on the side of your head yet? *Muchacho?*'

He grinned. '*Touché, touché*. All apologies.'

'Kurt Cobain,' I said. '1993. Or thereabouts.'

He blinked. 'Really? I would have said '95, but rock music has largely left me behind. Wireman got old, sad but true. As for the seizure thing . . . sorry, Edgar, I just don't believe it.'

He did, though. I could see it in his eyes. But before I could say anything else, he climbed down from the sawhorse and pointed north. 'Look! White van! I think the Forces of Cable TV have arrived!'

ii

I believed Wireman when he said he had no idea what Elizabeth Eastlake had been talking about on the answering machine tape after I played it for him. He continued to think that her concern for my daughter had something to do with her own long-deceased sisters. He professed to be completely puzzled about why she didn't want me to stockpile my pictures on the island. About that, he said, he didn't have a clue.

Joe and Rita Mean Dog moved in; the relentless barking of their menagerie commenced. The Baumgartens also moved in, and I often began to pass their boys playing Frisbee on the beach. They were just as Wireman had said: sturdy, handsome, and polite, one maybe eleven and the other maybe thirteen, with builds that would soon make them gigglebait among the junior high cheerleader set, if not already. They were always willing to share their Frisbee with me for a throw or two as I limped past, and the older – Jeff – usually called something encouraging like 'Yo, Mr Freemantle, nice chuck!'

A couple with a sports car moved into the house just south of Big Pink, and the distressing strains of Toby Keith began to waft to me around the cocktail hour. On the whole, I might have preferred Slipknot. The quartet of young people from Toledo had a golf cart they raced up and down the beach when they weren't playing volleyball or off on fishing expeditions.

Wireman was more than busy; he was a dervish. Luckily, he had help. One day Jack lent him a hand unclogging the Mean Dog lawn-sprinklers. A day or two later, I helped him push the Toledo visitors' golf cart out of a dune in which it had gotten stuck – those responsible had left it to go get a six-pack, and the tide was threatening to take it. My hip and leg were still mending, but there was nothing wrong with my remaining arm.

Bad hip and leg or not, I took Great Beach Walks. Some days – mostly when the fog came in during the late afternoon, first obliterating the Gulf with cold amnesia and then taking the houses, as well – I took pain pills from my diminishing stock. Most days I didn't. Wireman was rarely parked in his beach chair drinking green tea that February, but Elizabeth Eastlake was always in her parlor, she almost always knew who I was, and she usually had a book of poetry near to hand. It wasn't always Keillor's *Good Poems*, but that was the one she liked the best. I liked it, too. Merwin and Sexton and Frost, oh-my.

I did plenty of reading myself that February and March. I read more than I had in years – novels, short stories, three long non-fiction books about how we had stumbled into the Iraq mess (the short answer appeared to have W for a middle initial and a dick for a Vice President). But mostly what I did was paint. Every afternoon and evening I painted until I could barely lift my strengthening arm. Beachscapes, seascapes, still lifes, and sunsets, sunsets, sunsets.

177

But that fuse continued to smolder. The heat had been turned down but not off. The matter of Candy Brown wasn't the next thing, only the next obvious thing. And that didn't come until Valentine's Day. A hideous irony when you think of it.

Hideous.

iii

ifsogirl88 to EFree19
10:19 AM
February 3

Dear Daddy, It was great to hear you got a 'thumbs up' on your paintings! Hooray! ☺ And if they DO offer you a show, I'll catch the next plane and be there in my 'little black dress' (I have one, believe it or not). Got to stay put for now and study my butt off because – here is a secret – I'm hoping to surprise Carson when Spring Break rolls around in April. The Hummingbirds will be in Tennessee and Arkansas then (he sez the tour is off to a great start). I'm thinking that if I do okay on my mid-terms, I could catch up with the tour in either Memphis or Little Rock. What do you think?

Ilse

My misgivings about the Baptist Hummingbird hadn't faded, and what I thought was she was asking for trouble. But if she was making a mistake about him, it might be better for her to find out sooner rather than later. So – hoping to God *I* wasn't making a mistake – I e-mailed back and told her that sounded like an interesting idea, assuming she was okay on her coursework. (I couldn't bring myself to go balls-out and tell my beloved younger daughter that spending a week in the company of her boyfriend, even assuming said boyfriend was chaperoned by hardshell Baptists, was a *good* idea.) I also suggested it might be bad policy to share her plan with her mother. This brought a prompt response.

ifsogirl88 to EFree19
12:02 PM
February 3

Daddy Dearest: Do you think I've lost my freakin'
MIND???

Illy

No, I didn't think that . . . but if she caught her tenor doing the horizontal bop with one of the altos when she got to Little Rock, she was going to be one very unhappy If-So-Girl. I had no doubt that everything would then come out to her mother, engagement and all, and Pam would find a lot to say on the subject of my own sanity. I had already asked myself some questions on that score, and mostly decided to give myself a pass. When it comes to your kids, you find yourself making some weird calls from time to time and just hoping they turn out all right – calls *and* kids. Parenting is the greatest of hum-a-few-bars-and-I'll-fake-it skills.

Then there was Sandy Smith, the Realtor. On my answering machine, Elizabeth had said I must be one of those who believed in art for art's sake, or Duma Key would not have called me. What I wanted from Sandy was confirmation that the only thing calling me had been a glossy brochure, one that had probably been shown to potential renters with deep pockets all over the United States. Maybe all over the world.

The response I got wasn't what I had hoped for, but I'd be lying if I said I was *completely* surprised. That was my bad-memory year, after all. And then there's the desire to believe things happened a certain way; when it comes to the past we all stack the deck.

SmithRealty9505 to EFree19
2:17 PM
February 8

Dear Edgar: I am so glad you're enjoying the place. In answer to your question, the Salmon Point property wasn't the only brochure I sent you but one of nine detailing lease

opportunities in Florida and Jamaica. As I recall, Salmon Point was the only one you expressed interest in. In fact, I remember you saying, 'Don't dicker the deal, just do it.' Hope this helps.

Sandy

I read this message through twice, then murmured, 'Just do the deal and let the deal do you, *muchacha*.'

I couldn't remember the other brochures even now, but I remembered the one for Salmon Point. The folder it came in had been a bright pink. A *big* pink, you might say, and the words that caught my eye hadn't been *Salmon Point* but those below it, embossed in gold: YOUR SECRET GULFSIDE RETREAT. So maybe it had called me.

Maybe it had, after all.

iv

KamenDoc to EFree19
1:46 PM
February 10

Edgar: Long time no hear, as the deaf Indian said to the prodigal son (please forgive me; bad jokes are the only jokes I know). How goes the art? Concerning the MRI, I suggest you call the Center for Neurological Studies at Sarasota Memorial Hospital. The number is 941-555-5554.

Kamen

EFree19 to KamenDoc
2:19 PM
February 10

Kamen: Thanks for the referral. Center for Neurological Studies sounds pretty damned serious! But I will make the appointment very soon.

Edgar

180

KamenDoc to EFree19
4:55 PM
February 10

Soon should be soon enough. As long as you're not having seizures.

Kamen

He had punctuated 'as long as you're not having seizures' with one of those handy e-mail emoticons, this one a round laughing face with a mouthful of teeth. Having seen Wireman doing a pogo in the shadowy back seat of the rented van with his eyes pointing in different directions, I didn't feel like laughing myself. But I knew that, short of chains and a tractor hitch, I wouldn't be getting Wireman examined much before March fifteenth, unless he pitched a *grand mal* bitch. And of course, Wireman wasn't Xander Kamen's problem. I wasn't either, strictly speaking, and I was touched that he was still bothering. On impulse I clicked the REPLY button and typed:

EFree19 to KamenDoc
5:05 PM
February 10

Kamen: No seizures. I'm fine. Painting up a storm. I took some of my stuff to a Sarasota gallery, and one of the guys who owns the place had a look at it. I think he might offer me a show. If he does, and if I agree, would you come? It would be good to see a familiar face from the land of ice & snow.

Edgar

I was going to shut down the machine after that and make myself a sandwich, but the incoming-mail chime rang before I could.

181

KamenDoc to EFree19
5:09 PM
February 10

Name the date and I'm there.

I was smiling as I shut the computer down. And misting up a little, too.

v

A day later, I went to Nokomis with Wireman to pick up a new sinktrap for the folks at 17 (sports car; shitty country music) and some plastic fencing at the hardware store for the Mean Dogs. Wireman didn't need my help, and he certainly didn't need me limping around behind him in the Nokomis TruValue, but it was a crappy, rainy day, and I wanted to get off the island. We had lunch at Ophelia's and argued about rock and roll, which made it a cheerful outing. When I got back, the message light on my answering machine was blinking. It was Pam. 'Call me,' she said, and hung up.

I did, but first – this feels like a confession, and a cowardly one, at that – I went online, surfed to that day's Minneapolis *Star Tribune*, and clicked on OBITUARIES. I scrolled through the names quickly and made sure Thomas Riley wasn't one of them, knowing it proved nothing; he might have offed himself too late to make the morning line.

Sometimes she muted the phone and napped in the afternoon, in which case I'd get the answering machine and a little reprieve. Not this afternoon. It was Pam herself, soft but not warm: 'Hello.'

'It's me, Pam. Returning your call.'

'I suppose you were out sunning,' she said. 'It's snowing here. Snowing and as cold as a well-digger's belt-buckle.'

I relaxed a little. Tom wasn't dead. If Tom had been dead, we wouldn't be settling in for a little impromptu bitcharee.

'Actually, it's cold and rainy where I am,' I said.

'Good. I hope you catch bronchitis. Tom Riley stormed out of here this morning after calling me a meddlesome cunt and throwing a vase on the floor. I suppose I should be glad he didn't throw it at me.' Pam started to cry. She honked, then surprised me by laughing. It was bitter, but also surprisingly good-humored. 'When do you suppose your strange ability to induce my tears runs out?'

'Tell me what happened, Panda.'

'And no more of that. Call me that again and I'm hanging up. Then you can buzz Tom and ask *him* what happened. Probably that's what I ought to make you do, anyway. It would serve you right.'

I put my hand to my head and began to massage my temples: thumb in the left hollow, first two fingers in the right. It's sort of amazing that one hand can encompass so many dreams and so much pain. Not to mention the potential to hatch so much plain and fancy fuckery.

'Tell me, Pam. Please. I'll listen and not get angry.'

'Getting past that, are you? Give me a second.' There was a clunk as the phone went down, probably on the kitchen counter. For a moment I heard the distant babble of the TV and then it was gone. When she came back she said, 'All right, now I can hear myself think.' There was another mighty honk as she blew her nose once more. When she started talking again, she was composed, with no hint of tears in her voice.

'I asked Myra to call me when he got back home – Myra Devorkian, who lives across the street from him. I told her I was worried about his state of mind. No reason to keep that much to myself, was there?'

'No.'

'And bango! Myra said *she'd* been worried, too – she and Ben both. Said he was drinking too much, for one thing, and sometimes going in to his office with a ten o'clock shadow. Although she said he looked spiffy enough when he went off on his trip. Amazing how much neighbors see, even when they're not really close friends. Ben and Myra didn't know about . . . us, of course, but they knew damn well that Tom had been depressed.'

You think they didn't know, I didn't say.

'Anyway, long story short, I invited him over. There was a look in his eyes when he came in . . . this look . . . as if he thought maybe I intended to . . . you know . . .'

'Pick up where you left off,' I said.

'Am I telling this or are you?'

'Sorry.'

'Well, you're right. Of course you're right. I wanted to ask him into the kitchen for coffee, but we never got any farther than the hall. He wanted to kiss me.' She said this with a kind of defiant pride. 'I let him . . . once . . . but when it became obvious that he wanted more, I pushed him back and said I had something to say. He said he knew it was bad from the way I looked, but nothing could hurt the way I hurt him when I said we couldn't see each other any more. That's men for you – and they say *we're* the ones who know how to lay on the guilt.

'I said that just because we couldn't go on seeing each other romantically didn't mean I didn't still care about him. Then I said several people had told me he was acting strange – not like himself – and I put that together with him not taking his antidepressant pills and began to worry. I said I thought he was planning to kill himself.'

She stopped for a moment, then went on.

'Before he came, I never meant to say it right out like that. But it's funny – the minute he walked through the door I was almost positive, and when he kissed me I knew for a fact. His lips were cold. And dry. It was like kissing a corpse.'

'I'll bet,' I said, and tried to scratch my right arm.

'His face tightened up and I mean really. Every line smoothed out, and his mouth almost disappeared. He asked me who put an idea like that in my head. And then, before I could even answer, he said it was bullshit. That's the word he used, and it's not a Tom Riley word at all.'

She was right about that. The Tom I'd known in the old days wouldn't have said bullshit if he'd had a mouthful.

'I didn't want to give him any names – certainly not yours, because he would have thought I was crazy, and not Illy's, because I didn't know what he might say to her if—'

'I told you, Illy had nothing to do with—'

'Be quiet. I'm almost through. I just said these people who were talking about how funny he was acting didn't even know about the pills he's been taking since the second divorce, and how he quit taking them last May. He calls them stupid-pills. I said if he thought he was keeping everything that was wrong with him under wraps, he was mistaken. Then I said that if he did something to himself, I'd tell his mother and brother it was suicide, and it would break their hearts. That was your idea, Edgar, and it worked. I hope you're proud. That was when he broke my vase and called me a meddlesome cunt, see? He was as white as a sheet. I bet . . .' She swallowed. I could hear the click in her throat across all the miles. 'I bet he had the way he was going to do it all planned out.'

'I don't doubt it,' I said. 'What do you think he'll do now?'

'I don't know. I really don't.'

'Maybe I better call him.'

'Maybe you better not. Maybe finding out we talked would push him right over the edge.' With a touch of malice she added, 'Then *you'll* be the one losing sleep.'

It was a possibility I hadn't thought of, but she had a point. Tom and Wireman were alike in one way: both needed help and I couldn't drag them to it. An old *bon mot* bounced into my head, maybe apropos, maybe not: you can lead a whore to culture, but you can't make her think. Maybe Wireman could tell me who had said it. And when.

'So how did you know he meant to kill himself?' she asked. 'I want to know, and by God you're going to tell me before I hang up. I did my part and you're going to tell me.'

There it was, the question she hadn't asked before; she'd been too fixated on how I'd found out about her and Tom in the first place. Well, Wireman wasn't the only one with sayings; my father had a few, as well. One was, when a lie won't suffice, the truth will have to do.

'Since the accident, I've been painting,' I said. 'You know that.'

'So?'

I told her about the sketch I'd drawn of her, Max from Palm Desert, and Tom Riley. About some of my Internet explorations into the world of phantom limb phenomena. And about seeing Tom Riley standing at the head of the stairs in what I supposed was now my studio, naked except for his pajama pants, one eye gone, replaced by a socket filled with congealed gore.

When I finished, there was a long silence. I didn't break it. At last she said, in a new and cautious voice: 'Do you really believe that, Edgar – *any* of it?'

185

'Wireman, the guy from down the beach . . .' I stopped, infuriated in spite of myself. And not because I didn't have any words. Or not exactly. Was I going to tell her the guy from down the beach was an occasional telepath, so *he* believed me?

'What about the guy from down the beach, Edgar?' Her voice was calm and soft. I recognized it from the first month or so after my accident. It was her Edgar's-Going-Section-Eight voice.

'Nothing,' I said. 'It doesn't matter.'

'You need to call Dr Kamen and tell him about this new idea of yours,' she said. 'This idea that you're psychic. Don't e-mail him, *call* him. *Please.*'

'All right, Pam.' I felt very tired. Not to mention frustrated and pissed off.

'All right what?'

'All right, I'm hearing you. You're coming in loud and clear. No misunderstandings whatsoever. Perish the goddam thought. All I wanted was to save Tom Riley's life.'

To that she had no answer. And no rational explanation for what I had known about Tom, either. So that was where we left it. My thought as I hung up the phone was *No good deed goes unpunished.*

Maybe it was hers, too.

vi

I felt angry and lost. The dank, dreary weather didn't help. I tried to paint and couldn't. I went downstairs, took up one of my sketchpads, and found myself reduced to the sort of doodles I'd done in my other life while taking phone calls: cartoon shmoos with big ears. I was about to toss the pad aside in disgust when the phone rang. It was Wireman.

'Are you coming this afternoon?' he asked.

'Sure,' I said.

'I thought maybe with the rain—'

'I planned on creeping down in the car. I'm certainly not doing squat here.'

'Good. Just don't plan on Poetry Hour. She's in the fog.'

'Bad?'

'As bad as I've seen her. Disconnected. Drifting. Confused.' He took a deep breath and let it out. It was like listening to a gust of wind blow through the telephone. 'Listen, Edgar, I hate to ask this, but could I leave her with you for awhile? Forty-five minutes, tops. The Baumgartens have been having trouble with the sauna – it's the damned heater – and the guy coming out to fix it needs to show me a cut-off switch or something. And to sign his work-order, of course.'

'Not a problem.'

'You're a prince. I'd kiss you, but for those sore-raddled lips of yours.'

'Fuck you very much, Wireman.'

'Yeah, everyone loves me, it's my curse.'

'Pam called me. She talked to my friend Tom Riley.' Considering what the two of them had been up to it felt strange to be calling Tom a friend, but what the hell. 'I think she took the air out of his suicide plan.'

'That's good. So why do I hear lead in your voice?'

'She wanted to know how I knew.'

'Not how you knew she was bumping uglies with this guy, but—'

'How I diagnosed his suicidal depression from fifteen hundred miles away.'

'Ah! And what did you say?'

'Not having a good lawyer present, I was reduced to the truth.'

'And she thought you were *un poco loco.*'

'No, Wireman, she thought I was *muy loco.*'

'Does it matter?'

'No. But she's going to brood about this – believe me when I say Pam's U.S. Olympic Brooding Team material – and I'm afraid my good deed could explode in my younger daughter's face.'

'Assuming your wife's looking for someone to blame.'

'It's a safe assumption. I know her.'

'That would be bad.'

'It'd rock Ilse's world more than it deserves to be rocked. Tom's been like an uncle to her and Melinda their whole lives.'

'Then you'll have to convince your wife that you really saw what you saw, and your daughter had nothing to do with it.'

187

'How do I do *that*?'

'How about you tell her something about herself you have no way of knowing?'

'Wireman, you're crazy! I can't just *make* something like that happen!'

'How do you know? I have to get off the phone, *amigo* – by the sound, Miss Eastlake's lunch just went on the floor. I'll see you later?'

'Yeah,' I said. I was about to add goodbye, but he was already gone. I hung up, wondering where I had put Pam's gardening gloves, the ones that said HANDS OFF. Maybe if I had those, Wireman's idea might not turn out to be so crazy after all.

I looked for them all over the house and came up empty. Maybe I threw them away after making the *Friends with Benefits* drawing, but I couldn't remember doing it. I can't remember now. All I know is that I never saw them again.

vii

The room which Wireman and Elizabeth called the China Parlor was filled with a sad, subtropical winterlight that afternoon. The rain was heavier now, drumming against the walls and windows in waves, and a wind had gotten up, clattering through the palms surrounding *El Palacio* and sending shadows flying across the walls. For the first time since I'd been coming there, I could see no sense to the china figures on the long table; there were no *tableaux*, only a clutter of people, animals, and buildings. A unicorn and one of the blackface guys lay side-by-side next to the overturned school-house. If there was a story on the table today, it was a disaster movie. Near the Tara-style mansion stood a Sweet Owen cookie-tin. Wireman had explained the routine I should follow if Elizabeth called for it.

The lady herself was in her wheelchair, slumped a bit sideways, vacantly overseeing the disheveltry on her play-table, which was usually so neatly kept. She was wearing a blue dress that almost matched the enormous blue Chuck Taylors on her feet. Her slump had stretched the boat neck of the dress into a lopsided gawp that

188

revealed an ivory-colored slip-strap. I found myself wondering who had dressed her that morning, she or Wireman.

She spoke rationally at first, calling me by my correct name and enquiring after my health. She said goodbye to Wireman when he left for the Baumgartens' and asked him to please wear a hat and take an umbrella. All that was good. But when I brought her her snack from the kitchen fifteen minutes later, there had been a change. She was looking into the corner and I heard her murmur, 'Go back, go back, Tessie, you don't belong here. And make the big boy go away.'

Tessie. I knew that name. I used my thinking-sideways technique, looking for associations, and found one: a newspaper headline reading THEY ARE GONE. Tessie had been one of Elizabeth's twin sisters. Wireman had told me that. I heard him saying *The presumption is they drowned*, and a chill like a knife slipped into my side.

'Bring me that,' she said, pointing to the cookie-tin, and I did. From her pocket she drew a figurine wrapped in a hankie. She took the lid off the tin, gave me a look that combined slyness and confusion in a way that was hard to look at, then popped the figure inside. It made a soft hollow *bonk*. She fumbled the lid back on, pushing my hand away when I tried to help. Then she handed it to me.

'Do you know what to do with this?' she asked. 'Did . . . did . . .' I could see her struggling. The word was there, but dancing just out of reach. Mocking her. I could give it to her, but I remembered how furious it made me when people did that, and waited. 'Did *him* tell you what to do with it?'

'Yes.'

'Then what are you waiting for? *Take* the bitch.'

I carried the tin up one side of the tennis court to the little pond. The fish were jumping at the surface, a lot more excited by the rain than I was. There was a little pile of stones beside the bench, just as Wireman had said there would be. I tossed one in ('You might not think she could hear that, but her ears are very sharp,' Wireman had told me), being careful to avoid beaning one of the carp. Then I took the tin, with the figurine still inside, back into the house. But not into the China Parlor. I went into the kitchen, removed the lid, and pulled out the wrapped figure. This

189

hadn't been in Wireman's set of contingency instructions, but I was curious.

It was a china woman, but the face had been chipped away. There was only a ragged blank where it had been.

'*Who's there?*' Elizabeth shrieked, making me jump. I almost dropped the creepy little thing on the floor, where it surely would have shattered on the tiles.

'Just me, Elizabeth,' I called back, laying the figure on the counter.

'Edmund? Or Edgar, or whatever your name is?'

'Right.' I went back into the parlor.

'Did you take care of that business of mine?'

'Yes, ma'am, I sure did.'

'Have I had my snack yet?'

'Yes.'

'All right.' She sighed.

'Do you want something else? I'm sure I could—'

'No thanks, hon. I'm sure the train will be here soon, and you know I don't like to travel on a full stomach. I always end up in one of the backwards seats and with food in my stomach I should certainly be train-sick. Have you seen my tin, my Sweet Owen tin?'

'I think it was in the kitchen. Should I bring it?'

'Not on such a wet day,' she said. 'I thought I'd have you throw her in the pond, the pond would do, but I've changed my mind. It seems unnecessary on such a wet day. The quality of mercy is not strained, you know. It droppeth like the gentle rain.'

'From heaven,' I said.

'Yeah, yeah.' She flapped her hand as if that part were of no matter.

'Why don't you arrange your chinas, Elizabeth? They're all mixed up today.'

She cast a glance at the table, then looked at the window when an especially strong gust of wind slapped it with rain. 'Fuck,' she said. 'I'm so fucking confused.' And then, with a spite I would not have guessed she had in her: 'They all died and left me to *this*.'

I was the last one to be repulsed by her lapse into vulgarity; I understood it too well. Maybe the quality of mercy isn't strained, there are millions of us who live and die by the idea, but . . . we have things like this waiting. Yes.

She said, 'He never should have got that thing, but he didn't know.'

'What thing?'

'What thing,' she agreed, and nodded. 'I want the train. I want to get *out* of here before the big boy comes.'

After that we both lapsed into silence. Elizabeth closed her eyes and appeared to doze off in her wheelchair.

For something to do, I got out of my own chair, which would have looked at home in a gentlemen's club, and approached the table. I plucked up a china girl and boy, looked at them, then put them aside. I scratched absently at the arm that wasn't there, studying the senseless litter before me. There had to be at least a hundred figures on the polished length of oak. Maybe two hundred. Among them was a china woman with an old-fashioned cap on – a milk-maid's cap, I thought – but I didn't want her, either. The cap was wrong, and besides, she was too young. I found another woman with long painted hair, and she was better. That hair was a little too long and a little too dark, but—

No it wasn't, because Pam had been to the beauty parlor, some-times known as the Midlife Crisis Fountain of Youth.

I held the china figure, wishing I had a house to put her in and a book for her to read.

I tried to switch the figurine to my right hand – perfectly natural because my right hand was there, I could feel it – and it fell to the table with a clack. It didn't break, but Elizabeth's eyes opened. 'Dick! Was that the train? Did it whistle? Did it cry?'

'Not yet,' I said. 'Why don't you nap a little?'

'Oh, you'll find it on the second floor landing,' she said as if I had asked her something else, and closed her eyes again. 'Call me when the train comes. I'm so sick of this station. And watch for the big boy, that cuntlicker could be anywhere.'

'I will,' I said. My right arm itched horribly. I reached into my back pocket, hoping my notebook was there. It wasn't. I'd left it on the kitchen counter back at Big Pink. But that made me think of the *Palacio* kitchen. There was a notepad for messages on the counter where I'd left the tin. I hurried back, snatched up the pad, stuck it between my teeth, then almost ran back to the China Parlor, already pulling my Uni-ball pen from my breast pocket. I sat down in my wingback chair and began to sketch the china doll rapidly while the rain whipped the windows and Elizabeth sat leaning in her wheelchair across the table from me, dozing with her mouth ajar. The wind-driven shadows of the palms flew around the walls like bats.

It didn't take long, and I realized something as I worked: I was pouring the itch out through the tip of the pen, decanting it onto the page. The woman in my drawing was the china figure, but she was also Pam. The woman was Pam, but she was also the china figure. Her hair was longer than when I'd last seen her, and spread out on her shoulders. She was sitting in

(*the BURN, the CHAR*)

a chair. What chair? A rocking chair. Hadn't been any such item in our house when I left it, but there was now. Something was on the table beside her. I didn't know what it was at first, but it emerged from the tip of the pen and became a box with printing across the top. Sweet Owen? Did it say Sweet Owen? No, it said Grandma's. My Uni-ball put something on the table beside the box. An oatmeal cookie. Pam's favorite. While I was looking at it, the pen drew the book in Pam's hand. Couldn't read the title because the angle was wrong. By now my pen was adding lines between the window and her feet. She'd said it was snowing, but now the snow was over. The lines were meant to be sunrays.

I thought the picture was finished, but apparently there were two more things. My pen moved to the far left side of the paper and added the television, quick as a flash. New television, flat screen like Elizabeth's. And below it—

The pen finished and fell away. The itch was gone. My fingers were stiff. On the other side of the long table, Elizabeth's doze had deepened into real sleep. Once she might have been young and beautiful. Once she might have been some young man's dream baby. Now she was snoring with her mostly toothless mouth pointed at the ceiling. If there's a God, I think He needs to try a little harder.

viii

I had seen a phone in the library as well as the kitchen, and the library was closer to the China Parlor. I decided neither Wireman

192

nor Elizabeth would begrudge me a long-distance call to Minnesota. I picked up the phone, then paused with it curled to my chest. On a wall next to the suit of armor, highlighted by several cunning little pin-spots in the ceiling, was a display of antique weapons: a long-barreled muzzle-loader that looked of Revolutionary War vintage, a flintlock pistol, a derringer that would have been at home in a riverboat gambler's boot, a Winchester carbine. Mounted above the carbine was the gadget Elizabeth had been holding in her lap the day Ilse and I had seen her. To either side, making an inverted V, were four loads for the thing. You couldn't call them arrows; they were too short. Harpoonlets still seemed like the right word. Their tips were very bright, and looked very sharp.

I thought, *You could do some real damage with a thing like that.* Then I thought: *My father was a skin diver.*

I pushed it out of my mind and called what used to be home.

ix

'Hi, Pam, it's me again.'

'I don't want to talk to you any more, Edgar. We finished what we have to say.'

'Not quite. But this will be short. I have an old lady to look after. She's sleeping now, but I don't like to leave her long.'

Pam, curious in spite of herself: 'What old lady?'

'Her name's Elizabeth Eastlake. She's in her mid-eighties, and she's got a good start on Alzheimer's. Her principal caregiver is taking care of an electrical problem with someone's sauna, and I'm helping out.'

'Did you want a gold star to paste on the Helping Others page of your workbook?'

'No, I called to convince you I'm not crazy.' I had brought in my drawing. Now I crooked the handset between my shoulder and my ear so I could pick it up.

'Why do you care?'

'Because you're convinced that all this started with Ilse, and it didn't.'

'My God, you're unbelievable! If she called from Santa Fe and said she'd broken a shoelace, you'd fly out there to take her a new one!'

'I also don't like you thinking that I'm down here going insane when I'm not. So . . . are you listening?'

Only silence from the other end, but silence was good enough. She was listening.

'You're ten or maybe fifteen minutes out of the shower. I think that because your hair is down on the back of your housecoat. I guess you still don't like the hairdryer.'

'How—'

'I don't *know* how. You were sitting in a rocking chair when I called. You must have gotten it since the divorce. Reading a book and eating a cookie. A Grandma's oatmeal cookie. The sun's out now, and it's coming in the window. You have a new television, the kind with a flat screen.' I paused. 'And a cat. You got a cat. It's sleeping under the TV.'

Dead silence from her end. On my end the wind blew and the rain slapped the windows. I was about to ask her if she was there when she spoke again, in a dull voice that didn't sound like Pam at all. I had thought she was done hurting my heart, but I was wrong. 'Stop spying on me. If you ever loved me – stop spying on me.'

'Then stop blaming me,' I said in a hoarse, not-quite-breaking voice. Suddenly I remembered Ilse getting ready to go back to Brown, Ilse standing in the strong tropical sun outside the Delta terminal, looking up at me and saying, *You deserve to get better. Sometimes I wonder if you really believe that.* 'What's happened to me isn't my fault. The accident wasn't my fault and neither is this. I didn't ask for it.'

She screamed, '*Do you think I did?*'

I closed my eyes, begging something, anything, to keep me from giving back anger for anger. 'No, of course not.'

'*Then leave me out of it! Stop calling me! Stop SCARING me!*'

She hung up. I stood holding the phone to my ear. There was silence, then a loud click. It was followed by that distinctive Duma Key warbling hum. Today it sounded rather subaqueous. Maybe because of the rain. I hung the phone up and stood looking at the suit of armor. 'I think that went very well, Sir Lancelot,' I said.

No reply, which was exactly what I deserved.

194

I crossed the plant-lined main hall to the doorway of the China Parlor, looked in at Elizabeth, and saw she was sleeping in the same head-cocked position. Her snores, which had earlier struck me as pathetic in their naked antiquity, were now actually comforting; otherwise, it would have been too easy to imagine her sitting there dead with her neck broken. I wondered if I should wake her, and decided to let her sleep. Then I glanced right, toward the wide main staircase, and thought of her saying *Oh, you'll find it on the second floor landing.*

Find what?

Probably it had been just another bit of gibberish, but I had nothing better to do, so I walked down the hall that would have been a dogtrot in a humbler house – the rain tapping the glass ceiling – and then climbed the wide staircase. I stopped five risers from the top, staring, then slowly climbed the rest of the way. There was something, after all: an enormous black-and-white photograph in a frame of narrow banded gold. I asked Wireman later how a black-and-white from the nineteen-twenties could have been blown up to such a size – it had to have been at least five feet tall by four wide – with so little blurring. He said it had probably been taken with a Hasselblad, the finest non-digital camera ever made.

There were eight people in the photograph, standing on white sand with the Gulf of Mexico in the background. The man was tall and handsome and appeared to be in his mid-forties. He was wearing a black bathing singlet that consisted of a strap-style shirt and trunks that looked like the close-fitting underwear basketball players wear nowadays. Ranged on either side of him stood five girls, the oldest a ripe teenager, the youngest identical towheads that made me think of the Bobbsey Twins from my earliest adventures in reading. The twins were wearing identical bathing dresses with frilled skirts, and holding hands. In their free hands they clasped dangly-legged, apron-wearing Raggedy Ann dolls that made me think of Reba . . . and the dark yarn hair above the vacantly smiling faces of the twins' dolls was surely *RED*. In the crook of one arm, the man – John Eastlake, I had no doubt – held girl number six, the toddler who would eventually become the snoring crone below me. Behind the

195

white folks stood a young black woman of perhaps twenty-two, with her hair tied in a kerchief. She was holding a picnic basket, and judging from the way the not-inconsiderable muscles in her arms were bunched, it was heavy. Three bangled silver bracelets clung to one forearm.

Elizabeth was smiling and holding out her chubby little hands to whoever had taken this family portrait. No one else was smiling, although there might have been the ghost of one lurking around the corners of the man's mouth; he had a mustache, and that made it hard to tell. The young black nanny looked positively grim.

In the hand not occupied with supporting the toddler, John Eastlake held two items. One was a skin diver's facemask. The other was the harpoon pistol I had seen mounted on the wall of the library with the other weapons. The question, it seemed to me, was whether or not some rational Elizabeth had come out of the mental fog long enough to send me up here.

Before I could consider this further, the front door opened below me. 'I'm back!' Wireman called. 'Mission accomplished! Now who wants a drink?'

How to Draw a Picture (V)

Don't be afraid to experiment; find your muse and let her lead you. As her talent grew stronger, Elizabeth's muse became Noveen, the marvelous talking doll. Or so she thought. And by the time she discovered her mistake – by the time Noveen's voice changed – it was too late. But at first it must have been wonderful. Finding one's muse always is.

The cake, for instance.

Make it go on the floor, *Noveen says.* Make it go on the floor, Libbit!

And because she can, she does. She draws Nan Melda's cake on the floor. Splattered on the floor! Ha! And Nan Melda standing over it, hands on hips, disgusted.

And was Elizabeth ashamed when it actually happened? Ashamed and a little frightened? I think she was.

I know *she was. For children, meanness is usually funny only when it's imagined.*

Still, there were other games. Other experiments. Until finally, in '27 . . .

In Florida, all out-of-season hurricanes are called Alice. It's a kind of joke. But the one that came screaming in off the Gulf in March of that year should have been named Hurricane Elizabeth.

The doll whispered to her in a voice that must have sounded like the wind in the palms at night. Or the retreating tide grating through the shells under Big Pink. Whispering as little Libbit lingered on the porch of sleep. Telling her how much fun it would be to paint a big storm. And more.

Noveen says There are secret things. Buried treasures a big storm will uncover. Things Daddy would like to find and look at.

And that turned the trick. Elizabeth cared only a little about painting a storm, but pleasing her Daddy? That idea was irresistible.

Because Daddy was angry that year. Mad at Adie, who wouldn't go back to school even after her European Tour. Adie didn't care about meeting the right people or going to the right deb balls. She was besotted with

197

her Emery . . . who wasn't the Right Sort at all, in Daddy's view of things.

Daddy says He's not our kind, he's a Celluloid Collar, *and Adie says* He's *my* kind, no matter what collar, *and Daddy's furious.*

There were bitter arguments. Daddy mad at Adie and vicey-versey. Hannah and Maria mad at Adie for having a handsome boyfriend who was both Older and Below Her. The twins scared by all that mad. Libbit scared, too. Nan Melda declared over and over that if not for Tessie and Lo-Lo, she would have gone back to her people in Jacksonville long since.

Elizabeth drew these things, so I saw them.

The boil finally popped its top. Adie and her Unsuitable Young Man eloped off to Atlanta, where Emery had been promised work in the office of a competitor. Daddy was raging. The Big Meanies, home from the Braden School for the weekend, heard him on the telephone in his study, telling someone he'd have Emery Paulson brought back and horsewhipped within an inch of his life. He would have them both horsewhipped!

Then he says No, by God. Let it be what it is. She's made her bed; let her sleep in it.

After that came the storm. The Alice.

Libbit felt it coming. She felt the wind begin to rise and blow out of simple charcoal strokes as black as death. The size of the actual storm when it arrived — the pelting rain, the freight-train shriek of the gale — frightened her badly, as if she had whistled for a dog and gotten a wolf.

But then the wind died and the sun came out and everyone was all right. Better than all right, because in the Alice's aftermath, Adie and her Unsuitable Young Man were forgotten for a time. Elizabeth even heard Daddy humming as he and Mr Shannington cleaned up the wreckage in the front yard, Daddy driving the little red tractor and Mr Shannington throwing drowned palm-fronds and busted branches into the little trailer trundling along behind.

The doll whispered, the muse told its tale.

Elizabeth listened and painted the place off Hag's Rock that very day, the one where Noveen whispered the buried treasure now lay exposed.

Libbit begs her Daddy to go look, begs him begs him begs him. Daddy says NO, *Daddy says he's too tired, too stiff from all that yardwork.*

Nan Melda says Some time in the water might loosen you up, Mr Eastlake.

Nan Melda says I'll bring down a picnic lunch and the l'il girls.

And then Nan Melda says You know how she is now. If she say something's out there, then maybe . . .

So they went downbeach by Hag's Rock – Daddy in the swimsuit that no longer fit him, and Elizabeth, and the twins, and Nan Melda. Hannah and Maria were back in school, and Adie . . . but best not talk about her. Adie's IN DUTCH. *Nan Melda was carrying the red picnic basket. Inside was the lunch, sunhats for the girls, Elizabeth's drawing things, Daddy's spear-pistol, and a few harpoons for it.*

Daddy puts on his flippers and wades into the caldo *up to his knees and says* This is cold! It better not take long, Libbit. Tell me where this fabulous treasure lies.

Libbit says I will, but do you promise I can have the china dolly?

Daddy says Any doll is yours – fair salvage.

The muse saw it and the girl painted it. So their future is set.

9 – Candy Brown

i

Two nights later I painted the ship for the first time.

I called it *Girl and Ship* to begin with, then *Girl and Ship No. 1*, although neither was its real name; its real name was *Ilse and Ship No. 1*. It was the *Ship* series even more than what happened to Candy Brown that decided me on whether or not to show my work. If Nannuzzi wanted to do it, I'd go along. Not because I was seeking what Shakespeare called 'the bubble reputation' (I owe Wireman for that one), but because I came to understand that Elizabeth was right: it was better not to let work pile up on Duma Key.

The *Ship* paintings were good. Maybe great. They certainly felt that way when I finished them. They were also bad, powerful medicine. I think I knew that from the first one, executed during the small hours of Valentine's Day. During the last night of Tina Garibaldi's life.

ii

The dream wasn't exactly a nightmare, but it was vivid beyond my power to describe in words, although I captured some of the feeling on canvas. Not all, but some. Enough, maybe. It was sunset. In that dream and all the ones which followed, it was always sunset. Vast red light filled the west, reaching high to heaven, where it faded first to orange, then to a weird green. The Gulf was nearly dead calm, with only the smallest and glassiest of rollers crossing its surface like respiration. In the reflected sunset glare, it looked like a huge socket filled with blood.

Silhouetted against that furnace light was a three-masted derelict. The ship's rotted sails hung limp with red fire glaring through the holes and rips. There was no one alive on board. You only had to

201

look to know that. There was a feeling of hollow menace about the thing, as though it had housed some plague that had burned through the crew, leaving only this rotting corpse of wood, hemp, and sailcloth. I remember feeling that if a gull or pelican flew over it, the bird would drop dead on the deck with its feathers smoking.

Floating about forty yards away was a small rowboat. Sitting in it was a girl, her back to me. Her hair was red, but the hair was false − no live girl had tangled yarn hair like that. What gave away her identity was the dress she wore. It was covered with tic-tac-toe grids and the printed words I WIN, YOU WIN, over and over. Ilse had that dress when she was four or five . . . about the age of the twin girls in the family portrait I'd seen on the second floor landing of *El Palacio de Asesinos*.

I tried to shout, to warn her not to go near the derelict. I couldn't. I was helpless. In any case it didn't seem to matter. She only sat there in her sweet little rowboat on the mild red rollers, watching and wearing Illy's tic-tac-toe dress.

I fell out of my bed, and on my bad side. I cried out in pain and rolled over on my back, listening to the waves from outside and the soft grinding of the shells under the house. They told me where I was but did not comfort me. *I win*, they said. *I win, you win. You win, I win. The gun, I win. The fruit, you win. I win, you win.*

My missing arm seemed to burn. I had to put a stop to it or go crazy, and there was only one way to do that. I went upstairs and painted like a lunatic for the next three hours. I had no model on my table, no object in view out my window. Nor did I need any. It was all in my head. And as I worked, I realized this was what all the pictures had been struggling toward. Not the girl in the rowboat, necessarily; she was probably just an added attraction, a toehold in reality. It was the ship I had been after all along. The ship and the sunset. When I thought back, I realized the irony of that: *Hello*, the pencil-sketch I'd made on the day I came, had been the closest.

iii

I tumbled into bed around three-thirty and slept until nine. I woke feeling refreshed, cleaned out, brand-new. The weather was fine:

cloudless and warmer than it had been in a week. The Baumgartens were getting ready to return north, but I had a spirited game of Frisbee with their boys on the beach before they left. My appetite was high, my pain-level low. It was nice to feel like one of the guys again, even for an hour.

Elizabeth's weather had also cleared. I read her a number of poems while she arranged her chinas. Wireman was there, caught up for once and in good spirits. The world felt fine that day. It occurred to me only later that George 'Candy' Brown might well have been abducting twelve-year-old Tina Garibaldi at the same time I was reading Richard Wilbur's poem about laundry, 'Love Calls Us to the Things of the World,' to Elizabeth. I chose it because I happened to see an item in that day's paper saying it had become something of a Valentine's Day favorite. The Garibaldi kidnapping happened to be recorded. It occurred at exactly 3:16 p.m., according to the time-stamp on the tape, and that would have been just about the time I paused to sip from my glass of Wireman's green tea and unfold the Wilbur poem, which I had printed off the Internet.

There were closed-circuit cameras installed to watch the loading-dock areas behind the Crossroads Mall. To guard against pilferage, I suppose. What they caught in this case was the pilferage of a child's life. She comes into view crossing right to left, a slim kid dressed in jeans with a pack on her back. She was probably planning to duck into the mall before going the rest of the way home. On the tape, which the TV stations replayed obsessively, you see him emerge from a rampway and take her by the wrist. She turns her face up to his and appears to ask him a question. Brown nods in reply and leads her away. At first she's not struggling, but then – just before they disappear behind a Dumpster – she attempts to pull free. But he's still holding her firmly by the wrist when they disappear from the camera's view. He killed her less than six hours later, according to the county medical examiner, but judging by the terrible evidence of her body, those hours must have seemed very long to that little girl, who never harmed anyone. They must have seemed endless.

Outside the open window, The morning air is all awash with angels, Richard Wilbur writes in 'Love Calls Us to the Things of the World'. But no, Richard. No.

Those were only sheets.

203

iv

The Baumgartens departed. The Godfrey's dogs barked them goodbye. A Merry Maids crew went into the house where the Baumgartens had been staying and gave it a good cleaning. The Godfrey's dogs barked them hello (*and* goodbye). Tina Garibaldi's body was found in a ditch behind the Wilk Park Little League field, naked from the waist down and discarded like a bag of garbage. Her mother was shown on Channel 6 screaming and harrowing at her cheeks. The Kintners replaced the Baumgartens. The folks from Toledo vacated #39 and three pleasant old ladies from Michigan moved in. The old ladies laughed a lot and actually said *Yoo-hoo* when they saw me or Wireman coming. I have no idea if they put the newly installed Wi-Fi at #39 to use or not, but the first time I played Scrabble with them, they fed me my lunch. The Godfreys' dogs barked tirelessly when the old ladies went on their afternoon walks. A man who worked at the Sarasota E-Z Jet Wash called the police and said the guy on the Tina Garibaldi tape looked very much like one of his fellow car-washers, a guy named George Brown, known to everyone as Candy. Candy Brown had left work around 2:30 on Valentine's Day afternoon, this man said, and hadn't returned until the next morning. Claimed he hadn't felt well. The E-Z Jet Wash was only a block from the Crossroads Mall. Two days after Valentine's, I came into the *Palacio* kitchen and found Wireman sitting at the table with his head thrown back, shaking all over. When the shakes subsided, he told me he was fine. When I said he didn't look fine, he told me to keep my opinions to myself, speaking in a brusque tone that was unlike him. I held up three fingers and asked him how many he saw. He said three. I held up two and he said two. I decided – not without misgivings – to let it go. Again. I was not, after all, my Wireman's keeper. I painted *Girl and Ship Nos. 2* and *3*. In *No. 2*, the child in the rowboat was wearing Reba's polka-dotted blue dress, but I was pretty sure it was still Ilse. And in *No. 3* there was no doubt. Her hair had returned to the fine cornsilk I remembered from those days, and she was wearing a sailor-blouse with blue curlicue stitching around the collar that I had reason to remember very well: she'd been wearing it one Sunday when she'd fallen out of the apple tree in our back yard and broken her arm. In *No. 3* the ship had turned slightly, and I could read the first letters of its name on the prow in flaking paint: *PER*. I had no idea what the rest of the letters might be. That was also the first painting with John Eastlake's spear-pistol in it. It was lying loaded on one of the rowboat's seats. On the eighteenth of February, a friend of Jack's showed up to help with repairs to some of the rental properties. The Godfreys' dogs barked gregariously at him, inviting him to come on over any time he felt like having a chunk removed from his hip-hop-jeans-clad buttsky. Police questioned Candy Brown's wife (she also called him Candy, everyone called him Candy, he had probably invited Tina Garibaldi to call him Candy before torturing and killing her) about his whereabouts on the afternoon of Valentine's Day. She said maybe he was sick, but he hadn't been sick at home. He hadn't come home until eight o'clock or so that night. She said he had brought her a box of chocolates. She said he was an old sweetie about things like that. On the twenty-first of February, the country-music folks took their sports car and went boot-scootin back to the northern climes from whence they'd come. No one else moved in to take their place. Wireman said it signaled the turn of the snowbird ride. He said it always turned earlier on Duma Key, which had zero restaurants and tourist attractions (not even a lousy alligator farm!). The Godfreys' dogs barked ceaselessly, as if to proclaim the tide of winter vacationers might have turned, but it was a long way from out. On the same day the boot-scooters left Duma, the police showed up at Candy Brown's home in Sarasota with a search warrant. According to Channel 6, they took several items. A day later, the three old ladies at #39 once more fed me my lunch at Scrabble; I never so much as *sniffed* a Triple Word Score, but I did learn that *qiviut* is a word. When I got home and snapped on the TV, the BREAKING NEWS logo was on Channel 6, which is All Suncoast, All of the Time. Candy Brown had been arrested. According to 'sources close to the investigation', two of the items taken in the search of the Brown house were undergarments, one spotted with blood. DNA testing would follow as day follows night. Candy Brown didn't wait. The following day's newspaper quoted him as saying to police, 'I got high and did a terrible thing.' This was what I read as I drank my morning juice. Above the story was

The Picture, already as familiar to me as the photo of Kennedy being shot in Dallas. The Picture showed Candy with his hand locked on Tina Garibaldi's wrist, her face turned up to his questioningly. The telephone rang. I picked it up without looking at it and said hello. I was preoccupied with Tina Garibaldi. It was Wireman. He asked if maybe I could come down to the house for a little while. I said sure, of course, started to say goodbye, and then realized I was hearing something, not in his voice but just under it, that was a long way from normal. I asked him what was wrong.

'I seem to have gone blind in my left eye, *muchacho*.'

He laughed a little. It was a strange, lost sound.

'I knew it was coming, but it's still a shock. I suppose we'll all feel that way when we wake up d-d—' He drew a shuddering breath. 'Can you come? I tried to get Annmarie from Bay Area Private Nursing, but she's out on a call, and ... can you come, Edgar? Please?'

'I'll be right there. Just hang on, Wireman. Stay where you are and hang on.'

v

I hadn't had trouble with my own eyesight in weeks. The accident had caused some loss of peripheral vision and I tended to turn right to look at things I'd formerly picked up easily while looking straight ahead, but otherwise I was fine in the vision department. Going out to my anonymous rental Chevy, I wondered how I'd feel if that bloody redness started to creep over things again ... or if I woke up some morning with nothing but a black hole on one side of my world. That made me wonder how Wireman could have managed a laugh. Even a little one.

I had my hand on the Malibu's doorhandle when I remembered his saying that Annmarie Whistler, whom he depended upon to stay with Elizabeth when he had to be gone for any length of time, was on a call. I hurried back to the house and called Jack's mobile, praying that he'd answer and that he could come. He did, and he could. That was one for the home team.

206

vi

I drove off the island for the first time that morning, and I broke my cherry in a big way, joining the bumper-to-bumper northbound traffic on the Tamiami Trail. We were bound for Sarasota Memorial Hospital. This was on the recommendation of Elizabeth's doctor, who I'd called over Wireman's weak protests. And now Wireman kept asking me if *I* was all right, if I was sure I could do this, if it wouldn't have been better to let Jack drive him so I could stay with Elizabeth.

'I'm fine,' I said.

'Well, you look scared to death. I can see that much.' His right eye had shifted in my direction. His left tried to follow suit, but without much success. It was bloodshot, slightly upturned, and welling careless tears. 'You gonna freak out, *muchacho?*'

'No. Besides, you heard Elizabeth. If you hadn't gone on your own, she would have taken a broom and beaten you right out the door.'

He hadn't meant 'Miss Eastlake' to know there was anything wrong with him, but she'd been coming into the kitchen on her walker and overheard his end of our conversation. And besides, she had a little of what Wireman had. It went unacknowledged between us, but it was there.

'If they want to admit you—' I began.

'Oh, they'll want to, it's a fucking reflex with them, but it's not going to happen. If they could fix it, that would be different. I'm only going because Hadlock may be able to tell me that this isn't a permanent clusterfuck but just a temporary blip on the radar.' He smiled wanly.

'Wireman, what the hell's wrong with you?'

'All in good time, *muchacho.* What are you painting these days?'

'Never mind right now.'

'Oh dear,' Wireman said. 'Looks like I'm not the only one who's tired of questions. Did you know that during the winter months, one out of every forty regular users of the Tamiami Trail will have a vehicular mishap? It's true. And according to something I heard on the news the other day, the chances of an asteroid the size of the Houston Astrodome hitting the earth are actually better than the chances of—'

I reached for the radio and said, 'Why don't we have some music?'
'Good idea,' he said. 'But no fucking country.'

For a second I didn't understand, and then I remembered the recently departed boot-scooters. I found the area's loudest, dumbest rock station, which styles itself The Bone. There Nazareth was screaming its way through 'Hair of the Dog'.

'Ah, puke-on-your-shoes rock and roll,' Wireman said. 'Now you're talkin, *mi hijo.*'

vii

That was a long day. Any day you drop your bod onto the conveyor belt of modern medicine – especially as it's practiced in a city over-stuffed with elderly, often ailing winter visitors – you're in for a long day. We were there until six. They did indeed want to admit Wireman. He refused.

I spent most of my time in those purgatorial waiting rooms where the magazines are old, the cushions on the chairs are thin, and the TV is always bolted high in one corner. I sat, I listened to worried conversations compete with the TV-cackle, and every now and then I went to one of the areas where cell phones were allowed and used Wireman's to call Jack. Was she good? She was terrific. They were playing Parcheesi. Then reconfiguring China Town. The third time they were eating sandwiches and watching *Oprah*. The fourth time she was sleeping.

'Tell him she's made all her restroom calls,' Jack said. 'So far.'

I did. Wireman was pleased to hear it. And the conveyor belt trundled slowly along.

Three waiting rooms, one outside General Admitting, where Wireman refused to even take a clipboard with a form on it – possibly because he couldn't read it (I filled in the necessary information), one outside Neurology, where I met both Gene Hadlock, Elizabeth's doctor, and a pallid, goateed fellow named Herbert Principe. Dr Hadlock claimed that Principe was the best neurologist in Sarasota. Principe did not deny this, nor did he say shucks. The last waiting room was on the second floor, home of Big Fancy Equipment. Here Wireman was taken not to Magnetic Resonance

Imaging, a process with which I was very familiar, but instead to X-Ray at the far end of the hall, a room I imagined to be dusty and neglected in this modern age. Wireman gave me his Mary medallion to hold and I was left to wonder why Sarasota's best neurologist would resort to such old-fashioned technology. No one bothered to enlighten me.

The TVs in all three waiting rooms were tuned to Channel 6, where again and again I was subjected to The Picture: Candy Brown with his hand locked on Tina Garibaldi's wrist, her face turned up to his, frozen in a look that was terrible because anyone brought up in a halfway decent home knew, in his or her heart, exactly what it meant. You told your children be careful, *very* careful, that a stranger could mean danger, and maybe they believed it, but kids from nice homes had also been raised to believe safety was their birthright. So the eyes said *Sure, mister, tell me what I'm supposed to do.* The eyes said *You're the adult, I'm the kid, so tell me what you want.* The eyes said *I've been raised to respect my elders.* And most of all, what killed you, were the eyes saying *I've never been hurt before.*

I don't think that endless, looping coverage and near-constant repetition of The Picture accounts for everything that followed, but did it play a part? Yeah.

Sure it did.

viii

It was past dark when I finally drove out of the parking garage and turned south on the Trail, headed back toward Duma. At first I hardly thought about Wireman; I was totally absorbed in my driving, somehow positive this time my luck would run out and we would have an accident. Once we got past the Siesta Key turnoffs and the traffic thinned a little, I started to relax. When we got to the Crossroads Mall, Wireman said: 'Pull in.'

'Need something at The Gap? Joe Boxers? Couple of tee-shirts with pockets?'

'Don't be a smartass, just pull in. Park under a light.'

I parked under one of the lights and turned off the engine. I found it moderately creepy there, even though the lot was well over

209

half full and I knew that Candy Brown had taken Tina Garibaldi on the other side, the loading dock side.

'I guess I can tell this once,' Wireman said. 'And you deserve to hear. Because you've been good to me. And you've been good *for* me.'

'Right back atcha on that, Wireman.'

His hands were resting on a slim gray folder he had carried out of the hospital with him. His name was on the tab. He raised one finger off it to still me without looking at me – he was looking straight ahead, at the Bealls Department Store anchoring this end of the mall. 'I want to do this all at once. That work for you?'

'Sure.'

'My story is like . . .' He turned to me, suddenly animated. His left eye was bright red and weeping steadily, but at least now it was pointing at me along with the other one. '*Muchacho*, have you ever seen one of those happynews stories about a guy winning two or three hundred million bucks on the Powerball?'

'Everyone has.'

'They get him up on stage, they give him a great big fake cardboard check, and he says something which is almost always inarticulate, but that's good, in a situation like that inarticulate is the *point*, because picking all those numbers is fucking outrageous. Absurd. In a situation like that the best you can do is "I'm going to fucking Disney World." Are you with me so far?'

'So far, yeah.'

Wireman went back to studying the people going in and out of Bealls, behind which Tina Garibaldi had met Candy Brown to her pain and sorrow.

'I won *la lotería*, too. Only not in a good way. In fact, I'd say it was just about the world's worst way. The lawyering I did in my other life was in Omaha. I worked for a firm called Fineham, Dooling, and Allen. Wits – of which I considered myself one – sometimes called it Findum, Fuckum, and Forgettum. It was actually a great firm, honest as the day. We did good business, and I was well positioned there. I was a bachelor, and by that time – I was thirty-seven – I thought that was probably my lot in life. Then the circus came to town, Edgar. I mean an actual circus, one with big cats and aerialists. Most of the performers were of other nationalities, as

210

is often the case. The aerialist troupe and their families were from Mexico. One of the circus accountants, Julia Taveres, was also from Mexico. As well as keeping the books, she functioned as translator for the fliers.'

He gave her name the Spanish pronunciation – *Hulía*.

'I did not go to the circus. Wireman does the occasional rock-show; he doesn't do circuses. But here's the lottery again. Every few days, the circus's clerical staff would draw slips from a hat to see who'd go shopping for the office snacks – chips, dips, coffee, soda. One day in Omaha, Julia drew the marked slip. While coming back across the supermarket parking lot to the van, a produce truck entering the lot at a high rate of speed struck a line of shopping carts – you know how they stack them up?'

'Yes.'

'Okay. Bang! The carts roll thirty feet, strike Julia, break her leg. She was blindsided, had no chance to get out of the way. There happened to be a cop parked nearby, and he heard her screaming. He called an ambulance. He also Breathalyzed the produce truck driver. He blew a one-seven.'

'Is that bad?'

'Yes, *muchacho*. In Nebraska, a one-seven means do not collect two hundred dollars, go directly to drunk. Julia, on the advice of the doctor who saw her in the Emergency Room, came to us. There were thirty-five lawyers in Findum, Fuckum, and Forgettum back then, and Julia's personal-injury case could have ended up with any one of fifteen. I got it. Do you see the numbers starting to roll into place?'

'Yes.'

'I did more than represent her; I married her. She wins the suit and a large chunk of change. The circus rolls out of town, as circuses have a way of doing, only minus one accountant. Shall I tell you we were very much in love?'

'No,' I said. 'I hear it every time you say her name.'

'Thank you, Edgar. Thanks.' He sat there with his head bowed and his hands on his folder. Then he dragged a battered, bulging wallet from his hip pocket. I had no idea how he could bear to sit on such a rock. He flipped through the little windows meant for photograph and important documents, then stopped and slid out a photograph of a dark-haired, dark-eyed woman in a white sleeve-less blouse. She looked about thirty. She was a heart-stopper.

'*Mi Julia*,' he said. I started to hand the picture back and he shook his head. He was choosing another photo. I dreaded to see it. I took it, though, when he handed it over.

It was Julia Wireman in miniature. That same dark hair, framing a pale, perfect face. Those same dark solemn eyes.

'Esmeralda,' Wireman said. 'The other half of my heart.'

'Esmeralda,' I said. I thought the eyes looking out of this photograph and the eyes looking up at Candy Brown in The Picture were almost the same. But maybe all children's eyes are the same. My arm began to itch. The one that had been burnt up in a hospital incinerator. I scratched at it and got my ribs. No news there.

Wireman took the pictures back, kissed each with a brief, dry ardor that was terrible to see, and returned them to their transparent sleeves. It took him a little while, because his hands had picked up a tremble. And, I suppose, he was having trouble seeing. 'You actually don't even have to watch those old numbers, *amigo*. If you close your eyes you can hear them falling into place: *Click* and *click* and *click*. Some guys just strike lucky. *Hotcha!*' He popped his tongue against the roof of his mouth. The sound was shockingly loud in the little sedan.

'When Ez was three, Julia signed on part-time with an outfit called Work Fair, Immigration Solutions in downtown Omaha. She helped Spanish-speakers with and without green cards get jobs, and she helped start illegals who wanted citizenship on the right road. Just a little storefront outfit, low profile, but they did a lot more practical good than all the marches and sign-waving. In Wireman's humble opinion.'

He pressed his hands against his eyes and drew a deep, shuddering breath. Then he let his palms fall on top of the file-folder with a thump.

'When it happened, I was in Kansas City on business. Julia spent Monday to Thursday mornings at Work Fair. Ez went to a daycare. A good one. I could have sued and broken that place — beggared the women who ran it — but I didn't. Because even in my grief, I understood that what happened to Esmeralda could have happened to anyone's child. It's all just *la lotería, entiende*? Once our firm sued

212

a Venetian blind company – I wasn't personally involved – when a baby lying in his crib got hold of the draw-cord, swallowed it, and choked to death. The parents won and there was a payout, but their baby was just as dead, and if it hadn't been the cord, it might have been something else. A Matchbox car. The ID tag off the dog's collar. A marble.' Wireman shrugged. 'With Ez it was the marble. She pulled it down her throat during playtime and choked to death.'

'Wireman, Jesus! I'm so sorry!'

'She was still alive when they got her to the hospital. The woman from the daycare called both Julia's office and mine. She was babbling-crazy, insane. Julia went tearing out of Work Fair, got into her car, drove like hell. Three blocks from the hospital she had a head-on collision with an Omaha Public Works truck. She was killed instantly. By then our daughter had probably already been dead for twenty minutes. That Mary medallion you held for me . . . that was Julia's.'

He fell silent, and the silence spun out. I didn't fill it; there's nothing to say to a story like that. Eventually he resumed.

'Just another version of the Powerball. Five numbers, plus that all-important Bonus Number. Click, click, click, click, click. And then *clack* for good measure. Did I think such a thing could happen to me? No, *muchacho*, never in my wildest, and God punishes us for what we can't imagine. My mother and dad begged me to go see a psychiatrist, and for a little while – eight months after the funerals – I did indeed go. I was tired of floating through the world like a balloon tethered three feet over my own head.'

'I know the feeling,' I said.

'I know you do. We checked into hell on different shifts, you and me. And out again, I suppose, although my heels are still smoking. How about yours?'

'Yeah.'

'The psychiatrist . . . nice man, but I couldn't talk to him. With him I was inarticulate. With him I found myself grinning a lot. I kept expecting a cute chick in a bathing suit to trot out my big cardboard check. The audience would see it and applaud. And eventually a check *did* come. When we married, I'd taken out a joint life insurance policy. When Ez came, I added to it. So I really *did* win *la lotería*. Especially when you add in the compensation Julia

213

received from the accident in the supermarket parking lot. Which brings us to this.'

He held up the slim gray folder.

'The thought of suicide had been out there, circling closer and closer. The primary attraction was the idea that Julia and Esmeralda might also still be out there, waiting for me to catch up . . . but they might not wait forever. I'm not a conventionally religious man, but I think there's at least a chance that there *is* life after death, and that we survive as . . . you know, ourselves. But of course . . .' A wintry smile touched the sides of his mouth. 'Mostly I was just depressed. I had a gun in my safe. A .22. I bought it for home protection after Esmeralda was born. One night I sat down with it at the dining room table, and . . . I believe you might know this part of the story, *muchacho.*'

I raised one hand and seesawed it in a maybe *sí*, maybe *no* gesture.

'I sat down at the dining room table in my empty house. There was a bowl of fruit there, courtesy of the home shopper I employed. I put the gun on the table, and then I closed my eyes. I spun the bowl of fruit around two or three times. I told myself if I picked an apple out of the bowl, I'd put the gun to my temple and end my life. If it was an orange, however . . . then I'd take my lottery winnings and go to Disney World.'

'You could hear the refrigerator,' I said.

'That's right,' he said without surprise. 'I could hear the fridge – both the hum of the motor and the clunk of the ice-maker. I reached out and I picked an apple.'

'Did you cheat?'

Wireman smiled. 'A fair question. If you mean did I peek, the answer is no. If you mean did I memorize the geography of the fruit in the bowl . . .' He shrugged. '*Quién sabe?* In any case, I picked an apple: in Adam's fall, sinned we all. I didn't have to bite it or smell it; I could tell what it was by the skin. So without opening my eyes – or giving myself any chance to think – I picked up the gun and put it to my temple.' He mimed this with the hand I no longer had, cocking the thumb and placing the first finger against the small circular scar that his long, graying hair usually hid. 'My last thought was, "At least I won't have to listen to that refrigerator anymore, or eat one more gourmet shepherd's pie out of it." I don't remember any bang. Nevertheless, the whole world went white, and that was the end of Wireman's other life. Now . . . would you like the hallucinogenic shit?'

'Yes, please.'

'You want to see if it matches yours, don't you?'

'Yes.' And a question occurred to me. One of some import, maybe. 'Wireman, did you have any of these telepathic bursts . . . weird receptions . . . whatever you want to call them . . . *before* you came to Duma Key?' I was thinking of Monica Goldstein's dog, Gandalf, and how I seemed to have choked him with an arm I no longer had.

'Yes, two or three,' he said. 'I may tell you about them in time, Edgar, but I don't want to stick Jack with Miss Eastlake for too long. All other considerations aside, she's apt to be worried about me. She's a dear thing.'

I could have said that Jack — also sort of a dear thing — would probably be worried, too, but instead I only told him to go on.

'You often have a redness about you, *muchacho*,' Wireman said. 'I don't think it's an aura, exactly, and it's not exactly a thought . . . except when it is. I've gotten it from you as a word as well as a color on three or four occasions. And yes, once when I was off Duma Key. When we were at the Scoto.'

'When I was stuck for a word.'

'Were you? I don't remember.'

'Neither do I, but I'm sure that was it. *Red's* a mnemonic for me. A trigger. From a Reba McEntyre song, of all things. I found it almost by accident. And there's something else, I guess. When I forget stuff I tend to get . . . you know . . .'

'A little pissed off?'

I thought of how I'd taken Pam by the throat. How I'd tried to choke her.

'Yeah,' I said. 'You could say that.'

'Ah.'

'Anyway, I guess that red must have gotten out and stained my . . . my mental suit of clothes? Is that what it's like?'

'Close. And every time I sense that around you, *in* you, I think of waking up after putting a bullet in my temple and seeing the whole world was dark red. I thought I was in hell, that that was what hell was going to be like, an eternity of deepest scarlet.' He paused. 'Then I realized it was just the apple. It was lying right in front of me, maybe an inch from my eyes. It was on the floor and I was on the floor.'

'I'll be damned,' I said.

'Yes, that's what *I* thought, but it wasn't damnation, only an apple. "In Adam's fall, sinned we all." I said that out loud. Then I said, "Fruit-bowl." I remember everything that happened and everything that was said over the next ninety-six hours with perfect clarity. Every detail.' He laughed. 'Of course I know some of the things I remember aren't true, but I remember them with exquisite precision, all the same. No cross-examination could trip me up to this very day, not even concerning the pus-covered roaches I saw crawling out of old Jack Fineham's eyes, mouth, and nostrils.

'I had a hell of a headache, but once I got over the shock of the apple close-up, I felt pretty much okay otherwise. It was four in the morning. Six hours had gone by. I was lying in a puddle of congealed blood. It was caked on my right cheek like jelly. I remember sitting up and saying, "I'm a dandy in aspic" and trying to remember if aspic was some kind of jelly. I said, "No jelly in the fruit-bowl." And saying that seemed so rational it was like passing a sanity test. I began to doubt that I'd shot myself. It seemed more likely that I'd gone to sleep at the dining room table only *thinking* of shooting myself, fallen off my chair, and hit my head. That's where the blood came from. In fact, it seemed almost certain, given the fact that I was moving around and talking. I told myself to say something else. To say my mother's name. Instead I said, "Cash crop in the groun, lan'lord soon be roun."'

I nodded, excited. I had had similar experiences, not once but countless times, after coming out of my coma. Sit in the *buddy*, sit in the *chum*.

'Were you angry?'

'No, serene! Relieved! I could accept a little disorientation from a knock on the head. Only then I saw the gun on the floor. I picked it up and smelled the muzzle. There's no mistaking the smell of a recently fired gun. It's acrid, a smell with claws. Still, I held onto the falling-asleep-and-hitting-my-head idea until I got into the bathroom and saw the hole in my temple. Little round hole with a corona of singe-marks around it.' He laughed again, as people do when remembering some crazy boner they've pulled – forgetting to open the garage door, for instance, and then backing into it. 'That's when I heard the last number clicking into place, Edgar – the Powerball Number! And I knew I was going to Disney World, after all.'

'Or a reasonable facsimile,' I said. 'Christ, Wireman.'

'I tried to wash the powder-burns off, but bearing down with a facecloth hurt too much. It was like biting down on a bad tooth.'

Suddenly I understood why they'd X-rayed him instead of sticking him in the MRI machine. The bullet was still in his head.

'Wireman, can I ask you something?'

'All right.'

'Are a person's optic nerves . . . I don't know . . . bass-ackwards?'

'Indeed they are.'

'So that's why your *left* eye is fucked up. It's like . . .' For a moment the word wouldn't come, and I clenched my fists. Then it was there. 'It's like contracoup.'

'I guess so, yeah. I shot myself in the right side of my stupid head, but it's my left eye that's fucked up. I put a Band-Aid over the hole. And took some aspirin.'

I laughed. I couldn't help it. Wireman smiled and nodded.

'Then I went to bed and tried to sleep. I might as well have tried sleeping in the middle of a brass band. I didn't sleep for four days. I felt I would never sleep again. My mind was going four thousand miles an hour. This made cocaine seem like Xanax. I couldn't even lie still for long. I managed twenty minutes, then leaped up and put on a mariachi record. It was five-thirty in the morning. I spent thirty minutes on the exercise bike – first time I'd been on it since Julia and Ez died – showered, and went in to work.

'For the next three days I was a bird, I was a plane, I was Super Lawyer. My colleagues progressed from being worried about me to being scared for me to being scared for themselves – the *non sequiturs* were getting worse, and so was my tendency to lapse into both pidgin Spanish and a kind of Pépé LePew French – but there can be no doubt that I moved a mountain of paper during those days, and very little of it ever came back on the firm. I checked. The partners in the corner offices and the lawyers in the trenches were united in the belief that I was having a nervous breakdown, and in a sense they were right. It was an *organic* nervous breakdown. Several people tried to get me to go home, with no success. Dion Knightly, one of my good friends there, all but begged me to let him take me to see a doctor. Know what I told him?'

I shook my head.

'"Corn in the field, deal soon sealed." I remember it perfectly! Then I walked away. Except I was almost skipping. Walking was too slow for Wireman. I pulled two all-nighters. The third night, the security guard escorted me, protesting, from the premises. I informed him that a rigid penis has a million capillaries but not one scruple. I also told him he was a dandy in aspic, and that his father hated him.' Wireman brooded down at his folder briefly. 'The thing about his father got to him, I think. Actually I know it did.' He tapped his scarred temple. 'Weird radio, *amigo*. Weird radio.

'The next day I was called in to see Jack Fineham, the grand high rajah of our kingdom. I was ordered to take a leave of absence. Not asked, ordered. Jack opined that I'd come back too soon after "my unfortunate family reversals". I told him that was silly, I'd had no family reversals. "Say only that my wife and child et a rotten apple," I told him. "Say that, thou white-haired syndic, for it did be mortal full of bugs." That was when the roaches started to come out of his eyes and nose. And a couple from under his tongue, spilling white scum down his chin when they crawled over his lower lip.

'I started to scream. And I went for him. If not for the panic button on his desk – I didn't even know the paranoid old geezer had one – I might have killed him. Also, he could run surprisingly fast. I mean he *sped* around that office, Edgar. Must have been all those years of tennis and golf.' He mulled this for a moment. 'Still, I had both madness and youth on my side. I had laid hands on him by the time the posse burst in. It took half a dozen lawyers to haul me off him, and I tore his Paul Stuart suit-coat in half. Straight down the back.' He shook his head slowly back and forth. 'You should have heard that *hijo de puta* holler. And you should have heard *me*. The maddest shit you can imagine, including accusations – shouted at the top of my lungs – about his preference for ladies' underwear. And like the thing about the security guard's father, I think that may well have been true. Funny, no? And, crazy or not, valued legal mind or not, that was the end of my career at Findum, Fuckum, and Forgettum.'

'I'm sorry,' I said.

'*De nada*, all for the best,' he said in a businesslike tone. 'As the lawyers were wrestling me out of his office – which was trashed – I pitched a fit. The grandest of *grand mals*. If there hadn't been a legal aide handy with some medical training, I might have died right there. As it was, I was out cold for three days. And hey, I needed the sleep. So now . . .'

He opened the folder and handed me three X-rays. They weren't as good as the cortical slices produced by an MRI, but I had an informed layman's understanding of what I was looking at, thanks to my own experience.

'There it is, Edgar, a thing many claim does not exist: the brain of a lawyer. Have any pictures like these yourself?'

'Let's put it this way: if I'd wanted to fill a scrapbook . . .'

He grinned. 'But who'd want a scrapbook of shots like these? Do you see the slug?'

'Yes. You must have been holding the gun . . .' I held up my hand, tilting the finger at a pretty severe downward angle.

'That's about right. And it had to've been a partial misfire. There was enough bang to drive it through my skull-case and deflect the bullet downward at an even steeper angle. It burrowed into my brain and came to rest. But before it did, it created a kind of . . . I don't know . . .'

'Bow-wave?'

His eyes lit up. 'Exactly! Only the texture of brain-matter is more like calves' liver than water.'

'Euuuu. Nice.'

'I know. Wireman can be eloquent, he admits it. The slug created a downward bow-wave that caused edema and pressure on the optic chiasm. That's the brain's visual switching-point. Are you getting the richness of this? I shot myself in the temple and not only did I end up still alive, I ended up with the bullet causing problems in the equipment located back *here*.' He tapped the ridge of bone above his right ear. 'And the problems are getting worse because the slug's moving. It's at least a quarter-inch deeper in than two years ago.

Probably more. I didn't need Hadlock or Principe to give me that information; I can see it in these pictures for myself.'

'So let them operate on you, Wireman, and take it out. Jack and I will make sure Elizabeth's okay until you're back on your . . .' He was shaking his head. 'No? Why no?'

'It's too deep for surgery, *amigo*. That's why I didn't let them admit me. Did you think it was because I've got a Marlboro Man complex? No way. My days of *wanting* to be dead are over. I still miss my wife and my daughter, but now I've got Miss Eastlake to take care of, and I've come to love the Key. And there's you, Edgar. I want to know how your story comes out. Do I regret what I did? Sometimes *sí*, sometimes *no*. When it's *sí*, I remind myself I wasn't the same man then that I am now, and that I have to cut the old me some slack. That man was so hurt and lost he really wasn't responsible. This is my other life, and I try to look at my problems in it as . . . well . . . birth defects.'

'Wireman, that's bizarre.'

'Is it? Think of your own situation.'

I thought of my situation. I was a man who had choked his own wife and then forgot about it. A man who now slept with a doll in the other half of the bed. I decided to keep my opinions to myself.

'Dr Principe only wants to admit me because I'm an interesting case.'

'You don't know that.'

'But I *do*!' Wireman spoke with suppressed passion. 'I've met at least four Principes since I did this to myself. They're terrifyingly similar: brilliant but disassociative, incapable of empathy, really only one or two doors down from the sociopaths John D. MacDonald used to write about. Principe can't operate on me any more than he could on a patient who presents with a malignant tumor in that same location. With a tumor they could at least try radiation. A lead slug isn't amenable to that. Principe knows it, but he's fascinated. And sees nothing wrong with giving me a little false hope if it'll get me in a hospital bed where he can ask me if it hurts when he does . . . *this*. And later, when I'm dead, perhaps there'd be a paper in it for him. He can go to Cancún and drink wine coolers on the beach.'

'That's harsh.'

'Ain't in the same league as those Principe eyes – *those* are harsh. I get one look at em and want to run the other way while I still can. Which is pretty much what I did.'

I shook my head and let it go. 'So what's the outlook?'

'Why don't you get rolling? This place is starting to give me the willies. I just realized it's where that freako grabbed the little girl.'

'I could have told you that when we drove in.'

'Probably just as well you kept it to yourself.' He yawned. 'God, I'm tired.'

'It's stress.' I looked both ways, then turned back onto the Tamiami Trail. I still couldn't believe I was driving, but I was starting to like it.

'The outlook is not exactly rosy. I'm taking enough Doxepin and Zonegran now to choke a horse – those're anti-seizure drugs, and they've been working pretty well, but I knew I was in trouble that night we had dinner at Zoria's. I tried to deny it, but you know what they say: denial drowned Pharaoh and Moses led the Children of Israel free.'

'Uh . . . I think that was the Red Sea. Are there other drugs you can take? Stronger ones?'

'Principe certainly waved his prescription pad at me, but he wanted to offer Neurontin, and I won't even chance that.'

'Because of your job.'

'Right.'

'Wireman, you won't do Elizabeth any good if you go bat-blind.'

He didn't reply for a minute or two. The road, now all but deserted, unrolled in front of my headlights. Then he said, 'Blindness will soon be the least of my problems.'

I risked a sideways glance at him. 'You mean this could kill you?'

'Yes.' He spoke with a lack of drama that was very convincing. 'And Edgar?'

'What?'

'Before it does, and while I've still got one good eye left to see with, I'd like to look at some more of your work. Miss Eastlake wants to see some, too. She asked me to ask. You can use the car to haul em down to *El Palacio* – you seem to be doing admirably.'

The turn-off to Duma Key was ahead. I put on my blinker.

'I'll tell you what I think sometimes,' he said. 'I think that this run of fabulous luck I've been having has got to turn and run the other way. There's absolutely no statistical reason to think such a thing, but it's something to hold onto. You know?'

'I do,' I said. 'And Wireman?'

'Still here, *muchacho*.'

'You love the Key, but you also think something's wrong with the Key. What is it about this place?'

'I don't know what it is, but it's got something. Don't you think so?'

'Of course I do. You know I do. The day Ilse and I tried to drive down the road, we both got sick. Her worse than me.'

'And she's not the only one, according to the stories I've heard.'

'There are stories?'

'Oh yeah. The beach is okay, but inland . . .' He shook his head. 'I'm thinking it might be some kind of pollution in the water-table. The same something that makes the flora grow like a mad bastard in a climate where you need irrigation just to keep the frigging lawns from dying. I don't know. But it's best to stay clear. I think that might be especially true for young ladies who'd like to have children someday. The kind without birth defects.'

Now there was a nasty idea that hadn't occurred to me. I didn't say anything the rest of the way back.

ix

This is about memory, and few of mine from that winter are as clear as the one of arriving back at *El Palacio* that February night. The wings of the iron gate were open. Sitting between them in her wheelchair, just as she had been on the day Ilse and I had set out on our abortive exploration southward, was Elizabeth Eastlake. She didn't have the harpoon gun, but she was once more in her two-piece sweatsuit (this time with what looked like an old high-school jacket thrown over the top), and her big sneakers – looking black instead of blue in the wash of the Malibu's headlights – were propped on the chrome footrests. Beside her was her walker, and beside her walker stood Jack Cantori with a flashlight in his hand.

When she saw the car, she began struggling to her feet. Jack moved to restrain her. Then, when he saw she really meant it, he put the flashlight down on thc cobbles and helped. By the time I parked next to the gateway, Wireman was opening his door. The Malibu's headlights illuminated Jack and Elizabeth like actors on a stage. 'No, Miss Eastlake!' Wireman called. 'No, don't try to get up! I'll push you inside!'

She paid no attention. Jack helped her to her walker – or she led him to it – and she grasped the handles. Then she started thumping it toward the car. By then I was struggling out on the driver's side, fighting my bad right hip to escape, as I always did. I was standing beside the hood when she set the walker aside and held her arms out to him. The flesh above her elbows hung limp and dead, pale as dough in the headlights, but her feet were planted wide apart and her stance was sure. A breeze full of night perfumes blew back her hair, and I wasn't a bit surprised to see a scar – a very old one – denting the right side of her head. It could almost have been the twin of my own.

Wireman came around the open passenger door and just stood there for a second or two. I think he was deciding if he could still take comfort as well as give it. Then he went to her in a kind of bearlike, shambling walk, his head lowered, his long hair hiding his ears and swinging against his cheeks. She put her arms around him and pulled his head down on her considerable bosom. For a moment she swayed and I was alarmed, wide-set stance or no, but then she came straight again and I saw those gnarled, arthritis-twisted hands begin to rub his back, which had begun to heave.

I walked toward them, a little uncertainly, and her eyes turned toward me. They were perfectly clear. This wasn't the woman who had asked about when the train was coming, the one who had said she was so fucking confused. All her circuit-breakers were back in the ON positions. At least temporarily.

'We'll be fine,' she said. 'You can go home, Edgar.'

'But—'

'We'll be fine.' Rubbing his back with her gnarled fingers. Rubbing it with infinite tenderness. 'Wireman will push me inside. In just a minute. Won't you, Wireman?'

He nodded against her breast without lifting his head or making a sound.

I thought it over and decided to do what she wanted. 'That's fine, then. Goodnight, Elizabeth. Goodnight, Wireman. Come on, Jack.'

The walker was the kind equipped with a shelf. Jack put the flashlight on it, glanced at Wireman – still standing with his face hidden against the old woman's bosom – and then walked to the open passenger door of my car. 'Goodnight, ma'am.'

'Goodnight, young man. You are an impatient Parcheesi player, but you show promise. And Edgar?' She looked calmly back at me over Wireman's bent head, his heaving back. 'The water runs faster now. Soon come the rapids. Do you feel that?'

'Yes,' I said. I didn't know what she was talking about. I *did* know what she was talking about.

'Stay. Please stay on the Key, no matter what happens. We need you. *I* need you, and Duma Key needs you. Remember I said that, when I slip away again.'

'I will.'

'Look for Nan Melda's picnic basket. It's in the attic, I'm quite sure. It's red. You'll find it. They're inside.'

'What would that be, Elizabeth?'

She nodded. 'Yes. Goodnight, Edward.'

And as simply as that, I knew the slipping-away had begun once more. But Wireman would get her inside. Wireman would take care of her. But until he was able to, she would take care of them both. I left them standing on the cobbles beneath the gate arch, between the walker and the wheelchair, she with her arms around him, he with his head on her breast. That memory is clear.

Clear.

x

I was exhausted from the stress of driving – I think from spending the day among so many people after being alone for so long, too – but the thought of lying down, let alone going to sleep, was out of the question. I checked my e-mail and found communiqués from both my daughters. Melinda had come down with strep in Paris and was taking it as she always took illness – personally. Ilse had sent a link to the Asheville, North Carolina, *Citizen-Times*. I clicked on it and found a terrific review of The Hummingbirds, who had appeared at the First Baptist Church and had had the faithful shouting hallelujah. There was also a picture of Carson Jones and a very good-looking blonde standing in front of the rest of the group, their mouths open in song, their eyes locked. **Carson Jones and Bridget Andreisson duet on 'How Great Thou Art'**, read the caption. Hmmm. My If-So-Girl had written, 'I'm not a bit jealous.' Double-hmmmm.

I made myself a bologna and cheese sandwich (three months on Duma Key and I was still a go for bologna), then went upstairs. Looked at the *Girl and Ship* paintings that were really *Ilse and Ship*. Thought of Wireman asking me what I was painting these days. Thought of the long message Elizabeth had left on my answering machine. The anxiety in her voice. She'd said that I must take precautions.

I came to a sudden decision and went back downstairs, going as fast as I could without falling.

xi

Unlike Wireman, I don't lug my old swollen Lord Buxton around with me; I usually tuck one credit card, my driver's license, and a little fold of cash into my front pocket and call it good. The wallet was locked in a living room desk drawer. I took it out, thumbed through the business cards, and found the one with **SCOTO GALLERY** printed on it in raised gold letters. I got the after-hours recording I had expected. When Dario Nannuzzi had finished his little spiel and the beep had beeped, I said: 'Hello, Mr Nannuzzi, this is Edgar Freemantle from Duma Key. I'm the . . .' I paused briefly, wanting to say *guy* and knowing that wasn't what I was to him. 'I'm the artist who does the sunsets with the big shells and plants and things sitting on them. You spoke about possibly showing my work. If you're still interested, would you give me a call?' I recited my telephone number and hung up, feeling a little better. Feeling as if I'd done *something*, at least.

I got a beer out of the fridge and turned on the TV, thinking I might find a movie worth watching on HBO before turning in. The shells beneath the house had taken on a pleasant, lulling sound, their conversation tonight civilized and low-pitched.

225

They were drowned out by the voice of a man standing in a thicket of microphones. It was Channel 6, and the current star was Candy Brown's court-appointed lawyer. He must have held this videotaped press conference at approximately the same time Wireman was getting his head examined. The lawyer looked about fifty, and his hair was pulled back into a Barrister Ponytail, but there was nothing going-through-the-motions about him. He looked and sounded *invested*. He was telling the reporters that his client would plead not guilty by reason of insanity.

He said that Mr Brown was a drug addict, a porn-addicted sex addict, and a schizophrenic. Nothing about being powerless over ice cream and *Now That's What I Call Music* compilations, but of course the jury hadn't been empanelled yet. In addition to Channel 6's mike, I saw NBC, CBS, ABC, Fox, and CNN logos. Tina Garibaldi couldn't have gotten coverage like this winning a spelling bee or a science fair, not even for saving the family dog from a raging river, but get raped and murdered and you're nationwide, Swee'pea. Everyone knows your killer had your underpants in his bureau drawer.

'He comes by his addictions honestly,' the lawyer said. 'His mother and both his stepfathers were drug addicts. His childhood was a horror during which he was systematically beaten and sexually abused. He has spent time in institutions for mental illness. His wife is a good-hearted woman, but mentally challenged herself. He never should have been on the streets to begin with.'

He faced the cameras.

'This is Sarasota's crime, not George Brown's. My heart goes out to the Garibaldis, I weep for the Garibaldis' – he lifted his tearless face to the cameras, as if to somehow prove this – 'but taking George Brown's life up in Starke won't bring Tina Garibaldi back, and it won't fix the broken system that put this broken human being on the streets, unsupervised. That's my statement, thank you for listening, and now, if you'll excuse me—'

He started away, ignoring the shouted questions, and things might still have been all right – different, at least – if I'd turned off the TV or changed the channel right then. But I didn't. I watched the Channel 6 talking head back in the studio say, 'Royal Bonnier, a legal crusader who has won half a dozen supposedly unwinnable *pro bono* cases, said he would make every effort to exclude the following video, shot by a security camera behind Bealls Department Store, from the trial.'

And that damned thing started again. The kid crosses from right to left with the pack on her back. Brown emerges from the rampway and takes her by the wrist. She looks up at him and appears to ask him a question. And that was when the itch descended on my missing arm like a swarm of bees.

I cried out – in surprise as well as agony – and fell on the floor, knocking both the remote and my sandwich-plate onto the rug, scratching at what wasn't there. Or what I couldn't get at. I heard myself yelling at it to stop, *please* stop. But of course there was only one way to stop it. I got on my knees and crawled for the stairs, registering the crunch as one knee came down on the remote and broke it, but first changing the station. To CMT: Country Music Television. Alan Jackson was singing about murder on Music Row. Twice going up the stairs I clawed for the banister, that's how *there* my right hand was. I could actually feel the sweaty palm squeak on the wood before it passed through like smoke.

Somehow I got to the top and stumbled to my feet. I flicked all the light-switches up with my forearm and staggered to my easel at a half-assed run. There was a partly finished *Girl and Ship* on it. I heaved it aside without a look and slammed a fresh blank canvas in its place. I was breathing in hot little moans. Sweat was trickling out of my hair. I grabbed a wipe-off cloth and flapped it over my shoulder the way I'd flapped burp-rags over my shoulder when the girls were small. I stuck a brush in my teeth, put a second one behind my ear, started to grab a third, then picked up a pencil instead. The minute I started sketching, the monstrous itch in my arm began to abate. By midnight the picture was done and the itch was gone. Only it wasn't just a picture, not this one; this one was *The* Picture, and it was good, if I do say so myself. And I do. I really was a talented sonofabitch. It showed Candy Brown with his hand locked around Tina Garibaldi's wrist. It showed Tina looking up at him with those dark eyes, terrible in their innocency. I'd caught her look so perfectly that her parents would have taken one glance at the finished product and wanted to commit suicide. But her parents were never going to see this.

No, not this one.

My painting was an almost exact copy of the photograph that had been in every Florida newspaper at least once since February fifteenth, and probably in most papers across the United States. There was only one major difference. I'm sure Dario Nannuzzi would have seen it as a trademark touch – Edgar Freemantle the American Primitive fighting gamely past the cliché, struggling to reinvent Candy and Tina, that match made in hell – but Nannuzzi was never going to see this one, either.

I dropped my brushes back into their mayo jars. I was paint up to my elbow (and all down the left side of my face), but cleaning up was the last thing on my mind.

I was too hungry.

There was hamburger, but it wasn't thawed. Ditto the pork roast Jack had picked up at Morton's the previous week. And the rest of my current bologna stash had been supper. There was, however, an unopened box of Special K with Fruit and Yogurt. I started to pour some into a cereal bowl, but in my current state of raven-ousness, a cereal bowl looked roughly the size of a thimble. I shoved it aside so hard it bounced off the breadbox, got one of the mixing bowls from the cupboard over the stove instead, and dumped the whole box of cereal into it. I floated it with half a quart of milk, added seven or eight heaping tablespoons of sugar, then dug in, pausing only once to add more milk. I ate all of it, then sloshed off to bed, stopping at the TV to silence the current urban cowboy. I collapsed crosswise on the counterpane, and found myself eye-to-eye with Reba as the shells beneath Big Pink murmured.

What did you do? Reba asked. *What did you do this time, you nasty man?*

I tried to say *Nothing*, but I was asleep before the word could come out. And besides – I knew better.

xii

The phone woke me. I managed to push the right button on the second try and said something that vaguely resembled hello.

'*Muchacho*, wake up and come to breakfast!' Wireman cried. 'Steak

228

and eggs! It's a celebration!' He paused. 'At least I'm celebrating. Miss Eastlake's fogged out again.'

'What are we cele—' It hit me then, the only thing it possibly *could* be, and I snapped upright, tumbling Reba onto the floor. 'Did your vision come back?'

'It's not that good, I'm afraid, but it's still good. This is something all of Sarasota can celebrate. Candy Brown, *amigo*. The guards who do the morning count found him dead in his cell.'

For a moment that itch flashed down my right arm, and it was red.

'What are they saying?' I heard myself asking. 'Suicide?'

'Don't know, but either way – suicide or natural causes – he saved the state of Florida a lot of money and the parents the grief of a trial. Come on over and blow a noisemaker with me, what do you say?'

'Just let me get dressed,' I said. 'And wash.' I looked at my left arm. It was splattered with many colors. 'I was up late.'

'Painting?'

'No, banging Pamela Anderson.'

'Your fantasy life is sadly deprived, Edgar. I banged the Venus de Milo last night, and she had *arms*. Don't be too long. How do you like your *huevos*?'

'Oh. Scrambled. I'll be half an hour.'

'That's fine. I must say you don't sound very thrilled with my news bulletin.'

'I'm still trying to wake up. On the whole, I'd have to say I'm very glad he's dead.'

'Take a number and get in line,' he said, and hung up.

xiii

Because the remote was broken, I had to tune the TV manually, an antique skill but one I found I still possessed. On 6, All Tina, All the Time had been replaced by a new show: All Candy, All the Time. I turned the volume up to an earsplitting level and listened while I scrubbed the paint off.

George 'Candy' Brown appeared to have died in his sleep. A guard

229

who was interviewed said, 'The guy was the loudest snorer we ever had – we used to joke that the inmates would have killed him just for that, if he'd been in gen-pop.' A doctor said that sounded like sleep apnea and opined that Brown might have died from a resulting complication. He said such deaths in adults were uncommon but far from unheard-of.

Sleep apnea sounded like a good call to me, but I thought I had been the complication. With most of the paint washed off, I climbed the stairs to Little Pink for a look at my version of The Picture in the long light of morning. I didn't think it would be as good as I'd believed when I staggered downstairs to eat an entire box of cereal – it couldn't be, considering how fast I'd worked.

Only it was. There was Tina, dressed in jeans and a clean pink tee-shirt, with her pack on her back. There was Candy Brown, also dressed in jeans, with his hand upon her wrist. Her eyes were turned up to his and her mouth was slightly open, as if to ask a question – *What do you want, mister?* being the most likely. His eyes were looking down at her, and they were full of dark intent, but the rest of his face showed nothing at all, because the rest of his face wasn't there. I hadn't painted his mouth and nose.

Below the eyes, my version of Candy Brown was a perfect blank.

10 – The Bubble Reputation

i

I got on the plane that brought me to Florida wearing a heavy duffle coat, and I wore it that morning when I limped down the beach from Big Pink to *El Palacio de Asesinos*. It was cold, with a stiff wind blowing in from the Gulf, where the water looked like broken steel under an empty sky. If I had known that was to be the last cold day I'd ever experience on Duma Key, I might have relished it . . . but probably not. I had lost my knack for suffering the cold gladly.

In any case, I hardly knew where I was. I had my canvas collection pouch slung over my shoulder, because carrying it when I was on the beach was now second nature, but I never put a single shell or bit of flotsam in it. I just plodded along, swinging my bad leg without really feeling it, listening to the wind whistle past my ears without really hearing it, and watching the peeps scurry in and out of the surf without really seeing them.

I thought: *I killed him just as surely as I killed Monica Goldstein's dog. I know that sounds like bullshit, but—*

Only it *didn't* sound like bullshit.

It *wasn't* bullshit.

I had stopped his breath.

ii

There was a glassed-in sunporch on the south side of *El Palacio*. It looked toward the tangles of tropical overgrowth in one direction and out at the metallic blue of the Gulf in the other. Elizabeth was seated there in her wheelchair, with a breakfast tray attached to the arms. For the first time since I'd met her, she was strapped in. The

231

tray, littered with curds of scrambled egg and pieces of toast, looked like the aftermath of a toddler's meal. Wireman had even been feeding her juice from a sippy cup. The small table-model television in the corner was tuned to Channel 6. It was still All Candy, All of the Time. He was dead and Channel 6 was beating off on the body. He undoubtedly deserved no better, but it was still gruesome.

'I think she's finished,' Wireman said, 'but maybe you'd sit with her while I scramble you a couple and burn the toast.'

'Happy to, but you don't have to go to any trouble on my part. I worked late and had a bite afterward.' A bite. Sure. I'd spied the empty mixing bowl in the kitchen sink on my way out.

'It's no trouble. How's your leg this morning?'

'Not bad.' It was the truth. '*Et tu, Brute?*'

'I'm all right, thanks.' But he looked tired; his left eye was still red and drippy. 'This won't take five minutes.'

Elizabeth was almost completely AWOL. When I offered her the sippy cup, she took a little and then turned her head away. Her face looked ancient and bewildered in the unforgiving winterlight. I thought that we made quite a trio: the senile woman, the ex-lawyer with the slug in his brain, and the amputee ex-contractor. All with battle-scars on the right side of our heads. On TV, Candy Brown's lawyer — now ex-lawyer, I guess — was calling for a full investigation. Elizabeth perhaps spoke for all of Sarasota County on this issue by closing her eyes, slumping down against the restraining strap so that her considerable breastworks pushed up, and going to sleep.

Wireman came back in with eggs enough for both of us, and I ate with surprising gusto. Elizabeth began to snore. One thing was certain; if she had sleep apnea, she wouldn't die young.

'Missed a spot on your ear, *muchacho*,' Wireman said, and tapped the lobe of his own with his fork.

'Huh?'

'Paint. On your buggerlug.'

'Yeah,' I said. 'I'll be scrubbing it off everywhere for a couple of days. I splashed it around pretty good.'

'What were you painting in the middle of the night?'

'I don't want to talk about it right now.'

He shrugged and nodded. 'You're getting that artist thang going. That groove.'

232

'Don't start with me.'

'Matters have come to a sad pass when I offer respect and you hear sarcasm.'

'Sorry.'

He waved it away. 'Eat your *huevos*. Grow up big and strong like Wireman.'

I ate my *huevos*. Elizabeth snored. The TV chattered. Now it was Tina Garibaldi's aunt in the electronic center ring, a girl not much older than my daughter Melinda. She was saying that God had decided the State of Florida would be too slow and had punished 'that monster' Himself. I thought, *Got a point there*, muchacha, *only it wasn't God.*

'Turn that shit-carnival off,' I said.

He killed the tube, then turned to me attentively.

'Maybe you were right about the artist thang. I've decided to show my stuff at the Scoto, if that guy Nannuzzi still wants to show it.'

Wireman smiled and patted his hands together softly, so as not to wake Elizabeth. 'Excellent! Edgar seeks the bubble reputation! And why not? Just why the hell not?'

'I don't seek the bubble anything,' I said, wondering if that were completely true. 'But if they offer me a contract, would you come out of retirement long enough to look it over?'

His smile faded. 'I will if I'm around, but I don't know how long I'll be around.' He saw the look on my face and raised his hand. 'I ain't tuning up the Dead March yet, but ask yourself this, *mi amigo*: am I still the right man to take care of Miss Eastlake? In my current condition?'

And because that was a can of worms I didn't want to open – not this morning – I asked, 'How did you get the job in the first place?'

'Does it matter?'

'It might,' I said.

I was thinking of how I'd started my time on Duma Key with one assumption – that I had chosen the place – and had since come to believe that maybe it had chosen me. I had even wondered, usually lying in bed and listening to the shells whisper, if my accident had really been an accident. Of course it had been, *must* have been, but it was still easy to see similarities between mine and Julia Wireman's. I got the crane; she got the Public Works truck. But of course there are people – functioning human beings in most respects – who will tell you they've seen the face of Christ on a taco.

'Well,' he said, 'if you expect another long story, you can forget it. It takes a lot to story me out, but for the time being, the well's almost dry.' He looked at Elizabeth moodily. And perhaps with a shade of envy. 'I didn't sleep very well last night.'

'Short version, then.'

He shrugged. His febrile good cheer had disappeared like the foam on top of a glass of beer. His big shoulders were slumped forward, giving his chest a caved-in look.

'After Jack Fineham "furloughed" me, I decided Tampa was reasonably close to Disney World. Only when I got there, I was bored titless.'

'Sure you were,' I said.

'I also felt that some atonement was in order. I didn't want to go to Darfur or to New Orleans and work storefront *pro bono*, although that crossed my mind. I felt like maybe the little balls with the lottery numbers on them were still bouncing somewhere and one more was waiting to go up the pipe. The last number.'

'Yeah,' I said. A cold finger touched the base of my neck. Very lightly. 'One more number. I know the feeling.'

'*Sí, señor*, I know you do. I was waiting to do good, hoping to balance the books again. Because I felt they needed balancing. And one day I saw an ad in the Tampa *Tribune*. "Wanted, Companion for elderly lady and Caretaker for several premium island rental properties. Applicant must supply resume and recommendations to match excellent salary and benefits. This is a challenging position which the right person will find rewarding. Must be bonded." Well, I was bonded and I liked the sound of it. I interviewed with Miss Eastlake's lawyer. He told me the couple who'd previously filled the position had been called back to New England when the parent of one or the other had suffered a catastrophic accident.'

'And you got the job. What about—?' I pointed in the general direction of his temple.

'Never told him. He was dubious enough already – wondered, I think, why a legal beagle from Omaha would want to spend a year putting an old lady to bed and rattling the locks on houses that are empty most of the time – but Miss Eastlake . . .' He reached out and stroked her gnarled hand. 'We saw eye-to-eye from the first, didn't we, dear?'

She only snored, but I saw the look on Wireman's face and felt that cold finger touch the back of my neck again, a little more firmly this time. I felt it and knew: the three of us were here because something wanted us here. My knowing wasn't based on the kind of logic I'd grown up with and built my business on, but that was all right. Here on Duma I was a different person, and the only logic I needed was in my nerve-endings.

'I think the world of her, you know,' Wireman said. He picked up his napkin with a sigh, as though it were something heavy, and wiped his eyes. 'By the time I got here, all that crazy, febrile shit I told you about was gone. I was husked out, a gray man in a blue and sunny clime who could only read the newspaper in short bursts without getting a blinder of a headache. I was holding onto one basic idea: I had a debt to pay. Work to do. I'd find it and do it. After that I didn't care. Miss Eastlake didn't hire me, not really; she took me in. When I came here she wasn't like this, Edgar. She was bright, she was funny, she was haughty, flirty, capricious, demanding – she could hector me or humor me out of a blue mood if she chose to, and she often chose to.'

'She sounds smokin'.'

'She *was* smokin'. Another woman would have given in completely to the wheelchair by now. Not her. She hauls her hundred and eighty up on that walker and plods around this air-conditioned museum, the courtyard outside . . . she even used to enjoy target-shooting, sometimes with one of her father's old handguns, more often with that harpoon pistol, because it's got less kick. And because she says she likes the sound. You see her with that thing, and she really *does* look like the Bride of the Godfather.'

'That's how I first saw her,' I said.

'I took to her right away, and I've come to love her. Julia used to call me *mi compañero*. I think of that often when I'm with Miss Eastlake. She's *mi compañera, mi amiga*. She helped me find my heart when I thought my heart was gone.'

'I'd say you struck lucky.'

235

'Maybe *sí*, maybe *no*. Tell you this, it's going to be hard to leave her. What's she gonna do when a new person shows up? A new person won't know about how she likes to have her coffee at the end of the boardwalk in the morning . . . or about pretending to throw that fucking cookie-tin in the goldfish pond . . . and she won't be able to explain, because she's headed into the fog for good now.'

He turned to me, looking haggard and more than a little frantic.

'I'll write everything down, that's what I'll do – our whole routine. Morning to night. And you'll see that the new caretaker keeps to it. Won't you, Edgar? I mean, you like her, too, don't you? You wouldn't want to see her hurt. And Jack! Maybe he could pitch in a little. I know it's wrong to ask, but—'

A new thought struck him. He got to his feet and stared out at the water. He'd lost weight. The skin was so tight on his cheek-bones that it shone. His hair hung over his ears in clumps, badly needing a wash.

'If I die – and I could, I could go out in a wink just like *Señor* Brown – you'll have to take over here until the estate can find a new live-in. It won't be much of a hardship, you can paint right out here. The light's great, isn't it? The light's terrific!'

He was starting to scare me. 'Wireman—'

He whirled around and now his eyes were blazing, the left one seemingly through a net of blood. 'Promise, Edgar! We need a plan! If we don't have one, they'll cart her away and put her in a home and she'll be dead in a month! In a week! I know it! So promise!'

I thought he might be right. And I thought that if I wasn't able to take some of the pressure off his boiler, he was apt to have another seizure right in front of me. So I promised. Then I said, 'You may end up living a lot longer than you think, Wireman.'

'Sure. But I'll write everything down anyway. Just in case.'

iii

He once more offered me the *Palacio* golf cart for the return trip to Big Pink. I told him I'd be fine walking, but I wouldn't mind having a glass of juice before setting out.

236

Now I enjoy fresh-squeezed Florida oj as much as anyone, but I confess to having an ulterior motive that particular morning. He left me in the little receiving room at the beach end of *El Palacio's* glassed-in center hall. He used this room as an office, although how a man who couldn't read for more than five minutes at a stretch could deal with correspondence was beyond me. I guessed – and this touched me – that Elizabeth might have helped him, and quite a lot, before her own condition began to worsen.

Coming in for breakfast, I had glanced into this room and spied a certain gray folder lying on the closed lid of a laptop for which Wireman probably had little use these days. I flipped it open now and took one of the three X-rays.

'Big glass or little glass?' Wireman called from the kitchen, startling me so badly that I almost dropped the sheet in my hand.

'Medium's fine!' I called back. I tucked the X-ray film into my collection pouch and flipped the folder closed again. Five minutes later I was trudging back up the beach.

iv

I didn't like the idea of stealing from a friend – not even a single X-ray photograph. Nor did I like keeping silent about what I was sure I'd done to Candy Brown. I could have told him; after the Tom Riley business, he would have believed me. Even without that little twinkle of ESP, he would have believed me. That was the trouble, actually. Wireman wasn't stupid. If I could send Candy Brown to the Sarasota County Morgue with a paintbrush, then maybe I could do for a certain brain-damaged ex-lawyer what the doctors could not. But what if I couldn't? Better not to raise false hopes . . . at least outside of my own heart, where they were outrageously high.

By the time I got back to Big Pink, my hip was yelling. I slung my duffle coat into the closet, took a couple of Oxycontins, and saw the message-light on my answering machine was blinking.

It was Nannuzzi. He was delighted to hear from me. Yes indeed, he said, if the rest of my work was on a par with what he'd seen, the Scoto would be pleased and proud to sponsor an exhibition of my work, and before Easter, when the winter people went home. Would it be possible for him and one or more of his partners to come out, visit me in my studio, and look at some of my other completed work? They would be happy to bring a sample contract for me to look at.

It was good news – exciting news – but in a way it seemed to be happening on some other planet, to some other Edgar Freemantle. I saved the message, started to go upstairs with the pilfered X-ray, then stopped. Little Pink wasn't right because the *easel* wasn't right. Canvas and oil paints weren't right, either. Not for this.

I limped back down to my big living room. There was a stack of Artisan pads and several boxes of colored pencils on the coffee table, but they weren't right, either. There was a low, vague itching in my missing right arm, and for the first time I thought that I might really be able to do this . . . if I could find the right medium for the message, that was.

It occurred to me that a medium was also a person who took dictation from the Great Beyond, and that made me laugh. A little nervously, it's true.

I went into the bedroom, at first not sure what I was after. Then I looked at the closet and knew. The week before, I'd had Jack take me shopping – not at the Crossroads Mall but at one of the men's shops on St Armand's Circle – and I'd bought half a dozen shirts, the kind that button up the front. When she was a little kid, Ilse used to call them Big People Shirts. They were still in their cellophane bags. I tore the bags off, pulled out the pins, and tossed the shirts back into the closet, where they landed in a heap. I didn't want the shirts. What I wanted were the cardboard inserts.

Those bright white rectangles of cardboard.

I found a Sharpie in a pocket of my PowerBook carrying case. In my old life I'd hated Sharpies for both the smell of the ink and their tendency to smear. In this one I'd come to love the fat boldness of the lines they created, lines that seem to insist on their own absolute reality. I took the cardboard inserts, the Sharpie, and the X-ray of Wireman's brain out to the Florida room, where the light was bright and declamatory.

The itch in my missing arm deepened. By now it felt almost like a friend.

238

I didn't have the sort of light-box doctors stick X-rays and MRI scans on when they want to study them, but the Florida room's glass wall made a very acceptable substitute. I didn't even need Scotch tape. I was able to snap the X-ray into the crack between the glass and the chrome facing, and there it was, a thing many claimed did not exist: the brain of a lawyer. It floated against the Gulf. I stared at it for awhile, I don't know how long – two minutes? four? – fascinated by the way the blue water looked when viewed through the gray crenellations, how those folds changed the water to fog.

The slug was a black chip, slightly fragmented. It looked a little like a small ship. Like a rowboat floating on the *caldo*.

I began to draw. I had meant only to draw his brain intact – no slug – but it ended up being more than that. I went on and added the water, you see, because the picture seemed to demand it. Or my missing arm. Or maybe they were the same. It was just a suggestion of the Gulf, but it was there, and it was enough to be successful, because I really *was* a talented sonofabitch. It only took twenty minutes, and when I was done I had drawn a human brain floating on the Gulf of Mexico. It was, in a way, way cool.

It was also horrifying. It isn't a word I want to use about my own work, but it's unavoidable. As I took the X-ray down and compared it to my picture – slug in the science, no slug in the art – I realized something I perhaps should have seen much earlier. Certainly after I started the *Girl and Ship* series. What I was doing didn't work just because it played on the nerve-endings; it worked because people knew – on some level they really did know – that what they were looking at had come from a place beyond talent. The feeling those Duma pictures conveyed was horror, barely held in check. Horror waiting to happen. Inbound on rotted sails.

v

I was hungry again. I made myself a sandwich and ate it in front of my computer. I was catching up with The Hummingbirds – they had become quite the little obsession with me – when the phone rang. It was Wireman.

'My headache's gone,' he said.

'Do you always say hello like that?' I asked. 'Can I maybe expect your next call to begin "I just evacuated my bowels"?'

'Don't make light of this. My head has ached ever since I woke up on the dining room floor after shooting myself. Sometimes it's just background noise and sometimes it rings like New Year's Eve in hell, but it always aches. And then, half an hour ago, it just *quit*. I was making myself a cup of coffee and it *quit*. I couldn't believe it. At first I thought I was dead. I've been walking around on eggshells, waiting for it to come back and really wallop me with Maxwell's Silver Hammer, and it *hasn't*.'

'Lennon-McCartney,' I said. '1968. And don't tell me I'm wrong on that one.'

He didn't tell me anything. Not for a long time. But I could hear him breathing. Then, at last, he said: 'Did you do something, Edgar? Tell Wireman. Tell your Daddy.'

I thought about telling him I hadn't done a damn thing. Then I considered him checking his X-ray folder and finding one was gone. I also considered my sandwich, wounded but far from dead. 'What about your vision? Any change there?'

'Nope, the left lamp is still out. And according to Principe, it ain't coming back. Not in this life.'

Shit. But hadn't part of me known the job wasn't done? This morning's diddling with Sharpie and Cardboard had been nothing like the previous night's full-blown orgasm. I was tired. I didn't want to do anything more today but sit and stare at the Gulf. Watch the sun go down in the *caldo largo* without painting the fucking thing. Only this was Wireman. *Wireman*, goddammit.

'You still there, *muchacho*?'

'Yes,' I said. 'Can you get Annmarie Whistler for a few hours later today?'

'Why? What for?'

'So you can sit for your portrait,' I said. 'If your eye's still out, I guess I need the actual Wireman.'

'You *did* do something.' His voice was low. 'Did you paint me already? From memory?'

'Check the folder with your X-rays in it,' I said. 'Be here around four. I want to take a nap first. And bring something to eat. Painting makes me hungry.' I thought of amending that to *a certain kind of painting*, and didn't. I thought I'd said enough.

vi

I wasn't sure I'd be able to nap, but I did. The alarm roused me at three o'clock. I went up to Little Pink and considered my store of blank canvases. The biggest was five feet long by three wide, and this was the one I chose. I pulled my easel's support-strut to full extension and set up the blank canvas longways. That blank shape, like a white coffin on end, touched off a little flutter of excitement in my stomach and down my right arm. I flexed those fingers. I couldn't see them, but I could feel them opening and closing. I could feel the nails digging into the palm. They were long, those nails. They had grown since the accident and there was no way to cut them.

vii

I was cleaning my brushes when Wireman came striding up the beach in his shambling, bearlike gait, the peeps fleeing before him. He was wearing jeans and a sweater, no coat. The temperatures had begun to moderate.

He hollered a hello at the front door and I yelled for him to come on upstairs. He got most of the way and saw the big canvas on the easel. 'Holy shit, *amigo*, when you said portrait, I got the idea we were talking about a headshot.'

'That's sort of what I'm planning,' I said, 'but I'm afraid it's not going to be that realistic. I've already done a little advance work. Take a look.'

The pilfered X-ray and Sharpie sketch were on the bottom shelf of my workbench. I handed them to Wireman, then sat down again in front of my easel. The canvas waiting there was no longer completely blank and white. Three-quarters of the way up was a faintly drawn rectangle. I had made it by holding the shirt-cardboard against the canvas and running a No. 2 pencil around the edge.

241

Wireman said nothing for almost two minutes. He kept looking back and forth between the X-ray and the picture I had drawn from it. Then, in a voice almost too low to hear: 'What are we talking about here, *muchacho*? What are we saying?'

'We're not,' I said. 'Not yet. Hand me the shirt-cardboard.'

'Is that what this is?'

'Yes, and be careful. I need it. *We* need it. The X-ray doesn't matter anymore.'

He passed me the shirt-cardboard picture with a hand that wasn't quite steady.

'Now go over to the wall where the finished pictures are. Look at the one on the far left. In the corner.'

He went over, looked, and recoiled. 'Holy shit! When did you do this?'

'Last night.'

He picked it up and turned it toward the light streaming through the big window. He looked at Tina, who was looking up at the mouthless, noseless Candy Brown.

'No mouth, no nose, Brown dies, case closed,' Wireman said. His voice was no more than a whisper. 'Jesus Christ, I'd hate to be the *maricón de playa* who kicked sand in *your* face.' He set the picture back down and stepped away from it . . . carefully, like it might explode if it were joggled. 'What got into you? What *possessed* you?'

'Goddam good question,' I said. 'I almost didn't show you. But . . . considering what we're up to here . . .'

'What *are* we up to here?'

'Wireman, you know.'

He staggered a little bit, as if he were the one with the bad leg. And he had come over sweaty. His face shone with it. His left eye was still red, but maybe not *as* red. Of course that might only have been the Department of Wishful Thinking. 'Can you do it?'

'I can try,' I said. 'If you want me to.'

He nodded, then stripped off his sweater. 'Go for it.'

'I need you by the window, so the light falls on your face nice and strong as the sun starts going down. There's a stool in the kitchen you can sit on. How long have you got Annmarie for?'

'She said she could stay until eight, and she'll give Miss Eastlake dinner. I brought us lasagna. I'll put it in your oven at five-thirty.'

242

'Good.' By the time the lasagna was ready, the light would be gone, anyway. I could take some digital photos of Wireman, clip them to the easel, and work from those. I was a fast worker, but I already knew this was going to be a longer process – days, at least.

When Wireman came back upstairs with the stool, he stopped dead. 'What are you *doing*?'

'What does it look like I'm doing?'

'Cutting a hole in a perfectly good canvas.'

'Go to the head of the class.' I laid aside the cut rectangle, then picked up the cardboard insert with the floating brain on it. I went behind the easel. 'Help me glue this in place.'

'When did you figure all this out, *vato*?'

'I didn't,' I said.

'You didn't?' He was looking at me through the canvas, like a thousand lookie-loos I'd seen peering through a thousand peep-holes at construction sites in my other life.

'Nope. Something's kind of telling me as I go along. Come around to this side.'

With Wireman's help, the rest of the prep only took a couple of minutes. He blocked the rectangle with the shirt-cardboard. I fished a little tube of Elmer's Glue from my breast pocket, and began fixing it in place. When I came back around, it was perfect. Looked that way to me, anyway.

I pointed at Wireman's forehead. 'This is your brain,' I said. Then I pointed at my easel. 'This is your brain on canvas.'

He looked blank.

'It's a joke, Wireman.'

'I don't get it,' he said.

viii

We ate like football players that night. I asked Wireman if he was seeing any better and he shook his head regretfully. 'Things are still mighty black on the left side of my world, Edgar. Wish I could tell you different, but I can't.'

I played him Nannuzzi's message. Wireman laughed and pumped his fist. It was hard not to be touched by his pleasure, which bordered on glee. 'You're on your way, *muchacho* – this is your other life for sure. Can't wait to see you on the cover of *Time*.' He held his hands up, as if framing a cover.

'There's only one thing about it that worries me,' I said . . . and then had to laugh. Actually a lot of things about it worried me, including the fact that I had not the slightest idea what I was letting myself in for. 'My daughter may want to come. The one who visited me down here.'

'What's wrong with that? Most men would be delighted to have their daughters watch them turn pro. You going to eat that last piece of lasagna?'

We split it. Being of artistic temperament, I took the bigger half.

'I'd love her to come. But your boss-lady says Duma Key is no place for daughters, and I sort of believe her.'

'My boss-lady has Alzheimer's, and it's really starting to bite. The bad news about that is she doesn't know her ass from her elbow anymore. The good news is she meets new people every day. Including me.'

'She said the thing about daughters twice, and she wasn't fogged out either time.'

'And maybe she's right,' he said. 'Or possibly it's just a bee in Miss Eastlake's bonnet, based on the fact that a couple of her sisters died here when she was four.'

'Ilse vomited down the side of my car. When we got back here she was still so sick she could hardly walk.'

'She probably just ate the wrong thing on top of too much sun. Look – you don't want to take a chance and I respect that. So what you're going to do is put both daughters up in a good hotel where there's twenty-four-hour room service and the concierge sucks up harder than an Oreck. I suggest the Ritz-Carlton.'

'Both? Melinda won't be able to—'

He took a last bite of his lasagna and put it aside. 'You ain't looking at this straight, *muchacho*, but Wireman, grateful bastard that he is—'

'You've got nothing to be grateful for yet—'

'—will set you straight. Because I can't stand to see a bunch of needless worries steal away your happiness. And Jesus-Krispies, you *should* be happy. Do you know how many people there are on the west coast of Florida who'd kill for a show on Palm Avenue?'

'Wireman, did you just say Jesus-*Krispies*?'

'Don't change the subject.'

'They haven't exactly offered me a show yet.'

'They will. They ain't bringing a sample contract out here to the williwags just for shits and giggles. So listen to me, now. Are you listening?'

'Sure.'

'Once this show is scheduled – and it will be – you're going to do what any artist new on the scene would be expected to do: publicity. Interviews, starting with Mary Ire and going on from there to the newspapers and Channel 6. If they want to play up your missing arm, so much the better.' He did the framing thing with his hands again. 'Edgar Freemantle Bursts Upon the Suncoast Art Scene Like a Phoenix from the Smoking Ashes of Tragedy!'

'Smoke this, *amigo*,' I said, and gripped my crotch. But I couldn't help smiling.

Wireman took no notice of my vulgarity. He was on a roll. 'That missing *brazo* of yours gonna be golden.'

'Wireman, you are one cynical mongrel.'

He took this for the compliment it sort of was. He nodded and waved it aside magnanimously. 'I'll serve as your lawyer. You're going to pick the paintings; Nannuzzi consults. Nannuzzi sets the show arrangement; you consult. Sound about right?'

'I guess so, yeah. If that's how it's done.'

'It's how *this* is going to be done. And, Edgar – last but very far from least – you're going to call everyone you care for and invite them to your show.'

'But—'

'Yes,' he said, nodding. 'Everyone. Your shrink, your ex, both daughters, this guy Tom Riley, the woman who rehabbed you—'

'Kathi Green,' I said, bemused. 'Wireman, Tom won't come. No way in hell. Neither will Pam. And Lin's in France. With *strep*, for God's sake.'

Wireman took no notice. 'You mentioned a lawyer—'

'William Bozeman the Third. Bozie.'

'Invite him. Oh, your mom and dad, of course. Your sisters and brothers.'

'My parents are dead and I was an only child. Bozie . . .' I nodded. 'Bozie would come. But don't call him that, Wireman. Not to his face.'

'Call another lawyer Bozie? Do you think I'm stupid?' He considered. 'I shot myself in the head and didn't manage to kill myself, so you better not answer that.'

I wasn't paying much attention, because I was thinking. For the first time I understood that I could throw a coming-out party for my other life . . . *and people might show up.* The idea was both thrilling and daunting.

'They might *all* come, you know,' he said. 'Your ex, your globe-trotting daughter, and your suicidal accountant. Think of it – a mob of Michiganders.'

'Minnesotans.'

He shrugged and flipped up his hands, indicating they were both the same to him. Pretty snooty for a guy from Nebraska.

'I could charter a plane,' I said. 'A Gulfstream. Take a whole floor at the Ritz-Carlton. Blow a big wad. Why the fuck not?'

'That's right,' he said, and snickered. 'Really do the starving artist bit.'

'Yeah,' I said. 'Put out a sign in the window. "WILL WORK FOR TRUFFLES."'

Then we were both laughing.

ix

After our plates and glasses were in the dishwasher, I led him back upstairs, but just long enough so I could take half a dozen digital photos of him – big, charmless close-ups. I have taken a few good photographs in my life, but always by accident. I hate cameras, and the cameras seem to know it. When I was done, I told him he could go home and spell Annmarie. It was dark outside, and I offered him my Malibu.

'Gonna walk. The air will be good for me.' Then he pointed at the canvas. 'Can I take a look?'

'Actually, I'd rather you didn't.'

I thought he might protest, but he just nodded and went back downstairs, almost trotting. There was a new spring in his step — that was surely not my imagination. At the door he said, 'Call Nannuzzi in the morning. Don't let the grass grow under your heels.'

'All right. And you call me if anything changes with your . . .' I gestured at his face with my paint-stippled hand.

He grinned. 'You'll be the first to know. For the time being, I can settle for being headache-free.' The grin faded. 'Are you sure it won't come back?'

'I'm sure of nothing.'

'Yeah. Yeah, that's the human condition, ain't it? But I thank you for trying.' And before I knew he was going to do it, he had taken my hand and kissed the back of it. A gentle kiss in spite of the bristles on his upper lip. Then he told me *adiós* and was gone into the dark and the only sound was the sigh of the Gulf and the whispering conversation of the shells under the house. Then there was another sound. The phone was ringing.

x

It was Ilse, calling to chat. Yes, her classes were going fine, yes, she felt well — great, in fact — yes, she was calling her mother once a week and staying in touch with Lin by e-mail. In Ilse's opinion, Lin's strep was probably so much self-diagnosed bullcrap. I told her I was stunned by her generosity of feeling and she laughed.

I told her there was a possibility that I might be showing my work at a gallery in Sarasota, and she shrieked so loudly I had to hold the phone away from my ear.

'Daddy, that's *wonderful*! When? Can I come?'

'Sure, if you want to,' I said. 'I'm going to invite everybody.' This was a decision I hadn't entirely made until I heard myself telling her. 'We're thinking mid-April.'

'Shit! That's when I was planning to catch up with The Hummingbirds tour.' She paused. Thinking. Then: 'I can work them both in. A little tour of my own.'

247

'You think?'

'Yes, of course. You just give me the date and I am *there*.'

Tears pricked the backs of my eyelids. I don't know what it's like to have sons, but I'm sure it can't be as rewarding – as plain nice – as having daughters. 'I appreciate that, hon. Do you think . . . is there any possibility your sister might come?'

'You know what, I think she will,' Ilse said. 'She'll be crazy to see what you're doing that's got people in the know so excited. Will you get written up?'

'My friend Wireman thinks so. One-armed artist, and all that.'

'But you're just good, Daddy!'

I thanked her, then moved on to Carson Jones. Asked what she heard from him.

'He's fine,' she said.

'Really?'

'Sure – why?'

'I don't know. I just thought I heard a little cloud in your voice.'

She laughed ruefully. 'You know me too well. The fact is, they're SRO everyplace they play now – word's getting around. The tour was supposed to end on May fifteenth because four of the singers have other commitments, but the booking agent found three new ones. And Bridget Andreisson, who's become quite the star, got them to push back the start of her understudy pastorate in Arizona. Which was lucky.' Her voice flattened as she said this last, and became the voice of some adult woman I didn't know. 'So instead of finishing in mid-May, the tour has been extended to the end of June, with dates in the Midwest and a final concert at the Cow Palace in San Francisco. Some bigga-time, huh?' This was my phrase, used when Illy and Lin were little girls putting on what they called 'ballet super-shows' in the garage, but I couldn't recall ever saying it in that sad tone of not-quite-sarcasm.

'Are you worried about your guy and this Bridget?'

'No!' she said at once, and laughed. 'He says she has a great voice and he's lucky to be singing with her – they have two songs now instead of just one – but she's shallow and stuck-up. Also, he wishes she'd pop some Certs before he has to, you know, share a mike with her.'

I waited.

248

'Okay,' Ilse said at last.

'Okay what?'

'Okay, I'm worried.' A pause. 'A little bit, because he's with her on a bus every day and on stage with her every night and I'm here.' Another, longer pause. Then: 'And he doesn't sound the same when I talk to him on the phone. Almost . . . but not quite.'

'That could be your imagination.'

'Yes. It could. And in any case, if something's going on − nothing is, I'm sure nothing is − but if something *is*, better now rather than after . . . you know, than after we . . .'

'Yes,' I said, thinking that was so adult it hurt. I remembered finding the picture of them at the roadside stand with their arms around each other, and touching it with my missing right hand. Then rushing up to Little Pink with Reba clamped between my stump and my right side. A long time ago, that seemed. *I love you, Punkin!* 'Smiley' had written, but the picture I'd done that day with my Venus colored pencils (they also seemed a long time ago) had somehow mocked the idea of enduring love: the little girl in her little tennis dress, looking out at the enormous Gulf. Tennis balls all around her feet. More floating in on the incoming waves.

That girl had been Reba, but also Ilse, and . . . who else? Elizabeth Eastlake?

The idea came out of nowhere, but I thought yes.

The water runs faster now, Elizabeth had said. *Soon come the rapids. Do you feel that?*

I felt it.

'Daddy, are you there?'

'Yes,' I said again. 'Honey, be good to yourself, okay? And try not to get too spun up. My friend down here says in the end we wear out our worries. I sort of believe that.'

'You always make me feel better,' she said. 'That's why I call. I love you, Daddy.'

'I love you too.'

'How many bunches?'

How many years since she'd asked that? Twelve? Fourteen? It didn't matter, I remembered the answer.

'A million and one for under your pillow,' I said.

Then I said goodbye and hung up and thought that if Carson Jones hurt my daughter, I'd kill him. The thought made me smile a little, wondering how many fathers had had the same thought and made the same promise. But of all those fathers, I might be the only one who could kill a heedless, daughter-hurting suitor with a few strokes of a paintbrush.

xi

Dario Nannuzzi and one of his partners, Jimmy Yoshida, came out the very next day. Yoshida was a Japanese-American Dorian Gray. Getting out of Nannuzzi's Jaguar in my driveway, dressed in faded straight-leg jeans and an even more faded Rihanna Pon De Replay tee-shirt, long black hair blowing in the breeze off the Gulf, he looked eighteen. By the time he got to the end of the walk, he looked twenty-eight. When he shook my hand, up close and personal, I could see the lines tattooed around his eyes and mouth and put him somewhere in his late forties.

'Pleased to meet you,' he said. 'The gallery is still buzzing over your visit. Mary Ire has been back three times to ask when we're going to sign you up.'

'Come on in,' I said. 'Our friend down the beach – Wireman – has called me twice already to make sure I don't sign anything without him.'

Nannuzzi smiled. 'We're not in the business of cheating artists, Mr Freemantle.'

'Edgar, remember? Would you like some coffee?'

'Look first,' Jimmy Yoshida said. 'Coffee later.'

I took a breath. 'Fine. Come on upstairs.'

xii

I'd covered my portrait of Wireman (which was still little more than a vague shape with a brain floating in it three-quarters of the way up), and my picture of Tina Garibaldi and Candy Brown had gone bye-bye in the downstairs closet (along with *Friends with*

250

Benefits and the red-robe figure), but I had left my other stuff out. There was now enough to lean against two walls and part of a third; forty-one canvases in all, including five versions of *Girl and Ship*.

When their silence was more than I could bear, I broke it. 'Thanks for the tip on that Liquin stuff. It's great. What my daughters would call da bomb.'

Nannuzzi seemed not to have heard. He was going in one direction, Yoshida in the other. Neither asked about the big, sheet-draped canvas on the easel; I guessed that doing that might be considered poor etiquette in their world. Beneath us, the shells murmured. Somewhere, far off, a Jet-ski blatted. My right arm itched, but faint and very deep, telling me it wanted to paint but could wait – it knew the time would come. Before the sun went down. I'd paint and at first I would consult the photographs clipped to the sides of the easel and then something else would take over and the shells would grind louder and the chrome of the Gulf would change color, first to peach and then to pink and then to orange and finally to *RED*, and it would be well, it would be well, all manner of things would be well.

Nannuzzi and Yoshida met back by the stairs leading down from Little Pink. They conferred briefly, then came toward me. From the hip pocket of his jeans, Yoshida produced a business-size envelope with the words **SAMPLE CONTRACT/SCOTO GALLERY** neatly typed on the front. 'Here,' he said. 'Tell Mr Wireman we'll make any reasonable accommodation in order to represent your work.'

'Really?' I asked. 'Are you sure?'

Yoshida didn't smile. 'Yes, Edgar. We're sure.'

'Thank you,' I said. 'Thank you both.' I looked past Yoshida to Nannuzzi, who *was* smiling. 'Dario, I really appreciate this.'

Dario looked around at the paintings, gave a little laugh, then lifted his hands and dropped them. 'I think we should be the ones expressing appreciation, Edgar.'

'I'm impressed by their clarity,' Yoshida said. 'And their . . . I don't know, but . . . I think . . . *lucidity*. These images carry the viewer along without drowning him. The other thing that amazes me is how fast you've worked. You're unbottling.'

251

'I don't know that word.'

'Artists who begin late are sometimes said to unbottle,' Nannuzzi said. 'It's as if they're trying to make up for lost time. Still . . . forty paintings in a matter of months . . . of *weeks*, really . . .'

And you didn't even see the one that killed the child-murderer, I thought.

Dario laughed without much humor. 'Try not to let the place burn down, all right?'

'Yes – that would be bad. Assuming we make a deal, could I store some of my work at your gallery?'

'Of course,' Nannuzzi said.

'That's great.' Thinking I'd like to sign as soon as possible no matter what Wireman thought of the contract, just to get these pictures off the Key . . . and it wasn't fire I was worried about. Unbottling might be fairly common among artists who began later in life, but forty-one paintings on Duma Key were at least three dozen too many. I could feel their live presence in this room, like electricity in a bell jar.

Of course, Dario and Jimmy felt it, too. That was part of what made those fucking pictures so effective. They were *catching*.

xiii

I joined Wireman and Elizabeth for coffee at the end of *El Palacio's* boardwalk the next morning. I was down to nothing but aspirin to get going, and my Great Beach Walks were now a pleasure instead of a challenge. Especially since the weather had warmed up.

Elizabeth was in her wheelchair with the remains of a breakfast pastry scattered across her tray. It looked to me as if he'd also managed to get some juice and half a cup of coffee into her. She was staring out at the Gulf with an expression of stern disapproval, looking this morning more like Captain Bligh of HMS *Bounty* than a Mafia don's daughter.

'*Buenos días, mi amigo,*' Wireman said. And to Elizabeth: 'It's Edgar, Miss Eastlake. He came for sevens. Want to say hello?'

'Piss shit head rat,' she said. I think. In any case, she said it to the Gulf, which was still dark blue and mostly asleep.

'Still not so good, I take it,' I said.

252

'No. She's gone down before and come back up, but she's never gone down so far.'

'I still haven't brought her any of my pictures to look at.'

'No point right now.' He handed me a cup of black coffee. 'Here. Get your bad self around this.'

I passed him the envelope with the sample contract in it. As Wireman pulled it out, I turned to Elizabeth. 'Would you like some poems later today?' I asked her.

Nothing. She only looked out at the Gulf with that stony frown: Captain Bligh about to order someone strapped to the foremast and flogged raw.

For no reason at all, I asked: 'Was your father a skin diver, Elizabeth?'

She turned her head slightly and cut her ancient eyes in my direction. Her upper lip lifted in a dog's grin. There was a moment – it was brief, but seemed long – when I felt another person looking at me. Or not a person at all. An entity that was wearing Elizabeth Eastlake's old, doughy body like a sock. My right hand clenched briefly, and once more I felt nonexistent, too-long fingernails bite into a nonexistent palm. Then she looked back at the Gulf, simultaneously feeling across the tray until her fingers happened on a piece of the breakfast pastry, and I was calling myself an idiot who had to stop letting his nerves get the best of him. There were undoubtedly strange forces at work here, but not every shadow was a ghost.

'He was,' Wireman said absently, unfolding the contract. 'John Eastlake was a regular Ricou Browning – you know, the guy who played the Creature from the Black Lagoon back in the fifties.'

'Wireman, you're an artesian well of useless information.'

'Yeah, ain't I cool? Her old man didn't buy that harpoon pistol in a store, you know; Miss Eastlake says he had it commissioned. It probably ought to be in a museum.'

But I didn't care about John Eastlake's harpoon gun, not just then. 'Are you *reading* that contract?'

He dropped it on the tray and looked at me, bemused. 'I was trying.'

'And your left eye?'

'Nothing. But hey, no reason to be disappointed. The doctor *said*—'

'Do me a favor. Cover your left peeper.'

He did.

'What do you see?'

'You, Edgar. One *hombre muy feo.*'

'Yeah, yeah. Cover the right one.'

He did. 'Now I just see black. Only . . .' He paused. 'Maybe not *as* black.' He dropped his hand again. 'I can't tell for sure. These days I can't separate the truth from the wishful thinking.' He shook his head hard enough to make his hair fly, then thumped his forehead with the heel of his hand.

'Take it easy.'

'Easy for you to say.' He sat silent for a few moments, then picked the piece of breakfast pastry out of Elizabeth's hand and fed it to her. When it was tucked safely away in her mouth, he turned to me. 'Would you mind her while I go get something?'

'Happy to.'

He jogged up the boardwalk and I was left with Elizabeth. I tried feeding her one of the remaining pieces of breakfast pastry and she nibbled it out of my hand, bringing back a fleeting recollection of a rabbit I'd had when I was seven or eight. Mr Hitchens had been its name, although I no longer knew why – memory's a funny thing, isn't it? Her lips were toothless and soft, but not unpleasant. I stroked the side of her head, where her white hair – wiry, rather coarse – was pulled back toward a bun. It occurred to me that Wireman must comb that hair each morning, and make that bun. That Wireman must have dressed her this morning, including diapers, for surely she wasn't continent when she was like this. I wondered if he thought of Esmeralda when he pinned the pins or secured the ties. I wondered if he thought of Julia when he made the bun.

I picked up another piece of breakfast pastry. She opened her mouth obediently for it . . . but I hesitated. 'What's in the red picnic basket, Elizabeth? The one in the attic?'

She seemed to think. And hard. Then: 'Any old pipe-dip.' She hesitated. Shrugged. 'Any old pipe-dip Adie wants. Shoot!' And cackled. It was a startling, witchlike sound. I fed her the rest of her breakfast pastry, piece by piece, and asked no more questions.

xiv

When Wireman returned, he had a microcassette recorder. He handed it to me. 'I hate to ask you to put that contract on tape, but I have to. At least the damn thing's only two pages long. I'd like it back this afternoon, if that's possible.'

'It is. And if some of my pictures actually sell, you're on commission, my friend. Fifteen per cent. That should cover both legal and talent.'

He sat back in his chair, laughing and groaning at the same time. '*Por Dios!* Just when I thought I couldn't sink any lower in life, I become a fucking talent agent! Excuse the language, Miss Eastlake.'

She took no notice, only stared sternly out at the Gulf, where – at the farthest, bluest edge of vision – a tanker was dreaming north toward Tampa. It fascinated me at once. Boats on the Gulf had a way of doing that to me.

Then I forced my attention back to Wireman. 'You're responsible for all of this, so—'

'Bull*shit* you say!'

'—so you have to be prepared to stand up and take your cut like a man.'

'I'll take ten per cent, and that's probably too much. Take it, *muchacho*, or we start discussing eight.'

'All right. Ten it is.' I stuck out my hand and we shook over Elizabeth's crumb-littered tray. I put the little recorder in my pocket. 'And you'll let me know if there's any change in your . . .' I pointed at his red eye. Which really wasn't as red as it had been.

'Of course.' He picked up the contract. There were crumbs on it from Elizabeth's pastry. He brushed them off and handed it to me, then leaned forward, hands clasped between his knees, gazing at me over the imposing shelf of Elizabeth's bosom. 'If I had another X-ray, what would it show? That the slug was smaller? That it was gone?'

'I don't know.'

'Are you still working on my portrait?'

'Yes.'

'Don't stop, *muchacho*. Please don't stop.'

'I don't plan to. But don't get your hopes up too high, okay?'

'I won't.' Then another thought struck him, one that was eerily similar to Dario's stated concern. 'What do you think would happen if lightning struck Big Pink and it burned flat with that picture inside? What do you think would happen to me?'

I shook my head. I didn't want to think about it. I did think about asking Wireman if I could go up to *El Palacio*'s attic and look around for a certain picnic basket (it was *RED*), then decided not to. I was sure it was there, less sure that I wanted to know what was in it. There were strange things kicking around Duma Key, and I had reason to believe they weren't all nice things, and what I wanted to do about most of them was nothing. If I left them alone, then maybe they'd leave me alone. I'd send most of my pictures off-island to keep everything nice and peaceful; sell them, too, if people wanted to buy them. I could watch them go without a pang. I was passionate about them while I was working on them, but when they were done, they meant no more to me than the hard semi-circles of callus I'd sometimes sand off the sides of my great toes so my workboots wouldn't pinch at the end of a hot August day on some job site.

I'd hold back the *Girl and Ship* series, not out of any special affection, but because the series wasn't done; those paintings were still live flesh. I might show them and sell them later, but for now I meant to keep them right where they were, in Little Pink.

xv

There were no boats on the horizon by the time I got back to my place, and the urge to paint had passed for the time being. I used Wireman's micro-recorder instead, and put the sample contract on tape. I was no lawyer, but I'd seen and signed my share of legal paper in my other life, and this struck me as pretty simple.

That evening I took both the contract and the tape recorder back down to *El Palacio*. Wireman was making supper. Elizabeth was sitting in the China Parlor. The gimlet-eyed heron – which was a kind of unofficial housepet – stood on the walk outside, peering in with grim disapproval. The late-day sun filled the room with light. Yet it was *not* light. China Town was in disarray, the people

256

and animals tumbled here and there, the buildings scattered to the four corners of the bamboo table. The pillared plantation-house was actually overturned. In her chair beside it, wearing her Captain Bligh expression, Elizabeth seemed to dare me to put things right.

Wireman spoke from behind me, making me jump. 'If I try to set things back up in any kind of pattern, she sweeps it apart again. She's knocked a bunch to the floor and broken them.'

'Are they valuable?'

'Some, but that's really not the point. When she's herself, she knows every one of them. Knows and loves. If she comes around and asks where Bo Peep is . . . or the Coaling Man . . . and I have to tell her she broke them, she'll be sad all day.'

'If she comes around.'

'Yes. Well.'

'Think I'll head on home, Wireman.'

'Gonna paint?'

'That's the plan.' I turned to the disarray on the table. 'Wireman?'

'Right here, *vato*.'

'Why does she mess them up when she's like this?'

'I think . . . because she can't stand looking at what she's not.'

I started to turn around. He put a hand on my shoulder.

'I'd just as soon you didn't look at me just now,' he said. His voice was barely under control. 'I'm not myself just now. Go out the front door and then cut back through the courtyard, if you want to take the beach. Would you do that?'

I did that. And when I got back, I worked on his portrait. It was all right. By which I suppose I mean it was good. I could see his face in there, wanting to come out. Starting to rise. There was nothing special, but that was fine. It was always best when it was nothing special. I was happy, I remember that. I was at peace. The shells murmured. My right arm itched, but very low and deep. The window giving on the Gulf was a rectangle of blackness. Once I went downstairs and ate a sandwich. I turned on the radio and found The Bone: J. Geils doing 'Hold Your Lovin'. J. Geils was nothing special, only great − a gift from the gods of rock and roll. I painted and Wireman's face rose a little more. It was a ghost now. It was a ghost haunting the canvas. But it was a harmless ghost. If I turned around, Wireman wouldn't be standing at the head of the stairs where Tom Riley had been standing, and down the beach at *El Palacio de Asesinos*, the left side of Wireman's world was still dark; it was just a thing I knew. I painted. The radio played. Below the music, the shells whispered.

At some point I quit, showered, and went to bed. There were no dreams.

When I think back to my time on Duma Key, those days in February and March when I was working on Wireman's portrait seem like the best days.

xvi

Wireman called the next day at ten. I was already at my easel. 'Am I interrupting?'

'It's okay,' I said. 'I can use a break.' This was a lie.

'We missed you this morning.' A pause. 'Well, you know. I missed you. *She* . . .'

'Yeah,' I said.

'The contract's a bunny-hug. Very little to fuck with. It says you and the gallery split right down the middle, but I'm gonna cap that. Fifty-fifty shall not live after gross sales reach a quarter-mil. Once you pass that point, the split goes to sixty-forty, your favor.'

'Wireman, I'll never sell a quarter of a million dollars' worth of paintings!'

'I'm hoping they'll feel exactly the same way, *muchacho*, which is why I'm also going to propose that the split goes to seventy-thirty at half a million.'

'Plus a handjob from Miss Florida,' I said feebly. 'Get that in there.'

'Noted. The other thing is this one-hundred-and-eighty-day termination clause. It ought to be ninety. I don't foresee a problem there, but I think it's interesting. They're afraid some big New York gallery is going to swoop down and carry you off.'

'Anything else about the contract I should know?'

'Nope, and I sense you want to get back to work. I'll get in touch with Mr Yoshida about these changes.'

'Any change in your vision?'

'No, *amigo*. Wish I could say there was. But you keep painting.'

258

I was taking the phone away from my ear when he said, 'Did you happen to see the news this morning?'

'No, never turned it on. Why?'

'County coroner says Candy Brown died of congestive heart failure. Just thought you'd like to know.'

xvii

I painted. It was a slow go but far from a no go. Wireman swam into existence around the window where his brain swam on the Gulf. It was a younger Wireman than the one in the photos clipped to the sides of my easel, but that was okay; I consulted them less and less, and on the third day I took them down altogether. I didn't need them anymore. Still, I painted the way I supposed most other artists painted: as if it were a job instead of some speed-trip insanity that came and went in spasms. I did it with the radio on, now always tuned to The Bone.

On the fourth day, Wireman brought me a revised contract and told me I could sign. He said Nannuzzi wanted to photograph my paintings and make slides for a lecture at the Selby Library in Sarasota in mid-March, a month before my show opened. The lecture, Wireman said, would be attended by sixty or seventy art patrons from the Tampa-Sarasota area. I told him fine and signed the contract.

Dario came out that afternoon. I was impatient for him to click his pix and be gone so I could go back to work. Mostly to make conversation, I asked him who would be giving the lecture at the Selby Library.

Dario looked at me with one eyebrow cocked, as if I had made a joke. 'The one person in the world who is now conversant with your work,' he said. 'You.'

I gaped at him. 'I can't give a lecture! I don't know anything about art!'

He swept his arm at the paintings, which Jack and two part-timers from the Scoto were going to crate and transport to Sarasota the following week. They would remain crated, I assumed, in the storage area at the back of the gallery, until just before the show opened. 'These say different, my friend.'

259

'Dario, these people *know* stuff! They've taken courses! I'll bet most of them were art majors, for Christ's sake! What do you want me to do, stand up there and say *duh?*'

'That's pretty much what Jackson Pollock did when he talked about his work. Often while drunk. And it made him rich.' Dario came over to me and took me by the stump. That impressed me. Very few people will touch the stump of a limb; it's as if they believe, down deep, that amputation might be catching. 'Listen, my friend, these are important people. Not just because they have money, but because they're interested in new artists and each one knows three more who feel the same. After the lecture – *your* lecture – the talk will start. The kind of talk that almost always turns into that magical thing called "buzz".'

He paused, twiddling the strap of his camera and smiling a little.

'All you have to do is talk about how you began, and how you grew—'

'Dario, I don't *know* how I grew!'

'Then say that. Say anything! You're an *artist*, for God's sake!'

I left it at that. The threatened lecture still seemed distant to me, and I wanted him out of there. I wanted to turn on The Bone, pull the cloth off the painting on the easel, and go back to work on *Wireman Looks West*. Want the dirty-ass truth? The painting was no longer about some hypothetical magic trick. Now it was its own magic trick. I had become very selfish about it, and anything that might come after – a promised interview with Mary Ire, the lecture, the show itself – seemed to be not ahead of me but somehow far above me. The way rain on the surface of the Gulf must seem to a fish.

During that first week of March, it was all about daylight. Not sunset light but daylight. How it filled Little Pink and seemed to lift it. That week it was about the music from the radio, anything by the Allman Brothers, Molly Hatcher, Foghat. It was about J. J. Cale beginning 'Call Me the Breeze' by saying 'Here's another of your old rock n roll favorites; shuffle on down to Broadway,' and how when I turned the radio off and cleaned my brushes, I could hear the shells under the house. It was about the ghostface I saw, the one belonging to a younger man who had yet to see the view from Duma. There was a song – I think by Paul Simon – with the line *If I'd never loved, I never would have cried.* That was this face. It wasn't a real face, not quite real, but I was making it real. It was growing around the brain that was floating on the Gulf. I didn't need photographs anymore, because this was a face I knew. This one was a memory.

xviii

March fourth was hot all day, but I didn't bother turning on the air conditioning. I painted in nothing but a pair of gym shorts, with the sweat trickling down my face and sides. The telephone rang twice. The first time it was Wireman.

'We haven't seen much of you in these parts lately, Edgar. Come to supper?'

'I think I'm going to pass, Wireman. Thanks.'

'Painting, or tired of our society down here at *El Palacio*? Or both?'

'Just the painting part. I'm almost done. Any change in the vision department?'

'The left lamp is still out, but I bought an eyepatch for it, and when I wear it, I can read with my right eye for as long as fifteen minutes at a stretch. This is a great leap forward, and I think I owe it to you.'

'I don't know if you do or not,' I said. 'This isn't the same as the picture I did of Candy Brown and Tina Garibaldi. Or of my wife and her . . . her friends, for that matter. This time there's no *bam*. Do you know what I mean when I say *bam*?'

'Yes, *muchacho*.'

'But if something's going to happen, I think it'll happen soon. If not, you'll at least have a portrait of how you looked – *maybe* how you looked – when you were twenty-five.'

'Are you kiddin, *amigo*?'

'No.'

'I don't think I even remember what I looked like when I was twenty-five.'

'How's Elizabeth? Any change in her?'

He sighed. 'She seemed a little better yesterday morning, so I set

261

her up in the back parlor – there's a smaller table there, what I call the China Suburbs – and she threw a set of Wallendorf ballerinas on the floor. Smashed all eight. Irreplaceable, of course.'

'I'm sorry.'

'Last fall I never thought it could get this bad, and God punishes us for what we can't imagine.'

My second call came fifteen minutes later, and I threw my brush down on my work-table in exasperation. It was Jimmy Yoshida. It was hard to stay exasperated after being exposed to his excitement, which bordered on exuberance. He'd seen the slides, which he claimed were going to 'knock everyone on their asses'.

'That's wonderful,' I said. 'At my lecture I intend to tell them, "Get up off your asses" . . . and then walk out.'

He laughed as though this were the funniest thing he'd ever heard, then said, 'Mainly I called to ask if there are any pictures you want marked NFS – not for sale.'

Outside there was a rumble that sounded like a big, heavily loaded truck crossing a plank bridge. I looked toward the Gulf – where there were no plank bridges – and realized I'd heard thunder far off to the west.

'Edgar? Are you still there?'

'Still here,' I said. 'Assuming anyone wants to buy, you can sell everything but the *Girl and Ship* series.'

'Ah.'

'That sounded like a disappointed ah.'

'I was hoping to buy one of those for the gallery. I had my eye on *Number 2*.' And considering the terms of the contract, he would be buying it at a fifty per cent discount. *Not bad, lad*, my father might have said.

'That series isn't done yet. Maybe when the rest of them are painted.'

'How many more will there be?'

I'll keep painting them until I can read the fucking ghost-ship's name on the transom.

I might have said this aloud if more thunder hadn't rumbled out in the west. 'I guess I'll know when the time comes. Now, if you'll excuse me—'

'You're working. Sorry. I'll let you get back to it.'

When I killed the cordless, I considered whether or not I did want to go back to work. But . . . I was close. If I forged ahead, I might be able to finish tonight. And I sort of liked the idea of painting while a thunderstorm blew in from the Gulf.

God help me, the idea struck me as romantic.

So I turned up the radio, which I'd turned down to talk on the phone, and there was Axl Rose, screaming ever deeper into 'Welcome to the Jungle'. I picked up a brush and put it behind my ear. Then I picked up another and began to paint.

xix

The thunderheads stacked up, huge flatboats black on the bottom and bruise-purple through the middle. Every now and then lightning would flash inside them, and then they looked like brains filled with bad ideas. The Gulf lost its color and went dead. Sunset was a yellow band that flicked feeble orange and went out. Little Pink filled with gloom. The radio began to bray static with each burst of lightning. I paused long enough to turn it off, but I didn't turn on the lights.

I don't remember exactly when it stopped being me that was doing the painting . . . and to this day I'm not sure that it *ever* stopped being me; maybe *sí*, maybe *no*. All I know is that at some point I looked down and saw my right arm in the last of the failing daylight and the occasional stutters of lightning. The stump was tanned, the rest dead white. The muscles hung loose and flabby. There was no scar, no seam except the tan-line, but below there it itched like old dry fire. Then the lightning flashed again and there was no arm, there had never been an arm – not on Duma Key, at least – but the itch was still there, so bad it made you want to bite a piece out of something.

I turned back to the canvas and the second I did, the itch poured in that direction like water let out of a bag, and the frenzy fell on me. The storm dropped on the Key as the dark came down and I thought of certain circus acts where the guy throws knives blindfolded at a pretty girl spreadeagled on a spinning wooden platter, and I think I laughed because I was *painting* blindfold, or almost.

263

Every now and then the lightning would flash and Wireman would leap at me, Wireman at twenty-five, Wireman before Julia, before Esmeralda, before *la lotería*.

I win, you win.

A huge flash of lightning lit my window purple-white, and a great whooping gust of gale rode that electricity in from the Gulf, driving rain against the glass so hard I thought (in the part of my mind still capable of thought) that it must surely break. A munitions dump exploded directly overhead. And beneath me the murmur of the shells had become the gossip of dead things telling secrets in bone voices. How could I not have heard that before? Dead things, yes! A ship had come here, a ship of the dead with rotted sails, and it had offloaded living corpses. They were under this house, and the storm had brought them to life. I could see them pushing up through the boneyard blanket of the shells, pallid jellies with green hair and seagull eyes, crawling over each other in the dark and talking, talking, talking. Yes! Because they had a lot to catch up on, and who knew when the next storm might come and bring them to life again?

Yet still I painted. I did it in terror and in the dark, my arm moving up and down so that for a little while there I seemed to actually be *conducting* the storm. I couldn't have stopped. And at some point, *Wireman Looks West* was done. My right arm told me so. I slashed my initials – EF – in the lower left corner and then broke the brush in two, using both hands to do it. The pieces I dropped on the floor. I staggered away from my easel, crying out for whatever was going on to stop. And it would; surely it would; the picture was done and surely now it would.

I came to the head of the stairs and looked down, and there at the bottom were two small dripping figures. I thought: *Apple, orange.* I thought, *I win, you win.* Then the lightning flashed and I saw two girls of about six, surely twins and surely Elizabeth Eastlake's drowned sisters. They wore dresses that were plastered to their bodies. Their hair was plastered to their cheeks. Their faces were pale horrors.

I knew where they had come from. They had crawled out of the shells.

They started up the stairs toward me, hand in hand. Thunder

exploded a mile overhead. I tried to scream. I couldn't. I thought, *I am not seeing this*. I thought, *I am*.

'I can do this,' one of the girls said. She spoke in the voice of the shells.

'It was red,' the other girl said. She spoke in the voice of the shells. They were halfway up now. Their heads were little more than skulls with wet hair draggling down the sides.

'Sit in the *char*,' they said together, like girls chanting a skip-rope rhyme . . . but they spoke in the voice of the shells. 'Sit in the *burn*.'

They reached up for me with terrible fishbelly fingers.

I fainted at the head of the stairs.

xx

The telephone was ringing. That was my Telephone Winter.

I opened my eyes and groped for the bedside lamp, wanting light right away because I'd just had the worst nightmare of my life. Instead of finding the lamp, my fingers struck a wall. At the moment they did, I became aware that my head was cocked at a strange, painful angle against that same wall. Thunder rumbled – but faint and sullen; it was going-away thunder now – and that was enough to bring everything back with painful, frightening clarity. I wasn't in bed. I was in Little Pink. I had fainted because—

My eyes flew open. My ass was on the landing, my legs trailing down the stairs. I thought of the two drowned girls – no, it was more, it was an instant of total, brilliant recall – and shot to my feet without feeling my bad hip at all. My concentration was fixed entirely on the three light-switches at the head of the stairs, but even as my fingers found them I thought: *Won't work, the storm will have knocked out the power*.

But they *did* work, banishing the dark in the studio and the stairwell. I had a nasty moment when I saw sand and water at the foot of the stairs, but the light reached far enough for me to see that the front door had blown open.

Surely it had just blown open.

In the living room, the phone quit and the answering machine

265

kicked in. My recorded voice invited the caller to leave a message at the sound of the beep. The caller was Wireman.

'Edgar, where are you?' I was too disoriented to tell if I was hearing excitement, dismay, or terror in his voice. 'Call me, you need to call me *right away!*' And then a click.

I went downstairs one tentative step at a time, like a man in his eighties, and made the lights my first priority: living room, kitchen, both bedrooms, Florida room. I even turned on the lights in the bathrooms, reaching into the darkness to do it, bracing myself in case something cold and wet and draped in seaweed should reach back. Nothing did. With all the lights on, I relaxed enough to realize I was hungry again. Starving. It was the only time I felt that way after working on Wireman's portrait . . . but of course, that last session had been a lulu.

I stooped to examine the mess that had blown in through the open door. Just sand and water, the water already beading atop the wax my housekeeper used to keep the cypress gleaming. There was some dampness on the lower stair risers, which were carpeted, but dampness was all it was.

I wouldn't admit to myself that I'd been looking for footprints.

I went to the kitchen, made a chicken sandwich, and gobbled it standing at the counter. I grabbed a beer from the fridge to wash it down. When the sandwich was gone, I ate the remains of the previous day's salad, more or less floating in Newman's Own French. Then I went into the living room to call *El Palacio*. Wireman answered on the first ring. I was prepared to tell him I'd been outside, looking to see if the storm had done any damage to the house, but my whereabouts at the time of his call were the last thing on Wireman's mind. Wireman was crying and laughing.

'I can see! As well as ever! Left eye's as clear as a bell. I can't believe it, but—'

'Slow down, Wireman, I can barely make you out.'

He didn't slow down. Maybe he couldn't. 'A pain went through my bad eye at the height of the storm . . . pain like you wouldn't believe . . . like a hot wire . . . I thought we'd been struck by lightning, so help me God . . . I tore off the eyepatch . . . and I could see! Do you understand what I'm telling you? *I can see!*'

'Yes,' I said. 'I understand. That's wonderful.'

'Was it you? It was, wasn't it?'

I said, 'Maybe. Probably. I've got a painting for you. I'll bring it tomorrow.' I hesitated. 'I'd take good care of it, *amigo*. I don't think it matters what happens to them once they're done, but I also thought Kerry was gonna beat Bush.'

He laughed wildly. 'Oh, *verdad*, I heard that. Was it hard?'

A thought struck me before I could answer. 'Was the storm hard on Elizabeth?'

'Oh man, awful. They always scare her, but this one . . . she was in terror. Screaming about her sisters. Tessie and Lo-Lo, the ones who drowned back in the nineteen-twenties. She even had me going for awhile there . . . but it's over now. Are *you* okay? *Was* it hard?'

I looked at the scatterings of sand on the floor between the front door and the stairs. Surely no footprints there. If I thought I was seeing more than sand, that was just my fucking *artistic imagination*. 'A little. But it's all over now.'

I hoped that was true.

xxi

We talked for another five minutes . . . or rather Wireman talked. Babbled, actually. The last thing he said was that he was afraid to go to sleep. He was afraid he might wake up to discover he was blind in his left eye again. I told him I didn't think he had to worry about that, wished him a good night, and hung up. What *I* was worried about was waking up in the middle of the night to discover Tessie and Laura – Lo-Lo, to Elizabeth – sitting on either side of my bed.

One of them perhaps holding Reba on her damp lap.

I took another beer and went back upstairs. I approached the easel with my head down, staring at my feet, then looked up quickly, as if hoping to catch the portrait by surprise. Part of me – a rational part – expected to see it defaced by paint splattered from hell to breakfast, a partial Wireman obscured by the daubs and blotches I'd thrown at the canvas during the thunderstorm, when my only real light had been lightning. The rest of me knew better. The rest of

267

me knew that I'd been painting by some other light (just as blinded knife-throwers use some other sense to guide their hands). That part knew *Wireman Looks West* had turned out just fine, and that part was right.

In some ways it was the best work I did on Duma Key, because it was my most *rational* work – up until the end, remember, *Wireman Looks West* had been done in daylight. And by a man in his right mind. The ghost haunting my canvas had become a sweetheart of a face, young and calm and vulnerable. The hair was a fine clear black. A little smile lurked at the corners of the mouth; in the green eyes, as well. The eyebrows were thick and handsome. The forehead above them was broad, an open window where this man bent his thoughts toward the Gulf of Mexico. There was no slug in that visible brain. I could just as easily have taken away an aneurism or a malignant tumor. The cost of finishing the job had been high, but the bill had been paid.

The storm had faded to a few faint rumbles somewhere over the Florida panhandle. I thought I could sleep, and I could do it with the bedside lamp on if I wanted to; Reba would never tell. I could even sleep with her nestled in between my stump and my side. I'd done it before. And Wireman could see again. Although even that seemed beside the point right then. The point seemed to be that I had finally painted something great.

And it was mine.

I thought I could sleep on that.

How to Draw a Picture (VI)

Keep your focus. It's the difference between a good picture and just one more image cluttering up a world filled with them.

Elizabeth Eastlake was a demon when it came to focus; remember that she literally drew herself back into the world. And when the voice inhabiting Noveen told her about the treasure, she focused on that and drew pictures of it littered on the sandy floor of the Gulf. Once the storm had uncovered it, that entrancing strew was close enough to the surface so that the sun must have picked out gleams on it at midday – gleams that would have searched all the way to the surface.

She wanted to please her Daddy. All she wanted for herself was the china doll.

Daddy says Any doll is yours – fair salvage, *and God help him for that.*

She waded in beside him, up to her chubby knees, pointing, saying It's right out there. Swim n kick til I say stop.

He waded out farther while she stood there, and when he rolled forward, giving his body to the caldo, *his flippers looked to her the size of small rowboats. Later she would draw them just that way. He spat in his mask, rinsed it, and put it on. Popped the mouthpiece of his snorkel behind his lips. Went fin-trudging out into the sunny blue with his face in the water, his body merging with the moving sun-sparks that turned the glassy rollers to gold.*

I know all this. Elizabeth drew some and I drew some.

I win, you win.

She stood up to her knees in the water with Noveen tucked under her arm, watching, until Nan Melda, worried about the rip, hollered her back to what they called Shade Beach. Then they all stood together. Elizabeth shouted for John to stop. They saw his flippers go up as he made his first dive. He was down maybe forty seconds, then surfaced in a spray, spitting the snorkel's mouthpiece.

He says I'll be damned if there isn't something down there!

269

And when he came back to little Libbit, he hug her hug her hug her.

I knew it. I drew it. With the red picnic basket on a blanket nearby and the spear-gun sitting on top of the basket.

He went out again, and the next time he came in with an armload of antiquity held awkwardly against his chest. Later he would begin using Nan Melda's market basket, a lead weight in the bottom to pull it down more easily. Later still came a newspaper photo with much of the rescued rickrack — the 'treasure' — spread out before a smiling John Eastlake and his talented, fiercely focused daughter. But no china doll in that picture.

Because the china doll was special. It belonged to Libbit. It was her fair salvage.

Was it the doll-thing that drove Tessie and Lo-Lo to their deaths? That created the big boy? Just how much did Elizabeth have to do with it by then? Who was the artist, who the blank surface?

Some questions I have never answered to my own satisfaction, but I have drawn my own pictures and I know that when it comes to art, it's perfectly okay to paraphrase Nietzsche: if you keep your focus, eventually your focus will keep you. Sometimes without parole.

11 – The View from Duma

i

The next morning, early, Wireman and I stood in the Gulf – plenty cold enough to be an eye-popper – up to our shins. He had walked in, and I had followed without question. Without a single word. Both of us were holding coffee cups. He was wearing shorts; I had paused just long enough to roll my pants to my knees. Behind us, at the end of the boardwalk, Elizabeth slouched in her chair, looking grimly out at the horizon and grizzling down her chin. A large part of her breakfast still lay before her. She had eaten some, scattered the rest. Her hair was loose, blowing in a warm breeze from the south.

The water surged around us. Once I got used to it, I loved the silky feel of that surge: first the lift that made me feel as if I'd magically dieted off twelve pounds or so, then the backrun that pulled sand out from between my toes in small, tickling whirlpools. Seventy or eighty yards beyond us, two fat pelicans drew a line across the morning. Then they folded their wings and dropped like stones. One came up empty, but the other had breakfast in its bill. The small fish disappeared down the hatch even as the pelican rose. It was an ancient ballet, but no less pleasing for that. South and inland, where the green tangles rose, another bird cried 'Oh-oh! Oh-oh!' over and over.

Wireman turned toward me. He didn't look twenty-five, but he looked younger than at any time since I'd met him. There was no redness at all in his left eye, and it had lost that disjointed, I'm-looking-my-own-way cast. I had no doubt that it was seeing me; that it was seeing me very well.

'Anything I can ever do for you,' he said. 'Ever. In my life. You call, I come. You ask, I do. It's a blank check. Are you clear on that?'

'Yes,' I said. I was clear on something else, as well: when someone

271

offers you a blank check, you must never, ever cash it. That wasn't a thing I thought out. Sometimes understanding bypasses the brain and proceeds directly from the heart.

'All right, then,' he said. 'It's all I'm going to say.'

I heard snoring. I looked around and saw that Elizabeth's chin had sunk to her chest. One hand was fisted around a piece of toast. Her hair whirled around her head.

'She looks thinner,' I said.

'She's lost twenty pounds since New Year's. I'm slipping her those maxi-shakes – Ensure, they're called – once a day, but she won't always take em. What about you? Is it just too much work that's got you looking that way?'

'What way?'

'Like the Hound of the Baskervilles recently bit off your left asscheek. If it's overwork, maybe you ought to knock off and stretch out a little.' He shrugged. '"That's our opinion, we welcome yours," as they say on Channel 6.'

I stood where I was, feeling the lift and drop of the waves, and thinking about what I could tell Wireman. About how *much* I could tell Wireman. The answer seemed self-evident: all or nothing.

'I think I better fill you in on what happened last night. You just have to promise not to call for the men in the white coats.'

'All right.'

I told him about how I'd finished his portrait mostly in the dark. I told him about seeing my right arm and hand. Then seeing the two dead girls at the foot of the stairs and passing out. By the time I finished, we'd waded back out of the water and walked to where Elizabeth was snoring. Wireman began to clean her tray, sweeping the refuse into a bag he took from the pouch hanging on one arm of her chair.

'Nothing else?' he asked.

'That isn't enough?'

'I'm just asking.'

'Nothing else. I slept like a baby until six o'clock. Then I put you – the *painting* of you – in the back of the car and drove down here. When you're ready to see it, by the way—'

'All in good time. Think of a number between one and ten.'

'What?'

'Just humor me, *muchacho*.'

I thought of a number. 'Okay.'

He was silent for a moment, looking out at the Gulf. Then he said, 'Nine?'

'Nope. Seven.'

He nodded. 'Seven.' He drummed his fingers against his chest for a few moments, then dropped them into his lap. 'Yesterday I could have told you. Today I can't. My telepathy thing – that little twinkle – is gone. It's more than a fair trade. Wireman is as Wireman was, and Wireman says *muchas gracias*.'

'What's your point? Or did you have one?'

'I did. The point is you're not going crazy, if that's what you're afraid of. On Duma Key, broken people seem to be special people. When they cease being broken, they cease being special. Me, I'm mended. You're still broken, so you're still special.'

'I'm not sure what you're getting at.'

'Because you're trying to make a simple thing hard. Look in front of you, *muchacho*, what do you see?'

'The Gulf. What you call the *caldo largo*.'

'And what do you spend most of your time painting?'

'The Gulf. Sunsets on the Gulf.'

'And what is painting?'

'Painting is seeing, I guess.'

'No guess about it. And what is seeing on Duma Key?'

Feeling like a child reciting a lesson of which he's not quite sure, I said: '*Special* seeing?'

'Yes. So what do you think, Edgar? Were those dead girls there last night or not?'

I felt a chill up my back. 'Probably they were.'

'I think so, too. I think you saw the ghosts of her sisters.'

'I'm frightened of them.' I said this in a low voice.

'Edgar . . . I don't think ghosts can hurt people.'

'Maybe not ordinary people in an ordinary place,' I said.

He nodded, rather reluctantly. 'All right. So what do you want to do?'

'What I *don't* want to do is leave. I'm not done here yet.'

I wasn't just thinking of the show – the bubble reputation. There was more. I just didn't know what the more was. Not yet. If I'd

273

attempted putting it into words, it would have come out sounding stupid, like something written on a fortune cookie. Something with the word *fate* in it.

'Do you want to come down here to the *Palacio*? Move in with us?'

'No.' I thought that might make matters even worse, somehow. And besides, Big Pink was my place. I had fallen in love with it. 'But Wireman, will you see how much you can find out about the Eastlake family in general and those two girls in particular? If you can read again, then maybe you could dig around on the Internet—'

He gripped my arm. 'I'll dig like a motherfucker. Maybe you could do some good in that direction, as well. You're going to do an interview with Mary Ire, right?'

'Yes. They've scheduled it for the week after my so-called lecture.'

'Ask her about the Eastlakes. Maybe you'll hit the jackpot. Miss Eastlake was a big patron of the arts in her time.'

'Okay.'

He grasped the handles of the sleeping old woman's wheelchair and turned it around so it faced the orange roofs of the estate house again. 'Now let's go look at my portrait. I want to see what I looked like back when I still thought Jerry Garcia could save the world.'

ii

I'd parked my car in the courtyard, beside Elizabeth Eastlake's silver Vietnam War–era Mercedes-Benz. I slid the portrait from my much humbler Chevrolet, set it on end, and held it up for Wireman to look at. As he stood there silently regarding it, a strange thought occurred to me: I was like a tailor standing beside a mirror in a men's clothing store. Soon my customer would either tell me he liked the suit I'd made for him, or shake his head regretfully and say it wouldn't do.

Far off to the south, in what I was coming to think of as the Duma Jungle, that bird took up its warning 'Oh-oh!' cry again.

Finally I couldn't take it anymore. 'Say something, Wireman. Say anything.'

'I can't. I'm speechless.'

'You? Not possible.'

But when he looked up from the portrait, I realized it was true. He looked like someone had walloped him on the head with a hammer. I understood by then that what I was doing affected people, but none of those reactions were quite like Wireman's on that March morning.

What finally woke him up was a sharp knocking sound. It was Elizabeth. She was awake and rapping on her tray. 'Smoke!' she cried. 'Smoke! *Smoke!*' Some things survived even the fog of Alzheimer's, it seemed. The part of her brain that craved nicotine never decayed. She'd smoke until the end.

Wireman took a pack of American Spirits from the pocket of his shorts, shook one out, put it in his mouth, and lit it. Then he held it out to her. 'If I let you handle this yourself, are you going to light yourself on fire, Miss Eastlake?'

'*Smoke!*'

'That's not very encouraging, dear.'

But he gave it to her, and Alzheimer's or no Alzheimer's, she handled it like a pro, drawing in a deep drag and jetting it out through her nostrils. Then she settled back in her chair, looking for the moment not like Captain Bligh on the poop deck but FDR on the reviewing stand. All she needed was a cigarette-holder to clamp between her teeth. And, of course, some teeth.

Wireman returned his gaze to the portrait. 'You don't seriously mean to just give this away, do you? You can't. It's incredible work.'

'It's yours,' I said. 'No arguments.'

'You have to put it in your show.'

'I don't know if that's such a good idea—'

'You yourself said once they're done, any effect on the subject's probably over—'

'Yeah, *probably.*'

'Probably's good enough for me, and the Scoto's safer than this house. Edgar, this deserves to be seen. Hell, it *needs* to be seen.'

'Is it you, Wireman?' I was honestly curious.

'Yes. No.' He stood looking at it a moment longer. Then he turned to me. 'It's how I wanted to be. Maybe it's how I was, on the few best days of my best year.' He added, almost reluctantly: 'My most idealistic year.'

For a little while we said nothing, only looked at the portrait while Elizabeth puffed like a choo-choo train. An *old* choo-choo train.

Then Wireman said: 'There are many things I wonder about, Edgar. Since coming to Duma Key, I have more questions than a four-year-old at bedtime. But one thing I don't wonder about is why you want to stay here. If I could do something like this, I'd want to stay here forever.'

'Last year at this time I was doodling on phone pads while I was on hold,' I said.

'So you said. Tell me something, *muchacho*. Looking at this . . . and thinking of all the other ones you've done since you started . . . would you change the accident that took your arm? Would you change it, even if you could?'

I thought of painting in Little Pink while The Bone pumped out hardcore rock and roll in thick chunks. I thought of the Great Beach Walks. I even thought of the older Baumgarten kid yelling *Yo, Mr Freemantle, nice chuck!* when I spun the Frisbee back to him. Then I thought of waking up in that hospital bed, how dreadfully *hot* I had been, how scattered my thoughts had been, how sometimes I couldn't even remember my own name. The anger. The dawning realization (it came during *The Jerry Springer Show*) that part of my body was AWOL. I had started crying and had been unable to stop.

'I would change it back,' I said, 'in a heartbeat.'

'Ah,' he said. 'Just wondering.' And turned to take away Elizabeth's cigarette.

She immediately held out her hands like an infant who has been deprived of a toy. 'Smoke! *Smoke! SMOKE!*' Wireman butted the cigarette on the heel of his sandal and a moment later she quieted again, the cigarette forgotten now that her nicotine jones was satisfied.

'Stay with her while I put the painting in the front hall, would you?' Wireman asked.

'Sure,' I said. 'Wireman, I only meant—'

'I know. Your arm. The pain. Your wife. It was a stupid question. Obviously. Just let me put this painting safe, okay? Then the next time Jack comes, send him down here. We'll wrap it nice and he can take it to the Scoto. But I'm gonna scrawl NFS all over the packing before it goes to Sarasota. If you're giving it to me, this baby is *mine*. No screw-ups.'

In the jungle to the south, the bird took up its worried cry again: 'Oh-oh! Oh-oh! Oh-oh!'

I wanted to say something else to him, explain to him, but he was hurrying away. Besides, it had been his question. His stupid question.

iii

Jack Cantori took *Wireman Looks West* to the Scoto the following day, and Dario called me as soon as he had it out of the cardboard panels. He claimed to have never seen anything like it, and said he wanted to make it and the *Girl and Ship* paintings the centerpieces of the show. He and Jimmy believed the very fact that those works weren't for sale would hype interest. I told him fine. He asked me if I was getting ready for my lecture, and I told him I was thinking about it. He told me that was good, because the event was already stirring 'uncommon interest', and the circulars hadn't even gone out yet.

'Plus of course we'll be sending JPEG images to our e-listers,' he said.

'That's great,' I said, but it didn't feel great. During those first ten days of March, a curious lassitude stole over me. It didn't extend to work; I painted another sunset and another *Girl and Ship*. Each morning I walked on the beach with my pouch slung over my shoulder, prospecting for shells and any other interesting litter that might have washed up. I found a great many beer and soda cans (most worn as smooth and white as amnesia), a few prophylactics, a child's plastic raygun, and one bikini bottom. Zero tennis balls. I drank green tea with Wireman under the striped umbrella. I coaxed Elizabeth to eat tuna salad and macaroni salad, heavy on the mayo; I chivvied her into drinking Ensure 'milkshakes' through a straw. One day I sat on the boardwalk beside her wheelchair and sanded the mystic rings of yellow callus on her big old feet.

What I did not do was make any notes for my supposed 'art lecture', and when Dario called to say it had been switched to the

277

Public Library lecture space, which seated two hundred, I flatter myself that my offhand reply gave no clue as to how cold my blood ran.

Two hundred people meant four hundred eyes, all trained on me.

What I also did not do was write any invitations, make any move to reserve rooms for the nights of April fifteenth and sixteenth at the Ritz-Carlton in Sarasota, or reserve a Gulfstream to fly down a gaggle of friends and relatives from Minnesota.

The idea that any of them might want to see my daubings began to seem nutty.

The idea that Edgar Freemantle, who one year previous had been fighting with the St Paul Planning Committee about bedrock test drillings, might be giving an *art lecture* to a bunch of actual *art patrons* seemed absolutely insane.

The paintings seemed real enough, though, and the work was . . . God, the work was wonderful. When I stood before my easel in Little Pink at sunset, stripped to my gym shorts and listening to The Bone, watching *Girl and Ship No. 7* emerge from the white with eerie speed (like something sliding out of a fogbank), I felt totally awake and alive, a man in exactly the right place at exactly the right time, a ball that was a perfect fit for its socket. The ghostship had turned a little more; its name appeared to be the *Perse*. On a whim, I Googled this word, and found exactly one hit – probably a world's record. Perse was a private school in England, where the alumni were called Old Perseans. There was no mention of a School Ship, three-masted or otherwise.

In this latest version, the girl in the rowboat was wearing a green dress with straps that crossed over her bare back, and all around her, floating on the sullen water, were roses. It was a disturbing picture.

Walking on the beach, eating my lunch and drinking a beer, with Wireman or on my own, I was happy. When I was painting pictures I was happy. More than happy. When I was painting I felt filled up and fully realized in some basic way I had never understood before coming to Duma Key. But when I thought about the show at the Scoto and all the stuff that went into making an exhibition of new work successful, my mind went into lockdown. It was more than stage fright; this felt like outright panic.

I forgot things – like opening any e-mails from Dario, Jimmy, or

Alice Aucoin at the Scoto. If Jack asked me if I was excited about 'doing my thing' at the Selby Library's Geldbart Auditorium, I'd tell him oh-yeah, then ask him to gas up the Chevy in Osprey, and forget what he'd asked me. When Wireman asked if I'd talked to Alice Aucoin yet about how the various groupings were to be hung, I'd suggest we volley some tennis balls, because Elizabeth seemed to enjoy watching.

Then, about a week before the scheduled lecture, Wireman said he wanted to show me something he'd made. A little craftwork. 'Maybe you could give me your opinion as an artist,' he said.

There was a black folder lying on the table in the shade of the striped umbrella (Jack had mended the rip with a piece of electrician's tape). I opened it and took out what looked like a glossy brochure. On the front was one of my early efforts, *Sunset with Sophora*, and I was surprised at how professional it looked. Below the repro was this:

Dear Linnie: This is what I've been doing in Florida, and although I know you're awfully busy . . .

Below *awfully busy* was an arrow. I looked up at Wireman, who was watching me expressionlessly. Behind him, Elizabeth was staring at the Gulf. I didn't know if I was angry at his presumption or relieved by it. In truth, I felt both things. And I couldn't remember telling him I sometimes called my older daughter Linnie.

'You can use any type-font you want,' he said. 'This one's a little girly-girl for my taste, but my collaborator likes it. And the name in each salutation is interchangeable, of course. You can customize. That's the beauty of doing things like this on a computer.'

I didn't reply, just turned to the next page. Here was *Sunset with Witchgrass* on one side and *Girl and Ship No. 1* on the other. Running below the pictures was this:

. . . I hope you'll join me for an exhibition of my work, on the night of April 15th, at the Scoto Gallery, in Sarasota, Florida, 7 PM–10 PM. A First Class reservation in your name has been made on Air France Flight 22, departing Paris on the 15th at 8:25 AM and arriving in New York at 10:15 AM; you are also

reserved on Delta Flight 496, leaving New York's JFK on the 15th at 1:20 PM and arriving in Sarasota at 4:30 PM. A limousine will meet your flight and take you to the Ritz-Carlton, where your stay has been booked, with my compliments, for the nights of April 15th–April 17th.

There was another arrow below this. I looked up at Wireman, bewildered. He was still with the poker face, but I could see a pulse beating on the right side of his forehead. Later on he said, 'I knew I was putting our friendship on the line, but somebody had to do something, and by then it had become clear to me that it wasn't going to be you.'

I turned to the next page in the brochure. Two more of those amazing reproductions: *Sunset with Conch* on the left and an untitled sketch of my mailbox on the right. That was a very early one, done with Venus colored pencils, but I liked the flower growing up beside the wooden post – it was a brilliant yellow and black oxeye – and even the sketch looked good in reproduction, as if the man who'd done it knew his business. Or was getting to know it.

The copy here was brief.

If you can't come, I'll more than understand – Paris isn't just around the corner! – but I'm hoping that you will.

I was angry, but I wasn't stupid. Somebody had to take hold. Apparently Wireman had decided that was his job.

Ilse, I thought. *It's got to be Ilse who helped him with this.*

I expected to find another painting over the printed matter on the last page, but I didn't. What I saw there hurt my heart with surprise and love. Melinda was ever my hard girl, my project, but I had never loved her the less for that, and what I felt showed clearly in the black-and-white photo, which looked creased across the middle and dog-eared at two of its four corners. It had a right to look beat-up, because the Melinda standing next to me could have been no older than four. That made this snapshot at least eighteen years old. She was wearing jeans, cowboy boots, a Western-style shirt, and a straw hat. Had we just come back from Pleasant Hill Farms, where she sometimes rode a Shetland pony named Sugar? I thought so.

In any case, we were standing on the sidewalk in front of the little starter home we'd had in Brooklyn Park, me in faded jeans and a white tee-shirt with the short sleeves rolled up a turn and my hair combed back like a greaser. I had a can of Grain Belt beer in one hand and a smile on my face. Linnie had one hand hooked into the pocket of my jeans and a look of love – such love – on her upturned face that it made my throat ache. I smiled the way you do when you're about an inch away from bursting into tears. Below the picture it said:

If you want to keep current on who else is coming, you can call me at 941-555-6166, or Jerome Wireman at 941-555-8191, or your Mom. She'll be coming down with the Minnesota contingent, by the way, and will meet you at the hotel.

Hope you can come – love you either way, Pony Girl—

Dad

I closed the letter that was also a brochure that was also an invitation and sat staring silently down at it for a few moments. I did not entirely trust myself to speak.

'That's just a rough draft, of course.' Wireman sounded tentative. In other words, not like himself at all. 'If you hate it, I'll junk it and start again. No harm, no foul.'

'You didn't get that picture from Ilse,' I said.

'No, *muchacho*. Pam found it in one of her old photo albums.'

All at once everything made sense.

'How many times have you talked to her, *Jerome*?'

He winced. 'That hurts, but maybe you have a right. Probably half a dozen times. I started by telling her you were getting yourself in a jam down here, and that you were taking a lot of other people with you—'

'What the *fuck*!' I cried, stung.

'People who'd invested a lot of hope and trust in you, not to mention money—'

'I'm perfectly capable of refunding any money the people at the Scoto may have laid out on—'

'Shut up,' he said, and I had never heard such coldness in his voice. Or seen it in his eyes. 'You ain't an asshole, *muchacho*, so don't

281

act like one. Can you refund their trust? Can you refund their prestige, if the great new artist they've promised their customers doesn't materialize for either the lecture or the show?'

'Wireman, I can do the *show*, it's just the goddam *lecture—*'

'*They* don't know that!' he shouted. He had a hell of a shouting voice on him, a real courtroom bellow. Elizabeth took no notice, but peeps took off from the water's edge in a brown sheet. 'They have this funny idea that maybe on April fifteenth you'll be a *no-show*, or that you'll yank your stuff altogether and they'll have a bunch of empty rooms during the tenderloin of the tourist season, when they're used to doing a third of their yearly business.'

'They have no reason to think that,' I said, but my face was throbbing like a hot brick.

'No? How did you think about this kind of behavior in your other life, *amigo*? What conclusions did you draw about a supplier who contracted for cement and then didn't show up on the dime? Or a plumbing sub who got the job on a new bank and wasn't there on the day he was supposed to start? Did you feel real, I dunno, confident about guys like that? Did you believe their excuses?'

I said nothing.

'Dario sends you e-mails asking for decisions, he gets no answer. He and the others call on the phone and get vague replies like "I'll think about it." This would make them nervous if you were Jamie Wyeth or Dale Chihuly, and you're not. Basically you're just some guy who walked in off the street. So they call me, and I do the best I can – I'm your fuckin agent, after all – but I'm no artist, and neither are they, not really. We're like a bunch of cab-drivers trying to deliver a baby.'

'I get it,' I said.

'I wonder if you do.' He sighed. Big sigh. 'You say it's just stage fright about the lecture and you're going to go through with the show. I'm sure part of you believes that, but *amigo*, I gotta say that I think part of you has no *intention* of showing up at the Scoto Gallery on April fifteenth.'

'Wireman, that's just—'

'Bullshit? Is it? I call the Ritz-Carlton and ask if a Mr Freemantle has reserved any rooms for mid-April and get the big *non, non, Nannette*. So I take a deep breath and get in touch with your ex.

She's no longer in the phone book, but your Realtor gives me the number when I tell her it's sort of an emergency. And right away I discover Pam still cares about you. She actually wants to call and tell you that, but she's scared you'll blow her off.'

I gaped at him.

'The first thing we establish once we get past the introductions is Pam Freemantle knows zip and zoop about a big art exhibition five weeks hence by her ex-husband. The second thing – she makes a phone call while Wireman dangles on hold and does a crossword puzzle with his newly restored vision – is that her ex has done *bupkes* about chartering a plane, at least with the company she knows. Which leads us to discuss if, deep down, Edgar Freemantle has decided that when the time comes, he's just going to – in the words of my misspent youth – cry fuck it and crawl in the bucket.'

'No, you've got it all wrong,' I said, but these words came out in a listless drone that did not sound especially convincing. 'It's just that all the organizational stuff drives me crazy, and I kept . . . you know, putting it off.'

Wireman was relentless. If I'd been on the witness stand, I think I'd have been a little puddle of grease and tears by then; the judge would have called a recess to allow the bailiff time to either mop me up or buff me to a shine. 'Pam says if you subtracted the Freemantle Company buildings from the St Paul skyline, it would look like Des Moines in nineteen seventy-two.'

'Pam exaggerates.'

He took no notice. 'Am I supposed to believe that a guy who organized that much work couldn't organize some plane tickets and two dozen hotel rooms? Especially when he could reach out to an office staff that would absolutely love to hear from him?'

'They don't . . . I don't . . . they can't just . . .'

'Are you getting pissed?'

'No.' But I was. The old anger was back, wanting to raise its voice until it was shouting as loud as Axl Rose on The Bone. I raised my fingers to a spot just over my right eye, where a headache was starting up. There would be no painting for me today, and it was Wireman's fault. Wireman was to blame. For one moment I wished him blind. Not just half-blind but *blind* blind, and realized I could paint him that way. At that the anger collapsed.

283

Wireman saw my hand go to my head and let up a little. 'Look, most of the people she's contacted unofficially have already said hell yes, of course, they'd love to. Your old line foreman Angel Slobotnik told Pam he'd bring you a jar of pickles. She said he sounded thrilled.'

'Not pickles, pickled eggs,' I said, and Big Ainge's broad, flat, smiling face was for a moment almost close enough to touch. Angel, who had been right there beside me for twenty years, until a major heart attack sidelined him. Angel, whose most common response to any request, no matter how seemingly outrageous, was *Can do, boss.*

'Pam and I made the flight arrangements,' Wireman said. 'Not just for the people from Minneapolis–St Paul, but from other places, as well.' He tapped the brochure. 'The Air France and Delta Flights in here are real, and your daughter Melinda is really booked on em. She knows what's going on. So does Ilse. They're only waiting to be officially invited. Ilse wanted to call you, and Pam told her to wait. She says you have to pull the trigger on this, and whatever she may have been wrong about in the course of your marriage, *muchacho*, she's right about that.'

'All right,' I said. 'I'm hearing you.'

'Good. Now I want to talk to you about the lecture.'

I groaned.

'If you do a bunk on the lecture, you'll find it twice as hard to go to the opening-night party—'

I looked at him incredulously.

'What?' he asked. 'You disagree?'

'Do a bunk?' I asked. 'Do a *bunk*? What the fuck is that?'

'To cut and run,' he said, sounding slightly defensive. 'British slang. See for instance Evelyn Waugh, *Officers and Gentlemen*, 1952.'

'See my ass and your face,' I said. 'Edgar Freemantle, present day.'

He flipped me the bird, and just like that we were mostly okay again.

'You sent Pam the pictures, didn't you? You sent her the JPEG file.'

'I did.'

'How did she react?'

'She was blown away, *muchacho*.'

I sat silently, trying to imagine Pam blown away. I could do it, but the face I saw lighting up in surprise and wonder was a younger

284

face. It had been quite a few years since I'd been able to generate that sort of wind.

Elizabeth was dozing off, but her hair was flying against her cheeks and she pawed at them like a woman troubled by insects. I got up, took an elastic from the pouch on the arm of her wheelchair – there was always a good supply of them, in many bright colors – and pulled her hair back into a horsetail. The memories of doing this for Melinda and Ilse were sweet and terrible.

'Thank you, Edgar. Thank you, *mi amigo*.'

'So how do I do it?' I asked. I was holding my palms on the sides of Elizabeth's head, feeling the smoothness of her hair as I had often felt the smoothness of my daughters' after it had been shampooed; when memory takes its strongest hold, our own bodies become ghosts, haunting us with the gestures of our younger selves. 'How do I talk about a process that's at least partially supernatural?'

There. It was out. The root of the matter.

Yet Wireman looked calm. 'Edgar!' he exclaimed.

'Edgar *what?*'

The sonofabitch actually laughed. 'If you tell them that . . . *they will believe you.*'

I opened my mouth to refute this. Thought of Dalí's work. Thought of that wonderful Van Gogh picture, *Starry Night*. Thought of certain Andrew Wyeth paintings – not *Christina's World* but his interiors: spare rooms where the light is both sane and strange, as if coming from two directions at the same time. I closed my mouth again.

'I can't tell you just what to say,' Wireman said, 'but I can give you something like this.' He held up the brochure/invitation. 'I can give you a template.'

'That would help.'

'Yeah? Then listen.'

I listened.

iv

'Hello?'

I was sitting on the couch in the Florida room. My heart was beating heavily. This was one of those calls – everyone's made a few

285

– where you simultaneously hope it will go through the first time, so you can get it over with, and hope it won't, so you can put off some hard and probably painful conversation a little while longer.

I got Option One; Pam answered on the first ring. All I could hope was this conversation would go better than the last one. Than the last couple, in fact.

'Pam, it's Edgar.'

'Hello, Edgar,' she said cautiously. 'How are you?'

'I'm . . . all right. Good. I've been talking with my friend Wireman. He showed me the invitation the two of you worked up.' *The two of you worked up.* That sounded unfriendly. Conspiratorial, even. But what other way was there to put it?

'Yes?' Her voice was impossible to read.

I drew in a breath and jumped. God hates a coward, Wireman says. Among other things. 'I called to say thanks. I was being a horse's ass. Your jumping in like that was what I needed.'

The silence was long enough for me to wonder if maybe she'd quietly hung up at some point. Then she said, 'I'm still here, Eddie – I'm just picking myself up off the floor. I can't remember the last time you apologized to me.'

Had I apologized? Well . . . never mind. Close enough, maybe. 'Then I'm sorry about that, too,' I said.

'I owe you an apology myself,' she said, 'so I guess this one's a wash.'

'You? What do you have to apologize for?'

'Tom Riley called. Just two days ago. He's back on his meds. He's going to, I quote, "see someone" again – by which I assume he means a shrink – and he called to thank me for saving his life. Have you ever had someone call and thank you for that?'

'No.' Although I'd recently had someone call and thank me for saving his sight, so I kind of knew what she was talking about.

'It's quite an experience. "If not for you I'd be dead now." Those were his exact words. And I couldn't tell him he had you to thank, because it would have sounded crazy.'

It was as if a tight belt cinching my middle had suddenly been cut away. Sometimes things work out for the best. Sometimes they actually do. 'That's good, Pam.'

'I've been on to Ilse about this show of yours.'

'Yes, I—'

'Well, Illy and Lin both, but when I talked to Ilse, I turned the conversation toward Tom and I could tell right away that she doesn't know anything about what went on between the two of us. I was wrong about that, too. And showed a very unpleasant side of myself while I was at it.'

I realized, with alarm, that she was crying. 'Pam, listen.'

'I've shown *several* unlovely sides of myself, to several people, since you left me.'

I didn't leave you! I almost shouted. And it was close. Close enough to make sweat pop out on my forehead. *I didn't leave you, you asked for a divorce, you witting quench!*

What I said was 'Pam, that's enough.'

'But it was so hard to believe, even after you called and told me those other things. You know, about my new TV. And Puffball.'

I started to ask who Puffball was, then remembered the cat.

'I'm doing better, though. I've started going to church again. Can you believe that? And a therapist. I see her once a week.' She paused, then rushed on. 'She's good. She says a person can't close the door on the past, she can only make amends and go on. I understood that, but I didn't know how to start making amends to you, Eddie.'

'Pam, you don't owe me any—'

'My therapist says it isn't about what *you* think, it's about what *I* think.'

'I see.' That sounded a lot like the old Pam, so maybe she'd found the right therapist.

'And then your friend Wireman called and told me you needed help . . . and he sent me those pictures. I can't wait to see the actual things. I mean, I knew you had *some* talent, because you used to draw those little books for Lin when she was so sick that year—'

'I did?' I remembered Melinda's sick year; she'd had one infection after another, culminating in a massive bout of diarrhea, probably brought on by too many antibiotics, that had landed her in the hospital for a week. She lost ten pounds that spring. If not for summer vacation – and her own grade-A intelligence – she would have needed to repeat the second grade. But I couldn't remember drawing any little books.

'Freddy the Fish? Carla the Crab? Donald the Timid Deer?'

Donald the Timid Deer rang a very faint bell, way down deep, but . . . 'No,' I said.

'Angel thought you should try to get them published, don't you remember? But *these* . . . my God. Did you know you could do it?'

'No. I started thinking something might be there when I was at the place on Lake Phalen, but it's gone farther than I thought it would.' I thought of *Wireman Looks West* and the mouthless, noseless Candy Brown and thought I'd just uttered the understatement of the century.

'Eddie, will you let me do the rest of the invitations the way I did the sample? I can customize them, make them nice.'

'Pa—' Almost *Panda* again. 'Pam, I can't ask you to do that.'

'I want to.'

'Yeah? Then okay.'

'I'll write them and e-mail them to Mr Wireman. You can check them over before he prints them. He's quite a jewel, your Mr Wireman.'

'Yes,' I said. 'He is. The two of you really ganged up on me.'

'We did, didn't we?' She sounded delighted. 'You needed it. Only you have to do something for me.'

'What?'

'You have to call the girls, because they're going *crazy*, Ilse in particular. Okay?'

'Okay. And Pam?'

'What, hon?' I'm sure she said it without thinking, without knowing how it could cut. Ah, well – she probably felt the same when she heard my pet name for her coming up from Florida, growing colder with every mile it sped north.

'Thanks,' I said.

'Totally welcome.'

It was only quarter to eleven when we said goodbye and hung up. Time never went faster that winter than it did during my evenings in Little Pink – standing at my easel, I'd wonder how the colors in the west could possibly fade so fast – and it never went slower than it did that morning, when I made the phone calls I'd been putting off. I swallowed them one after the other, like medicine.

I looked at the cordless sitting in my lap. 'Fuck you, phone,' I said, and started dialing again.

288

v

'Scoto Gallery, this is Alice.'

A cheery voice I'd come to know well over the last ten days.

'Hi, Alice, it's Edgar Freemantle.'

'Yes, Edgar?' Cheery became cautious. Had that cautious note been there before? Had I just ignored it?

I said, 'If you have a couple of minutes, I wonder if we could talk about ordering the slides at the lecture.'

'*Yes,* Edgar, we certainly could.' The relief was palpable. It made me feel like a hero. Of course it also made me feel like a rat.

'Have you got a pad handy?'

'You bet your tailfeathers!'

'Okay. Basically, we're going to want them in chronological order—'

'But I don't *know* the chronology, I've been trying to tell you th—'

'I know, and I'm going to give it to you now, but listen, Alice: the first slide *won't* be chronological. The first should be of *Roses Grow from Shells.* Have you got that?'

'*Roses Grow from Shells.* I've got it.' For only the second time since meeting me, Alice sounded genuinely happy that we were talking.

'Now, the pencil sketches,' I said.

We talked for the next half an hour.

vi

'*Oui, allô?*'

For a moment I said nothing. The French threw me a little. The fact that it was a young man's voice threw me more.

'*Allô, allô?*' Impatient now. '*Qui est à l'appareil?*'

'Mmm, maybe I have the wrong number,' I said, feeling not just like an asshole but a monolingual American asshole. 'I was trying to reach Melinda Freemantle.'

'*D'accord,* you have the right number.' Then, off a little: 'Melinda! *C'est ton papa, je crois, chérie.*'

The phone went down with a clunk. I had a momentary image

– very clear, very politically incorrect, and very likely brought on by Pam's mention of the cartoon books I'd once drawn for a little sick girl – of a large talking skunk in a beret, Monsieur Pépé LePew, strutting around my daughter's *pension* (if that was the word for a bedsitter-type apartment in Paris) with wavy aroma lines rising from his white-striped back.

Then Melinda was there, sounding uncharacteristically flustered. 'Dad? Daddy? Is everything all right?'

'Everything's fine,' I said. 'Is that your roommate?' It was a joke, but I realized from her uncharacteristic silence that I had unwittingly hit the nail on the head. 'It's not a big deal, Linnie. I was just—'

'—goofin wit me, right.' It was impossible to tell if she was amused or exasperated. The connection was good but not that good. 'He is, actually.' The subtext of that one to come through loud and clear: *Want to make something of it?*

I most assuredly did not want to make something of it. 'Well, I'm glad you made a friend. Does he wear a beret?'

To my immense relief, she laughed. With Lin, it was impossible to tell which way a joke was going to go, because her sense of humor was as unreliable as an April afternoon. She called: '*Ric! Mon papa . . .*' Something I didn't catch, then: '*. . . si tu portes un béret!*'

There was faint male laughter. *Ah, Edgar,* I thought. *Even overseas you lay them in the aisles, you* père fou.

'Daddy, *are* you all right?'

'Fine. How's your strep?'

'All better, thanks.'

'I just got off the phone with your mother. You're going to get an official invitation to this show I'm having, but she says you'll come and I'm thrilled.'

'*You're* thrilled? Mom sent me some of the pictures and I can't wait. When did you learn to *do* that?'

This seemed to be the question of the hour. 'Down here.'

'They're *amazing.* Are the others as good?'

'You'll have to come and see for yourself.'

'Could Ric come?'

'Does he have a passport?'

'Yes . . .'

290

'Will he promise not to poke ze fun at your old man?'

'He's very respectful of his elders.'

'Then assuming the flights aren't sold out and you don't mind sleeping two to a room – I assume that's not a problem – then of course he can come.'

She squealed so loudly it hurt my ear, but I didn't take the telephone away. It had been a long time since I'd said or done anything to make Linnie Freemantle squeal like that. 'Thank you, Daddy – that's great!'

'It'll be nice to meet Ric. Maybe I'll steal his beret. I'm an artist now, after all.'

'I'll tell him you said that.' Her voice changed. 'Have you talked to Ilse yet?'

'No, why?'

'When you do, don't say anything about Ric coming, okay? Let me do that.'

'I hadn't planned to.'

'Because she and Carson . . . she said she told you about him . . .'

'She did.'

'Well, I'm pretty sure there's a problem there. Illy says she's "thinking things over". That's a direct quote. Ric's not surprised. He says you should never trust a person who prays in public. All I know is she sounds a lot more grown up than my baby sister used to.'

Same goes for you, Lin, I thought. I had a momentary image of how she'd looked at seven, when she'd been so sick Pam and I both thought she might die on us, although we'd never said so aloud. Back then Melinda had been all big dark eyes, pale cheeks, and lank hair. Once I remember thinking *Skull on a stick* and hating myself for the thought. And hating myself more for knowing, in the deep reaches of my heart, that if one of them had to sicken that way, I was glad it had been her. I always tried to believe that I loved both my daughters with the same weight and intensity, but it wasn't true. Maybe it is for some parents – I think it was for Pam – but it never was for me. And did Melinda know?

Of course she did.

'Are you taking care of yourself?' I asked her.

'Yes, Daddy.' I could almost see her rolling her eyes.

'Continue to do so. And get here safe.'

'Daddy?' A pause. 'I love you.'

I smiled. 'How many bunches?'

'A million and one for under your pillow,' she said, as if humoring a child. That was all right. I sat there for a little while, looking out at the water, rubbing absently at my eyes, then made what I hoped would be the day's last call.

vii

It was noon by then, and I didn't really expect to get her; I thought she'd be out eating lunch with friends. Only like Pam, she answered on the first ring. Her hello was oddly cautious, and I had a sudden clear intuition: she thought I was Carson Jones, calling either to beg for another chance or to explain. To explain yet again. That was a hunch I never verified, but then, I never had to. Some things you simply know are true.

'Hey, If-So-Girl, whatcha doon?'

Her voice brightened immediately. 'Daddy!'

'How are you, hon?'

'I'm fine, Daddy, but not as fine as you — did I tell you they were good? I mean, did I *tell* you, or what?'

'You told me,' I said, grinning in spite of myself. She might have sounded older to Lin, but after that first tentative hello, she sounded to me like the same old Illy, bubbling over like a Coke float.

'Mom said you were dragging your feet, but she was going to team up with this friend you made down there and get you cranking. I *loved* it! She sounded just like the old days!' She paused to draw breath, and when she spoke again, she didn't sound so giddy. 'Well . . . not quite, but it'll do.'

'Know what you mean, jellybean.'

'Daddy, you're so amazing. This is a comeback and a *half.*'

'How much is all this sugar going to cost me?'

'*Millions,*' she said, and laughed.

'Still planning to drop in on The Hummingbirds tour?' I tried to sound just interested. Not particularly concerned with my almost-twenty-year-old daughter's love life.

'No,' she said, 'I think that's off.' Only five words, and little ones at that, but in those five words I heard the different, older Illy, one who might in the not-so-distant future be at home in a business suit and pantyhose and pumps with practical three-quarter heels, who might wear her hair tied back at the nape of her neck during the day and perhaps carry a briefcase down airport concourses instead of wearing a Gapsack on her back. Not an If-So-Girl any longer; you could strike any *if* from this vision. The *girl* as well.

'The whole thing, or—'

'That remains to be seen.'

'I don't mean to pry, honey. It's just that enquiring Dads—'

'—want to know, of course they do, but I can't help you this time. All I know right now is that I still love him – or at least I think I do – and I miss him, but he's got to make a choice.'

At this point, Pam would have asked *Between you and the girl he's been singing with?* What I asked was, 'Are you eating?'

She burst into peals of merry laughter.

'Answer the question, Illy.'

'Like a damn pig!'

'Then why aren't you out to lunch now?'

'A bunch of us are going to have a picnic in the park, that's why. Complete with anthro study notes and Frisbee. I'm bringing the cheese and French bread. And I'm late.'

'Okay. As long as you're eating and not brooding in your tent.'

'Eating well, brooding moderately.' Her voice changed again, became the adult one. The abrupt switches back and forth were disconcerting. 'Sometimes I lie awake a little, and then I think of you down there. Do you lie awake?'

'Sometimes. Not as much now.'

'Daddy, was marrying Mom a mistake you made? That she made? Or was it just an accident?'

'It wasn't an accident and it wasn't a mistake. Twenty-four good years, two fine daughters, and we're still talking. It wasn't a mistake, Illy.'

'You wouldn't change it?'

People kept asking me that question. 'No.'

'If you could go back . . . would you?'

I paused, but not long. Sometimes there's no time to decide what's the best answer. Sometimes you can only give the true answer. 'No, honey.'

'Okay. But I miss you, Dad.'

'I miss you, too.'

'Sometimes I miss the old times, too. When things were less complicated.' She paused. I could have spoken – wanted to – but kept silent. Sometimes silence is best. 'Dad, do people ever deserve second chances?'

I thought of my own second chance. How I had survived an accident that should have killed me. And I was doing more than just hanging out, it seemed. I felt a rush of gratitude. 'All the time.'

'Thanks, Daddy. I can't wait to see you.'

'Back atcha. You'll get an official invitation soon.'

'Okay. I really have to go. Love you.'

'Love you, too.'

I sat for a moment with the phone at my ear after she hung up, listening to the nothing. 'Do the day and let the day do you,' I said. Then the dial tone kicked in, and I decided I had one more call to make, after all.

viii

This time when Alice Aucoin came to the phone, she sounded a lot more lively and a lot less cautious. I thought that was a nice change.

'Alice, we never talked about a name for the show,' I said.

'I was sort of assuming you meant to call it "Roses Grow from Shells",' she said. 'That's good. Very evocative.'

'It is,' I said, looking out to the Florida room and the Gulf beyond. The water was a brilliant blue-white plate; I had to squint against the glare. 'But it's not quite right.'

'You have one you like better, I take it?'

'Yes, I think so. I want to call it "The View from Duma". What do you think?'

Her response was immediate. 'I think it sings.'

So did I.

ix

I had sweat through my LOSE IT IN THE VIRGIN ISLANDS tee-shirt in spite of Big Pink's efficient air conditioning, and I was more exhausted than a brisk walk to *El Palacio* and back left me these days. My ear felt hot and throbby from the telephone. I felt uneasy about Ilse – the way parents are always uneasy about the problems of their children, I suppose, once they're too old to be called home when it starts to get dark and the baths are being drawn – but I also felt satisfied with the work I'd put in, the way I used to feel after a good day on a hard construction job.

I didn't feel particularly hungry, but I made myself slop a few tablespoons of tuna salad onto a lettuce leaf and washed it down with a glass of milk. Whole milk – bad for the heart, good for the bones. *I guess that one's a wash*, Pam would have said. I turned on the kitchen TV and learned that Candy Brown's wife was suing the City of Sarasota over her husband's death, claiming negligence. *Good luck on that one, sweetheart*, I thought. The local meteorologist said the hurricane season might start earlier than ever. And the Devil Rays had gotten their low-rent asses kicked by the Red Sox in an exhibition game – welcome to baseball reality, boys.

I considered dessert (I had Jell-O Pudding, sometimes known as The Last Resort of the Single Man), then just put my plate in the sink and limped off to the bedroom for a nap. I considered setting the alarm, then didn't bother; I'd probably only doze. Even if I actually slept, the light would wake me up in an hour or so, when it got over to the western side of the house and came angling in the bedroom window.

So thinking, I lay down and slept until six o'clock that evening.

x

There was no question of supper; I didn't even consider it. Below me the shells were whispering *paint, paint*.

I went upstairs to Little Pink like a man in a dream, wearing only my undershorts. I turned on The Bone, set *Girl and Ship No. 7* against the wall, and put a fresh canvas – not as big as the one

295

I'd used for *Wireman Looks West*, but big – on my easel. My missing arm was itching, but this no longer bothered me the way it had at first; the truth was, I'd almost come to look forward to it.

Shark Puppy was on the radio: 'Dig'. Excellent song. Excellent lyrics. *Life is more than love and pleasure.*

I remember clearly how the whole world seemed to be waiting for me to begin – that was how much power I felt running through me while the guitars screamed and the shells murmured.

I came here to dig for treasure.

Treasure, yes. Loot.

I painted until the sun was gone and the moon cast its bitter rind of white light over the water and after that was gone, too.

And the next night.

And the next.

And the next.

Girl and Ship No. 8.

If you want to play you gotta pay.

I unbottled.

xi

The sight of Dario in a suit and a tie, with his lush hair tamed and combed straight back from his forehead, scared me even more than the murmuring audience that filled Geldbart Auditorium, where the lights had just been turned down to half . . . except for the spotlight shining down on the lectern standing at center stage, that was. The fact that Dario himself was nervous – going to the podium he had nearly dropped his note-cards – scared me even worse.

'Good evening, my name is Dario Nannuzzi,' he said. 'I am co-curator, and chief buyer at the Scoto Gallery on Palm Avenue. More importantly, I have been a part of the Sarasota art community for thirty years, and I hope you will excuse my brief descent into what some might call Bobbittry when I say there is no finer art community in America.'

This brought enthusiastic applause from an audience which – as Wireman said later – might know the difference between Monet and Manet, but apparently didn't have a clue that there was a difference between George Babbitt and John Bobbitt. Standing in the wings, suffering through that purgatory only frightened main speakers experience as their introducers wind their slow and peristaltic courses, I hardly noticed.

Dario shifted his top file-card to the bottom, once again nearly dropped the whole stack, recovered, and looked out at his audience again. 'I hardly know where to begin, but to my relief I need say very little, for true talent seems to blaze up from nowhere, and serves as its own introduction.'

That said, he proceeded to introduce me for the next ten minutes as I stood in the wings with my one lousy page of notes clutched in my remaining hand. Names went past like floats in a parade. A few, like Edward Hopper and Salvador Dalí, I knew. Others, like Yves Tanguy and Kay Sage, I didn't. Each unknown name made me feel more of an impostor. The fear I felt was no longer mental; it clamped a deep and stinking hold in my bowels. I felt like I needed to pass gas, but I was afraid I might load my pants instead. And that wasn't the worst. Every word I had prepared had gone out of my mind except for the very first line, which was hideously appropriate: *My name is Edgar Freemantle, and I have no idea how I wound up here.* It was supposed to elicit a chuckle. It wouldn't, I knew that now, but at least it was true.

While Dario droned on – Joan Miró this, Breton's Surrealist Manifesto that – a terrified ex-contractor stood with his pathetic page of notes clutched in his cold fist. My tongue was a dead slug that might croak but would speak no coherent word, not to two hundred art mavens, many of whom held advanced degrees, some of whom were motherfucking *professors*. Worst of all was my brain. It was a dry socket waiting to be filled with pointless, flailing anger: the words might not come, but the rage was always on tap.

'Enough!' Dario cried cheerily, striking fresh terror into my pounding heart and sending a cramp rolling through my miserable basement regions – terror above, barely held-in shit below. What a lovely combination. 'It has been fifteen years since the Scoto added a new artist to its crowded spring calendar, and we have never introduced one in whom there has been greater interest. I think the

297

slides you are about to see and the talk you are about to hear will explain our interest and excitement.'

He paused dramatically. I felt a poison dew of sweat spring out on my brow and wiped it off. The arm that I lifted seemed to weigh fifty pounds.

'Ladies and gentlemen, Mr Edgar Freemantle, lately of Minneapolis–St Paul, now of Duma Key.'

They applauded. It sounded like an artillery barrage going off. I commanded myself to run away. I commanded myself to faint. I did neither. Like a man in a dream – but not a good one – I walked onstage. Everything seemed to be happening slowly. I saw that every seat was taken but *no* seat was taken because they were on their feet, they were giving me a standing O. High above me, on the domed ceiling, angels flew in airy disregard of the earthly matters below, and how I wished I was one of them. Dario stood beside the podium, hand outstretched. It was the wrong one; in his own nervousness he had extended his right, and so my return handshake was awkward and bass-ackwards. My notes were crumpled briefly between our palms, then tore. *Look what you did, you asshole,* I thought – and for one terrible moment I was afraid I'd said it aloud for the mike to pick up and broadcast all over the room. I was aware of how bright the spotlight was as Dario left me there on my lonely perch. I was aware of the microphone on its flexible chrome rod, and thinking it looked like a cobra rising out of a snake-charmer's basket. I was aware of bright points of light shining on that chrome, and on the rim of the water glass, and on the neck of the Evian bottle next to the water glass. I was aware that the applause was starting to taper off; some of the people were resuming their seats. Soon an expectant silence would replace the applause. They would wait for me to begin. Only I had nothing to say. Even my opening line had left my head. They would wait and the silence would stretch out. There would be a few nervous coughs, and then the murmuring would start. Because they were assholes. Just a bunch of lookie-loo assholes with rubber necks. And if I managed anything, it would be an angry torrent of words that would sound like the outburst of a man suffering from Tourette's.

I'd just call for the first slide. Maybe I could do that much and the pictures would carry me. I'd have to hope they would. Only when I looked at my page of notes, I saw that not only was it torn straight down the middle, my sweat had blurred the jottings so badly I could no longer make them out. Either that or stress had created a short circuit between my eyes and my brain. And what *was* the first slide, anyway? A mailbox painting? *Sunset with Sophora?* I was almost positive neither of those was right.

Now everyone was sitting. The applause was finished. It was time for the American Primitive to open his mouth and ululate. Three rows back, sitting on the aisle, was that nozzy birch Mary Ire, with what looked like a porthand shad open on her lap. I looked for Wireman. He'd gotten me into this, but I bore him no anus. I only wanted to apologize with my eyes for what was coming.

I'll be in the front row, he'd said. *Dead center.*

And he was. Jack, my housekeeper Juanita, Jimmy Yoshida, and Alice Aucoin were sitting on Wireman's left. And on his right, on the aisle—

The man on the aisle had to be a hallucination. I blinked, but he was still there. A vast face, dark and calm. A figure crammed so tightly into the plush auditorium seat it seemed it might take a crowbar to get him out again: Xander Kamen, peering up at me through his enormous horn-rimmed glasses and looking more like a minor god than ever. Obesity had canceled his lap, but balanced on the bulge of his belly was a ribbon-garnished gift box about three feet long. He saw my surprise – my shock – and made a gesture: not a wave but an odd, beneficent salute, putting the tips of his fingers first to his massive brow, then to his lips, then holding his hand out to me with the fingers spread. I could see the pallor of his palm. He smiled up at me, as if his presence here in the first row of the Geldbart Auditorium next to my friend Wireman were the most natural thing in the world. His large lips formed four words, one after the other: *You can do this.*

And maybe I could. If I thought away from this moment. If I thought sideways.

I thought of Wireman – Wireman looking west, to be exact – and my opening line came back to me.

I nodded to Kamen. Kamen nodded back. Then I looked at the audience and saw they were just people. All the angels were over

299

our heads, and they were now flying in the dark. As for demons, most were probably in my mind.

'Hello—' I began, then recoiled at the way my voice boomed out from the microphone. The audience laughed, but the sound didn't make me angry, as it would have a minute before. It was only laughter, and goodnatured.

I can do this.

'Hello,' I said again. 'My name is Edgar Freemantle, and I'm probably not going to be very good at this. In my other life I was in the building trade. I knew I was good at that, because I landed jobs. In my current life I paint pictures. But nobody said anything about public speaking.'

This time the laughter was a little freer and a little more general.

'I was going to start by saying I have no idea how I wound up here, but actually I do. And that's good, because it's all I have to tell. You see, I don't know anything about art history, art theory, or even art appreciation. Some of you probably know Mary Ire.'

This brought a chuckle, as if I'd said *Some of you may have heard of Andy Warhol.* The lady herself looked around, preening a little, her back ramrod straight.

'When I first brought some of my paintings into the Scoto Gallery, Ms Ire saw them and called me an American primitive. I sort of resented that, because I change my underwear every morning and brush my teeth every night before I go to bed—'

Another burst of laughter. My legs were just legs again, not cement, and now that I felt capable of running away, I no longer wanted or needed to. It was possible they'd hate my pictures, but that was all right because *I* didn't hate them. Let them have their little laugh, their little boo-and-hiss, their little gasp of distaste (or their little yawn), if that was what they wanted to do; when it was over, I could go back and paint more.

And if they loved them? Same deal.

'But if she meant I'm someone who's doing something he doesn't understand, that he can't express in words because no one ever taught him the right terms, then she's right.'

Kamen was nodding and looking pleased. And so, by God, was Mary Ire.

'So all that leaves is the story of how I got here – the bridge I walked over to get from my other life to the one I'm living these days.'

Kamen was patting his meaty hands together soundlessly. That made me feel good. Having him there made me feel good. I don't know exactly what would have happened if he hadn't've been, but I think it would have been what Wireman calls *mucho feo* – very ugly.

'But I have to keep it simple, because my friend Wireman says that when it comes to the past, we all stack the deck, and I believe that's true. Tell too much and you find yourself . . . mmm . . . I don't know . . . telling the past you wished for?'

I looked down and saw Wireman was nodding.

'Yeah, I think so, the one you wished for. So simply put, what happened is this: I had an accident at a job site. Bad accident. There was this crane, you see, and it crushed the pickup truck I was in, and it crushed me, as well. I lost my right arm and I almost lost my life. I was married, but my marriage broke up. I was at my wits' end. This is a thing I see more clearly now; I only knew then that I felt very, very bad. Another friend, a man named Xander Kamen, asked me one day if anything made me happy. That was something . . .'

I paused. Kamen looked up intently from the first row with the long gift-box balanced on his non-lap. I remembered him that day at Lake Phalen – the tatty briefcase, the cold autumn sunshine coming and going in diagonal stripes across the living room floor. I remembered thinking about suicide, and the myriad roads leading into the dark: turnpikes and secondary highways and shaggy little forgotten lanes.

The silence was spinning out, but I no longer dreaded it. And my audience seemed not to mind. It was natural for my mind to wander. I was an *artist*.

'The idea of happiness – at least as it applied to me – was something I hadn't thought of in a long time,' I said. 'I thought of supporting my family, and after I started my own company, I thought of not letting down the people who worked for me. I also thought of becoming a success, and worked for it, mostly because so many people expected me to fail. Then the accident happened. Everything changed. I discovered I had no—'

I reached out for the word I wanted, groping with both hands, although they only saw one. And, perhaps, a twitch of the old stump inside its pinned-up sleeve.

'I had no resources to fall back on. As far as happiness went . . .' I shrugged. 'I told my friend Kamen that I used to draw, but I hadn't done it in a long time. He suggested I take it up again, and when I asked why, he said because I needed hedges against the night. I didn't understand what he meant then, because I was lost and confused and in pain. I understand it better now. People say night falls, but down here it rises. It rises out of the Gulf, after sunset's done. Seeing that happen amazed me.'

I was also amazed at my own unplanned eloquence. My right arm was quiet throughout. My right arm was just a stump inside a pinned-up sleeve.

'Could we have the lights all the way down? Including mine, please?'

Alice was running the board herself, and wasted no time. The spotlight in which I had been standing dimmed to a whisper. The auditorium was swallowed in gloom.

I said, 'What I discovered, crossing the bridge between my two lives, is that sometimes beauty grows in spite of all expectations. But that's not a very original idea, is it? It's really just a platitude . . . sort of like a Florida sunset. Nevertheless, it happens to be the truth, and the truth deserves to be spoken . . . *if* you can say it in a new way. I tried to put it in a picture. Alice, could we have the first slide, please?'

It shone out on the large screen to my right, nine feet wide and seven feet high: a trio of gigantic lush roses growing from a bed of dark pink shells. They were dark because they were below the house, in the shadow of the house. The audience drew in its breath, a sound like a brief but loud gust of wind. I heard that and knew it wasn't just Wireman and the folks at the Scoto who understood. Who saw. They gasped the way people do when they have been blindsided by something completely unexpected.

Then they began to applaud. It went on for almost a full minute. I stood there gripping the left side of the podium, listening, dazed.

The rest of the presentation took about twenty-five minutes, but I remember very little of it. I was like a man conducting a slide-show in a dream. I kept expecting to wake up in my hospital bed, hot and shot through with pain, roaring for morphine.

xii

That dreamlike feeling persisted through the post-lecture reception at the Scoto. I had no sooner finished my first glass of champagne (bigger than a thimble, but not much) before a second was thrust into my hand. I was toasted by people I didn't know. There were shouts of 'Hear, hear!' and one cry of 'Maestro!' I looked around for my new friends and didn't see them anywhere.

Not that there was much time to look. The congratulations seemed endless, both on my talk and on the slides. At least I didn't have to deal with any extended critiques of my technique, because the actual painting (plus a few sketches in colored pencil for good measure) were squirreled away in two of the large back rooms, safely under lock and key. And the secret of avoiding getting smashed at your reception if you're a one-armed man, I was discovering, was to constantly keep a bacon-wrapped shrimp in your remaining paw.

Mary Ire came by and asked if we were still on for our interview.

'Sure,' I said. 'Although I don't know what else I can tell you. I think I said it all this evening.'

'Oh, we'll think of a few things,' she said, and damned if she didn't tip me a wink from behind her nineteen-fifties-style cat's-eye glasses as she handed her champagne flute back to one of the circulating waiters. 'Day after tomorrow. À bientôt, monsieur.'

'You bet,' I said, restraining an urge to tell her that if she was going to speak French, she'd have to wait until I was wearing my Manet beret. She wafted off, kissing Dario on one cheek before slipping out into the fragrant March night.

Jack came over, snagging a couple of champagne flutes on the way. Juanita, my housekeeper, looking trim and chic in a little pink suit, was with him. She took a skewered shrimp, but refused the champagne. He held out the glass to me instead, waiting until I swallowed the last of my hors d'oeuvre and took it. Then he clinked his own against it.

303

'Congrats, boss – you rocked the house.'

'Thanks, Jack. A critic I can actually understand.' I swallowed the champagne (a swallow per flute is all there was) and turned to Juanita. 'You look absolutely beautiful.'

'*Gracias*, Mr Edgar,' she said, and glanced around. 'These pictures are nice, but yours are much better.'

'Thank you.'

Jack handed Juanita another shrimp. 'Will you excuse us a couple of seconds?'

'Of course.'

Jack drew me to the side of a splashy Gerstein sculpture. 'Mr Kamen asked Wireman if they could stay behind a little at the libe after the joint cleared out.'

'He did?' I felt a tickle of concern. 'Why?'

'Well, he spent most of the day getting down here, and he said that him and airplane heads really don't get along.' Jack grinned. 'He told Wireman he'd been sitting on something all day and sorta wanted to climb down off it in peace.'

I burst out laughing. Yet I was also touched. It couldn't be easy for a man of Kamen's size to travel on public transport . . . and now that I really considered the matter, I guessed it would be impossible for him to sit down in one of those paltry airplane bathrooms at all. To stand up and take a leak? Maybe. Barely. But not sit down. He simply wouldn't fit.

'Anyway, Wireman thought Mr Kamen deserved a T-O. Said you'd understand.'

'I do,' I said, and beckoned Juanita over. She looked too lonely standing there by herself in what was probably her best outfit while the culture vultures ebbed and flowed around her. I gave her a hug and she smiled up at me. And just as I was finally persuading her to take one of the glasses of champagne (my use of the word *pequeño* for small made her giggle, so I assumed it wasn't quite right), Wireman and Kamen – the latter still holding the gift-box – came in. Kamen lit up at the sight of me, and that did me more good than several rounds of applause, even with a standing O thrown in.

I took a champagne flute from a passing tray, cut through the crowd, and handed it to him. Then I slipped my arm around as much of his bulk as I could and gave him a hug. He hugged back hard enough to make my still tender ribs squall.

'Edgar, you look terrific. I'm so glad. God is good, my friend. God is good.'

'So are you,' I said. 'How'd you happen to turn up in Sarasota? Was it Wireman?' I turned to my *compadre* of the striped umbrella. 'It was, wasn't it? You called and asked Kamen if he'd be the Mystery Guest at my lecture.'

Wireman shook his head. 'I called *Pam*. I was in a panic, *muchacho,* because I could see you were freaking out about the gig. She said that after your accident you listened to Dr Kamen when you wouldn't listen to anyone else. So I called him. I never thought he'd come on such short notice, but . . . here he is.'

'Not only am I here, I brought you a gift from your daughters,' he said, and handed me the box. 'Although you'll have to make do with what I had in stock, because I didn't have time to shop. I fear you may be disappointed.'

I suddenly knew what the present was, and my mouth went dry. Nevertheless I lodged the box under my stump, pulled away the ribbon, and tore off the paper. I was barely aware of Juanita taking it. Inside was a narrow cardboard box that looked to me like a child's coffin. Of course. What else would it look like? Stamped on the lid was **MADE IN THE DOMINICAN REPUBLIC**.

'Classy, Doc,' Wireman said.

'I didn't have time to do something nicer, I'm afraid,' Kamen replied.

Their voices seemed to come from far away. Juanita removed the box-top. I think Jack took that. And then Reba was looking up at me, this time in a red dress instead of a blue one, but the polka-dots were the same; so were the shiny black Mary Janes, the lifeless red hair and the blue eyes that said *Oouuu, you nasty man! I been in here all this time!*

Still from a great distance, Kamen was saying: 'Ilse was the one who called and suggested a doll as a present. This was after she and her sister talked on the phone.'

Of course it was Ilse, I thought. I was aware of the steady murmur of conversation in the gallery, like the sound of the shells under Big Pink. My *Oh gosh, how nice* smile was still nailed to my face, but if

305

someone had poked me in the back just then, I might have screamed. *Ilse is the one who's been on Duma Key. Who's been down the road that leads past* El Palacio.

As shrewd as he was, I don't think Kamen had any idea that anything was wrong – but of course he'd been traveling all day and was far from his best. Wireman, however, was looking at me with his head cocked slightly to one side and his brow furrowed. And by then, I think Wireman knew me better than Dr Kamen ever had.

'She knew you already had one,' Kamen was saying. 'She thought a pair would remind you of both daughters, and Melinda agreed. But of course, Lucys are all I have—'

'Lucys?' Wireman asked, taking the doll. Her pink rag-stuffed legs dangled. Her shallow eyes stared.

'They look like Lucille Ball, don't you think? I give them to some of my patients, and of course they give them their own names. What did you name yours, Edgar?'

For a moment the old frost descended on my brain and I thought *Rhonda Robin Rachel, sit in the buddy, sit in the chum, sit in the fucking CHAR.* Then I thought, *It was RED.*

'Reba,' I said. 'Just like the country singer.'

'And do you still have her?' Kamen asked. 'Ilse said you did.'

'Oh, yes,' I said, and remembered Wireman talking about the Powerball, how you could close your eyes and hear the numbers falling into place: *Click* and *click* and *click.* I thought I could hear that now. The night I'd finished *Wireman Looks West,* I'd had visitors at Big Pink, little refugees seeking shelter from the storm. Elizabeth's drowned sisters, Tessie and Laura Eastlake. Now I was meant to have twins in Big Pink again, and why?

Because something had reached out, that was why. Something had reached out and put the idea in my daughter's head. This was the next click of the wheel, the next Ping-Pong ball to pop out of the basket.

'Edgar?' Wireman asked. 'Are you all right, *muchacho?*'

'Yes,' I said, and smiled. The world came swimming back, in all its light and color. I made myself take the doll from Juanita, who was looking at it with puzzlement. It was a hard thing to do, but I managed. 'Thank you, Dr Kamen. Xander.'

He shrugged and spread his hands. 'Thank your girls, Ilse in particular.'

'I will. Who's ready for another glass of champagne?'

They all were. I replaced my new doll in her box, promising myself two things. One was that neither of my daughters would ever know how badly seeing the damned thing had frightened me. The other promise was that I knew two sisters – two *living* sisters – who were never, ever, going to set foot on Duma Key at the same time. Or ever, if I could help it.

That was one promise that I kept.

12 – Another Florida

i

'All right, Edgar, I think we're almost finished.'

Maybe she saw something on my face, because Mary laughed. 'Has it been that awful?'

'No,' I said, and it hadn't been, really, although her questions about my technique had made me feel uncomfortable. What it came down to was I looked at things, then slopped on the paint. That was my technique. And influences? What could I say? The light. It always came down to the light, both in the pictures I liked to look at and the ones I liked to paint. What it did to the surface of things, and what it seemed to suggest about what was inside, hunting a way out. But that didn't sound scholarly; to my ears it sounded goofy.

'Okay,' she said, 'last subject: how many more paintings are there?'

We were sitting in Mary Ire's penthouse apartment on Davis Islands, a tony Tampa enclave which looked to me like the art deco capital of the world. The living room was a vast, nearly empty space with a couch at one end and two slingback chairs at the other. There were no books, but then, there was no TV, either. On the east wall, where it would catch the early light, was a large David Hockney. Mary and I were at opposite ends of the couch. She had her shorthand pad in her lap. There was an ashtray perched beside her on the arm of the sofa. Between us was a big silver Wollensak tape-recorder. It had to be fifty years old, but the reels turned soundlessly. German engineering, baby.

Mary wore no make-up, but her lips were coated with clear goo that made them shine. Her hair was tied up in a careless, coming-apart twist that looked simultaneously elegant and slatternly. She smoked English Ovals and sipped what looked like straight Scotch from a Waterford tumbler (she offered me a drink and seemed disappointed when I opted for bottled water). She wore tailored cotton

309

slacks. Her face looked old, used, and sexy. Its best days might have been around the time *Bonnie and Clyde* was playing in theaters, but her eyes were still breathtaking, even with lines at the corners, cracks in the eyelids, and no make-up to enhance them. They were Sophia Loren eyes.

'You showed twenty-two slides at the Selby. Nine were of pencil-sketches. Very interesting, but small. And eleven paintings, because there were actually three slides of *Wireman Looks West*, two close-ups and the wide-angle. So how many other paintings are there? How many will you be showing at the Scoto next month?'

'Well,' I said, 'I can't say for sure, because I'm painting all the time, but I think right now there are about . . . twenty more.'

'Twenty,' she said, softly and tonelessly. 'Twenty more.'

Something about the way she was looking at me made me uncomfortable and I shifted around. The sofa creaked. 'I think the actual number might be twenty-one.' Of course there were a few pictures I wasn't counting. *Friends with Benefits*, for instance. The one I sometimes thought of as *Candy Brown Loses His Breath*. And the red-robe sketch.

'So. Over thirty in all.'

I did the addition in my head and shifted around some more. 'I guess so.'

'And you have no idea how amazing that is. I can see by your face that you don't.' She got up, dumped her ashtray in a waste-basket behind the couch, then stood looking at the Hockney with her hands in the pockets of her expensive slacks. The painting showed a cube of a house and a blue swimming pool. Beside the pool was a ripe teenager in a black tank suit. She was all breasts and long tanned legs and dark hair. She wore dark glasses, and a tiny sun blazed in each lens.

'Is that an original?' I asked.

'Yes indeed,' she said, without turning. 'The girl in the swimsuit is an original, too. Mary Ire, circa 1962. Gidget in Tampa.' She turned to me, her face fierce. 'Turn that tape recorder off. The interview is over.'

I turned it off.

'I want you to listen to me. Will you?'

'Of course.'

310

'There are artists who labor for months over a single painting of half the quality your work shows. Of course many spend their mornings getting over the excesses of the night before. But *you* . . . you're producing these things like a man working on an assembly line. Like a magazine illustrator or a . . . I don't know . . . a comic-book artist!'

'I grew up believing folks were supposed to work hard at what they do – I think that's all it is. When I had my own company, I worked much longer hours, because the hardest boss a man can ever have is himself.'

She nodded. 'Not true for everyone, but when it is true, it's *really* true. I know.'

'I just carried that . . . you know, that ethic . . . over to what I do now. And it's all right. Hell, it's better than all right. I turn on the radio . . . it's like I go into a daze . . . and I paint . . .' I was blushing. 'I'm not trying to set the world's land-speed record, or anything—'

'I *know* that,' she said. 'Tell me, do you block?'

'Block?' I knew what the word meant in a football context; otherwise, I was drawing a blank. 'What's that?'

'Never mind. In *Wireman Looks West* – which is staggering, by the way, that *brain* – how did you set the features?'

'I took some pictures,' I said.

'I'm sure you did, darling, but when you got ready to paint the portrait, how did you set the features?'

'I . . . well, I—'

'Did you use the third-eye rule?'

'Third-eye rule? I never heard of any third-eye rule.'

She smiled at me kindly. 'In order to get the right spacing between a subject's eyes, painters will often imagine or even block a third eye between the two actual ones. What about the mouth? Did you center it using the ears?'

'No . . . that is, I didn't know you were supposed to do that.' Now it felt as if I were blushing all over my body.

'Relax,' she said. 'I'm not suggesting y'all start following a bunch of bullshit art school rules after breaking them so spectacularly. It's just . . .' She shook her head. 'Thirty paintings since last November? No, it's even less time than that, because you didn't start painting right away.'

311

'Of course not, I had to get some art supplies first,' I said, and Mary laughed herself into a coughing fit that she washed away with a sip of Scotch.

'If thirty paintings in three months is what almost getting crushed to death does,' she said when she could talk again, 'maybe I ought to find me a crane.'

'You wouldn't want to,' I said. 'Believe me.' I got up, went to the window, and looked down on Adalia Street. 'This is some place you've got here.'

She joined me, and we looked out together. The sidewalk café directly across and seven stories below might have been airlifted in from New Orleans. Or Paris. A woman strolled up the sidewalk eating what looked like a baguette, the hem of her red skirt swirling. Somewhere someone was playing a twelve-bar guitar blues, every note ringing clear. 'Tell me something, Edgar – when you look out there, does what you see interest you as an artist or as the builder you used to be?'

'Both,' I said.

She laughed. 'Fair enough. Davis Islands is entirely artificial – the brainchild of a man named Dave Davis. He was Jay Gatsby, Florida-style. Have you heard of him?'

I shook my head.

'That just proves that fame's a fleeting thing. During the Roaring Twenties, Davis was a god down here on the Suncoast.'

She waved an arm at the tangled streets below; the bangles on her scrawny wrist jangled; somewhere not too distant, a church-bell marked the hour of two.

'He dredged the whole thing from swampland at the mouth of the Hillsborough River. Talked the Tampa city fathers into moving both the hospital and the radio station here, back when radio was a bigger deal than health care. He built strange and beautiful apart-ment complexes in a time when the concept of an apartment complex was unknown. He put up hotels and swank nightclubs. He threw the dough around, married a beauty contest winner, divorced her, married her again. He was worth millions when a million dollars was worth what twelve million is today. And one of his best friends lived just down the coast on Duma Key. John Eastlake. Familiar with that name?'

'Of course. I've met his daughter. My friend Wireman takes care of her.'

Mary lit a fresh cigarette. 'Well, both Dave and John were as rich as Croesus – Dave with his land and building speculations, John with his mills – but Davis was a peacock and Eastlake was more of a plain brown wren. Just as well for him, because you know what happens to peacocks, don't you?'

'They get their tailfeathers chopped off?'

She took a drag on her latest cigarette, then pointed the fingers holding it at me as she jetted smoke from her nostrils. 'That would be correct, sir. In 1925, the Florida Land Bust hit this state like a brick on a soap bubble. Dave Davis had invested pretty much everything he had in what you see out there.' She waved at the zig-zaggy streets and pink buildings. 'In 1926, Davis was owed four million bucks on various successful ventures and collected something like thirty thousand.'

It had been awhile since I'd ridden on the tiger's neck – which was what my father called over-extending your resources to the point where you had to start juggling your creditors and getting creative with your paperwork – and I'd never ridden that far up, even in The Freemantle Company's early, desperate days. I felt for Dave Davis, long dead though he must be.

'How much of his own debts could he cover? Any?'

'He managed at first. Those were boom years in other parts of the country.'

'You know a lot about this.'

'Suncoast art is my passion, Edgar. Suncoast history is my hobby.'

'I see. So Davis survived the Land Bust.'

'For a short while. I imagine he sold his stocks on the bull market to cover his first round of losses. And friends helped him.'

'Eastlake?'

'John Eastlake was a major angel, and that's aside from any of Dave's bootleg hooch he may have stored out on the Key from time to time.'

'Did he do that?' I asked.

'*Maybe*, I said. That was another time and another Florida. You hear all sorts of colorful Prohibition-era booze-running stories if you live down here awhile. Booze or no booze, Davis would have been flat broke by Easter of '26 without John Eastlake. John was no playboy, didn't go nightclubbing and cathousing like Davis and some of Davis's other friends, but he'd been a widower since 1923, and I'm guessing that old Dave might have helped a pal with a gal from time to time when his pal was feeling lonely. But by the summer of '26, Dave's debts were just too high. Not even his old pals could save him.'

'So he disappeared one dark night.'

'He disappeared, but not by the dark of the moon. That was not the Davis style. In October of 1926, less than a month after Hurricane Esther knocked the living hell out of his life's work, he sailed for Europe with a bodyguard and *his* new gal-pal, who happened to be a Mack Sennett bathing beauty. The gal-pal and the bodyguard got to Gay Paree, but Dave Davis never did. He disappeared at sea, without a trace.'

'This is a true story you're telling me?'

She raised her right hand in the Boy Scout salute – the image slightly marred by the cigarette smoldering between her first two fingers. 'True blue. In November of '26, there was a memorial service right over there.' She pointed toward where the Gulf twinkled between two bright pink art deco buildings. 'At least four hundred people attended, many of them, I understand, the sort of women who were partial to ostrich feathers. One of the speakers was John Eastlake. He tossed a wreath of tropical flowers into the water.'

She sighed, and I caught a waft of her breath. I had no doubt that the lady could hold her liquor; I also had no doubt that she was well on her way to squiffy if not outright drunk this afternoon.

'Eastlake was undoubtedly sad about the passing of his friend,' she said, 'but I bet he was congratulating himself on surviving Esther. I bet they all were. Little did he know he'd be throwing more wreaths into the water less than six months later. Not just one daughter gone but two. Three, I suppose, if you count the eldest. She eloped to Atlanta. With a foreman from one of Daddy's mills, if memory serves. Although that's hardly the same as losing two in the Gulf. God, that must have been hard.'

'THEY ARE GONE,' I said, remembering the headline Wireman had quoted.

She glanced at me sharply. 'So you've done some research of your own.'

'Not me, Wireman. He was curious about the woman he was working for. I don't think he knows about the connection to this Dave Davis.'

She looked thoughtful. 'I wonder how much Elizabeth herself remembers?'

'These days she doesn't even remember her own name,' I said.

Mary gave me another look, then turned from the window, got her ashtray, and put out her cigarette. 'Alzheimer's? I'd heard rumors.'

'Yes.'

'I'm goddam sorry to hear it. I got the more lurid details of the Dave Davis story from her, you know. In better days. I used to see her all the time, on the circuit. And I interviewed most of the artists who stayed at Salmon Point. Only you call it something else, don't you?'

'Big Pink.'

She smiled. 'I knew it was something cute.'

'How many artists stayed there?'

'Lots. They came to lecture in Sarasota or Venice, and perhaps to paint for awhile – although those who stayed at Salmon Point did precious little of that. For most of Elizabeth's guests, their time on Duma Key amounted to little more than a free vacation.'

'She provided the place gratis?'

'Oh, yes,' she said, smiling rather ironically. 'The Sarasota Arts Council paid the honoraria for their lectures, and Elizabeth usually provided the lodging – Big Pink, née Salmon Point. But you didn't get that deal, did you? Perhaps next time. Especially since you actually *work* there. I could name half a dozen artists who stayed in your house and never so much as wet a brush.' She marched to the sofa, lifted her glass, and had a sip. No – a swallow.

'Elizabeth has a Dalí sketch that was done at Big Pink,' I said. 'That I saw with my own eyes.'

Mary's eyes gleamed. 'Oh, yes, well. Dalí. Dalí *loved* it there, but not even he stayed long . . . although before he left, the son of a bitch goosed me. Do you know what Elizabeth told me after he left?'

I shook my head. Of course I didn't, but I wanted to hear.

315

'He said it was "too rich". Does that strike a chord with you, Edgar?'

I smiled. 'Why do you suppose Elizabeth turned Big Pink into an artist's retreat? Was she always a patron of the arts?'

She looked surprised. 'Your friend didn't tell you? Perhaps he doesn't know. According to local legend, Elizabeth was once an artist of some note herself.'

'What do you mean, according to local legend?'

'There's a story – for all I know it's pure myth – that she was a child prodigy. That she painted beautifully, while very young, and then just stopped.'

'Did you ever ask her?'

'Of course, silly man. Asking people things is what I do.' She was swaying a bit on her feet now, the Sophia Loren eyes noticeably bloodshot.

'What did she say?'

'That there was nothing to it. She said, "Those who can, do. And those who can't, *support* those who can. Like us, Mary."'

'Sounds good to me,' I said.

'Yes, it did to me, too,' Mary said, taking another sip from her Waterford tumbler. 'The only problem I had with it was I didn't believe it.'

'Why not?'

'I don't know, I just didn't. I had an old friend named Aggie Winterborn who used to do the advice-to-the-lovelorn column in the Tampa *Trib*, and I happened to mention the story once to her. This was around the time Dalí was favoring the Suncoast with his presence, maybe 1980. We were in a bar somewhere – in those days we were always in a bar somewhere – and the conversation had turned to how legends are built. I mentioned the story of how Elizabeth had supposedly been a baby Rembrandt as an example of that, and Aggie – long dead, God rest her – said she didn't think that was a legend, she thought it was the truth, or a version of it. She said she'd seen a newspaper story about it.'

'Did you ever check?' I asked.

'Of course I did. I don't write everything I know' – she tipped me a wink – 'but I like to *know* everything.'

'What did you find?'

316

'Nothing. Not in the *Tribune*, not in the Sarasota or Venice papers, either. So maybe it *was* just a story. Hell, maybe all that stuff about her father storing Dave Davis's whiskey on Duma Key was just a story, too. But . . . I'd've bet money on Aggie Winterborn's memory. And Elizabeth had a look on her face when I asked her about it.'

'What kind of look?'

'An I'm-not-telling-*you* look. But all that's a long time ago, much booze under the bridge since, and you can't ask her about it now, can you? Not if she's as bad as you say.'

'No, but maybe she'll come back. Wireman says she has before.'

'We'll hope,' Mary said. 'She's a rarity, you know. Florida's full of old people – they don't call it God's waiting room for nothing – but precious few of em grew up here. The Suncoast Elizabeth remembers – *remembered* – really was another Florida. Not the hurry-scurry sprawl we have now, with the domed stadiums and the turn-pikes going everywhere, and not the one I grew up in, either. Mine was the John D. MacDonald Florida, back when people in Sarasota still knew their neighbors and the Tamiami Trail was a honky-tonk. Back then people sometimes still came home from church to find alligators in their swimming pools and bobcats rooting in their trash.'

She was actually *very* drunk, I realized . . . but that didn't make her uninteresting.

'The Florida Elizabeth and her sisters grew up in was the one that existed after the Indians were gone but before old Mr White Man had fully conshol . . . consolidated his hold. Your little island would have looked very different to you. I've seen the pictures. It was cabbage palms covered in strangler fig and gumbo limbo and slash pine inland; it was liveoak and mangrove in the few places the ground was wet. There was Cherokee bean and inkberry low on the ground, but none of that jungle shit that's growing out there now. The beaches are the only thing that's the same, and the sea oats, of course . . . like the hem of a skirt. The drawbridge was there at the north end, but there was just one house.'

'What caused all that growth?' I asked. 'Do you have any idea? I mean three quarters of the island is buried in it.'

She might not have heard. 'Just the one house,' she repeated. 'Sitting up there on the little rise of ground toward the south end and looking like something you'd see on the Gracious Homes Tour in Charleston or Mobile. Pillars and a crushed gravel drive. You had your grand view of the Gulf to the west; your grand view of the Florida coast looking east. Not that there was much to see; just Venice. Village of Venice. Sleepy li'l village.' She heard how she sounded and pulled herself together. 'Excuse me, Edgar. Please. I don't do this every day. Really, you should take my . . . my excitement . . . as a compliment.'

'I do.'

'Twenty years ago I would have tried to get you into bed instead of drinking myself stupid. Maybe even ten. As it is, I can only hope I haven't scared you away for good.'

'No such luck.'

She laughed, a caw both barren and cheery. 'Then I hope you'll come back soon. I make a mean red gumbo. But right now . . .' She put an arm around me and led me to the door. Her body was thin and hot and rock-hard beneath her clothes. Her gait was just south of steady. 'Right now I think it's time for you to go and for me to take my afternoon siesta. I regret to say I need it.'

I stepped out into the hall, then turned back. 'Mary, did you ever hear Elizabeth speak of the deaths of her twin sisters? She would have been four or five. Old enough to remember something so traumatic.'

'Never,' Mary said. 'Never once.'

ii

There were a dozen or so chairs lined up outside the lobby doors, in what was a thin but comfortable band of shade at quarter past two in the afternoon. Half a dozen oldsters were sitting there, watching the traffic on Adalia Street. Jack was also there, but he was neither watching the traffic nor admiring the passing ladies. He was tipped back against the pink stucco and reading *Mortuary Science for Dummies*. He marked his place and got up as soon as he saw me.

'Great choice for this state,' I said, nodding at the book with the trademark google-eyed nerd on the cover.

'I've got to pick a career sometime,' he said, 'and the way you're moving lately, I don't think this job is going to last much longer.'

'Don't hurry me,' I said, feeling in my pocket to make sure I had my little bottle of aspirin. I did.

'Actually,' Jack said, 'that's just what I'm going to do.'

'Have you got someplace you have to be?' I asked, limping down the cement walk beside him and into the sunshine. It was hot. There's spring on the west coast of Florida, but it only stops for a cup of coffee before heading north to do the heavy work.

'No, but you've got a four o'clock appointment with Dr Hadlock in Sarasota. I think we can just make it, if the traffic's kind.'

I stopped him with a hand on the shoulder. 'Elizabeth's doctor? What are you talking about?'

'For a physical. Word on the street is you've been putting it off, boss.'

'Wireman did this,' I muttered, and ran my hand through my hair. 'Wireman the doctor-hater. I'll never let him hear the end of it. You're my witness, Jack, I will *never*—'

'Nope, he said you'd say that,' Jack said. He tugged me back into motion. 'Come on, come on, we'll never beat the rush hour traffic if we don't get rolling.'

'Who? If Wireman didn't make the appointment, then who?'

'Your other friend. The big black dude. Man, I liked him, he was totally chilly.'

We'd reached the Malibu and Jack opened the passenger door for me, but for a moment I just stood there looking at him, thunderstruck. '*Kamen?*'

'Yep. Him and Dr Hadlock got talking at your reception after the lecture, and Dr Kamen just happened to mention that he was concerned because you still hadn't had the checkup you'd been promising to get. Dr Hadlock volunteered to give you one.'

'Volunteered,' I said.

Jack nodded, smiling in the bright Florida sunshine. Impossibly young, with a canary-yellow copy of *Mortuary Science for Dummies* tucked under his arm. 'Hadlock told Dr Kamen they couldn't let anything happen to such an important newly-discovered talent. And just for the record, I agree.'

'Thanks a pantload, Jack.'

He laughed. 'You're a trip, Edgar.'

'May I assume I'm also chilly?'

319

'Yup, you're a bad refrigerator. Get in, and let's get back over the bridge while we still can.'

iii

As it happened, we got to Dr Hadlock's Beneva Road office on the dot. Freemantle's Theorem of Office Waiting states that one must add thirty minutes to the time of one's appointment to arrive at the time one is actually seen, but in this case I was pleasantly surprised. The receptionist called my name at only ten past the hour and ushered me into a cheerful examination room where a poster to my left depicted a heart drowning in fat and one to my right showed a lung that looked charbroiled. The eye-chart directly ahead was a relief, even though I wasn't much good after the sixth line.

A nurse came in, put a thermometer under my tongue, took my pulse, wrapped a blood pressure cuff around my arm, inflated it, studied the readout. When I asked her how I was doing, she smiled noncommittally and said, 'You pass.' Then she drew blood. After that I retired to the bathroom with a plastic cup, sending Kamen bitter vibes as I unzipped my fly. A one-armed man can provide a urine sample, but the potential for accidents is greatly magnified.

When I returned to the exam room, the nurse was gone. She had left a folder with my name on it. Beside the folder was a red pen. My stump gave a twinge. Without thinking about what I was doing, I took the pen and put it in my pants pocket. There was a blue Bic clipped to my shirt pocket. I took it out and put it where the red pen had been lying.

And what are you going to say when she comes back? I asked myself. *That the Pen Fairy came in and decided to make a swap?*

Before I could answer that question – or consider why I had stolen the red pen to begin with – Gene Hadlock came in and offered his hand. His left hand . . . which in my case was the right one. I found I liked him quite a lot better when he was divorced from Principe, the goateed neurologist. He was about sixty, a little on the pudgy side, with a white mustache of the toothbrush variety and a pleasant examining-table manner. He had me strip down to my shorts and examined my right leg and side at some length. He prodded me in several places, enquiring about the level of pain. He asked me what I was taking for painkillers and seemed surprised when I told him I was getting by on aspirin.

'I'm going to examine your stump,' he said. 'That all right?'

'Yes. Just take it easy.'

'I'll do my best.'

I sat with my left hand resting on my bare left thigh, looking at the eye-chart as he grasped my shoulder with one hand and cupped my stump in the other. The seventh line on the chart looked like **AGODSED**. A god said what? I wondered.

From somewhere, very distant, I felt faint pressure. 'Hurt?'

'No.'

'Okay. No, don't look down, just keep looking straight ahead. Do you feel my hand?'

'Uh-huh. Way off. Pressure.' But no twinge. Why would there be? The arm that was no longer there had wanted the pen, and the pen was in my pocket, so now the arm was asleep again.

'And how about this, Edgar? May I call you Edgar?'

'Anything but late to dinner. The same. Pressure. Faint.'

'Now you can look.'

I looked. One hand was still on my shoulder, but the other was at his side. Nowhere near the stump. 'Oops.'

'Not at all, phantom sensations in the stump of a limb are normal. I'm just surprised at the rate of healing. And the lack of pain. I squeezed pretty darn hard to begin with. This is all good.' He cupped the stump again and pushed upward. 'Does that give pain?'

It did – a dull, low sparkle, vaguely hot. 'A little,' I said.

'If it didn't I'd be worried.' He let go. 'Look at the eye-chart again, all right?'

I did as he asked, and decided that all-important seventh line was **AGOCSEO**. Which made more sense because it made no sense.

'How many fingers am I touching you with, Edgar?'

'Don't know.' It didn't feel like he was touching me at all.

'Now?'

'Don't know.'

'And now.'

'Three.' He was almost up to my collarbone. And I had an idea

– crazy but very strong – that I would have been able to feel his fingers everywhere on the stump if I'd been in one of my painting frenzies. In fact, I would have been able to feel his fingers in the air below the stump. And I think *he* would have been able to feel *me* . . . which would no doubt have caused the good doctor to run screaming from the room.

He went on – first to my leg, then my head. He listened to my heart, looked into my eyes, and did a bunch of other doctorly things. When he'd exhausted most of the possibilities, he told me to get dressed and meet him at the end of the hall.

This turned out to be a pleasantly littered little office. Hadlock sat behind the desk and leaned back in his chair. There were pictures on one wall. Some, I assumed, were of the doctor's family, but there were also shots of him shaking hands with George Bush the First and Maury Povich (intellectual equals, in my book), and one of him with an amazingly vigorous and pretty Elizabeth Eastlake. They were holding tennis rackets, and I recognized the court. It was the one at *El Palacio*.

'I imagine you'd like to get back to Duma and get off that hip, wouldn't you?' Hadlock asked. 'Must hurt by this time of the day, and I bet it's all three witches from *Macbeth* when the weather's damp. If you want a prescription for Percocet or Vicodin—'

'No, I'm fine with the aspirin,' I said. I'd labored to get off the hard stuff and wasn't going back on it at this point, pain or no pain.

'Your recovery is remarkable,' Hadlock said. 'I don't think you need me to tell you how lucky you are not to be in a wheelchair for the rest of your life, very likely steering yourself around by blowing into a straw.'

'I'm lucky to be alive at all,' I said. 'Can I assume you didn't find anything dire?'

'Pending blood and urine, I'd say you're good to go. I'm happy to order X-rays on your rightside injuries and your head, if you've got symptoms that concern you, but—'

'I don't.' I had symptoms, and they concerned me, but I didn't think X-rays would pinpoint the cause. Or causes.

He nodded. 'The reason I went over your stump so carefully was because you don't wear a prosthesis. I thought you might be

322

experiencing tenderness. Or there might be signs of infection. But all seems well.'

'I guess I'm just not ready.'

'That's fine. More than fine. Considering the work you're doing, I'd have to say "If it ain't broke, don't fix it" applies here. Your paintings . . . remarkable. I can't wait to see them on display at the Scoto. I'm bringing my wife. She's very excited.'

'That's great,' I said. 'Thank you.' This sounded limp, at least to my own ears, but I still hadn't figured out how to respond to such compliments.

'Having you turn up as an actual paying tenant at Salmon Point is sad and ironic,' Hadlock said. 'For years – you might know this – Elizabeth reserved that house as an artist's retreat. Then she became ill and allowed it to be listed as just another rental property, although she *did* insist that whoever took it would have to lease it for three months or longer. She didn't want any Spring Breakers partying in there. Not where Salvador Dalí and James Bama once laid down their storied heads.'

'I can't say that I blame her. It's a special place.'

'Yes, but few of the famous artists who stayed there did anything special. Then the second "regular" tenant comes along – a building contractor from Minneapolis recovering from an accident, and . . . well. Elizabeth must be very gratified.'

'In the building biz, we called that laying it on with a trowel, Dr Hadlock.'

'Gene,' he said. 'And the people who were at your lecture didn't think so. You were marvelous. I only wish Elizabeth could have been there. How she would have *preened.*'

'Maybe she'll make the opening.'

Very slowly, Gene Hadlock shook his head. 'I doubt that. She's fought the Alzheimer's tooth and nail, but there comes a time when the disease simply wins. Not because the patient is weak but because it's a physical condition, like MS. Or cancer. Once the symptoms begin to manifest, usually as a loss of short-term memory, a clock begins to run. I think Elizabeth's time may be up, and I'm very sorry. It's clear to me, I think it was clear to everyone at the lecture, that all this fuss makes you uncomfortable—'

'You can say that again.'

'—but if she'd been there, she would have enjoyed it *for* you. I've known her most of my life, and I can tell you she would have supervised everything, including the hanging of each and every picture in the gallery.'

'I wish I'd known her then,' I said.

'She was amazing. When she was forty-five and I was twenty, we won the mixed doubles amateur tennis tournament at The Colony on Longboat Key. I was home from college on semester break. I've still got the cup. I imagine she's still got hers, somewhere.'

That made me think of something – *You'll find it, I'm sure* – but before I could chase that memory to its source, something else occurred to me. Something much more recent.

'Dr Hadlock – Gene – did Elizabeth herself ever paint? Or draw?'

'Elizabeth? Never.' And he smiled.

'You're sure of that.'

'You bet. I asked her once, and I remember the occasion very well. It was when Norman Rockwell was in town to lecture. He didn't stay at your place, either; he stayed at the Ritz. Norman Rockwell, pipe and all!' Gene Hadlock shook his head, smiling more widely now. 'Ye gods, what a controversy *that* was, the *howling* when the Arts Council announced Mr *Saturday Evening Post* was coming. It was Elizabeth's idea and she loved the hubbub it caused, said they could have filled Ben Hill Griffin Stadium—' He saw my blank look. 'The University of Florida. "The swamp where only Gators come out alive"?'

'If you're talking football, my interest begins with the Vikings and ends with the Packers.'

'The point is, I asked her about her own artistic abilities during the Rockwell uproar – and he did indeed sell out; not the Geldbart, either, but City Center. Elizabeth laughed and said she could hardly draw stick figures. In fact, she used a sports metaphor, which is probably why I thought of the Gators. She said she was like one of those wealthy college alumni, except she was interested in art instead of football. She said, "If you can't be an athlete, hon, be an athletic supporter. And if you can't be an artist, feed em, care for em, and make sure they have a place to come in out of the rain." But artistic talent herself? Absolutely none.'

I thought of telling him about Mary Ire's friend Aggie Winterborn.

324

Then I touched the red pen in my pocket and decided not to. I decided what I wanted to do was to get back to Duma Key and paint. *Girl and Ship No. 8* was the most ambitious of the series, also the largest and the most complex, and it was almost done.

I stood up and offered my hand. 'Thank you for everything.'

'Not at all. And if you change your mind and want something a little stronger for the pain—'

iv

The drawbridge to the Key was up to allow some rich guy's toy to wallow through the pass to the Gulf side. Jack sat behind the wheel of the Malibu, admiring the girl in the green bikini who was sunning on the foredeck. The Bone was on the radio. An ad for some motorcycle dealership ended (The Bone was big on motor-cycle sales and various mortgage services), and The Who came on: 'Magic Bus.' My stump began to tingle, then to itch. And that itch spread slowly downward, sleepy but deep. Very deep. I inched the volume up a tick, then reached into my pocket and pulled out the stolen pen. Not blue; not black; it was *red*. I admired it for a moment in the late sun. Then I thumbed open the glove compartment and pawed around.

'Help you find something, boss?'

'Nope. Keep your eye on yonder honey. I'm doin fine.'

I pulled out a coupon for a free Checkers NASCAR Burger – *Ya Gotta Eat!*, the coupon proclaimed. I turned it over. The flip side was blank. I drew quickly and without thinking. It was done before the song was. Underneath my small picture I printed five letters. The picture was similar to the doodles I'd done in my other life while dickering (usually with some dickhead) on the phone. The letters spelled *PERSE*, the name of my mystery ship. Only I didn't think that was how you said it. I could have added an accent over the *E*, but that would turn it into something that sounded like *Persay*, and I didn't think that was right, either.

'What's that?' Jack asked, looking over, then answered his own question. 'Little red picnic basket. Cute. But what's a Purse?'

'You say it *persie*.'

325

'I'll take your word for it.' The barrier at our end of the draw-bridge went up and Jack rolled across onto Duma Key.

I looked at the little red picnic basket I'd drawn – only I thought you called this kind, the kind with wicker sides, a hamper – and wondered why it looked so familiar. Then I realized it didn't, not exactly. It was the *phrase* that was familiar. *Look for Nan Somebody's picnic basket*, Elizabeth had said on the night I brought Wireman back from Sarasota Memorial. The last night I had seen her *compos mentis*, I realized now. *It's in the attic. It's red.* And: *You'll find it, I'm sure.* And: *They're inside.* Only when I had asked her what she was talking about, she hadn't been able to tell me. She had slipped away.

It's in the attic. It's red.

'Of course it is,' I said. 'Everything is.'

'What, Edgar?'

'Nothing,' I said, looking at the stolen pen. 'Just thinking out loud.'

v

Girl and Ship No. 8 – the last in the series, I felt almost sure – really *was* done, but I stood considering it in the lengthening light with my shirt off and The Bone blasting 'Copperhead Road'. I had worked on it longer than any of the others – had come to realize that in many ways it summed up the others – and it was disturbing. That was why I covered it with a piece of sheet at the end of my sessions. Now, looking at it with what I hoped was a dispassionate eye, I realized disturbing was probably the wrong word; that baby was fucking terrifying. Looking at it was like looking at a mind turned sideways.

And maybe it would never be *completely* done. Certainly there was still room for a red picnic basket. I could hang it over the *Perse's* bowsprit. What the hell, why not? The damned thing was crammed with figures and details as it was. Always room for one more.

I was reaching out a brush loaded with what could have been blood to do just that when the phone rang. I almost let it go – surely would have done, if I'd been in one of my painting trances

326

– but I wasn't. The picnic basket was only meant to be a grace note, and I had already added others. I put the brush back and picked up the phone. It was Wireman, and he sounded excited.

'She had a clear patch late this afternoon, Edgar! It might not mean anything – I'm trying to keep my hopes low – but I've seen this before. First one clear interval, then another, then another, then they start to merge together and she's herself again, at least for awhile.'

'She knows who she is? Where she is?'

'Not now, but for half an hour or so, starting around five-thirty, she knew that stuff and who I was, too. Listen, *muchacho* – she lit her own damn cigarette!'

'I'll be sure to tell the Surgeon General,' I said, but I was thinking. Five-thirty. Right around the time Jack and I had been waiting for the drawbridge. Around the time I'd felt that urge to draw.

'Did she want anything besides a cigarette?'

'She asked for food. But before that, she asked to go to the China Village. She wanted her chinas, Edgar! Do you know how long it's been?'

I did, actually. And it was good to hear him excited on her behalf.

'She started to fade after I got her there, though. She looked around and asked me where Percy was. She said she wanted Percy, that Percy needed to go in the cookie-tin.'

I looked at my painting. At my ship. It was mine now, all right. My *Perse*. I licked my lips, which suddenly felt leathery. The way they always had when I first woke up after the accident. When some of the time I couldn't remember who I was. Do you know what's queer? Remembering forgetting. It's like looking into a hall of mirrors. 'Which one is Percy?'

'Damned if I know. When she wants me to throw the cookie-tin in the goldfish pond, she always insists on putting a girl china in it. Usually the shepherdess with her face chipped off.'

'Did she say anything else?'

'She wanted food, I told you. Tomato soup. And peaches. By then she'd stopped looking at the chinas, and she was getting confused again.'

Had she gotten confused because Percy wasn't there? Or the *Perse*? Maybe ... but if she'd ever had a china boat, I'd never seen it. I thought – not for the first time – that Perse was a funny word. You couldn't trust it. It kept changing.

Wireman said, 'At one point she told me the table was leaking.'

'And was it?'

There was a brief pause. Then he said, not very humorously: 'Are we having a little joke at Wireman's expense, *mi amigo?*'

'No, I'm curious. What did she say? Exactly?'

'Just that. "The table is leaking." But her chinas are on a table-table, as you well know, not a water-table.'

'Calm down. Don't lose your good thoughts.'

'I'm trying not to, but I have to say you seem a little off your conversational game, Edster.'

'Don't call me Edster, it sounds like a vintage Ford. You brought her soup, and she was . . . what? Gone again?'

'Pretty much, yeah. She'd broken a couple of her china figures on the floor – a horse and a rodeo girl.' He sighed.

'Did she say "It's leaking" before or after you brought her the food?'

'After, before, what does it matter?'

'I don't know,' I said. 'Which was it?'

'Before. I think. Yes, before. Afterward, she'd pretty much lost interest in everything, including chucking the Sweet Owen tin into the pond for the umpteenth time. I brought the soup in her favorite mug, but she pushed it away so hard she slopped some on her poor old arm. She didn't even seem to feel it. Edgar, why are you asking these questions? What do you know?' He was pacing around with the cell phone to his ear. I could see him doing it.

'Nothing. I'm feeling around in the dark, for Chrissake.'

'Yeah? Which arm you doing it with?'

That stopped me for a moment, but we had come too far and shared too much for lies, even when the truth was nuts. 'My right one.'

'All right,' he said. 'All right, Edgar. I wish I knew what was going on, that's all. Because *something* is.'

'*Maybe* something is. How is she now?'

'Sleeping. And I'm interrupting you. You're working.'

'No,' I said, and tossed the brush aside. 'I think this is done, and

I think I'm also done for awhile. Just walking and shelling for me between now and the show.'

'Noble aspirations, but I don't think you can do it. Not a worka-holic like you.'

'I think you're wrong.'

'Okay, I'm wrong. Won't be the first time. Are you going to come down and visit with us tomorrow? I want you to see it if she lights up again.'

'Count on it. And maybe we could hit a few tennis balls.'

'Fine by me.'

'Wireman, there's one other thing. Did Elizabeth ever paint?'

He laughed. 'Who knows? I asked her once and she said she could hardly draw stick figures. She said her interest in the arts wasn't much different from the interest some wealthy alumni have in football and basketball. She joked about it, said—'

'If you can't be an athlete, be an athletic supporter.'

'Exactly. How'd you know?'

'It's an old one,' I said. 'See you tomorrow.'

I hung up and stood where I was, watching the long light of evening fire up a Gulf sunset I had no urge to paint. They were the same words she'd used with Gene Hadlock. And I had no doubt that if I asked others, I'd hear the same anecdote once or twice or a dozen times: *She said I can't even draw stick figures, she said if you can't be an athlete, be an athletic supporter.* And why? Because an honest woman may occasionally goof the truth, but a good liar never varies her story.

I hadn't asked him about the red picnic basket, but I told myself that was all right; if it was in the attic of *El Palacio*, it would still be there the next day, and the day after that. I told myself there was time. Of course, that's what we always tell ourselves, isn't it? We can't imagine time running out, and God punishes us for what we can't imagine.

I looked at *Ship and Girl No. 8* with something approaching distaste and threw the cover-sheet over it. I never added the red picnic hamper to the bowsprit; I never put a brush to that particu-lar painting again – the final mad descendent of my first sketch in Big Pink, the one I'd named *Hello. No. 8* may have been the best thing I ever did, but in a strange way, I almost forgot it. Until the show, that was. After that I could never forget it.

vi

The picnic basket.

That damned red picnic basket full of her drawings.

How that haunts me.

Even now, four years later, I find myself playing the what-if game, wondering how much would have changed if I'd pushed everything else aside and gone hunting for it. It *was* found − by Jack Cantori − but by then it was too late.

And maybe − I can't say for sure − it wouldn't have changed anything, because some force was at work, both on Duma Key and inside Edgar Freemantle. Can I say that force brought me there? No. Can I say it didn't? No, I can't say that, either. But by the time March became April, it had begun to gain strength and ever so stealthily extend its reach. *The water runs faster now,* Elizabeth had told me. *Soon come the rapids.* And they did come.

That basket.

Elizabeth's damned picnic basket.

It was *red.*

vii

Wireman's hope that Elizabeth was coming around began to seem unjustified. She remained a muttering lump in her wheelchair, every now and then stirring enough to cry out for a cigarette in the cracked voice of an aging parrot. He hired Annmarie Whistler away from Bay Area Private Nursing to come in and help him four days a week. The extra help might have eased Wireman's workload, but it did little to comfort him; he was heartsore.

But that was something I only glimpsed from the corner of my eye as April rolled in, sunny and hot. Because, speaking of hot . . . there I was.

Once Mary Ire's interview was published, I became a local celebrity. Why not? Artist was good, especially in the Sarasota area. Artist Who Used to Build Banks and Then Turned His Back on Mammon was better. One-Armed Artist of Blazing Talent was the absolute Golden Motherfucker. Dario and Jimmy scheduled a number of follow-up interviews, including one with Channel 6. I emerged from their Sarasota studio with a blinding headache and a complimentary CHANNEL 6 SUNCOAST WEATHER-WATCHER bumper sticker, which I ended up plastering on one of the **MEAN DOGS** sawhorses. Don't ask me why.

I also took over the Florida end of the travel-and-hospitality arrangements. Wireman was by then too busy trying to get Elizabeth to ingest anything but cigarette smoke. I found myself consulting with Pam every two or three days about the guest-list from Minnesota and travel arrangements from other parts of the country. Ilse called twice. I thought she was making an effort to sound cheerful, but I could have been wrong. My attempts to find out how her love-life was progressing were kindly but firmly blocked. Melinda called – to ask for my hat-size, of all things. When I asked why, she wouldn't tell. Fifteen minutes after she hung up, I realized: she and her French *ami* really were buying me a fucking beret. I burst out laughing.

An AP reporter from Tampa came to Sarasota – he wanted to come to Duma, but I didn't like the idea of a reporter tramping around in Big Pink, listening to what I now thought of as my shells. He interviewed me at the Scoto instead, while a photographer took pictures of three carefully selected paintings: *Roses Grow from Shells, Sunset with Sophora*, and *Duma Road*. I was wearing a Casey Key Fish House tee-shirt, and a photo of me – baseball cap on backwards and one short sleeve empty except for a nub of stump – ran nationwide. After that, my telephone rang off the hook. Angel Slobotnik called and talked for twenty minutes. At one point, he said he always knew I had it in me. 'What?' I asked. His reply was 'Bullshit, boss,' and we laughed like maniacs. Kathi Green called; I heard all about her new boyfriend (not so good) and her new self-help program (wonderful). I told her about how Kamen had shown up at the lecture and saved my ass. By the end of that call she was crying and saying she'd never had such a gutty, come-from-behind patient. Then she said when she saw me she was going to tell me to drop and give her fifty sit-ups. That sounded like the old Kathi. To top it all off, Todd Jamieson, the doctor who had probably saved me from a decade or two as a human rutabaga, sent me a bottle of champagne with a card reading, *Cannot wait to see your work.*

331

If Wireman had bet me on whether or not I'd get bored and pick up a brush again before the show, he would have lost. When I wasn't getting ready for my big moment, I was walking, reading, or sleeping. I mentioned this to him on one of the rare afternoons when we were together at the end of *El Palacio*'s boardwalk, drinking green tea under the striped umbrella. This was less than a week before the show.

'I'm glad,' he said simply. 'You needed to rest.'

'What about you, Wireman? How are you doing?'

'Not great, but I will survive – Gloria Gaynor, 1978. It's sadness, mostly.' He sighed. 'I'm going to lose her. I kidded myself that maybe she was coming back, but . . . I'm going to lose her. It's not like Julia and Esmeralda, thank God, but it still weighs on me.'

'I'm sorry.' I laid my hand over his. 'For her *and* for you.'

'Thanks.' He looked out at the waves. 'Sometimes I think she won't die at all.'

'No?'

'No. I think the Walrus and the Carpenter will come for her, instead. That they'll just lead her away like they did those trusting Oysters. Lead her away down the beach. Do you remember what the Walrus says?'

I shook my head.

'"It seems a shame to play them such a trick, After we've brought them out so far, And made them trot so quick."' He swiped an arm across his face. 'Look at me, *muchacho*, crying just like the Walrus. Ain't I stupid.'

'No,' I said.

'I hate to face the idea that this time she's gone for good, that the best part of her went off down the beach with the Walrus and the Carpenter and there's nothing left but a fat old piece of suet that hasn't quite forgotten how to breathe yet.'

I said nothing. He wiped his eyes again with his forearm and drew in a long, watery breath. Then he said, 'I looked into the story of John Eastlake, and how his daughters were drowned, and what happened after – do you remember asking me to do that?'

I did, but it seemed long ago, and unimportant. What I think now is that something *wanted* it to seem that way to me.

'I went surfing around on the Internet and came up with a good deal from the local newspapers and a couple of memoirs that are available for download. One of them – I shit you not, *muchacho* – is called *Boat Trips and Beeswax, A Girlhood in Nokomis*, by Stephanie Weider Gravel-Miller.'

'Sounds like quite a trip down memory lane.'

'It was. She talks about "the happy darkies, picking oranges and singing simple songs of praise in their mellifluous voices." '

'I guess that was before Jay-Z.'

'Got that right. Even better, I talked to Chris Shannington, over on Casey Key – you've almost certainly seen him. Colorful old geezer who walks everyplace with this gnarled briarwood cane, almost as tall as he is, and a big straw hat on his head. His father, Ellis Shannington, was John Eastlake's gardener. According to Chris, it was Ellis who took Maria and Hannah, Elizabeth's two older sisters, back to the Braden School ten days or so after the drowning. He said, "Those chirrun were heartbroken for the babby-uns." '

Wireman's imitation of the old man's southern accent was eerily good, and I found myself for some reason thinking of the Walrus and the Carpenter again, walking up the beach with the little Oysters. The only part of the poem I could remember clearly was the Carpenter telling them they'd had a pleasant run, but of course the Oysters couldn't answer, for they'd been eaten – every one.

'Do you want to hear this now?' Wireman asked.

'Have you got time to tell me now?'

'Sure. Annmarie's got the duty until seven, although as a matter of practical fact, we share it most days. Why don't we walk up to the house? I've got a file. There isn't much in it, but there's at least one picture that's worth looking at. Chris Shannington had it in a box of his father's things. I walked up to the Casey Key Public Library with him and copied it.' He paused. 'It's a picture of Heron's Roost.'

'As it was back then, you mean?'

We had started to stroll back up the boardwalk, but Wireman stopped. 'No, *amigo*, you misunderstand. I'm talking about the *original* Heron's Roost. *El Palacio* is the *second* Roost, built almost twenty-five years after the little girls drowned. By then, John Eastlake's ten or twenty million had grown to a hundred and fifty million or so. War Is Good Business, Invest Your Son.'

333

'Vietnam protest movement, 1969,' I said. 'Often seen in tandem with A Woman Needs a Man Like a Fish Needs a Bicycle.'

'Good, *amigo*,' Wireman said. He waved a hand toward the riotous greenery that began just south of us. 'The first Heron's Roost was out there, back when the world was young and flappers said *poop-oopie-doop*.'

I thought of Mary Ire, not just tiddly or squiffy but downright drunk, saying *Just the one house, sitting up there and looking like something you'd see on the Gracious Homes Tour in Charleston or Mobile.*

'What happened to it?' I asked.

'So far as I know, nothing but time and decay,' he said. 'When John Eastlake gave up on recovering the bodies of his twins, he gave up on Duma Key, too. He paid off most of the help, packed his traps, took the three daughters who remained to him, got in his Rolls-Royce – he really had one – and drove away. A novel F. Scott Fitzgerald never wrote, that's what Chris Shannington said. Told me Eastlake was never at peace until Elizabeth brought him back here.'

'Do you think that's something Shannington actually knows, or just a story he's gotten used to hearing himself tell?'

'*Quién sabe?*' Wireman said. He stopped again and waved toward the southern end of Duma Key. 'No overgrowth back then. You could see the original house from the mainland and vice-versa. And so far as I know, *amigo*, the house is still there. Whatever's left of it. Sitting and rotting.' He reached the kitchen door and looked at me, unsmiling. '*That* would be something to paint, wouldn't it? A ghost-ship on dry land.'

'Maybe,' I said. 'Maybe it would.'

viii

He took me into the library with the suit of armor in the corner and the museum-quality weapons on the wall. There, on the table next to the telephone, was a folder marked JOHN EASTLAKE/ HERON'S ROOST I. He opened it and removed a photograph showing a house that bore an unmistakable similarity to the one we were in – the similarity, say, of first cousins. Yet there was one basic difference between the two, and the similarities – the same

334

basic footprint for both houses, I thought, and the same roof of bright orange Spanish tile – only underlined it.

The current *Palacio* hid from the world behind a high wall broken by only a single gate – there wasn't even a tradesman's entrance. It had a beautiful interior courtyard which few people other than Wireman, Annmarie, the pool girl, and the twice-weekly gardener ever saw; it was like the body of a beautiful woman hidden under a shapeless piece of clothing.

The first Heron's Roost was very different. Like Elizabeth's mansion in China Town, it featured half a dozen pillars and a broad, welcoming verandah. It had a wide drive sweeping boldly up to it, splitting what looked like two acres of lawn. Not a gravel drive, either, as Mary Ire had told me, but rosy crushed shells. The original had invited the world in. Its successor – *El Palacio* – told the world to stay the hell out. Ilse had seen that at once, and so had I, but that day we had been looking from the road. Since then my view had changed, and with good reason: I had gotten used to seeing it from the beach. To coming upon it from its unarmored side.

The first Heron's Roost had also been higher, three stories in front and four in back, so – if it really did stand on a rise, as Mary had said – people on the top floor would have had a breathtaking three-hundred-and-sixty-degree view of the Gulf, the mainland, Casey Key, and Don Pedro Island. Not bad. But the lawn looked strangely ragged – unkempt – and there were holes in the line of ornamental palms dancing like hula girls on either side of the house. I looked closer and saw that some of the upper windows had been boarded up. The roofline had a strangely unbalanced look, too. It took a second to realize why. There was a chimney at the east end. There should have been another at the west end, but there wasn't.

'Was this taken after they left?' I asked.

He shook his head. 'According to Shannington, it was snapped in March of 1927, before the little girls drowned, when everyone was still happy and well. That isn't dilapidation you see, it's storm-damage. From an Alice.'

'Which is what?'

'Hurricane season officially starts June fifteenth down here and lasts about five months. Out-of-season storms with torrential rains and high winds . . . as far as the old-timers are concerned, they're all Alice. As in Hurricane Alice. It's kind of a joke.'

'You're making that up.'

'Nope. Esther – the big one in '26 – missed Duma completely, but the Alice in March of '27 hit it pretty much dead-on. Then it blew inland and drowned in the Glades. It did the damage you see in this picture – not much, really; blew down some palms, knocked out some glass, tore up the lawn. But in another way, its effects are still being felt. Because it seems pretty certain it was that Alice that led to the drowning deaths of Tessie and Laura, and that led to everything else. Including you and me standing here now.'

'Explain.'

'Remember this?'

He took another photo from his folder, and I certainly did remember it. The big one was on the second-floor landing of the main staircase. This was a smaller, sharper copy. It was the Eastlake family, with John Eastlake wearing a black bathing singlet and looking like a Hollywood B-list actor who might have specialized in detective movies and jungle epics. He was holding Elizabeth. One hand cupped her plump little bottom. The other held that harpoon pistol, and a face-mask with an attached snorkel.

'Judging just by Elizabeth, I'm going to guess this might have been taken around 1925,' Wireman said. 'She looks two, going on three. And Adriana' – he tapped the eldest – 'looks like she might be seventeen going on thirty-four, wouldn't you say?'

Indeed. Seventeen and ripe, even in her it-covers-damn-near-everything bathing suit.

'She's already got that sulky, pouty I-want-to-be-somewhere-else look, too,' Wireman said. 'I wonder just how surprised her father was when she up and eloped with one of his plant managers. And I wonder if he wasn't, in his heart of hearts, glad to see her go.' He put on his Chris Shannington drawl. 'Run off to Atlanta with a boy in a tie and an eyeshade.' Then he quit it. I guessed the subject of little dead girls, even ones lost eighty years ago, was still a tender one with him. 'She and her new hubby came back, but by then it was just a hunt for the bodies.'

I tapped the grim-faced black nanny. 'Who was this?'

'Melda or Tilda or maybe even, God save us, Hecuba, according to Chris Shannington. His father knew, but Chris no longer remembers.'

'Nice bracelets.'

He glanced at them without much interest. 'If you say so.'

'Maybe John Eastlake was sleeping with her,' I said. 'Maybe the bracelets were a little present.'

'*Quién sabe?* Rich widower, young woman – it's been known to happen.'

I tapped the picnic basket, which the young black woman was holding with both hands, her arms bunched as though it was heavy. Heavier than just a few sandwiches could account for, you'd think . . . but maybe there was a whole chicken in there. And maybe a few bottles of beer for ole massa, as well – a little reward after he'd finished his day's dives. 'What color would you say that hamper is? Dark brown? Or is it red?'

Wireman gave me a strange look. 'In a black-and-white photograph, it's hard to tell.'

'Tell me how the storm led to the deaths of the little girls.'

He opened the folder again and handed me an old news story with an accompanying photograph. 'This is from the Venice *Gondolier*, March 28th, 1927. I got the original info on the net. Jack Cantori called the paper, got someone to make a copy and shoot me a fax. Jack's terrific, by the way.'

'No argument there,' I said. I studied the photo. 'Who are these girls? No – don't tell me. The one on his left's Maria. Hannah's on his right.'

'A-plus. Hannah's the one with breasts. She was fourteen in '27.'

We studied the fax sheet in silence for a few moments. E-mail would have been better. The fax had annoying dark vertical lines running through it, blurring some of the print, but the headline was clear enough: **STORM PROVES TREASURE-HUNTING BOON TO AMATEUR DIVER**. And the picture was clear enough, too. Eastlake's hairline had receded a little. As if to compensate, his narrow bandleader's mustache was now closer to a walrus. And although he was still wearing the same black bathing singlet, it was now under severe stress . . . and actually popped under one arm, I thought, although the picture's resolution wasn't quite good enough to be certain. It appeared Dad Eastlake had packed on some

337

pork between 1925 and 1927 – the B-movie actor would have trouble getting roles if he didn't start skipping desserts and doing more work in the gym. The girls flanking him weren't as sloe-eyed-sexy as their big sister – you looked at Adriana and thought about hot afternoons in a haymow, you looked at these two and wondered if they were getting their schoolwork done – but they were pretty in a not-quite-there-yet way, and their excitement shone out in the picture. Sure it did.

Because, spread before them on the sand, was treasure.

'I can't make it all out, and the damn caption's blurry,' I complained.

'There's a magnifying glass in the desk, but let me save you a headache.' Wireman picked up a pen and pointed with the tip. 'That's a medicine bottle, and that there is a musket-ball – or so Eastlake claims in the story. Maria's got her hand on what appears to be a boot . . . or the remains of one. Next to the boot—'

'Pair of spectacles,' I said. 'And . . . a necklace-chain?'

'The story claims it's a bracelet. I don't know. All I could swear to is a metal loop of some kind, overgrown with crud. But the older girl's definitely holding out an earring.'

I scanned the story. In addition to the stuff on view, Eastlake had found various eating utensils . . . four cups he claimed were 'Italianate' . . . a trivet . . . a box of gears (whatever that might mean) . . . and nails without number. He had also found half a China Man. Not a Chinaman; a China Man. It wasn't pictured, at least not that I could see. The story said Eastlake had been diving on the eroded reefs west of Duma Key for fifteen years, sometimes to fish, often just to relax. He said he had found all sorts of litter, but nothing of interest. He said that the Alice (he called it that) had generated some remarkably big waves, and they must have shifted the sand inside the reef just enough to reveal what he called 'a dumping field'.

'He doesn't call it a wreck,' I said.

'It wasn't,' Wireman said. 'There was no boat. He didn't find one, and neither did the dozens of people who helped him try to recover the bodies of his little girls. Only detritus. They would have found a wreck if there was a wreck to find; the water on the southwest end of the Key is no more than twenty-five feet deep all the way out to what remains of Kitt Reef, and it's pretty clear now. Back then it was like turquoise glass.'

338

'Any theories about how it came to be there?'

'Sure. The best is that some boat close to foundering came blowing in a hundred, two hundred, three hundred years before, shedding shit as it came. Or maybe the crew was tossing stuff overboard to stay afloat. They made repairs after the storm was over and went on their way. It would explain why there was a swath of detritus for Eastlake to find, and also why none of it was particularly valuable. Treasure would have stayed with the ship.'

'And the reef wouldn't have ripped the keel out of a boat that got blown in here back in the 1700s? Or 1600s?'

Wireman shrugged. 'Chris Shannington says no one knows what the geography of Kitt Reef might have been a hundred and fifty years ago.'

I looked at the spread-out loot. The smiling middle daughters. The smiling Daddy, who was soon going to have to buy himself a new bathing costume. And I suddenly decided he hadn't been sleeping with the nanny. No. Even a mistress would have told him he couldn't have a newspaper photo of himself taken in that old thing. She would have found a tactful reason, but the real one was right in front of me, after all these years; even with less-than-perfect vision in my right eye, I could see it. He was too fat. Only he didn't see it, and his daughters didn't see it, either. Loving eyes did not see.

Too fat. Something there, wasn't there? Some A that practically demanded a B.

'I'm surprised he talked about what he found at all,' I said. 'If you happened on stuff like this today and then blabbed to Channel 6, half of Florida would show up in their little putt-putts, hunting for doubloons and pieces of eight with metal detectors.'

'Ah, but this was another Florida,' Wireman said, and I remembered Mary Ire using the same phrase. 'John Eastlake was a rich man, and Duma Key was his private preserve. Besides, there were no doubloons, no pieces of eight – just moderately interesting junk uncovered by a freak storm. For weeks he went down and dived where that debris was scattered on the floor of the Gulf – and it was close in, according to Shannington; at low tide, you could practically wade to it. And sure, he was probably keeping an eye out for valuables. He was a rich man, but I don't think that vaccinates a man against the treasure-bug.'

'No,' I said. 'I'm sure it doesn't.'

'The nanny would have gone with him on his treasure-hunting expeditions. The three still-at-home girls, too: the twins and Elizabeth. Maria and Hannah were back at their boarding school in Bradenton, and big sis had run off to Atlanta. Eastlake and his little ones probably had picnics down there.'

'How often?' I began to see where this was going.

'Often. Maybe every day while the debris field was at its richest. They wore a path from the house to what was called Shade Beach. It was half a mile, if that.'

'A path two adventurous little girls could follow on their own.'

'And one day did. To everyone's sorrow.' He swept the pictures back into the folder. 'There's a story here, *muchacho,* and I suppose it's marginally more interesting than a little girl swallowing a marble, but a tragedy is a tragedy, and at the bottom, all tragedies are stupid. Give me a choice and I'll take *A Midsummer Night's Dream* over *Hamlet* every time. Any fool with steady hands and a working set of lungs can build up a house of cards and then blow it down, but it takes a genius to make people laugh.'

He brooded a moment.

'What probably happened is that one day in April of 1927, when Tessie and Laura were supposed to be napping, they decided to get up, sneak down the path, and go hunting for treasure at Shade Beach. Probably they meant to do no more than wade in as far as their knees, which is all they were permitted to do – one of the stories quotes John Eastlake as saying that, and Adriana backed him up.'

'The married daughter who came back.'

'Right. She and her new husband returned a day or two before the search for the bodies was officially called off. That's according to Shannington. Anyway, one of the little girls maybe saw something gleaming a little further out and started to flounder. Then—'

'Then her sister tried to save her.' Yes, I could see it. Only I saw Lin and Ilse as they'd been when they were small. Not twins, but for three or four golden years nearly inseparable.

Wireman nodded. 'And then the rip took em both. Had to've been that way, *amigo;* that's why the bodies weren't found. Off they went, heigh-ho for the *caldo largo.*'

I opened my mouth to ask him what he meant by the rip, then remembered a painting by Winslow Homer, romantic but of undeniable power: *Undertow*.

The intercom on the wall beeped, startling us both. Wireman struck the folder with his arm as he turned around, knocking photocopies and faxes everywhere.

'Mr Wireman!' It was Annmarie Whistler. 'Mr Wireman, are you there?'

'I'm here,' Wireman said.

'Mr Wireman?' She sounded agitated. Then, as if to herself: 'Jesus, where *are* you?'

'The fucking button,' he muttered, and went to the wall unit, not quite running. He pushed the button. 'I'm here. What's wrong? What's happened? Did she fall?'

'No!' Annmarie cried. 'She's awake! Awake and *aware*! She's asking for you! Can you come?'

'Right away,' he said, and turned to me, grinning. 'Do you hear that, Edgar? Come on!' He paused. 'What are you looking at?'

'These,' I said, and held out the two pictures of Eastlake in his bathing dress: the one where he was surrounded by all his daughters, and the one taken two years later, where he was flanked by just Maria and Hannah.

'Never mind em now – didn't you hear her? Miss Eastlake is *back*!' He booked for the door. I dropped his folder on the library table and followed him. I had made the connection – but only because I'd spent the last few months cultivating the art of seeing. Cultivating it strenuously.

'Wireman!' I called. He'd gone the length of the dogtrot and was halfway up the staircase. I was limping as fast as I could and he was still pulling away. He waited for me, not very patiently. 'Who told him the debris field was there?'

'Eastlake? I assume he stumbled on it while pursuing his diving hobby.'

'I don't think so – he hadn't been in that bathing suit for a long time. Diving and snorkeling may have been his hobby in the early twenties, but I think that around 1925, eating dinner became his chief diversion. So who told him?'

Annmarie came out of a door near the end of the hall. There

341

was a goofy, unbelieving grin on her face that made her look half her forty years.

'Come on,' she said. 'This is wonderful.'

'Is she—'

'She is,' came Elizabeth's cracked but unmistakable voice. 'Come in here, Wireman, and let me see your face while I still know it.'

ix

I lingered in the hall with Annmarie, not sure what to do, looking at the knickknacks and the big old Frederic Remington at the far end – Indians on ponies. Then Wireman called for me. His voice was impatient and rough with tears.

The room was dim. The shades had all been drawn. Air conditioning whispered through a vent somewhere above us. There was a table next to her bed with a lamp on it. The shade was green glass. The bed was the hospital kind, and cranked up so she could almost sit. The lamp put her in a soft spotlight, with her hair loose on the shoulders of a pink dressing gown. Wireman sat beside her, holding her hands. Above her bed was the only painting in the room, a fine print of Edward Hopper's *Eleven a.m.*, an archetype of loneliness waiting patiently at the window for some change, any change.

Somewhere a clock was ticking.

She looked at me and smiled. I saw three things in her face. They hit me one after the other like stones, each one heavier than the last. The first was how much weight she'd lost. The second was that she looked horribly tired. The third was that she hadn't long to live.

'Edward,' she said.

'No—' I began, but when she raised one hand (the flesh hanging down in a snow-white bag above her elbow), I stilled at once. Because here was a fourth thing to see, and it hit hardest of all – not a stone but a boulder. I was looking at myself. This was what people had seen in the aftermath of my accident, when I was trying to sweep together the poor scattered bits of my memory – all that treasure that looked like trash when it was spread out in such ugly, naked fashion. I thought of how I had forgotten my doll's name, and I knew what was coming next.

342

'I can do this,' she said.

'I know you can,' I said.

'You brought Wireman back from the hospital,' she said.

'Yes.'

'I was so afraid they'd keep him. And I would be alone.'

I didn't reply to this.

'Are you Edmund?' she asked timidly.

'Miss Eastlake, don't tax yourself,' Wireman said gently. 'This is—'

'Hush, Wireman,' I said. 'She can do this.'

'You paint,' she said.

'Yes.'

'Have you painted the ship yet?'

A curious thing happened to my stomach. It didn't sink so much as it seemed to disappear and leave a void between my heart and the rest of my guts. My knees tried to buckle. The steel in my hip went hot. The back of my neck went cold. And warm, prickling fire ran up the arm that wasn't there.

'Yes,' I said. 'Again and again and again.'

'You're Edgar,' she said.

'Yes, Elizabeth. I'm Edgar. Good for you, honey.'

She smiled. I guessed no one had called her honey in a long time. 'My mind is like a tablecloth with a great big hole burned into it.' She turned to Wireman. '*Muy divertido, sí?*'

'You need to rest,' he said. 'In fact, you need to *dormir como un tronco.*'

She smiled faintly. 'Like a log. Yes. And I think when I wake up, I'll still be here. For a little while.' She lifted his hands to her face and kissed them. 'I love you, Wireman.'

'I love you, too, Miss Eastlake,' he said. Good for him.

'Edgar? . . . Is it Edgar?'

'What do you think, Elizabeth?'

'Yes, of course it is. You're to have a show? Is that how we left things before my last . . .' She drooped her eyelids, as if to mime sleep.

'Yes, at the Scoto Gallery. You really need to rest.'

'Is it soon? Your show?'

'In less than a week.'

'Your paintings . . . the ship paintings . . . are they on the mainland? At the gallery?'

343

Wireman and I exchanged a look. He shrugged.

'Yes,' I said.

'Good.' She smiled. 'I'll rest, then. Everything else can wait . . . until after you have your show. Your moment in the sun. Are you selling them? The ship pictures?'

Wireman and I exchanged another look, and the message in his eyes was very clear: *Don't upset her.*

'They're marked NFS, Elizabeth. That means—'

'I know what it means, Edgar, I didn't fall out of an orange tree yesterday.' Inside their deep pockets of wrinkles, caught in a face that was receding toward death, her eyes flashed. 'Sell them. However many there are, *you must sell them*. And however hard it is for you. Break them up, send them to the four winds. Do you understand me?'

'Yes.'

'Will you do it?'

I didn't know if I would or not, but I recognized her signs of growing agitation from my own not-so-distant past. 'Yes.' At that point, I would have promised her to jump to the moon in seven-league boots, if it would have eased her mind.

'Even then they may not be safe,' she mused in an almost-horrified voice.

'Stop, now,' I said, and patted her hand. 'Stop thinking about this.'

'All right. We'll talk more after your show. The three of us. I'll be stronger . . . clearer . . . and you, Edgar, will be able to pay attention. Do you have daughters? I seem to remember that you do.'

'Yes, and they're staying on the mainland with their mother. At the Ritz. That's already arranged.'

She smiled, but the corners drooped almost at once. It was as if her mouth were melting. 'Crank me down, Wireman. I've been in the swamp . . . forty days and forty nights . . . so it feels . . . and I'm tired.'

He cranked her down, and Annmarie came in with something in a glass on a tray. No chance Elizabeth was going to drink any of it; she had already corked off. Over her head, the loneliest girl in the world sat in a chair and looked out the window forever, face hidden by the fall of her hair, naked but for a pair of shoes.

x

For me, sleep was long in coming that night. It was after midnight before I finally slipped away. The tide had withdrawn, and the whispered conversation under the house had ceased. That didn't stop the whispered voices in my head, however.

Another Florida, Mary Ire whispered. *That was another Florida.*

Sell them. However many there are, you must sell them. That was Elizabeth, of course.

The *grown* Elizabeth. I heard another version of her, however, and because I had to make this voice up, what I heard was Ilse's voice as it had been as a child.

There's treasure, Daddy, this voice said. *You can get it if you put on your mask and snorkel. I can show you where to look.*

I drew a picture.

xi

I was up with the dawn. I thought I could go to sleep again, but not until I took one of the few Oxycontin pills I still had put aside, and until I made a telephone call. I took the pill, then dialed the Scoto and got the answering machine – there wouldn't be a living person in the gallery for hours yet. Artistic types aren't morning people.

I pushed 11 for Dario Nannuzzi's extension, and after the beep I said: 'Dario, it's Edgar. I've changed my mind about the *Girl and Ship* series. I want to sell them after all, okay? The only *caveat* is that they should all go to different people, if possible. Thanks.'

I hung up and went back to bed. Lay there for fifteen minutes watching the overhead fan turn lazily and listening to the shells whisper beneath me. The pill was working, but I wasn't drifting off. And I knew why.

I knew exactly why.

I got up again, hit redial, listened to the recorded message, then punched in Dario's extension one more time. His recorded voice invited me to leave a message at the beep. 'Except for *No. 8*,' I said. 'That one is still NFS.'

345

And *why* was it NFS?

Not because it was genius, although I think it was. Not even because when I looked at it, it was – for me – like listening to the darkest part of my heart telling its tale. It was because I felt that something had let me live just to paint it, and that to sell it would be to deny my own life, and all the pain I had undergone to reclaim it.

Yeah, that.

'That one's mine, Dario,' I said.

Then I went back to bed, and that time I slept.

How to Draw a Picture (VII)

Remember that 'seeing is believing' puts the cart before the horse. Art is the concrete artifact of faith and expectation, the realization of a world that would otherwise be little more than a veil of pointless consciousness stretched over a gulf of mystery. And besides — if you don't believe what you see, who will believe your art?

The trouble after the treasure all had to do with belief. Elizabeth was fiercely talented, but she was only a child — and with children, faith is a given. It's part of the standard equipment. Nor are children, even the talented ones (especially the talented ones), in full possession of their faculties. Their reason still sleeps, and the sleep of reason breeds monsters.

Here's a picture I never painted:

*Identical twins in identical jumpers, except one is red, with an **L** on the front, and the other is blue, with a **T**. The girls are holding hands as they run along the path that leads to Shade Beach. They call it that because for most of the day it's in the shadow of Hag's Rock. There are tear-tracks on their pale round faces, but they will soon be gone because by now they are too terrorized to cry.*

If you can believe this, you can see the rest.

A giant crow flies slowly past them, upside-down, its wings outstretched. It speaks to them in their Daddy's voice.

Lo-Lo falls and cuts her knees on the shells. Tessie pulls her to her feet. They run on. It isn't the upside-down talking crow they are afraid of, nor the way the sky sometimes lenses from blue to a sunset red before going back to blue; it is the thing behind them.

The big boy.

Even with its fangs it still looks a little like one of the funny frogs Libbit used to draw, but this one is ever so much bigger, and real enough to cast a shadow. Real enough to stink and shake the ground each time it jumps. They have been frightened by all sorts of things since Daddy found the treasure, and Libbit says they dassn't come out of their room at night, or

347

even look out their windows, but this is day, and the thing behind them is too real not to be believed, and it is gaining.

The next time it's Tessie who falls and Lo-Lo who pulls her up, casting a terrified glance behind her at the thing chasing them. It's surrounded by dancing bugs it sometimes licks out of the air. Lo-Lo can see Tessie in one bulging, stupid eye. She herself is in the other.

They burst onto the beach gasping and out of breath and now there's nowhere to go but the water. Except maybe there is, because the boat is back again, the one they have seen more and more frequently in the last few weeks. Libbit says the boat isn't what it seems, but now it's a floating white dream of safety, and besides — there is no choice. The big boy is almost at their heels.

It came out of the swimming pool just after they finished playing Adie's Wedding in Rampopo, the baby-house on the side lawn (today Lo-Lo got to play Adie). Sometimes Libbit can make these awful things go away by scribbling on her pad, but now Libbit is sleeping — she has had a great many troubled nights lately.

The big boy leaps off the path and onto the beach, spraying sand all around. Its bulging eyes stare. Its fragile white belly, so full of noisome guts, bulges. Its throat throbs.

The two girls, standing with their hands linked and their feet in the running boil of what Daddy calls the little surf, look at each other. Then they look at the ship, swinging at anchor with its sails furled and shining. It looks even closer, as if it has moved in to rescue them.

Lo-Lo says We have to.

Tessie says But I can't SWIM!

You can dogpaddle!

The big boy leaps. They can hear its guts slash when it lands. They sound like wet garbage in a barrel of water. The blue fades from the sky and then the sky bleeds red. Then, slowly, it changes back again. It's been that kind of day. And haven't they known this kind of day was coming? Haven't they seen it in Libbit's haunted eyes? Nan Melda knows; even Daddy knows, and he's not here all the time. Today he's in Tampa, and when they look at the greenish-white horror that's almost upon them, they know that Tampa might as well be the far side of the moon. They are on their own.

Tessie grips Lo-Lo's shoulder with cold fingers. What about the rip?

But Lo-Lo shakes her head. The rip is good! The rip will take us to the boat!

There's no more time to talk. The frog-thing is getting ready to leap again. And they understand that, while it cannot be real, somehow it is. It can kill them. Better to chance the water. They turn, still holding hands, and throw themselves into the caldo. *They fix their eyes on the slim white swallow swinging at anchor close to them. Surely they will be hauled aboard, and someone will use the ship-to-shore to call the Roost. 'Netted us a pair of mermaids,' they'll say. 'You know anyone who wants em?'*

The rip parts their hands. It is ruthless, and Lo-Lo actually drowns first because she fights harder. Tessie hears her cry out twice. First for help. Then, giving up, her sister's name.

Meanwhile, a vagary of the rip is sweeping Tessie straight for the ship, and holding her up at the same time. For a few magical moments it's as though she's on a surfboard, and her weak dogpaddle seems to be propelling her like an outboard motor. Then, just before a colder current reaches up and coils around her ankles, she sees the ship change into—

Here's a picture I did paint, not once but again and again and again:

The whiteness of the hull doesn't exactly disappear; it is sucked inward like blood fleeing the cheek of a terrified man. The ropes fray. The bright-work dulls. The glass in the windows of the aft cabin bursts outward. A junkheap clutter appears on the decking, rolling into existence from fore to aft. Except it was there all along. Tessie just didn't see it. Now she sees.

Now she believes.

A creature comes from belowdecks. It creeps to the railing, where it stares down at the girl. It is a slumped thing in a hooded red robe. Hair that might not be hair at all flutters dankly around a melted face. Yellow hands grip splintered, punky wood. Then, one lifts slowly.

And waves to the girl who will soon be GONE.

It says Come to me, child.

And, drowning, Tessie Eastlake thinks It's a WOMAN!

She sinks. And does she feel still-warm hands, those of her freshly dead sister, gripping her calves and pulling her down?

Yes, of course. Of course she does.

Believing is also feeling.

Any artist will tell you so.

13 – The Show

i

Someday, if your life is long and your thinking machinery stays in gear, you'll live to remember the last good thing that ever happened to you. That's not pessimism talking, just logic. I hope I haven't run out of good things yet – there would be no purpose in living if I believed I had – but it's been a long time between. I remember the last one clearly. It happened a little over four years ago, on the evening of April fifteenth, at the Scoto Gallery. It was between seven forty-five and eight o'clock, and the shadows on Palm Avenue were beginning to take on the first faint tinges of blue. I know the time, because I kept checking my watch. The Scoto was already packed – to the legal limit and probably a little beyond – but my family hadn't arrived. I had seen Pam and Illy earlier in the day, and Wireman had assured me that Melinda's flight was on time, but so far that evening there hadn't been a sign of them. Or a call.

In the alcove to my left, where both the bar and eight of the *Sunset With* pictures had drawn a crowd, a trio from the local music conservatory was tinkling through a funereal version of 'My Funny Valentine'. Mary Ire (holding a glass of champagne but sober so far) was expatiating on something artistic to an attentive little crowd. To the right was a bigger room, featuring a buffet. On one wall in there was *Roses Grow from Shells* and a painting called *I See the Moon*; on another, three views of Duma Road. I'd observed several people taking photographs of these with their camera-phones, although a sign on a tripod just inside the door announced that all photography was *verboten*.

I mentioned this to Jimmy Yoshida in passing, and he nodded, seeming not angry or even irritated, but rather bemused. 'There are a great many people here I either don't associate with the art scene

351

or don't recognize at all,' he said. 'The size of this crowd is outside of my experience.'

'Is that a bad thing?'

'God, no! But after years of fighting to keep our corporate heads above water, it feels strange to be carried along this way.'

The Scoto's center gallery was large, which was a good thing that night. In spite of the food, drink, and music in the smaller rooms, the center seemed to be where most of the visitors eventually gravitated. The *Girl and Ship* series had been mounted there on almost invisible cords, directly down the center of the room. *Wireman Looks West* was on the wall at the far end. That one and *Girl and Ship No. 8* were the only paintings in the show which I had stickered NFS, *Wireman* because the painting was his, *No. 8* because I simply couldn't sell it.

'We keepin you up, boss?' Angel Slobotnik said from my left, as oblivious to his wife's elbow as ever.

'No,' I said. 'I was never more awake in my life, I just—'

A man in a suit that had to've cost two grand stuck out his hand. 'Henry Vestick, Mr Freemantle, First Sarasota Bank and Trust. Private Accounts. These are just marvelous. I am *stunned*. I am *amazed*.'

'Thank you,' I said, thinking he'd left out YOU MUST NOT STOP. 'Very kind.'

A business card appeared between his fingers. It was like watching a street-busker do a magic trick. Or would have been, if street-buskers wore Armani suits. 'If there's anything I can do ... I've written my phone numbers on the back – home, cell, office.'

'Very kind,' I repeated. I couldn't think of anything else to say, and really, what did Mr Vestick think I was going to do? Call him at home and thank him again? Ask him for a loan and offer him a painting as collateral?

'May I bring my wife over later and introduce her?' he asked, and I saw a look in his eyes. It wasn't exactly like the look that had been in Wireman's when he realized that I'd put the blocks to Candy Brown, but it was close. As if Vestick were a little afraid of me.

'Of course,' I said, and he slipped away.

'You used to build branch banks for guys like that and then have to fight em when they didn't want to pay the overage,' Angel said. He was in a blue off-the-rack suit and looked on the verge of bursting out of it in nine different directions, like The Incredible Hulk. 'Back then he woulda thought you were just some moke tryin to mess up his day. Now he looks at you like you could shit gold belt-buckles.'

'Angel, you stop!' Helen Slobotnik cried, simultaneously throwing another elbow and grabbing for his glass of champagne. He held it serenely out of her reach.

'Tell her it's the truth, boss!'

'I think it sort of is,' I said.

And it wasn't only the banker I was getting that look from. The women . . . jeez. When my eyes met theirs, I caught a softening, a speculation, as if they were wondering how I might hold them with only the one arm. That was probably crazy, but—

I was grabbed from behind, almost yanked off my feet. My own glass of champagne would have spilled, but Angel snatched it deftly. I turned, and there was Kathi Green, smiling at me. She'd left the Rehab Gestapo far behind, at least for tonight; she was wearing a short, shimmery green dress that clung to every well-maintained inch of her, and in her heels she stood almost to my forehead. Standing beside her, towering over her, was Kamen. His enormous eyes swam benevolently behind his horn-rimmed glasses.

'Jesus, Kathi!' I cried. 'What would you've done if you'd knocked me over?'

'Made you give me fifty,' she said, smiling more widely than ever. Her eyes were full of tears. 'Toldja that on the phone. Look at your tan, you handsome boy.' The tears spilled over and she hugged me.

I hugged back, then shook hands with Kamen. His hand swallowed mine whole.

'Your plane is the way for men my size to fly,' he said, and people turned in his direction. He had one of those deep James Earl Jones voices that can make supermarket circulars sound like the Book of Isaiah. 'I enjoyed myself to the *max*, Edgar.'

'It's not really mine, but thank you,' I said. 'Have either of you—'

'Mr Freemantle?'

It was a lovely redhead whose generously freckled breasts were in danger of tumbling from the top of a fragile pink dress. She had big green eyes. She looked about my daughter Melinda's age. Before I could say anything, she reached out and gently grasped my fingers.

353

'I just wanted to touch the hand that painted those pictures,' she said. 'Those wonderful, *freaky* pictures. God, you're *amazing*.' She lifted my hand and kissed it. Then she pressed it to one of her breasts. I could feel the rough pebble of the nipple through a thin gauze of chiffon. Then she was gone into the crowd.

'Does that happen often?' Kamen asked, and at the same moment Kathi asked, 'So how's divorce treating you, Edgar?' They looked at each other for a moment, then burst out laughing.

I understood what they were laughing at – Edgar's Elvis moment – but to me it just seemed weird. The rooms of the Scoto began to look a little like chambers in an undersea grotto, and I realized I could paint it that way: undersea rooms with paintings on their walls, paintings that were being looked at by schooling peoplefish while Neptune's Trio burbled 'Octopus's Garden'.

Far too weird. I wanted Wireman and Jack – also not here yet – but even more, I wanted my people. Illy most of all. If I had them, maybe this would start to feel like reality again. I glanced toward the door.

'If you're looking for Pam and the girls, I expect they'll be right along,' Kamen said. 'Melinda had a problem with her dress and went up to change at the last minute.'

Melinda, I thought. *Of course, it would be Mel—*

And that was when I saw them, threading their way through the crowd of artistic gawkers, looking very northern and out of place amid the tans. Tom Riley and William Bozeman III – the immortal Bozie – paced behind them in dark suits. They stopped to look at three of the early sketches, which Dario had set up near the door in a triptych. It was Ilse who saw me first. She cried '*DADDY!*' and then cut through the crowd like a PT boat with her sister just behind her. Lin was tugging a tall young man in her wake. Pam waved, and also started toward me.

I left Kamen, Kathi, and the Slobotniks, Angel still holding my drink. Someone began, 'Pardon me, Mr Freemantle, I wonder if I could ask—' but I paid no attention. In that moment all I could see was Ilse's glowing face and joyous eyes.

We met in front of the sign reading **THE SCOTO GALLERY PRESENTS 'THE VIEW FROM DUMA'. PAINTINGS AND SKETCHES BY EDGAR FREEMANTLE**. I was aware that she was wearing a powder-blue dress I had never seen before, and that with her hair up and what seemed like a swan's length of neck showing, she looked startlingly adult. I was aware of an immense, almost overpowering love for her, and gratitude that she felt the same for me – it was in her eyes. Then I was holding her.

A moment later, Melinda was there with her young man standing behind her (and above her – he was one long, tall helicopter). I didn't have an arm for her and her sister both, but she had one for me; she grabbed me and kissed the side of my face. 'Bonsoir, Dad, congratulations!'

Then Pam was in front of me, the woman I had called a quitting birch not so long ago. She was wearing a dark blue pants suit, a light blue silk blouse, and a string of pearls. Sensible earrings. Sensible but good-looking low heels. Full Minnesota if ever I had seen it. She was obviously frightened to death by all the people and the strange environment, but there was a hopeful smile on her face just the same. Pam had been many things in the course of our marriage, but hopeless was never one of them.

'Edgar?' Pam asked in a small voice. 'Are we still friends?'

'You better believe it,' I said. I only kissed her briefly, but hugged her as thoroughly as a one-armed man can do it. Ilse was holding onto me on one side; Melinda had the other, squeezing hard enough to hurt my ribs, but I didn't care. As if from a great distance, I heard the room erupt in spontaneous applause.

'You look good,' Pam whispered in my ear. 'No, you look wonderful. I'm not sure I would have known you on the street.'

I stepped back a little, looking at her. 'You look pretty fine yourself.'

She laughed, blushing, a stranger with whom I had once spent my nights. 'Make-up covers a multitude of sins.'

'Daddy, this is Ric Doussault,' Melinda said.

'Bonsoir and congratulations, Monsieur Freemantle,' Ric said. He was holding a plain white box. He now held it out. 'From Linnie and me. Un cadeau. The gift?'

I knew what un cadeau was, of course; the real revelation was the exotic lilt his accent gave to my daughter's nickname. It made me understand in a way nothing else could that she was now more his than mine.

355

It seemed to me that the majority of the people in the gallery had gathered around to watch me open my present. Tom Riley had made it almost to Pam's shoulder. Bozie was next to him. From just behind them, Margaret Bozeman skated me a kiss from the heel of her palm. Next to her was Todd Jamieson, the doctor who had saved my life . . . two sets of aunts and uncles . . . Rudy Rudnick, my old secretary . . . Kamen, of course, he was impossible to miss . . . and Kathi by his side. They had all come, everyone but Wireman and Jack, and I was beginning to wonder if something had happened to keep them away. But for the moment that seemed secondary. I thought of waking up in my hospital bed, confused and separated from everything by unremitting pain, then I looked around at this and wondered how things could possibly have changed so completely. All these people had come back into my life for one night. I didn't want to cry, but I was pretty sure I was going to; I could feel myself starting to dissolve like a tissue in a cloudburst.

'Open it, Daddy!' Ilse said. I could smell her perfume, something sweet and fresh.

'Open it! Open it!' Good-natured voices from the packed circle watching us.

I opened the box. Pulled out some white tissue paper and uncovered what I had expected . . . although I had expected something jokey, and this was no joke. The beret Melinda and Ric had brought me from France was dark red velvet, and smooth as silk to the touch. It had not come cheap.

'This is too nice,' I said.

'No, Daddy,' Melinda said. 'Not nice enough. We only hope it fits.'

I took it out of the box and held it up. The audience *ohh-ed* appreciatively. Melinda and Ric looked at each other happily, and Pam – who felt Lin somehow never get her proper share of affection or approval from me (and she was probably right) – gave me a look that was positively radiant. Then I put the beret on. It was a perfect fit. Melinda reached up, made one tiny adjustment, faced the watching audience, turned her palms outward to me, and said: '*Voici mon père, ce magnifique artiste!*' They burst into applause and cries of *Bravo!* Ilse kissed me. She was crying and laughing. I remember the white vulnerability of her neck and the feel of her lips, just above my jaw.

I was the belle of the ball and I had my family around me. There was light and champagne and music. It happened four years ago, on the evening of April fifteenth, between seven forty-five and eight o'clock, while the shadows on Palm Avenue were just beginning to take on the first faint tinges of blue. This is a memory I keep.

ii

I toured them around, with Tom and Bozie and the rest of the Minnesota crowd tagging after. Many of those present might have been first-time gallery attendees, but they were polite enough to give us some space.

Melinda paused for a full minute in front of *Sunset with Sophora*, then turned to me, almost accusingly. 'If you could do this all along, Dad, why in God's name did you waste thirty years of your life putting up County Extension buildings?'

'Melinda Jean!' Pam said, but absently. She was looking toward the center room, where the *Girl and Ship* paintings hung suspended.

'Well, it's true,' Melinda said. 'Isn't it?'

'Honey, I didn't know.'

'How can you have something this big inside you and not know?' she demanded.

I didn't have an answer for that, but Alice Aucoin rescued me. 'Edgar, Dario wondered if you could step into Jimmy's office for a few minutes? I'll be happy to escort your family into the main room and you can join them there.'

'Okay . . . what do they want?'

'Don't worry, they're all smiling,' she said, and smiled herself.

'Go on, Edgar,' Pam said. And, to Alice: 'I'm used to him being called away. When we were married, it was a way of life.'

'Dad, what does this red circle on top of the frame mean?' Ilse asked.

'That it's sold, dear,' Alice said.

I paused to look at *Sunset with Sophora* as I started away, and . . .

357

sure enough, there was a little red circle on the upper right corner of the frame. That was a good thing – it was nice to know the crowd here was composed of more than just lookers drawn by the novelty of a one-armed dauber – but I still felt a pang, and wondered if it was normal to feel that way. I had no way of telling. I didn't know any other artists to ask.

iii

Dario and Jimmy Yoshida were in the office; so was a man I'd never met before. Dario introduced him to me as Jacob Rosenblatt, the accountant who kept the Scoto's books in trim. My heart sank a little as I shook his hand, turning my own to do it because he offered the wrong one, as so many people do. Ah, but it's a righties' world.

'Dario, are we in trouble here?' I asked.

Dario placed a silver champagne bucket on Jimmy's desk. In it, reclining on a bed of crushed ice, was a bottle of Perrier-Jouët. The stuff they were serving in the gallery was good, but not this good. The cork had been recently drawn; there was still faint breath drifting from the bottle's green mouth. 'Does this look like trouble?' he asked. 'I would have had Alice ask your family in, as well, but the office is too freaking small. Two people who *should* be here right now are Wireman and Jack Cantori. Where the hell are they? I thought they were coming together.'

'So did I. Did you try Elizabeth Eastlake's house? Heron's Roost?'

'Of course,' Dario said. 'Got nothing but the answering machine.'

'Not even Elizabeth's nurse? Annmarie?'

He shook his head. 'Just the answering machine.'

I started having visions of Sarasota Memorial. 'I don't like the sound of that.'

'Perhaps the three of them are on their way here right now,' Rosenblatt said.

'I think that's unlikely. She's gotten very frail and short of breath. Can't even use her walker anymore.'

'I'm sure the situation will resolve itself,' Jimmy said. 'Meanwhile, we should raise a glass.'

358

'*Must* raise a glass, Edgar,' Dario added.

'Thanks, you guys, that's very kind, and I'd be happy to have a drink with you, but my family's outside and I want to walk around with them while they look at the rest of my pictures, if that's all right.'

Jimmy said, 'Understandable, but—'

Dario interrupted, speaking quietly. 'Edgar, the show's a sell.'

I looked at him. 'Beg your pardon?'

'We didn't think you'd had a chance to get around and see all the red dots,' Jimmy said. He was smiling, his color so high he might have been blushing. 'Every painting and sketch that *was* for sale *has* been sold.'

Jacob Rosenblatt, the accountant, said: 'Thirty paintings and fourteen sketches. It's unheard-of.'

'But . . .' My lips felt numb. I watched as Dario turned and this time took a tray of glasses from the shelf behind the desk. They were in the same floral pattern as the Perrier-Jouët bottle. 'But the price you put on *Girl and Ship No. 7* was forty thousand dollars!'

From the pocket of his plain black suit, Rosenblatt took a curl of paper that had to have come from an adding machine. 'The paintings fetched four hundred and eighty-seven thousand dollars, the sketches an additional nineteen. The total comes to a little over half a million dollars. It's the greatest sum the Scoto has ever taken in during the exhibition of a single artist's work. An amazing coup. Congratulations.'

'*All* of them?' I said in a voice so tiny I could hardly hear it myself. I looked at Dario as he put a champagne glass in my hand.

He nodded. 'If you had decided to sell *Girl and Ship No. 8*, I believe that one alone would have fetched a hundred thousand dollars.'

'Twice that,' Jimmy said.

'To Edgar Freemantle, at the start of his brilliant career!' Rosenblatt said, and raised his glass. We raised our glasses and drank, not knowing that my brilliant career was, for all practical purposes, at an end.

We caught a break there, *muchacho*.

359

iv

Tom Riley fell in beside me as I moved back through the crowd toward my family, smiling and shaking conversational gambits as fast as I could. 'Boss, these are incredible,' he said, 'but they're a little spooky, too.'

'I guess that's a compliment,' I said. The truth was, talking to Tom felt spooky, knowing what I did about him.

'It's definitely a compliment,' he said. 'Listen, you're headed for your family. I'll take a hike.' And he started to do just that, but I grabbed him by the elbow.

'Stick with me,' I said. 'Together we can repel all boarders. On my own, I may not get to Pam and the girls until nine o'clock.'

He laughed. Old Tommy looked good. He'd added some pounds since that day at Lake Phalen, but I'd read that antidepressants sometimes do that, especially to men. On him, a little more weight was okay. The hollows under his eyes had filled in.

'How've you been, Tom?'

'Well . . . in truth . . . depressed.' He lifted one hand in the air, as if to wave off a commiseration I hadn't offered. 'It's a chemical imbalance thing, and it's a bitch getting used to the pills. They muddy up your thinking at first – they did mine, anyway. I went off them awhile, but I'm back on now and life's looking better. It's either the fake endorphins kicking in or the effect of springtime in The Land of a Billion Lakes.'

'And The Freemantle Company?'

'The books are in the black, but it's not the same without you. I came down here thinking I might pitch you on coming back. Then I got a look at what you're doing and realized your days in the building biz are probably done.'

'I think so, yeah.'

He gestured toward the canvases in the main room. 'What are they, really? I mean, no bullshit. Because – I wouldn't say this to very many people – they remind me of the way life was inside my head when I wasn't taking my pills.'

'They're just make-believe,' I said. 'Shadows.'

'I know about shadows,' he said. 'You just want to be careful they don't grow teeth. Because they can. Then, sometimes when you

360

reach for the light-switch to make them go away, you discover the power's out.'

'But you're better now.'

'Yes,' he said. 'Pam had a lot to do with that. Can I tell you something about her you might already know?'

'Sure,' I said, only hoping he wasn't going to share the fact that she sometimes laughed way down in her throat when she came.

'She has great insight but little kindness,' Tom said. 'It's a weirdly cruel mix.'

I said nothing . . . but not necessarily because I thought he was wrong.

'She gave me a brisk talking-to about taking care of myself not so long ago, and it hit home.'

'Yeah?'

'Yeah. And from the look of her, you might be in for a talking-to yourself, Edgar. I think I might find your friend Kamen and engage him in a bit of a discourse. Excuse me.'

The girls and Ric were staring up at *Wireman Looks West* and chattering animatedly. Pam, however, was positioned about halfway down the line of *Girl and Ship* paintings, which hung like movie posters, and she looked disturbed. Not angry, exactly, just disturbed. Confused. She beckoned me over, and once I was there, she didn't waste time.

'Is the little girl in these pictures Ilse?' She pointed up at *No. 1*. 'I thought at first this one with the red hair was supposed to be the doll Dr Kamen gave you after your accident, but Ilse had a tic-tac-toe dress like that when she was little. I bought it at Rompers. And *this* one—' Now she pointed at *No. 3*. 'I swear this is the dress she just had to have to start first grade in – the one she was wearing when she broke her damn arm that night after the stock car races!'

Well, there you were. I remembered the broken arm as having come after church, but that was only a minor misstep in the grand dance of memory. There were more important things. One was that Pam was in a unique position to see through most of the smoke and mirrors that critics like to call art – at least in my case she was. In that way, and probably in a great many others, she was still my wife. It seemed that in the end, only time could issue a divorce decree. And that the decree would be partial at best.

361

I turned her toward me. We were being watched by a great many people, and I suppose to them it looked like an embrace. And in a way, it was. I got one glimpse of her wide, startled eyes, and then I was whispering in her ear.

'Yes, the girl in the rowboat is Ilse. I never meant her to be there, because I never meant *anything*. I never even knew I was going to paint these pictures until I started doing them. And because she's back-to, no one else is ever going to know unless you or I tell them. And I won't. But—' I pulled back. Her eyes were still wide, her lips parted as if to receive a kiss. 'What did *Ilse* say?'

'The oddest thing.' She took me by the sleeve and pulled me down to *No. 7* and *No. 8*. In both of these, Rowboat Girl was wearing the green dress with straps that crossed over her bare back. 'She said you must be reading her mind, because she ordered a dress like that from Newport News just this spring.'

She looked back at the pictures. I stood silently beside her and let her look.

'I don't like these, Edgar. They're not like the others, and I don't like them.'

I thought of Tom Riley saying, *Your ex has great insight but little kindness.*

Pam lowered her voice. 'You don't know something about Illy that you shouldn't, do you? The way you knew about—'

'No,' I said, but I was more troubled by the *Girl and Ship* series than ever. Some of it was seeing them all hung in a line; the accumulated weirdness was like a punch.

Sell them. That was Elizabeth's opinion. *However many there are, you must sell them.*

And I could understand why she thought so. I did not like seeing my daughter, not even in the guise of the child she had long outgrown, in such close proximity to that rotted sheerhulk. And in a way, I was surprised that perplexity and disquiet were all Pam felt. But of course, the paintings hadn't had a chance to work on her yet.

And they were no longer on Duma Key.

The young people joined us, Ric and Melinda with their arms around each other. 'Daddy, you're a genius,' Melinda said. 'Ric thinks so, too, don't you, Ric?'

'Actually,' Ric said, 'I do. I came prepared to be . . . polite. Instead I am struggling for the words to say I am amazed.'

'That's very kind,' I said. '*Merci.*'

'I'm so proud of you, Dad,' Illy said, and hugged me.

Pam rolled her eyes, and in that instant I could cheerfully have whacked her one. Instead I folded Ilse into my arms and kissed the top of her head. As I did, Mary Ire's voice rose from the front of the Scoto in a cigarette-hoarsened shout that was full of amazed disbelief. '*Libby Eastlake! I don't believe my god-damned eyes!*'

It was my ears I didn't believe, but when a spontaneous spatter of applause erupted from the doorway, where the real aficionados had gathered to chat and take a little fresh evening air, I understood why Jack and Wireman had been late.

v

'What?' Pam asked. '*What?*' I had her on one side and Illy on the other as I moved toward the door; Linnie and Ric bobbed along in our wake. The applause grew louder. People turned toward the door and craned to see. 'Who is it, Edgar?'

'My best friends on the island.' Then, to Ilse: 'One of them's the lady from down the road, remember her? She turned out to be the Daughter of the Godfather instead of the Bride. Her name's Elizabeth Eastlake, and she's a sweetheart.'

Ilse's eyes were shining with excitement. 'The old gal in the big blue sneakers!'

The crowd – many of them still applauding – parted for us, and I saw the three of them in the reception area, where two tables with a punchbowl on each had been set up. My eyes began to sting and a lump rose in my throat. Jack was dressed in a slate gray suit. With his usually unruly surfer's thatch tamed, he looked like either a junior executive in the Bank of America or an especially tall seventh grader on Careers Day. Wireman, pushing Elizabeth's chair, was wearing faded, beltless jeans and a round-collared white linen shirt that emphasized his deep tan. His hair was combed back, and I realized for the first time that he was good-looking the way Harrison Ford was in his late forties.

But it was Elizabeth who stole the show, Elizabeth who elicited the applause, even from the newbies who hadn't the slightest idea who she was. She was wearing a black pantsuit of dull rough cotton, loose but elegant. Her hair was up and held with a gauzy snood that flashed like diamonds beneath the gallery's downlighters. From her neck hung an ivory scrimshaw pendant on a gold chain, and on her feet were not big blue Frankenstein sneakers but elegant pumps of darkest scarlet. Between the second and third fingers of her gnarled left hand was an unlit cigarette in a gold-chased holder.

She looked left and right, smiling. When Mary came to the chair, Wireman stopped pushing long enough for the younger woman to kiss Elizabeth's cheek and whisper in her ear. Elizabeth listened, nodded, then whispered back. Mary cawed laughter, then caressed Elizabeth's arm.

Someone brushed by me. It was Jacob Rosenblatt, the accountant, his eyes wet and his nose red. Dario and Jimmy were behind him. Rosenblatt knelt by her wheelchair, his bony knees cracking like starter pistols, and cried, 'Miss Eastlake! Oh, Miss Eastlake, so long we're not seeing you, and now . . . oh, what a wonderful surprise!'

'And you, Jake,' she said, and cradled his bald head to her bosom. It looked like a very large egg lying there. 'Handsome as Bogart!' She saw me . . . and winked. I winked back, but it wasn't easy to keep my happy face on. She looked haggard, dreadfully tired in spite of her smile.

I raised my eyes to Wireman's, and he gave the tiniest of shrugs. *She insisted*, it said. I switched my gaze to Jack and got much the same.

Rosenblatt, meanwhile, was rummaging in his pockets. At last he came up with a book of matches so battered it looked as if it might have entered the United States without a passport at Ellis Island. He opened it and tore one out.

'I thought smoking was against the rules in all these public buildings now,' Elizabeth said.

Rosenblatt struggled. Color rose up his neck. I almost expected his head to explode. Finally he exclaimed: '*Fuck* the rules, Miss Eastlake!'

'*BRAVISSIMO!*' Mary shouted, laughing and throwing her hands to the ceiling, and at this there was another round of applause. A greater one came when Rosenblatt finally got the ancient match to ignite and held it out to Elizabeth, who placed her cigarette-holder between her lips.

'Who is she really, Daddy?' Ilse asked softly. 'Besides the little old lady who lives down the lane, I mean?'

I said, 'According to reports, at one time she *was* the Sarasota art scene.'

'I don't understand why that gives her the right to muck up *our* lungs with *her* cigarette smoke,' Linnie said. The vertical line was returning between her brows.

Ric smiled. 'Oh, *chérie*, this after all the bars we—'

'*This* is not *there*,' she said, the vertical line deepening, and I thought, *Ric, you may be French, but you have a lot to learn about this particular American woman.*

Alice Aucoin murmured to Dario, and from his pocket, Dario produced an Altoids tin. He dumped the mints into the palm of his hand and gave Alice the tin. Alice gave it to Elizabeth, who thanked her and tapped her cigarette ash into it.

Pam watched, fascinated, then turned to me. 'What does *she* think of your pictures?'

'I don't know,' I said. 'She hasn't seen them.'

Elizabeth was beckoning to me. 'Will you introduce me to your family, Edgar?'

I did, beginning with Pam and ending with Ric. Jack and Wireman also shook hands with Pam and the girls.

'After all the calls, I'm pleased to meet you in the flesh,' Wireman told Pam.

'The same goes back to you,' Pam said, sizing him up. She must have liked what she saw, because she smiled – and it was the real one, the one that lights her whole face. 'We did it, didn't we? He didn't make it easy, but we did it.'

'Art is never easy, young woman,' Elizabeth said.

Pam looked down at her, still smiling the genuine smile – the one I'd fallen in love with. 'Do you know how long it's been since anyone called me young woman?'

'Ah, but to me you look very young and beautiful,' Elizabeth said . . . and was this the woman who had been little more than a muttering lump of cheese slumped in her wheelchair only a week ago? Tonight that seemed hard to believe. Tired as she looked, it seemed impossible to believe. 'But not as young and beautiful as your daughters. Girls, your father is — by all accounts — a very talented fellow.'

'We're very proud of him,' Melinda said, twisting her necklace.

Elizabeth smiled at her, then turned to me. 'I should like to see the work and judge for myself. Will you indulge me, Edgar?'

'I'd be happy to.' I meant it, but I was damned nervous, as well. Part of me was afraid to receive her opinion. That part was afraid she might shake her head and deliver her verdict with the bluntness to which her age entitled her: *Facile . . . colorful . . . certainly lots of energy . . . but perhaps not up to much. In the end.*

Wireman moved to grasp the handles of her chair, but she shook her head. 'No — let Edgar push me, Wireman. Let him *tour* me.' She plucked the half-smoked cigarette from the holder, those gnarled fingers doing the job with surprising dexterity, and crushed it out on the bottom of the tin. 'And the young lady's right — I think we've all had quite enough of *this* reek.'

Melinda had the grace to blush. Elizabeth offered the tin to Rosenblatt, who took it with a smile and a nod. I have wondered since then — I know it's morbid, but yes, I've wondered — if she would have smoked more of it if she had known it was to be her last.

vi

Even those who didn't know John Eastlake's surviving daughter from a hole in the wall understood that a Personage had come among them, and the tidal flow which had moved toward the reception area at the sound of Mary Ire's exuberant shout now reversed itself as I rolled the wheelchair into the alcove where most of the *Sunset With* pictures had been hung. Wireman and Pam walked on my left; Ilse and Jack were on my right, Ilse giving the wheelchair's handle on that side little helping taps to make sure it stayed on course. Melinda and Ric were behind us, Kamen, Tom Riley, and Bozie behind them. Behind that trio came seemingly everyone else in the gallery.

I wasn't sure there would be room to get her chair in between the makeshift bar set-up and the wall, but there was, just. I started to push it down that narrow aisle, grateful that we'd at least be leaving the rest of the retinue behind us, when Elizabeth cried: '*Stop!*'

I stopped at once. 'Elizabeth, are you all right?'

'Just a minute, honey – hush.'

We sat there, looking at the paintings on the wall. After a little bit, she fetched a sigh and said, 'Wireman, do you have a Kleenex?'

He had a handkerchief, which he unfolded and handed to her.

'Come around here, Edgar,' she said. 'Come where I can see you.'

I managed to get around between the wheelchair and the bar, with the bartender bracing the table to make sure it didn't tip over.

'Are you able to kneel down, so we can be face to face?'

I was able. My Great Beach Walks were paying dividends. She clutched her cigarette holder – both foolish and somehow magnificent – in one hand, Wireman's handkerchief in the other. Her eyes were damp.

'You read me poems because Wireman couldn't. Do you remember that?'

'Yes, ma'am.' Of course I remembered. Those had been sweet interludes.

'If I were to say "Speak, memory" to you, you'd think of the man – I can't recall his name – who wrote *Lolita*, wouldn't you?'

I had no idea who she was talking about, but I nodded.

'But there's a poem, too. I can't remember who wrote it, but it begins, "Speak, memory, that I may not forget the taste of roses nor the sound of ashes in the wind; That I may once more taste the green cup of the sea." Does it move you? Yes, I see it does.'

The hand with the cigarette holder in it opened. Then it reached out and caressed my hair. The idea occurred to me (and has since recurred) that all my struggle to live and regain a semblance of myself may have been paid back by no more than the touch of that old woman's hand. The eroded smoothness of the palm. The bent strength of those fingers.

'Art is memory, Edgar. There is no simpler way to say it. The clearer the memory, the better the art. The purer. These paintings – they break my heart and then make it new again. How glad I am to know they were done at Salmon Point. No matter what.' She lifted the hand she'd caressed my head with. 'Tell me what you call that one.'

'*Sunset with Sophora.*'

'And these are . . . what? *Sunset with Conch, Numbers 1* through *4*?'

I smiled. 'Well, there were sixteen of them, actually, starting with colored pencil-sketches. Some of those are out front. I picked the best oils for in here. They're surreal, I know, but—'

'They're not surreal, they're classical. Any fool can see that. They contain all the elements: earth . . . air . . . water . . . fire.'

I saw Wireman mouth: *Don't tire her out!*

'Why don't I give you a quick tour of the rest and then get you a cold drink?' I asked her, and now Wireman was nodding and giving me a thumb-and-forefinger circle. 'It's hot in here, even with the air conditioning.'

'Fine,' she said. 'I *am* a little tired. But Edgar?'

'Yes?'

'Save the ship paintings for the last. After them I'll *need* a drink. Perhaps in the office. Just one, but something stiffer than Co'-Cola.'

'You've got it,' I said, and edged my way back to the rear of the chair.

'Ten minutes,' Wireman whispered in my ear. 'No more. I'd want to get her out before Gene Hadlock shows up, if possible. He sees her, he's going to shit a brick. And you know who he'll throw it at.'

'Ten,' I said, and rolled Elizabeth into the buffet room to look at the paintings in there. The crowd was still following. Mary Ire had begun taking notes. Ilse slipped one hand into the crook of my elbow and smiled at me. I smiled back, but I was having that I'm-in-a-dream feeling again. The kind that may tilt you into a nightmare at any moment.

Elizabeth exclaimed over *I See the Moon* and the Duma Road series, but it was the way she reached her hands out to *Roses Grow from Shells*, as if to embrace it, that gave me goosebumps. She lowered her arms again and looked over her shoulder at me. 'That's the essence of it,' she said. 'The essence of Duma. Why those who've lived there awhile can never really leave. Even if their heads carry

368

their bodies away, their hearts stay.' She looked at the picture again and nodded. '*Roses Grow from Shells*. That is correct.'

'Thank you, Elizabeth.'

'No, Edgar – thank *you*.'

I glanced back for Wireman and saw him talking to that other lawyer from my other life. They seemed to be getting along famously. I only hoped Wireman wouldn't slip and call him Bozie. Then I turned to Elizabeth again. She was still looking at *Roses Grow from Shells*, and wiping her eyes.

'I love this,' she said, 'but we should move along.'

After she'd seen the other paintings and sketches in the buffet room, she said, as if to herself: 'Of course I knew someone would come. But I never would have guessed it would be someone who could produce works of such power and sweetness.'

Jack tapped me on the shoulder, then leaned close to murmur in my ear. 'Dr Hadlock has entered the building. Wireman wants you to speed this up if you can.'

The main gallery – where the *Girl and Ship* paintings hung – was on the way to the office, and Elizabeth could leave by the loading door in back after having her drink; it would actually be more convenient for her wheelchair. Hadlock could accompany her, if he so desired. But I dreaded taking her past the *Ship* series, and it was no longer her critical opinion I was worried about.

'Come on,' she said, and clicked her amethyst ring on the arm of her wheelchair. 'Let's look at them. No hesitating.'

'All right,' I said, and began pushing her toward the main gallery.

'Are you all right, Eddie?' Pam asked in a low voice.

'Fine,' I said.

'You're not. What's wrong?'

I only shook my head. We were in the main room now. The pictures were suspended at a height of about six feet; the room was otherwise open. The walls, covered with coarse brown stuff that looked like burlap, were bare except for *Wireman Looks West*. I rolled Elizabeth's chair slowly along. The wheels were soundless on the pale blue carpet. The murmur of the crowd behind us had either stopped or my ears had filtered it out. I seemed to see the paintings for the first time, and they looked oddly like stills culled from a strip of movie film. Each image was a little clearer, a little more in focus, but always essentially the same, always the ship I had first glimpsed in a dream. It was always sunset, and the light filling the west was always a titanic red anvil that spread blood across the water and infected the sky. The ship was a three-masted corpse, something that had floated in from a plaguehouse of the dead. Its sails were rags. Its deck was deserted. There was something horrible in every angular line, and although it was impossible to say just what, you feared for the little girl alone in her rowboat, the little girl who first appeared in a tic-tac-toe dress, the little girl afloat on the wine-dark Gulf.

In that first version, the angle of the deathship was wrong to see anything of the name. In *Girl and Ship No. 2*, the angle had improved but the little girl (still with the false red hair and now also wearing Reba's polka-dotted dress) blocked out all but the letter *P*. In *No. 3, P* had become *PER* and Reba had pretty clearly become Ilse, even back-to. John Eastlake's spear-pistol lay in the rowboat.

If Elizabeth recognized this, she gave no indication. I pushed her slowly up the line as the ship bulked larger and closer, its black masts looming like fingers, its sails sagging like dead flesh. The furnace sky glared through the holes in the canvas. Now the name on the transom was *PERSE*. There might have been more – there was room for more – but if so, it was hidden by shadows. In *Girl and Ship No. 6* (the ship now looming over the rowboat), the little girl was wearing what appeared to be a blue singlet with a yellow stripe around the neck. Her hair in that one was orange-ish; it was the only Rowboat Girl whose identity I wasn't sure of. Maybe it was Ilse, since the others were . . . but I wasn't entirely convinced. In this one the first few rose-petals had begun to appear on the water (plus one single yellow-green tennis ball with the letters **DUNL** visible on it), and an odd assortment of geegaws were heaped on deck: a tall mirror (which, reflecting the sunset, appeared filled with blood), a child's rocking horse, a steamer trunk, a pile of shoes. These same objects appeared in *No. 7* and *No. 8,* where they had been joined by several others – a young girl's bicycle leaning against the foremast, a pile of tires stacked on the stern, a great hourglass at midships. This last also reflected the sun and appeared to be full of blood instead of sand. In *Girl and Ship No. 8* there were more rose petals floating between the rowboat and the *Perse*. There were more tennis balls, too, at least half a dozen. And a rotting garland of flowers hung around the neck of the rocking horse. I could almost smell the stench of their perfume on the still air.

'Dear *God,*' Elizabeth whispered. 'She has grown so strong.' There had been color in her face but now it was all gone. She didn't look eighty-five; she looked two hundred.

Who? I tried to ask, but nothing came out.

'Ma'am . . . Miss Eastlake . . . you shouldn't tax yourself,' Pam said.

I cleared my throat. 'Can you get her a glass of water?'

'I will, Dad,' Illy said.

Elizabeth was still staring at *Girl and Ship No. 8.* 'How many of those . . . those *souvenirs* . . . do you recognize?' she asked.

'I don't . . . my imagination . . .' I fell silent. The girl in the rowboat of *No. 8* was no souvenir, but she *was* Ilse. The green dress, with its bare back and crisscrossing straps, had seemed jarringly sexy for a little girl, but now I knew why: it was a dress Ilse had bought recently, from a mail order catalogue, and Ilse was no longer a little girl. Otherwise, the tennis balls were still a mystery to me, the mirror meant nothing, nor did the stack of tires. And I didn't know for a fact that the bicycle leaning against the foremast had been Tina Garibaldi's, but I feared it . . . and my heart was somehow sure of it.

Elizabeth's hand, dreadfully cold, settled on my wrist. 'There's no bullet on the frame of this last one.'

'I don't know what you're—'

Her grip tightened. 'You *do.* You know *exactly* what I mean. The show is a *sell,* Edgar, do you think I'm blind? A bullet on the frame of every painting we've looked at – including *No. 6,* the one with my sister Adie in the rowboat – but not this one!'

I looked back toward *No. 6,* where Rowboat Girl had orange hair. 'That's your *sister?*'

She paid no attention. I don't think she even heard me. All her attention was bent upon *Girl and Ship No. 8.* 'What do you mean to do? Take it back? *Do you mean to take it back to Duma?*' Her voice rang out in the quiet of the gallery.

'Ma'am . . . Miss Eastlake . . . you really shouldn't excite yourself this way,' Pam said.

371

Elizabeth's eyes blazed in the hanging flesh of her face. Her nails dug into the scant meat of my wrist. 'And what? Put it next to another one you've already started?'

'I haven't started another—' Or had I? My memory was playing me again, as it often did in moments of stress. If someone had at that moment demanded that I speak the name of my older daughter's French boyfriend, I probably would have said René. As in Magritte. The dream had tilted, all right; here was the nightmare, right on schedule.

'*The one where the rowboat is empty?*'

Before I could say anything, Gene Hadlock shoved through the crowd, followed by Wireman, followed by Ilse, holding a glass of water.

'Elizabeth, we should go,' Hadlock said.

He reached for her arm. Elizabeth swept his hand away. On the follow-through she struck the glass Ilse was starting to proffer and it went flying, hitting one of the bare walls and shattering. Someone cried out and some woman, incredibly, laughed.

'Do you see the rocking horse, Edgar?' she held out her hand. It was trembling badly. Her nails had been painted coral pink, probably by Annmarie. 'That belonged to my sisters, Tessie and Laura. They loved it. They dragged that damned thing with them everywhere. It was outside Rampopo – the baby playhouse on the side lawn – after they drowned. My father couldn't bear to look at it. He had it thrown into the water at the memorial service. Along with the garland, of course. The one around the horse's neck.'

Silence except for the tearing rasp of her breath. Mary Ire staring with big eyes, her obsessive note-taking at an end, the pad hanging forgotten in one hand by her side. Her other hand had gone to her mouth. Then Wireman pointed to a door that was quite cleverly concealed in more of the brown burlappy stuff. Hadlock nodded. And suddenly Jack was there, and it was actually Jack who took charge. 'Have you out in a jiff, Miz Eastlake,' he said. 'No worries.' He seized the handles of her wheelchair.

'*Look at the ship's wake!*' Elizabeth shouted at me as she was borne out of the public eye for the last time. '*For Christ's sake, don't you see what you've painted?*'

I looked. So did my family.

'There's nothing there,' Melinda said. She looked mistrustfully toward the office door, which was just closing behind Jack and Elizabeth. 'Is she dotty, or what?'

Illy was standing on tiptoe, craning for a closer look. 'Daddy,' she said hesitantly. 'Are those faces? Faces in the water?'

'No,' I said, surprised at the steadiness of my own voice. 'All you're seeing is an idea she put in your head. Will you guys excuse me for a minute?'

'Of course,' Pam said.

'May I be of assistance, Edgar?' Kamen asked in his booming basso.

I smiled. I was surprised at how easily that came, too. Shock has its purposes, it seems. 'Thanks, but no. Her doctor's in with her.'

I hurried toward the office door, resisting an urge to look back. Melinda hadn't seen it; Ilse had. My guess was that not many people would, even if it were pointed out to them . . . and even then, most would dismiss it as either coincidence or a small artistic wink.

Those faces.

Those screaming drowned faces in the ship's sunset wake.

Tessie and Laura were there, most certainly, but others as well, just below them where the red faded to green and the green to black.

One might be a carrot-topped girl in an old-fashioned singlet-style bathing suit: Elizabeth's oldest sister, Adriana.

vii

Wireman was giving her sips of what looked like Perrier while Rosenblatt fussed at her side, literally wringing his hands. The office seemed packed with people. It was hotter than the gallery, and getting hotter.

'I want you all out!' Hadlock said. 'Everyone but Wireman! Now! Right now!'

Elizabeth pushed aside the glass with the back of her hand. 'Edgar,' she said in a husky voice. 'Edgar stays.'

'No, Edgar goes,' Hadlock said. 'You've excited yourself quite en—'

His hand was in front of her. She seized it and squeezed it. With some force, it seemed, because Hadlock's eyes widened.

'*Stays.*' It was only a whisper, but a powerful one.

People began to leave. I heard Dario telling the crowd gathered outside that everything was fine, Miss Eastlake felt a little faint but her doctor was with her and she was recovering. Jack was going out the door when Elizabeth called, 'Young man!' He turned.

'Don't forget,' she told him.

He gave her a brief grin and knocked off a salute. 'No, ma'am, I sure won't.'

'I should have trusted you in the first place,' she said, and Jack went out. Then, in a lower voice, as if her strength were fading: 'He's a good boy.'

'Trusted him for what?' Wireman asked her.

'To search the attic for a certain picnic basket,' she said. 'In the picture on the landing, Nan Melda is holding it.' She looked at me reproachfully.

'I'm sorry,' I said. 'I remember you telling me, but I just . . . I got painting, and . . .'

'I don't blame you,' she said. Her eyes had receded deep in their sockets. 'I should have known. It's her power. The same power that drew you here in the first place.' She looked at Wireman. 'And you.'

'Elizabeth, that's enough,' Hadlock said. 'I want to take you to the hospital and run some tests. Run some fluids into you while I'm at it. Get you some rest—'

'I'll be getting all the rest I need very soon now,' she told him, and smiled. The smile exposed a large and rather gruesome ring of dentures. Her eyes returned to me. 'Trixie pixie nixie,' she said. 'To her it's all a game. All our sorrow. And she's awake again.' Her hand, very cold, settled on my forearm. 'Edgar, *she's awake!*'

'Who? Elizabeth, who? Perse?'

She shuddered backward in her chair. It was as if an electrical current were passing through her. The hand on my arm tightened. Her coral nails punched through my skin, leaving a quartet of red crescents. Her mouth opened, exposing her teeth this time in a snarl instead of a smile. Her head went backward and I heard something in there snap.

'*Catch the chair before it goes over!*' Wireman roared, but I couldn't – I had only one arm, and Elizabeth was clutching it. Was docked in it.

Hadlock grabbed one of the push-handles and the chair skittered

374

sideways instead of toppling backwards. It struck Jimmy Yoshida's desk. Now Elizabeth was in full seizure mode, jittering back and forth in her chair like a puppet. The snood came loose from her hair and flailed, sparkling, in the light of the overhead flourescents. Her feet jerked and one of her scarlet pumps went flying off. *The angels want to wear my red shoes*, I thought, and as if the line had summoned it, blood burst from her nose and mouth.

'*Hold her!*' Hadlock shouted, and Wireman threw himself across the arms of the chair.

She did this, I thought coldly. *Perse. Whoever she is.*

'I've got her!' Wireman said. 'Call 911, doc, for Christ's sake!'

Hadlock hurried around the desk, picked up the phone, dialed, listened. 'Fuck! I just get more dial-tone!'

I snatched it from him. 'You must have to dial 9 for an outside line,' I said, and did it with the phone cradled between my ear and shoulder. And when the calm-voiced woman on the other end asked me the nature of my emergency, I was able to tell her. It was the address I couldn't remember. I couldn't even remember the name of the gallery.

I handed the phone to Hadlock and went back around the desk to Wireman.

'Christ Jesus,' he said. 'I *knew* we shouldn't have brought her, I *knew* . . . but she was so fucking *insistent*.'

'Is she out?' I looked at her, slumped in her chair. Her eyes were open, but they looked vacantly at a point in the far corner. 'Elizabeth?' There was no response.

'Was it a stroke?' Wireman asked. 'I never knew they could be so *violent*.'

'That was no stroke. Something shut her up. Go to the hospital with her—'

'Of course I'll—'

'And if she says anything else, *listen*.'

Hadlock came back. 'They're waiting for her at the hospital. An ambulance will be here any minute.' He stared hard at Wireman, and then his look softened. 'Oh, all right,' he said.

'Oh all right?' Wireman asked. 'What does that mean, oh all right?'

'It means if something like this was going to happen,' Hadlock said, 'where do you think she would have *wanted* it to happen? At home in bed, or in one of the galleries where she spent so many happy days and nights?'

Wireman took in a deep, shaky breath, let it out, nodded, then knelt beside her and began to brush at her hair. Elizabeth's face was patchy-red in places, and bloated, as if she were having an extreme allergic reaction.

Hadlock bent and tilted her head back, trying to ease her terrible rasping. Not long after, we heard the approaching warble of the ambulance.

viii

The show dragged on and I stuck it out, partly because of all the effort Dario, Jimmy, and Alice had put into the thing, but mostly for Elizabeth. I thought it was what she would have wanted. My moment in the sun, she'd called it.

I didn't go to the celebratory dinner afterwards, though. I made my excuses, then sent Pam and the girls on with Kamen, Kathi, and some others from Minneapolis. Watching them pull away, I realized I hadn't made arrangements for a ride to the hospital. While I was standing there in front of the gallery, wondering if Alice Aucoin had left yet, a beat-to-shit old Mercedes pulled up beside me, and the passenger window slid down.

'Get in,' Mary Ire said. 'If you're going to Sarasota Memorial, I'll drop you off.' She saw me hesitate and smiled crookedly. 'Mary's had very little to drink tonight, I assure you, and in any case, the Sarasota traffic goes from clogged to almost zero after ten p.m. – the old folks take their Scotch and Prozac and then curl up to watch Bill O'Reilly on TiVo.'

I got in. The door clunked when it shut, and for one alarming moment I thought my ass was going to keep descending until it was actually on Palm Avenue. Finally my downward motion stopped. 'Listen, Edgar,' she said, then hesitated. 'Can I still call you Edgar?'

'Of course.'

She nodded. 'Lovely. I couldn't remember with perfect clarity what sort of terms we parted on. Sometimes when I drink too much . . .' She shrugged her bony shoulders.

'We're fine,' I said.

'Good. As for Elizabeth . . . not so good. Is it?'

I shook my head, not trusting myself to speak. The streets were almost deserted, as promised. The sidewalks were dead empty.

'She and Jake Rosenblatt were a thing for awhile. It was pretty serious.'

'What happened?'

Mary shrugged. 'Can't say for sure. If you forced me to guess, I'd say that in the end she was just too used to being her own mistress to be anyone else's. Other than on a part-time basis, that is. But Jake never got over her.'

I remembered him saying *Fuck the rules, Miss Eastlake!* and wondered what he had called her in bed. Surely not Miss Eastlake. It was a sad and useless bit of speculation.

'Maybe this is for the best,' Mary said. 'She was guttering. If you'd known her in her prime, Edgar, you'd know she wasn't the sort of woman who'd want to go out that way.'

'I wish I had known her in her prime.'

'Can I do anything for your family?'

'No,' I said. 'They're having dinner with Dario and Jimmy and the whole state of Minnesota. I'll join them later if I can – maybe for dessert – and I'm booked into the Ritz, where they're all staying. If nothing else, I'll see them in the morning.'

'That's nice. *They* seemed nice. And understanding.'

Pam actually seemed more understanding now than before the divorce. Of course now I was down here painting and not up there yelling at her. Or trying to staff her with a butter-fife.

'I'm going to praise your show to the skies, Edgar. I doubt if that means much to you tonight, but perhaps it will later on. The paintings are just extraordinary.'

'Thank you.'

Ahead, the lights of the hospital were twinkling in the dark. There was a Waffle House right next door. It was probably good business for the cardiac unit.

'Will you give Libby my love, if she's in any condition to take note of such things?'

'Sure.'

'And I have something for you. It's in the glove compartment.

377

Manila envelope. I was going to use it to bait the hook for a follow-up interview, but fuck it.'

I had some problems with the old car's glove compartment button, but finally the little door fell open like a corpse's mouth. There was a lot more than a manila envelope in there – a geologist could have taken core-samples probably going back to 1965 – but the envelope was in front, and it had my name printed on it.

As she pulled up in front of the hospital, in a spot marked 5 MINUTES PICK-UP AND DROP-OFF, Mary said: 'Prepare to be amazed. I was. An old copy-editor friend of mine chased that down for me – she's older than Libby, but still sharp.'

I bent back the clasps and slid out two Xeroxed sheets of an ancient newspaper story. 'That,' Mary said, 'is from the Port Charlotte *Weekly Echo*. June of 1925. It's got to be the story my friend Aggie saw, and the reason I could never find it is because I never looked as far south as Port Charlotte. Also, the *Weekly Echo* gave up the ghost in 1931.'

The streetlight beneath which she'd parked wasn't good enough for the fine print, but I could read the headline and see the picture. I looked for a long time.

'It means something to you, doesn't it?' she asked.

'Yes. I just don't know what.'

'If you figure it out, will you tell me?'

'All right,' I said. 'You might even believe it. But Mary . . . this is one story you'll never print. Thanks for the ride. And thanks for coming to my show.'

'Both my pleasure. Remember to give Libby my love.'

'I will.'

But I never did. I had seen Elizabeth Eastlake for the last time.

ix

The ICU nurse on duty told me that Elizabeth was in surgery. When I asked for what, she told me she wasn't sure. I looked around the waiting room.

'If you're looking for Mr Wireman, I believe he went to the cafeteria for coffee,' the nurse said. 'That's on the fourth floor.'

'Thanks.' I started away, then turned back. 'Is Dr Hadlock part of the surgical team?'

'I don't think so,' she said, 'but he's observing.'

I thanked her again and went in search of Wireman. I found him in a far corner of the caff, sitting in front of a paper cup about the size of a World War II mortar shell. Except for a scattering of nurses and orderlies and one tense-looking family group in another corner of the room, we had the place to ourselves. Most of the chairs were upended on the tables, and a tired-looking lady in red rayon was working out with a mop. An iPod hung in a sling between her breasts.

'*Hola, mi vato,*' Wireman said, and gave me a wan smile. His hair, neatly combed back when he made his entrance with Elizabeth and Jack, had fallen down around his ears, and there were dark circles around his eyes. 'Why don't you grab yourself a cup of coffee? It tastes like factory-made shit, but it do prop up a person's eyelids.'

'No, thanks. Just let me borrow a sip of yours.' I had three aspirin in my pants pocket. I fished them out and swallowed them with some of Wireman's coffee.

He wrinkled his nose. 'In with all your germy change. That's nasty.'

'I have a strong immune system. How is she?'

'Not good.' He looked at me bleakly.

'Did she come around at all in the ambulance? Say anything else?'

'She did.'

'What?'

From the pocket of his linen shirt, Wireman took an invitation to my show, with **THE VIEW FROM DUMA** printed on one side. On the other he'd scrawled three notes. They jagged up and down – from the motion of the ambulance, I assumed – but I could read them:

'*The table is leaking.*'

'*You will want to but you mustn't.*'

'*Drown her back to sleep.*'

They were all spooky, but that last one made the flesh on my arms prickle.

'Nothing else?' I asked, handing the invitation back.

'She said my name a couple of times. She knew me. And she said yours, Edgar.'

'Have a look at this,' I said, and slid the manila envelope across the table.

He asked where I'd gotten it and I told him. He said it all seemed a little convenient, and I shrugged. I was remembering something Elizabeth had said to me – *The water runs faster now. Soon come the rapids*. Well, the rapids were here. I had a feeling this was only the start of the white water.

My hip was starting to feel a little better, its late-night sobbing down to mere sniffles. According to popular wisdom, a dog is a man's best friend, but I would vote for aspirin. I pulled my chair around the table and sat next to Wireman, where I could read the headline: **DUMA KEY TOT BLOSSOMS FOLLOWING SPILL – IS SHE A CHILD PRODIGY?** Beneath was a photograph. In it was a man I knew well in a bathing suit I knew well: John Eastlake in his slimmer, trimmer incarnation. He was smiling, and holding up a smiling little girl. It was Elizabeth, looking the same age as in the family portrait of Daddy and His Girls, only now she was holding out a drawing to the camera in both hands and wearing a gauze bandage wrapped around her head. There was another, much older girl in the picture – big sister Adriana, and yes, she could have been a carrot-top – but to begin with, Wireman and I paid little attention to her. Or to John Eastlake. Or even to the toddler with the bandage around her head.

'Holy wow,' Wireman said.

The picture was of a horse looking over a fence rail. It wore an unlikely (and un-equine) smile. In the foreground, back-to, was a little girl with lots of golden ringlets, holding out a carrot the size of a shotgun for the smiling horse to eat. To either side, bracketing the picture almost like theater curtains, were palm trees. Above were puffy white clouds and a great big sun, shooting off happy-rays of light.

It was a child's picture, but the talent that had created it was beyond doubt. The horse had a *joie de vivre* that made the smile the punchline of a cheerful joke. You could put a dozen art students in a room, tell them to execute a happy horse, and I was willing to bet not one of them would be able to match the success of that picture. Even the oversized carrot felt not like a mistake but part of the giggle, an intensifier, an artistic steroid.

'It's *not* a joke,' I muttered, bending closer . . . only bending closer did no good. I was seeing this picture through four aggravating levels of obfuscation: the photograph, the newspaper reproduction of the photograph, the Xerox of the newspaper reproduction of the photograph . . . and time itself. Over eighty years of it, if I had the math right.

'What's not a joke?' Wireman asked.

'The way the size of the horse is exaggerated. And the carrot. Even the sunrays. It's a child's cry of glee, Wireman!'

'A hoax is what it is. Got to be. She would have been *two!* A child of two can't even make stick-figures and call em mommy and daddy, can she?'

'Was what happened to Candy Brown a hoax? Or what about the bullet that used to be in your brain? The one that's now gone?'

He was silent.

I tapped **CHILD PRODIGY**. 'Look, they even had the right fancy term for it. Do you suppose if she'd been poor and black, they would have called her **PICKANINNY FREAK** and stuck her in a sideshow somewhere? Because I sort of do.'

'If she'd been poor and black, she never would have made the paper at all. Or fallen out of a pony-trap to begin with.'

'Is that what hap—' I stopped, my eye caught by the blurry photograph again. Now it was big sis I was looking at. Adriana.

'What?' Wireman asked, and his tone was *What now?*

'Her bathing suit. Look familiar to you?'

'I can't see very much, just the top. Elizabeth's holding her picture out in front of the rest.'

'What about the part you can see?'

He looked for a long time. 'Wish I had a magnifying glass.'

'That would probably make it worse instead of better.'

'All right, *muchacho*, it *does* look vaguely familiar . . . but maybe that's just an idea you put in my head.'

'In all the *Girl and Ship* paintings, there was only one Rowboat Girl I was never sure of: the one in *No. 6.* The one with the orangey hair, the one in the blue singlet with the yellow stripe around the neck.' I tapped Adriana's blurred image in the photocopy Mary Ire had given me. 'This is the girl. This is the swimming suit. I'm sure of it. So was Elizabeth.'

'What are we saying here?' Wireman asked. He was skimming

381

the print, rubbing at his temples as he did so. I asked if his eye was bothering him.

'No. This is just so . . . so fucking . . .' He looked up at me, eyes big, still rubbing his temples. 'She fell out of the goddam pony-trap and hit her head on a rock, or so it says here. Woke up in the doctor's infirmary just as they were getting ready to transport her to the hospital in St Pete. Seizures thereafter. It says, "The seizures continue for Baby Elizabeth, although they are moderating and seem to do her no lasting harm." And she started painting pictures!'

I said, 'The accident must have happened right after the big group portrait was taken, because she looks exactly the same, and they change fast at that age.'

Wireman seemed not to notice. 'We're all in the same rowboat,' he said.

I started to ask him what he meant, then realized I didn't have to. 'Sí, señor,' I said.

'She fell on her head. I shot myself in the head. *You* got your head crushed by a payloader.'

'Crane.'

He waved his hand as if to indicate this made no difference. Then he used the hand to grip my surviving wrist. His fingers were cold. 'I have questions, *muchacho*. How come she stopped painting? And how come I never started?'

'I can't say for certain why she stopped. Maybe she forgot — blocked it out — or maybe she deliberately lied and denied. As for you, your talent's empathy. And on Duma Key, empathy got raised to telepathy.'

'That's bullshi . . .' He trailed off.

I waited.

'No,' he said. 'No. It's not. But it's also completely gone. Want to know something, *amigo*?'

'Sure.'

He cocked a thumb at the tense family group across the room from us. They had gone back to their discussion. Pop was now shaking his finger at Mom. Or maybe it was Sis. 'A couple of months ago, I could have told you what that hoopdedoo was about. Now all I could do is make an educated guess.'

'And probably come out in much the same place,' I said. 'Would you trade one for the other in any case? Your eyesight for the occasional thoughtwave?'

'God, no!' he said, then looked around the caff with an ironic, despairing, head-cocked smile. 'I can't believe we're having this discussion, you know. I keep thinking I'll wake up and it'll all be as you were, Private Wireman, assume the position.'

I looked him in the eye. 'Ain't gonna happen.'

x

According to the *Weekly Echo*, Baby Elizabeth (as she was referred to almost throughout) began her artistic endeavors on the very first day of her at-home convalescence. She quickly went on, 'gaining skill and prowess with each passing hour, it seemed to her amazed father.' She started with colored pencils ('Sound familiar?' Wireman asked), before progressing to a box of watercolors the bemused John Eastlake brought home from Venice.

In the three months following her accident, much of it spent in bed, she had done literally hundreds of watercolors, turning them out at a rate John Eastlake and the other girls found a little frightening. (If 'Nan Melda' had an opinion, it wasn't offered in print.) Eastlake tried to slow her down – on doctor's orders – but this was counterproductive. It caused fretfulness, crying fits, insomnia, bouts of fever. Baby Elizabeth said when she couldn't draw or paint, 'her head hurted'. Her father said that when she did paint, 'She ate like one of the horses she liked to draw.' The article's author, one M. Rickert, seemed to find this endearing. Recalling my own eating binges, I found it all too familiar.

I was going over the muddy print for the third time, with Wireman where my right arm would have been, if I'd had a right arm, when the door opened and Gene Hadlock came in. He was still wearing the black tie and bright pink shirt he'd had on at the show, although the tie had been pulled down and the collar was loosened. He was still wearing green scrub pants and green bootees over his shoes. His head was down. When he looked up I saw a face that was as long and sad as an old bloodhound's.

'Eleven-nineteen,' he said. 'There was never really a chance.' Wireman put his face in his hands.

xi

I got to the Ritz at quarter to one in the morning, limping with fatigue and not wanting to be there. I wanted to be in my bedroom at Big Pink. I wanted to lie in the middle of my bed, push the strange new doll to the floor as I had the ornamental pillows, and hug Reba to me. I wanted to lie there and look at the turning fan. Most of all, I wanted to listen to the whispered conversation of the shells under the house as I drifted off to sleep.

Instead I had this lobby to deal with: too ornate, too full of people and music (cocktail piano even at this hour), most of all, too bright. Still, my family was here. I had missed the celebratory dinner. I would not miss the celebratory breakfast.

I asked the clerk for my key. He gave it to me, along with a stack of messages. I opened them one after another. Most were congratulations. The one from Ilse was different. It read: *Are you okay? If I don't see you by 8 a.m., I'm coming to find you. Fair warning.*

At the very bottom was one from Pam. The note itself was only four words long: *I know she died.* Everything else that needed saying was expressed by the enclosure. It was her room key.

xii

I stood outside 847 five minutes later with the key in my hand. I'd move it toward the slot, then move my finger toward the doorbell, then look back toward the elevators. I must have stood that way for five minutes or more, too exhausted to make up my mind, and might have stood there even longer if I hadn't heard the elevator doors open, followed by the sound of tipsy convivial laughter. I was afraid it would turn out to be someone I knew – Tom and Bozie, or Big Ainge and his wife. Maybe even Lin and Ric. In the end I hadn't booked the entire floor, but I'd taken most of it.

I pushed the key into the lock. It was the electronic kind you didn't even have to turn. A green light came on, and as the laughter from down the hall came closer, I slipped inside.

I had ordered her a suite, and the living room was big. There had apparently been a before-show party, because there were two room-service tables and lots of plates with the remains of canapés on them. I spotted two — no, three champagne buckets. Two of the bottles were sticking bottoms-up, dead soldiers. The third appeared to still be alive, although on life support.

That made me think of Elizabeth again. I saw her sitting beside her China Village, looking like Katharine Hepburn in *Woman of the Year*, saying *See how I've put the children outside the schoolhouse! Do come see!*

Pain is the biggest power of love. That's what Wireman says.

I threaded my way around chairs where my nearest and dearest had sat, talking and laughing and — I was sure of it — toasting my hard work and good fortune. I took the last champagne bottle from the pool in which it sat, held it up to the wall-length picture-window showcasing Sarasota Bay, and said: 'Here's to you, Elizabeth. *Hasta la vista, mi amada.*'

'What does *amada* mean?'

I turned. Pam was standing in the bedroom doorway. She was wearing a blue nightgown I didn't remember. Her hair was down. It hadn't been so long since Ilse was in junior high school. It touched her shoulders.

'It means darling,' I said. 'I learned it from Wireman. He was married to a Mexican woman.'

'Was?'

'She died. Who told you about Elizabeth?'

'The young man who works for you. I asked him to call if there was news. I'm so sorry.'

I smiled. I tried to put the champagne bottle back and missed the bucket. Hell, I missed the table. The bottle hit the carpet and rolled. Once the Daughter of the Godfather had been a child, holding out her picture of a smiling horse for a photographer's camera, the photographer probably some jazzy guy wearing a straw hat and arm garters. Then she had been an old woman jittering away the last of her life in a wheelchair while her snood came loose and flailed from one final hairpin under the fluorescent lights of an art gallery office. And the time between? It probably seemed like no more than a nod or the wave of a hand to the clear blue sky. In the end we all go smash to the floor.

Pam held out her arms. There was a full moon shining in through the big window, and by its light I could see the rose tattoo on the swell of her breast. Something else new and different . . . but the breast was familiar. I knew it well. 'Come here,' she said.

I came. I struck one of the room-service tables with my bad hip, gave a muttering cry, and stumbled the last two steps into her arms, thinking this was a nice reunion, we were both going to land on the carpet, me on top of her. Maybe I could even break a couple of her ribs. It was certainly possible; I'd put on twenty pounds since coming to Duma Key.

But she was strong. I forgot that. She held my weight, at first bracing against the side of the bedroom door, then standing up straight with me in her arms. I put my own arm around her and laid my cheek on her shoulder, just breathing in the scent of her.

Wireman! I woke up early and I've been having such a wonderful time with my chinas!

'Come on, Eddie, you're tired. Come to bed.'

She led me into the bedroom. The window in here was smaller, the moonlight thinner, but the window was open and I could hear the constant sigh of the water.

'Are you sure—'

'Hush.'

I'm sure I've been told your name but it escapes me, so much does now.

'I never meant to hurt you. I'm so sorry—'

She put two fingers against my lips. 'I don't want your sorry.'

We sat side by side on the bed in the shadows. 'What *do* you want?'

She showed me with a kiss. Her breath was warm and tasted of champagne. For a little while I forgot about Elizabeth and Wireman, picnic baskets, and Duma Key. For a little while there was just she and I, like the old days. The two-armed days. For a little while after that I slept – until the first light came creeping. The loss of memory isn't always the problem; sometimes – maybe even often – it's the solution.

How to Draw a Picture (VIII)

Be brave. Don't be afraid to draw the secret things. No one said art was always a zephyr; sometimes it's a hurricane. Even then you must not hesitate or change course. Because if you tell yourself the great lie of bad art – that you are in charge – your chance at the truth will be lost. The truth isn't always pretty. Sometimes the truth is the big boy.

The little ones say It's Libbit's frog. A frog with *teef.*

And sometimes it's something even worse. Something like Charley in his bright blue breeches.

Or HER.

Here is a picture of little Libbit with her finger to her lips. She says Shhhh. *She says* If you talk she'll hear, so shhhh. *She says* Bad things can happen, and upside-down talking birds are just the first and least, so shhhh. If you try to run, something awful may come out of the cypress and gumbo limbo and catch you on the road. There are even worse things in the water down at Shade Beach – worse than the big boy, worse than Charley who moves so quick. They're in the water, waiting to drown you. And not even drowning is the end, no, not even drowning. So shhhh.

But for the true artist, the truth will insist. Libbit Eastlake can hush her mouth, but not her paints and pencils.

There's only one person she dares talk to, and only one place she can do it – only one place at Heron's Roost where HER *hold seems to fail. She makes Nan Melda go there with her. And tries to explain how this happened, how the talent demanded the truth and the truth slithered out of her grasp. She tries to explain how the drawings have taken over her life and how she has come to hate the little china doll Daddy found with the rest of the treasure – the little china woman who was Libbit's fair salvage. She tries to explain her deepest fear: if they don't do something, the twins may not be the only ones to die, only the first ones. And the deaths may not end on Duma Key.*

She gathers all her courage (and for a child who is little more than a

387

baby, she must have had a great lot of it) and tells the whole truth, mad as it is. First about how she made the hurricane, but that it wasn't her idea – it was HER *idea.*

I think Nan Melda believes it. Because she's seen the big boy? Because she's seen Charley?

I think she saw both.

The truth has to come out, that's the basis of art. But that's not to say the world must see it.

Nan Melda says Where yo new doll now? The china doll?

Libbit says In my special treasure-box. My heart-box.

Nan Melda says And what her name?

Libbit says Her name is Perse.

Nan Melda says Percy a boy's name.

And Libbit says I can't help it. Her name is Perse. That's the truth. *And she says* Perse has a ship. It looks nice but it's not nice. It's bad. What are we going to do, Nanny?

Nan Melda thinks about it as they stand there in the one safe place. And I believe she knew what needed to be done. She might not have been an art critic – no Mary Ire – but I think she knew. The bravery is in the doing, *not in the* showing. *The truth can be hidden away again, if it's too terrible for the world to look at. And it happens. I'm sure it happens all the time.*

I think every artist worth a damn has a red picnic basket.

14 – The Red Basket

i

'Share your pool, mister?'

It was Ilse, in green shorts and matching halter. Her feet were bare, her face without makeup and puffy with sleep. Her hair was yanked back in a ponytail, the way she'd worn it when she was eleven, and if not for the fullness of her breasts, she could have passed for that eleven-year-old.

'Any time,' I said.

She sat beside me on the tiled lip of the pool. We were about halfway down, my butt on **5** and hers on **FT**.

'You're up early,' I said, but this didn't surprise me. Illy had always been our restless one.

'I was worried about you. Especially when Mr Wireman called Jack to say that nice old woman died. It was Jack who told us. We were still at dinner.'

'I know.'

'I'm so sorry.' She put her head on my shoulder. 'And on your special night, too.'

I put my arm around her.

'Anyway, I only slept a couple of hours, and then got up because it was light. And when I looked out, who should I see sitting beside the pool but my father, all by himself?'

'Couldn't sleep anymore. I just hope I didn't wake your m—' I stopped, aware of Ilse's large, round eyes. 'Don't go getting any ideas, Miss Cookie. It was strictly comfort.'

It had *not* been strictly comfort, but what it had been was something I wasn't prepared to explore with my daughter. Or myself, for that matter.

She slumped a little, then straightened and looked at me, head tilted, the beginnings of a smile at the corners of her mouth.

'If you have hopes, that's your business,' I said. 'But I would advise you not to get them up. I'm always going to care for her, but sometimes people go too far to turn back. I think . . . I'm pretty sure that's the case with us.'

She looked back at the still surface of the pool, the little smile at the corners of her mouth dying away. I hated seeing it go, but maybe it was for the best. 'All right, then.'

That left me free to move on to other matters. I didn't want to, but I was still her father and she was in many ways still a child. Which meant that, no matter how badly I felt about Elizabeth Eastlake this morning, or how confused I might be about my own situation, I still had certain duties to fulfill.

'Need to ask you something, Illy.'

'Okay, sure.'

'Are you not wearing the ring because you don't want your mother to see it and go nuclear . . . which I would fully understand . . . or because you and Carson—'

'I sent it back,' she said in a flat and toneless voice. Then she giggled, and a stone rolled off my heart. 'But I sent it UPS, and I insured it.'

'So . . . it's over?'

'Well . . . never say never.' Her feet were in the water and she kicked them slowly back and forth. 'Carson doesn't *want* it to be, so he says. I'm not sure I do, either. At least not without seeing how we do face to face. The phone or e-mail really isn't the way to talk something like this out. Plus, I want to see if the attraction is still there, and if so, how much.' She glanced sideways, a little anxiously. 'That doesn't gross you out, does it?'

'No, honey.'

'Can I ask you something?'

'Yes.'

'How many second chances did you give Mom?'

I smiled. 'Over the course of the marriage? I'd say two hundred or so.'

'And how many did she give you?'

'About the same.'

'Did you ever . . .' She stopped. 'I can't ask you that.'

I looked at the pool, aware of a very middle-class flush rising in

390

my cheeks. 'Since we're having this discussion at six in the morning and not even the pool boy's here yet, and since I think I know what your problem with Carson Jones is, you can ask. The answer is no. Not even once. But if I'm dead honest, I have to say that was more luck than stone-ass righteousness. There were times when I came close, and once when it was probably only luck or fate or providence that kept in from happening. I don't think the marriage would have ended if the . . . the accident had happened, I think there are worse offenses against a partner, but they don't call it cheating for nothing. One slip can be excused as human fallibility. Two can be excused as human frailty. After that—' I shrugged.

'He says it was just once.' Her voice was little more than a whisper. Her feet had slowed to a dreamy underwater drift. 'He said she started coming on to him. And finally . . . you know.'

Sure. It happens that way all the time. In books and movies, anyway. Maybe sometimes in real life, too. Just because it sounded like a self-serving lie didn't mean it was.

'The girl he sings with?'

Ilse nodded. 'Bridget Andreisson.'

'She of the bad breath.'

Faint smile.

'I seem to remember you telling me not too long ago that he'd have to make a choice.'

A long silence. Then: 'It's complicated.'

It always is. Ask any drunk in a bar who's been thrown out by his wife. I kept quiet.

'He told her he doesn't want to see her anymore. And the duets are off. I know that for a fact, because I checked some of the latest reviews on the Internet.' She colored faintly at this, although I didn't blame her for checking. I would have checked, too. 'When Mr Fredericks – he's the tour director – threatened to send him home, Carson told him he could if he wanted to, but he wasn't singing with that holy blond bitch anymore.'

'Were those his exact words?'

She smiled brilliantly. 'He's a *Baptist,* Daddy, I'm interpreting. Anyway, Carson stood his ground and Mr Fredericks relented. For me, that's a mark in his favor.'

Yes, I thought, *but he's still a cheater who calls himself Smiley.*

391

I took her hand. 'What's your next move?'

She sighed. The ponytail made her look eleven; the sigh made her sound forty. 'I don't know. I'm at a loss.'

'Then let me help you. Will you do that?'

'All right.'

'For the time being, stay away from him,' I said, and I discovered I wanted that with all my heart. But there was more. When I thought of the *Girl and Ship* paintings – especially the girl in the rowboat – I wanted to tell her not to talk to strangers, keep her hairdryer away from the bathtub, and jog only at the college track. *Never across Roger Williams Park at dusk.*

She was looking at me quizzically, and I managed to get myself in gear again. 'Go right back to school—'

'I wanted to talk to you about that—'

I nodded, but squeezed her arm to show her I wasn't quite finished. 'Finish your semester. Make your grades. Let Carson finish the tour. Get perspective, *then* get together . . . understand what I'm saying?'

'Yes . . .' She understood, but didn't sound convinced.

'When you do get together, do it on neutral ground. And I don't mean to embarrass you, but it's still just the two of us, so I'm going to say this. Bed is not neutral ground.'

She looked down at her swimming feet. I reached out and turned her face to mine.

'When the issues aren't resolved, bed is a battleground. I wouldn't even have dinner with the guy until you know where you stand with him. Meet in . . . I don't know . . . Boston. Sit on a park bench and work it out. Get it clear in your mind and make sure it's clear in his. *Then* have dinner. Do a Red Sox game. Or go to bed, if you think it's the right thing. Just because I don't want to think about your sex-life doesn't mean I don't think you should have one.'

She relieved me considerably by laughing. At the sound, a waiter who still looked half-asleep came out to ask us if we wanted coffee. We said we did. When he went to get it, Ilse said: 'All right, Daddy. Point taken. I was going to tell you that I'm going back this afternoon, anyway. I have an Anthro prelim at the end of the week, and there are a bunch of us who've formed a little study group. We call ourselves the Survivors' Club.' She regarded me anxiously. 'Would

392

that be okay? I know you were planning on a couple of days, but now there's this thing with your friend—'

'No, honey, that's fine.' I kissed the tip of her nose, thinking that if I was close up, she wouldn't see how pleased I was – pleased that she'd come for the show, pleased that we'd had some time together this morning, pleased most of all that she would be a thousand miles north of Duma Key by the time the sun went down tonight. Assuming she could get a flight reservation, that was. 'And as for Carson?'

She sat quiet for perhaps an entire minute, swinging her bare feet back and forth through the water. Then she stood up and took my arm, helping me to my feet. 'I think you're right. I'll say that if he's serious about our relationship, he'll just have to put everything on hold until July 4th.'

Now that her decision was made, her eyes were bright again.

'That'll get me to the end of the semester and a month of summer vacation besides. It'll get him through to his last show at the Cow Palace, plus plenty of time to figure out if he's as finished with Blondie as he thinks he is. Does it suit you, father dear?'

'Down to the ground.'

'Here comes the coffee,' she said. 'Now the question is, how long until breakfast?'

ii

Wireman wasn't at the morning-after breakfast, but he had reserved the Bay Island Room from eight to ten. I presided over two dozen friends and family members, most from Minnesota. It was one of those events people remember and talk about for decades, partly because of encountering so many familiar faces in an exotic setting, partly because the emotional atmosphere was so volatile.

On the one hand, there was a very palpable sense of Home Town Boy Makes Good. They had sensed it at the show, and their judgment was confirmed in the morning papers. The reviews in the Sarasota *Herald Tribune* and the Venice *Gondolier* were great, but short. Mary Ire's piece in the Tampa *Trib*, on the other hand, took up nearly a whole page and was lyrical. She must have written most

393

of it ahead of time. She called me 'a major new American talent'. My mother – always a bit of a sourpuss – would have said, *Take that and a dime and you can wipe your ass in comfort.* Of course that was her saying forty years ago, when a dime bought more than it does today.

Elizabeth, of course, was the other hand. There was no death-notice for her, but a boxed item had been added to the page of the Tampa paper carrying Mary's review: **WELL-KNOWN ART PATRON STRICKEN AT FREEMANTLE SHOW.** The story, just two paragraphs long, stated that Elizabeth Eastlake, a long-time fixture on the Sarasota art scene and resident of Duma Key, had suffered an apparent seizure not long after arriving at the Scoto Gallery and had been taken by ambulance to Sarasota Memorial Hospital. No word of her condition was available at press time.

My Minnesota people knew that on the night of my triumph, a good friend had died. There would be bursts of laughter and occasional raillery, then glances in my direction to see if I minded. By nine-thirty, the scrambled eggs I'd eaten were sitting like lead in my stomach, and I was getting one of my headaches – the first in almost a month.

I excused myself to go upstairs. I'd left a small bag in the room I hadn't slept in. The shaving kit contained several foil packets of Zomig, a migraine medication. It wouldn't stop a full-blown Force 5, but it usually worked if I took a dose early enough. I swallowed one with a Coke from the bar fridge, started to leave, and saw the light on the phone flashing. I almost left it, then realized the message might be from Wireman.

It turned out there were half a dozen messages. The first four were more congratulations, which fell on my aching head like pellets of hail on a tin roof. By the time I got to Jimmy's – he was the fourth – I had begun punching the 6-button on the keypad, which hurried me on to the next message. I was in no mood to be stroked.

The fifth message was indeed from Jerome Wireman. He sounded tired and stunned. 'Edgar, I know you've got a couple of days earmarked for family and friends, and I hate like hell to ask you this, but can we get together at your place this afternoon? We need to talk, and I mean really. Jack spent the night here with me at *El*

Palacio – he didn't want me to be alone, that's one helluva good kid – and we were up early, hunting for that red basket she was on about, and . . . well, we found it. Better late than never, right? She wanted you to have it, so Jack took it over to Big Pink. The house was unlocked, and listen, Edgar . . . someone's been inside.'

Silence on the line, but I could hear him breathing. Then:

'Jack's severely freaked, and you got to prepare for a shock, *muchacho*. Though you may already have an idea—'

There was a beep, and then the sixth message started. It was still Wireman, now rather pissed off, which made him sound more like himself.

'Fucking short-ass message tape! *Chinche pedorra! Ay!* Edgar, Jack and I are going over to Abbot-Wexler. They're . . .' A brief pause as he worked to keep it together. '. . . the funeral home she wanted. I'll be back by one. You really ought to wait for us before you go in your house. It isn't trashed or anything, but I want to be with you when you look in that basket and when you see what got left in your studio upstairs. I don't like to be mysterious, but Wireman ain't putting this shit on a message-tape anybody might listen to. And there's one more thing. One of her lawyers called. Left a message on the machine – Jack and I were still up in the fucking attic. He says I'm her sole beneficiary.' A pause. '*La lotería.*' A pause. 'I get everything.' A pause. 'Fuck *me.*'

That was all.

iii

I punched 0 for the hotel operator. After a short wait, she gave me the number of the Abbot-Wexler Funeral Parlor. I dialed it. A robot answered, offering me a truly amazing array of death-oriented services ('For Casket Showroom, push 5'). I waited it out – the offer for an actual human being always comes last these days, a booby-prize for boobs who can't cope with the twenty-first century – and while I waited I thought about Wireman's message. The house unlocked? Really? My post-accident memory was unreliable, of course, but habit wasn't. Big Pink did not belong to me, and I had been taught since earliest childhood to take especial care of what

395

belonged to others. I was pretty sure I had locked the house. So if someone had been inside, why hadn't the door been forced?

I thought for just a moment of two little girls in wet dresses — little girls with decayed faces who spoke in the grating voice of the shells under the house — and then pushed the image away with a shudder. They had been only imagination, surely, the vision of an overstrained mind. And even if they had been something more . . . ghosts didn't have to unlock doors, did they? They simply passed right through, or drifted up through the floorboards.

'. . . 0 if you need help.'

By God, I had almost missed my cue. I pushed 0, and after a few bars of something that sounded vaguely like 'Abide with Me', a professionally soothing voice asked if it could help me. I suppressed an irrational and very strong urge to say: *It's my arm! It's never had a decent burial!* and hang up. Instead, cradling the phone and rubbing a spot over my right eyebrow, I asked if Jerome Wireman was there.

'May I ask which deceased he represents?'

A nightmare image rose before me: a silent courtroom of the dead, and Wireman saying *Your Honor, I object.*

'Elizabeth Eastlake,' I said.

'Ah, of course.' The voice warmed, became provisionally human. 'He and his young friend have stepped out — they were going to work on Ms Eastlake's obituary, I believe. I may have a message for you. Will you hold?'

I held. 'Abide with Me' resumed. Digger the Undertaker eventually returned. 'Mr Wireman asks if you would join him and . . . uh . . . Mr Candoori, if possible, at your place on Duma Key at two this afternoon. It says, "If you arrive first, please wait outside." Have you got that?'

'I do. You don't know if he'll be back?'

'No, he didn't say.'

I thanked him and hung up. If Wireman had a cell phone, I'd never seen him carrying it, and I didn't have the number in any case, but Jack had one. I dug the number out of my wallet and dialed it. It diverted to voicemail on the first ring, which told me it was either turned off or dead, either because Jack had forgotten to charge it or because he hadn't paid the bill. Either one was possible.

Jack's severely freaked, and you got to prepare for a shock.

I want to be with you when you look in that basket.

But I already had a pretty good idea about what was in the basket, and I doubted if Wireman had been surprised, either.

Not really.

iv

The Minnesota Mafia was silent around the long table in the Bay Island Room, and even before Pam stood up, I realized they had been doing more than talking about me while I was gone. They had been holding a meeting.

'We're going back,' Pam said. 'That is, most of us are. The Slobotniks had plans to visit Disney World when they came down, the Jamiesons are going on to Miami—'

'And we're going with them, Daddy,' Melinda said. She was holding Ric's arm. 'We can get a flight back to Orly from there that's actually cheaper than the one you booked.'

'I think we could stand the expense,' I said, but I smiled. I felt the strangest mixture of relief, disappointment, and fear. At the same time I could feel the bands that had been tightening in my head come unlocked and start dropping away. The incipient headache was gone, just like that. It could have been the Zomig, but the stuff usually doesn't work that fast, even with a caffeine-laced drink to give it a boost.

'Have you heard from your friend Wireman this morning?' Kamen rumbled.

'Yes,' I said. 'He left a message on my machine.'

'And how is he doing?'

Well. That was a long story, wasn't it? 'He's coping, doing the funeral parlor thing . . . and Jack's helping . . . but he's rocky.'

'Go help him,' Tom Riley said. 'That's your job for the day.'

'Yes, indeed,' Bozie added. 'You're grieving yourself, Edgar. You don't need to be playing host right now.'

'I called the airport,' Pam said, as if I had protested – which I hadn't. 'The Gulfstream's standing by. And the concierge is helping to make the other travel arrangements. In the meantime, we've still got this morning. The question is, what do we do with it?'

We ended up doing what I had planned: we visited the John and Mable Ringling Museum of Art.

And I wore my beret.

v

Early that afternoon, I found myself standing in the boarding area at Dolphin Aviation, kissing my friends and relatives goodbye, or shaking their hands, or hugging them, or all three. Melinda, Ric, and the Jamiesons were already gone.

Kathi Green the Rehab Queen kissed me with her usual ferocity. 'You take care of yourself, Edgar,' she said. 'I love your paintings, but I'm much more proud of the way you're walking. You've made amazing progress. I'd like to parade you in front of my latest generation of crybabies.'

'You're tough, Kathi.'

'Not so tough,' she said, wiping her eyes. 'Truth is, I'm a freakin marshmallow.'

Then Kamen was towering over me. 'If you need help, get in touch ASAP.'

'Yep,' I said. 'You be the KamenDoc.'

Kamen smiled. It was like having God smile on you. 'I don't think all's right with you yet, Edgar. I can only hope it will *be* right. No one deserves more to land with the shiny side up and the rubber side down.'

I hugged him. A one-armed hug, but he made up for it.

I walked out to the plane beside Pam. We stood at the foot of the boarding stairs while the others got on. She was holding my hand in both of hers, looking up at me.

'I'm only going to kiss you on the cheek, Edgar. Illy's watching and I don't want her to get the wrong idea.'

She did so, then said, 'I'm worried about you. There's a white look around your eyes that I don't like.'

'Elizabeth—'

She shook her head a tiny bit. 'It was there last night, even before she came to the gallery. Even when you were at your happiest. A white look. I don't know how to describe it any better than that.

I only saw it once before, back in 1992, when it looked for a little while like you might miss that balloon payment and lose the business.'

The jet engines were whining and a hot breeze was blowing her hair around her face, tumbling her careful beauty-shop curls into something younger and more natural. 'Can I ask you something, Eddie?'

'Of course.'

'Could you paint anywhere? Or does it have to be here?'

'Anywhere, I think. But it would be different somewhere else.'

She was looking at me fixedly. Almost pleadingly. 'Just the same, a change might be good. You need to lose that white look. I'm not talking about coming back to Minnesota, necessarily, just going . . . somewhere else. Will you think about it?'

'Yes.' But not until I saw what was in the red picnic basket. And not until I'd made at least one trip to the south end of the Key. And I thought I could do that. Because *Ilse* was the one who'd gotten sick, not me. All I'd had was one of my red-tinged flash-backs to the accident. And that phantom itch.

'Be well, Edgar. I don't know exactly what's become of you, but there's still enough of the old you to love.' She stood on tiptoe in her white sandals — bought specially for this trip, I had no doubt — and planted another soft kiss on my stubbly cheek.

'Thank you,' I said. 'Thank you for last night.'

'No thanks required,' she said. 'It was sweet.'

She squeezed my hand. Then she was up the stairs and gone.

vi

Outside Delta departures again. This time without Jack.

'Just you and me, Miss Cookie,' I said. 'Looks like we closed down the bar.'

Then I saw she was crying and wrapped my arm around her.

'Daddy, I wish I could stay here with you.'

'Go back, honey. Study for your test and knock the hell out of it. I'll see you soon.'

She pulled back. Looked at me anxiously. 'You'll be okay?'

399

'Yes. And you be okay, too.'

'I will. I will.'

I hugged her again. 'Go on. Check in. Buy magazines. Watch CNN. Fly well.'

'All right, Daddy. It was amazing.'

'*You're* amazing.'

She gave me a hearty smack on the mouth – to make up for the one her mother had held back on, perhaps – and went in through the sliding doors. She turned back once and waved to me, by then little more than a girl-shape behind the polarized glass. I wish with all my heart that I could have seen her better, because I never saw her again.

vii

From the Ringling Art Museum I had left messages for Wireman – one at the funeral home and one on *El Palacio*'s answering machine – saying I'd be back around three, and asking him to meet me there. I also asked him to tell Jack that if Jack was old enough to vote and party with FSU sorority girls, he was old enough to take care of his damned cell phone.

It was actually close to three-thirty when I arrived back on the Key, but both Jack's car and Elizabeth's vintage silver Benz were parked on the cracked square to the right of Big Pink, and the two of them were sitting on my back stoop, drinking iced tea. Jack was still wearing his gray suit, but his hair was once more in its customary disarray and he was wearing a Devil Rays tee under his jacket. Wireman was wearing black jeans and a white shirt, open at the collar; a Nebraska Cornhuskers gimme cap was cocked back on his head.

I parked, got out, and stretched, trying to get my bad hip in gear. They stood up and came to meet me, neither of them smiling.

'Everyone gone, *amigo*?' Wireman asked.

'Everyone but my Aunt Jean and Uncle Ben,' I said. 'They're veteran freeloaders, dedicated to squeezing a good thing to the very last drop.'

Jack smiled without much humor. 'Every family's got a few,' he said.

400

'How are you?' I asked Wireman.

'About Elizabeth I'm okay. Hadlock said it was probably for the best this way, and I suppose he's right. Her leaving me what may amount to a hundred and sixty million dollars in cash, securities, and properties . . .' He shook his head. 'That's different. Maybe someday I'll have the luxury of trying to get my head around it, but right now . . .'

'Right now something's going on.'

'*Sí, señor.* And it's very weird.'

'How much have you told Jack?'

Wireman looked a bit uncomfortable. 'Well, I tell you what, *amigo.* Once I started, it was damn hard to find a reasonable stopping place.'

'He told me all of it,' Jack said. 'Or so he claims. Including what he thinks you did about restoring his eyesight, and what you think you did to Candy Brown.' He paused. 'And the two little girls you saw.'

'Are you okay with the Candy Brown thing?' I asked.

'If it was up to me, I'd give you a medal. And the people of Sarasota would probably give you your own float in the Memorial Day parade.' Jack stuffed his hands in his pockets. 'But if you told me last fall that stuff like this could happen outside of M. Night Shyamalan movies, I would have laughed.'

'What about last week?' I asked.

Jack thought about it. On the other side of Big Pink, the waves came steadily in. Under my living room and bedroom, the shells would be talking. 'No,' he said. 'Probably wouldn't've laughed then. I knew from the first there was something about you, Edgar. You got here, and . . .' He ran the fingers of his two hands together, lacing them. And I thought that was right. That was how it had been. Like the fingers of two hands lacing together. And the fact that I only had one hand had never mattered.

Not here.

'What are you saying, *hermano?*' Wireman asked.

Jack shrugged. 'Edgar and Duma. Duma and Edgar. It was like they were waiting for each other.' He looked embarrassed, but not unsure.

I cocked a thumb at my house. 'Let's go in.'

401

'Tell him about finding the basket first,' Wireman said to Jack.

Jack shrugged. 'Wasn't no thing; didn't take twenty minutes. It was sitting up on top of some old bureau at the far end of the attic. Light from one of the vents to the outside was shining in on it. Like it *wanted* to be found.' He glanced at Wireman, who nodded agreement. 'Anyway, we took it down to the kitchen and looked inside. It was heavier than hell.'

Jack talking about the heaviness of the basket made me think of how Melda, the housekeeper, had been holding it in the family portrait: with her arms bunched. Apparently it had been heavy back then, too.

'Wireman told me to bring the basket down here and leave it for you, since I had a key . . . only I didn't need a key. Place was unlocked.'

'Was the door actually open?'

'Nope. What I did first was turn my key and actually lock it again. Gave me a hell of a surprise.'

'Come on,' Wireman said, leading the way. 'Show and Tell time.'

There was a fair amount of Florida Gulf Coast scattered on the hardwood floor of the entry: sand, small shells, a couple of sophora husks, and a few bits of dried sawgrass. There were also tracks. The sneaker-prints were Jack's. It was the others that made my skin freckle with goosebumps. I made out three sets, one large and two small. The small ones were the tracks of children. All of those feet had been bare.

'Do you see how they go up the stairs, fading as they go?' Jack said.

'Yes,' I said. My voice sounded faint and faraway to my own ears.

'I walked beside them, because I didn't want to mess them up,' Jack said. 'If I'd known then what Wireman told me while we were waiting for you, I don't think I could have gone up at all.'

'I don't blame you,' I said.

'But there was no one there,' Jack said. 'Just . . . well, you'll see. And look.' He led me to the side of the stairs. The ninth riser was on our eye-level, and with the light striking across it, I could see, very faintly, the tracks of small bare feet pointing the other way.

Jack said, 'This looks pretty clear to me. The kids went up to your studio, then came back down again. The adult stayed by the front door, probably as lookout . . . although if this was the middle of the night, there probably wasn't much to look out *for*. Have you been setting the burglar alarm?'

'No,' I said, not quite meeting his eye. 'I can't remember the numbers. I keep them on a slip of paper in my wallet, but each time I came through the door turned into a race against time, me versus that fucking beeper on the wall—'

'It's okay.' Wireman gripped my shoulder. 'These burglars didn't take; they left.'

'You don't really believe Miss Eastlake's dead sisters paid you another visit, do you?' Jack asked.

'Actually,' I said, 'I think they did.' I thought that would sound stupid in the bright light of an April afternoon, with a ton of sunlight pouring down and reflecting off the Gulf, but it didn't.

'In *Scooby Doo*, it would turn out to be the crazy librarian,' Jack said. 'You know, trying to scare you off the Key so he could keep the treasure for himself.'

'If only,' I said.

'Suppose those small tracks *were* made by Tessie and Laura Eastlake,' Wireman said. 'Who made the bigger ones?'

Neither of us replied.

'Let's go upstairs,' I said at last. 'I want to look in the basket.'

We went up (avoiding the tracks – not to preserve them, but simply because none of us wanted to step on them) to Little Pink. The picnic basket, looking just like the one I'd drawn with the red pen I'd pilfered from Gene Hadlock's examining room, was sitting on the carpet, but my eyes were drawn first to my easel.

'You can believe I beat a hasty retreat when I saw *that*,' Jack said.

I could believe it, but I felt no urge to retreat. Quite the opposite. I was drawn forward instead, like an iron bolt to a magnet. A fresh canvas had been set up there and then, sometime in the dead of night – maybe while Elizabeth had been dying, maybe while I'd been having sex with Pam for the last time, maybe while I'd been sleeping beside her – a finger had dipped into my paint. Whose finger? I didn't know. What color? That was obvious: red.

403

The letters that staggered and draggled and dripped their way across the canvas were *red*. And accusing. They almost seemed to shout.

where our sister

viii

'Found art,' I said in a dry, rattlebox voice that hardly sounded like my own.

'Is that what it is?' Wireman asked.

'Sure.' The letters seemed to waver in front of me, and I wiped my eyes. 'Graffiti art. They'd love it at the Scoto.'

'Maybe, but that's some creepy shit,' Jack said. 'I hate it.'

So did I. And it was my studio, goddammit, *mine*. I had a lease. I snatched the canvas off the easel, momentarily expecting it to burn my fingers. It didn't. It was just a canvas, after all, one I'd stretched myself. I put it against the wall, facing in. 'Is that better?'

'It is, actually,' Jack said, and Wireman nodded. 'Edgar . . . if those little girls were here . . . can ghosts write on canvas?'

'If they can move Ouija board planchettes and write in window-frost, I imagine they could write on a canvas,' I said. Then, rather reluctantly, I added: 'But I don't see ghosts unlocking my front door. Or putting a canvas up on the easel to begin with.'

'There wasn't a canvas there?' Wireman asked.

'I'm pretty sure not. The blank ones are all racked in the corner.'

'Who's the sister?' Jack wanted to know. 'Who's the sister they're asking about?'

'It must be Elizabeth,' I said. 'She was the only sister left.'

'Bullshit,' Wireman said. 'If Tessie and Laura were on the ever-popular other side of the veil, they wouldn't have any problem

404

locating sister Elizabeth; she was right here on Duma Key for over fifty-five years, and Duma was the only place *they* ever knew.'

'What about the others?' I asked.

'Maria and Hannah both died,' Wireman said. 'Hannah in the seventies, in New York – Ossining, I think – and Maria in the early eighties, somewhere out west. Both married, Maria a couple of times. I know that from Chris Shannington, not Miss Eastlake. She sometimes talked about her father, but hardly ever about her sisters. She cut herself off from the rest of her family after she and John came back to Duma in 1951.'

where our sister?

'And Adriana? What about her?'

He shrugged. '*Quién sabe?* History ate her up. Shannington thinks she and her new husband probably went back to Atlanta after the search for the babby-uns was called off; they weren't here for the memorial service.'

'She might have blamed Daddy for what happened,' Jack said.

Wireman nodded. 'Or maybe she just couldn't stand to hang around.'

I remembered Adriana's pouty I-want-to-be-somewhere-else look in the family portrait and thought Wireman might be onto something there.

'In any case,' Wireman went on, 'she has to be dead, too. If she was alive, she'd be almost a hundred. Odds of that are mighty slim.'

where our sister?

Wireman gripped my arm and turned me to face him. His face looked drawn and old. '*Muchacho*, if something supernatural killed Miss Eastlake in order to shut her up, maybe we ought to take the hint and get off Duma Key.'

'I think it might be too late for that,' I said.

'Why?'

'Because she's awake again. Elizabeth said so before she died.'

'Who's awake?'

'Perse,' I said.

'Who is that?'

'I don't know,' I said. 'But I think we're supposed to drown her back to sleep.'

ix

The picnic basket had been scarlet when it was new, and had faded only a little over its long life, perhaps because so much of it had been spent tucked away in the attic. I began by hefting one of the handles. The damn thing was pretty heavy, all right; I guessed about twenty pounds. The wicker on the bottom, although tightly woven, had sagged down some. I set it back on the carpet, pushed the thin wooden carry-handles down to either side, and flipped back the lid on hinges that squeaked slightly.

There were colored pencils, most of which had been sharpened down to stubs. And there were drawings made by a certain child prodigy well over eighty years ago. A little girl who'd fallen out of a pony-trap at the age of two and banged her head and awakened with seizures and a magical ability to draw. I knew this even though the drawing on the first page wasn't a drawing at all – not really, but this:

I flicked it up. Beneath was this:

After that, the pictures *became* pictures, growing in technique and sophistication with a speed that was beyond belief. Unless, that was, you happened to be a guy like Edgar Freemantle, who had done little more than doodle until an accident on a building site had taken his arm, crushed his skull, and nearly ended his life.

She had drawn fields. Palms. The beach. A gigantic black face, round as a basketball, with a smiling red mouth – probably Melda the housekeeper, although this Melda looked like an overgrown child in extreme close-up. Then more animals – raccoons, a turtle, a deer, a bobcat – that were naturally sized, but walking on the Gulf or flying through the air. I found a heron, executed in perfect detail, standing on the balcony railing of the house she had grown

406

up in. Directly below it was another watercolor of the same bird, only this time it was hovering upside-down over the swimming pool. The gimlet eyes staring out of the picture were the same shade as the pool itself. *She was doing what I've been doing*, I thought, and my skin began to creep again. *Trying to reinvent the ordinary, make it new by turning it into a dream.*

Would Dario, Jimmy, and Alice cream their jeans if they saw these? I thought there was no doubt.

Here were two little girls – Tessie and Laura, surely – with great big pumpkin smiles that deliberately overran the edges of their faces.

Here was a Daddy bigger than the house beside which he stood – had to be the first Heron's Roost – smoking a cigar the size of a rocket. A smoke-ring circled the moon overhead.

Here were two girls in dark green jumpers on a dirt road with schoolbooks balanced on their heads the way some African native girls balanced their pots: Maria and Hannah, no doubt. Behind them came a line of frogs. In defiance of perspective, the frogs grew larger rather than smaller.

Next came Elizabeth's *Smiling Horses* phase. There were a dozen or more. I leafed through them, then turned back to one and tapped it. 'This is the one that was in the newspaper article.'

Wireman said, 'Go a little deeper. You ain't seen nuthin yet.'

More horses . . . more family, rendered in pencil or charcoal or in jolly watercolors, the family members almost always with their hands linked like paperdolls . . . then a storm, the water in the swimming pool lashed into waves, the fronds of a palm pulled into ragged banners by the wind.

There were well over a hundred pictures in all. She might only have been a child, but she had also been unbottling. Two or three more storm pictures . . . maybe the Alice that had uncovered Eastlake's treasure-trove, maybe just a big thunderstorm, it was impossible to say for sure . . . then the Gulf . . . the Gulf again, this time with flying fish the size of dolphins . . . the Gulf with pelicans that appeared to have rainbows in their mouths . . . the Gulf at sunset . . . and . . .

I stopped, my breath caught in my throat.

Compared with many of the others I'd gone through, this one was dead simple, just the silhouette of a ship against the dying light, caught at the tipping-point between day and dark, but its simplicity was what gave it its power. Certainly I'd thought so when I drew the same thing on my first night in Big Pink. Here was the same cable, stretched taut between the bow and what might in Elizabeth's time have been called a Marconi tower, creating a brilliant orange triangle. Here was the same upward shading of light, orange to blue. There was even the same scribbly, not-quite-careless overlay of color that made the ship – skinnier than mine had been – look like a phantom out there, trudging its way north.

'I drew this,' I said faintly.

'I know,' Wireman said. 'I've seen it. You called it *Hello*.'

I thumbed deeper, hurrying through big bunches of watercolors and colored pencil drawings, knowing what I would eventually find. And yes, near the bottom I came to Elizabeth's first picture of the *Perse*. Only she had drawn it new, a slim three-masted beauty with sails furled, standing in on the blue-green waters of the Gulf beneath a trademark Elizabeth Eastlake sun, the kind that shoots off long happy-rays of light. It was a wonderful piece of work, almost begging for a calypso soundtrack.

But unlike her other paintings, it also felt false.

'Keep going, *muchacho*.'

The ship . . . the ship . . . family, four of them, anyway, standing on the beach with their hands linked like paperdolls and those big Elizabeth happysmiles . . . the ship . . . the house, with what looked like a Negro lawn jockey standing on its head . . . the ship, that gorgeous white swallow . . . John Eastlake . . .

John Eastlake *screaming* . . . blood running from his nose and one eye . . .

I stared at it, mesmerized. It was a child's watercolor, but it had been executed with hellish skill. It depicted a man who looked insane with terror, grief, or both.

'My *God*,' I said.

'One more, *muchacho*,' Wireman said. 'One more to go.'

I flicked back the picture of the screaming man. Old dried watercolors rattled like bones. Beneath the screaming father was the ship again, only this time it really was my ship, my *Perse*. Elizabeth had painted it at night, and not with a brush – I could still see the ancient dried prints of her child's fingers in the swirls of gray and black. This time it was as if she had finally seen through the *Perse's* disguise. The boards were splintered, the sails drooping and full of holes. Around her, blue in the light of a moon that did not smile or send out happy-rays, hundreds of skeleton arms rose from the water in a dripping salute. And standing on the foredeck was a baggy, pallid thing, vaguely female, wearing a decayed something that might have been a cloak, a winding shroud . . . or a robe. It was the red-robe, *my* red-robe, only seen from the front. Three empty sockets peered from its head, and its grin outran the sides of its face in a crazy jumble of lips and teeth. It was far more horrible than my *Girl and Ship* paintings, because it went straight to the heart of the matter without any pause for the mind to catch up. *This is everything awful,* it said. *This is everything you ever feared to find waiting in the dark. See how its grin races off its face in the moonlight. See how the drowned salute it.*

'Christ,' I said, looking up at Wireman. 'When, do you think? After her sisters—?'

'Must have been. Must have been her way of coping with it, don't you think?'

'I don't know,' I said. Part of me was trying to think of my own girls, and part of me was trying not to. 'I don't know how a kid – any kid – could come up with something like that.'

'Race memory,' Wireman said. 'That's what the Jungians would say.'

'And how did I end up painting this same fucking ship? Maybe this same fucking *creature*, only from the back? Do the Jungians have any theories about that?'

'It doesn't say *Perse* on Elizabeth's,' Jack pointed out.

'She would have been four,' I said. 'I doubt if the name would have made much of an impression on her.' I thought of her earlier pictures – the ones where this boat had been a beautiful white lie she had believed for a little while. 'Especially once she saw what it really was.'

'You talk as if it were real,' Wireman said.

My mouth was very dry. I went to the bathroom, drew myself a glass of water, and drank it down. 'I don't know what I believe about this,' I said, 'but I have a general rule of thumb in life, Wireman. If one person sees a thing, it could be a hallucination. If two people

409

see it, chances of reality improve exponentially. Elizabeth and I both saw the *Perse*.'

'In your *imaginations*,' Wireman said. 'In your *imaginations* you saw it.'

I pointed to Wireman's face and said, 'You've seen what my imagination can do.'

He didn't reply, but he nodded. He was very pale.

'You said, "Once she saw what it really was," ' Jack said. 'If the boat in that picture is real, what is it, exactly?'

'I think you know,' Wireman said. 'I think we all do; it's pretty damned hard to miss. We're just afraid to say it out loud. Go on, Jack. God hates a coward.'

'Okay, it's a ship of the dead,' Jack said. His voice was flat in my clean, well-lighted studio. He put his hands to his head and raked his fingers slowly through his hair, making it wilder than ever. 'But I'll tell you something, you guys: – if that's what's coming for me in the end, I sort of wish I'd never been born in the first place.'

x

I set the thick stack of drawings and watercolors aside on the carpet, delighted to get the last two out of my sight. Then I looked at what had been under her pictures, weighing the picnic basket down.

It was ammo for the spear-pistol. I lifted one of the stubby harpoons out. It was about fifteen inches long, and quite heavy. The shaft was steel, not aluminum – I wasn't sure aluminum had even been used in the nineteen-twenties. The business-end was triple-bladed, and although the blades were tarnished, they looked sharp. I touched the ball of my finger to one, and a tiny bead of blood appeared on the skin instantly.

'You ought to disinfect that,' Jack said.

'Yes indeed,' I said. I turned the thing over in the afternoon sun, sending reflections bounding around the walls. The short harpoon had its own ugly beauty, a paradox perhaps reserved exclusively for certain weapons of efficiency.

'This wouldn't go very far in water,' I said. 'Not as heavy as it is.'

'You'd be surprised,' Wireman said. 'The gun fires off a spring *and* a CO_2 cartridge. She bangs pretty good. And back in those days, short range was enough. The Gulf teemed with fish, even close in. If Eastlake wanted to shoot something, he could usually do it at point blank range.'

'I don't understand these tips,' I said.

Wireman said, 'Nor do I. She had at least a dozen harpoons, including four mounted on the wall in the library, and none of them are like these.'

Jack had gone into the bathroom and come back with a bottle of hydrogen peroxide. Now he took the harpoon I was holding and examined the triple-bladed tip. 'What is it? Silver?'

Wireman made his thumb and forefinger into a gun and pointed it at him. 'Hold your cards, but Wireman thinks you have scored a Bingo.'

'And you don't *get* that?' Jack asked.

Wireman and I looked at each other, then at Jack again.

'You haven't been watching the right movies,' he said. 'Silver bullets are what you use to kill werewolves. I don't know if silver works on vampires or not, but obviously *somebody* thought it did. Or that it might.'

'If you're suggesting Tessie and Laura Eastlake are vampires,' Wireman said, 'they must have built up a hell of a thirst since 1927.' He looked at me, expecting corroboration.

'I think Jack's onto something,' I said. I took the bottle of peroxide, dipped the finger I'd pricked into it, and splashed the bottle up and down a couple of times.

'Man-law,' Jack said, grimacing.

'Not unless you were planning to drink it,' I said, and after a moment's consideration Jack and I both burst out laughing.

'Huh?' Wireman asked. 'I don't get it.'

'Never mind,' Jack said, still grinning. Then he grew serious again. 'But there are no such things as vampires, Edgar. There could be ghosts, I'll give you that much – I think almost everyone believes there could be ghosts – but there's no such thing as vampires.' He brightened as an idea struck him. 'Besides, it takes a vampire to make a vampire. The Eastlake twins *drowned*.'

I picked up the short harpoon again, turning it from side to side,

411

making the reflection from the tarnished tip tumble along the wall. 'Still, this is suggestive.'

'Really,' Jack agreed.

'So's the unlocked door you found when you brought the picnic basket,' I said. 'The tracks. The canvas that was lifted out of the rack and put onto the easel.'

'You saying it was the crazy librarian after all, *amigo?*'

'No. Just that . . .' My voice cracked, broke. I had to take another sip of water before I could say what needed saying. 'Just that maybe vampires aren't the only things that come back from the dead.'

'What are you talking about?' Jack asked. 'Zombies?'

I thought of the *Perse* with her rotting sails. 'Let's say deserters.'

xi

'Are you sure you want to be here alone tonight, Edgar?' Wireman asked. 'Because I'm not sure it's such a great idea. Especially with that stack of old pictures for company.' He sighed. 'You have succeeded in giving Wireman a first-class case of the willies.'

We were sitting out in the Florida room, watching the sun start its long, slow decline toward the horizon. I had produced cheese and crackers.

'I'm not sure this will work otherwise,' I said. 'Think of me as a gunslinger of the art world. I paint alone, podner.'

Jack looked at me over a fresh glass of iced tea. 'You're planning to *paint?*'

'Well – sketch. It's what I know how to do.' And when I thought back to a certain pair of gardening gloves – HANDS printed on the back of one, OFF on the back of the other – I thought sketching would be enough, especially if I did it with little Elizabeth Eastlake's colored pencils.

I swung around to Wireman. 'You have the funeral parlor tonight, correct?'

Wireman glanced at his watch and heaved a sigh. 'Correct. From six until eight. There's another visitation tomorrow from noon until two. Relatives from afar will come to bare their teeth at the usurping interloper. That would be me. Then the final act, day after tomorrow.

Funeral at the Unitarian Universalist Church in Osprey. That's at ten. Followed by cremation at Abbot-Wexler. Burny-burny, hot-hot-hot.'

Jack grimaced. 'Gross me *out*.'

Wireman nodded. '*Death* is gross, son. Remember what we sang as children? "The worms crawl in, the worms crawl out, and the pus runs out like shaving cream."'

'Classy,' I said.

'Yep,' Wireman agreed. He selected another cracker, looked at it, then threw it violently back onto the tray. It bounced onto the floor. 'This is nuts. The whole thing.'

Jack picked up the cracker, seemed to consider eating it, then put it aside. Perhaps he had decided eating crackers off a Florida room floor violated another man-law. Probably it did. There are so many.

I said to Wireman, 'When you come back from the funeral parlor tonight, you check in on me, okay?'

'Yes.'

'If I tell you I'm fine, to just go on home, you do it.'

'Don't interrupt you if you're communing with your muse. Or the spirits.'

I nodded, because he wasn't that far off. Then I turned to Jack. 'And you're staying at *El Palacio* while Wireman's at the funeral parlor, right?'

'Sure, if that's what you guys want.' He looked a little uneasy about it, and I didn't blame him. It was a big house, Elizabeth had lived in it a long time, and it was where her memory was freshest. I would have been uneasy, too, if I hadn't been sure the spooks on Duma Key were elsewhere.

'If I call you, come on the run.'

'I will. Call me on the house phone or my cell phone.'

'You sure your cell phone's working?'

He looked slightly shamefaced. 'Battery was a little flat, is all. I got it charged in my car.'

Wireman said, 'I wish I understood better why you feel like you have to keep fooling with this, Edgar.'

'Because it's not over. For years it was. For years Elizabeth lived here very quietly, first with her father and then on her own. She had her charities, she had her friends, she played tennis, she played bridge – so Mary Ire told me – and most of all, she had the Suncoast art scene. It was the quiet, rewarding life of an elderly woman with lots of money and few bad habits other than her cigarettes. Then things started to change. *La lotería.* You said it yourself, Wireman.'

'You really think something's been making all this happen,' he said. Not with disbelief; with awe.

'It's what *you* believe,' I said.

'Sometimes I do. It isn't what I *want* to believe. That there's something with a reach so long . . . with eyesight keen enough to see you . . . me . . . God knows who or what else . . .'

'I don't like it either,' I said, but that was far from the truth. The truth was I hated it. 'I don't like the idea that something may have actually reached out and killed Elizabeth – maybe scared her to death – just to shut her up.'

'And you think you can find out what's going on from those pictures.'

'Some, yes. How much I won't know until I try.'

'And then?'

'It depends. Almost certainly a trip to the south end of the Key. There's unfinished business there.'

Jack put down his tea-glass. 'What unfinished business?'

I shook my head. 'Don't know. Her pictures may tell me.'

'Just as long as you don't get in over your head and discover you can't get back to shore,' Wireman said. 'That's what happened to those two little girls.'

'I know it,' I said.

Jack pointed his finger at me. 'Take care of yourself. Man-law.'

I nodded and pointed back. 'Man-law.'

15 – Intruder

i

Twenty minutes later I sat in Little Pink with my sketch-pad on my lap and the red picnic basket beside me. Directly ahead, filling the western-facing window with light, was the Gulf. Far below me was the murmur of the shells. I had set my easel aside and covered my paint-splattered work-table with a piece of toweling. I laid the remains of her freshly sharpened colored pencils on top of it. There wasn't much left of those pencils, which were fat and somehow antique, but I thought there'd be enough. I was ready.

'Bullshit I am,' I said. I was never going to be ready for this, and part of me was hoping nothing would happen. I thought something would, though. I thought that was why Elizabeth had wanted me to find her drawings. But how much of what was inside the red basket did she actually remember? My guess was that Elizabeth had forgotten most of what had happened to her when she was a child even before the Alzheimer's came along to complicate things. Because forgetting isn't always involuntary. Sometimes it's *willed*.

Who would want to remember something so awful that it had made your father scream until he bled? Better to stop drawing completely. To just go cold turkey. Better to tell people you can hardly even draw stick figures, that when it comes to art you're like wealthy alums who support their college sports teams: if you can't be an athlete, be an athletic supporter. Better to put it out of your mind completely, and in your old age, creeping senility will take care of the rest.

Oh, some of that old ability may still remain – like scar-tissue on the *dura* of the brain from an old injury (caused by falling out of a pony-trap, let's say) – and you might have to find ways to let that out once in awhile, to express it like a build-up of pus from

415

an infection that will never quite heal. So you get interested in other people's art. You become, in fact, a *patron* of the arts. And if that's still not enough? Why, maybe you begin to collect china figures and buildings. You begin to build yourself a China Town. No one will call creating such *tableaux* art, but it's certainly imaginative, and the regular exercise of the imagination – its visual aspect in particular – is enough to make it stop.

Make what stop?

The itch, of course.

That damnable itch.

I scratched at my right arm, passed through it, and for the ten thousandth time found only my ribs. I flipped back the cover of my pad to the first sheet.

Start with a blank surface.

It called to me, as I was sure such blank sheets had once called to her.

Fill me up. Because white is the absence of memory, the color of can't remember. Make. Show. Draw. And when you do, the itch will go away. For awhile the confusion will subside.

Please stay on the Key, she had said. *No matter what happens. We need you.*

I thought that might be true.

I sketched quickly. Just a few strokes. Something that could have been a cart. Or possibly a pony-trap, standing still and waiting for the pony.

'They lived here happily enough,' I told the empty studio. 'Father and daughters. Then Elizabeth fell out of the pony-trap and started to draw, the off-season hurricane exposed the debris field, the little girls drowned. Then the rest of them pop off to Miami, and the trouble stops. And, when they came back nearly twenty-five years later . . .'

Beneath the pony-trap I printed **FINE**. Paused. Added **AGAIN. FINE AGAIN.**

Fine, the shells whispered far below. *Fine again.*

Yes, they had been fine, John and Elizabeth had been fine. And after John died, Elizabeth had continued being fine. Fine with her art shows. Fine with her chinas. Then things had for some reason begun to change again. I didn't know if the deaths of Wireman's wife and daughter had been a part of that change, but I thought they might have been. And about his arrival and mine on Duma Key I thought there was no question. I had no rational reason for believing that, but I did.

Things on Duma Key had been okay ... then strange ... then for a long time they'd been okay again. And now ...

She's awake.

The table is leaking.

If I wanted to know what was happening now, I had to know what had happened then. Dangerous or not, I *had* to.

ii

I picked up her first drawing, which wasn't a drawing at all but just an uncertain line running across the middle of the paper. I took it in my left hand, closed my eyes, and then pretended I was touching it with my right, just as I had with Pam's HANDS OFF gardening gloves. I tried to see my right fingers running over that hesitant line. I could – sort of – but I felt a kind of despair. Did I mean to do this with all of the pictures? There had to be twelve dozen, and that was a conservative estimate. Also, I wasn't exactly being over-whelmed with psychic information.

Take it easy. Rome wasn't built in an hour.

I decided a little Radio Free Bone couldn't hurt and might help. I got up, holding the ancient piece of paper in my right hand, and of course it went fluttering to the floor because there *was* no right hand. I bent to pick it up, thinking I had the saying wrong, the saying was *Rome wasn't built in a* day.

But Melda says nour.

I stopped, holding the sheet of paper in my left hand. The hand the crane hadn't been able to get to. Was that an actual memory, something that had come drifting out of the picture, or just some-thing I'd made up? Just my mind, trying to be obliging?

'It's not a picture,' I said, looking at the hesitant line.

No, but it tried to be a picture.

My ass went back onto the seat of my chair with a thump. It wasn't a voluntary act of sitting; it was more a case of my knees

417

losing their lock and letting go. I looked at the line, then out the window. From the Gulf to the line. From the line to the Gulf.

She had tried to draw the horizon. It had been her first thing. *Yes.*

I picked up my pad and seized one of her pencils. It didn't matter which one as long as it was hers. It felt too big, too fat, in my hand. It also felt just right. I began to draw.

On Duma Key, it was what I did best.

iii

I sketched a child sitting on a potty chair. Her head was bandaged. She had a drinking glass in one hand. Her other arm was slung around her father's neck. He was wearing a strap-style undershirt and had shaving cream on his cheeks. Standing in the background, just a shadow, was the housekeeper. No bracelets in this sketch, because she didn't always wear them, but the kerchief was wrapped around her head, the knot in front. Nan Melda, the closest thing to a mother Libbit ever knew.

Libbit?

Yes, that was what they called her. What she called herself. Libbit, little Libbit.

'The littlest one of all,' I murmured, and flicked back the first page of the sketch-pad. The pencil – too short, too fat, unused for over three-quarters of a century – was the perfect tool, the perfect *channel*. It began to move again.

I sketched the little girl in a room. Books appeared on the wall behind her and it was a study. Daddy's study. The bandage was wound around her head. She was at a desk. She was wearing what looked like a housecoat. She had a

(*ben-cil*)

pencil in her hand. One of the colored pencils? Probably not – not then, not yet – but it didn't matter. She had found her thing, her focus, her *métier*. And how hungry it made her! How ravenous!

She thinks I will have more paper, please.

She thinks I am ELIZABETH.

'She literally drew herself back into the world,' I said, and my

418

body broke out in gooseflesh from head to toe – for hadn't I done the same? Hadn't I done *exactly* the same, here on Duma Key?

I had more work to do. I thought it was going to be a long and exhausting evening, but I felt I was on the verge of great discoveries, and what I felt wasn't fright – not then – but a kind of copper-mouthed excitement.

I bent down and picked up Elizabeth's third drawing. The fourth. The fifth. The sixth. Moving with greater and greater speed. Sometimes I stopped to draw, but mostly I didn't have to. The pictures were forming in my head, now, and the reason I didn't have to put them down on paper seemed clear to me: Elizabeth had already done that work, long ago, when she had been recovering from the accident that nearly killed her.

In the happy days before Noveen began to talk.

iv

At one point during my interview with Mary Ire, she said discovering in my middle age that I could paint with the best of them must have been like having someone give me the keys to a souped-up muscle car – a Roadrunner or a GTO. I said yes, it was like that. At another point she said it must have been like having someone give me the keys to a fully furnished house. A mansion, really. I said yes, like that, too. And if she had gone on? Said it must have been like inheriting a million shares of Microsoft stock, or being elected ruler for life of some oil-rich (and peaceful) emirate in the mideast? I would have said yeah, sure, you bet. To soothe her. Because those questions were *about* her. I could see the longing look in her eyes when she asked them. They were the eyes of a kid who knows the closest she's ever going to get to realizing her dream of the high trapeze is sitting on the bleachers at the Saturday matinee performance. She was a critic, and lots of critics who aren't called to do what they write about grow jealous and mean and small in their disappointment. Mary wasn't like that. Mary still loved it all. She drank whiskey from a water-glass and wanted to know what it was like when Tinkerbell flew out of nowhere and tapped you on the shoulder and you discovered that, even though you were on the

419

wrinkle-neck side of fifty, you had suddenly gained the ability to fly past the face of the moon. So even though it wasn't like having a fast car or being handed the keys to a fully furnished house, I told her it was. Because you *can't* tell anyone what it's like. You can only talk around it until everyone's exhausted and it's time to go to sleep.

But Elizabeth had known what it was like.

It was in her drawings, then in her paintings.

It was like being given a tongue when you had been mute. And more. Better. It was like being given back your memory, and a person's memory is everything, really. Memory is identity. It's *you*. Even from that first line – that incredibly *brave* first line meant to show where the Gulf met the sky – she had understood that seeing and memory were interchangeable, and had set out to mend herself.

Perse hadn't been in it. Not at first.

I was sure of that.

v

For the next four hours, I slipped in and out of Libbit's world. It was a wonderful, frightening place to be. Sometimes I scribbled words – *The gift is always hungry, start with what you know* – but mostly it was pictures. Pictures were the real language we shared.

I understood her family's quick arc from amazement to acceptance to boredom. It had happened partly because the girl was so prolific, maybe more because she was part of *them*, she was their little Libbit, and there's always that feeling that no good can come out of Nazareth, isn't there? But their boredom only made her hunger stronger. She looked for new ways to wow them, sought new ways of seeing.

And found them, God help her.

I drew birds flying upside-down, and animals walking on the swimming pool.

I drew a horse with a smile so big it ran off the sides of its face. I thought it was right around then that Perse had entered the picture. Only—

'Only Libbit didn't *know* it was Perse,' I said. 'She thought—'

420

I thumbed back through her drawings, almost to the beginning. To the round black face with the smiling mouth. At first glance I had dismissed this one as Elizabeth's portrait of Nan Melda, but I should have known better – it was a child's face, not a woman's. A *doll's* face. Suddenly my hand was printing NOVEEN beside it in strokes so hard that Elizabeth's old canary-yellow pencil snapped on the last stroke of the second N. I threw it on the floor and grabbed another.

It was Noveen that Perse had spoken through first, so as not to frighten her little genius. What could be less threatening than a little black girl-dolly who smiled and wore a red kerchief around her head, just like the beloved Nan Melda?

And was Elizabeth shocked or frightened when the doll began to speak on its own? I didn't think so. She might have been fiercely talented in that one narrow way, but she was still only a child of three.

Noveen told her things to draw, and Elizabeth—

I grabbed my sketch-pad again. Drew a cake lying on the floor. *Splattered* on the floor. Little Libbit thought that prank was Noveen's idea, but it had been Perse, testing Elizabeth's power. Perse experimenting as I had experimented, trying to find out how powerful this new tool might be.

Next had come the Alice.

Because, her doll whispered, there was treasure and a storm would uncover it.

So not an Alice at all, not really. And not an Elizabeth, because she *hadn't* been Elizabeth yet – not to her family, not to herself. The big blow of '27 had been Hurricane Libbit.

Because Daddy would like finding a treasure. And because Daddy needed to think of something besides—

'She's made her bed,' I said in a harsh voice that didn't sound like my own. 'Let her sleep in it.'

—besides how mad he was at Adie for running off with Emery, that Celluloid Collar.

Yes. That was how it had been on the south end of Duma Key, back in '27.

I drew John Eastlake – only it was just his fins showing against the sky, and the tip of his snorkel, and a shadow beneath. John Eastlake diving for treasure.

Diving for his youngest daughter's new doll, although he probably didn't believe it.

Beside one flipper I printed the words **FAIR SALVAGE**.

The images rose in my mind, clearer and clearer, as if they had been waiting all these years to be liberated, and I wondered briefly if every painting (and every implement used to make them), from those on the walls of caves in central Asia to the *Mona Lisa,* held such hidden memories of their making and makers, encoded in their strokes like DNA.

Swim n kick til I say stop.

I added Elizabeth to the picture of Diving Daddy, standing up to her chubby knees in the water, Noveen tucked under her arm. Libbit almost could have been the doll-girl in the sketch Ilse had demanded – the one I had titled *The End of the Game.*

And after he saw all those things, he hug me hug me hug me.

I made a hurried little sketch of John Eastlake doing just that, his facemask pushed up on top of his head. The picnic basket was nearby, on a blanket, and the spear-gun was resting on top of it.

He hug me hug me hug me.

Draw her, a voice whispered. *Draw Elizabeth's fair salvage. Draw Perse.*

But I wouldn't. I was afraid of what I might see. And what it might do to me.

And what about Daddy? What about John? How much had *he* known?

I flipped through her drawings to the picture of John Eastlake screaming, with blood running from his nose and one eye. He had known plenty. Probably too late, but he had known.

What exactly *had* happened to Tessie and Lo-Lo?

And to Perse, to shut her up for all those years?

What exactly was she? Not a doll, that much seemed sure.

I could have gone on – a picture of Tessie and Lo-Lo running down a path, some path, hand-in-hand, was already asking to be drawn – but I was beginning to come out of my half-trance and was scared almost to death. Besides, I thought I knew enough to be going on with; Wireman could help me figure out the rest, I was almost sure of it. I closed my sketch-pad. I put down that long-gone little girl's brown pencil – now just a nubbin – and realized

I was hungry. Ravenous, in fact. But that kind of hangover wasn't new to me, and there was plenty to eat in the refrigerator.

vi

I went downstairs slowly, my head spinning with images – an upside-down heron with blue gimlet eyes, the smiling horses, the boat-size swim-fins on Daddy's feet – and I didn't bother with the living room lights. There was no need to; by April I could have navigated the route from the foot of the stairs to the kitchen in pitch blackness. By then I had made that solitary house with its chin jutting over the edge of the water my own, and in spite of everything, I couldn't imagine leaving it. Halfway across the room I stopped, looking out through the Florida room to the Gulf.

There, riding at anchor no more than a hundred yards from the beach, clear and unmistakable in the light of a quarter-moon and a million stars, was the *Perse*. Her sails had been furled, but nets of rope sagged from her ancient masts like spiderwebs. *The shrouds*, I thought. *Those are its shrouds.* She bobbed up and down like a long dead child's rotten toy. The decks were empty, so far as I could see – of both life and souvenirs – but who knew what might be belowdecks?

I was going to faint. At the same instant I realized this, I realized why: I had stopped breathing. I told myself to inhale, but for one terrible second, nothing happened. My chest remained as flat as a page in a closed book. When it rose at last, I heard a whooping sound. That was me, struggling to go on with life in a conscious state. I blew out the air I had just taken in and inhaled more, a little less noisily. Black specks flocked in front of my eyes in the dimness, then faded. I expected the ship out there to do the same – surely it had to be a hallucination – but it remained, perhaps a hundred and twenty feet long and a little less than half that in the beam. Bobbing on the waves. Rocking from side to side just a little, too. Bowsprit wagging like a finger, seeming to say *Ouuu, you nasty man, you're in for it n—*

I slapped myself across the face hard enough to bring water to my left eye and the ship was still right there. I realized that if it *was*

423

there – truly there – then Jack would be able to see it from the boardwalk at *El Palacio*. There was a phone on the far side of the living room, but from where I was standing, the one on the kitchen counter was closer. And it had the advantage of being right under the light switches. I wanted lights, especially the ones in the kitchen, those good hard fluorescents. I backed out of the living room, not taking my eyes off the ship, and hit all three switches with the back of my hand. The lights came on, and I lost sight of the *Perse* – of everything beyond the Florida room – in their bright, no-nonsense glare. I reached for the phone, then stopped.

There was a man in my kitchen. He was standing by my refrigerator. He was wearing soaked rags that might once have been blue jeans and the kind of shirt that's called a boat-neck. What appeared to be moss was growing on his throat, cheeks, forehead, and forearms. The right side of his skull was crushed in. Petals of bone protruded through the lank foliage of his dark hair. One of his eyes – the right – was gone. What remained was a spongy socket. The other was an alien, disheartening silver that had nothing to do with humanity. His feet were bare, swollen, purple, and burst through to the bone at the ankles.

It grinned at me, lips splitting as they drew back, revealing two lines of yellow teeth set into old black gums. It raised its right arm, and here I saw what must have been another relic of the *Perse*. It was a manacle. One old and rusty circlet was clamped around the thing's wrist. The other one hung open like a loose jaw.

The other one was for me.

It emitted a loose hissing sound, perhaps all its decayed vocal cords could produce, and began to walk toward me under the bright no-nonsense fluorescents. It left footprints on the hardwood floor. It cast a shadow. I could hear a faint creaking and saw it was wearing a soaked leather belt – rotten, but for the time being, still holding.

A queer soft paralysis had come over me. I was conscious, but I couldn't run even though I understood what that open manacle meant, and what this thing was: a one-man press gang. He would clamp me and take me aboard yonder frigate, or schooner, or barquentine, or whatever-the-hell-it-was. I would become part of the crew. And while there might not be cabin boys on the *Perse*, I

424

thought there were at least two cabin *girls*, one named Tessie and one named Lo-Lo.

You have to run. At least clock it one with the phone, for Christ's sake!

But I couldn't. I was like a bird hypnotized by a snake. The best I could do was to take one numb step backward into the living room . . . then another . . . then a third. Now I was in the shadows again. It stood in the kitchen doorway with the white light of the fluorescents striking across its damp and rotted face and throwing its shadow across the living room carpet. Still grinning. I considered closing my eyes and trying to wish it away, but that wasn't going to work; I could *smell* it, like a Dumpster behind a restaurant that specializes in fish dinners. And—

'Time to go, Edgar.'

—it could talk, after all. The words were slushy but understandable.

It took a step into the living room. I took another of my numb steps backward, knowing in my heart it would do no good, that compensation wasn't enough, that when it got tired of playing it would simply dart forward and clamp that iron manacle on my wrist and drag me, screaming, down to the water, down to the *caldo largo*, and the last sound I'd hear on the living side would be the grating conversation of the shells under the house. Then the water would fill my ears.

I took another step back just the same, not sure I was even moving toward the door, only hoping, then another . . . and a hand fell on my shoulder.

I shrieked.

vii

'What the *fuck* is that thing?' Wireman whispered in my ear.

'I don't know,' I said, and I was sobbing. Sobbing with fear. 'Yes I do. I *do* know. Look out at the Gulf, Wireman.'

'I can't. I don't dare take my eyes off it.'

But the thing in the doorway had seen Wireman now – Wireman who'd come in through the open door just as it had itself, Wireman who had arrived like the cavalry in a John Wayne Western – and

425

had stopped three steps inside the living room, its head slightly lowered, the manacle swinging back and forth from its outstretched arm.

'Christ,' Wireman said. 'That ship! The one in the paintings!'

'Go on,' the thing said. 'We have no business with you. Go on, and you may live.'

'It's lying,' I said.

'Tell me something I don't know,' Wireman said, then raised his voice. He was standing just behind me, and he almost blew out my eardrum. '*Leave! You're trespassing!*'

The drowned young man made no reply, but it was every bit as fast as I had feared. At one moment it was standing three steps inside the living room. At the next it was right in front of me, and I had only the vaguest, flickering impression of it crossing the distance between. Its smell – rot and seaweed and dead fish turning to soup in the sun – bloomed and became overwhelming. I felt its hands, freezing cold, close over my forearm, and cried out in shock and horror. It wasn't the cold, it was how *soft* they were. How *flabby*. That one silver eye peered at me, seeming to drill into my brain, and for a moment there was a sensation of being filled with pure darkness. Then the manacle clamped on my wrist with a flat hard clacking sound.

'*Wireman!*' I screamed, but Wireman was gone. He was running away from me, across the room, as fast as he could.

The drowned thing and I were chained together. It dragged me toward the door.

viii

Wireman was back just before the dead man could pull me over the threshold. He had something in his hand that looked like a blunt dagger. For a moment I thought it must be one of the silver harpoons, but that was only a powerful bit of wishful thinking; the silver harpoons were upstairs with the red picnic basket. 'Hey!' he said. 'Hey, you! Yeah, I'm talking to you! *Cojudo de puta madre!*'

Its head snapped around as fast as the head of a snake about to

426

strike. Wireman was almost as fast. Holding the blunt object in both hands, he drove it into the thing's face, striking home just above the right eye-socket. The thing shrieked, a sound that went through my head like shards of glass. I saw Wireman wince and stagger back; saw him struggle to hold onto his weapon and drop it to the sandy floor of the entryway. It didn't matter. The man-thing which had seemed so solid spun into insubstantiality, clothes and all. I felt the manacle around my wrist also lose its solidity. For a moment I could still see it and then it was only water, dripping onto my sneakers and the carpet. There was a larger wet patch where the demon sailor had been only a moment before.

I felt thicker warmth on my face and wiped blood from my nose and off my upper lip. Wireman had fallen over a hassock. I helped him up and saw his nose was bleeding, too. A line of blood also ran down the side of his throat from his left ear. It rose and fell with the rapid beat of his heart.

'Christ, that *scream*,' he said. 'My eyes are watering and my ears are ringing like a motherfucker. Can you hear me, Edgar?'

'Yes,' I said. 'Are you all right?'

'Other than thinking I just saw a dead guy disappear in fucking front of me? I guess so.' He bent down, picked the blunt cylinder off the floor, and kissed it. 'Glory be to God for dappled things,' he said, then barked laughter. 'Even when they're not dappled.'

It was a candlestick. The tip, where you were supposed to stick your candle, looked dark, as if it had touched something very hot instead of something cold and wet.

'There are candles in all Miss Eastlake's rentals, because we lose the power out here all the time,' Wireman said. 'We have a gennie at the big house, but the other places don't, not even this one. But unlike the smaller houses, this one *does* have candlesticks from the big house, and they just happen to be silver.'

'And you remembered that,' I said. Marveled, really.

He shrugged, then looked at the Gulf. So did I. There was nothing there but moonlight and starlight on the water. For now, at least.

Wireman gripped my wrist. His fingers closed over it where the manacle had been, and my heart jumped. 'What?' I said, not liking the new fear I saw in his face.

'Jack,' he said. 'Jack's alone at *El Palacio*.'

We took Wireman's car. In my terror, I'd never noticed the headlights or heard it pull in beside my own.

ix

Jack was okay. There had been a few calls from old friends of Elizabeth's, but the last one had come at quarter of nine, an hour and a half before we came bursting in, bloody and wide-eyed, Wireman still waving the candlestick. There had been no intruders at *El Palacio*, and Jack hadn't seen the ship that had been anchored for awhile in the Gulf off Big Pink. Jack had been eating microwave popcorn and watching *Beverly Hills Cop* on an old videotape.

He listened to our story with mounting amazement, but no real disbelief; this was a young man, I had to remind myself, that had been raised on shows like *The X-Files* and *Lost*. Besides, it fit with what he'd been told earlier. When we were done, he took the candlestick from Wireman and examined the tip, which looked like the burnt filament in a dead lightbulb.

'Why didn't it come for me?' he asked. 'I was alone, and totally unprepared.'

'I don't want to bruise your self-esteem,' I said, 'but I don't think you're exactly a priority to whoever's running this show.'

Jack was looking at the narrow red mark on my wrist. 'Edgar, is that where—'

I nodded.

'Fuck,' Jack said in a low voice.

'Have you figured out what's going on?' Wireman asked me. 'If she sent that thing after you, she must think you have, or that you're close.'

'I don't think anyone will ever know all of it,' I said, 'but I know who that thing was when it was alive.'

'Who?' Jack was staring at me with wide eyes. We were standing in the kitchen and Jack was still holding the candlestick. Now he put it aside on the counter.

'Emery Paulson. Adriana Eastlake's husband. They came back from Atlanta to help with the search after Tessie and Laura went missing,

428

that much is true, but they never left Duma Key again. Perse saw to that.'

x

We went into the parlor where I had first met Elizabeth Eastlake. The long, low table was still there, but now it was empty. Its polished surface struck me as a pitch-perfect mockery of life.

'Where are they?' I asked Wireman. 'Where are her chinas? Where's the Village?'

'I boxed everything up and put it in the summer-kitchen,' he said, pointing vaguely. 'No real reason, I just . . . I just couldn't . . . *muchacho*, would you like some green tea? Or a beer?'

I asked for water. Jack said he'd take a beer, if that was all right. Wireman set off to get them. He made it as far as the hallway before starting to cry. They were big, noisy sobs, the kind you can't stifle no matter how hard you try.

Jack and I looked at each other, then looked away. We said nothing.

xi

He was gone a lot longer than it usually takes to get two cans of beer and a glass of water, but when he came back, he had regained his composure.

'Sorry,' he said. 'I don't usually lose someone I love and poke a candlestick in a vampire's face in the same week. Usually it's one or the other.' He shrugged his shoulders in an effort at insouciance. It was unsuccessful, but I had to give him points for trying.

'They're not vampires,' I said.

'Then what are they?' he asked. 'Expatiate.'

'I can only tell you what her pictures told me. You have to remember that, no matter how talented she might have been, she was still only a child.' I hesitated, then shook my head. 'Not even that. Hardly more than a baby. Perse was . . . I guess you'd say Perse was her spirit-guide.'

Wireman cracked his beer, sipped it, then leaned forward. 'And

429

what about you? Is Perse your spirit-guide, as well? Has she been intensifying what *you* do?'

'Of course she has,' I said. 'She's been testing the limits of my ability and extending them – I'm sure that's what Candy Brown was about. And she's been picking my material. That's what the *Girl and Ship* paintings were about.'

'And the rest of your stuff?' Jack asked.

'Mostly mine, I think. But some of it—' I stopped, suddenly struck by a terrible idea. I put my glass aside and almost knocked it over. 'Oh Christ.'

'What?' Wireman asked. 'For God's sake, what?'

'You need to get your little red book of phone numbers. Right now.'

He went and got it, then handed me the cordless telephone. I sat for a moment with it in my lap, not sure who to call first. Then I knew. But there is one rule of modern life even more ironclad than the one which states that there's never a cop around when you need one: when you really need a human being, you always get the answering machine.

That's what I got at Dario Nannuzzi's home, at Jimmy Yoshida's, at Alice Aucoin's.

'*Fuck!*' I cried, slamming the disconnect button with my thumb when Alice's recorded voice started in with 'I'm sorry I'm not here to take your call right now, but—'

'They're probably still celebrating,' Wireman said. 'Give it time, *amigo*, and it'll all quiet down.'

'I don't *have* time!' I said. 'Fuck! Shit! *Fuck!*'

He put a hand on mine, and spoke soothingly. 'What is it, Edgar? What's wrong?'

'The pictures are dangerous! Maybe not all, but some, for sure!'

He thought about it, then nodded. 'Okay. Let's think about this. The most dangerous ones are probably the *Girl and Ship* series, right?'

'Yes. I'm sure that's the case.'

'They're almost certainly still at the gallery, waiting to be framed and shipped.'

Shipped. Dear God, *shipped*. Even the word was scary. 'I can't let that happen.'

'*Muchacho*, getting sidetracked is what you can't let happen.'

He didn't understand this wasn't a sidetrack. Perse could whistle up a great wind when she wanted to.

But she needed help.

I found the number of the Scoto and dialed it. I thought it was just possible that someone might be there, even at quarter of eleven on the night after the big shindig. But the ironclad rule held, and I got the machine. I waited impatiently, then pressed 9 to leave a general message.

'Listen, you guys,' I said, 'this is Edgar. I don't want you to send *any* of the paintings or drawings out until I tell you, okay? *Not a single one.* Just put a hold on em for a few days. Use any excuse you have to, but do it. Please. It's very important.'

I broke the connection and looked at Wireman. 'Will they?'

'Considering your demonstrated earning power? You bet. And you just spared yourself a long, involved conversation. Now can we get back to—'

'Not yet.' My family and friends would be the most vulnerable, and the fact that they'd gone their separate ways afforded me no comfort. Perse had already demonstrated that her reach was long. And I had started meddling. I thought she was angry with me, or frightened of me, or both.

My first impulse was to call Pam, but then I remembered what Wireman had said about sparing myself a long, involved conversation. I consulted my own untrustworthy memory instead of Wireman's little book . . . and for once, under pressure, it came through.

But I'll get his answering machine, I thought. And I did, but at first I didn't know it.

'Hello, Edgar.' Tom Riley's voice, but not Tom's voice. It was dead of emotion. *It's the drugs he takes*, I thought . . . although that deadness hadn't been there at the Scoto.

'Tom, listen and don't say anyth—'

But the voice went on. That dead voice. 'She'll kill you, you know. You and all your friends. The way she's killed me. Only I'm still alive.'

I staggered on my feet.

'*Edgar!*' Wireman said sharply. 'Edgar, what's wrong?'

431

'Shut up,' I said. 'I need to hear.'

The message seemed to be over, but I could still hear him breathing. Slow, shallow respiration coming from Minnesota. Then he resumed.

'Being dead is better,' he said. 'Now I have to go and kill Pam.'

'Tom!' I shouted at the message. 'Tom, *wake up!*'

'After we're dead we're going to be married. It's to be a ship-board wedding. *She* promised.'

'*Tom!*' Wireman and Jack crowding in, one gripping my arm, the other gripping my stump. I hardly noticed.

And then:

'Leave a message at the beep.'

The beep came and then the line went silent.

I didn't hang up the phone; I dropped it. I turned to Wireman. 'Tom Riley's gone to kill my wife,' I said. And then went on, although the words didn't feel like mine: 'He may have done it already.'

xii

Wireman didn't ask for an explanation, just told me to call her. I put the telephone back to my ear, but couldn't remember the number. Wireman read it to me, but I couldn't punch it in; the bad side of my vision had, for the first time in weeks, come over all red.

Jack did it for me.

I stood listening to the phone ring in Mendota Heights, waiting for Pam's bright, impersonal voice on the answering machine – a message saying she was in Florida but would return calls soon. Pam who was no longer in Florida, but who might be lying dead on her kitchen floor, with Tom Riley next to her, just as dead. This vision was so clear I could see blood on the cabinets, and on the knife in Tom's stiffening hand.

One ring . . . two . . . three . . . the next would kick the answering machine into life . . .

'Hello?' It was Pam. She sounded breathless.

'Pam!' I shouted. 'Jesus Christ, is it actually you? Answer me!'

432

'Edgar? Who told you?' She sounded totally bewildered. And still breathless. Or maybe not. That was a Pam-voice I knew: slightly foggy, the way she sounded when she had a cold, or when she was . . .

'Pam, are you crying?' And then, belatedly: 'Told me what?'

'About Tom Riley,' she said. 'I thought you might be his brother. Or – please, God, no – his mother.'

'What about Tom?'

'He was fine on the trip back,' she said, 'laughing and showing off his new sketch, playing cards in the back of the plane with Kamen and some of the others.' Now she *did* start to cry, big sobs like static, her words coming in between. It was an ugly sound, but it was also beautiful. Because it was alive. 'He was *fine*. And then, tonight, he killed himself. The papers will probably call it an accident, but it was suicide. That's what Bozie says. Bozie has a friend on the cops who called and told him, and then he called me. Tom drove into a retaining wall at seventy miles an hour or more. No skid-marks. This was on Route 23, which means he was probably on his way here.'

I understood everything, and I didn't need any phantom arm to tell me, either. There was something Perse wanted, because she was angry with me. Angry? *Furious*. Only Tom had had a moment of sanity – a moment of *courage* – and had taken a quick detour into a concrete cliff.

Wireman was making crazy what's-going-on gestures in front of my face. I turned away from him.

'Panda, he saved your life.'

'What?'

'I know what I know,' I said. 'The sketch he was showing off in the plane . . . it was one of mine, right?'

'Yes . . . he was so proud . . . Edgar, *what are you*—'

'Did it have a name? Did the sketch have a name? Do you know?'

'It was called *Hello*. He kept saying, "Don't look much like Minnesota dere" . . . doing that dumb Yooper thing of his . . .' A pause, and I didn't break in because I was trying to think. Then: 'This is your special kind of knowing. Isn't it?'

Hello, I was thinking. Yes, of course. The first sketch I'd done in

Big Pink had also been one of the powerful ones. And Tom had bought it.

Goddamned *Hello*.

Wireman took the phone from me, gently but firmly.

'Pam? It's Wireman. Is Tom Riley . . . ?' He listened, nodding. His voice was very calm, very soothing. It was a voice I'd heard him use with Elizabeth. 'All right . . . yes . . . yes, Edgar's fine, I'm fine, we're all fine down here. Sorry about Mr Riley, of course. Only you need to do something for us, and it's extremely important. I'm going to put you on speaker.' He pushed a button I hadn't even noticed before. 'Are you still there?'

'Yes . . .' Her voice was tinny but clear. And she was getting herself under control.

'How many of Edgar's family and friends bought pictures?'

She considered. 'Nobody in the family bought any of the actual *paintings*, I'm sure of that.'

I breathed a sigh of relief.

'I think they were sort of hoping – or maybe expecting's the word – that in time . . . on the right birthday, or maybe at Christmas . . .'

'I understand. So they didn't get anything.'

'I didn't say that. Melinda's boyfriend also bought one of the sketches. What's this about? *What's wrong with the pictures?*'

Ric. My heart jumped. 'Pam, this is Edgar. Did Melinda and Ric take the sketch with them?'

'With all those airplanes, including transatlantic? He asked that it be framed and shipped. I don't think she knows. It was of flowers done in colored pencils.'

'So that one's still at the Scoto.'

'Yes.'

'And you're sure nobody else in the family bought paintings.'

She took maybe ten seconds to consider. It was agony. At last she said, 'No. I'm positive.' *You better be, Panda,* I thought. 'But Angel and Helen Slobotnik bought one. *Mailbox with Flowers,* I believe it's called.'

I knew the one she was talking about. It was actually titled *Mailbox with Oxeyes*. And I thought that one was harmless, I thought that one was probably all mine, but still . . .

'They didn't take it, did they?'

434

'No, because they were going to Orlando first, fly home from there. They also asked that it be framed and shipped.' No questions now, only answers. She sounded younger – like the Pam I had married, the one who'd kept my books back in those pre-Tom days. 'Your surgeon – can't remember his name—'

'Todd Jamieson.' I said it automatically. If I'd paused to think, I wouldn't have been able to remember.

'Yes, him. He also bought a painting, and arranged for shipment. He wanted one of those spooky *Girl and Ship* ones, but they were spoken for. He settled for a conch-shell floating on the water.'

Which could be trouble. All the surreal ones could be trouble.

'Bozie bought two of the sketches, and Kamen bought one. Kathi Green wanted one, but said she couldn't afford it.' A pause. 'I thought her husband was sort of a dork.'

I would have given her one if she'd asked, I thought.

Wireman spoke up again. 'Listen to me now, Pam. You've got work to do.'

'All right.' A little fog still in her voice, but mostly sharp. Mostly right there.

'You need to call Bozeman and Kamen. Do it right away.'

'Okay.'

'Tell them to burn those sketches.'

A slight pause, then: 'Burn the sketches, okay, got it.'

'As soon as we're off the phone,' I put in.

A touch of annoyance: 'I said I got that, Eddie.'

'Tell them I'll reimburse them their purchase price times two, or give them different sketches, whichever they want, but that those sketches aren't safe. They *are not safe*. Have you got that?'

'Yep, I'll do it right now.' And she finally asked a question. *The* question. 'Eddie, did that *Hello* picture kill Tom?'

'Yes. I need a callback.'

I gave her the phone number. Pam sounded like she was crying again, but still repeated it back perfectly.

'Pam, thank you,' Wireman said.

'Yeah,' Jack added. 'Thanks, Mrs Freemantle.'

I thought she'd ask who that was, but she didn't. 'Edgar, do you promise the girls will be okay?'

'If they didn't take any of my pictures with them, they'll be fine.'

435

'Yes,' she said. 'Your goddamned pictures. I'll call back.'

And she was gone, without a goodbye.

'Better?' Wireman asked when I hung up.

'I don't know,' I said. 'I hope to God it is.' I pressed the heel of my hand first against my left eye, then against my right. 'But it doesn't *feel* better. It doesn't feel *fixed*.'

xiii

We were quiet for a minute. Then Wireman asked, 'Was Elizabeth falling out of that pony-trap really an accident? What's your best guess?'

I tried to clear my mind. This stuff was important, too.

'My best guess is that it was. When she woke up, she suffered from amnesia, aphasia, and God knows what else as a result of brain injuries that were beyond diagnosis in 1925. Painting was more than her therapy; she was a genuine prodigy, and she was her own first great artwork. The housekeeper – Nan Melda – was also amazed. There was that story in the paper, and presumably everyone who read it was amazed over breakfast . . . but you know how people are—'

'What amazes you at breakfast is forgotten by lunch,' Wireman said.

'Jesus,' Jack said, 'if I'm as cynical as you two when I get old, I think I'll turn in my badge.'

'That's Jesus-*Krispies* to you, son,' Wireman said, and actually laughed. It was a stunned sound, but *there*. And that was good.

'Everyone's interest began to wane,' I said. 'And that was probably true for Elizabeth, as well. I mean, who gets bored quicker than a three-year-old?'

'Only puppies and parakeets,' Wireman said.

'A creative burn at three,' Jack said, bemused. 'Fucking awesome concept.'

'So she started to . . . to . . .' I stopped, for a moment unable to go on.

'Edgar?' Wireman asked quietly. 'All right?'

I wasn't, but I had to be. If I wasn't, Tom would only be the

436

beginning. 'It's just that he looked good at the gallery. *Good*, you know? Like he'd put it all together again. If not for *her* meddling—'

'I know,' Wireman said. 'Drink some of your water, *muchacho*.'

I drank some of my water, and forced myself back to the business at hand. 'She started to experiment. She went from pencils to fingerpaints to watercolors in – I think – a period of *weeks*. Plus some of the pictures in the picnic basket were done in fountain-pen, and I'm pretty sure some were done with house-paint, which I'd been meaning to try myself. It has a look when it dries—'

'Save it for your art-class, *muchacho*,' Wireman said.

'Yeah. Yeah.' I drank some more water. I was starting to get back on track. 'She started to experiment with different media, too. If that's the right word; I think it is. Chalk on brick. Sand-drawings on the beach. One day she painted Tessie's face on the kitchen counter in melted ice cream.'

Jack was leaning forward, hands clasped between his muscular thighs, frowning. 'Edgar . . . this isn't just blue-sky? You *saw* this?'

'In a way. Sometimes it *was* actual seeing. Sometimes it was more like a . . . a wave that came out of her pictures, and from using her pencils.'

'But you know it's true.'

'I know.'

'She didn't care if the pictures lasted or not?' Wireman asked.

'No. The *doing* mattered more. She experimented with media, and then she started to experiment with reality. To change it. And *that's* when Perse heard her, I think, when she started messing with reality. Heard her and woke up. Woke up and started calling.'

'Perse was with the rest of that junk Eastlake found, wasn't she?' Wireman asked.

'Elizabeth thought it was a doll. The best doll ever. But they couldn't be together until she was strong enough.'

'Which *she* are you talking about?' Jack asked. 'Perse or the little girl?'

'Probably both. Elizabeth was just a kid. And Perse . . . Perse had been asleep for a long time. Sleeping under the sand, full fathom five.'

'Very poetic,' Jack said, 'but I don't know exactly what you're talking about.'

'Neither do I,' I said. 'Because *her* I don't see. If Elizabeth drew pictures of Perse, she destroyed them. I find it suggestive that she turned to collecting china figures in her old age, but maybe that's just a coincidence. What I know is that Perse established a line of communication with the child, first through her drawings, then through her up-to-then favorite doll, Noveen. And Perse instituted a kind of . . . well, exercise program. I don't know what else you'd call it. She persuaded Elizabeth to draw things, and those things would happen in the real world.'

'She's been playing the same game with you, then,' Jack said. 'Candy Brown.'

'And my eye,' Wireman said. 'Don't forget fixing my eye.'

'I'd like to think that was all me,' I said . . . but had it been? 'There *have* been other things, though. Small things, mostly . . . using some of my pictures as a crystal ball . . .' I trailed off. I didn't really want to go there, because that road led back to Tom. Tom who should have been fixed.

'Tell us the rest of what you found out from her pictures,' Wireman said.

'All right. Start with that out-of-season hurricane. Elizabeth summoned it up, probably with help from Perse.'

'You've *got* to be shitting me,' Jack said.

'Perse told Elizabeth where the debris was, and Elizabeth told her father. Among the litter was a . . . let's say there was a china figure, maybe a foot high, of a beautiful woman.' Yes, I could see that. Not the details, but the figure. And the empty, pupil-less pearls that were her eyes. 'It was Elizabeth's prize, her fair salvage, and once it was out of the water, it *really* went to work.'

Jack spoke very softly. 'Where would a thing like that have come from to begin with, Edgar?'

A phrase rose to my lips, from where I don't know, only that it wasn't my own: *There were elder gods in those days; kings and queens they were.* I didn't say it. I didn't want to hear it, not even in that well-lighted room, so I only shook my head.

'I don't know. And I don't know what country's flag that ship might have been flying when it blew in here, maybe scraping its hull open on the top of Kitt Reef and spilling some of its cargo. I don't know much of anything for sure . . . but I think that Perse has a ship of her own, and once she was free of the water and completely welded to Elizabeth Eastlake's powerful child's mind, she was able to call it.'

'A ship of the dead,' Wireman said. His face was childlike with fear and wonder. Outside, a wind shook the massed foliage in the courtyard; the rhododendrons nodded their heads and we could hear the steady, sleepy sound of the waves pounding the shore. I had loved that sound ever since coming to Duma Key, and I still loved it, but now it frightened me, too. 'A ship called . . . what? *Persephone?*'

'If you like,' I said. 'It's certainly crossed my mind that Perse was Elizabeth's way of trying to say that. It doesn't matter; we're not talking Greek mythology here. We're talking about something far older and more monstrous. Hungry, too. That much it does have in common with vampires. Only hungry for souls, not blood. At least that's what I think. Elizabeth had her new "doll" for no more than a month, and God knows what life was like at the first Heron's Roost during that time, but it couldn't have been good.'

'Did Eastlake have the silver harpoons made then?' Wireman asked.

'I can't tell you. There's so much I don't know, because what I do know comes from Elizabeth, and she was little more than an infant. I have no sense of what happened in *her* other life, because by then she'd quit drawing. And if she remembered the time when she did—'

'She was doing her best to forget it,' Jack finished.

Wireman looked glum. 'By the end, she was well on her way to forgetting everything.'

I said, 'Remember the pictures where everybody seems to be wearing these big, loopy drug-addict grins? That was Elizabeth, trying to re-make the world she remembered. The pre-Perse world. A happier one. In the days before her twin sisters drowned, she was one scared kid, but she was afraid to say anything, because she felt that the things going wrong were all her fault.'

'What things?' It was Jack.

'I don't know exactly, but there's one picture of an old-timey Negro lawn jockey standing on his head, and I think that stands for everything. I think that for Elizabeth, in those last days, *everything* seemed to be standing on its head.' There was more than that to the lawn jockey – I was almost positive – but I didn't know what, and this probably wasn't the time to chase after it, anyway. 'I think in the days before and just after Tessie and Laura drowned, the family might almost have been prisoners at Heron's Roost.'

'And only Elizabeth would have known why?' Wireman asked.

'I don't know.' I shrugged. 'Nan Melda might have known some of it. *Probably* knew some of it.'

'Who was at that house during the period after the treasure-find and before the drownings?' Jack asked.

I thought about it. 'I suppose Maria and Hannah might have come home from school for a weekend or two, and Eastlake could have been away on business for part of March and April. The ones who were *surely* there that whole time were Elizabeth, Tessie, Laura, and Nan Melda. And Elizabeth tried to draw her new "friend" out of existence.' I licked my lips. They were very dry. 'She did it with her colored pencils, the ones in the basket. This was just before Tessie and Laura drowned. Maybe the night before. Because their drownings were punishment, right? The way Tom killing Pam was supposed to be *my* punishment, for prying. I mean, you see that?'

'Christ almighty,' Jack whispered. Wireman was very pale.

'Until then, I don't think Elizabeth understood.' I thought about this, then shrugged. 'Hell, I can't remember how much *I* understood when I was four. But until then probably the worst thing that had ever happened to her in her life – other than falling out of that pony-trap, and I'll bet she didn't even remember that – was getting turned over her Daddy's knee and paddled or having her hand slapped for trying to take one of Nan Melda's jam tarts before they were cooled. What did she know about the nature of evil? All she knew was that Perse was naughty, Perse was a bad doll instead of a good doll, she was out of control and getting out-of-controller all the time, she had to be sent away. So Libbet sat down with her pencils and some drawing paper and told herself, "I can do this. If I go slow and do my best work, I can do this." ' I stopped and passed my hand over my eyes. 'I think that's right, but you have to take it with a grain of salt. It could be mixed up with what I remember about myself. My mind playing more tricks. More stupid fucking pet tricks.'

'Take it easy, *muchacho*,' Wireman said. 'Go slow. She tried to draw Perse out of existence. How does one do a thing like that?'

'Draw and then erase.'

'Perse didn't let her?'

'Perse didn't know, I'm almost sure of it. Because Elizabeth was able to hide what she meant to do. If you ask me how, I can't tell you. If you ask me if it was her own idea – something she thought up by herself at the age of four—'

'Not beyond belief,' Wireman said. 'In a way, it's four-year-old thinking.'

'I don't understand how she could have kept it from this Perse,' Jack said. 'I mean . . . a little kid?'

'I don't know, either,' I said.

'In any case, it didn't work,' Wireman said.

'No. It didn't. I think she made the drawing, and I'm sure she did it in pencil, and I think when she was done, she erased the whole thing. It probably would have killed a human being the way I killed Candy Brown, but Perse wasn't human. All it did was make her angry. She paid Elizabeth back by taking the twins, whom she idolized. Tessie and Laura didn't go down that path to the Shade Beach to look for more treasure. They were driven. They ended up in the water, and they were lost.'

'Only not for good,' Wireman said, and I knew he was thinking of certain small footprints. Not to mention the thing that had been in my kitchen.

'No,' I agreed. 'Not for good.'

The wind blew again, this time hard enough to send something thudding against the Gulf side of the house. We all jumped.

'How did it get this Emery Paulson?' Jack asked.

'I don't know,' I said.

'And Adriana,' Wireman said. 'Did Perse get her, too?'

'I don't know,' I said. 'Maybe.' Reluctantly I added: 'Probably.'

'We haven't seen Adriana,' Wireman said. 'There's that.'

'Not yet,' I said.

'But the little girls drowned,' Jack said. Like he was trying to get it straight. 'This Perse-thing lured them into the water. Or something.'

'Yes,' I said. 'Or something.'

441

'But then there was a search. Outsiders.'

'There had to be, Jack,' Wireman said. 'People knew they were gone. Shannington, for one.'

'I know that,' Jack said. 'It's what I'm saying. So Elizabeth and her Dad and the housekeeper just dummied up?'

'What other choice?' I asked. 'Was John Eastlake going to tell forty or fifty volunteers "The boogeylady took my daughters, look for the boogeylady?" He might not even have known. Although he must have found out at some point.' I was thinking of the picture of him screaming. Screaming and bleeding.

'*What other choice* covers it for me,' Wireman said. 'I want to know what happened after the search was over. Just before she died, Miss Eastlake said something about drowning her back to sleep. Did she mean Perse? And if she did, how does a thing like that work?'

I shook my head. 'Don't know.'

'*Why* don't you know?'

'Because the rest of the answers are on the south end of the island,' I said. 'At whatever's left of the original Heron's Roost. And I think that's where Perse is, too.'

'All right, then,' Wireman said. 'Unless we're prepared to vacate Duma posthaste, it seems to me that we ought to go there.'

'Based on what happened to Tom, we don't even have that choice,' I said. 'I sold a lot of paintings, and the guys at the Scoto won't hold them forever.'

'Buy them back,' Jack suggested. Not that I hadn't already thought of that myself.

Wireman shook his head. 'Plenty of the owners won't want to sell, not even at twice the price. And a story like this wouldn't convince them.'

To this, no one said anything.

'But she's not quite as strong in daylight,' I said. 'I'd suggest nine o'clock.'

'Fine by me,' Jack said, and stood up. 'I'll be here at quarter of. Right now I'm going back across the bridge to Sarasota.' *The bridge.* That started an idea knocking around in my head.

'You're welcome to stay here,' Wireman said.

'After *this* conversation?' Jack raised his eyebrows. 'With all due respect, dude, no way. But I'll be here tomorrow.'

442

'Long pants and boots arc the order of the day,' Wireman said. 'It'll be overgrown down there, and there could be snakes.' He scrubbed a hand up the side of his face. 'Looks like I might be missing tomorrow's viewing at Abbot-Wexler. Miss Eastlake's relatives will have to bare their teeth at each other. What a pity . . . hey, Jack.'

Jack had started for the door. Now he turned back.

'You don't happen to have any of Edgar's art, do you?'

'Mmm . . . well . . .'

'Fess up. Confession's good for the soul, *compañero*.'

'One sketch,' Jack said. He shuffled his feet, and I thought he was blushing. 'Pen and ink. On the back of an envelope. A palm tree. I . . . ah . . . I fished it out of the trash basket one day. Sorry, Edgar. My bad.'

'S'okay, but burn it,' I said. 'Maybe I'll be able to give you another one when all this is over.' *If it ever is*, I thought but didn't add.

Jack nodded. 'Okay. You want a ride back to Big Pink?'

'I'll stay here with Wireman,' I said, 'but I *do* want to go back to Big Pink first.'

'Don't tell me,' Jack said. 'Jammies and a toothbrush.'

'No,' I said. 'Picnic basket and those silver har—'

The telephone rang, and we all looked at each other. I think I knew right away that it was bad news; I felt that sinking as my stomach turned into an elevator. It rang again. I looked at Wireman, but Wireman just looked at me. He knew, too. I picked it up.

'It's me.' Pam, heavy-voiced. 'Brace yourself, Edgar.'

When someone says something like that, you always try to fasten some kind of mental safety belt. But it rarely works. Most people don't have one.

'Spill it.'

'I got Bozie at home and told him what you said. He started asking questions, which was no surprise, but I told him I was in a hurry and didn't have any answers anyway, so – short form – he agreed to do as you asked. "For old times' sake," he said.'

That sinking sensation was getting worse.

'After that I tried Ilse. I wasn't sure I'd reach her, but she just got in. She sounded tired, but she's back, and she's okay. I'll check on Linnie tomorrow, when—'

'Pam—'

'I'm getting to it. After Illy I called Kamen. Someone answered on the second or third ring, and I started my spiel. I thought I was talking to him.' She paused. 'It was his brother. He said Kamen stopped in Starbucks for a latte on his way back from the airport. Had a heart attack while he was waiting in line. The EMTs transported him to the hospital, but it was only a formality. The brother said Kamen was DRT – dead right there. He asked me why I was calling, and I said it didn't matter now. Was that all right?'

'Yes.' I didn't think Kamen's sketch would have any effect on the brother, or anyone else; I thought its work was done. 'Thank you.'

'If it's any consolation, it *could* have been a coincidence – he was a hell of a nice guy, but he was also packing a lot of extra pounds. Anyone who looked at him could see that.'

'You could be right.' Although I knew she wasn't. 'I'll talk to you soon.'

'All right.' She hesitated. 'Take care of yourself, Eddie.'

'You too. Lock your doors tonight, and set the alarm.'

'I always do.'

She broke the connection. On the other side of the house, the surf was disputing with the night. My right arm was itching. I thought: *If I could get at you, I believe I'd cut you off all over again. Partly to stop the damage you can do, but mostly just to shut you up.*

But of course it wasn't my gone arm, or the hand which had once lived at the end of it, that was the problem; the problem was the woman-thing in the red robe, using me like some kind of fucked-up Ouija board.

'What?' Wireman asked. 'Don't keep us in suspense, *muchacho*, what?'

'Kamen,' I said. 'Heart attack. Dead.'

I thought of all the pictures stored at the Scoto, pictures that were sold. They'd be safe for a little while where they were, but in the end, money talks and bullshit walks. That wasn't even a man-law, it was the motherfucking American way.

'Come on, Edgar,' Jack said. 'I'll run you to your place, then drive you back here.'

444

xiv

I won't say our trip upstairs to Little Pink was exactly serene (I had the silver candlestick, and carried it at port arms all the time we were inside), but it was uneventful. The only spirits in the place were the agitated voices of the shells. I put the drawings back in the red picnic basket. Jack snagged the handles and carried it downstairs. I had his back the whole way, and locked Big Pink's door behind us. Much good *that* would do.

While we were riding back to *El Palacio*, a thought occurred to me . . . or recurred. I'd left my digital Nikon behind and didn't want to go back for it, but—

'Jack, do you have a Polaroid camera?'

'Sure,' he said. 'A One-Shot. It's what my Dad calls "old but serviceable." Why?'

'When you come tomorrow, I want you to stop for awhile on the Casey Key side of the drawbridge. Take a few Polaroids of the birds and the boats, okay?'

'Okay . . .'

'And sneak in a couple of the drawbridge itself, especially the lifting machinery.'

'Why? What do you want them for?'

'I'm going to sketch the drawbridge with the machinery gone,' I said. 'And I'm going to do it when I hear the horn that means it's up to let a boat go through. I don't think the motor and the hydraulics will really disappear, but with luck I can fuck it up badly enough to keep everybody off for awhile. Car-traffic, anyway.'

'Are you serious? You really think you can sabotage the bridge?'

'Given how often it breaks down on its own, that should be easy.' I looked again at the dark water and thought of Tom Riley, who should have been fixed. Who *had* been fixed, dammit. 'I only wish I could draw myself a good night's sleep.'

How to Draw a Picture (IX)

Look for the picture inside the picture. It's not always easy to see, but it's always there. And if you miss it, you can miss the world. I know that better than anyone, because when I looked at the picture of Carson Jones and my daughter – of Smiley and his Punkin – I thought I knew what I was looking for and missed the truth. Because I didn't trust him? Yes, but that's almost funny. The truth was, I wouldn't have trusted any man who presumed to claim my darling, my favored one, my Ilse.

I found a picture of him alone before I found the one of them together, but I told myself I didn't want the solo shot, that one wouldn't do me any good, if I wanted to know his intentions toward my daughter I had to touch them as a couple with my magic hand.

I was already making assumptions, you see. Bad ones.

If I'd touched the first one, really searched the first one – Carson Jones dressed in his Twins shirt, Carson alone – things might have been different. I might have sensed his essential harmlessness. Almost certainly would have. But I ignored that one. And I never asked myself why, if he was a danger to her, I had then drawn her alone, looking out at all those floating tennis balls.

Because the little girl in the tennis dress was her, of course. Almost all the girls I drew and painted during my time on Duma Key were, even the ones that masqueraded as Reba, or Libbit, or – in one case – as Adriana.

There was only one female exception: the red-robe.

Her.

When I touched the photograph of Ilse and her boyfriend, I had sensed death – I didn't admit it to myself at the time, but it was true. My missing hand sensed death, impending like rain in clouds.

I assumed Carson Jones meant my daughter harm, and that was why I wanted her to stay away from him. But he was never the problem. Perse wanted to make me stop – was, I think, desperate to make me stop once I found Libbit's old drawings and pencils – but Carson Jones was never Perse's weapon. Even poor Tom Riley was only a stopgap, a make-do.

447

The picture was there, but I made a wrong assumption, and missed the truth: the death I felt wasn't coming from him. It was hanging over her.

And part of me must have known I missed it.

Why else had I drawn those damned tennis balls?

16 – The End of the Game

i

Wireman offered a Lunesta to help me sleep. I was sorely tempted, but declined. I took one of the silver harpoons, however, and Wireman did likewise. With his hairy belly sloping slightly over his blue boxers and one of John Eastlake's specialty items in his right hand, he looked like some amusing Real Guy version of Cupid. The wind had gotten up even higher; it roared along the sides of the house and whistled around the corners.

'Bedroom doors open, right?' he asked.

'Check.'

'And if something happens in the night, holler like hell.'

'Roger that, Houston. You do the same.'

'Is Jack going to be all right, Edgar?'

'If he burns the sketch, he'll be fine.'

'You doing okay with what happened to your friends?'

Kamen, who taught me to think sideways. Tom, who had told me not to give up the home field advantage. Was I doing okay with what happened to my friends?

Well, yes and no. I felt sad and stunned, but I'd be a liar if I didn't say I also felt a certain low and slinking relief; humans are, in some ways, such complete shits. Because Kamen and Tom, although close, stood just outside the charmed circle of those who really mattered to me. *Those* people Perse hadn't been able to touch. And if we moved fast, Kamen and Tom would be our only casualties.

'*Muchacho?*'

'Yeah,' I said, feeling called back from a great distance. 'Yeah, I'm okay. Call me if you need me, Wireman, and don't hesitate. I don't expect to get many winks.'

449

ii

I lay looking up at the ceiling with the silver harpoon beside me on the bedtable. I listened to the steady rush of the wind and the steady tumble of the surf. I remember thinking, *This is going to be a long night.* Then sleep took me.

I dreamed of little Libbit's sisters. Not the Big Meanies; the twins.

The twins were running.

The big boy was chasing them.

It had *TEEF*.

iii

I woke with most of my body on the floor but one leg – my left – still propped on the bed and fast asleep. Outside, the wind and surf continued to roar. Inside, my heart was pounding almost as hard as the waves breaking on the beach. I could still see Tessie going down – drowning while those soft and implacable hands clasped her calves. It was perfectly clear, a hellish painting inside my head.

But it wasn't the dream of the little girls fleeing the frog-thing that was making my heart pound, not the dream that caused me to wake up on the floor with my mouth tasting like copper and every nerve seeming to burn. It was, rather, the way you wake from a bad dream realizing that you forgot something important: to turn off the stove, for instance, and now the house is filled with the smell of gas.

I pulled my foot off the bed and it hit the floor in a burst of pins and needles. I rubbed it, grimacing. At first it was like rubbing a block of wood, but then that numb sensation started to leave. The sensation that I'd forgotten something vital did not.

But what? I had some hopes that our expedition to the south end of the Key might put an end to the whole nasty, festering business. The biggest hurdle, after all, was belief itself, and as long as we didn't backslide in the bright Florida sunshine tomorrow, we were over that one. It was possible we might see upside-down birds, or that a gigantic hop-frog monstrosity like the one in my dream might try to bar our way, but I had an idea those were essentially wraiths

– excellent for dealing with six-year-old girls, not so good against grown men, especially when armed with silver-tipped harpoons.

And, of course, I would have my pad and pencils.

I thought Perse was now afraid of me and my newfound talent. Alone, still not recovered from my near-death experience (still suicidal, in fact), I might have been an asset instead of a problem. Because in spite of all his big talk, that Edgar Freemantle really hadn't had another life; that Edgar had just switched the backdrop of his invalid's existence from pines to palms. But once I had friends again . . . saw what was all around me and reached out to it . . .

Then I'd become dangerous. I don't know exactly what she had in mind – other than regaining her place in the world, that is – but she must have thought that when it came to mischief-making, the potential for a talented one-armed artist was great. I could have sent poison paintings all over the globe, by God! But now I had turned in her hand, just as Libbit had. Now I was something first to be stopped, then discarded.

'You're a little late for that, bitch,' I whispered.

So why did I still smell gas?

The paintings – especially the most dangerous ones, the *Girl and Ship* series – were safely under lock and key, and off-island, just as Elizabeth had wished. According to Pam, nobody in our circle of family and friends had taken sketches except for Bozie, Tom, and Xander Kamen. It was too late for Tom and Kamen, and I'd have given a great deal to change that, but Bozie had promised to burn his, so *that* was all right. Even Jack was covered, because he'd owned up to his little act of thievery. It had been smart of Wireman to ask him, I thought. I was only surprised he hadn't asked if I'd given Jack some artwork myse—

My breath turned to glass in my throat. *Now* I knew what I'd forgotten. Now, in this deep crease of the night with the wind roaring outside. I'd been so fixated on the goddam show that I'd never thought much about who I might have given work to *before* the show.

Can I have it?

My memory, still apt to be so balky, sometimes surprised me with bursts of Technicolor brilliance. It provided one now. I saw Ilse standing barefoot in Little Pink, dressed in shorts and a shell top.

451

She was standing by my easel. I had to ask her to move so I could see the picture she was so taken with. The picture I didn't even remember doing.

Can I have it?

When she stood aside, I saw a little girl in a tennis dress. Her back was turned, but she was the focus of the picture. The red hair marked her as Reba, my little love, that girlfriend from my other life. Yet she was also Ilse – Rowboat Ilse – and Elizabeth's big sister Adriana as well, for that was Adie's tennis dress, the one with the fine blue loops along the hem. (I couldn't know this, but I did; it was news that had come whispering up from Elizabeth's pictures – pictures done when she was still known as Libbit.)

Can I have it? This is the one I want.

Or the one something *wanted* her to want.

I tried Ilse, Pam had said. *I wasn't sure I'd reach her, but she just got in.*

All around the doll-girl's feet were tennis balls. Others floated shoreward on the mild waves.

She sounded tired, but she's okay.

Was she? Was she really? I had given her that damned picture. She was my Miss Cookie, and I could refuse her nothing. I had even named it for her, because she said artists had to name their pictures. *The End of the Game,* I'd told her, and now that clanged in my head like a bell.

iv

There was no phone extension in the guest bedroom, so I crept out into the hall with my silver harpoon clutched in one hand. In spite of my need to get through to Ilse as soon as possible, I took a moment to peer in through the open doorway across the hall. Wireman was lying on his back like a beached whale, snoring peacefully. His own silver harpoon was beside him, along with a glass of water.

I went past the family portrait, down the stairs, and into the kitchen. Here the rush of the wind and the roar of the surf was louder than ever. I picked up the phone and heard . . . nothing.

Of course. Did you think Perse would neglect the phones?

Then I looked at the handset and saw buttons for two lines. In the kitchen, at least, just picking up the phone wasn't enough. I said a little prayer under my breath, pushed the button marked LINE 1, and was rewarded with a dial tone. I moved my thumb to the button, then realized I couldn't remember Ilse's telephone number. My address book was back at Big Pink, and her telephone number had gone entirely out of my head.

v

The phone began to make a sirening sound. It was small – I had laid the handset down on the counter – but it seemed loud in the shadowy kitchen, and it made me think of bad things. Police cars responding to acts of violence. Ambulances rushing to the scenes of accidents.

I pushed the cut-off button, then leaned my head against the chilly brushed-steel front of *El Palacio's* big refrigerator. In front of me was a magnet reading FAT IS THE NEW THIN. Right, and dead was the new alive. Next to the magnet was a magnetized pad-holder and a stub of pencil on a string.

I pushed the LINE 1 button again and dialed 411. The automated operator welcomed me to Verizon Directory Assistance and asked me for city and state. I said 'Providence, Rhode Island,' enunciating as though on stage. So far, so good, but the robot choked on *Ilse* no matter how carefully I enunciated. It rolled me over to a human operator, who checked and told me what I had already suspected: Ilse's number was unpublished. I told the operator I was calling my daughter, and the call was important. The operator said I could talk to a supervisor, who would probably be willing to make an enquiry call on my behalf, but not until eight a.m. eastern time. I looked at the clock on the microwave. It was 2:04.

I hung up and closed my eyes. I could wake up Wireman, see if he had Ilse in his little red address book, but I had a gnawing intuition even that might take too long.

'I can do this,' I said, but with no real hope.

Of course you can, Kamen said. *What is your weight?*

453

It was a hundred and seventy-four, up from an all-time adult low of one-fifty. I saw these numbers in my mind: **174150**. The numbers were *red*. Then five of them turned green, one after the other. Without opening my eyes, I seized the stub of the pencil and wrote them on the pad: 40175.

And what is your Social Security number? Kamen enquired further.

It appeared in darkness, bright red numbers. Four of them turned green, and I added them to what I had already scrawled. When I opened my eyes I had printed 401759082 in a drunken, downward-tending sprawl on the pad.

It was right, I recognized it, but I was still missing a number.

It doesn't matter, the Kamen inside my head told me. *Keypad phones are an amazing gift to the memory-challenged. If you clear your mind and punch what you already have, you'll hit the last number with no problem. It's muscle memory.*

Hoping he was right, I opened LINE 1 again and punched in the area code for Rhode Island and then 759–082. My finger never hesitated. It punched the last number, and somewhere in Providence, a phone began to ring.

vi

'Hel-lo? . . . Who . . . zit?'

For a moment I was sure I'd blown the number after all. The voice was female, but sounded older than my daughter. Much. And medicated. But I resisted my initial impulse to say 'Wrong number' and hang up. *She sounded tired,* Pam had said, but if this was Ilse, she sounded more than tired; she sounded weary unto death.

'Ilse?'

No answer for a long time. I began to think the disembodied someone in Providence had hung up. I realized I was sweating, and heavily enough so I could smell myself, like a monkey on a branch. Then the same little refrain:

'Hel-lo? . . . Who . . . zit?'

'Ilse!'

Nothing. I sensed her getting ready to hang up. Outside the wind was roaring and the surf was pounding.

'Miss Cookie!' I shouted. 'Miss Cookie, don't you dare hang up this phone!'

That got through. 'Dad . . . dee?' There was a world of wonder in that broken word.

'Yeah, honey – Dad.'

'If you're really Daddy . . .' A long pause. I could see her in her own kitchen, barefoot (as she had been that day in Little Pink, looking at the picture of the doll and the floating tennis balls), head down, hair hanging around her face. Distracted, maybe almost to the point of madness. And for the first time I began to hate Perse as well as fear her.

'Ilse . . . Miss Cookie . . . I want you to listen to me—'

'Tell me my screen name.' There was a certain shocked cunning in the voice now. 'If you're really my Daddy, tell me my screen name.'

And if I didn't, I realized, she'd hang up. Because something had been at her. Something had been fooling her, pawing her over, drawing its webs around her. Only not an it. *She.*

Illy's screen name.

For a moment I couldn't remember that, either.

You can do this, Kamen said, but Kamen was dead.

'You're not . . . my Daddy,' said the distracted girl on the other end of the line, and again she was on the verge of hanging up.

Think sideways, Kamen advised calmly.

Even then, I thought, without knowing why I was thinking it. *Even then, even later, even now, even so—*

'You're not my Daddy, you're *her*,' Ilse said. That drugged and dragging voice, so unlike her. 'My Daddy's dead. I saw it in a dream. Goodb—'

'*If so!*' I shouted, not caring if I woke Wireman or not. Not even thinking about Wireman. '*You're If-So-Girl!*'

A long pause from the other end. Then: 'What's the rest of it?'

I had another moment of horrible blankness, and then I thought: *Alicia Keyes, keys on a piano—*

'88,' I said. 'You're If-So-Girl88.'

There was a long, long pause. It seemed forever. Then she began to cry.

vii

'Daddy, she said you were dead. That was the one thing I believed. Not just because I dreamed it but because Mom called and said Tom died. I dreamed you were sad and walked into the Gulf. I dreamed the undertow took you and you drowned.'

'I didn't drown, Ilse. I'm okay, I promise you.'

The story came out in fragments and bursts, interrupted by tears and digressions. It was clear to me that hearing my voice had steadied her but not cured her. She was wandering, strangely unfixed in time; she referred to the show at the Scoto as if it had occurred at least a week ago, and interrupted herself once to tell me that a friend of hers had been arrested for 'cropping'. This made her laugh wildly, as if she were drunk or stoned. When I asked her what cropping was, she told me it didn't matter. She said it might even have been part of her dream. Now she sounded sober again. Sober . . . but not *right*. She said the *she* was a voice in her head, but it also came from the drains and the toilet.

Wireman came in at some point during our conversation, turned on the kitchen fluorescents, and sat down at the table with his harpoon in front of him. He said nothing, only listened to my end.

Ilse said she had begun to feel strange – 'eerie-feary' was what she actually said – from the first moment she came back into her apartment. At first it was just a spaced-out feeling, but soon she was experiencing nausea, as well – the kind she'd felt the day we had tried to prospect south along Duma Key's only road. It had gotten worse and worse. A woman spoke to her from the sink, told her that her father was dead. Ilse said she'd gone out for a walk to clear her head after that, but decided to come right back.

'It must be those Lovecraft stories I read for my Senior English Project,' she said. 'I kept thinking someone was following me. That woman.'

Back in the apartment, she'd started to cook some oatmeal, thinking it might settle her stomach, but the very sight of it when it started to thicken nauseated her – every time she stirred it, she seemed to *see* things in it. Skulls. The faces of screaming children. Then a woman's face. The woman had too many eyes, Ilse said. The

456

woman in the oatmeal said her father was dead and her mother didn't know yet, but when she did, she would have a party.

'So I went and lied down,' she said, unconsciously reverting to the diction of childhood, 'and that's when I dreamed the woman was right and you were dead, Daddy.'

I thought of asking her when her mother had called, but I doubted if she'd remember, and it didn't matter, anyway. But, my God, hadn't Pam sensed anything wrong besides tiredness, especially in light of my phone call? Was she deaf? Surely I wasn't the only one who could hear this confusion in Ilse's voice, this *weariness*. But maybe she hadn't been so bad when Pam called. Perse was powerful, but that didn't mean it still didn't take her time to work. Especially at a distance.

'Ilse, do you still have the picture I gave you? The one of the little girl and the tennis balls? *The End of the Game,* I called it.'

'That's another funny thing,' she said. I had a sense of her *trying* to be coherent, the way a drunk pulled over by a traffic cop will try to sound sober. 'I meant to get it framed, but I didn't get around to it, so I tacked it on the wall of the big room with a Pushpin. You know, the living room/kitchen. I gave you tea there.'

'Yes.' I'd never been in her Providence apartment.

'Where I could look . . . look at it . . . but then when I camed back . . . hnn . . .'

'Are you going to sleep? Don't go to sleep on me, Miss Cookie.'

'Not sleeping . . .' But her voice was fading.

'Ilse! Wake up! *Wake the fuck up!'*

'Daddy!' Sounding shocked. But also fully awake again.

'What happened to the picture? What was different about it when you came back?'

'It was in the bed'oom. I guess I must have moved it myself – it's even stuck on the same red Pushpin – but I don't remember doing it. I guess I wanted it closer to me. Isn't that funny?'

No, I didn't think it was funny.

'I wouldn't want to live if you were dead, Daddy,' she said. 'I'd want to be dead, too. As dead as . . . as . . . as dead as a marble!' And she laughed. I thought of Wireman's daughter and did not.

'Listen to me carefully, Ilse. It's important that you do as I say. Will you do that?'

457

'Yes, Daddy. As long as it doesn't take too long. I'm . . .' The sound of a yawn. '. . . tired. I might be able to sleep, now that I know you're all right.'

Yes, she'd be able to sleep. Right under *The End of the Game*, hanging from its red Pushpin. And she'd wake up thinking that the dream had been this conversation, the reality her father's suicide on Duma Key.

Perse had done this. That hag. That *bitch*.

The rage was back, just like that. As if it had never been away. But I couldn't let it fuck up my thinking; couldn't even let it show in my voice, or Ilse might think it was aimed at her. I clamped the phone between my ear and shoulder. Then I reached out and grasped the slim chrome neck of the sink faucet. I closed my fist around it.

'This won't take long, hon. But you have to do it. Then you can go to sleep.'

Wireman sat perfectly still at the table, watching me. Outside, the surf hammered.

'What kind of stove do you have, Miss Cookie?'

'Gas. Gas stove.' She laughed again.

'Good. Get the picture and throw it in the oven. Then close the door and turn the oven on. High as it will go. Burn that thing.'

'No, Daddy!' Wide awake again, as shocked as when I'd said *fuck*, if not more so. 'I *love* that picture!'

'I know, honey, but it's the picture that's making you feel the way you do.' I started to say something else, then stopped. If it *was* the sketch — and it was, of course it was — then I wouldn't need to hammer it home. She'd know as well as I did. Instead of speaking I throttled the faucet back and forth, wishing with all my heart it was the bitch-hag's throat.

'Daddy! Do you really think—'

'I don't think, I know. Get the picture, Ilse. I'm going to hold the phone. Get it and stick it in the oven and *burn* it. Do it right now.'

'I . . . okay. Hold on.'

There was a clunk as the phone went down.

Wireman said, 'Is she doing it?'

458

Before I could reply, there was a snap. It was followed by a spout of cold water that drenched me to the elbow. I looked at the faucet in my hand, then at the ragged place where it had broken off. I dropped it in the sink. Water was spouting from the stump.

'I think she is,' I said. And then: 'Sorry.'

'*De nada.*' He dropped to his knees, opened the cupboard beneath the sink, reached in past the wastebasket and the stash of garbage bags. He turned something, and the gusher spouting from the broken faucet started to die. 'You don't know your own strength, *muchacho.* Or maybe you do.'

'Sorry,' I said again. But I wasn't. My palm was bleeding from a shallow cut, but I felt better. Clearer. It occurred to me that once upon a time, that faucet could have been my wife's neck. No wonder she had divorced me.

We sat in the kitchen and waited. The second hand on the clock above the stove made one very slow trip around the dial, started another. The water coming from the broken faucet was down to a bare rivulet. Then, very faintly, I heard Ilse, calling: 'I'm back ... I've got it ... I—' Then she screamed. I couldn't tell if it was surprise, pain, or both.

'Ilse!' I shouted. '*Ilse!*'

Wireman stood up fast, bumping his hip against the side of the sink. He raised his open hands to me. I shook my head – *Don't know.* Now I could feel sweat running down my cheeks, although the kitchen wasn't particularly warm.

I was wondering what to do next – who to call – when Ilse came back on the phone. She sounded exhausted. She also sounded like herself. Finally like herself. 'Jesus Christ in the morning,' she said.

'What happened?' I had to restrain myself from shouting. 'Illy, *what happened?*'

'It's gone. It caught fire and burned. I watched it through the window. It's nothing but ashes. I have to get a Band-Aid on the back of my hand, Dad. You were right. There was something really, really wrong with it.' She laughed shakily. 'Damn thing didn't want to go in. It folded itself over and ...' That shaky laugh again. 'I'd call it a paper-cut, but it doesn't *look* like a paper-cut, and it didn't feel like one. It feels like a bite. I think it bit me.'

viii

The important thing for me was that she was all right. The important thing for her was that I was. We were fine. Or so the foolish artist thought. I told her I'd call tomorrow.

'Illy? One more thing.'

'Yes, Dad.' She sounded totally awake and in charge of herself again.

'Go to the stove. Is there an oven light?'

'Yes.'

'Turn it on. Tell me what you see.'

'You'll have to hold on, then – the cordless is in the bedroom.' There was another pause, shorter. Then she came back and said, 'Ashes.'

'Good,' I said.

'Daddy, what about the rest of your pictures? Are they all like this one?'

'I'm taking care of it, honey. It's a story for another day.'

'All right. Thank you, Daddy. You're still my hero. I love you.'

'I love you, too.'

That was the last time we spoke, and neither of us knew. We never know, do we? At least we ended by exchanging our love. I have that. It's not much, but it's something. Others have it worse. I tell myself that on the long nights when I can't sleep.

Others have it worse.

ix

I slumped down across from Wireman and propped my head on my hand. 'I'm sweating like a pig.'

'Busting Miss Eastlake's sink might've had something to do with that.'

'I'm sor—'

'Say it again and I'll smack you,' he said. 'You did fine. It's not every man who gets to save his daughter's life. Believe me when I say that I envy you. Do you want a beer?'

'I'd throw it up all over the table. Got milk?'

He checked the fridge. 'No milk, but we *are* go for Half-n-Half.'
'Give me a shot of that.'

'You're a sick, sick puppydick, Edgar.' But he gave me a shot of Half-n-Half in a juice glass, and I tossed it off. Then we went back upstairs, moving slowly, clutching our stubby silver-tipped arrows like aging jungle warriors.

I went back into the guest bedroom, lay down, and once more gazed up at the ceiling. My hand hurt, but that was okay. She'd cut hers; I'd cut mine. It fit, somehow.

The table is leaking, I thought.

Drown her to sleep, I thought.

And something else – Elizabeth had said something else, as well. Before I could remember what it was, I remembered something much more important: Ilse had burned *The End of the Game* in her gas oven and had suffered no more than a cut – or maybe a bite – on the back of her hand.

Should have told her to disinfect that, I thought. *Should disinfect mine, too.*

I slept. And this time there was no giant dream-frog to warn me.

                                    x

A thud woke me as the sun was rising. The wind was still up – higher than ever – and it had blown one of Wireman's beach chairs against the side of the house. Or maybe the gay umbrella beneath which we had shared our first drink – iced green tea, very cooling.

I pulled on my jeans and left everything else lying on the floor, including the harpoon with the silver tip. I didn't think Emery Paulson would be back to visit me, not by daylight. I checked on Wireman, but that was only a formality; I could hear him snoring and whistling away. He was once more on his back, arms thrown wide.

I went downstairs to the kitchen and shook my head over the broken faucet and the juice glass with the dried Half-n-Half scum on its sides. I found a bigger glass in a cupboard and filled it with oj. I took it out on the back porch. The wind blowing in from the Gulf was strong but warm, lifting my sweaty hair back from my brow and temples. It felt good. Soothing. I decided to walk to the beach and drink my juice there.

I stopped three-quarters of the way down the boardwalk, about to take a sip of my juice. The glass was tipped, and some of it splattered on one bare foot. I barely noticed.

Out there on the Gulf, riding in toward shore on one of the large, wind-driven waves, was a bright green tennis ball.

It means nothing, I told myself, but that wouldn't hold water. It meant everything, and I knew it from the moment I saw it. I tossed the glass into the sea oats and broke into a lunging lurch – the Edgar Freemantle version of running that year.

It took me fifteen seconds to reach the end of the boardwalk, maybe even less, but in that time I saw three more tennis balls floating in on the tide. Then six, then eight. Most were off to my right – to the north.

I wasn't watching where I was going and plunged off the end of the boardwalk into thin air, arms whirling. I hit the sand still running and might have stayed up if I'd landed on my good leg, but I didn't. A zigzag of pain corkscrewed up my bad one, shin to knee to hip, and I went sprawling in the sand. Six inches in front of my nose was one of those damned tennis balls, its fuzz soaked flat.

DUNLOP was printed on the side, the letters as black as damnation.

I struggled to my feet, looking wildly out at the Gulf. There were only a few incoming balls in front of *El Palacio*, but farther north, near Big Pink, I saw a green flotilla – a hundred at least, probably many more.

It means nothing. She's safe. She burned the picture and she's asleep in her apartment a thousand miles from here, safe and sound.

'It means *nothing*,' I said, but now the wind blowing my hair back felt cold instead of warm. I began to limp toward Big Pink, down where the sand was wet and packed and shining. The peeps flew up in front of me in clouds. Every now and then an incoming wave would drop a tennis ball at my feet. There were lots of them now, scattered on the wet hardpack. Then I came to a burst-open crate reading *DUNLOP TENNIS BALLS* and *FACTORY REJECTS NO CANS*. It was surrounded by floating, bobbing tennis balls.

I broke into a run.

I unlocked the door and left my keys hanging in the lock. Lurched to the phone and saw the message light blinking. I pushed the PLAY button. The robot's expressionless male voice told me that this message had been received at 6:48 a.m., which meant I had missed it by less than half an hour. Then Pam's voice burst out of the speaker. I bent my head, the way you'd bend your head to try and keep a burst of jagged glass fragments from flying directly into your face.

'Edgar, the police called and they say Illy's dead! They say a woman named Mary Ire came to her apartment and killed her! One of your *friends*! One of your *art friends* from *Florida* has killed our *daughter*!' She burst into a storm of harsh and ugly weeping . . . then laughed. It was horrible, that laugh. I felt as if one of those flying shards of glass had cut into my face. 'Call me, you bastard. Call and explain yourself. *You said she'd be SAFE!*'

Then more crying. It was cut off by a click. Next came the hum of an open line.

I reached out and pushed the OFF button, silencing it.

I walked into the Florida room and looked at the tennis balls, still bobbing in on the waves. I felt doubled, like a man watching a man.

The dead twins had left a message in my studio – *Where our sister?* Had Illy been the sister they meant?

I could almost hear the hag laughing and see her nodding.

'Are you here, Perse?' I asked.

The wind rushed in through the screens. The waves crashed on the shore with metronome-like regularity. Birds flew over the water, crying. On the beach I could see another burst-open tennis ball crate, already half-buried in the sand. Treasure from the sea; fair salvage from the *caldo*. She was watching, all right. Waiting for me to break down. I was quite sure of it. Her – what? her guardians? – might sleep in the daytime, but not her.

'I win, you win,' I said. 'But you think you got your lasties, don't you? Clever Perse.'

Of course she was clever. She'd been playing the game for a long time. I had an idea she'd been old when the Children of Israel were still grubbing in the gardens of Egypt. Sometimes she slept, but now she was awake.

And her reach was long.

My phone began to ring. I went back in, still feeling like two Edgars, one earthbound, the other floating above the earthbound Edgar's head, and picked it up. It was Dario. He sounded upset.

'Edgar? What's this shit about not releasing the paintings to—'

'Not now, Dario,' I said. 'Hush.' I broke the connection and called Pam. Now that I wasn't thinking about it, the numbers came with no problem whatsoever; that marvelous muscle memory thing took over completely. It occurred to me that human beings might be better off if that was the only kind of memory they had.

Pam was calmer. I don't know what she'd taken, but it was already working. We talked for twenty minutes. She wept through most of the conversation, and was intermittently accusatory, but when I made no effort to defend myself, her anger collapsed into grief and bewilderment. I got the salient points, or so I thought then. There was one very salient point that we both were missing, but as a wise man once said, 'You can't hit em if you can't see em,' and the police representative who called Pam didn't think to tell her what Mary Ire had brought to our daughter's Providence apartment.

Besides the gun, that was. The Beretta.

'The police say she must have driven, and almost nonstop,' Pam said dully. 'She never could have gotten a gun like that on an airplane. Why did she do it? Was it another fucking *painting*?'

'Of course it was,' I said. 'She bought one. I never thought of that. I never thought of *her*. Not once. It was Illy's fucking *boyfriend* I was worried about.'

Speaking very calmly, my ex-wife — that's what she surely was now — said: '*You* did this.'

Yes. I had. I should have realized Mary Ire would buy at least one painting, and that she'd probably want a canvas from the *Girl and Ship* series — the most toxic of all. Nor would she have wanted the Scoto to store it, not when she lived right up the road in Tampa. For all I knew, she might have had it in the trunk of her beat-up Mercedes when she dropped me at the hospital. From there she could have gone right to her place on Davis Islands to get her home protection automatic. Hell, it would have been on her way north.

464

That part I should have at least guessed. I had met her, after all, and I knew what she thought of my work.

'Pam, something very bad is happening on this island. I—'

'Do you think I care about that, Edgar? Or about why that woman did it? You got our daughter killed. I don't ever want to talk to you again, I don't want to *see* you again, and I'd rather poke out my eyes than ever have to look at another picture of yours. You should have died when that crane hit you.' There was an awful thoughtfulness in her voice. 'That would have been a happy ending.'

There was a moment of silence, then once more the hum of an open line. I considered throwing the whole works across the room and against the wall, but the Edgar floating over my head said no. The Edgar floating over my head said that would perhaps give Perse too much pleasure. So I hung it up gently instead, and then for a minute I just stood there swaying on my feet, alive while my nineteen-year-old daughter was dead, not shot after all but drowned in her own bathtub by a mad art critic.

Then, slowly, I walked back out through the door. I left it open. There seemed no reason to lock it now. There was a broom meant for sweeping sand off the walk leaning against the side of the house. I looked at it and my right arm began to itch. I lifted my right hand and held it in front of my eyes. It wasn't there, but when I opened it and closed it, I could feel it flex. I could also feel a couple of long nails biting into my palm. The others felt short and ragged. They must have broken off. Somewhere – perhaps on the carpet upstairs in Little Pink – were a couple of ghost fingernails.

'Go away,' I told it. 'I don't want you anymore, go away and be dead.'

It didn't. It wouldn't. Like the arm to which it had once been attached, the hand itched and throbbed and ached and refused to leave me.

'Then go find my daughter,' I said, and the tears began to flow. 'Bring her back, why don't you? Bring her to me. I'll paint anything you want, just bring her to me.'

Nothing. I was just a one-armed man with a phantom itch. The only ghost was his own, drifting around just over his head, observing all this.

The creeping in my flesh grew worse. I picked the broom up,

weeping now not just from grief but also from the horrible discomfort of that unreachable itch, then realized I couldn't do what I needed to do – a one-armed man can't snap a broomhandle over his knee. I leaned it against the house again and stomped it with my good leg. There was a snap, and the bristle end went flying. I held the jagged end up in front of my streaming eyes and nodded. It would do.

I went around the corner of the house toward the beach, a distant part of my mind registering the loud conversation of the shells beneath Big Pink as the waves dashed into the darkness there and then withdrew.

I had one fleeting thought as I reached the wet and shining hardpack, dotted here and there with tennis balls: The third thing Elizabeth had said to Wireman was *You will want to, but you mustn't.*

'Too late,' I said, and then the string tethering the Edgar over my head broke. He floated away, and for a little while I knew no more.

17 – The South End of the Key

i

I next remember Wireman coming along and picking me up. I remember walking a few steps, then recalling that Ilse was dead and collapsing to my knees. And the most shameful thing was that, even though I was heartbroken, I was also hungry. Starving.

I remember Wireman helping me in through the open door and telling me it was all a bad dream, that I'd been having the horrors, and when I told him no, it was true, Mary Ire had done it, Mary Ire had drowned Ilse in Ilse's own bathtub, he had laughed and said that now he knew it was a dream. For one horrible moment I believed him.

I pointed to the answering machine. 'Play the message,' I said, and went into the kitchen. Staggered into the kitchen. When Pam started in again – *Edgar, the police called and they say Illy's dead!* – I was eating fistfuls of Frosted Mini-Wheats straight from the box. I had a queer sense of being part of a prepared slide. Soon I would be placed under a microscope and studied. In the other room, the message ended. Wireman cursed and played it again. I kept eating cereal. The time I'd spent on the beach before Wireman came along was missing. That part of my memory was as blank as my early hospital stay after my accident.

I took a final handful of cereal, crammed it into my mouth, and swallowed. It stuck in my throat, and that was good. That was fine. I hoped it would choke me. I *deserved* to choke. Then it slid down. I went shuffle-limping back into the living room. Wireman was standing beside the answering machine, wide-eyed.

'Edgar . . . *muchacho* . . . what in God's name—?'

'One of the paintings,' I said, and kept on shuffling. Now that I had something in my stomach, I wanted some more oblivion. If only for a little while. Only it was more than wanting, actually; it

467

was needing. I had broken the broomhandle . . . then Wireman came along. What was in the ellipsis? I didn't know.

I decided I didn't *want* to know.

'The paintings . . . ?'

'Mary Ire bought one. I'm sure it was one from the *Girl and Ship* series. And she took it with her. We should have known. *I* should have known. Wireman, I need to lie down. I need to sleep. Two hours, okay? Then wake me and we'll go to the south end.'

'Edgar, you can't . . . I don't expect you to after . . .'

I stopped to look at him. It felt as though my head weighed a hundred pounds, but I managed. '*She* doesn't expect me to, either, but this ends today. Two hours.'

Big Pink's open door faced east, and the morning sun struck brightly across Wireman's face, lighting a compassion so strong I could barely look at it. 'Okay, *muchacho*. Two hours.'

'In the meantime, try to keep everyone clear.' I don't know if he heard that last part or not. I was facing into my bedroom by then, and the words were trailing away. I fell onto my bed, and there was Reba. For a moment I considered throwing her across the room, as I had considered throwing the phone. Instead I gathered her to me and pressed my face against her boneless body and began to cry. I was still crying when I fell asleep.

ii

'Wake up.' Someone was shaking me. 'Wake up, Edgar. If we're going to do this, we have to get rolling.'

'I dunno – I'm not sure he's going to come around.' That voice was Jack's.

'Edgar!' Wireman slapped first one side of my face, then the other. Not gently, either. Bright light struck my closed eyes, flooding my world with red. I tried to get away from all these stimuli – there were bad things waiting on the other side of my eyelids – but Wireman wouldn't let me. '*Muchacho!* Wake up! It's ten past eleven!'

That got through. I sat up and looked at him. He was holding the bedside lamp in front of my face, so close I could feel the heat from the bulb. Jack was standing behind him. The realization that

Ilse was dead my Illy – struck at my heart, but I pushed it away. '*Eleven!* Wireman, I told you two hours! What if some of Elizabeth's relatives decide to—'

'Easy, *muchacho*. I called the funeral home and told them to keep everyone off Duma. I said that all three of us had come down with German measles. Very contagious. I also called Dario and told him about your daughter. Everything with the pictures is on hold, at least for now. I doubt if that's a priority with you, but—'

'Of course it is.' I got to my feet and rubbed my hand over my face. 'Perse doesn't get to do any more damage than she already has.'

'I'm sorry, Edgar,' Jack said. 'So damn sorry for your loss. I know that doesn't carry much water, but—'

'It does,' I said, and maybe in time it would. If I kept saying it; if I kept reaching out. My accident really taught me just one thing: the only way to go on is to go on. To say *I can do this* even when you know you can't.

I saw that one of them had brought the rest of my clothes, but for today's work I'd want the boots in the closet instead of the sneakers at the foot of the bed. Jack was wearing Georgia Giants and a long-sleeved shirt; that was good.

'Wireman, will you put on coffee?' I asked.

'Do we have time?'

'We'll have to make time. There's stuff I need, but what I need first is to wake up. You guys can use a little fuel, too, maybe. Jack, help me with my boots, would you?'

Wireman left for the kitchen. Jack knelt, eased on my boots, and tied them for me. 'How much do you know?' I asked him.

'More than I want to,' he said. 'But I don't understand any of it. I talked to that woman – Mary Ire? – at your show. I *liked* her.'

'I did, too.'

'Wireman called your wife while you were sleeping. She wouldn't talk to him very long, so then he called some guy he met at your show – Mr Bozeman?'

'Tell me.'

'Edgar, are you sure—'

'Tell me.' Pam's version had been broken and fragmentary, and even that was no longer clear in my mind – the details were obscured

469

by an image of Ilse's hair floating on the surface of an overflowing bathtub. That might or might not be accurate, but it was hellishly bright, hellishly *particular*, and it had blotted out almost everything else.

'Mr Bozeman said the police found no sign of forced entry, so they think your daughter must have let her in, even thought it was the middle of the night—'

'Or Mary just hit buzzers until somebody else let her in.' My missing arm itched. It was a deep itch. Sleepy. Dreamy, almost. 'Then she walked up to Illy's apartment and rang the bell. Let's say that she pretended to be someone else.'

'Edgar, are you guessing, or—'

'Let's say she pretended to be from a gospel group called The Hummingbirds, and let's say she called through the door that something bad had happened to Carson Jones.'

'Who's—'

'Only she calls him Smiley, and that's the convincer.'

Wireman was back. So was the floating Edgar. Edgar-down-below saw all the mundane things of a sunshiny Florida morning on Duma Key. Edgar-over-my-head saw more. Not everything; just enough to be too much.

'What happened then, Edgar?' Wireman asked. He spoke very softly. 'What do you think?'

'Let's say that Illy opens the door, and when she does, she finds a woman pointing a gun at her. She knows this woman from somewhere, but she's been through one bad scare already that night, she's disoriented, and she can't place her – her memory chokes. Maybe it's just as well. Mary tells her to turn around, and when she does . . . when she does that . . .' I began to cry again.

'Edgar, man, don't,' Jack said. He was almost crying himself. 'This is just guesswork.'

'It's not guesswork,' Wireman said. 'Let him talk.'

'But why do we need to know—'

'Jack . . . *muchacho* . . . we don't *know* what we need to know. So let the man talk.'

I heard their voices, but from far away.

'Let's say Mary hit her with the gun when she turned around.' I wiped my cheeks with the heel of my hand. 'Let's say she hit her

470

several times, four or five. In the movies, you get clopped once and you're out like a light. In real life, I doubt if it's like that.'

'No,' Wireman murmured, and of course this game of let's-say turned out to be all too accurate. My If-So-Girl's skull had been fractured in three places from repeated overhand blows, and she bled a great deal.

Mary dragged her. The blood-trail led across the living room/kitchen (the smell of the burnt sketch very likely still hanging in the air) and down the short hallway between the bedroom and the nook that served as Illy's study. In the bathroom at the end of the hall, Mary filled the tub and in it she drowned my unconscious daughter like an orphan kitten. When the job was done, Mary went into the living room, sat down on the sofa, and shot herself in the mouth. The bullet exited the top of her skull, splattering her ideas about art, along with a good deal of her hair, on the living room wall behind her. It was then just shy of four a.m. The man downstairs was an insomniac who knew the gunshot for what it was and called the police.

'Why drown her?' Wireman asked. 'I don't understand that.'

Because it's Perse's way, I thought.

'We're not going to think about that right now,' I said. 'All right?'

He reached out and squeezed my remaining hand. 'All right, Edgar.'

And if we get this business done, maybe we'll never have to, I thought.

But I *had* drawn my daughter. I was sure of it. I'd drawn her on the beach.

My dead daughter. My drowned daughter. Drawn in sand for the waves to take.

You will want to, Elizabeth had said, *but you mustn't*.

Oh, but Elizabeth.

Sometimes we have no choice.

iii

We swallowed strong coffee in Big Pink's sunny kitchen until sweat was standing out on our cheeks. I took three aspirin, adding another

471

layer of caffeine, then sent Jack to get two Artisan pads. And I told him to sharpen every colored pencil he could find while he was upstairs.

Wireman filled a plastic carry-sack with supplies from the fridge: carrot stubs, cucumber strips, a six-pack of Pepsi, three large bottles of Evian water, some roast beef, and one of Jack's Astronaut Chickens, still in its see-thru capsule.

'Surprised you can even think of food,' he said, with the tiniest touch of reproach.

'Food doesn't interest me in the slightest,' I said, 'but I may have to draw stuff. In fact, I'm *positive* I'll have to draw stuff. And that seems to burn calories by the carload.'

Jack returned with the drawing gear. I pawed it over, then sent him back upstairs for art-gum erasers. I suspected there would be more stuff I'd want – isn't there always? – but I couldn't think what it might be. I glanced at the clock. It was ten to twelve.

'Did you Polaroid the drawbridge?' I asked Jack. 'Please tell me you did.'

'Yeah, but I thought . . . the German measles story . . .'

'Let me see the photos,' I said.

Jack reached into his back pocket and produced some Polaroids. He shuffled through them and handed me four, which I dealt out on the kitchen table like a short hand of solitaire. I grabbed one of the Artisan pads and quickly began sketching the photo that showed the cogs and chains under the opening drawbridge – it was just a dinky little one-lane thing – the most clearly. My right arm continued to itch: a low, sleepy crawl.

'The German measles story was genius,' I said. 'It will keep almost everyone away. But almost isn't good enough. Mary wouldn't have stayed away from my daughter if someone had told her Illy had chicken p— *Fuck!*' My eyes had blurred, and a line that should have been true wandered off into falsehood.

'Take it easy, Edgar,' Wireman said.

I glanced at the clock. 11:58 now. The drawbridge would go up at noon; it always did. I blinked away the tears and went back to my sketch. Machinery spun itself into existence from the point of the Venus Black, and even now, with Ilse gone, the fascination of seeing something real emerge from nothing – like a shape drifting out of a fogbank – stole over me. And why not? When better? It was refuge.

'If she's got someone to attack us with and the drawbridge is out of commission, she'll just send them around to the Don Pedro Island footbridge,' Wireman said.

Without looking up from my drawing, I said: 'Maybe not. A lot of people don't know about the Sunshine Walkway, and I'm positive Perse doesn't.'

'Why?'

'Because it was built in the fifties, you told me that, and she was sleeping then.'

He considered this a moment, then said, 'You think she can be beaten, don't you?'

'Yes, I do. Not killed, maybe, but put back to sleep.'

'Do you know how?'

Find the leak in the table and fix it, I almost said . . . but that made no sense.

'Not yet. There are more of Libbit's pictures at the other house. The one at the south end of the key. They'll tell us where Perse is and tell me what to do.'

'How do you know there are more?'

Because there have to be, I would have said, but just then the noon horn went. A quarter of a mile down the road, the drawbridge between Duma Key and Casey Key – the only north link between us and the coast – was going up. I counted to twenty, putting *Mississippi* between each number as I had when I was a child. Then I erased the biggest cog in my drawing. There was a sensation when I did it – in the missing arm, yes, but also centered between and just above my eyes – of doing some lovely piece of precision work.

'Okay,' I said.

'Can we go now?' Wireman asked.

'Not quite yet,' I said.

He glanced at the clock, then back at me. 'I thought you were in a hurry, *amigo*. And given what we saw in here last night, I know that I am. So what else?'

'I need to draw you both,' I said.

473

iv

'I'd love to have you do a picture of me, Edgar,' Jack said, 'and I'm sure my mom would be totally blissed out – but I think Wireman's right. We ought to get going.'

'Have you ever been to the south end of the Key, Jack?'

'Uh, no.'

Of that I'd been almost sure. But as I tore the picture of the drawbridge machinery off the top of my pad, I looked at Wireman. In spite of the lead that now seemed to be lining my heart and emotions, I found that this was something I really wanted to know. 'What about you? Ever been down to the original Heron's Roost for a little poke-and-pry?'

'Actually, no.' Wireman went to the window and looked out. 'Drawbridge is still up – I can see the western leaf against the sky from here. So far, so good.'

I was not to be diverted so easily. 'Why not?'

'Miss Eastlake advised against it,' he said, still not turning from the window. 'She said the environment was bad. Groundwater, flora, even the air. She said the Army Air Corps did testing off the south end of Duma during World War II and managed to poison that end of the island, which is probably why the foliage grows so rank in most places. She said the poison oak is maybe the worst in America – worse than syphilis before penicillin is how she put it. Takes years to get rid of, if you rub up against it. Looks like it's gone, then it comes back. And it's everywhere. So she said.'

This was mildly interesting, but Wireman still hadn't actually answered my question. So I asked it again.

'She also claimed there are snakes,' he said, finally turning around. 'I have a horror of snakes. Have ever since I was a little boy and woke up one morning on a camping trip with my folks to discover I was sharing my sleeping bag with a milkie. It had actually worked its way into my undershirt. It sprayed me with musk. I thought I was fucking poisoned. Are you satisfied?'

'Yes,' I said. 'Did you tell her that story before or after she told you about the snake infestation on the south end?'

Stiffly, he said: 'I don't remember.' Then he sighed. 'Probably before. I see what you're saying – she wanted to keep me away.'

I didn't say it, you did, I thought. What I said was, 'It's mostly Jack I'm worried about. But it's better to be safe.'

'*Me?*' Jack looked startled. 'I don't have anything against snakes. And I know what poison oak and poison ivy look like. I was a Boy Scout.'

'Trust me on this,' I said, and began to sketch him. I worked quickly, resisting the urge to go into detail . . . as part of me seemed to want to do. While I was working, the first angry car horn began to honk on the coast side of the drawbridge.

'Sounds to me like the drawbridge is stuck again,' Jack said.

'Yes,' I agreed, not looking up from my drawing.

v

I sped along even more quickly with Wireman's sketch, but I again found myself having to fight the urge to fall into the work . . . because when I was in the work, the pain and grief were at bay. The work was like a drug. But there would be only so much daylight, and I didn't want to meet Emery again any more than Wireman did. What I wanted was for this to be over and for the three of us to be off-island – *far* off-island – by the time those sunset colors started to rise out of the Gulf.

'Okay,' I said. I had done Jack in blue and Wireman in blaze orange. Neither was perfect, but I thought both sketches caught the essentials. 'There's just one more thing.'

Wireman groaned. '*Edgar!*'

'Nothing I need to draw,' I said, and flipped the cover of the pad closed on the two sketches. 'Just smile for the artist, Wireman. But before you do, think of something that makes you feel particularly good.'

'Are you serious?'

'As a heart attack.'

His brow furrowed . . . then smoothed out. He smiled. As always, it lit up his whole face and made him a new man.

I turned to Jack. 'Now you.'

And because I really did feel that he was the more important of the two, I watched him very closely when he did.

475

vi

We didn't have a four-wheel drive, but Elizabeth's old Mercedes sedan seemed a reasonable substitute; it was built like a tank. We drove to *El Palacio* in Jack's car, and parked just inside the gate. Jack and I switched our supplies over to the SEL 500. Wireman's job was the picnic basket.

'A few other things while you're in there, if you can,' I said. 'Bug-spray, and a really good flashlight. Have you got one of those?'

He nodded. 'There's an eight-cell job in the gardening shed. It's a searchlight.'

'Good. And Wireman?'

He gave me a *what now* look – the exasperated kind you do mostly with your eyebrows – but said nothing.

'The spear pistol?'

He actually grinned. '*Sí, señor. Para fijacióno.*'

While he was gone, I stood leaning against the Mercedes, looking at the tennis court. The door at the far end had been left open. Elizabeth's semi-domesticated heron was inside, standing by the net. It looked at me with accusing blue eyes.

'Edgar?' Jack touched my elbow. 'Okay?'

I was not okay, and wouldn't be okay for a long time again. But . . .

I can do this, I thought. *I have to do this. She does not get to win.*

'Fine,' I said.

'I don't like it that you're so pale. You look like you did when you first came here.' Jack's voice cracked on the last couple of words.

'I'm fine,' I said again, and briefly cupped the back of his neck. I realized that, other than shaking his hand, it was probably the only time I had touched him.

Wireman came out clutching the handles of the picnic basket in both hands. He had three long-billed hats stacked on his head. John Eastlake's harpoon pistol was tucked under his arm. 'Flashlight's in the basket,' he said. 'Ditto Deep Woods Off, and three pairs of gardening gloves I found in the shed.'

'Brilliant,' I said.

'*Sí*. But it's quarter of one, Edgar. If we're going, can we please go?'

476

I looked at the heron on the tennis court. It stood by the net, as still as a hand on a broken clock, and looked back at me pitilessly. That was all right; it is, for the most part, a pitiless world.

'Yes,' I said. 'Let's go.'

vii

Now I had memory. It was no longer in perfect working order, and to this day I sometimes get confused about names and the order in which certain things happened, but every moment of our expedition to the house at the south end of Duma Key remains clear in my mind – like the first movie that ever amazed me or the first painting that ever took my breath away (*The Hailstorm,* by Thomas Hart Benton). Yet at first I felt cold, divorced from it all, like a slightly jaded patron of the arts looking at a picture in a second-rate museum. It wasn't until Jack found the doll inside the staircase going up to nowhere that I started to realize I was *in* the picture instead of just looking at it. And that there was no going back for any of us unless we could stop her. I knew she was strong; if she could reach all the way to Omaha and Minneapolis to get what she wanted, then all the way to Providence to keep it, of course she was strong. And still I underestimated her. Until we were actually in that house at the south end of Duma Key, I didn't realize how strong Perse was.

viii

I wanted Jack to drive, and Wireman to sit in the back seat. When Wireman asked why, I said I had my reasons, and I thought they'd become apparent in short order. 'And if I'm wrong about that,' I added, 'no one will be any more delighted than me.'

Jack backed onto the road and turned south. More out of curiosity than anything else, I punched on the radio and was rewarded with Billy Ray Cyrus, bellowing about his achy breaky heart. Jack groaned and reached for it, probably meaning to find The Bone. Before he could, Billy Ray was swallowed in a burst of deafening static.

'*Jesus, turn it off!*' Wireman yelped.

But first I turned it down. Reducing the volume made no difference. If anything, the static grew louder. I could feel it rattling the fillings of my teeth, and I punched the OFF button before my eardrums could start bleeding.

'What was *that*?' Jack asked. He had pulled over. His eyes were wide.

'Call it bad environment, why don't you,' I said. 'A little something left over from those Army Air Corps tests sixty years ago.'

'Very funny,' Wireman said.

Jack was looking at the radio. 'I want to try it again.'

'Be my guest,' I told him, and placed my hand over my left ear.

Jack pushed the power button. The static that came roaring out of the Mercedes's four speakers this time seemed as loud as a jet fighter's engine. Even with my palm over one ear, it ripped through my head. I thought I heard Wireman yell, but I wasn't sure.

Jack pushed the power button again and the hellish blizzard of noise cut out. 'I think we should skip the tunes,' he said.

'Wireman? All right?' My voice seemed to be coming from far away, through a steady low ringing noise.

'Rockin,' he said.

ix

Jack might have made it a little way beyond the point where Ilse got sick; maybe not. It was hard to tell once the growth got high. The road narrowed to a stripe, its surface humped and buckled by the roots running beneath it. The foliage had interlaced above us, blotting out most of the sky. It was like being in a living tunnel. The windows were rolled up, but even so, the car was filling with a green and fecund jungle smell.

Jack tested the old Mercedes's springs on a particularly egregious pothole, thumped up over a ridge in the pavement on the far side, then slammed to a stop and put the transmission in PARK.

'I'm sorry,' he said. His mouth was quivering and his eyes were too big. 'I'm—'

I knew perfectly well what he was.

Jack fumbled open the door, leaned out, and vomited. I'd thought the smell of the jungle (that's what it was once you were a mile past *El Palacio*) was strong in the car, but what came rolling in with the door open was ten times headier, thick and green and viciously alive. Yet I did not hear a single bird calling in that mass of junk foliage. The only sound was Jack losing his breakfast.

Then his lunch. At last he collapsed back against the seat. He thought *I* looked like a snowbird again? That was sort of funny, because on that early afternoon in mid-April, Jack Cantori was as pale as March in Minnesota. Instead of twenty-one, he looked a sickly forty-five. *It must have been the tuna salad*, Ilse had said, but it hadn't been the tuna. Something from the sea, all right, but not the tuna.

'I'm sorry,' he said. 'I don't know what's wrong with me. The smell, I guess – that rotten jungle smell—' His chest hitched, he made a *gurk* sound deep in his throat, and leaned out the door again. That time he missed his hold on the steering wheel, and if I hadn't grabbed him by the collar and yanked him back, he would have gone sprawling face-first into his own whoop.

He leaned back, eyes closed, face wet with sweat, panting rapidly.

'We better take him back to *El Palacio*,' Wireman said. 'I don't like to lose the time – hell, I don't like to lose *him* – but this shit ain't right.'

'As far as Perse's concerned, it's *exactly* right,' I said. Now my bad leg was itching almost as much as my arm. It felt like electricity. 'It's her little poison belt. How about you, Wireman? How's your gut?'

'Fine, but my bad eye – the one that used to be bad – is itching like a bastard, and my head's kind of humming. Probably from that damn radio.'

'It's not the radio. And the reason it's getting to Jack and not to us is because we've been . . . well . . . call it immunized. Sort of ironic, isn't it?'

Behind the wheel, Jack groaned.

'What can you do for him, *muchacho*? Anything?'

'I think so. I hope so.'

I had my pads on my lap and my pencils and erasers in a belt-pack. Now I flipped to the picture of Jack and found one of my art-gum erasers. I took away his mouth and the lower arcs of his eyes, all the way up to the corners. The itching in my right arm was fiercer than ever, and I actually had no doubt that what I planned to do would work. I summoned up the memory of Jack's smile in my kitchen – the one I'd asked him to give me while thinking of something particularly good – and drew it quickly with my Midnight Blue pencil. It took no more than thirty seconds (the eyes were really the key, when it comes to smiles, they always are), but those few lines changed the whole *idea* of Jack Cantori's face.

And I got something I hadn't expected. As I drew, I saw him kissing a girl in a bikini. No, more than saw. I could feel her smooth skin, even a few little grains of sand nestling in the hollow at the small of her back. I could smell her shampoo and taste a faint ghost of salt on her lips. I knew her name was Caitlin and he called her Kate.

I put my pencil back in the little belt-pack and zipped it closed. 'Jack?' Speaking quietly. His eyes were closed, and sweat still stood out on his cheeks and forehead, but I thought his breathing had slowed. 'How are you now? Any better?'

'Yeah,' he said without opening his eyes. 'What'd you do?'

'Well, as long as it's just the three of us, we might as well call it what it is: magic. A little counterspell I tossed your way.'

Wireman reached over my shoulder, picked up the pad, studied the picture, and nodded. 'I'm beginning to believe she should have left you alone, *muchacho*.'

I said, 'It was my daughter she should have left alone.'

x

We stayed where we were for five minutes, letting Jack get his second wind. At last he said he felt able to go on. His color was back. I wondered if we would have run into the same problems if we had gone around by water.

'Wireman, have you seen any fishing boats anchored off the south end of the Key?'

He considered. 'You know, I haven't. They usually stay on the Don Pedro side of the strait. That's odd, isn't it?'

480

'It's not odd, it's fucking sinister,' Jack said. 'Like this road.' It was down to nothing but a strip. Seagrape and banyan branches scraped along the sides of the slowly trundling Mercedes, making hellish *screee*-ing sounds. The road, lumped upward with tunneling roots and broken down to gravel and potholes in some places, continued to bend inland, and now it had also begun to climb.

We crept along, mile after slow mile, with the leaves and branches slapping and whacking. I kept expecting the road to break down entirely, but the thick interlacing foliage overhead had protected it from the elements to some degree, and it never quite did. The banyans gave way to an oppressive forest of Brazilian Peppers, and there we saw our first wildlife: a huge bobcat that stood for a moment in the rubbly remains of the road, hissing at us with its ears laid flat, then fled into the underbrush. A little farther on, a dozen plump black caterpillars fell onto the windshield and burst open, spreading gummy guts that the wipers and washer-fluid could do little to clear; they only spread the remains around until looking out through the windshield was like looking out of an eye with a cataract on it.

I told Jack to stop. I got out, opened the trunk, and found a little supply of clean rags. I used one to wipe the windshield, being careful to don a pair of the gloves Wireman had found – I was already wearing a hat. But so far as I could tell, they were only caterpillars; messy, but not supernatural.

'Not bad,' Jack said from the open driver's-side window. 'Now I'll pop the hood so you can check the—' He stopped, looking beyond me.

I turned. The road was down to little more than a path, cluttered with old chunks of asphalt and overgrown with Creeping Oxeye. Crossing it about thirty yards up was a line of five frogs the size of Cocker Spaniel puppies. The first three were a brilliant solid green that rarely if ever occurs in nature; the fourth was blue; the fifth was a faded orange that might once have been red. They were smiling, but there was something fixed and weary about those smiles. They were hopping slowly, as if their hoppers were almost busted. Like the bobcat, they reached the underbrush and disappeared into it.

'What the blue fuck were *those?*' Jack asked.

481

'Ghosts,' I said. 'Leftovers from a little girl's powerful imagination. And they won't last much longer, from the look of them.' I got back in. 'Go on, Jack. Let's ride while we can.'

He began to creep forward again. I asked Wireman what time it was.

'A little past two.'

We were able to ride all the way to the gate of the first Heron's Roost. I never would have bet on it, but we did. The foliage closed in one final time – banyans and scrub pines choked with gray beards of Spanish Moss – but Jack bulled the Mercedes through, and all at once the undergrowth drew back. Here the elements had washed the tar away completely and the end of the road was only a rutty memory, but it was good enough for the Mercedes, which jounced and bucketed up a long hill toward two stone pillars. A great unruly hedge, easily eighteen feet high and God knew how thick, ran away from the pillars on either side; it had also begun to spread fat green fingers down the hill toward the jungle growth. There were gates, but they stood rusty and halfway open. I didn't think the Mercedes would quite fit.

This last stretch of road was flanked on both sides by ancient Australian pines of imposing height. I looked for upside-down birds and saw none. I saw none of the rightside-up variety, either, for that matter, although I could now hear the faint buzz of insects.

Jack stopped at the gate and looked at us apologetically. 'This old girl ain't fitting through that.'

We got out. Wireman paused to look at the ancient, lichen-encrusted plaques fixed to the pillars. The one on the left said HERON'S ROOST. The one on the right said EASTLAKE, but below it something else had been scratched, as if with the point of a knife. Once it might have been hard to read, but the lichen growing from the little cuts gouged in the metal made it stand out: **Abyssus abyssum invocat.**

'Any idea what that means?' I asked Wireman.

'Indeed I do. It's a warning often given to new lawyers after they pass their bar exams. The liberal translation is "One misstep leads to another". The *literal* translation is "Hell invokes Hell".' He looked at me bleakly, then back at the message below the family name. 'I have an idea that might have been John Eastlake's final verdict before leaving this version of Heron's Roost forever.'

Jack reached out to touch the jagged motto, then seemed to think better of it.

Wireman did it for him. 'The verdict, gentlemen . . . and rendered in the law's own language. Come on. Sunset at 7:15, give or take, and daylight's a fleeting thing. We take turns with the picnic basket. It's one heavy *puta*.'

xi

But before we went anywhere, we paused inside the gate for a good look at Elizabeth's first home on Duma Key. My immediate reaction was dismay. Somewhere in the back of my mind had been a clear narrative thread: we'd enter the house, go upstairs, and find what had been Elizabeth's bedroom in those long-ago days when she'd been known as Libbit. There my missing arm, sometimes known as Edgar Freemantle's Divine Psychic Dowser, would lead me to a left-behind steamer trunk (or perhaps only a humble crate). Inside would be more drawings, the *missing* drawings, the ones that would tell me where Perse was and solve the riddle of the leaky table. All before sundown.

A pretty tale, and only one problem with it: the top half of Heron's Roost no longer existed. The house was on an exposed knoll, and its upper stories had been torn completely away in some long-ago storm. The ground floor still stood, but it was engulfed in gray-green vines which had also swarmed up the pillars in front. Spanish Moss hung from the eaves, turning the veranda into a cave. The house was ringed with shattered orange tiles, all that remained of the roof. They poked up like giants' teeth from the swale of weeds that had replaced the lawn. The last twenty-five yards of the shell drive had been buried in strangler fig. So had the tennis court and what might once have been a child's playhouse. More vines crept up the sides of the long, barnlike outbuilding behind the court and scrabbled along what remained of the playhouse's shingles.

'What's *that*?' Jack was pointing between the tennis court and the main house. There a long rectangle of evil black soup simmered in

483

the afternoon sun. Most of the bug-drone seemed to be coming from that direction.

'Now? I'd call it a tarpit,' Wireman said. 'Back in the Roaring Twenties, I imagine the Eastlake family called it their swimming pool.'

'Imagine taking a dip in *that*,' Jack said, and shuddered.

The pool was surrounded by willows. Behind it was another thick stand of Brazilian Peppers, and—

'Wireman, are those *banana* trees?' I asked.

'Yep,' he said. 'And probably full of snakes. Ugh. Look on the west side, Edgar.'

On the Gulf side of Heron's Roost, the snarl of weeds, vines, and creepers that had once been John Eastlake's lawn gave way to sea oats. The breeze was good and the view was better, making me realize that the one thing you rarely got in Florida was height. Here we had just enough to make it seem like the Gulf of Mexico was at our feet. Don Pedro Island was to our left, Casey Key dreaming away in a blue-gray haze to our right.

'Drawbridge is still up,' Jack said, sounding amused. 'They're really having problems this time.'

'Wireman,' I said. 'Look down there, along that old path. Do you see there?'

He followed my pointing finger. 'The rock outcropping? Sure, I see it. Not coral, I don't think, although I'd have to get a little closer to be sure – what about it?'

'Quit being a geologist for a minute and just *look*. What do you see?'

He looked. They both did. It was Jack who got it first. 'A profile?' Then he said it again, without the hesitation. 'A profile.'

I nodded. 'We can only see the forehead, the indentation of the eye-socket, and the top of the nose from here, but I bet if we were on the beach, we'd see a mouth, as well. Or what passed for one. That's Hag's Rock. And Shade Beach right below it, I'll bet you anything. Where John Eastlake went on his treasure-hunting expeditions.'

'And where the twins drowned,' Wireman added. 'That's the path they walked to get there. Only . . .'

He fell silent. The breeze tugged at our hair. We looked at the path, still visible after all these years. Little feet going down to swim hadn't done that. A footpath between Heron's Roost and Shade Beach would have disappeared in five years, maybe only two.

'That's no path,' Jack said, reading my mind. 'That used to be a *road*. Not paved, but a road, just the same. Why would anybody want a road between their house and the beach, when it couldn't have been more than a ten-minute walk?'

Wireman shook his head. 'Don't know.'

'Edgar?'

'Not a clue.'

'Maybe he found more stuff on the bottom than just a few trinkets,' Jack said.

'Maybe, but—' I caught movement in the tail of my eye – something dark – and turned toward the house. I saw nothing.

'What is it?' Wireman asked.

'Probably nerves,' I said.

The breeze, which had been coming at us from the Gulf, switched slightly and puffed out of the south instead. It brought a stench of putridity with it.

Jack recoiled, grimacing. 'What the fuck is *that*!'

'Perfume from the pool would be my guess,' Wireman said. 'Jack, I love the smell of sludge in the morning.'

'Yeah, but it's afternoon.'

Wireman gave him a *duh* look, then turned to me. 'What do you think, *muchacho*? On we go?'

I took a quick inventory. Wireman had the red basket; Jack had the bag with the food in it; I had my art supplies. I wasn't sure just what we were going to do if the rest of Elizabeth's drawings had blown away in the storm that had torn the roof off the ruin just ahead (or if there *were* no more pictures), but we had come this far and we had to do something. Ilse insisted on that, from my bones and heart.

'Yes,' I said. 'On we go.'

xii

We had reached the point where the driveway began to be over-grown with strangler fig when I saw that black thing go flickering

485

through the high tangle of weeds to the right of the house. This time Jack saw it, too.

'Someone's there,' he said.

'I didn't see anyone,' Wireman said. He set down the picnic basket and armed sweat from his brow. 'Switch with me awhile, Jack. You take the basket and I'll take the food. You're young and strong. Wireman's old and used up. He'll die soo— *holy shit what's that!*'

He staggered back from the basket and would have fallen if I hadn't caught him around the waist. Jack shouted with surprise and horror.

The man came bursting from the undergrowth just ahead on our left. There was no way he could have been there – Jack and I had glimpsed him fifty yards away only seconds before – but he was. He was a black man but not a human being. We never mistook him for an actual human being. For one thing, his legs, cocked and clad in blue breeches, did not move as he passed in front of us. Nor did he stir the thick mat of strangler fig springing up all around him. Yet his lips grinned; his eyes rolled with jolly malevolence. He wore a peaked cap with a button on top, and that was somehow the worst.

I thought if I had to look at that cap for long, it would drive me mad.

The thing disappeared into the grass on our right, a black man in blue breeches, about five and a half feet tall. The grass was no more than five feet high, and simple mathematics said he had no business disappearing into it, but he did.

A moment later he – *it* – was on the porch, grinning at us like De Ole Family Retainer, and then, with no pause, he – *it* – was at the bottom of the steps, and once more darting into the weeds, grinning at us all the time.

Grinning at us from beneath its cap.

Its cap was *RED*.

Jack turned to flee. There was nothing on his face but mindless, blabbering panic. I let go of Wireman to grab him, and if Wireman had also decided to flee, I think that would have been the end of our expedition; I had only the one arm, after all, and couldn't restrain them both. Couldn't restrain either of them, if they really meant to turn tail.

Terrified as I was, I never even came close to running. And

Wireman, God bless him, stood his ground, watching with his mouth hung open as the black man next appeared from the grove of banana trees between the pool and the outbuilding.

I got Jack by the belt and yanked him back. I couldn't slap him in the face – I had no hand to slap with – and so I settled for shouting. '*It's not real! It's her nightmare!*'

'Her . . . nightmare?' Something like comprehension dawned in Jack's eyes. Or maybe just a little consciousness. I'd settle for that.

'Her nightmare, her boogeyman, whatever she was afraid of when the lights went out,' I said. 'It's just another ghost, Jack.'

'How do you know?'

'For one thing, it's flickering like an old movie,' Wireman said. 'Look at it.'

The black man was gone, then there again, this time in front of the rust-encrusted ladder leading up to the pool's diving platform. It grinned at us from beneath its red cap. Its shirt, I saw, was as blue as its breeches. It slid from place to place with its unmoving legs always cocked in the same position, like a figure in a shooting gallery. It was gone again, then appeared on the porch. A moment later it was in the driveway, almost directly in front of us. Looking at it made my head hurt, and it still made me afraid . . . but only because *she* had been afraid. Libbit.

The next time it showed itself, it was on the double-rutted path to the Shade Beach, and this time we could see the Gulf shining through its blouse and breeches. It winked out of sight, and Wireman began to laugh hysterically.

'What?' Jack turned to him. Almost turned *on* him. '*What?*'

'It's a fuckin *lawn jockey!*' Wireman said, laughing harder than ever. 'One of those black lawn jockeys that are now so politically *verboten*, blown up to three, maybe four times its normal size! Elizabeth's boogeyman was the house lawn jockey!'

He tried to say more, but couldn't. He leaned over, laughing so hard he had to brace his hands on his knees. I saw the joke, but couldn't share it . . . and not only because my daughter was dead in Rhode Island. Wireman was only laughing now because at first he had been as frightened as Jack and I, as frightened as Libbit must have been. And why had she been frightened? Because someone, quite likely by accident, had put the wrong idea in her imaginative little head. My money was on Nan Melda, and – maybe – a bedtime story meant only to soothe a child who was still fretful from her head injury. Maybe even insomniac. Only this bedtime story had lodged in the wrong place, and grown TEEF.

Mr Blue Breeches wasn't like the frogs we'd seen back on the road, either. Those had been *all* Elizabeth, and there'd been no malevolence about them. The lawn jockey, however . . . he might originally have come from little Libbit's battered head, but I had an idea that Perse had long since appropriated him for her own purposes. If anyone got this close to Elizabeth's first home, there it was, all ready to scare the intruder away. Into a stay at the nearest lunatic asylum, maybe.

Which meant there might be something here to find, after all.

Jack looked nervously toward where the sunken path – which really did look as if it had been big enough to accommodate a cart or even a truck, once upon a time – dropped down and out of sight. 'Will it be back?'

'It doesn't matter, *muchacho*,' Wireman said. 'It's not real. That picnic basket, on the other hand, needs to be carried. So mush. On, you huskies.'

'Just looking at it made me feel like I was losing my mind,' Jack said. 'Do you understand that, Edgar?'

'Of course. Libbit had a very powerful imagination, back in the day.'

'What *happened* to it, then?'

'She forgot how to use it.'

'Jesus,' Jack said. 'That's horrible.'

'Yes. And I think that kind of forgetting is easy. Which is even more horrible.'

Jack bent down, picked up the basket, then looked at Wireman. 'What's *in* here? Gold bars?'

Wireman grabbed the bag of food and smiled serenely. 'I packed a few extras.'

We worked our way up the overgrown driveway, keeping an eye out for the lawn jockey. It did not return. At the top of the porch steps, Jack set the picnic basket down with a little sigh of relief. From behind us came a flurry and flutter of wings.

We turned and saw a heron alight on the driveway. It could have been the same one that had been giving me the cold-eye from *El Palacio*'s tennis court. Certainly the gaze was the same: blue and sharp and without an ounce of pity.

'Is that real?' Wireman asked. 'What do you think, Edgar?'

'It's real,' I said.

'How do you know?'

I could have pointed out that the heron was casting a shadow, but for all I knew, the lawn jockey had been casting one, as well; I had been too amazed to notice. 'I just do. Come on, let's go inside. And don't bother knocking. This isn't a social call.'

xiii

'Uh, this could be a problem,' Jack said.

The veranda was deeply shadowed by mats of hanging Spanish Moss, but once our eyes had adjusted to the gloom, we could see a thick and rusty chain encircling the double doors. Not one but two padlocks hung down from it. The chain had been run through hooks on either jamb.

Wireman stepped forward for a closer look. 'You know,' he said, 'Jack and I might be able to snap one or both of those hooks right off. They've seen better days.'

'Better *years*,' Jack said.

'Maybe,' I said, 'but the doors themselves are almost certainly locked, and if you go rattling chains and snapping hooks, you're going to disturb the neighbors.'

'Neighbors?' Wireman asked.

I pointed straight up. Wireman and Jack followed my finger and saw what I already had: a large colony of brown bats sleeping in what looked like a vast hanging cloud of cobweb. I glanced down and saw the porch was not just coated but plated with guano. It made me very glad I was wearing a hat.

When I looked up again, Jack Cantori was at the foot of the steps. 'No way, baby,' he said. 'Call me a chicken, call me a candy-ass, call me any name in the book, I'm not going there. With Wireman it's snakes. With me it's bats. Once—' He looked like he had more to say, maybe a lot, but didn't know how to say it. He

489

took another step back, instead. I had a moment to contemplate the eccentricity of fear: what the weird jockey hadn't been able to accomplish (close, but that only counts in horseshoes), a colony of sleeping brown bats had. For Jack, at least.

Wireman said, 'They can carry rabies, *muchacho* – did you know that?'

I nodded. 'I think we should look for the tradesman's entrance.'

xiv

We made our way slowly along the side of the house, Jack in the lead and carrying the red picnic basket. His shirt was dark with sweat, but he no longer showed the slightest sign of nausea. He should have; probably we all should have. The stench from the pool was nearly overpowering. Thigh-high grass whickered against our pants; stiff fiddlewood stems poked at our ankles. There were windows, but unless Jack wanted to try standing on Wireman's shoulders, they were all too high.

'What time is it?' Jack puffed.

'Time for you to move a little faster, *mi amigo*,' Wireman said. 'You want me to spell you on that basket?'

'Sure,' Jack said, sounding really out of temper for the first time since I'd met him. 'Then you can have a heart attack and me and the boss can try out our CPR technique.'

'Are you suggesting I'm not in shape?'

'In shape, but I still put you fifty pounds into the cardiac danger zone.'

'Quit it,' I said. 'Both of you.'

'Put it down, son,' Wireman said. 'Put that *cesto de puta madre* down and I'll carry it the rest of the way.'

'No. Forget it.'

Something black moved in the corner of my eye. I almost didn't look. I thought it was the lawn jockey again, this time darting alongside the pool. Or skimming its buggy, smelly surface. Thank God I decided to make sure.

Wireman, meanwhile, was glowering at Jack. His manhood had been impugned. 'I want to spell you.'

490

A piece of the pool's turgid nastiness had come alive. It detached itself from the blackness and flopped onto the cracked, weed-sprouting concrete lip, splattering muck about itself in a dirty starburst.

'No, Wireman, I got it.'

A piece of nastiness with eyes.

'Jack, I'm telling you for the last time.'

Then I saw the tail, and realized what I was looking at.

'And I'm telling *you*—'

'Wireman,' I said, and grabbed his shoulder.

'*No*, Edgar, I can do this.'

I can do this. How those words clanged in my head. I forced myself to speak slowly, loudly, and emphatically.

'Wireman, shut up. There's an alligator. It just came out of the pool.'

Wireman was afraid of snakes, Jack was afraid of bats. I had no idea I was afraid of alligators until I saw that chunk of prehistoric darkness separate itself from the decaying stew in the old pool and come for us, first across the overgrown concrete (brushing aside the last surviving, tipped-over lawn chair as it did) and then sliding into the weeds and vines trailing down from the nearest Brazilian Peppers. I caught one glimpse of its snout wrinkling back, one black eye squeezing shut in what could have been a wink, and then there was only its dripping back protruding here and there through the shivering greenery, like a submarine that's three-quarters under. It was coming for us, and after telling Wireman, I could do no more. Grayness came over my sight. I leaned back against the old warped boards of Heron's Roost. They were warm. I leaned there and waited to be eaten by the twelve-foot-long horror that lived in John Eastlake's old swimming pool.

Wireman never hesitated. He stripped the red basket from Jack's hands, dropped it on the ground, and knelt beside it, flipping back one end as he did so. He reached in and produced the largest handgun I had ever seen outside of a motion picture. Kneeling there in the high grass with the open picnic basket in front of him, Wireman gripped it in both hands. I had a good angle on his face, and I thought then and still think now that he looked perfectly serene . . . especially for a man facing what could be seen as a snake writ large. He waited.

'*Shoot it!*' Jack screamed.

Wireman waited. And beyond him, I saw the heron. It was floating in the air above the long, overgrown utility building behind the tennis court. It was floating upside down.

'Wireman?' I said. 'Safety catch?'

'*Caray,*' he murmured, and flicked something with his thumb. A red spot high on the pistol's handgrip winked out of view. He never took his eyes from the high grass, which had now begun to shake. Then it parted, and the alligator came at him. I had seen them on the Discovery Channel and *National Geographic* specials, but nothing prepared me for how fast that thing could move on those stub-legs. The grass had brushed most of the mud from its rudiment of a face, and I could see its enormous smile.

'*Now!*' Jack screamed.

Wireman shot. The report was tremendous – it went rolling away like something solid, something made of stone – and the result was tremendous, as well. The top half of the alligator's head came off in a cloud of mud, blood, and flesh. It didn't slow down; to the contrary, those stubby legs seemed to speed up as it ran off the last thirty feet or so. I could hear the grass whickering harshly along its plated sides.

The barrel of the gun rose with the recoil. Wireman let it. I've never seen calm like that, and it still amazes me. When the gun came back to dead level, the alligator was no more than fifteen feet away. He fired again, and the second bullet lifted the thing's front half to the sky, revealing a greenish-white belly. For a moment it seemed to be dancing on its tail, like a happy gator in a Disney cartoon.

'*Yahh, you ugly bastard!*' Jack screamed. '*Fuck ya mutha! Fuck ya GRANDmutha!*'

The gun again rose with the recoil. Once again, Wireman let it. The alligator thumped down on its side, belly exposed, the stubs of its legs thrashing, its tail whipping and tearing up grass and earth in clots. When the muzzle came back level, Wireman pulled the trigger again, and the center of the thing's belly seemed to disintegrate. All at once the ragged, flattened circle in which it lay was mostly red instead of green.

I looked for the heron. The heron was gone.

Wireman got up, and I saw he was shaking. He walked toward the alligator – although not quite within the radius of the still-whipping tail – and pumped two more rounds into it. The tail gave a final convulsive whack against the ground, the body a final jerk, and then it was still.

He turned to Jack and held up the automatic in a shaking hand. 'Desert Eagle, .357,' he said. 'One big old handgun, made by badass Hebrews – James McMurtry, two thousand-six. Mostly what added the weight to the basket was the ammo. I tossed in all the clips I had. That was about a dozen.'

Jack walked over to him, embraced him, then kissed him on both cheeks. 'I'll carry that basket to Cleveland if you want, and never say a word.'

'At least you won't have to carry the gun,' Wireman said. 'From now on, sweet old Betsy McCall goes in my belt.' And he put it there, after loading a fresh clip and carefully re-engaging the safety. This took him two tries, because of his shaking hands.

I came over to him and also kissed him on each cheek.

'Oh gosh,' he said. 'Wireman no longer feels Spanish. Wireman is beginning to feel positively French.'

'How do you happen to have a gun in the first place?' I asked.

'It was Miss Eastlake's idea, after the last cocaine skirmish in Tampa – St Pete.' He turned to Jack. 'You remember, don't you?'

'Yeah. Four dead.'

'Anyway, Miss Eastlake suggested I get a gun for home protection. I got a big one. She and I even did some target practice together.' He smiled. 'She was good, and she didn't mind the noise, but she *hated* the recoil.' He looked at the splattered alligator. 'I guess it did the job. What next, *muchacho?*'

'Around back, but . . . did either of you see that heron?'

Jack shook his head. So did Wireman, looking bemused.

'*I* saw it,' I told him. 'And if I see it again . . . or if either of you do . . . I want you to shoot it, Jerome.'

Wireman raised his eyebrows but said nothing. We resumed our tramp along the east side of the deserted estate.

XV

Finding a way in through the back turned out not to be a problem: there *was* no back. All but the most easterly corner of the mansion had been torn off, probably in the same storm that had taken the top stories. Standing there, looking into the overgrown ruin of what had once been a kitchen and pantry, I realized that Heron's Roost was little more than a moss-festooned façade.

'We can get in from here,' Jack said doubtfully, 'but I'm not sure I trust the floor. What do you think, Edgar?'

'I don't know,' I said. I felt very tired. Maybe it was only spent adrenaline from our encounter with the alligator, but it felt like more than that to me. It felt like defeat. There had been too many years, too many storms. And a little girl's drawings were ephemeral things to start with. 'What time *is* it, Wireman? Without the bull-shit, if you please.'

He looked at his watch. 'Two-thirty. What do you say, *muchacho*? Go in?'

'I don't know,' I repeated.

'Well, I do,' he said. 'I killed a fucking alligator to get here; I'm not leaving without at least a look around the old homestead. The pantry floor looks solid, and it's the closest to the ground. Come on, you two, let's pile up some shit to stand on. A couple of those beams should do. Jack, you can go first, then help me. We'll pull Edgar up together.'

And that's how we did it, dirty and disheveled and out of breath, scrambling first into the pantry and going from there into the house itself, looking around with wonder, feeling like time travelers, tourists in a world that had ended over eighty years before.

18 – Noveen

i

The house stank of decaying wood, old plaster, and moldy fabric. There was also an underlying greenish odor. Some of the furniture was left – ruined by time and slumped by moisture – but the fine old wallpaper in the parlor hung in strips, and there was a huge paper nest, ancient and silent, clinging to the ceiling in the rotting front hall. Below it, dead wasps lay in a foot-deep hill on the warped cypress floorboards. Somewhere, in what remained of the upstairs, water was dripping, one isolated drop at a time.

'The cypress and redwood in this place would have been worth a fortune if somebody had come up and got it before it went to hell,' Jack said. He bent down, seized the end of a protruding board, and pulled. It came up, bent almost like taffy, then broke off – not with a snap but a listless *crump*. A few woodlice came strolling from the rectangular hole below it. The smell that puffed up was dank and dark.

'No scavenge, no salvage, and nobody up here partying hearty,' Wireman said. 'No discarded condoms or step-ins, not a single JOE LOVES DEBBIE spray-painted on a wall. I don't think anyone's been up here since John chained the door and drove away for the last time. I know that's hard to believe—'

'No,' I said. 'It's not. The Heron's Roost at this end of the Key has belonged to Perse since 1927. John knew it, and made sure to keep it that way when he wrote his will. Elizabeth did the same. But it's not a shrine.' I looked into the room opposite the formal parlor. It might once have been a study. An old rolltop desk sat in a puddle of stinking water. There were bookshelves, but they stood empty. 'It's a tomb.'

'So where do we look for these drawings?' Jack asked.

'I have no idea,' I said. 'I don't even . . .' A chunk of plaster lay

495

in the doorway, and I kicked it. I wanted to send it flying, but it was too old and wet; it only disintegrated. 'I don't think there *are* any more drawings. Not now that I see the place.'

I glanced around again, smelling the wet reek.

'You could be right, but I don't trust you,' Wireman said. 'Because, *muchacho*, you're in mourning. And that makes a man tired. You're listening to the voice of experience.'

Jack went into the study, squishing across damp boards to get to the old rolltop. A drop of water plinked down on the visor of his cap, and he looked up. 'Ceiling's caving in,' he said. 'There was probably at least one bathroom overhead, maybe two, and maybe a roof cistern to catch rainwater, back in the day. I can see a hanging pipe. One of these years it's gonna come all the way down, and this desk will go bye-bye.'

'Just make sure you don't go bye-bye, Jack,' Wireman said.

'It's the floor I'm worried about right now,' he said. 'Feels mushy as hell.'

'Come back, then,' I said.

'In a minute. Let me check this, first.'

He ran the drawers, one after the other. 'Nothing,' he said. 'Nothing . . . more nothing . . . nothing . . .' He paused. 'Here's something. A note. Handwritten.'

'Let's see it,' Wireman said.

Jack brought it to him, taking big, careful steps until he got past the wet part of the floor. I read over Wireman's shoulder. The note was scrawled on plain white paper in a big flat man's hand:

August 19, '26

Johnny — You want, you get. This is the last of the good stuff, & just for you, My Lad. The 'champers' aint my best ever but 'What The Hell.' Single-malt's OK. CC for the 'common herd' (ha-ha). 5 Ken in the keg. And as you asked, Table X 2, and in cera. I take no credit, just struck lucky, but it really is the last. Thanks for everything, Pal. See you when I get back this side of the puddle.

DD

Wireman touched *Table X 2* and said, 'The table is leaking. Does the rest of this mean anything to you, Edgar?'

496

It did, but for a moment my damned sick memory refused to give it up. *I can do this*, I thought . . . and then thought sideways. First to Ilse saying *Share your pool, mister?*, and that hurt, but I let it because that was the way in. What followed was the memory of another girl dressed for another pool. This girl was all breasts and long legs in a black tank suit, she was Mary Ire as Hockney had painted her – *Gidget in Tampa*, she had called her younger self – and then I had it. I let out a breath I hadn't known I was holding.

'DD was Dave Davis,' I said. 'In the Roaring Twenties he was a Suncoast mogul.'

'How do you know that?'

'Mary Ire told me,' I said, and a cold part of me that would probably never warm up again could appreciate the irony; life is a wheel, and if you wait long enough, it always comes back around to where it started. 'Davis was friends with John Eastlake, and apparently supplied Eastlake with plenty of good liquor.'

'Champers,' Jack said. 'That's champagne, right?'

Wireman said, 'Good for you, Jack, but I want to know what Table is. And *cera*.'

'It's Spanish,' Jack said. 'You should know that.'

Wireman cocked an eyebrow at him. 'You're thinking of *será* – with an *s*. As in *que será, será*.'

'Doris Day, 1956,' I said. 'The future's not ours to see.' *And a good thing, too*, I thought. 'One thing I'm pretty sure of is that Davis was right when he said this was the last delivery.' I tapped the date: August 19th. 'The guy sailed for Europe in October of 1926 and never came back. He disappeared at sea – or so Mary Ire told me.'

'And *cera*?' Wireman asked.

'Let it go for now,' I said. 'But it's strange – just this one piece of paper.'

'A little odd, maybe, but not completely strange,' Wireman said. 'If you were a widower with young daughters, would you want to take your bootlegger's last receipt with you into your new life?'

I considered it, and decided he had a point. 'No . . . but I'd probably destroy it, along with my stash of French postcards.'

Wireman shrugged. 'We'll never know how much incriminating paperwork he *did* destroy . . . or how little. Except for having a little

497

drinkie now and then with his pals, his hands may have been relatively clean. But, *muchacho* . . .' He put a hand on my shoulder. 'The paper *is* real. We *do* have it. And if something's out to get us, maybe something else is looking out for us . . . just a little. Isn't that possible?'

'It would be nice to think so, anyway. Let's see if there's anything else.'

ii

It seemed at first there wasn't. We poked around all the downstairs rooms and found nothing but near-disaster when my foot plunged through the flooring in what must once have been the dining room. Wireman and Jack were quick, however, and at least it was my bad leg that went down; I had my good one to brace myself with.

There was no hope of checking above ground-level. The staircase went all the way up, but beyond the landing and a single ragged length of rail beside it, there was only blue sky and the waving fronds of one tall cabbage palm. The second floor was a remnant, the third complete toast. We started back toward the kitchen and our makeshift step-down to the outside world with nothing to show for our exploration but an ancient note announcing a booze delivery. I had an idea what *cera* might mean, but without knowing where Perse was, the idea was useless.

And she was here.

She was close.

Why else make it so fucking hard to *get* here?

Wireman was in the lead, and he stopped so suddenly I ran into him. Jack ran into me, whacking me in the butt with the picnic basket.

'We need to check the stairs,' Wireman said. He spoke in the tone of a man who can't believe he has been such a dumb cluck.

'I beg pardon?' I asked.

'We need to check the stairs for a ha-ha. I should have thought of that first thing. I must be losing it.'

'What's a ha-ha?' I asked.

Wireman was turning back. 'The one at *El Palacio* is four steps up from the bottom of the main staircase. The idea — she said it was her father's – was to have it close to the front door in case of fire. There's a lockbox inside it, and nothing much inside the lockbox now but a few old souvenirs and some pictures, but once she kept her will and her best pieces of jewelry in there. Then she told her lawyer. Big mistake. He insisted she move all that stuff to a safe deposit box in Sarasota.'

We were at the foot of the stairs now, back near the hill of dead wasps. The stink of the house was thick around us. He turned to me, his eyes gleaming. '*Muchacho*, she also kept a few very valuable china figures in that box.' He surveyed the wreck of the staircase, leading up to nothing but senseless shattery and blue sky beyond. 'You don't suppose . . . if Perse *is* something like a china figure that John fished off the bottom of the Gulf . . . you don't suppose she's hidden right here, in the stairs?'

'I think anything's possible. Be careful. *Very.*'

'I'll bet you anything that there's a ha-ha,' he said. 'We repeat what we learn as children.'

He brushed away the dead wasps with his boot – they made a whispery, papery sound – and then knelt at the foot of the stairs. He examined the first stair riser, then the second, then the third. When he got to the fourth, he said: 'Jack, give me the flashlight.'

iii

It was easy to tell myself that Perse wasn't hiding in a secret compartment under the stairs – that would be too easy – but I remembered the chinas Elizabeth liked to secrete in her Sweet Owen cookie-tin and felt my pulse speed up as Jack rummaged in the picnic basket and brought out the monster flashlight with the stainless steel barrel. He slapped it into Wireman's hand like a nurse handing a doctor an instrument at the operating table.

When Wireman trained the light on the stair, I saw the minute gleam of gold: tiny hinges set at the far end of the tread. 'Okay,' he said, and handed back the flashlight. 'Put the beam on the edge of the tread.'

Jack did as told. Wireman reached for the lip of the riser, which was meant to swing up on those tiny hinges.

'Wireman, just a minute,' I said.

He turned to me.

'Sniff it first,' I said.

'Say *what*?'

'Sniff it. Tell me if it smells wet.'

He sniffed the stair with the hinges at the back, then turned to me again. 'A little damp, maybe, but *everything* in here smells that way. Want to be a little more specific?'

'Just open it very slowly, okay? Jack, shine the light directly inside. Look for wetness, both of you.'

'Why, Edgar?' Jack asked.

'Because the Table is leaking, she said so. If you see a ceramic container – a bottle, a jug, a keg – that's her. It'll almost certainly be cracked, and maybe broken wide open.'

Wireman pulled in a breath, then let it out. 'Okay. As the mathemetician said when he divided by zero, here goes nothing.'

He tried to lift the stair, with no result.

'It's locked. I see a tiny slot . . . must have been a hell of a small key—'

'I've got a Swiss Army knife,' Jack offered.

'Just a minute,' Wireman said, and I saw his lips tighten down as he applied upward pressure with his fingertips. A vein stood out in the hollow of his temple.

'Wireman,' I started, 'be carefu—'

Before I could finish, the lock – old and tiny and undoubtedly rotted with rust – snapped. The stair-tread flew up and tore off at the hinges. Wireman tumbled backward. Jack caught him, and then I caught Jack in a clumsy one-armed hug. The big flashlight hit the floor but didn't break; its bright beam rolled, spotlighting that grisly pile of dead wasps.

'Holy shit,' Wireman said, regaining his feet. 'Larry, Curly, and Moe.'

Jack picked up the flashlight and shone it into the hole in the stairs.

'What?' I asked. 'Anything? Nothing? Talk!'

'Something, but it's not a ceramic bottle,' he said. 'It's a metal box. Looks like a candy box, only bigger.' He bent down.

'Maybe you better not,' Wireman said.

500

But it was too late for that. Jack reached in all the way up to his elbow, and for one moment I was sure his face would lengthen in a scream as something battened on his arm and yanked him down to the shoulder. Then he straightened again. In his hand he held a heart-shaped tin box. He held it out to us. On the top, barely visible beneath speckles of rust, was a pink-cheeked angel. Below that, in old-fashioned script, these painted words:

ELIZABETH
HER THINGS

Jack looked at us questioningly.

'Go on,' I said. It wasn't Perse – I was positive of that now. I felt both disappointed and relieved. 'You found it; go on and open it.'

'It's the drawings,' Wireman said. 'It must be.'

I thought so, too. But it wasn't. What Jack lifted out of the rusty old heart-shaped box was Libbit's dolly, and seeing Noveen was like coming home.

Ouuuu, her black eyes and scarlet smiling mouth seemed to be saying. *Ouuu, I been in there all that time, you nasty man.*

iv

When I saw her come out of that box like a disinterred corpse out of a crypt, I felt a terrible, helpless horror come stealing through me, beginning at the heart and radiating outward, threatening to first loosen all my muscles and then unknit them completely.

'Edgar?' Wireman asked sharply. 'All right?'

I did my best to get hold of myself. Mostly it was the thing's toothless smile. Like the jockey's cap, that smile was *red*. And as with the jockey's cap, I felt that if I looked at it too long, it would drive me mad. That smile seemed to insist that everything which had happened in my new life was a dream I was having in some hospital ICU while machines kept my twisted body alive a little while longer . . . and maybe that was good, for the best, because it meant nothing had happened to Ilse.

'Edgar?' When Jack stepped toward me, the doll in his hand bobbed in its own grotesque parody of concern. 'You're not going to faint, are you?'

'No,' I said. 'Let me see that.' And when he tried to pass it to me: 'I don't want to take it. Just hold it up.'

He did as I asked, and I understood at once why I'd had that feeling of instant recognition, that sense of coming home. Not because of Reba or her more recent companion – although all three were ragdolls, there was that similarity. No, it was because I had seen her before, in several of Elizabeth's drawings. At first I'd assumed she was Nan Melda. That was wrong, but—

'Nan Melda gave this to her,' I said.

'Sure,' Wireman agreed. 'And it must have been her favorite, because it was the only one she ever drew. The question is, why did she leave it behind when the family left Heron's Roost? Why did she lock it away?'

'Sometimes dolls fall out of favor,' I said. I was looking at that red and smiling mouth. Still red after all these years. Red like the place memories went to hide when you were wounded and couldn't think straight. 'Sometimes dolls get scary.'

'Her pictures talked to you, Edgar,' Wireman said. He waggled the doll, then handed it to Jack. 'What about her? Will the doll tell you what we want to know?'

'Noveen,' I said. 'Her name's Noveen. And I wish I could say yes, but only Elizabeth's pencils and pictures speak to me.'

'How do you know?'

A good question. How *did* I know?

'I just do. I bet she could have talked to *you*, Wireman. Before I fixed you. When you still had that little twinkle.'

'Too late now,' Wireman said. He rummaged in the food-stash, found the cucumber strips, and ate a couple. 'So what do we do? Go back? Because I have an idea that if we go back, *'chacho*, we'll never summon the testicular fortitude to return.'

I thought he was right. And meanwhile, the afternoon was passing all around us.

Jack was sitting on the stairs, his butt on a riser two or three above the ha-ha. He was holding the doll on his knee. Sunshine fell through the shattered top of the house and dusted them with light. They were strangely evocative, would have made a terrific painting: *Young Man and Doll*. The way he was holding Noveen reminded me of something, but I couldn't put my finger on just what. Noveen's black shoebutton eyes seemed to look at me, almost smugly. *I seen a lot, you nasty man. I seen it all. I know it all. Too bad I'm not a picture you can touch with your phantom hand, ain't it?*

Yes. It was.

'There was a time when *I* could have made her talk,' Jack said.

Wireman looked puzzled, but I felt that little *click* you get when a connection you've been trying to make finally goes through. Now I knew why the way he was holding the doll looked so familiar.

'Into ventriloquism, were you?' I hoped I sounded casual, but my heart was starting to bump against my ribs again. I had an idea that here at the south end of Duma Key, many things were possible. Even in broad daylight.

'Yeah,' Jack said with a smile that was half-embarrassed, half-reminiscent. 'I bought a book about it when I was only eight, and stuck with it mostly because my Dad said it was like throwing money away, I gave up on everything.' He shrugged, and Noveen bobbed a bit on his leg. As if she were also trying to shrug. 'I never got *great* at it, but I got good enough to win the sixth-grade Talent Competition. My Dad hung the medal on his office wall. That meant a lot to me.'

'Yeah,' Wireman said. 'There's nothing like an atta-boy from a doubtful dad.'

Jack smiled, and as always, it illuminated his whole face. He shifted a little, and Noveen shifted with him. 'Best thing, though? I was a shy kid, and ventriloquism broke me out a little. It got easier to talk to people — I'd sort of pretend I was Morton. My dummy, you know. Morton was a wiseass who'd say anything to anybody.'

'They all are,' I said. 'It's a rule, I think.'

'Then I got into junior high, and ventriloquism started to seem like a nerd talent compared to skateboarding, so I gave it up. I don't know what happened to the book. *Throw Your Voice*, it was called.'

We were silent. The house breathed dankly around us. A little

503

while ago, Wireman had killed a charging alligator. I could hardly believe that now, even though my ears were still ringing from the gunshots.

Then Wireman said: 'I want to hear you do it. Make her say, "*Buenos días, amigos, mi nombre es Noveen,* and *la mesa* is leaking."'

Jack laughed. 'Yeah, right.'

'No – I'm serious.'

'I can't. If you don't do it for awhile, you forget how.'

And from my own research, I knew he could be right. In the matter of learned skills, memory comes to a fork in the road. Down one branch are the it's-like-riding-a-bicycle skills; things which, once learned, are almost never forgotten. But the creative, ever-changing forebrain skills have to be practiced almost daily, and they are easily damaged or destroyed. Jack was saying ventriloquism was like that. And while I had no reason to doubt him – it involved creating a new personality, after all, as well as throwing one's voice – I said: 'Give it a try.'

'What?' He looked at me. Smiling. Puzzled.

'Go on, take a shot.'

'I told you, I can't—'

'Try, anyway.'

'Edgar, I have no idea what she would sound like even if I *could* still throw my voice.'

'Yeah, but you've got her on your knee, and it's just us chickens, so go ahead.'

'Well, shit.' He blew hair off his forehead. 'What do you want her to say?'

Wireman said, very quietly indeed: 'Why don't we just see what comes out?'

v

Jack sat with Noveen on his knee for a moment longer, their heads in the sun, little bits of disturbed dust from the stairs and the ancient hall carpet floating around their faces. Then he shifted his grip so that his fingers were on the doll's rudiment of a neck and her cloth shoulders. Her head came up.

'Hello, boys,' Jack said, only he was trying not to move his lips and it came out *Hello, oys.*

He shook his head; the disturbed dust flew. 'Wait a minute,' he said. 'That sucks.'

'Got all the time in the world,' I told him. I think I sounded calm, but my heart was thudding harder than ever. Part of what I was feeling was fear for Jack. If this worked, it might be dangerous for him.

He stretched out his throat and used his free hand to massage his Adam's apple. He looked like a tenor getting ready to sing. Or like a bird, I thought. A Gospel Hummingbird, maybe. Then he said, 'Hello, boys.' It was better, but—

'No,' he said. 'Shit-on-toast. Sounds like that old blond chick, Mae West. Wait.'

He massaged his throat again. He was looking up into the cascading bright as he did it, and I'm not sure he knew that his other hand – the one on the doll – was moving. Noveen looked first at me, then at Wireman, then back at me. Black shoebutton eyes. Black beribboned hair cascading around a chocolate-cookie face. Red **O** of a mouth. An *Ouuu, you nasty man* mouth if ever there was one.

Wireman's hand gripped mine. It was cold.

'Hello, boys,' Noveen said, and although Jack's Adam's apple bobbed up and down, his lips barely moved on the *b* at all.

'Hey! How was that?'

'Good,' Wireman said, sounding as calm as I didn't feel. 'Have her say something else.'

'I get paid extra for this, don't I, boss?'

'Sure,' I said. 'Time and a ha—'

'Ain't you gone draw nuthin?' Noveen asked, looking at me with those round black eyes. They really were shoebuttons, I was almost sure of it.

'I have nothing to draw,' I said. 'Noveen.'

'I tell you sumpin you c'n draw. Whereat yo pad?' Jack was now looking off to the side, into the shadows leading to the ruined parlor, bemused, eyes distant. He looked neither conscious nor unconscious; he looked someplace between.

Wireman let go of me and reached into the food-bag, where I had stowed the two Artisan pads. He handed me one. Jack's hand

505

flexed a bit, and Noveen appeared to bend her head slightly to study it as I first flipped back the cover and then unzipped the pouch that held my pencils. I took one.

'Naw, naw. Use one of hers.'

I rummaged again, and took out Libbit's pale green. It was the only one still long enough to afford a decent grip. It must not have been her favorite color. Or maybe it was just that Duma's greens were darker.

'All right, now what?'

'Draw me in the kitchen. Put me up agin the breadbox, that do fine.'

'On the counter, do you mean?'

'Think I was talkin bout on the flo?'

'Christ,' Wireman muttered. The voice had been changing steadily with each exchange; now it wasn't Jack's at all. And whose was it, given the fact that in its prime the only ventriloquism available to make the doll speak had been provided by a little girl's imagination? I thought it had been Nan Melda's then, and that we were listening to a version of that voice now.

As soon as I began to work, the itch swept down my missing arm, defining it, making it *there*. I sketched her sitting against an old-fashioned breadbox, then drew her legs dangling over the edge of the counter. With no pause or hesitation – something deep inside me, where the pictures came from, said that to hesitate would be to break the spell while it was still forming, while it was still fragile – I went on and drew the little girl standing beside the counter. Standing beside the counter and looking up. Little four-year-old girl in a pinafore. I could not have told you what a pinafore was before I drew one over little Libbit's dress as she stood there in the kitchen beside her doll, as she stood there looking up, as she stood there—

Shhhhh—

—with one finger to her lips.

Now, moving quicker than ever, the pencil racing, I added Nan Melda, seeing her for the first time outside that photograph where she was holding the red picnic basket bunched in her arms. Nan Melda bent over the little girl, her face set and angry.

No, not angry—

506

vi

Scared.

That's what Nan Melda is, scared near to death. She knows something is going on, Libbit knows something is going on, and the twins know, too – Tessie and Lo-Lo are as scared as she is. Even that fool Shannington knows something's wrong. That's why he's taken to staying away as much as he can, preferring to work on the farm shoreside instead of coming out to the Key.

And the Mister? When he's here, the Mister's too mad about Adie, who's run off to Atlanta, to see what's right in front of his eyes.

At first Nan Melda thought what was in front of her eyes was just her own imagination, picking up on the baby-uns' games; surely she never really saw no pelicans or herons flying upside-down, or the hosses smiling at her when Shannington brought over the two-team from Nokomis to give the girls a ride. And she guessed she knew why the little ones were scairt of Charley; there might be mysteries on Duma now, but that ain't one of em. That was her own fault, although she meant well—

vii

'Charley!' I said. 'His name's Charley!'

Noveen cawed her laughing assent.

I took the other pad out of the food-sack – almost *ripped* it out – and threw back the cover so savagely that I tore it half off. I groped among the pencils and found the stub of Libbit's black. I wanted black for this side-drawing, and there was just enough to pinch between my thumb and finger.

'Edgar,' Wireman said. 'For a minute there I thought I saw . . . it looked like—'

'Shut up!' Noveen cried. 'Ne'mine no mojo arm! You gone want to see this, I bet!'

I drew quickly, and the jockey came out of the white like a figure out of heavy fog. It was quick, the strokes careless and hurried, but the essence was there: the knowing eyes and the broad lips that might have been grinning with either mirth or malevolence. I had no time to color the shirt and the breeches, but I fumbled for the

507

pencil stamped Plain Red (one of mine) along its barrel and added the awful cap, scribbling it in. And once the cap was there you knew what that grin really was: a nightmare.

'Show me!' Noveen cried. 'I want to see if y'got it right!'

I held the picture up to the doll, who now sat straight on Jack's leg while Jack slumped against the wall beside the staircase, looking off into the parlor.

'Yep,' Noveen said. 'That's the bugger who scared Melda's girls. Mos' certainly.'

'What—?' Wireman began, and shook his head. 'I'm lost.'

'Melda seen the frog, too,' Noveen said. 'The one the babbies call the big boy. The one wit d'*teef*. That's when Melda finally corner Libbit in d'kitchen. To make her talk.'

'At first Melda thought the stuff about Charley was just little kids scaring each other, didn't she?'

Noveen cawed again, but her shoebutton eyes stared with what could have been horror. Of course, eyes like that can look like anything you want them to, can't they? 'That's right, sugar. But when she seen ole Big Boy down there at the foot of the lawn, crossin the driveway and goin into the trees . . .'

Jack's hand flexed. Noveen's head shook slowly back and forth, indicating the collapse of Nan Melda's defenses.

I shuffled the pad with Charley the jockey on it to the bottom and went back to the picture of the kitchen: Nan Melda looking down, the little girl looking up with her finger on her lips – *Shhhh!* – and the doll bearing silent witness from her place against the breadbox. 'Do you see it?' I asked Wireman. 'Do you understand?'

'Sort of . . .'

'Sugar-candy was mos'ly done, once *she* was out,' Noveen said. 'Thass what it come down to.'

'Maybe at first Melda thought Shannington was moving the lawn jockey around as a kind of joke – because he knew the three little girls were scared of it.'

'Why in God's name would they be?' Wireman asked.

Noveen said nothing, so I passed my missing hand over the Noveen in my drawing – the Noveen leaning against the breadbox – and then the one on Jack's knee spoke up. As I sort of knew she would.

508

'Nanny din' mean nothin bad. She knew they 'us scairt of Charley – this 'us befo the bad things started – an so she tole em a bedtime story to try an make it better. Made it worse instead, as sometimes happens with small chirrun. Then the bad woman come – the bad white woman from the sea – n dat bitch made it worse still. She made Libbit draw Charley alive, for a joke. She had other jokes, too.'

I threw back the sheet with Libbit going *Shhhh*, seized my Burnt Umber from my pack – now it didn't seem to matter whose pencils I used – and sketched the kitchen again. Here was the table, with Noveen lying on her side, one arm cast up over her head, as if in supplication. Here was Libbit, now wearing a sundress and an expression of dismay achieved in no more than half a dozen racing lines. And here was Nan Melda, backing away from the open breadbox and screaming, because inside—

'Is that a rat?' Wireman asked.

'Big ole blind woodchuck,' Noveen said. 'Same thing as Charley, really. She got Libbit to draw it in the breadbox, and it *was* in the breadbox. A joke. Libbit 'us sorry, but the bad water-woman? Nuh-uh. She *never* sorry.'

'And Elizabeth – Libbit – *had* to draw,' I said. 'Didn't she?'

'You know *dat*,' Noveen said. 'Don't you?'

I did. Because the gift is hungry.

viii

Once upon a time, a little girl fell and did her head wrong in just the right way. And that allowed something – something female – to reach out and make contact with her. The amazing drawings that followed had been the come-on, the carrot dangling at the end of the stick. There had been smiling horses and troops of rainbow-colored frogs. But once Perse was out – what had Noveen said? – sugar-candy was mos'ly done. Libbit Eastlake's talent had turned in her hand like a knife. Except it was no longer really *her* hand. Her father didn't know. Adie was gone. Maria and Hannah were away at the Braden School. The twins couldn't understand. But Nan Melda began to suspect, and . . .

I flipped back and looked at the little girl with the finger on her lips.

She's listening, so shhhh. If you talk, she'll hear, so shhhh. Bad things can happen, and worse things are waiting. Terrible things in the Gulf, waiting to drown you and take you to a ship where you'll live something that's not life. And if I try to tell? Then the bad things may happen to all of us, and all at once.

Wireman was perfectly still beside me. Only his eyes moved, sometimes looking at Noveen, sometimes looking at the pallid arm that flickered in and out of view on the right side of my body.

'But there was a safe place, wasn't there?' I asked. 'A place where she could talk. Where?'

'You know,' Noveen said.

'No, I—'

'Yessir, you do. You sho do. You only forgot awhile. Draw it and you see.'

Yes, she was right. Drawing was how I'd re-invented myself. In that way, Libbit

(*where our sister*)

was my kin. For both of us, drawing was how we remembered how to remember.

I flipped to a clean sheet. 'Do I have to use one of her pencils?' I asked.

'Not no mo. You be fine with any.'

So I rummaged in my pack, found my Indigo, and began drawing. I drew the Eastlake swimming pool with no hesitation – it was like giving up thought and allowing muscle memory to punch in a phone number. I drew it as it had been when it had been bright and new and full of clean water. The pool, where for some reason Perse's hold slipped and her hearing failed.

I drew Nan Melda, up to her shins, and Libbit up to her waist, with Noveen tucked under her arm and her pinafore floating around her. Words floated out of my strokes.

Where yo new doll now? The china doll?

In my special treasure-box. My heart-box.

So it *had* been there, at least for awhile.

And what her name?

Her name is Perse.

510

Percy a boy's name.

And Libbit, firm and sure: *I can't help it. Her name is Perse.*

All right den. And you say she can't hear us here.

I don't think so . . .

That's good. You say you c'n make things come. But listen to me, child—

ix

'Oh my God,' I said. 'It wasn't Elizabeth's idea. It was *never* Elizabeth's idea. We should have known.'

I looked up from the picture I had drawn of Nan Melda and Libbit standing in the pool. I realized, in a distant way, that I was very hungry.

'What are you talking about, Edgar?' Wireman asked.

'Getting rid of Perse was Nan Melda's idea.' I turned to Noveen, still sitting on Jack's knee. 'I'm right, aren't I?'

Noveen said nothing, so I passed my right hand over the figures in my swimming-pool drawing. For a moment I saw that hand, long fingernails and all.

'Nanny didn't know no better,' Noveen said an instant later from Jack's leg. 'And Libbit be trustin Nanny.'

'Of course she did,' Wireman said. 'Melda was almost the child's mother.'

I had visualized the drawing and erasing as happening in Elizabeth's room, but now I knew better. It had happened at the pool. Perhaps even *in* the pool. Because the pool had been, for some reason, safe. Or so little Libbit had believed.

Noveen said, 'It din' make Perse gone, but it sholy did get her attention. I think it *hoit* dat bitch.' The voice sounded tired now, croaky, and I could see Jack's Adam's apple sliding up and down in his throat again. 'I *hope* it did!'

'Yes,' I said. 'Probably it did. So . . . what came next?' But I knew. Not the details, but I knew. The logic was grim and irrefutable. 'Perse took her revenge on the twins. And Elizabeth and Nan Melda knew. They knew what they did. Nan Melda knew what *she* did.'

'She knew,' Noveen said. It was still a female voice, but it was edging closer to Jack's all the time. Whatever the spell was, it wouldn't hold much longer. 'She held on until the Mister found their tracks down on Shade Beach – tracks goin into the water – but after that she couldn't hold on no longer. She felt she got her babby-uns killed.'

'Did she see the ship?' I asked.

'Seen it that night. You cain't see that boat at night and not believe.'

I thought of my *Girl and Ship* paintings and knew that was the truth.

'But even before the Mister rung the high sheriff on the s'change to say his twins was missin and probably drownded, Perse done spoke to Libbit. Tole her how it was. An' Libbit tole Nanny.'

The doll slumped, its round cookie-face seeming to study the heart-shaped box from which it had been exhumed.

'Told her what, Noveen?' Wireman asked. 'I don't understand.'

Noveen said nothing. Jack, I thought, looked exhausted even though he hadn't moved at all.

I answered for Noveen. 'Perse said, "Try to get rid of me again and the twins are just the beginning. Try again and I'll take your whole family, one by one, and save you for last." Isn't that right?'

Jack's fingers flexed. Noveen's rag head nodded slowly up and down.

Wireman licked his lips. 'That doll,' he said. 'Exactly whose ghost is it?'

'There are no ghosts here, Wireman,' I said.

Jack moaned.

'I don't know what he's been doing, *amigo*, but he's done,' Wireman said.

'Yes, but we're not.' I reached for the doll – the one that had gone everywhere with the child artist. And as I did, Noveen spoke to me for the last time, in a voice that was half hers and half Jack's, as if both of them were struggling to come through at the same time.

'Nuh-uh, not *dat* hand – you need dat hand to draw wit'.'

And so I reached out the arm I used to lift Monica Goldstein's dying dog out of the street six months ago, in another life and universe. I used that hand to grasp Elizabeth Eastlake's doll and lift it off Jack's knee.

512

'Edgar?' Jack said, straightening up. 'Edgar, how in *hell* did you get your—'

—*arm back*, I suppose he said, but I don't know for sure; I didn't hear the finish. What I saw were those black eyes and that black maw of a mouth ringed with red. Noveen. All these years she had been down there in the double dark – under the stair and in the tin box – waiting to spill her secrets, and her lipstick had stayed fresh all the while.

Are you set? she whispered inside my head, and that voice wasn't Noveen's, wasn't Nan Melda's (I was sure of that), wasn't even Elizabeth's; that was all Reba. *You all set and ready to draw, you nasty man? Are you ready to see the rest? Are you ready to see it all?*

I wasn't . . . but I would have to be.

For Ilse.

'Show me your pictures,' I whispered, and that red mouth swallowed me whole.

How to Draw a Picture (X)

Be prepared to see it all. If you want to create — God help you if you do, God help you if you can — don't you dare commit the immorality of stopping on the surface. Go deep and take your fair salvage. Do it no matter how much it hurts.

You can draw two little girls — twins — but anyone can do that. Don't stop there just because the rest is a nightmare. Do not neglect to add the fact that they are standing thigh-deep in water that should be over their heads. A witness — Emery Paulson, for instance — could see this if he looked, but so many people aren't prepared to see what is right in front of their eyes.

Until, of course, it's too late.

He's come down to the beach to smoke a cigar. He can do this on the back porch or on the veranda, but some strong compulsion has urged him down the rutted road Adie calls Drunkard's Boulevard and then down the steeper, sandy path to the beach. This voice has suggested his cigar will taste better here. He can sit on a fallen log the waves have cast up and watch the after-ashes of the sunset, as orange fades to tangerine and the stars go blue. The Gulf will look pleasant in such light, the voice suggests, even if the Gulf has had the bad taste to mark the beginning of his marriage by swallowing two of his beloved's little sisters.

But there's more to watch than just a sunset, it seems. There's a ship out there. It's an old-fashioned one, a pretty, slim-bulled thing with three masts and furled sails. Instead of sitting on the log, he walks down the beach to where the dry sand becomes wet and firm and packed, marveling at that swallow-shape against the fading sunset. Some trick of the air makes it seem as if the day's last red is shining right through the hull.

He is thinking this when the first cry comes, chiming in his head like a silver bell: Emery!

And then comes another: Emery, help! The undertow! The rip!

That is when he sees the girls, and his heart gives a springing leap. It seems to rise all the way to his throat before falling back into place, where it dashes double-time. The unlit cigar tumbles from his fingers.

515

Two little girls, and they look just the same. They appear to be wearing identical jumpers, and although Emery should not be able to distinguish colors in this dying light, he can: one jumper is red, with an **L** *on the front; the other is blue, with a* **T**.

The rip! *the girl with the* **T** *on her jumper calls, holding out her arms in supplication.*

The undertow! *calls the girl with the* **L**.

And although neither girl appears to be in the slightest danger of drowning, Emery doesn't hesitate. His joy won't let him hesitate, nor his bright certainty that this is a miracle opportunity: when he turns up with the twins, his previously distant father-in-law will change his tune in a hurry. And the silver chimes those voices ring in his head, they urge him forward, too. He rushes to rescue Adie's sisters, to gather the lost girls in and splash with them to shore.

Emery! *That's Tessie, her eyes dark in her china-pale face . . . but her lips are* red.

Emery, hurry! *That's Laura, with her dripping white hands held out to him and her lank curls pasted against her white cheeks.*

He cries I'm coming, girls! Hold on!

Splashing toward them, now up to his shins, now his knees.

He cries Fight it! *as though they are doing anything but standing there in water that is only thigh-deep on them, although he's now up to his own thighs and he's six feet and two inches tall.*

The water of the Gulf – still chilly in mid-April – is up to his chest when he reaches them, when he reaches out to them, and when they seize him with hands that are stronger than any little girls' hands should be; by the time he's close enough to see the silvery gleam in their glazed eyes and smell the salty, dead-fish aroma coming from their rotting hair, it's too late. He struggles, his cries of joy and his entreaties to fight the undertow turning first to yells of protest and then to screams of horror, but by then it is far too late. The screams do not last long, in any case. Their small hands have become cold claws digging deep into his flesh as they pull him deeper, and the water fills his mouth, drowning his screams. He sees the ship against the last cold ashes of the sunset, and – how did he not see it before? how did he not know? – realizes it is a hulk, a plague ship, a deathship. Something is waiting for him there, something in a shroud, and he would scream if he could, but now the water fills his eyes and there are other hands, ones that feel like nothing but stripped radiations of bone, closing around his ankles. A talon pulls off a shoe, then tweaks a toe . . . as if it means to play 'This little piggy went to market' with him as he drowns.

As Emery Paulson drowns.

19 – April of '27

i

Someone was yelling in the dark. It sounded like *Make him stop screaming*. Then there was a flat hard whacking sound and the dark lit up deep red, first on one side, then in the back. The red rolled toward the front of the darkness like a cloud of blood in water.

'You hit him too hard,' someone said. Was that Jack?

'Boss? Hey, boss!' Somebody was shaking me, so I still had a body. Probably that was good. Jack was shaking me. Jack *who?* I could get it, but I had to think sideways. His name was like someone on The Weather Channel—

More shaking. Rougher. '*Muchacho!* You there?'

My head bonked something, and I opened my eyes. Jack Cantori was kneeling to my left, his face tight and scared. It was Wireman in front of me, on his feet but bending over, shaking me like a daiquiri. The doll was lying face-down on my lap. I batted her aside with a grunt of disgust – oh you nasty man, indeed. Noveen landed in the pile of dead wasps with a papery rustle.

Suddenly the places she'd taken me began to come back: hell's own tour. The path to Shade Beach that Adriana Eastlake had called (much to her father's fury) Drunkard's Boulevard. The beach itself, and the horrible things that had happened there. The pool. The cistern.

'His eyes are open,' Jack said. 'Thank God. Edgar, do you hear me?'

'Yes,' I said. My voice was hoarse from screaming. I wanted food, but first I wanted to pour something down my burning throat. 'Thirsty – can you help a brother out?'

Wireman handed me one of the big bottles of Evian water. I shook my head. 'Pepsi.'

'You sure, *muchacho?* Water might be—'

519

'Pepsi. Caffeine.' That wasn't the only reason, but it would do.

Wireman put the Evian back and gave me a Pepsi. It was warm, but I chugged half of it, burped, then drank again. I looked around and saw only my friends and a length of dirty hallway. That was not good. In fact, it was terrible. My hand – I was definitely back to one again – was stiff and throbbing, as if I had been using it steadily for at least two hours, so where were the drawings? I was terrified that without the drawings, everything would fade the way dreams do upon waking. And I had risked more than my life for that information. I had risked my sanity.

I struggled, trying to get to my feet. A bolt of pain went through my head where I'd bumped it against the wall. 'Where are the pictures? Please tell me there are pictures!'

'Relax, *muchacho*, right here.' Wireman stepped aside and showed me a semi-tidy stack of Artisan sheets. 'You were drawing like a madman, tearing them off your pad as you went. I took em and stacked em up.'

'All right. Good. I need to eat. I'm starving.' And this felt like the literal truth.

Jack looked around uneasily. The front corridor, which had been filled with afternoon light when I took Noveen from Jack and went bye-bye down a black hole, was now dimmer. Not dark – not yet, and when I looked up I could see the sky overhead was still blue – but it was clear that the afternoon was either gone or almost gone.

'What time is it?' I asked.

'Quarter past five,' Wireman said. He didn't have to glance at his watch, which told me he'd been keeping close track. 'Sunset's still a couple of hours away. Give or take. So if they only come out at night—'

'I think they do. That's enough time, and I still need to eat. We can get out of this ruin. We're done with the house. We may need a ladder, though.'

Wireman raised his eyebrows but didn't ask; he only said, 'If there is one, it's probably in the barn. Which seems to have stood up to Father Time pretty well, actually.'

'What about the doll?' Jack asked. 'Noveen?'

'Put her back in Elizabeth's heart-box and bring her along,' I said. 'She deserves a place at *El Palacio*, with the rest of Elizabeth's things.'

'What's our next stop, Edgar?' Wireman asked.

'I'll show you, but one thing first.' I pointed to the gun in his belt. 'That thing's still loaded, right?'

'Absolutely. Fresh clip.'

'If the heron comes back, I still want you to shoot it. Make it a priority.'

'Why?'

'Because it's her,' I said. 'Perse's been using it to watch us.'

ii

We left the ruin the way we'd entered it and found a Florida early evening full of clear light. The sky above was cloudless. The sun cast a brilliant silver sheen across the Gulf. In another hour or so that track would begin to tarnish and turn to gold, but not yet.

We trudged along the remains of Drunkard's Boulevard, Jack carrying the picnic basket, Wireman the bag containing the food and the Artisan pads. I had my drawings. Sea oats whispered at our pants legs. Our shadows trailed long behind us toward the wreck of the mansion. Far ahead, a pelican saw a fish, folded its wings, and dropped like a dive-bomber. We did not see the heron, nor were we visited by Charley the Lawn Jockey. But when we reached the crest of the ridge, where the path had once sloped down along dunes that were now eroded and steep, we saw something else.

We saw the *Perse*.

She lay at anchor three hundred yards out. Her spotless sails were furled. She rolled from side to side on the swell, ticking like a clock. From here we could read the entire name painted on her starboard side: *Persephone*. She appeared deserted, and I was sure she was – in the daytime, the dead stayed dead. But Perse wasn't dead. Worse luck for us.

'My God, it could have sailed right out of your paintings,' Jack breathed. There was a stone bench to the right of the path, barely visible for the bushes growing around it and the vines snaking over its flat seat. He dropped onto it, gaping out at the boat.

521

'No,' I said. 'I painted the truth. You're seeing the mask it wears in the daytime.'

Wireman stood beside Jack, shading his eyes against the sun. Then he turned to me. 'Do they see it over on Don Pedro? They don't, do they?'

'Maybe some do,' I said. 'The terminally ill, the schizos currently ditching their medicine . . .' That made me think of Tom. 'But it's here for us, not them. We're meant to leave Duma Key on it tonight. The road will be closed to us once the sun goes down. The living dead may all be out there on *Persephone*, but there are *things* in the jungle. Some — like the lawn jockey — are things that Elizabeth created as a little girl. There are others that have come since Perse woke up again.' I paused. I didn't like to say the rest, but I did. I had to. 'I imagine I'm responsible for some of those. Every man has his nightmares.'

I thought of the skeleton arms reaching up in the moonlight.

'So,' Wireman said harshly. 'The plan is for us to leave by boat, is it?'

'Yes.'

'Press gang? Like in jolly old England?'

'Pretty much.'

'I can't do that,' Jack said. 'I get seasick.'

I smiled and sat down beside him. 'Sea voyages aren't in the plan, Jack.'

'Good.'

'Can you open that chicken for me, and tear me off a leg?'

He did as I asked, and they watched, fascinated, as I devoured first one leg, then the other. I asked if anyone wanted the breast, and when they both said no, I ate that, too. Halfway through it I thought of my daughter, lying pale and dead in Rhode Island. I kept on eating, doing it methodically, wiping my greasy hands on my jeans between bites. Ilse would have understood. Not Pam and probably not Lin, but Illy? Yes. I was frightened of what lay ahead, but I knew Perse was frightened, too. If she hadn't been, she would not have tried so hard to keep us out. On the contrary, she would have welcomed us in.

'Time's wasting, *muchacho*,' Wireman said. 'Daylight fleets.'

'I know,' I said. 'And my daughter's dead forever. I'm still starving, though. Is there anything sweet? Cake? Cookies? A motherfucking HoHo?'

There wasn't. I settled for another Pepsi and a few cucumber strips dipped in ranch dressing, which to me has always looked and tasted like slightly sweetened snot. At least my headache was fading. The images that had come to me in the dark – the ones that had been waiting all those years inside Noveen's rag-stuffed head – were also fading, but I had my own pictures to refresh them. I wiped my hands a final time and put the stack of torn and wrinkled sheets on my lap: the family album from hell.

'Keep an eye out for that heron,' I told Wireman.

He looked around, glanced at the deserted ship ticking back and forth out there on the mild swell, then looked back at me. 'Wouldn't the spear-pistol be better for Big Bird? With one of the silver harpoons attached?'

'No. The heron's something she just rides, the way a man rides a horse. She'd probably like it if we wasted one of the silvertips on it, but Perse is done getting what she likes.' I smiled without humor. 'That part of the lady's career is over.'

iii

Wireman made Jack get up so he could strip the vines from the bench. Then we sat there, three unlikely warriors, two in their fifties and one barely out of his teens, overlooking the Gulf of Mexico on one side and a ruined mansion on the other. The red basket and mostly depleted food-bag were at our feet. I thought I had twenty minutes to tell them what I knew, even half an hour, and that would still leave enough time.

I hoped.

'Elizabeth's connection with Perse was closer than mine,' I said. 'Much more *intense* than mine. I don't know how she stood it. Once she had the china figure, she saw everything, whether she was there or not. And she drew everything. But the worst pictures she burned before she left this place.'

'Like the picture of the hurricane?' Wireman asked.

'Yes. I think she was afraid of their power, and she was right to

523

be afraid. But she saw it all. And the doll stored it all up. Like a psychic camera. In most cases, I just saw what Elizabeth saw and drew what Elizabeth drew. Do you understand that?'

They both nodded.

'Start with this path, which was once a road. It went from Shade Beach to the barn.' I pointed to the long, vine-coated outbuilding where I hoped we would find a ladder. 'I don't think the bootlegger who wore it into the coral was Dave Davis, but I'm confident he was one of Davis's business associates, and that a fair amount of hooch came onto the Florida Suncoast by way of Duma Key. From Shade Beach to John Eastlake's barn, then across to the mainland. Mostly top-shelf stuff headed for a couple of jazz clubs in Sarasota and Venice, stored as a favor to Davis.'

Wireman glanced at the declining sun, then at his watch. 'Does this have any bearing on our current situation, *muchacho*? I assume it does.'

'You bet.' I produced a drawing of a keg with a fat screw-lid bung on top. The word TABLE had been sketched in a semi-circle on the side, with SCOTLAND below it, in another semi-circle. It was ragged work; I drew far better than I printed. 'Whiskey, gents.'

Jack indicated a vague, humanoid scribble on the keg between TABLE and SCOTLAND. The figure had been executed in orange, and one foot was raised behind it. 'Who's the chick in the dress?'

'That's not a dress, it's a kilt. It's supposed to be a highlander.'

Wireman raised his shaggy brows. 'Won't win any awards for that one, *muchacho*.'

'Elizabeth put Perse in some sort of midget whiskey barrel,' Jack mused. 'Or maybe it was Elizabeth and Nan Melda—'

I shook my head. 'Just Elizabeth.'

'How big was this thing?'

I held my hands about two feet from each other, considered, then moved them a little farther apart.

Jack nodded, but he was frowning, too. 'She put the china figure in and screwed the cap back on. Or put the plug in the jug. And drowned Perse to sleep. Which seems fucked up to me, boss. She was underwater when she started *calling* to Elizabeth, for God's sake. On the bottom of the Gulf!'

'Leave that for now.' I put the sketch of the whiskey barrel on the bottom of the stack and showed them the next one. It was Nan Melda, using the telephone in the parlor. There was something furtive about the tilt of her head and the hunch of her shoulders, only a quick stroke or two, but it said all that needed to be said about how southern folk felt back in 1927 about black housekeepers using the parlor phone, even in an emergency.

'We thought Adie and Emery read about it in the paper and came back, but the Atlanta papers probably didn't even cover the drowning of two little girls in Florida. When Nan Melda was sure the twins were missing, she called Eastlake – the Mister – on the mainland to give him the bad news. Then she called where Adie was staying with her new husband.'

Wireman pounded his fist on his leg. 'Adie told her Nanny where she was staying! Of course she did!'

I nodded. 'The newlyweds had to've caught a train that very night, because they were home before dark the next day.'

'By then the two middle daughters must have been home, too,' Jack said.

'Yep, the whole family,' I said. 'And the water out there . . .' I gestured toward where the slim white ship rode at anchor, waiting for dark. 'It was covered with small boats. The hunt for the bodies went on for at least three days, although they all knew those girls had to be dead. I imagine the last thing on John Eastlake's mind was trying to figure out how his eldest daughter and her husband got the news. All he could think during those days was his lost twins.'

'THEY ARE GONE,' Wireman murmured. '*Pobre hombre.*'

I held up the next picture. Here were three people standing on the veranda of Heron's Roost, waving, as a big old touring car motored down the crushed shell driveway toward the stone posts and the sane world beyond. I had sketched in a scattering of palms and some banana trees, but no hedge; the hedge did not exist in 1927.

In the rear window of the touring car, two small white ovals were looking back. I touched each in turn. 'Maria and Hannah,' I said. 'Going back to the Braden School.'

Jack said, 'That's a little cold, don't you think?'

I shook my head. 'I don't, actually. Children don't mourn like adults.'

Jack nodded. 'Yeah. I guess. But I'm surprised . . .' He fell silent.

'What?' I asked. 'What surprises you?'

'That Perse let them go,' Jack said.

'She didn't, not really. They were only going to Bradenton.'

Wireman tapped the sketch. 'Where's Elizabeth in this?'

'Everywhere,' I said. 'We're looking through her eyes.'

iv

'There's not much more, but the rest is pretty bad.'

I showed them the next sketch. It was as hurried as the other ones, and the male figure in it was depicted back-to, but I had no doubt it was the living version of the thing that had clamped a manacle on my wrist in the kitchen of Big Pink. We were looking down on him. Jack looked from the picture to Shade Beach, now eroded to a mere strip, then back to the picture. Finally he looked at me.

'Here?' he asked in a low voice. 'The point of view in this one is from right here?'

'Yes.'

'That's Emery,' Wireman said, touching the figure. His voice was even lower than Jack's. Sweat had sprung up on his brow.

'Yes.'

'The thing that was in your house.'

'Yes.'

He moved his finger. 'And those are Tessie and Laura?'

'Tessie and Lo-Lo. Yes.'

'They . . . what? Lured him in? Like sirens in one of those old Greek fairy-tales?'

'Yes.'

'This really happened,' Jack said. As if to get the sense of it.

'It really did,' I agreed. 'Never doubt her strength.'

Wireman looked toward the sun, which was nearer the horizon than ever. Its track had begun to tarnish at last. 'Then finish up, *muchacho*, quick as you can. So we can do our business and get the hell out of here.'

'I don't have much more to tell you, anyway,' I said. I shuffled

526

through a number of sketches that were little more than vague scribbles. 'The real heroine was Nan Melda, and we don't even know her last name.'

I showed them one of the half-finished sketches: Nan Melda, recognizable by the kerchief around her head and a perfunctory dash of color across the brow and one cheek, talking to a young woman in the front hallway. Noveen was propped nearby, on a table that was nothing but six or eight lines with a quick oval shape to bind them together.

'Here she is, telling Adriana some tall tale about Emery, after he disappeared. That he was called suddenly back to Atlanta? That he went to Tampa to get a surprise wedding present? I don't know. Anything to keep Adie in the house, or close by.'

'Nan Melda was playing for time,' Jack said.

'It was all she could do.' I pointed toward the crowding jungle overgrowth between us and the north end of the Key, growth that had no business being there – not, at least, without a team of horti-culturalists working overtime to provide its upkeep. 'All that wasn't there in 1927, but *Elizabeth* was here, and she was at the peak of her talents. I don't think anyone trying to use the road that went off-island would have stood a chance. God knows what Perse had made Elizabeth draw into existence between here and the draw-bridge.'

'Adriana was supposed to be next?' Wireman asked.

'Then John. Maria and Hannah after them. Because Perse meant to have all of them except – maybe – Elizabeth herself. Nan Melda must have known she could only hold Adie a single day. But a day was all she needed.'

I showed them another picture. Although much more hurried, it was once again Nan Melda and Libbit standing in the shallow end of the pool. Noveen lay on the edge with one rag arm trailing in the water. And beside Noveen, sitting on its fat belly, was a wide-mouth ceramic keg with TABLE printed on the side in a semi-circle.

'Nan Melda told Libbit what she had to do. And she told Libbit she had to do it no matter what she saw in her head or how loud Perse screamed for her to stop . . . because she *would* scream, Nan Melda said, if she found out. She said they'd just have to hope Perse found out too late to make any difference. And then Melda said . . .'

I stopped. The track of the lowering sun was growing brighter and brighter. I had to go on, but it was hard now. It was very, very hard.

'What, *muchacho*?' Wireman said gently. 'What did she say?'

'She said that *she* might scream, too. And Adie. And her Daddy. But she couldn't stop. "Dassn't stop, child," she said. "Dassn't stop or it's all for nothing." ' As if of its own accord, my hand plucked the Venus Black from my pocket and scrawled two words beneath the primitive drawing of the girl and the woman in the swimming pool:

dassn't stop

My eyes blurred with tears. I dropped the pencil into the sea oats and wiped the tears away. So far as I know, that pencil is still where I dropped it.

'Edgar, what about the silver-tipped harpoons?' Jack asked. 'You never said anything about them.'

'There weren't any magic goddam harpoons,' I said tiredly. 'They must have come years later, when Eastlake and Elizabeth returned to Duma Key. God knows which of them got the idea, and whichever one it was may not have even been completely sure why it seemed important.'

'But . . .' Jack was frowning again. 'If they didn't have the silver harpoons in 1927 . . . then how . . .'

'No silver harpoons, Jack, but plenty of water.'

'I still don't follow that. Perse *came* from the water. She's *of* water.' He looked at the ship, as if to make sure it was still there. It was.

'Right. But at the pool, *her hold slipped*. Elizabeth knew it, but didn't understand the implications. Why would she? She was just a child.'

'Oh, fuck,' Wireman said. He slapped his forehead. 'The swimming pool. Fresh water. It was a freshwater pool. Fresh as opposed to salt.'

I pointed a finger at him.

Wireman touched the picture I'd drawn of the ceramic keg sitting beside the doll. 'This keg was an *empty*? Which they filled from the pool?'

'I have no doubt.' I shuffled the swimming-pool sketch aside and showed them the next one. The perspective was again from almost exactly where we were sitting. Above the horizon, a just-risen sickle

528

moon shone between the masts of a rotting ship I hoped I would never have to draw again. And on the beach, at the edge of the water—

'Christ, that's awful,' Wireman said. 'I can't even see it clearly and it's still awful.'

My right arm was itching, throbbing. *Burning.* I reached down and touched the picture with the hand I hoped I would never have to see again . . . although I was afraid I might.

'I can see it for all of us,' I said.

How to Draw a Picture (XI)

Don't quit until the picture's complete. I can't tell you if that's the cardinal rule of art or not, I'm no teacher, but I believe those six words sum up all I've been trying to tell you. Talent is a wonderful thing, but it won't carry a quitter. And there always comes a time – if the work is sincere, if it comes from that magic place where thought, memory, and emotion all merge – when you will want to quit, when you will think that if you put your pencil down your eye will dull, your memory will lapse, and the pain will end. I know all this from the last picture I drew that day – the one of the gathering on the beach. It was only a sketch, but I think that when you're mapping hell, a sketch is all you need.

I started with Adriana.

All day long she has been frantic about Em, her emotions ranging from wild anger at him to fear for him. It has even crossed her mind that Daddy has Done Something Rash, although that seems unlikely; his grief has made him torpid and unresponsive ever since the search ended.

When sunset comes and there's still no sign of Em, you'd think she'd become more nervous than ever, but instead she grows calm, almost cheerful. She tells Nan Melda that Em will be back directly, she's sure of it. She feels it in her bones and hears it in her head, where it sounds like a small, chiming bell. She supposes that bell is what they mean by 'woman's intuition', and you don't become fully aware of it until you're married. She tells Nanny this, too.

Nan Melda nods and smiles, but she watches Adie narrowly. She's been watching her all day. The girl's man is gone for good, Libbit has told her this and Melda believes her, but Melda also believes that the rest of the family may be saved . . . that she herself may be saved.

Much, however, depends on Libbit herself.

Nan Melda goes up to check on her remaining babby-un, touching the bracelets on her left arm as she climbs the stairs. The silver bracelets are from her Mama, and Melda wears them to church every Sunday. Perhaps that's why she took them from her special-things box today, slipping them

531

on and pushing them up until they stuck on the swell of her forearm instead of letting them dangle loose above her wrist. Perhaps she wanted to feel a little closer to her Mama, to borrow a little of Mama's quiet strength, or perhaps she just wanted the association of something holy.

Libbit is in her room, drawing. She is drawing her family, Tessie and Lo-Lo very much included. The eight of them (Nan Melda is also family, as far as Libbit is concerned) stand on the beach where they have spent so many happy times swimming and picnicking and building sand castles, their hands linked like paper dolls and great big smiles running off the sides of their faces. It's as if she thinks she can draw them back to life and happiness by the pure force of her will.

Nan Melda could almost believe it possible. The child is powerful. Re-creating life, however, is beyond her. Re-creating real life is even beyond the thing from the Gulf. Nan Melda's eyes drift to Libbit's special-things box before going back to Libbit herself again. She has only seen the figurine that came from the Gulf once, a tiny woman in a faded pink wrap that might once have been scarlet and a hood from which hair spills, hiding her brow.

She asks Libbit if everything is all right. It's all she dares to say, as far as she dares to go. If there really is a third eye hidden under the curls of the thing in the box — a far-seeing mojo eye — it is impossible to be too careful.

Libbit says Good. I just drawin, Nan Melda.

Has she forgotten what she's supposed to do? Nan Melda can only hope she hasn't. She has to go back downstairs now, and keep an eye on Adie. Her man will be calling for her soon.

Part of her cannot believe this is happening; part of her feels as if her whole life has been a preparation for it.

Melda says You may hear me call yo Daddy. If I do, you want to go pick up those things you lef by the pool. Don't leave em out all night for the dew t'git at.

Still drawing, not looking up. But then she says something that gladdens Melda's frightened heart. No'm. I'll take Perse. Then I won't be scared if it's dark.

Melda says You take whoever you want, jus' bring in Noveen, she still out there.

It's all she has time for, all she dares when she thinks about that special probing mojo eye, and how it might be trying to see inside her head.

532

Melda touches her bracelets again as she goes downstairs. She is very glad she had them on while she was in Libbit's room, even though the little china woman was put away in the tin box.

She is just in time to see the swirl of Adie's dress at the end of the back hall as Adie turns into the kitchen.

It is time. This is going to play out.

Instead of following Adie to the kitchen, Melda runs down the front hall to the Mister's study, where, for the first time in the seven years she's worked for the family, she enters without knocking. The Mister is sitting behind his desk with his tie off and his collar undone and his braces hanging down in slack loops. He has the folding gold-framed pictures of Tessie and Lo-Lo in his hands. He looks up at her, his eyes red in a face that is already thinner. He doesn't seem surprised that his housekeeper should come bursting in unannounced; he has the air of a man beyond surprise, beyond shock, but of course this will turn out not to be so.

He says What is it, Melda Lou?

She says You got to come right away.

He looks at her from his streaming eyes with a calm and infuriating stupidity. Come where?

She says To the beach. And bring at-ere.

She points to the harpoon pistol, which hangs on the wall, along with several short harpoons. The tips are steel, not silver, and the shafts are heavy. She knows; hasn't she carried them in the basket enough times?

He says What are you talking about?

She says I cain't be taking time to explain. You got to come to the beach right now, less you want to lose another one.

He goes. He doesn't ask which daughter, or inquire again why he should want the harpoon pistol; he just snatches it off the wall, takes two of the harpoons in his other hand, and strides out through the open study door, first beside Melda and then ahead of her. By the time he reaches the kitchen, where Melda has last seen Adie, he's at a full-out run and she is falling behind even though she's running herself, holding her skirts before her in both hands. And is she surprised by this sudden break in his torpor, this sudden galvanizing action? No. Because, despite the blanket of his grief, the Mister has also known that something here is wrong and going wronger all the time.

The back door stands open. An evening breeze frisks in, stirring it back farther on its hinges . . . only now it's actually a night breeze. Sunset is

533

dying. There will still be light on Shade Beach, but here at Heron's Roost, dark has already come. Melda dashes across the back porch and sees the Mister already on the path to the beach. He's only a shadow. She looks around for Libbit, but of course she doesn't see her; if Libbit is doing what she is supposed to be doing, then she's already on her way to the swimming pool with her heart-box under her arm.

The heart-box with the monster inside it.

She runs after the Mister and catches him at the bench, where the path drops down to the beach. He is standing there, frozen. In the west, the last of the sunset is a sullen orange line that will soon be gone, but there is enough light for her to see Adie at the edge of the water, and the man who is wading to greet her.

Adriana screams Emery! *She sounds mad with joy, as if he's been gone a year instead of a day.*

Melda shouts No, Ade, keep away from him! *from beside the frozen, gaping man, but she knows Adie will pay no attention, and she doesn't; Adie runs to her husband.*

John Eastlake says What − *and that's all.*

He's broken free of his torpor long enough to run this far, but now he's frozen again. Is it because he sees the two other forms, farther out but also wading toward shore? Wading in water that should be over their heads? Melda thinks not. She thinks he is still staring at his oldest daughter as the dim figure of the man coming out of the water reaches for her with his dripping arms and lays hold of her neck with his dripping hands, first choking off her glad cries and then dragging her into the surge.

Out there in the Gulf, waiting, ticking back and forth on the mild swell like a clock that tells time in years and centuries rather than minutes and hours, is the black hulk of Perse's ship.

Melda grabs the Mister's arm, sinking her hand deep into the bicep, and speaks to him as she has never spoken to a white man in her life.

She says Give a help, you son of a bitch! 'Fore he drownds her!

She yanks him forward. He comes. She doesn't wait to see if he keeps on or freezes up again, and she has forgotten all about Libbit; all she can think about is Adie. She has to stop the Emery-thing from dragging her into the water, and she has to do it before the dead babby-uns can get there to help him.

She cries Turn loose! Turn loose of her!

Flying down the beach with her skirt belling out behind. Emery has

534

gotten Adie in almost up to her waist. Adie is now fighting, but she's also choking. Melda flounders toward them and throws herself on the pallid corpse who has his wife by the throat. He screams when Melda's left arm, the one with the bracelets on it, touches him. It is a bubbling sound, as if his throat is full of water. He writhes in Melda's grip like a fish, and she rakes him with her fingernails. Flesh sloughs away beneath them with sickening ease, but no blood flows from the pale wounds. His eyes roll in their sockets, and they are like the eyes of a dead carp in the moonlight.

He pushes Adriana away so he can grapple with the harpy that has attacked him, the harpy with the cold, repelling fire on its arm.

Adie wails No, Nanny, stop, you're hurting him!

Adie flounders forward to pull Melda off, or at least separate them, and that's the moment when John Eastlake, standing shin-deep in the Gulf, fires the harpoon pistol. The triple-bladed bit takes his oldest daughter high in the throat, and she stands bolt-upright, with two inches of steel poking out in front of her and four more jutting out behind, just below the base of her skull.

John Eastlake shrieks Adie, no! Adie, I DIDN'T MEAN TO!

Adie turns toward the sound of her father's voice and actually begins to walk toward him, and that is all Nan Melda has time to see. Adie's dead husband is trying to tear itself free of her grip, but she doesn't want to let it go; she wants to end its terrible half-life and perhaps by doing so warn off the two baby-horrors before they can get too close. And she thinks (so far as she can *think) that she can do that, because she has seen a smoldering scorch-mark on the thing's pale, wet cheek and understands that her bracelet has made it.*

Her silver bracelet.

The thing reaches for her, its wrinkled mouth yawning in what might be either fear or fury. Behind her, John Eastlake is screaming his daughter's name, over and over.

Melda snarls You done this! *and when the Emery thing seizes her, she lets it.*

You and the bitch been runnin you, *she would add, but its white hands close on her throat as they closed on poor Adie's, and she can only gurgle. Her left arm is free, however, the one with the bracelets on it, and that arm feels very powerful. She draws it back and swings it forward in a great arc, connecting with the right side of the Emery-thing's head.*

The result is spectacular. The creature's skull caves in under the blow, as if a little immersion had turned that hard cage to candy. But it's still hard, all right; one of the shards that comes poking through the mat of Emery's hair slashes her forearm deep, and blood goes pattering down into the water that surges around them.

Two shadows pass her, one on her left, one on her right.

Lo-Lo cries Daddy! *in her new silver voice.*

Tessie cries Daddy, help us!

The Emery-thing is trying to get away from Melda now, floundering and splashing, wanting no more to do with her. Melda jabs the thumb of her powerful left hand in its right eye, feeling something cold, like toad-guts under a rock, come squishing out. Then she whirls around, staggering, as the rip tries to pull her feet from under her.

She reaches out with her left hand and seizes Lo-Lo by the scruff of her neck and pulls her backward. 'You ain't!' she grunts, and Lo-Lo comes flailing with a cry of surprise and agony . . . and no cry like that ever came from no little girl's throat, Melda knows.

John howls Melda, stop it!

He's kneeling in the last thin run of the surf with Adie before him. The harpoon's shaft juts up from her throat.

Melda, leave my girls alone!

She has no time to listen, although she spares a thought for Libbit — why has Libbit not drowned the china figure? Or did it not work? Has the thing Libbit calls Percy stopped her somehow? Melda knows it's all too possible; Libbit is powerful, but Libbit is still only a child.

No time to think of that. She reaches out for the other undead, for Tessie, but her right hand isn't like her left, there's no silver to guard it, and Tessie turns with a snarl and bites. Melda is aware of thin shooting pain but not that two fingers and part of a third have been bitten off and now float in the water beside the pallid child. There's too much adrenaline whipping through her for that.

Over the top of the hill, where the bootleggers sometimes tote pallets laden with liquor, a small sickle moon rises, casting further thin radiance on this nightmare. By its light, Melda sees Tessie turn back to her father; sees Tessie hold out her arms again.

Daddy! Daddy, please help us! Nan Melda's gone crazy!

Melda doesn't think. She reaches across her body and seizes the child by hair she has washed and braided a thousand times.

John Eastlake screams MELDA, NO!

Then, as he picks up the dropped harpoon pistol and casts about on the sand near his dead daughter's body for the remaining shaft, another voice calls. This one comes from behind Melda, from the ship anchored out there on the caldo.

It says You should never have interfered with me.

Melda, still holding the Tessie-thing by the hair (it fights and kicks, but she's hardly aware of it), spins clumsily in the water and sees her, *standing at the rail of her ship in her cloak of red. Her hood is down, and Melda sees she is not even close to human, she is something* other, *something beyond human understanding. In the moonlight her face is ghastly and full of knowing.*

Rising from the water, thin skeleton arms salute her.

The breeze blows apart the snakes of her hair; Melda sees the third eye in Perse's forehead; sees it seeing her, *and all will to resist is snuffed out in an instant.*

At that moment, however, the head of the bitch-goddess snaps around as if she has heard something or someone tiptoeing up behind her.

She cries What?

And then: No! Put that down! Put it down! YOU CAN'T DO THAT!

But apparently Libbit can — and has — because the shape of the thing at the ship's rail wavers, turns watery . . . and then becomes nothing but moonlight. The skeleton arms slither back beneath the water and are gone.

The Emery-thing is gone, too — disappeared — but the twins shriek together in shared pain and desolation at their abandonment.

Melda cries to the Mister It's goan be all right!

She turns the one she's had by the hair a-loose. She doesn't think it will want anything to do with the living, not now, not for awhile.

She cries Libbit's done done it! She—

John Eastlake shrieks GET YOUR HANDS OFF MY DAUGHTERS, YOU BAD NIGGER!

And he fires the harpoon pistol for the second time.

Do you see it strike home, piercing Nan Melda through? If so, the picture is complete.

Ah, God — the picture is complete.

537

20 – Perse

i

The picture – not the last full-blown Edgar Freemantle work of art, but the second-to-last – showed John Eastlake kneeling on Shade Beach with his dead daughter beside him and the sickle moon, just risen above the horizon, behind him. Nan Melda stood thigh-deep in the water, with one little girl on either side of her; their damp, upturned faces were drawn long in expressions of terror and rage. The shaft of one of those short harpoons protruded from between the woman's breasts. Her hands were clasped upon it as she looked unbelievingly at the man whose daughters she had tried so hard to protect, the man who had called her a bad nigger before taking her life.

'He screamed,' I said. 'He screamed until his nose bled. Until he bled from one eye. It's a wonder he didn't scream himself into a cerebral hemorrhage.'

'There's no one on the ship,' Jack said. 'Not in this drawing, at least.'

'No. Perse was gone. What Nan Melda hoped for actually happened. The business on the beach distracted the bitch just long enough for Libbit to take care of her. To drown her to sleep.' I tapped Nan Melda's left arm, where I had drawn two quick arcs and made one tiny crisscross to indicate a reflection of weak moonlight. 'And mostly because something told her to put on her mother's silver bracelets. Silver, like a certain candlestick.' I looked at Wireman. 'So maybe there *is* something on the bright side of the equation, looking out for us a little.'

He nodded, then pointed to the sun. In another moment or two, it would touch the horizon, and the track of light beating across to us, now yellow, would deepen to pure gold. 'But dark is when the bad things come out to play. Where is the china Perse now? Any idea where it ended up after all this on the beach?'

539

'I don't know *exactly* what happened after Eastlake killed Nan Melda, but I've got the general gist. Elizabeth . . .' I shrugged. 'She'd shot her bolt, at least for awhile. Hit overload. Her father must've heard her screaming, and that's probably the only thing that could still bring him around. He must have remembered that, no matter how awful things were, he still had a live daughter at Heron's Roost. He might even have remembered that he had two more thirty or forty miles away. Which left him with a mess to clean up.'

Jack pointed silently at the horizon, where the sun was now touching.

'I know, Jack, but we're closer than you think.' I shuffled the last sheet of paper to the top of the pile. It was the barest of sketches, but there was no mistaking that knowing smile. It was Charley the Lawn Jockey. I got to my feet and turned them away from the Gulf and the waiting ship, which was now silhouetted, black against gold. 'Do you see it?' I asked them. '*I* saw it, on our way up from the house. The *real* jockey statue, I mean, not the projection we saw on our way in.'

They looked. 'I don't,' Wireman said, 'and I think I would if it was there, *muchacho*. I know the grass is high, but that red cap should still stand out. Unless it's in one of the banana groves.'

'Got it!' Jack cried, and actually laughed.

'The fuck you *do*,' Wireman said, stung. Then: 'Where?'

'Behind the tennis court.'

Wireman looked there, started to say he still didn't see it, then stopped. 'I'll be a son of a bitch,' he said. 'The Christing thing's upside-down, isn't it?'

'Yes. And since it has no actual feet to stick up, that's the square iron base you see. Charley marks the spot, *amigos*. But first we need to go to the barn.'

ii

I had no premonition of what was waiting for us inside the long, overgrown outbuilding, which was dark and stifling hot, and no idea that Wireman had drawn the Desert Eagle automatic until it went off.

The doors were the kind that slide open on tracks, but these would never slide again; they were rusted in place eight feet apart, and had been for decades. Gray-green Spanish Moss dangled down like a curtain, obscuring the top of the gap between the doors.

'What we're looking f—' I began, and that was when the heron came flapping out with its blue eyes blazing, its long neck stretched forward, and its yellow beak snapping. It was getting itself into flight as soon as it cleared the doors, and I had no doubt that its target was my eyes. Then the Desert Eagle roared, and the bird's mad blue glare disappeared along with the rest of its head, in a fine spray of blood. It hit me, light as a bundle of wires wrapped around a hollow core, then dropped at my feet. At the same instant I heard a high, silver scream of fury in my head.

It wasn't just me, either. Wireman winced. Jack dropped the handles of the picnic basket and jammed the heels of his hands against his ears. Then it was gone.

'One dead heron,' Wireman said, his voice not quite steady. He prodded the bundle of feathers, then flipped it off my boots. 'For God's sake, don't tell Fish and Wildlife. Shooting one of these'd probably cost me fifty grand and five years in jail.'

'How did you know?' I asked.

He shrugged. 'What does it matter? You told me to shoot it if I saw it. You Lone Ranger, me Tonto.'

'But you had the gun out.'

'I had what Nan Melda might have called "an intuition" when she was putting on her Mama's silver bracelets,' Wireman said, unsmiling. 'Something's keeping an eye on us, all right, leave it at that. And after what happened to your daughter, I'd say we're owed a little help. But we have to do our part.'

'Just keep your shootin iron handy while we do it,' I said.

'Oh, you can count on that.'

'And Jack? Can you figure out how to load the speargun?'

No problem there. We were a go for speargun.

iii

The interior of the barn was dark, and not just because the ridge of land between us and the Gulf cut off the direct light of the setting sun. There was still plenty of light in the sky, and there were plenty of cracks and chinks in the slate roof, but the vines had overgrown them. What light did enter from above was green and deep and untrustworthy.

The outbuilding's central area was empty save for an ancient tractor sitting wheelless on the massive stumps of its axles, but in one of the equipment stalls, the light of our powerful flashlight picked out a few rusty, left-over tools and a wooden ladder leaning against the back wall. It was filthy and depressingly short. Jack tried climbing it while Wireman trained the light on him. He bounced up and down on the second rung, and we heard a warning creak.

'Stop bouncing on it and set it out by the door,' I said. 'It's a ladder, not a trampoline.'

'I dunno,' he said. 'Florida's not the ideal climate for preserving wooden ladders.'

'Beggars can't be choosers,' Wireman said.

Jack picked it up, grimacing at the dust and dead insects that showered down from the six filthy steps. 'Easy for you to say. You won't be the one climbing on it, not at your weight.'

'I'm the marksman of the group, *niño*,' Wireman said. 'Each to his own job.' He was striving for airy, but he sounded strained and looked tired. 'Where are the rest of the ceramic keglets, Edgar? Because I'm not seeing them.'

'Maybe in back,' I said.

I was right. There were perhaps ten of the ceramic Table Whiskey 'keglets' at the very back of the outbuilding. I say *perhaps* because it was hard to tell. They had been smashed to bits.

iv

Surrounding the bigger chunks of white ceramic, and mixed in with them, were glittering heaps and sprays of glass. To the right of this pile were two old-fashioned wooden handcarts, both overturned. To the left, leaning against the wall, was a sledgehammer with a rusty business-end and patches of moss growing up the handle.

'Someone had a container-smashing party,' Wireman said. 'Who do you think? Em?'

'Maybe,' I said. 'Probably.'

For the first time I started to wonder if she was going to beat us after all. We had some daylight left, but less than I had expected and far less than I was comfortable with. And now . . . in what were we going to drown her china simulacrum? A fucking Evian water bottle? It wasn't a bad idea, in a way – they were plastic, and according to the environmentalists, the damned things are going to last forever – but a china figure would never fit through the hole in the top.

'So what's the fallback position?' Wireman asked. 'The gas tank of that old John Deere? Will that do?'

The thought of trying to drown Perse in the old tractor's gas tank made me cold all over. It was probably nothing but rusty lace. 'No. I don't think that will work.'

He must have heard something close to panic in my voice, because he gripped my arm. 'Take it easy. We'll think of something.'

'Sure, but what?'

'We'll take her back up to Heron's Roost, that's all. There'll be something there.'

But in my mind's eye I kept seeing how the storms had dealt with the mansion that had once dominated this end of Duma Key, turning it into little more than a façade. Then I wondered how many containers we actually *would* find there, especially with just forty minutes or so before dark came and the *Perse* sent a landing-party to end our meddling. God, to have forgotten such an elementary item as a water-tight container!

'Fuck!' I said. I kicked a pile of shards and sent them flying. '*Fuck!*'

'Easy, *vato*. That won't help.'

No, it wouldn't. And she'd like me angry, wouldn't she? The old angry Edgar would be easy to manipulate. I tried to get hold of myself, but the *I can do this* mantra wasn't working. Still, it was all I had. And what do you do when you can't use anger to fall back on? You admit the truth.

'All right,' I said. 'But I don't have a clue.'

'Relax, Edgar,' Jack said, and he was smiling. 'That part's gonna be okay.'

'Why? What do you mean?'

'Trust me on this,' he said.

v

As we stood looking at Charley the Lawn Jockey in light that was now taking on a definite purple cast, a nonsense couplet from an old Dave Van Ronk blues occurred to me: '*Mama bought a chicken, thought it was a duck; Sat it on the table with the legs stickin up.*' Charley wasn't a chicken or a duck, but his legs, ending not in shoes but a dark iron pedestal, were indeed sticking up. His head, however, was gone. It had crashed down through a square of ancient moss- and vine-covered boards.

'What's that, *muchacho*?' Wireman asked. 'Do you know?'

'I'm pretty sure it's a cistern,' I said. 'I'm hoping not a septic tank.'

Wireman shook his head. 'He wouldn't have put them in a shitheap no matter how bad his mental state was. Never in a million years.'

Jack looked from Wireman to me, his young face full of horror. 'Adriana's down there? And the nanny?'

'Yes,' I said. 'I thought you understood that. But the most important thing is that *Perse's* down there. And the reason I think it's a cistern is—'

'Elizabeth would have insisted on making sure the bitch was in a watery grave,' Wireman said grimly. 'A *fresh*-watery one.'

vi

Charley was heavy, and the boards covering the hole in the high grass were more rotten than the steps of the ladder. Of course they were; unlike the ladder, the wooden cap had been directly exposed to the elements. We worked carefully in spite of the thickening shadows, not knowing how deep it was beneath. At last I was able to push the troublesome jockey far enough to one side so that Wireman and Jack could grab the slightly cocked blue legs. I stepped onto the rotted wooden cap in doing so; someone had to, and I was the lightest. It bent under my weight, gave out a long, warning groan, puffed up sour air.

'Get off it, Edgar!' Wireman yelled, and at the same instant Jack cried, 'Grab it, oh whore, it's gonna fall through!'

They seized Charley as I stepped off the sagging cap, Wireman around the bent knees and Jack around the waist. For a moment I thought it was going to drop through anyway, dragging them both along. Then they gave a combined shout of effort and tumbled over backward with the lawn jockey on top of them. Its grinning face and red cap were covered with huge lumbering beetles. Several dropped off onto Jack's straining face, and one fell directly into Wireman's mouth. He screamed, spat it out, and leaped to his feet, still spitting and rubbing his lips. Jack was beside him a moment later, dancing around him in a circle and brushing the bugs off his shirt.

'Water!' Wireman bellowed. 'Gimme the water, one of em got in my *mouth*, I could feel it crawling on my fucking *tongue!*'

'No water,' I said, rummaging in the considerably depleted bag. Now on my knees, I could smell the air rising through the ragged hole in the cap far better than I wanted to. It was like air from a newly breached tomb. Which, of course, it was. 'Pepsi.'

'Cheeseburger, cheeseburger, Pepsi,' Jack said. 'No Coke.' He laughed dazedly.

I handed Wireman a can of soda. He stared at it unbelievingly for a moment, then raked back the pull tab. He took a mouthful, spat it out in a brown and foamy spray, took another, then spat that one out. The rest of the can he drank in four long swallows.

'*Ay, caramba,*' he said. 'You're a hard man, Van Gogh.'

I was looking at Jack. 'What do you think? Can we shift it?'

Jack studied it, then fell on his knees and began to tear away the vines clinging to the sides. 'Yeah,' he said. 'But we gotta get rid of this shit.'

'We should have brought a crowbar,' Wireman said. He was still spitting. I didn't blame him.

'Wouldn't have helped, I don't think,' Jack said. 'The wood's too rotted. Help me, Wireman.' And when I fell on my knees beside him: 'Don't bother, boss. This is a job for guys with two arms.'

I felt another flash of anger at that – the old anger was very close now – and quelled it as best I could. I watched them work their way around the circular cap, tearing away the vines and the weeds as the light faded from the sky. A single bird cruised by with its wings folded. It was upside-down. You saw something like that and felt like checking into the nearest nuthouse. Preferably for a long stay.

545

The two of them were working opposite each other, and as Wireman neared the place where Jack had begun and Jack neared the place where Wireman had begun, I said: 'Is that speargun loaded, Jack?'

He looked up. 'Yes. Why?'

'Because this is going to be a photo finish after all.'

vii

Jack and Wireman knelt on one side of the cap. I knelt on the other. Above us, the sky had deepened to an indigo that would soon be violet. 'My count,' Wireman said. '*Uno . . . dos . . . TRES!*' They pulled and I pushed as well as I could with my remaining arm. That was pretty well, because my remaining arm had grown strong during my months on Duma Key. For a moment the cap resisted. Then it slid toward Wireman and Jack, revealing a crescent of darkness – a black and welcoming smile. This thickened to a half-moon, then a full circle.

Jack stood up. So did Wireman. He was checking his hands for more bugs. 'I know how you feel,' I said, 'but I don't think we have time for you to do a full delousing.'

'Point taken, but unless you've chewed on one of those *maricones*, you *don't* know how I feel.'

'Tell us what to do, boss,' Jack said. He was looking uneasily into the pit, from which that sallow stench was still issuing.

'Wireman, you have fired the speargun – right?'

'Yes, at targets. With Miss Eastlake. Didn't I say I was the marksman of the group?'

'Then you're on guard. Jack, shine that light.'

I could see by his face that he didn't want to, but there was no choice – until this was done, there'd be no going back. And if it wasn't done, there'd never be any going back.

Not by the land route, at least.

He picked up the long-barreled flashlight, clicked it on, and shone the powerful beam down into the hole. 'Ah, God,' he whispered.

It was indeed a cistern lined with coral rock, but at some point during the last eighty years the ground had shifted, a fissure had opened – probably at the very bottom – and the water inside had leaked out. What we saw in the flashlight's beam was a damp, moss-lined gullet eight or ten feet deep and about five feet in diameter. Lying at the bottom, entwined in an embrace that had lasted eighty years, were two skeletons dressed in rotten rags. Beetles crawled busily around them. Whitish toads – small boys – hopped on the bones. A harpoon lay beside one skeleton. The tip of the second harpoon was still buried in Nan Melda's yellowing spine.

The light began to sway. Because the young man holding it was swaying.

'Don't you faint on us, Jack!' I said sharply. 'That's an order!'

'I'm okay, boss.' But his eyes were huge, glassy, and behind the flashlight – still not quite steady in his hand – his face was parchment white. 'Really.'

'Good. Shine it down there again. No, left. A little more . . . *there*.'

It was one of the Table Whiskey kegs, now little more than a hump under a heavy shag of moss. One of those white toads was crouched on it. It looked up at me, lids nictitating malevolently.

Wireman glanced at his watch. 'We have . . . I'm thinking maybe fifteen minutes before sundown. Could be a little more, could be less. So . . . ?'

'So Jack puts the ladder into the hole, and down I go.'

'Edgar . . . *mi amigo* . . . you have just one arm.'

'She took my daughter. She murdered Ilse. You know this is my job.'

'All right.' Wireman looked at Jack. 'Which leaves the watertight container question.'

'Don't worry,' he said, then picked up the ladder and handed me the flash. 'Shine it down there, Edgar. I need both hands for what I'm doing.'

It seemed to take him forever to get the ladder placed to his satisfaction, but finally the feet were on the bottom, between the bones of Nan Melda's outstretched arm (I could still see the silver bracelets, although now overgrown with moss) and one of Adie's legs. The ladder was really very short, and the top rung was two feet below ground-level. That was all right; Jack could steady me to begin with. I thought of asking him again about the container for the china figure, then didn't. He seemed completely at ease on that score, and I decided to trust him all the way. It was really too late to do otherwise.

In my head a voice, very low, almost meditative, said: *Stop now and I'll let you go free.*

'Never,' I said.

Wireman looked at me without surprise. 'You heard it, too, huh?'

viii

I lay on my stomach and backed into the hole. Jack gripped my shoulders. Wireman stood beside him with the loaded harpoon pistol in his hands and the three extra silvertips stuck in his belt. Between them, the flashlight lay on the ground, spraying a bright light into a tangle of uprooted weeds and vines.

The stench of the cistern was very strong, and I felt a tickling on my shin as something scurried up my leg. I should have tucked my pants cuffs into the tops of my boots, but it was a little late to go back and start over.

'Do you feel the ladder?' Jack asked. 'Are you there yet?'

'No, I . . .' Then my foot touched the top rung. 'There it is. Hang on.'

'I've gotcha, don't worry.'

Come down here and I'll kill you.

'Go on and try,' I said. 'I'm coming for you, you birch, so take your best shot.'

I felt Jack's hands tighten spasmodically on my shoulders. 'Jesus, boss, are you s—'

'I'm sure. Just hold on.'

There were half a dozen rungs on the ladder. Jack was able to hold onto my shoulders until I'd gotten down three, and then I was chest-deep. He offered me the flashlight. I shook my head. 'Use it to spot me.'

'You don't get it. You don't need it for light, you need it for *her.*'

For a minute I still didn't get it.

'Unscrew the lens cap. Take out the batteries. Put her inside. I'll hand you down the water.'

Wireman laughed without humor. 'Wireman likes it, *niño.*' Then

548

he bent to me. 'Now go on. Bitch or birch, drown her and let's have done with her.'

ix

The fourth rung snapped. The ladder tilted, and I fell off with the flashlight still clamped between my side and my stump, first shining up at the darkening sky, then illuminating lumps of coral coated with moss. My head connected with one of these and I saw stars. A moment later I was lying on a jagged bed of bones and staring into Adriana Eastlake Paulson's eternal grin. One of those pallid toads leaped at me from between her mossy teeth and I batted at it with the barrel of the flashlight.

'Muchacho!' Wireman shouted, and Jack added, 'Boss, are you all right!'

I was bleeding from the scalp – I could feel it running down my face in warm streams – but I thought I was okay; certainly I had been through worse in the Land of a Thousand Lakes. And the ladder, although aslant, was still standing. I looked to my right and there was the moss-covered Table Whiskey keg we'd come all this way to find. There were two toads on it now instead of one. They saw me looking and leaped into my face, eyes bulging, mouths gaping. I had no doubt that Perse wished they had teeth, like Elizabeth's big boy. Ah, the good old days.

'I'm okay,' I said, batting the toads away and struggling to sit up. Bones broke beneath me and all around me. Except . . . no. They didn't break. They were too old and damp to break. They first bent, then popped. 'Send down the water. It's okay to drop it in the bag, just try not to hit me in the head with it.'

I looked at Nan Melda.

I'm going to take your silver bracelets, I told her, *but it's not stealing. If you're somewhere close and can see what I'm doing, I hope you'll think of it as sharing. A kind of passing-on.*

I slipped them off her remains and put them on my own left wrist, raising my arm and letting gravity slide them up to the catch-point. Above me, Jack was hanging head-down into the cistern. 'Watch out, Edgar!'

549

The bag came down. One of the bones I'd broken in my fall punched through the plastic and water came trickling out. I yelled in fright and anger, opened the bag, looked inside. Only a single plastic bottle had been punctured. The other two were still whole. I turned to the moss-covered ceramic keg, slipped my hand into the thicket of slime under it, and worked it free. It didn't want to come, but the thing inside had taken my daughter and I meant to have it. Finally it rolled toward me, and when it did, a good-sized chunk of coral slipped away on the other side of it and thudded to the muddy bottom of the cistern.

I shone the light on the keg. There was only a thin scum of moss on the side that had been facing the wall, and I could see the highlander in his kilt, one foot raised behind him as he did his fling. I could also see a jagged crack running straight down the keg's curved side. That chunk of coral had made it when it fell out of the wall. The keg which Libbit had filled from the swimming pool back in 1927 had been leaking ever since that chunk had struck it, and now it was almost dry.

I could hear something rattling inside.

I'll kill you if you don't stop, but if you do, I'll let you go. You and your friends.

I felt my lips skin back in a grin. And had Pam seen a grin like that when my hand closed around her neck? Of course she had. 'You shouldn't have killed my daughter.'

Stop now or I'll take the other one, too.

Wireman called down, and the desperation in his voice was naked. 'Venus just popped, *amigo*. I take that as a bad sign.'

I was sitting against one damp wall, with coral poking into my back and bones poking into my side. Movement was restricted, and in some other country my hip was throbbing badly – not screaming yet, but probably soon. I had no idea how I was supposed to climb the ladder again in such condition, but I was too angry to worry about it.

'Pardon me, Miss Cookie,' I murmured to Adie, and stuck the butt of the flashlight in her bony mouth. Then I took the ceramic keg in both hands . . . because both hands were there. I bent my good leg, pushing bones and muck to either side with the heel of my boot, lifted the keg into the dusty beam of light, and brought it down on my upraised knee. It cracked again, releasing a little flood of sludgy water, but didn't break.

Perse screamed inside it and I felt my nose begin to bleed. And the light from the flash changed. It turned *red*. In that scarlet glow, the skulls of Adie Paulson and Nan Melda gaped and grinned at me. I looked at the moss-covered walls of this filthy throat into which I'd climbed of my own free will and saw other faces: Pam's . . . Mary Ire's, twisted in rage as she brought the butt of her gun down on Ilse's head . . . Kamen's, filled with terminal surprise as he dropped with his thunderclap heart attack . . . Tom, twisting the wheel of his car to send it hurtling into concrete at seventy miles an hour.

Worst of all, I saw Monica Goldstein, screaming *You killed my doggy!*

'Edgar, what's happening?' That was Jack, a thousand miles away.

I thought of Shark Puppy on The Bone, singing 'Dig'. I thought of telling Tom, *That man died in his pick-up.*

Then put me in your pocket and we'll go together, she said. *We'll sail together into your* real *other life, and all the cities of the world will be at your feet. You'll live long . . . I can arrange that . . . and you'll be the artist of the age. They'll rank you with Goya. With Leonardo.*

'Edgar?' There was panic in Wireman's voice. 'People are coming from the beach side. I think I hear them. This is bad, *muchacho*.'

You don't need them. We don't need them. They're nothing but . . . nothing but crew.

Nothing but crew. At that, the red rage descended over my mind even as my right hand began to slip out of existence again. But before it could go completely . . . before I lost my grip on either my fury or the damned cracked keg . . .

'Stick it up your friend, you dump birch,' I said, and raised the keg over my throbbing, upthrust knee again. 'Stick it in the buddy.' I brought it down as hard as I could on that bony knob. There was a pain, but less than I had been prepared for . . . and in the end, that's usually the way, don't you think? 'Stick it up your fucking *chum*.'

The keg didn't break; already cracked, it simply burst, showering my jeans with murky wetness from the inch or so of water that

551

had still been left inside. And a small china figure tumbled out: a woman wrapped in a cloak and a hood. The hand clasping the edges of the cloak together at her neck was not really a hand at all, but a claw. I snatched the thing up. I had no time to study it – they were coming now, I had no doubt of that, coming for Wireman and Jack – but there was long enough to see that Perse was extraordinarily beautiful. If, that was, you could ignore the claw hand and the disquieting hint of a third eye beneath the hair that had tumbled out from beneath her hood and over her brow. The thing was also extremely delicate, almost translucent. Except when I tried to snap it between my hands, it was like trying to snap steel.

'*Edgar!*' Jack screamed.

'Keep them back!' I snapped. 'You have to keep them back!'

I tucked her into the breast pocket of my shirt, and immediately felt a sickening warmth begin to spread through to my skin. And it was *thrumming*. My untrustworthy mojo arm was gone again, so I stuck a bottle of Evian water between my side and my stump, then spun off the cap. I repeated this clumsy and time-consuming process with the other bottle.

From overhead, Wireman cried out in a voice that was almost steady: 'Stay back! This is tipped with silver! I'll use it!'

The response to this was clear, even at the bottom of the cistern. '*Do you think you can reload fast enough to shoot all three of us?*'

'No, Emery,' Wireman responded. He spoke as if to a child, and his voice had firmed all the way. I never loved him so much as I did then. 'I'll settle for you.'

Now came the hard part, the terrible part.

I began unscrewing the cap of the flashlight. On the second turn, the light went out and I was in nearly perfect darkness. I dumped the D-batteries from the flashlight's steel sleeve, then fumbled for the first bottle of Evian. My fingers closed on it, and I poured it in, working by feel. I had no idea how much the flashlight would hold, and thought one bottle would fill it all the way to the top. I was wrong. I was reaching for the second one when full night must have come to Duma Key. I say that because that was when the china figure in my pocket came to life.

x

Any time I doubt that last mad passage in the cistern, all I have to do is look at the traffic-jam of white scars on the left side of my chest. Anyone seeing me naked wouldn't notice them particularly; because of my accident, I am a roadmap of scars, and that small white bundle tends to get lost among the gaudier ones. But these were made by the teeth of a living doll. One that chewed through my shirt and skin and into the muscle beneath.

One that meant to chew all the way to my heart.

xi

I almost knocked the second bottle of water over before managing to pick it up. That was mostly from surprise, but there was plenty of pain as well, and I cried out. I felt fresh blood begin to flow, this time running down inside my shirt to the crease between my torso and my belly. She was twisting in my pocket, *writhing* in my pocket, her teeth sinking in and biting and *plowing*, digging deeper, deeper. I had to tear her out, and I ripped away a good chunk of bloody shirt and flesh with her. The figure had lost that smooth, cool feel. It was hot now, and writhing in my hand.

'*Come on!*' Wireman yelled from up above. '*Come on, you want it?*'

She sank her tiny china teeth, sharp as needles, into the webbing of flesh between my thumb and first finger. I howled. She might have gotten away then in spite of all my fury and determination, but Nan Melda's bracelets slid down, and I could feel her cringing away from them, deeper into my palm. One leg actually slithered out between my second finger and my ring finger. I squeezed all my fingers together, pinning it. Pinning *her*. Her movements grew sluggish. I can't swear that one of the bracelets was touching her – it was pitch black – but I'm almost positive it was.

From above me came the hollow compressed-air *CHOW* of the harpoon pistol, and then a scream that seemed to rip through my brains. Below it – *behind* it – I could hear Wireman shouting, 'Get in back of me, Jack! Take one of the—' Then no more, just the

553

sound of grunting cries from my friends and the angry, unearthly laughter of two long-dead children.

I had the flashlight's barrel clasped between my knees, and I didn't need anyone to tell me that anything could go wrong in the dark, especially for a one-armed man. I would have only one chance. Under conditions like that, it's best not to hesitate.

No! Stop! Don't do th—

I dropped her in, and one result was immediate: above me, the children's angry laughter turned to shrieks of surprised horror. Then I heard Jack. He sounded hysterical and half-insane, but I was never so glad to hear anyone in my life.

'That's right, go on and run! Before your fucking ship sails and leaves you behind!'

Now I had a delicate problem. I had taken hold of the flashlight in my remaining hand, and she was inside . . . but the cap was somewhere in here with me, and I couldn't see it. Nor did I have another hand to feel around with.

'Wireman!' I called. 'Wireman, are you there?'

After a moment long enough to first seed four kinds of fear and then start them growing, he answered: 'Yeah, *muchacho*. Still here.'

'All right?'

'One of em scratched me and it ought to be disinfected, but otherwise, yeah. Basically I think we both are.'

'Jack, can you come down here? I need a hand.' And then, sitting there crooked among the bones with the water-filled shell of the flashlight held up like the Statue of Liberty's torch, I began to laugh.

Some things are just so true you have to.

xii

My eyes had adjusted enough for me to make out a dark shape seeming to float down the side of the cistern – Jack, descending the ladder. The sleeve of the flashlight was thrumming in my hand – weak, but definitely thrumming. I pictured a woman drowning in a narrow steel tank and pushed the image away. It was too much like what had happened to Ilse, and the monster I had imprisoned was nothing like Ilse.

554

'There's a rung missing,' I said. 'If you don't want to die down here, you want to be careful as hell.'

'I can't die tonight,' he said in a thin and shaking voice I never would have identified as his. 'I have a date tomorrow.'

'Congratulations.'

'Thank y—'

He missed the rung. The ladder shifted. For a moment I was sure he was going to come down on top of me, on top of the upheld flashlight. The water would spill out, *she* would spill out, and it all would have been for nothing.

'What's happening?' Wireman shouted from above us. '*What the fuck's happening?*'

Jack settled back against the wall, one hand gripping a lucky chunk of coral that he happened to find at the last crucial second. I could see one of his legs plunged down like a piston to the next intact rung, and there was a healthy ripping sound. 'Man,' he whispered. 'Man oh man oh fucking man.'

'*What's happening?*' Wireman nearly roared.

'Jack Cantori ripped out the seat of his pants,' I said. 'Now shut up a minute. Jack, you're almost there. She's in the flashlight, but I've only got the one hand and I can't pick up the cap. You have to come down and find it. I don't care if you step on me, just don't bump the flashlight. Okay?'

'O-Okay. Jesus, Edgar, I thought I was gonna go ass over teapot.'

'So did I. Come down now. But slowly.'

He came down, first stepping on my thigh – it hurt – and then putting his foot on one of the empty Evian bottles. It crackled. Then he stepped on something that broke with a damp pop, like a defective noisemaker.

'Edgar, what was *that?*' He sounded on the verge of tears. 'What—'

'Nothing.' I was pretty sure it had been Adie's skull. His hip thumped the flashlight. Cold water slopped over my wrist. Inside the metal sleeve, something bumped and turned. Inside my head, a terrible black-green eye – the color of water at the depth just before all light fails – also turned. It looked at my most secret thoughts, at the place where anger surpasses rage and becomes homicide. It saw . . . then *bit* down. The way a woman would bite into a plum. I will never forget the sensation.

555

'Watch it, Jack – close quarters. Like a midget submarine. Careful as you can.'

'I'm freaking out, boss. Little touch of claustrophobia.'

'Take a deep breath. You can do this. We'll be out soon. Do you have matches?'

He didn't. Nor a lighter. Jack might not be averse to six beers on a Saturday night, but his lungs were smoke-free. Thus there ensued a long, nightmarish space of minutes – Wireman says no more than four, but to me it seemed thirty, thirty at least – during which Jack knelt, felt among the bones, stood, moved a little, knelt again, felt again. My arm was getting tired. My hand was going numb. Blood continued to run from the wounds on my chest, either because they were slow in clotting or because they weren't clotting at all. But my hand was the worst. All feeling was leaving it, and soon I began to believe I was no longer holding the flashlight sleeve at all, because I couldn't see it and I was losing the sense of it against my skin. The feeling of weight in my hand had been swallowed by the tired throb of my muscles. I had to fight the urge to rap the metal sleeve against the side of the cistern to make sure I still had it, even though I knew if I did, I might drop it. I began to think that the cap must be lost in the maze of bones and bone fragments, and Jack would never find it without a light.

'What's happening?' Wireman called.

'Getting there!' I called back. Blood dribbled into my left eye, stinging, and I blinked it away. I tried to think of Illy, my If-So-Girl, and was horrified to realize I couldn't remember her face. 'Little slag, little horrock, we're working it out.'

'What?'

'*Snag!* Little snag, little hold-up! You fucking deaf, Wearman?'

Was the flashlight sleeve tilting? I feared it was. Water could be running over my hand and I might now be too numb to feel it. But if the sleeve *wasn't* tilting and I tried to correct, I'd make matters worse.

If water's running out, her head will be above the surface again in a matter of seconds. And then it'll be all over. You know that, right?

I knew. I sat in the dark with my arm up, afraid to do anything. Bleeding and waiting. Time had been cancelled and memory was a ghost.

'Here it is,' Jack said at last. 'It's caught in someone's ribs. Wait . . . got it.'

'Thank God,' I said. 'Thank Christ.' I could see him in front of me, a dim shape with one knee between my awkwardly bent legs, planted in the litter of disarranged bones that had once been part of John Eastlake's eldest daughter. I held the flashlight sleeve out. 'Screw it on. Gently does it, because I can't hold it straight much longer.'

'Luckily,' he said, 'I have two hands.' And he put one of his over mine, steadying the water-filled flashlight as he began screwing the cap back on. He paused only once, to ask me why I was crying.

'Relief,' I said. 'Go on. Finish. Hurry.'

When it was done, I took the capped flashlight from him. It wasn't as heavy as when it had been filled with D-cells, but I didn't care about that. What I cared about was making sure that the lid was screwed down tight. It seemed to be. I told Jack to have Wireman check it again when he got back up.

'Will do,' he said.

'And try not to break any more rungs. I'm going to need them all.'

'You get past the broken one, Edgar, and we'll haul you the rest of the way.'

'Okay, and I won't tell anyone you tore out the seat of your pants.'

At that he actually laughed. I watched the dark shape of him go up the ladder, taking a big stride to get past the broken rung. I had a moment of doubt accompanied by a terrible vision of tiny china hands unscrewing the flashlight cap from the inside – yes, even though I was sure the fresh water had immobilized her – but Jack didn't cry out or come tumbling back down, and the bad moment passed. There was a circle of brighter darkness above my head, and eventually he reached it.

When he was up and out, Wireman called down: 'Now you, *muchacho.*'

'In a minute,' I said. 'Are your girlfriends gone?'

'Ran away. Shore leave over, I guess.'

'And Emery?'

'That you need to see for yourself, I think. Come on up.'

557

I repeated, 'In a minute.'

I leaned my head back against the moss-slimy coral, closed my eyes, and reached out. I kept reaching until I touched something smooth and round. Then my first two fingers slipped into an indentation that was almost certainly an eyesocket. And since I was sure it had been Adriana's skull Jack had crushed—

All's ending as well as can be at this end of the island, I told Nan Melda. *And this isn't much of a grave, but you may not be in it much longer, my dear.*

'May I keep your bracelets? There might be more to do.'

Yes. I was afraid I had another thing coming.

'Edgar?' Wireman sounded worried. 'Who you talking to?'

'The one who really stopped her,' I said.

And because the one who really stopped her did not tell me she would have her bracelets back, I kept them on and began the slow and painful work of getting to my feet. Dislodged bone-fragments and bits of moss-encrusted ceramic showered down around my feet. My left knee – my good one – felt swollen and tight against the torn cloth of my pants. My head was throbbing and my chest was on fire. The ladder looked at least a mile high, but I could see the dark shapes of Jack and Wireman hanging over the rim of the cistern, waiting to grab me when – *if* – I managed to haul myself into grabbing-range.

I thought: *There's a three-quarter moon tonight, and I can't see it until I get out of this hole in the ground.*

So I got started.

xiii

The moon had risen fat and yellow above the eastern horizon, casting its glow on the lush jungle growth that overbore the south end of the key and gilding the east side of John Eastlake's ruined mansion, where he had once lived with his housekeeper and his six girls – happily enough, I suppose, before Libbit's tumble from the pony-trap changed things.

It also gilded the ancient, coral-encrusted skeleton that lay on the mattress of trampled vines Jack and Wireman had uprooted to free the cistern cap. Looking at Emery Paulson's remains, a snatch of Shakespeare from my high school days recurred, and I spoke it aloud: 'Full fathom five thy father lies . . . those are pearls that were his eyes.'

Jack shivered violently, as if stroked by a keen wet wind. He actually clutched himself. This time he got it.

Wireman bent and picked up one thin, trailing arm. It snapped in three without a sound. Emery Paulson had been in the *caldo* a long, long time. There was a harpoon sticking through the shelly harp of his ribs. Wireman retrieved it now, having to work the tip free of the ground in order to take it back.

'How'd you keep the Twins from Hell off you with the spearpistol unloaded?' I asked.

Wireman jabbed the harpoon in his hand like a dagger.

Jack nodded. 'Yeah. I grabbed one out of his belt and did the same. I don't know how long it would have worked over the long haul, though – they were like mad dogs.'

Wireman replaced the silver-tipped harpoon he'd used on Emery in his belt. 'Speaking of the long haul, we might consider another storage container for your new doll. What do you think, Edgar?'

He was right. Somehow I couldn't imagine Perse spending the next eighty years in the barrel of a Garrity flashlight. I was already wondering how thin the shield between the battery case and the lens housing might be. And the rock that had fallen out of the cistern wall and cracked the Table Whiskey keg: had that been an accident . . . or a final victory of mind over matter after years of patient work? Perse's version of digging through the wall of her cell with a sharpened spoonhandle?

Still, the flashlight had served its purpose. God bless Jack Cantori's practical mind. No – that was too chintzy. God bless *Jack*.

'There's a custom silversmith in Sarasota,' Wireman said, '*Mexicano muy talentoso*. Miss Eastlake has – had – a few pieces of his stuff. I bet I could commission him to make a watertight tube big enough to hold the flashlight. That'd give us what insurance companies and football coaches call double coverage. It'd be pricey, but so what? Barring probate snags, I'm going to be an extremely wealthy man. Caught a break there, *muchacho*.'

'*La lotería*,' I said, without thinking.

559

'*Sí*,' he said. '*La* goddam *lotería*. Come on, Jack. Help me tip Emery into the cistern.'

Jack grimaced. 'Okay, but I . . . I really don't want to touch it.'

'I'll help with Emery,' I said. 'You hold onto the flashlight. Wireman? Let's do this.'

The two of us rolled Emery into the hole, then threw in the pieces of him that broke off – or as many as we could find. I still remember his stony coral grin as he tumbled into the dark to join his bride. And sometimes, of course, I dream about it. In these dreams I hear Adie and Em calling up to me from the dark, asking me if I wouldn't like to come down and join them. And sometimes in those dreams I do. Sometimes I throw myself into that dark and stinking throat just to make an end to my memories.

These are the dreams from which I wake up screaming, thrashing at the dark with a hand that is no longer there.

xiv

Wireman and Jack slid the cap into position again, and then we went back to Elizabeth's Mercedes. That was a slow, painful walk, and by the end of it I really wasn't walking at all; I was lurching. It was as if the clock had been rolled back to the previous October. I was already thinking of the few Oxycontin tablets I had waiting for me back at Big Pink. I would have three, I decided. Three would do more than kill the pain; with luck they would also pound me into at least a few hours of sleep.

Both of my friends asked if I didn't want to sling an arm around them. I refused. This wasn't going to be my last walk tonight; I had made up my mind about that. I still didn't have the last piece of the puzzle, but I had an idea. What had Elizabeth told Wireman? *You will want to but you mustn't.*

Too late, too late, too late.

The idea wasn't clear. What was clear was the sound of the shells. You could hear that sound from anywhere inside Big Pink, but to get the full effect, you really had to come up on the place from outside. That was when they sounded the most like voices. So many nights I had wasted painting when I could have been listening.

Tonight I would listen.

Outside the pillars, Wireman paused. 'Abyssus abyssum invocat,' he said.

'Hell invokes Hell,' Jack said, and sighed.

Wireman looked at me. 'Think we'll have any trouble negotiating the road home?'

'Now? No.'

'And are we done here?'

'We are.'

'Will we ever come again?'

'No,' I said. I looked at the ruined house, dreaming in the moonlight. Its secrets were out. I realized we'd left little Libbit's heart-shaped box behind, but maybe that was for the best. Let it stay here. 'No one will come here anymore.'

Jack looked at me, curious and a little afraid. 'How can you know that?'

'I know,' I said.

21 – The Shells by Moonlight

i

We had no trouble negotiating the road home. The smell was still there, but it was better now – partly because a good wind was getting up, blowing in off the Gulf, and partly because it was just . . . better now.

The courtyard lights of *El Palacio* were on a timer, and they looked wonderful, twinkling out of the dark. Inside the house, Wireman went methodically from room to room, turning on more lights. Turning on *all* the lights, until the house where Elizabeth had spent most of her life glowed like an ocean-liner coming into port at midnight.

When *El Palacio* was lit to the max, we took turns in the shower, passing the water-filled flashlight from hand to hand like a baton as we did so. Someone was always holding it. Wireman went first, then Jack, then me. After showering, each of us was inspected by the other two, then scrubbed with hydrogen peroxide where any skin was broken. I was the worst, and when I finally put my clothes back on, I stung all over.

I was finishing with my boots, laboriously tying them one-handed, when Wireman came into the guest bedroom looking grave. 'There's a message you need to hear on the machine downstairs. From the Tampa Police. Here, let me help you.'

He went down on one knee before me and began tightening my laces. I saw without surprise that the gray in his hair had advanced . . . and suddenly a bolt of alarm went through me. I reached out and grabbed his meaty shoulder. 'The flashlight! Does Jack—'

'Relax. He's sitting in Miss Eastlake's old China Parlor, and he's got it on his lap.'

I hurried, nevertheless. I don't know what I expected to find – the room empty, the unscrewed flashlight lying on the rug in a

563

puddle of dampness, maybe, or Jack sex-changed into the three-eyed, claw-handed bitch that had come falling out of the old cracked keg – but he was only sitting there with the flashlight, looking troubled. I asked if he was all right. And I took a good look at his eyes. If he was going . . . wrong . . . I thought I'd see it in his eyes.

'I'm fine. But that message from the cop . . .' He shook his head.

'Well, let's hear it.'

A man identifying himself as Detective Samson said that he was trying to reach both Edgar Freemantle and Jerome Wireman, to ask some questions about Mary Ire. He particularly wanted to speak to Mr Freemantle, if he had not left for Rhode Island or Minnesota – where, Samson understood, the body of his daughter was being transported for burial.

'I'm sure Mr Freemantle is in a state of bereavement,' Samson said, 'and I'm sure these are really Providence P.D.'s questions, but we know Mr Freemantle did a newspaper interview with the Ire woman recently, and I volunteered to talk with him and yourself, Mr Wireman, if possible. I can tell you over the phone what Providence is most curious about, if this message tape doesn't run out . . .' It didn't. And the last piece fell into place.

ii

'Edgar, this is crazy,' Jack said. It was the third time he'd said it, and he was beginning to sound desperate. 'Totally nuts.' He turned to Wireman. 'You tell him!'

'Un poco loco,' Wireman agreed, but I knew the difference between poco and muy even if Jack didn't.

We were standing in the courtyard, between Jack's sedan and Elizabeth's old Mercedes. The moon had risen higher; so had the wind. The surf was pounding the shore, and a mile away, the shells under Big Pink would be discussing all sorts of strange things: muy asustador. 'But I think I could talk all night and still not change his mind.'

'Because you know I'm right,' I said.

'Tu perdón, amigo, you might be right,' he said. 'I'll tell you one

564

thing: Wireman intends to get down on his fat and aging knees and pray you are.'

Jack looked at the flashlight in my hand. 'At least don't take *that*,' he said. 'Excuse my French, boss, but you're fucking crazy to take that!'

'I know what I'm doing,' I said, hoping to God it was true. 'And stay here, both of you. Don't try to follow me.' I raised the flashlight and pointed it at Wireman. 'You're on your honor.'

'All right, Edgar. My honor's a tattered thing, but I swear on it. One practical question: are you sure two Tylenol will be enough to get you down the beach to your house on your feet, or are you going to wind up doing the Crawly-Gator?'

'I'll get there upright.'

'And you'll call when you do.'

'I'll call.'

He opened his arms then, and I stepped into them. He kissed me on both cheeks. 'I love you, Edgar,' he said. 'You're a hell of a man. *Sano como una manzana*.'

'What does that one mean?'

He shrugged. 'Stay healthy. I think.'

Jack offered his hand – the left one, the boy was a learner – and then decided a hug was in order, after all. In my ear he whispered, 'Give me the flashlight, boss.'

In his I whispered back: 'Can't. Sorry.'

I started along the path to the back of the house, the one that would take me to the boardwalk. At the end of that boardwalk, a thousand or so years ago, I'd met the big man I was now leaving behind. He had been sitting under a striped umbrella. He had offered me iced green tea, very cooling. And he had said, *So – the limping stranger arriveth at last.*

And now he goeth, I thought.

I turned back. They were watching me.

'*Muchacho!*' Wireman called.

I thought he was going to ask me to come back so we could think about this a little more, talk it over a little more. But I had underestimated him.

'*Vaya con Dios, mi hombre.*'

I gave him a final wave and walked around the corner of the house.

iii

So then I took my last Great Beach Walk, as limping and painful as my first ones along that shell-littered shore. Only those had been by the rosy light of early morning, when the world was at its most still, the only things moving the mild lap of the waves and the brown clouds of peeps that fled before me. This was different. Tonight the wind roared and the waves raged, not alighting on the shore but committing suicide on it. The rollers further out were painted chrome, and several times I thought I saw the *Perse* from the corner of my eye, but each time I turned to look, there was nothing. Tonight there was nothing on my part of the Gulf but moonlight.

I lurched along, flashlight gripped in my hand, thinking of the day I had walked here with Ilse. She had asked me if this was the most beautiful place on earth and I had assured her that no, there were at least three others that were more beautiful . . . but I couldn't remember what I'd told her those others were, only that they were hard to spell. What I remembered most clearly was her saying I deserved a beautiful place, and time to rest. Time to heal.

Tears started to come then, and I let them. I had the flashlight in the hand I could have used to wipe them away, so I just let them come.

iv

I heard Big Pink before I actually saw it. The shells under the house had never been so loud. I walked a little farther, then stopped. It was just ahead of me now, a black shape where the stars were blotted out. Another forty or fifty slow, limping paces, and moonlight began to fill in the details. All the lights were out, even the ones I almost always left on in the kitchen and Florida room. That could have been a power outage caused by the wind, but I didn't think that was it.

I realized the shells were talking in a voice I recognized. I should have; it was my own. Had I always known that? I suppose I had. On some level, unless we're mad, I think most of us know the various voices of our own imaginations.

And of our memories, of course. They have voices, too. Ask anyone who has ever lost a limb or a child or a long-cherished dream. Ask anyone who blames himself for a bad decision, usually made in a raw instant (an instant that is most commonly *red*). Our memories have voices, too. Often sad ones that clamor like raised arms in the dark.

I walked on, leaving tracks behind me that featured one dragging foot. The blacked-out hulk of Big Pink grew closer. It wasn't ruined like Heron's Roost, but tonight it was haunted. Tonight there was a ghost waiting. Or maybe something a little more solid.

The wind gusted and I looked left, into its pushing force. The ship was out there now, all right, lightless and silent, its sails so many flapping rags in the wind, waiting.

Might as well go, the shells said as I stood in the moonlight, now less than twenty yards from my house. *Wipe the blackboard clean — it can be done, no one knows it better than you — and just sail away. Leave this sadness behind. If you want to play you gotta pay. And the best part?*

'The best part is I don't have to go alone,' I said.

The wind gusted. The shells murmured. And from the blackness under the house, where that bony bed lay six feet deep, a darker shadow slipped free and stepped into the moonlight. It stood bent over for a moment, as if considering, and then began to come toward me.

She began to come toward me. But not Perse; Perse had been drowned to sleep.

Ilse.

v

She didn't walk; I didn't expect her to walk. She shambled. It was a miracle — a black one — that she could move at all.

After that last phone call with Pam (you couldn't call it a conversation, exactly), I'd gone out Big Pink's back door and snapped the handle off the broom I used to sweep sand from the walk leading to the mailbox. Then I'd gone around to the beach, down to where the sand was wet and shining. I hadn't remembered what came after that, because I didn't want to. Obviously. Only now I did, now I had to, because now my handiwork was standing in front of me. It was Ilse, yet not Ilse. Her face was there, then it blurred and it wasn't. Her form was there, then it slipped toward shapelessness before firming up again. Little pieces of dead sea oats and bits of shell dropped from her cheeks and chest and hips and legs as she moved. The moonlight picked out an eye that was heartbreakingly clear, heartbreakingly *hers*, and then it was gone, only to reappear again, shining in the moonlight.

The Ilse shambling toward me was made of sand.

'Daddy,' she said. Her voice was dry, with a grating undertone – as if there were shells caught in there somewhere. I supposed there were.

You will want to, but you mustn't, Elizabeth had said . . . but sometimes we can't help ourselves.

The sand-girl held out her arm. The wind gusted and the fingers at the end of the hand blurred as fine grains blew off them and thinned them to bones. More sand skirled up from around her and the hand fattened again. Her features shifted like a landscape under rapidly passing summer clouds. It was fascinating . . . hypnotic.

'Give me the flashlight,' she said. 'Then we'll go on board together. On the ship I can be the way you remember me. Or . . . you don't have to remember anything.'

The waves were on the march. Under the stars they roared in, one after the other. Under the moon. Under Big Pink, the shells spoke loudly: my voice, arguing with itself. Bring the buddy. I win. Sit in the chum. You win. Here in front of me stood Ilse made of sand, a shifting houri by the light of a three-quarter moon, her features never the same from one second to the next. Now she was Illy at nine; now she was Illy at fifteen, headed out on her first real date; now she was Illy as she'd looked getting off the plane in December, Illy the college girl with an engagement ring on her finger. Here stood the one I'd always loved the best – wasn't that why Perse had killed her? – with her hand held out for the flashlight. The flashlight was my boarding pass for a long cruise on forgetful seas. Of course that part might be a lie . . . but sometimes we have to take a chance. And usually we do. As Wireman says, we fool ourselves so much we could do it for a living.

'Mary brought salt with her,' I said. 'Bags and bags of salt. She put it in the tub. The police want to know why. But they'd never believe the truth, would they?'

She stood before me with the thundering, incoming waves behind her. She stood there blowing away and re-forming from the sand beneath her, around her. She stood there and said nothing, only holding her arm outstretched to take what she had come for.

'Drawing you in the sand wasn't enough. Even Mary drowning you wasn't enough. She had to drown you in salt water.' I glanced down at the flashlight. 'Perse told her just what to do. From my picture.'

'Give it to me, Daddy,' the shifting sand-girl said. Her hand was still held out. Only with the wind blowing, sometimes it was a claw. Even with sand feeding up from the beach to keep it plump, sometimes it was a claw. 'Give it to me and we can go.'

I sighed. Some things were inevitable, after all. 'All right.' I took a step toward her. Another of Wireman's sayings occurred to me: *In the end we wear out our worries.* 'All right, Miss Cookie. But it'll cost you.'

'Cost me what?' Her voice was the sound of sand against a window. The grating sound of the shells. But it was also Ilse's voice. My If-So-Girl.

'Just a kiss,' I said, 'while I'm still alive to feel it.' I smiled. I couldn't feel my lips – they were numb – but I could feel the muscles around them stretching. Just a little. 'I suppose it will be a sandy one, but I'll pretend you've been playing on the beach. Making castles.'

'All right, Daddy.'

She came closer, moving in a queer shamble-drift that wasn't walking, and up close the illusion collapsed entirely. It was like bringing a painting close to your eyes and watching as the scene – portrait, landscape, still life – collapses into nothing but strokes of color, most with the marks of the brush still embedded in them. Ilse's features disappeared. What I saw where they had been was nothing but a furious cyclone of sand and tiny bits of shell. What I smelled wasn't skin and hair but only salt water.

Pallid arms reached for me. Membranes of sand smoked off them in the wind. The moon shone through them. I held up the flashlight. It was short. And its barrel was plastic rather than stainless steel.

'You might want a look at this before you go giving away kisses, though,' I said. 'It came from the glove compartment of Jack Cantori's car. The one with Perse inside is locked in Elizabeth's safe.'

The thing froze, and when it did, the wind off the Gulf tore away the last semblance of humanity. In that moment I was confronting nothing but a whirling sand-devil. I took no chances, however; it had been a long day, and I had no intention of taking chances, especially if my daughter were somewhere . . . well, somewhere else . . . and waiting for her final rest. I swung my arm as hard as I could, the flashlight clamped in my fist and Nan Melda's silver bracelets sliding down my arm to my wrist. I had cleaned them carefully in the kitchen sink at *El Palacio*, and they jingled.

I had one of the silver-tipped harpoons stuck in my belt, behind my left hip, for good measure, but I didn't need it. The sand-devil exploded outward and upward. A scream of rage and pain went through my head. Thank God it was brief, or I think it would have torn me apart. Then there was nothing but the sound of the shells under Big Pink and a brief dimming of the stars over the dunes to my right as the last of the sand blew away in a disorganized flurry. The Gulf was once more empty except for the moon-gilded rollers, marching in toward shore. The *Perse* had gone, if it had ever been there.

The strength ran out of my legs and I sat down with a thump. Maybe I'd end up doing the Crawly-Gator the rest of the way, after all. If so, Big Pink wasn't far. Right now I thought I'd just sit here and listen to the shells. Rest a little. Then maybe I'd be able to get up and walk those last twenty yards or so, go in, and call Wireman. Tell him I was all right. Tell him it was done, that Jack could come and pick me up.

But for now I would just sit here and listen to the shells, which no longer seemed to be talking in my voice, or anyone else's. Now I would just sit here by myself on the sand, and look out at the Gulf, and think about my daughter, Ilse Marie Freemantle, who had weighed six pounds and four ounces at birth, whose first word had been *dog,* who had once brought home a large brown balloon crayoned on a piece of construction paper, shouting exultantly, 'I drawed a pitcher of you, Daddy!'

Ilse Marie Freemantle.

I remember her well.

22 – June

i

I piloted the skiff out to the middle of Lake Phalen and killed the motor. We drifted toward the little orange marker I'd left there. A few pleasure boats buzzed back and forth on the glass-smooth surface, but no sailboats; the day was perfectly still. There were a few kids in the playground area, a few people in the picnic area, and a few on the nearest hiking trail skirting the water. On the whole, though, for a lake that's actually within the city limits, the area was almost empty.

Wireman – looking strangely un-Florida in a fisherman's hat and a Vikings pullover – commented on this.

'School's still in,' I said. 'Give it another couple of weeks and there'll be boats buzzing everywhere.'

He looked uneasy. 'Does that make this the right place for her, *muchacho*? I mean, if a fisherman should net her up—'

'No nets allowed on Lake Phalen,' I said, 'and there are few rods and reels. This lake is pretty much for pleasure-boaters. And swimmers, in close to shore.' I bent and picked up the cylinder the Sarasota silversmith had made. It was three feet long, with a screw-down top at one end. It was filled with fresh water, and the water-filled flashlight was inside that. Perse was sealed in double darkness, and sleeping in a double blanket of fresh water. Soon she would be sleeping even deeper.

'This is a beautiful thing,' I said.

'That it is,' Wireman agreed, watching the afternoon sun flash from the cylinder as I turned it over in my hand. 'And nothing on it to catch a hook. Although I'd still feel easier about dumping it in a lake up around the Canadian border.'

'Where someone really *might* come along dragging a net,' I said. 'Hide in plain sight – it's not a bad policy.'

573

Three young women in a sportabout went buzzing by. They waved. We waved back. One of them yelled, '*We love cute guys!*' and all three of them laughed.

Wireman tipped them a smiling salute, then turned back to me. 'How deep is it out here? Do you know? That little orange flag suggests you do.'

'Well, I'll tell you. I did a little research on Lake Phalen – probably overdue, since Pam and I have owned the place on Aster Lane going on twenty-five years. The average depth is ninety-one feet . . . except out here, where there's a fissure.'

Wireman relaxed and pushed his cap back a little from his brow. 'Ah, Edgar. Wireman thinks you're still *el zorro* – still the fox.'

'Maybe *sí*, maybe *no*, but there's three hundred and eighty feet of water under that little orange flag. Three hundred and eighty at least. A hell of a lot better than a twelve-foot cistern thumbed into a coral splinter on the edge of the Gulf of Mexico.'

'Amen.'

'You look well, Wireman. Rested.'

He shrugged. 'That Gulfstream's the way to fly. No standing in line at security, no pawing through your carry-on to make sure you didn't turn your little shitass can of Foamy into a bomb. And for once in my life I managed to fly north without a stop at fucking Atlanta. Thanks . . . although I could have afforded it myself, it looks like.'

'You settled with Elizabeth's relatives, I take it?'

'Yep. Took your suggestion. Offered them the house and the north end of the Key in exchange for the cash and securities. They thought that was a hell of a deal, and I could see their lawyers thinking, "Wireman is a lawyer, and today he has a fool for a client."'

'Guess I ain't the only *zorro* in this boat.'

'I'll end up with over eighty million bucks in liquid assets. Plus various keepsakes from the house. Including Miss Eastlake's Sweet Owen cookie-tin. Think she was trying to tell me something with that, *'chacho*?'

I thought of Elizabeth popping various china figures into the tin and then insisting Wireman throw it in the goldfish pond. Of course she had been trying to tell him something.

'The rels got the north end of Duma Key, development value . . . well, sky's the limit. Ninety million?'

574

'Or so they think.'

'Yes,' he agreed, turning somber. 'So they think.' We sat in silence for a little while. He took the cylinder from me. I could see my face in its side, but distorted by the curve. I didn't mind looking at it that way, but I very rarely look at myself in a mirror anymore. It's not that I've aged; I don't care for the Freemantle fellow's eyes these days. They have seen too much.

'How's your wife and daughter?'

'Pam's out in California with her mother. Melinda's back in France. She stayed with Pam for awhile after Illy's funeral, but then she went back. I think it was the right call. She's getting on with it.'

'What about you, Edgar? Are you getting on with it?'

'I don't know. Didn't Scott Fitzgerald say there are no second acts in American life?'

'Yep, but he was a washed-up drunk when he said it.' Wireman put the cylinder at his feet and leaned forward. 'Listen to me, Edgar, and listen good. There are actually five acts, and not just in American lives – in every life that's fully lived. Same as in every Shakespearian play, tragedy and comedy alike. Because that's what our lives are made up of – comedy and tragedy.'

'For me, the yuks have been in short supply just lately,' I said.

'Yeah,' he agreed, 'but Act Three has potential. I'm in Mexico now. Told you, right? Beautiful little mountain town called Tamazunchale.'

I gave it a try.

'You like the way it rolls off your tongue. Wireman can see that you do.'

I smiled. 'It do have a certain ring to it.'

'There's this rundown hotel for sale there, and I'm thinking about buying it. It'd take three years of losses to put that kind of operation on a paying basis, but I've got a fat money-belt these days. I *could* use a partner who knows something about building and maintenance, though. Of course, if you're still concentrating on matters artistic . . .'

'I think you know better.'

'Then what do you say? Let us marry our fortunes together.'

'Simon and Garfunkel, 1969,' I said. 'Or thereabouts. I don't

575

know, Wireman. I can't decide now. I do have one more picture to paint.'

'Indeed you do. Just how big is this storm going to be?'

'Dunno. But Channel Six is gonna love it.'

'Plenty of warning, though, right? Property damage is fine, but no one gets killed.'

'No one gets killed,' I agreed, hoping this would be true, but once that phantom limb was given free rein, all bets were off. That's why my second career had to end. But there *would* be this one final picture, because I meant to be fully avenged. And not just for Illy; for Perse's other victims, as well.

'Do you hear from Jack?' Wireman asked.

'Just about every week. He's going to FSU in Tallahassee in the fall. My treat. In the meantime, he and his Mom are moving down the coast to Port Charlotte.'

'Was that also your treat?'

'Actually . . . yes.' Since Jack's father died of Crohn's Disease, he and his mother had had a bit of a tough skate.

'And your idea?'

'Right again.'

'So you think Port Charlotte's going to be far enough south to be safe.'

'I think so.'

'And north? What about Tampa?'

'Rain-showers at most. It's going to be a small storm. Small but powerful.'

'A tight little Alice. Like the one in 1927.'

'Yes.'

We sat looking at each other, and the girls cruised by again in their sportabout, laughing louder and waving more enthusiastically than before. Sweet bird of youth, flying on afternoon wine coolers. We saluted them.

When they were gone, Wireman said: 'Miss Eastlake's surviving relatives are never going to have to worry about getting building permits for their new property, are they?'

'I don't think so, no.'

He thought it over, then nodded. 'Good. Send the whole island to Davy Jones's locker. Works for me.' He picked up the silver cylinder, turned his attention to the little orange flag over the fissure that splits the middle of Lake Phalen, then looked back at me. 'Want to say any final words, *muchacho?*'

'Yes,' I said, 'but not many.'

'Get em ready, then.' Wireman turned on his knees and held the silver cylinder out. The sun sparkled on it for what I hoped would be the final time in at least a thousand years . . . but I had an idea Perse was good at finding her way to the surface. That she had done it before, and would again. Even from Minnesota, she would somehow find the *caldo.*

I said the words I'd been holding in my mind. '*Sleep forever.*'

Wireman's fingers opened. There was a small splash. We leaned over the side of the boat and watched the silver cylinder slide smoothly out of sight with one final glimmer of sunlight to mark its descent.

ii

Wireman stayed that night, and the next. We ate rare steaks, drank green tea in the afternoon, and talked about anything but old times. Then I took him to the airport, where he'd fly to Houston. There he planned to rent a car and drive south. See some of the country, he said.

I offered to go with him as far as security, and he shook his head. 'You shouldn't have to watch as Wireman removes his shoes for a business school graduate,' he said. 'This is where we say *adiós,* Edgar.'

'Wireman—' I said, and could say no more. My throat was filled with tears.

He pulled me into his arms and kissed me firmly on both cheeks. 'Listen, Edgar. It's time for Act Three. Do you understand me?'

'Yes,' I said.

'Come down to Mexico when you're ready. And if you want to.'

'I'll think about it.'

'You do that. *Con Dios, mi amigo; siempre con Dios.*'

'And you, Wireman. And you.'

I watched him walk away with his tote-bag slung over one shoulder. I had a sudden brilliant memory of his voice the night

Emery had attacked me in Big Pink, of Wireman shouting *cojudo de puta madre* just before driving the candlestick into the dead thing's face. He had been magnificent. I willed him to turn back one final time . . . and he did. Must have caught a thought, my mother would have said. Or had an intuition. That's what Nan Melda would have said.

He saw me still standing there and his face lit in a grin. 'Do the day, Edgar!' he cried. People turned to look, startled.

'And let the day do you!' I called back.

He saluted me, laughing, then walked into the jetway. And of course I *did* eventually come south to his little town, but although he's always alive for me in his sayings – I never think of them in anything but the present tense – I never saw the man himself again. He died of a heart attack two months later, in Tamazunchale's open-air market, while dickering for fresh tomatoes. I thought there would be time, but we always think stuff like that, don't we? We fool ourselves so much we could do it for a living.

iii

Back at the place on Aster Lane, my easel stood in the living room, where the light was good. The canvas on it was covered with a piece of toweling. Beside it, on the table with my oil paints, were several aerial photos of Duma Key, but I'd hardly glanced at them; I saw Duma in my dreams, and still do.

I tossed the towel on the couch. In the foreground of my painting – my last painting – stood Big Pink, rendered so realistically I could almost hear the shells grating beneath it with each incoming wave.

Propped against one of the pilings, the perfect surreal touch, were two red-headed dolls, sitting side by side. On the left was Reba. On the right was Fancy, the one Kamen had fetched from Minnesota. The one that had been Illy's idea. The Gulf, usually so blue during my time on Duma Key, I had painted a dull and ominous green. Overhead, the sky was filled with black clouds; they massed to the top of the canvas and out of sight.

My right arm began to itch, and that remembered sensation of power began to flow first into me and then through me. I could see my picture almost with the eye of a god . . . or a goddess. I could give this up, but it would not be easy.

When I made pictures, I fell in love with the world.

When I made pictures, I felt whole.

I painted awhile, then put the brush aside. I mixed brown and yellow together with the ball of my thumb, then skimmed it over the painted beach . . . oh so lightly . . . and a haze of sand lifted, as if on the first hesitant puff of air.

On Duma Key, beneath the black sky of an inriding June storm, a wind began to rise.

How to Draw a Picture (XII)

Know when you're finished, and when you are, put your pencil or your paintbrush down. All the rest is only life.

February 2006 – June 2007

Afterthoughts

I have taken liberties with the geography of Florida's west coast, and with its history, as well. Although Dave Davis was real, and did indeed disappear, he is used here fictionally.

And no one in Florida calls out-of-season storms 'Alices' except me.

I want to thank my wife, the novelist Tabitha King, who read this book in an early draft and suggested valuable changes; the Sweet Owen cookie-tin was only one of them.

I want to thank Russ Dorr, my old medical friend, who patiently explained both Broca's area and the physics of contracoup injuries.

I also want to thank Chuck Verrill, who edited the book with his usual combination of gentleness and ruthlessness.

Teddy Rosenbaum, my friend and copy-editor: *muchas gracias*.

And you, my old friend Constant Reader; always you.

Stephen King
Bangor, Maine